Your book has strength, particularly in the way you depict the ambiguity of whites. Your passion shows. I like your real quotes from newspapers.

Probably the most historically correct novel I have ever read.

I traveled through Chattanooga many times. I felt like I was there!

I like how each chapter is a page turner! This chapter made me feel as if I was reading from the journal. Your book gets "gooder and gooder"!

This is a home run for you. This book is like waiting for dessert after dinner. You tease me continuously with each chapter.

Can they all be my favorite chapters! I love your book!

I'm reading along and Ka-boom! Real genius! "We shall, in the end, Walela, be pushed and pushed until we tumble off the end of the earth and fall into discarded mountains of white meaningless paper." You have a habit of finishing a paragraph with a concluding sentence that is profound! Mountains of white meaningless paper...all the treaties written on paper were full of lies and deceit. You perfected the craft of imagery. Bravo!

I liked how tastefully you described the scene at the river. My book club friends would enjoy reading this. Cassie is my favorite character. My favorite scene was Cassie's brother on his first deer hunt. I felt like I was right there in the woods running along-side him.

Barney, this is the best writing ever! "Ben was completely unaware of his moral transformation. The crisp black and white principles of youth he had allowed to blend with the colorless ethics of law and politics coating his soul with multiple layers of indistinct grey protecting him from identifying truth or detecting a lie. Unknown to himself, Ben had become a puppet—a caricature, faintly resembling his previous self—controlled by political marionettes whose strings attached directly to his compromised integrity, all sustained by hollow promises of money, power and pleasure."

Wow! Ben is in denial, trying to justify this horror. Well written. The poem *One Day in May* was a fitting end.

I was disappointment because I finished the book. I didn't want the book to end. Something you only find with a good story teller.

I have thoroughly enjoyed your book, every chapter! I always know I have read an exceptional book when the story does not end at the last page but continues on in my mind and your book has done that for me.

I am totally in awe. What a tremendous accomplishment. I knew when you told us the title it would be good. It was better than good.

Other Books by Barney Beard

Chapter Books

The Incredible Adventure of the Eight Cousins- (Award Winner)
The Horrible Word Hole
The Great Alphabet Adventure
The Bow Window

Fun Books for Early Reading

Luke's Great Adventure Begins
Carter Finds His Imagination
Quinn's Great Adventure
Oliver Learns to Read
Oliver and Quinn Travel in Space
Luke and Carter's Winter Adventure
Melody and Connor: Christmas with Grammy
Melody and Connor: Their Visit with Grammy
Luke and Carter: Their Summer Adventure

Odds and Ends by Barney

Letters to My Grandchildren
The Adventures of Bouncy
Our Favorite Nursery Rhymes
The Official Rules of Canasta
Golf for Beginners-(Double Award Winner)
Golf for Beginners: Left Hand Version

A White Killing Frost

The Vanishment

When does the thief legally own that which he stole?

A Historical Novel by
Barney Beard
1st Edition

ISBN-13:978-0996432832
ISBN-10:0996432833

Copyright © 2017-2018 by Barney Beard

All right reserved under International and Pan American Copyright Conventions. No part of this publication may be reproduced or transmitted in any form or by any means, electronic or mechanical, including photocopy, recording, or any information storage and retrieval system, without the prior written permission of the author.

Contact:
Barney Beard
P.O. Box 5, Lady Lake, Florida 32159

Dedicated to my constant parents

Alyce Helene
and
Samuel Emerson Beard

who provided a loving home every day of my life
and taught me to read at an early age.
If I had one wish, it would be they could read this book.

Acknowledgements

There are dozens of people I must acknowledge for their generous assistance.

Cassie, my dear friend, was the original inspiration for this work. One afternoon after a long conversation at her dining table this story came to me almost fully formed. After an initial attempt at a screen play, this novel was the happy result of her influence.

There is a long list of others without which this book would have never happened:

Dr. Vicki Rozema, who gave me professional advice about the Trail of Tears, especially in Tennessee.

Dr. Steven Burt, who helped me in numerous ways with numerous literary professionals.

My dear Beth, my muse, who has been reading, researching and encouraging from the conception.

Connie, who has tirelessly corrected typos, run-on sentences, dangling participles and nonsensical paragraphs.

Thanks to my many friends, advanced readers and encouragers who graciously read my novel, generously shared their comments, were unhesitating in both praise and constructive criticism and who found hundreds and hundreds of typos—humiliating typos put into my manuscript in the dead of night by sadistic, unscrupulous, wicked typo-gremlins who revel in the public embarrassment of would-be authors.

Thanks to:
Patsy, Kari, Peggy, Martha, Hal, Judi, Joanna, Linda, Lee, Nancy, Kathleen, Les, Fred and Cindy and Gaila.

Many thanks to the others who I've unfortunately forgotten and left off this list. No doubt they will be angry with me for forgetting their names and their hard work on my behalf. If I have forgotten your hard work, please forgive my mental lapse. I have a good memory, it's just a bit short these days. Send me a scathing letter and remind me of my unfortunate oversight. I will include you in my next corrected version. I promise.

Barney Beard

Preface

The history you are about to read is taken from the pages of the personal journal of a precocious Cherokee girl. It is a journal she kept meticulously from 1820 to 1838. During those years the little girl you will get to know as Cassie grows into a woman.

She writes of her life, loves and the political milieu surrounding the turbulent last years of the Cherokee Nation in Georgia before their deportation en masse in 1838.

The newspaper articles are exact quotes from extant archives with references and were invaluable source documents.

Historical figures and events have been verified to the best of my ability. Cassie's journal speaks for itself.

This is Cassie's story. I commend it to you.

The Author

Table of Contents

Copied from the *Georgia Journal Newspaper*
9 March 1829 – page 2

"The benevolent and enlightened policy which the Government has invariably pursued towards its Indian neighbors ought to quiet the fears of the Cherokees on the subject of their territorial rights...."

Prologue

The summer sun bestows its glorious bounty. We preserve the soil's succulent gifts for the icy months. Days grow short. One morning we wake. The frozen ground crunches under our feet. Everything green has died, covered by a white killing frost.

Chapter I

Where We Keep Our Indians

Chapter 1

"Greg, why does this landscape look so different from the farmland we've driven by until now? What's going on?"

"It looks different because that's where we keep our Indians," Greg said.

"What do you mean, 'that's where we keep our Indians'? Is it a prison or something? Who keeps Indians? What are you talking about, Greg? Are you making fun of me?"

"No, I'm not making fun of you, Katie," Greg said, with a little chuckle. "I don't mean anything bad—not at all. That's just the way people out here talk about the Indians and their reservations. It's meant to be humorous. That's all. That's the Cherokee reservation we're passing and there are others. We keep a lot of different Indians out here."

I could hear Greg laughing under his breath. He kept his eyes on the road or he would have seen the dirty look I gave him. His answer to my question, intended to be humorous, hit me the wrong way.

"Greg, what an ugly thing to say," I shot back. "How would it sound if someone said, 'that's where we keep our women', or 'that's where we keep our black people'?"

"We don't mean anything bad, Katie. Honest, we don't," Greg said, smiling as if he were teasing me.

I wouldn't give up. I answered in a curt voice, "How would it sound if I said 'that's where we keep our Mexicans' or 'that's where we keep our Japanese people', like we did in WWII? What would you think about that? That was bad, wasn't it?"

I was on a roll. Greg was listening patiently and grinning like a cat. I felt like he was patronizing me, but I was persistent.

"I don't like the sound of what you said at all. I thought we fought a war to defeat that very idea. How can you say something like that as if it were just a big joke? I don't understand, Greg. Why do you keep laughing at me?"

"I didn't mean it like that, Katie. You're taking me the wrong way," Greg answered. "I didn't mean to start a fuss. My remark was meant to be funny. I'm not laughing at you."

"I don't think you're funny."

"You're taking me all wrong," Greg said, once again defending himself. "We like Indians out here. We don't have anything against Indians—nobody does."

"It didn't sound like that to me," I said.

Greg answered patiently with a jovial tone and a silly grin.

"Out of context, the remark could sound a bit bigoted, I guess, but that's what people say out here, Katie. It's what they've always said. We don't mean anything nasty. We're certainly not racist and we're not bigots. We're good folks."

I was pouting a little and thinking about what he was saying. The more I thought about his remark the more curious I became about what lay behind it. I realized I didn't know a thing about Indians.

"We got all kinds of Indians out here, Katie. We got Cherokee, Choctaw, Chickasaw, Pawnee, Cheyenne, Apache and more tribes I can't remember or pronounce. The east end of Oklahoma is full of Indians. They have their little towns and capitals. I guess what I said doesn't sound good when you think about it, but I don't mean to hurt anyone's feelings. We're good people out here, Katie—about as patriotic as you can get. The country people here are conservative and the salt of the earth. Everyone out here likes Indians— always have. Indians are different from white folks, but we like them."

I could feel myself becoming tense as I tried to sort out Greg's remark and his continuing self-justification. The more he explained and defended himself, the more bigoted he sounded.

Greg is a good man. I knew he was telling me how people thought but I was unprepared for his remark and less prepared for his defense. I was angry at myself for being surprised and snapping at my boyfriend. Up to this point, Greg and I had been having a great time on our trip west.

Greg's phrase kept ringing in my mind. I was determined to understand what was behind Greg's remark. I turned my back to Greg as much as I could. I wanted him to know the conversation was over. I needed to think. It was going to be all picture and no sound.

I watched the passing landscape and wondered what I was seeing. His remark echoed and I wanted to make sure when I finally did speak to him I didn't say something stupid. I stared out the window with my arms folded. I knew nothing about Oklahoma, Indians, their reservations, their culture or their history—not a thing—not a blessed thing.

I've lived in Walker County, Georgia all my life—way up in the northwest corner of the state. I went to primary school in Rock Spring and high school in Lafayette. I studied Georgia history, but at the moment I couldn't recall a thing I learned about Indians—nothing. Everything I remember about Indians I've learned from Hollywood. About all I know about Georgia history is a man named Button Gwinnett signed the Declaration of Independence and Savannah was our first big town. I know of no Indian reservations in Georgia. I know there had been Indian occupation before Georgia was colonized by Europeans, but I don't know where the Indians came from, where they lived, where they went or why they disappeared. I've never met an Indian in my life. None lived in our community—not one I knew of. When I was growing up listening to the old folks around where we lived, I never heard anyone talk about Indians—much less a place to keep them. What was I missing? Why had Greg's offhand remark put me in such a mental tizzy? I felt ignorant and confused.

As I thought more about it, I realized when Greg said, 'it's where we keep our Indians' he had clearly implied, 'it's where we white people keep our Indians'. I guess that's what disturbed me most. No matter how much he denied being racist, on examination his remark was about as racist as one could get. At the moment I had an irrational dislike of my boyfriend because of that single statement, and I didn't like that emotion either. Greg was a good man. I wanted to be fair.

Why was I surprised by the humorous terminology white folks used for Indian reservations in Oklahoma? Why did it upset me? Why should I care?

I'm a journalist. I'm educated and well read. I'm supposed to know things. I didn't like feeling uninformed and unable to connect the dots.

I laughed at myself. Greg couldn't construct three consecutive complete sentences. He didn't know the difference between a verb and an adverb and he probably thought a thesaurus was some kind of extinct dinosaur. Maybe I was pouting because my happy-go-lucky, business major boyfriend knew more about United States history than I did.

Arms still folded, I finally turned towards Greg. I spoke in a sharp, staccato voice.

"Can we visit the Cherokee reservation?"

"Of course we can, Katie. It's not a prison. It's part of the United States just like the rest of Oklahoma. We can go anywhere we want to out here."

3

I think Greg was enjoying the conversation and his morning drive. He wasn't upset or tense in the least.

"I want to see the place where you keep your Indians," I said sarcastically.

Greg laughed. I think he was teasing me on purpose and enjoying it. I didn't like his condescending attitude. It made me feel inferior.

"Tahlequah is just a bit north of here. That would be a good place to visit if you want to see a reservation and learn some things about the Cherokee. There's some historical stuff to see and you can read the roadside markers and such and get a feel for the reservation. They have good restaurants, if you like southern cooking. We could be there in two shakes if you want to go? It's up to you."

"Yes, let's go. Can we go now, today, right now?"

"Of course we can. It's your trip, my dear," Greg answered.

"I want to go now," I said petulantly.

"It's your project, Katie. I'm just your limo driver and the chairman of your entertainment committee. I'll take you wherever you want to go."

Greg laughed again. His easy-going nature and his friendly laugh was one of the things that made him attractive.

"I want to go to Tahlequah," I said. "I want to see what's there. I want to see an Indian reservation."

"No problem, Katie. We can be in Tahlequah for lunch and I'm hungry. If you ask a lot of questions as you usually do we won't make it to Mom and Dad's today, but that's alright with me. I don't care when we get there. I'm on vacation."

Greg squinted at the big road sign ahead.

"I think it's Highway 82 to Park Hill and then it's just a few miles north to Tahlequah if I remember right. You want to stay the night, Katie?"

My arms were still folded and my legs curled up under me in the passenger seat. Greg's remark was circling around and around in my mind like an out of control race car. I couldn't stop myself from thinking.

"Sure, let's stay the night. I've never been on an Indian reservation and the fact that it's the Cherokee capital is interesting. We don't have Indians in Georgia. I wonder why that is?"

I was thinking out loud and talking to myself.

"Well, we got plenty of them out here," Greg answered.

I couldn't believe how he kept on and on and how he always referred to Indians as 'them'.

"I'll call Momma and tell her we'll get there sometime tomorrow afternoon," Greg said. "I suggest you get online and get us a reservation at a nice motel."

He suddenly laughed louder than before—a big belly laugh.

"Get a reservation on the reservation. How appropriate, don't you think, Katie? We need to have a reservation to stay on the reservation."

Greg kept laughing. I was liking him less and less.

"Ok, that's fine. I'll get us a reservation," I answered tersely.

Despite myself, I giggled at his reservation joke. It was clever and Greg is a good guy at heart. I knew he would never intentionally be hateful toward anybody. He's a good man.

"No problem. I'll get us a reservation on the reservation," I said. "How do you spell Tahlequah?" I asked, screwing my face into a question mark.

"Look at that road sign there on your side. There it is, spelled out for you. Forty-two miles to Tahlequah. We'll be there in less than an hour."

Greg made a right turn onto Highway 82 and headed my Camry north into the heart of the Cherokee Indian reservation. I began wondering what kind of adventure lay ahead.

As Greg drove, I made reservations at the Red Bird Bed and Breakfast near downtown and set the GPS. I thought it would be better to spend the night in a nice bed and breakfast than a cheap motel where they never wash the bedspread. I detest cheap motels. Even non-smoking rooms smell of stale cigarette smoke and the carpets turn the bottom of my socks black.

The bed and breakfast advertised itself within easy walking distance of the historical section of town. A visit to the Cherokee reservation would be a welcome interlude for my summer research trip. I had a funny feeling that visiting Tahlequah was exactly what I was supposed to be doing. Why I knew that, I don't know.

I sat in the passenger seat with my back to Greg and my arms crossed. It was once again all picture and no sound. Greg knows my moods and knows it's best to ignore me when my arms are crossed. My mind was flying from one thought to the next as I stared out at the passing landscape.

My entire life's experience with Indians was limited to a few Hollywood movies like *The Searchers*, *Last of the Mohicans* and old re-runs of *Cheyenne*, *Lone Ranger*, *Gene Autry*, *Roy Rogers* and other old cowboy films my parents and grandparents used to watch when I was little.

I was perplexed. There are dozens and dozens of Indian place names in my part of Georgia but no Indians—none that I knew about. Why was that? I had never really thought about that before. Where did the Indians go when they left Georgia? When did they leave? Did they simply vanish one day?

I understood the origin of English place names like Knoxville, Dalton, Gainesville, Cleveland, Rome and Nashville but how did white, English speaking folk come up with names like Chattanooga, Hiwassee, Chickamauga, Chattooga, Ocoee and Ocmulgee?

Were there Indians in Georgia in the past? Of course there were. I knew that. The entire south had a history of Indian occupation, but I had no facts to call on from my school days. Was I sick that day when my Georgia history professor covered Indians? As hard as I searched my memory, I had no knowledge of pre-colonial Georgia. I was wondering if I was just plain ignorant or was bored in class and wasn't listening.

As Greg drove us towards Tahlequah, the place names from back home began swirling through my mind. Where did these strange, impossible-to-spell names come from? What mystery did they contain? Why was I thinking about them in the first place?

I currently lived in Chattanooga not far from Chickamauga Dam which is on the Tennessee River. I had driven by the Ocoee and Tellico Rivers and the gorgeous Nantahala River just over in North Carolina. I had held a little job just over the state line in Catoosa County, Georgia and farther south I had some relatives in Chattooga County and east of that was Cherokee County, but none of these places had Indians.

Not far from Chattanooga I remember driving by the little town of Rising Fawn in a beautiful valley tucked up against the side of the mountain. I always thought Rising Fawn the most beautiful English translation of an Indian name I had ever heard.

Georgia had rivers like the Altamaha, Chattahoochee, Oconee, Ocmulgee and the beautiful Hiwassee. Georgia had Indian names everywhere but no Indians. In Walker, Dade, Catoosa, Chattooga, Murray and Whitfield counties white folks owned all the farmland. Without exception, all the farmers I knew were white with European ancestry—mostly English, I imagine. I began to wonder about that. When did my part of the world turn from red to white? Had Walker County always been white?

It suddenly came to mind how my great-grandfather had been a lifeguard at the Lake Winnepesaukah Amusement Park in Rossville. Why would anyone give an amusement park near Rossville, Georgia a name like that? It was an Indian name. It had to be. I've been to the park many times through the years and never gave its name a second thought. My father told me the park filled their old swimming pool with concrete where his teenage father, my great-grandfather, had been lifeguard before WWII. They put the beautiful antique carousel that came from old Grant Park in Atlanta on top of the old concrete-filled swimming pool. I think the carousel is still there. I like going to Lake Winnie. It's a lot of fun. I remember the cotton candy that stuck all over my face and riding the Ferris wheel that frightened my socks off when I was little.

Why would white people use difficult to pronounce and impossible to spell Indian place names? Why wasn't it Lake Smith or Lake Vanderbilt Amusement Park? Why did they name it Lake Winnepesaukah?

I was confused. I told myself I was wasting my time being overly concerned about irrelevant history, but the other side of my mind was curious. I wanted answers but I didn't even know the questions. That's the very reason I'm in journalism. I'm always wanting to know why, who, what, when and where. I'm always curious about the back story. My nose was itching. My grandmother told me when my nose was itching it meant someone was coming.

Why did I know so little about our past? I continued thinking as I watched the Oklahoma landscape go by. Why did my knowledge of history have a complete void between the Revolutionary War and the Civil War? I had an eighty-year historical gap in my memory. I tried to think of just one important event in our American history between 1800 and 1860. All I came up with was the Battle of New Orleans in 1814 and if it wasn't for the old Johnny Horton song, I wouldn't have known that. The only mental peg that came to mind was, *'In 1814 we took a little trip, along with Colonel Jackson down the mighty Mississip', we took a little bacon an' we took a little beans and we fought the bloody British at the town of New Orleans'.*

Did nothing happen of significance between 1800 and 1860 and the beginning of the Civil War? Do I need to give Johnny Horton credit for my entire historical knowledge of this time period?

During the last couple of weeks I've gathered some wonderful stories for my writing project—stories portraying a marvelous kaleidoscope of diverse Americana. Each vignette I gathered fit comfortably with what I know about

7

our country, my white European cultural view and the modern education I'm receiving at the University of Tennessee at Chattanooga.

As I sat curled up on the car seat watching the reservation pass by I felt a growing disquiet. I was looking at something that didn't fit my comfortable view of America—not by a long shot. My growing emotional uneasiness was all because of Greg's offhand remark. Why was that?

There was more to this. I was certain. My journalism training was gradually kicking in and I began to systematize my questions. I could smell a story, a good story, in Greg's flippant, chauvinistic comment. The dozens of questions swirling in my mind made me think of my mother's patient interrogation techniques when I was a girl. When I had been up to something naughty, I always knew I would run out of answers long before my persistent mother would run out of questions. That thought made me smile. I've become my mother.

I felt a determination growing inside of me to understand—to know more about this whole thing with the Indians, our American history and the curious place names I was so familiar with in my part of the world.

My journalism professor said I could sense a compelling story the way animals feel the invisible approach of a storm, even though the sky is blue. I had that feeling now. I was onto something. Something yet to be discovered was looming just beyond my mental horizon. I had no idea what it was, but I knew it was interesting and it was out there waiting on me—beckoning.

What is it that has hijacked my day and is drawing me to Tahlequah? Is there a storm brewing perhaps? Have I allowed Greg's narrow-minded remark to redirect my summer project—turn me in a direction I had not planned—a direction I would have never planned? I wonder?

How could I grow up where I did in northwest Georgia, be well-read, be working on my master's degree in journalism and have so many nagging questions?

Maybe I'll get some answers in Tahlequah.

Chapter II

Katie Meets the Old Woman

Chapter 2

I kept my back turned to Greg and didn't say another word until we arrived in Tahlequah. We drove straight to the bed and breakfast. Our room was clean, smelled nice, was delightfully decorated and was even lovelier than the photographs. The hand-stitched quilt on the king-size, solid maple antique bed made me feel like I was at my grandmother's. I was five months pregnant and the added comfort was welcome.

Without unpacking we immediately left for the restaurant. We were starving and I was anxious to begin answering questions. I wanted to sniff for a story. Somehow, I knew this day would be special.

I was curious about some signage which I guessed used Cherokee script, and I noticed several interesting locations I marked to visit later. We decided to skip fast food and sample the authentic Cherokee fare advertised on a local mom and pop billboard. Once inside, it turned out the menu wasn't unusual, at least not for me being raised in the South. Their specialties were fried chicken, real mashed potatoes, turnip greens, green beans cooked with fatback, white gravy made with the drippings from the fried chicken—all the foods I learned to love at my grandma's house and still find tasty.

The Kentucky Wonders were some of the best I've ever eaten and the country-style ham was perfect. I love authentic country-style ham, the kind my grandfather used to preserve right on his farm. I avoid cheap ham—the kind the USDA allows to be injected with water. Why our government allows meat packing companies to inject pork with water I'll never know. I guess it's the same reason they allow wood pulp in Parmesan cheese.

After we ordered I watched the busy employees crossing the worn green and white tiled floor that ran throughout the dining room and through the swinging doors into the kitchen. One older waitress seemed not to be so busy. She was short, shorter than I am, had grey hair, dark eyes and a wrinkled face. Her complexion and facial features made me think she was probably Cherokee. She had deep facial wrinkles, especially around her mouth—wrinkles I've noticed only in long-time cigarette smokers.

9

There was a kindness about her I liked and I thought she might be a good person to ask about a story. I got her attention and she came to our table with a smile. I asked if she was Cherokee. She said she was. I told her I was gathering stories and politely requested if I could ask a few questions later and maybe have her tell me about something interesting that happened in the restaurant or a personal story about Tahlequah. She shook her head no.

She glanced down at the green tile floor and then back at me.

"Yes, ma'am, I know what you mean, but I'm not a story teller. My grandma has stories. She'll talk to you about anything. She's got lots of stories. She would talk to you—all day long if you want to."

She laughed out loud when she said that. The waitress paused and I could see she was thinking.

"I'm getting off for lunch in a bit and if you two want you can follow me home and I'll introduce you to my grandma," the waitress said. "She never goes anywhere and she'd be tickled to talk to you. She don't have many visitors and talkin' to you would do her good."

"Yes, I would like to meet your grandmother," I said.

"Our house is three minutes from here," the waitress said. "You two can talk to my grandmother while I have my lunch and you'll get all the stories you want, I fancy."

"Yes, we would like that," I told her again.

"I hope you have plenty of time," the waitress added. "She'll talk all day once you get her started. I'll come and get you when you've finished your lunch if you want to do that."

As the waitress walked away she laughed again, "Yep, I think you'll get all the story tellin' you want, young lady."

We finished our lunch and paid the bill to a bored employee at the cash register. Greg and I followed the waitress into the unpaved driveway of a small, sturdy two-bedroom wood frame house badly in need of a coat of paint. Three huge spreading white oaks shaded the little wooden-sided house and most of the sparse lawn. The lawn wasn't much more than isolated patches of scraggly grass gone to seed. The small, unkempt flower beds on either side of the front steps were mostly weeds. As we walked up to the porch, I noticed dead limbs and leaves banked up in the valley of the rusty tin roof, streaked with years of corrosion. We followed the waitress up the three creaky, unpainted wooden steps onto the front porch whose only furniture was an old rocking chair and two straight back chairs—nothing else. The two sash windows on either side of the front door were opaque with dust. The old screen door didn't quite fit the frame and the rusty screen had been pushed through beside the handle.

I was excited. I'm always eager as I prepare to listen to someone's story. We followed the waitress inside. The front door was held open by a large, heavy antique brass doorstop in the shape of an elephant at least a foot tall. It was quite a work of art—stunning in fact. I wondered how the magnificent elephant got here and where it came from. The small living area was neat and tidy. It was furnished with an old-fashioned three-piece stuffed suite covered with neat, clean, tucked-in white bed sheets concealing the lumpy, worn cushions underneath.

"Elisi, I've got company for you. I met this lady at the restaurant who writes about other people's stories. I told her you like to tell stories, so I brought her to meet you. I figured you would enjoy the company," the waitress said to her grandmother in a louder than normal voice.

"Have you got time to tell her a story or two or do you want her to come back another time?"

Before her granddaughter had finished speaking, the old woman stood with a pleasant smile and friendly eyes and extended her hand.

"It's a pleasure to meet you two. I'm Maude Bliss Allen. Have a seat and make yourself at home."

She pronounced each of her three names distinctly.

"You can call me Maude or Grandma. You can call me elisi if we become friends and I invite you over for dinner."

She laughed easily and continued almost without taking a breath.

"You've met my granddaughter, Kari. She's really Karen, but she's been Kari since she was a baby. Sit you two down and you're both welcome. Make yourself at home."

The waitress was right. The old woman was a talker. She spoke quickly and allowed us no time to respond between sentences.

Greg and I sat on the couch and listened. This was going to be interesting.

"Forgive my old house," the old woman continued. "Kari wants us to sell and move into an apartment or build us a new house out from town somewhere but I like living here in my old home place close to everything. It needs a lot of work but I like it here. I been here since the day I was born and I don't think I'd be happy nowhere else. I like this old house under the same trees that were here when my elisi was born. I got a picture of her holding me by that middle white oak out front. Whoever took the picture was standing on the porch steps. That old tree is about the same size now as in the old

11

photograph—interesting, isn't it? I grew a whole lot faster than those trees, didn't I? I reckon they'll be here when I'm gone. I love this place. I'll show you that old photograph if you want. When I'm gone Kari can move into a new apartment, but this place is home and always will be, I reckon."

Her granddaughter smiled but said nothing. I knew I was in the right place to hear stories. The old woman was wearing a faded blue cotton print dress that fell to her ankles and old, black flats with heavy, black support hose. Her eyes were dark like her granddaughter's. Her coarse white hair, tinged with yellow, was pulled back in a severe bun. Her back was bent forward because of a hump that made me think she had some kind of chronic spinal arthritis. The hump looked exactly as if she had a small pillow tucked into the top of the back of her dress. She stood as tall as she could with a cane in her left hand and her chin jutting forward. She looked directly at me for a few moments over the top of her old gold-rimmed glasses with a beautiful smile and dark perceptive eyes.

"Of course I have time for a story, dear. I always have time for stories. What's your name, child?"

Greg and I introduced ourselves. We dutifully began working through the required small talk—where we were from and why we were out here and where we were staying. Her granddaughter was right. Her grandmother did like to talk.

The old woman's granddaughter stood and interrupted as she walked towards their little kitchen in the back.

"Y'all pardon me. I'm going for a cigarette and make myself a sandwich and then I have to get back to the restaurant. I always come home in the afternoon for my lunch before the evenin' rush. I been workin' at the restaurant for twenty years and I hate their food. Y'all go ahead and talk. I'll eat anywhere in town but not where I work. I'd rather have cold bologna here than steak there. If you'll pardon me, their kitchen stinks. I hate the food there. Don't tell 'em I said that. I'll put on a pot of tea. Y'all talk and I'll be back in a minute or two."

She laughed and disappeared into the kitchen. We heard the screen door open and shut and smelled the cigarette smoke that drifted through the house.

"I hear you're quite a storyteller, Mrs. Allen. I'm a journalism major and I love to record people's stories. That's what I'm doing this summer—recording people's stories. I'm writing a book of stories—of first-hand Americana to finish my university degree and today is my very first visit to an Indian reservation."

The old woman was watching me. She was not only a talker, but I could tell she was a good listener. She didn't miss a thing.

"This is all new to me," I said. "We don't have Indians or reservations in Georgia. I'm sure there are some interesting stories here in Tahlequah."

I smiled and the old woman smiled back. Once again I couldn't help but notice her eyes, alert and penetrating, as if she were looking into my mind.

"No, young lady. Ain't no Indians in Georgia—at least not on a reservation. There's lots of us Cherokee scattered all over the United States and there's Cherokee folk the world over makin' an honest livin'. We're pretty much everywhere. I heard there are over three hundred thousand of us registered Cherokee now. That's quite a bunch of us, ain't it?"

"Yes, ma'am. It is."

"Lots of folks left the reservation but my people stayed. We like it here. We was always homebodies I guess, but I got relatives all over. I got a nephew who's an architect in Chicago, another nephew who's a mathematics professor at Vanderbilt and a niece who works for the government in DC. I really don't know what she does. She says she can't tell me much about her job or where she goes but she showed me the gun she carries for work with one of them laser sights on it like they got on NCIS. I guess you can figure out what she does for the government. Yep, we're scattered all around and a whole bunch of us are still out here, 'cept for those who stayed in North Carolina. They're the Eastern Cherokee and we're the Western Cherokee."

I was amazed how the old woman managed to speak so fast and breathe at the same time. I was loving listening to her.

"You're right, dear. Ain't no Cherokee reservations in Georgia. Ask me and I'll tell you why, if you want to know."

When she said that, it was as if her manner changed. She looked straight into my eyes and paused for a moment. I was going to tell her I wanted to know why there were no Indians in Georgia, but she continued speaking before I could ask. I didn't want to interrupt. This was going to be a one-sided conversation, but that was fine with me. I had come to listen.

"Yep, I have stories. My momma told me stories. Elisi told me stories. Elisi told me stories her momma told her and I remember them all. I mostly tell other people's stories. I don't have too many of my own. I guess our family was so poor about the only thing we ever had was stories. You're in a good business, dear. You could make a living right here in Tahlequah writing down people's stories, I reckon. We got plenty of stories."

I was listening and taking notes as fast as I could and occasionally jotting down questions I would ask later if we had time.

"We Cherokee are in Oklahoma now," the old woman continued breathlessly, "but I got cousins in North Carolina—ain't seen 'em in years and years—don't guess I ever will now. I won't never get in an airplane and I sure ain't goin' to ride all that way in a car—no sir."

I was amazed how the old woman talked almost without breathing. I was loving it.

"We got lots of stories about how we got here from back east. I suspect those are the stories you want to hear? Am I right?"

"Yes, ma'am. I would like that."

"We got stories how the government took our land and then took more after the war and how they keep tryin' to take more and more from us. Ever' year they come up with some new scheme to git more of our land. If you'll pardon me, dear, I hate the damned government. I read that the Federal Government owns sixty-three percent of all land west of the Mississippi and they're wantin' more. Imagine that—sixty-three percent. I don't know why they keep wantin' to take more. I guess the greedy white bastards in Washington want it all. That's the way they are, ain't they? They always been that way. They took everything we had back there and they won't be happy till they take everything we have out here."

The old woman paused and looked at the floor for a moment and gave a little laugh. She raised her eyes and looked straight at me with a quiet smile.

"Forgive me, dear. I didn't mean to be rude or use bad language—it just popped out. I'm sorry. I got carried away, didn't I?"

"That's quite alright, Mrs. Allen. We're enjoying listening to you."

"Thank you, dear. I don't often have a chance to speak my mind. I was usin' bad language to make a point, Katie. There ain't many folks who want to know what an old wore-out woman like me thinks. I appreciate you two comin' by today. You made my day, I can tell you. Your comin' by makes me feel special and once again, forgive me for usin' bad language. My momma would've give me a lickin' if she'd heard me say those words. She would've slapped my jaws for me."

I was going to respond but once again I didn't have time to say one word.

"You didn't come here to hear me complain, did you? You want to hear a story, don't you?"

"Yes, ma'am. Any kind of story you want to tell would be fine with me."

"Well, how about this," the old woman said. "The famous Mr. Ed is buried right here in Tahlequah. I can still hear his old television theme song," she continued with a broad smile, "and I can close my eyes right now and hear Mr. Ed sayin' on our little black and white TV all them years ago at the beginnin' of his show, '*Hello—I'm Mr. Ed*'. I can hear Mr. Ed shouting in his distinctive TV horse voice, '*Willlll---bbbbburrrr*'."

She laughed and laughed until tears ran down her cheeks. She paused, took off her glasses and wiped her eyes with a white lace handkerchief she had tucked up her sleeve. When she regained her composure, she leaned over and patted my knee.

"I'm so sorry dear. You're much too young for that story. You don't have any idea who Mr. Ed is, do you?"

"No ma'am. I don't think I know who you're talking about. Was Mr. Ed a famous actor or perhaps a cowboy celebrity? The name sounds familiar. I know the man that used to be on the late-night talk show with Johnny Carson was named Ed."

The old woman laughed again even louder than before. Her eyes danced with humor and she once again wiped the tears from her cheeks with her handkerchief and the back of her hand.

"Oh my dear, no. That's the wrong Ed. The fellow on the Johnny Carson Show was Ed McMahon. I watched Johnny Carson ever' night. I didn't figure you would know who Mr. Ed was. I hate to laugh at your expense dear, but the Mr. Ed I'm talkin' about, the one that's buried here in Tahlequah, was a TV actor. He was quite a celebrity in his day and you're right. He did have his own TV show. Ever'body knew Mr. Ed."

"Please forgive me, dear," she continued, "I haven't had so much pleasure at someone else's expense in a long time. I guess ever' now and then even an old woman like me needs a good laugh. Forgive me dear for laughing at you."

She patted my knee affectionately once again.

"Things change, don't they, Katie? It don't take people long to forget. When I was young, ever'body knew Mr. Ed. He's a thing of the past now—part of last century—an old relic like me."

The old woman sighed and continued, "Mr. Ed was a Hollywood star—a big star. He was a talkin' horse, dear. He was a tall, beautiful palomino 'bout sixteen hands. He was the star of his own television show in the sixties called *Mr. Ed*. I didn't figure you would know about it. You're much too young. I never see it on the television anymore. Mr. Ed is buried right here in Tahlequah. Things change, don't they dear?"

Again, she kept talking and didn't give me time to answer her rhetorical question.

"I don't figure you're interested in a story about a dead talkin' horse, dear. What kind of stories are you lookin' for young lady? I'm proud you came by to see me. I been expectin' you all morning."

"You were expecting us?"

"Yes, ma'am. I been expectin' you all morning," the old woman said looking straight into my eyes.

"I knew you was comin'. I got all dressed, put on my best stockings and straightened the livin' room just for you."

My mind was whirling. I was shocked. Before I could ask how that was possible and before the old woman could say more, Kari returned with the tea tray.

The tea service was gorgeous—quite unexpected and out of place in this old house—like the antique brass elephant doorstop holding open the front door. The teapot, the four cups, saucers, the sugar bowl and the small milk pitcher all matched and were classically elegant, obviously antique and looked expensive—very expensive. The workmanship was exquisite, the colors vibrant and the overall presentation timeless.

Kari asked her grandmother to move the yellow plastic flower arrangement from the middle of the old coffee table. She carefully set the tray between us. The delightful tea service looked out of place on the garish, green plastic serving tray next to the old couch covered in bed sheets and the coffee table with cigarette burns along the edges. Store-bought chocolate chip cookies were arranged neatly on a cracked china plate that didn't match the tea set. The old woman asked us how we preferred our tea and she carefully poured out without a word. Once we had our cup of tea and were settled back, the old woman spoke again. She never took her eyes from my face. After our introduction, Greg never said another word. I knew he was bored, but he can be patient.

The old woman's manner had become strange as if she and I were the only ones in the room. I didn't feel uncomfortable, not one bit, but I did feel as if there was something unusual about the day, the house and this old woman. One minute I was zipping down I-40 towards Fort Sill at seventy-five miles an hour intending to spend a quiet day with Greg's parents and the next minute I was drinking tea on an Indian reservation in an old house with an old woman I had never met.

I wanted to ask her why she was expecting us, but she began talking again and I didn't want to interrupt. I was determined to be patient and listen.

"Well, I got more stories. How about the story of this tea set?" the old woman said. "Would you like to hear that story, dear? I promise I won't laugh at you again."

"Oh my, yes, I love that kind of story. That's exactly the kind of thing I want to hear," I answered, and sat forward on the edge of the old stuffed chair as I carefully balanced my teacup and saucer on my knee. I love the moment a person begins their story in earnest. I've learned one never knows where someone's story will lead.

The old woman began, "The tea service we're drinking from came here to Oklahoma with my family on the Trail of Tears in 1838. Have you heard of the Trail of Tears, my dear?"

I nodded. I had heard of the Trail of Tears but knew little about it.

"The story is," she continued, "this tea service came with my great-great grandmother and was a gift from a friend of hers during that journey. That's pretty much all I know. Not much of a story, is it? I don't know where it was made or where it came from and I don't really know who the friend was. I can't imagine them having too many tea parties on the Trail of Tears, can you?"

"No, ma'am."

She didn't smile as she said that last sentence.

"I've always wondered how they managed to carry this tea set on their back eight-hundred miles over bad roads without breakin' it into little pieces. We never use it much—never have. I guess that's why it's still in one piece. Elisi had a strange custom we kids always thought. She never used this tea service except when a stranger visited, like you two. That's why we have it out today, because you're strangers. We never used it when it was just us and we still don't. We asked her why we only got it out when we had visitors, but she said that's what her elisi did. 'We must put out our best for strangers,' was all she ever said. I always took her to mean we Cherokee know what it's like to be away from home and in need of a friend and a nice cup of tea served by someone who cares. We thought about having it appraised, but that's silly, don't you think? We'll never sell it. Do you like it?"

"I love it. It's gorgeous," I said, and I meant it.

The old woman paused and took a sip of the strong tea and looked at me again over the top of her glasses.

"It's so delicate," I said, "and I adore the design and the colors and the gold trim around the edges. I don't think I've ever seen china quite like this in my life. It's obviously hand-made and hand-painted. I wouldn't be surprised if this gold around the edges isn't real gold leaf. This service wasn't mass produced by machines in a modern factory."

The old woman held her cup up and examined it carefully.

"It's beautiful, isn't it? I've loved it since I was a little girl."

I examined the delicate cup and saucer in my hand with new interest and decided I had better be extra careful. It made me nervous to know how old this cup was and that it was irreplaceable. It dawned on me this teacup was probably the oldest thing I had ever held in my hand. My inquisitive nature was aroused. Where did this tea service come from? Where was it manufactured? When? Who owned it? Who gave it to whom? How did it arrive in Tahlequah? I wanted to know the story. I should have been a detective. I would be a good one. I brought my mind back to task.

"This is a charming tea service, ma'am. Thank you so much for sharing the story. We can probably find out where this tea service was manufactured quite easily. Would you like to know where and when it was made and approximately what it's worth?"

"Oh my, yes, I would like that," the old woman answered quickly. "Could you discover those things after all these years? I'm sure it's over a hundred fifty years old. Do you know about antique china? Are you an expert in china tea sets, young lady, as well as bein' a journalist?"

"No, ma'am," I answered. "I don't know much about antiques, but if you will allow me to take some photos, I can do an online search. With photographs of the markings on the bottom of the pieces, I'm guessing I can tell you within a few years the date of manufacture and precisely where it was made and probably by whom, no matter where it came from. Have you ever watched *Antiques Roadshow*?"

"No, ma'am. I never watch that show," the old woman answered. "I don't watch much TV. I watch *Jeopardy* and *NCIS*. I like Mark Harmon, don't you? He's as cute as he can be. I watch all the *NCIS* re-runs and I watch the *TCM* channel. I like most everything that's as old as I am. I love old black and white movies and I watch some re-runs of the old shows, but most everything else on TV these days is a waste. I hate reality shows—dumbest things I ever saw and I detest the news. It's all bad news from mornin' to night, isn't it? They repeat the bad stuff over and over all day—nothin' but bad news—never any good news—not like Paul Harvey. I decided a long time ago I've heard enough bad news to last me forever. I don't need no more bad news. I don't want to fill my mind with misery from morning till night. And then if they ain't filling my mind with bad news they're tryin' to sell me some worthless thing I don't need. No, I don't watch much TV."

"I agree," I answered, with a chuckle. "I don't watch a lot of TV and I try to never watch TV news."

The old woman and I laughed together.

"With all that bad news on TV it ain't no wonder there's so many depressed people. I never watch the weather, neither. It's nice to wake up not knowing what our weather will be. I like surprises."

The old woman finally paused a moment and caught her breath and continued, "But I would love to know where my tea service came from. Oh, yes, I would love to know if you could find that information, Katie."

The old woman stared at the cup and saucer in her hand. I took a couple of dozen photos from different angles and close-ups of the markings on the bottom of the tea pot, the cups and saucers. It was a delicate and beautiful service and the research would be fun.

"Do you see these little blue crossed swords on the bottom of the pieces, Mrs. Allen?" I said. "These marks, according to what I have learned watching *Antiques Roadshow*, will tell us exactly who the manufacturer is and where and when these pieces were made, but I'll have to do some research online to discover details. It'll be fun and no problem at all, but I'll have to get back to you later."

The old woman marveled that I could use my phone to take pictures like a camera and that I could find the necessary information so easily on the internet. I took a couple of photographs of her and her granddaughter and showed her how my new phone worked.

"I'll find out what I can and send you the information. It won't take more than a few days after I get back," I told her.

"Thank you, my dear. That would be nice," the old woman said quietly.

"I'll do that first thing when I get back to Chattanooga," I said, and put my phone away. "I would like to hear some more of your stories before I leave. The reason I came to Tahlequah today is because I don't know anything about the Cherokee or their history. I was born and raised in northwest Georgia and I'm going to university just over the state line in Chattanooga, but I really don't know much about the Trail of Tears. I thought it would be a good idea to see if I could learn some Cherokee history firsthand. I'm interested in any story you might wish to share, but I would like to know why you said you were expecting me? I don't understand how that could be possible."

The old woman sighed and chuckled to herself and patted my knee again.

"Be patient my dear", she said, "and I'll tell you in a minute why I was expectin' you. No offense, but you folks who moved into our country don't ever think about us or about our Trail of Tears, do you? We been erased back East—out-of-sight and out-of-mind, you might say. I've always wondered how folks could live right where we used to live and not know about us, but things change, don't they? In the '60's ever'body knew who Mr. Ed was, but nobody knows who he is now. We used to be the Principle People but not now. I ain't surprised you don't know about us. Things change. That's what elisi used to say all the time and she was right. Of course, white folks never did care much for us Indians. They're the principle people now, aren't they?"

The old woman continued without a pause, "You asked me why there ain't no Indians in Georgia, Katie. I didn't avoid your question, my dear. I was just waitin' for the right time to answer. First thing is, when we want to speak proper we don't usually call ourselves Indians. Nowadays Indians are folks who live in India, aren't they dear, but you know that."

"Yes ma'am. I knew that. I didn't mean to be offensive," I said apologetically.

"I ain't offended, my dear," the old woman answered sweetly, "but we ain't from India and that means we're not Indians. We're Cherokee. Most folks these days call us Native Americans. Ever'body has to be politically correct, don't they? I prefer to think of myself as an old Cherokee woman who's been here for a long time. Truth is, my people have always lived here in what you call America. By the look of you—your people were English. My people was here waitin' when yours got off the boat. Somehow, my dear, I don't think my people ever thought of themselves as Native American, indigenous, First Nations or Aborigines. English folk are always trying to put a handle on anybody who ain't like them. The English like puttin' other folks in their place, don't they? They never bothered to call us by our name or even find out what our name was. The truth is we're the people who have lived here for a thousand years, Katie, and your people came from somewhere else."

"We called ourselves the Principle People—Aniyunwiya. Even the name Cherokee ain't a name we gave ourselves. Cherokee is an English corruption white folks got from the Creeks."

"I didn't know that," I said.

"Things change, don't they Katie? Before your people came, we spoke Cherokee. Today, me and you are talkin' in a language your people brought from England not so very long ago. Yep, things change," the old woman said, staring at her tea cup and saucer. "Yep, things change."

She looked up, leaned over and patted me affectionately on the knee once again. She gave me a broad smile. She was kindhearted. I could tell she wanted to make sure I wasn't offended by her correction of my loose terminology.

I wasn't offended. Her mannerisms reminded me of my own grandmother and how ultra-sensitive she was to the feelings of others.

"I ain't mad at you, Katie, an' I don't mean to hurt your feelin's for you callin' me an Indian. Everbody calls us Indians. We call ourselves Indians sometimes—hard not to. We're used to it. It's ok. When white folks first came, they thought this was India and called us Indians. They got it wrong, didn't they?"

"Yes ma'am. They did," I answered softly.

"I laugh when I think how white folks celebrate Columbus Day sayin' a disoriented Italian sailor who didn't know where he was discovered America," she continued. "We don't think much of Columbus, his day or the government that celebrates it. We think he invaded. They think Columbus found Europeans a new home, but that's another story, isn't it?

She paused again and patted my knee affectionately like I was a little puppy. I loved it.

"Forgive me, dear. Forgive me," she said without a pause. "I'll be up on my soap box before you know it. I don't want to make you mad at me. You'd think I was runnin' for mayor, wouldn't you? I know there ain't no Cherokee in Georgia and I know why. You're sweet for listenin' patiently to an old woman babble on like I'm doin' and not interruptin'. Some white folks would get mad at what I'm sayin'. I don't have much company and I guess I'm lonely. Thank you for being so polite with me."

"You're welcome, Mrs. Allen, and I love listening to you. I would never be angry with you. Say whatever it is that's on your mind. I can't tell you how interested I am in what you have to say."

The old woman laughed, "Well, Katie, these days 'bout the only thing that don't ache on my old body is my jawbone—so I guess that's why I talk so much. Talkin' is the only thing I do that don't hurt."

She laughed again when she said that and paused and stared into my eyes over the tops of her old, worn, gold-rimmed glasses—glasses that seemed to always be halfway down her nose exposing her clear bright eyes—eyes full of intelligence and kindness. She continued her lecture. I was fascinated.

"Do you still want me to tell you about Georgia and why there ain't no Cherokee there, Katie? I ain't made you mad, have I?"

I laughed and answered quickly, "Mrs. Allen, I'm privileged to be here and listen to your stories. I promise to write about my visit here today and the stories you've shared. You haven't made me angry—of course not."

"Ok, if you want to hear my stories, I'll keep goin'," the old woman said, and she took a deep breath.

"They took our country away from us, Katie—our whole country back east where you live now—what you call Georgia. White folks took every bit of it and deported us out here in '38 lock, stock and barrel. Bet you didn't know that, did you? We were forced to leave. We didn't leave by choice. Before '38, we Cherokee was in Georgia, Alabama, Tennessee and North Carolina, too. We were happy there. It was our home. It had been our home for a very long time. The Great Spirit Himself gave it to us. Then one day in May white soldiers rounded up ever' Cherokee family and brought us out here 'cause they wanted our land."

The old woman had just gotten into the beginning of her story about the Cherokee and already I had goosebumps. I was definitely in the right place.

"Their motives weren't complicated," the old woman continued. "They wanted our land. They took it and forced us out here to Oklahoma. This was the end of the earth in those days. Oklahoma didn't even have a name. I guess they would've pushed us right off the end of the world if they could've found the edge. They thought they was getting' rid of us when they brought us out here. But then they changed their mind after a while and took back most of what we had been given. White folks don't like us much, if you don't mind me sayin'."

She paused again and patted my knee.

"I don't mean you, dear, and I don't mean to offend, but if you don't know anything about that you need to read some history, don't you?"

"Yes, ma'am. I do need to read some history. I'll do that as soon as I get back to Chattanooga."

The old woman continued, "Personally, I find history books borin'—real borin'. They ain't nothing as boring as history books. Nobody likes to read that old stuff, do they? History is just one borin' thing after another with all those dates and names. I never can remember dates no matter how careful I read. When I was younger, I would read half a page in a history book and go to sleep. Maybe that's why nobody knows about those days and, anyways, who wants to talk to an old woman like me and listen to dusty ole' tales? Readin' history is as dreary as lickin' old carpet, ain't it? Worse than watchin' black and white re-runs?"

Suddenly she perked up and sat taller. I noticed her eyes sparkling over her glasses that had once again slipped down to the end of her nose as she looked into my eyes without blinking.

"But, my dear," she continued, "a well-told tale is another matter entirely, isn't it? Everybody loves stories. That's the way to learn history, ain't it? Ever'body's got time for gossip. You're in the story business. You know what I mean, don't you?"

"Yes ma'am. I know exactly what you mean. I love to read and I love to write and I love to record other people's stories. Everyone loves stories. That's why I'm here today. I think all humans have inside them an insatiable desire for story. That's what keeps TV and the publishing houses in business. How else could they sell all those tabloids and magazines at the checkout."

"You're right, dear," Kari's grandmother said with energy. "Everbody loves to hear a good story. Sometimes I think TV watchin' has made us lazy. Now-a-days we get our stories from TV instead of our imagination—instead of from books—instead of usin' our mind. We've become oversized children with an undersized vocabulary. Our heads have become soft. We need our stories spoon fed by our TV picture books. Our eyes are gettin' bigger and our brains smaller. I think television keeps us in mental kindergarten, don't you?"

Her eyes lit up as she said that. She looked directly into my face again searching my eyes to see if I understood. We connected. She was a lot smarter than she let on and I knew she didn't have an undersized vocabulary. She wasn't as uneducated as she made herself appear. I suspected her country girl vernacular and her intentional misuse of verb tenses and plurals was assumed for my benefit and used as a cover-up for an intelligent, penetrating mind. She was sharp—very sharp.

"Yes, ma'am," I answered. "That's exactly what TV does to us. My parents taught me to read when I was little—long before I went to school."

"Good for your parents, Katie."

She paused for a moment and looked at the floor and then back at me. "Katie, I'm eighty-eight years old. I was born right here in the back room of this old house in '27. My mother was born in that same room way back in '92.

It seems like yesterday I brought Kari's mother into the world in that same room in '48. Kari was born in a clinic in town in '66."

The old woman paused for a moment.

"Elisi was born after the Civil War in Park Hill. When elisi married edudu, her brothers came over and built this house for her. Nice strong house, ain't it?"

"Yes, ma'am. It is," I answered. "It's quite sturdy."

"This old house has been through many a twister, I can tell you," she said. "We put the roof back on a couple of times, but the house always stood."

"Oh yes, my dear, I've heard lots of stories right here in this old house— right here in this room and out on the porch in them old rockers watching the sun set behind the trees. I've heard stories how my great-grandma, elisi's mother, walked the Trail of Tears when she was just a girl. Now that's history, ain't it? That's a story you won't hear folks tell where you're from. All I know is elisi's mother was born somewhere in Cherokee Country in what you folks call Georgia—couldn't be too awful far from where you grew up. Soldiers brought her and her momma here in '38. Now, how would that be for a story? Would you like to hear about that?"

"Oh my, yes, I would love to hear that story. Oh yes, please," I begged. "And you say your family is from Georgia?"

I was so pleased to be here listening to Mrs. Allen and her stories. I could tell this day would be the highlight of my summer story gathering.

"We didn't call it Georgia, dear," Mrs. Allen said. "My people came from Cherokee Country—not Georgia. There ain't no difference now but there was then. We had our own nation with our own borders. Bet you didn't know that, did you?"

"No, ma'am. I didn't know that," I answered.

"We had our own written language, government, constitution and newspaper. We was civilized, just like whites folks."

When she said the word civilized she gave it a little extra stress and laughed out loud. I couldn't help but laugh with her even though I didn't understand what was behind her humor.

"Yep, we was civilized but the white folks still got rid of us. Folks on the whiteside called their country Georgia—after some king in England, but we didn't call our country Georgia. Georgia is an English name—ain't got nothin' to do with us. We had our own beautiful country given to us by our Great Spirit. The English kept takin' it piece by piece. They said our land was theirs—that their king had given them our country. They kept takin' till they finally took it all."

I was afraid to interrupt, comment or ask a question. I could tell this woman was speaking from her heart—probably saying what every Cherokee man and woman knew out here in Oklahoma. I didn't want to interrupt her flowing train of thought.

"After they took our country they made it part of Georgia," she continued. "That's all I know, dear. Don't know the village where my great-grandma was born. I guess this story is short, like the story about the tea set, there's not much more to tell. I've often thought about our country back east where you live now. I imagined what it would have been like in those days when my great-grandma was a little girl. I never met my great-grandmother. She died before I was born, but elisi, my grandmother, told me stories she heard from her elisi. I know those stories. All I know is my people lived there in Cherokee Country."

The old woman finally paused for a moment and stared out the window, obviously thinking about the story she was recounting. I imagined she was remembering things she had heard many times in this very room.

"My elisi's grandmother was five when she left Ross's Landing. I think Ross's Landing is near Chattanooga, isn't it, dear?"

"Yes ma'am. It's in Chattanooga right on the Tennessee River. I've been there many times and my university is close to that part of town."

"I never been out of Oklahoma," she answered. "I never been to Oklahoma City and I don't want to go, I can tell you. It's too busy. Too many folks and too many cars. I like it right here, thank you. I go to the grocery store, the post office and the Dollar Store. Kari an' I like John's Hickory House. We go ever' week. They got the best ribs. People come from all over for their ribs. I get half a rack or Kari an' I split a full rack. When I finish eatin' ribs, the bones are so clean you'd think I washed 'em in the sink. I don't waste nothin."

She laughed again with her lovely musical laugh, leaned over almost in my face with a big grin and patted my knee once more. I couldn't help but like this old woman who was pretending to be uneducated by using the vernacular she grew up with. She was anything but uneducated.

"Their slaw ain't as good as mine but all the other sides are good. I love their fried okra. My word, do I love okra. You can ask Kari. I always get okra and she gets mac an' cheese. We go at least once a week, but I never been

25

back east, dear. I don't reckon I'll ever go back there now. You'll just have to tell me about it, won't you, Katie?"

Once again, she took a breath and continued talking before I could ask a question or make a comment. Her granddaughter was right. She did love to talk. The longer she talked the more her face took on a far-away look as she rehearsed the old stories she had heard as a child.

"Elisi told me the stories her elisi told her about the Trail of Tears. She remembers it being hot summertime—dry and dusty. She remembered walkin' barefoot for weeks and weeks with lots of other families. The soldiers made them walk all day long ever' day. They were hungry and there were lots of sick folks, she said—and people dying. She remembers men digging graves. They never camped near any towns. They had a few tents and blankets but ever'body slept on the ground. The white soldiers gave them the same food ever' day—corn meal and salt pork. She remembered bein' terrified of big white men with their big hats lookin' down at them from high up on their mean horses. She dreamed about soldiers on horses her whole life—nightmares. She dreamed the big horses would chase the children through the woods. When the horses caught them, they would gobble up the little children with their big white teeth. What a terrible dream."

I was mesmerized. I had never heard a story like this. As the old woman talked, her visual focus drifted to some unseen place as if she were there, far beyond the horizon—beyond time itself, as she stared through the walls of her old house, reliving each sentence of the narrative she had heard from her grandmother. As she related the stories, I knew she was communicating the sights, sounds and emotions of the Trail of Tears with such an accuracy that I imagined her great-grandmother sitting there before me—rehearsing the story from actual memory. I loved it. Mrs. Allen was a skilled storyteller. I could learn a lot from this woman.

"There was wagons to carry the oldest and sickest, but the rest walked. The soldiers didn't leave nobody behind. We all had to go—ever' last one of us. A new broom sweeps clean, don't it—especially a new white broom—in Georgia. Even though she was only five, she walked barefoot the whole way—ever' step of eight hundred miles. Imagine that, Katie."

I wanted to comment, but I was afraid I would interrupt this marvelous recounting of what she had heard when she was a girl. I kept my mouth shut.

She continued, "Sometimes I dream about walkin' barefoot all that way, even though I never been there. Can you imagine soldiers makin' kids and old folks walk eight hundred miles barefoot?"

"No ma'am. I couldn't imagine that."

"Nobody never told you that story back in Georgia, did they, Katie?" she asked.

"No ma'am. I never heard stories like that when I was growing up. This is all new to me. I didn't know any of this."

"I don't reckon white folks want to tell their grandkids they're livin' on farms they stole from us. They don't want to talk about what they did to the folks they stole it from. They didn't like us much, did they?"

As I listened to the old woman, I couldn't imagine in my wildest dreams our own United States Army forcing children and their grey-headed grandparents at gunpoint to walk eight hundred miles barefoot just to take their land. It sounded like some macabre account of war in the Pacific during WWII.

There must have been mitigating circumstances? What she described would be prosecuted as war crimes today. Our government wouldn't do something like that, would they? I felt a growing nausea. This was the first time I had actually thought about what happened on the Trail of Tears.

She continued, "The soldiers kept us away from white towns and farms. I guess the government didn't want white folks to see what they was doin', like it was a big secret. My great-grandmother remembered her momma being pregnant and walkin' the whole way. According to our old family Bible, she delivered just a few weeks after they arrived in Park Hill. One of their friends died in childbirth on the trail, poor thing. Those were hard times Katie—hard times—the hardest of times. Elisi said she heard her elisi say that watchin' the woman die on the side of the road stuck in her mind her whole life. She cried herself to sleep thinkin' about the blue-bottles on the poor dead woman's eyes. I've dreamed about that myself. I'll probably dream about it again tonight, after tellin' you this. She said lots of kids and old folks died before they ever reached Oklahoma—dozens and dozens."

She patted me on the knee again and smiled, but her mind was still fixed in that faraway time. Her tone and her choice of pronouns made it sound as if it was she herself experiencing the deportation.

"If we got sick and couldn't walk the soldiers piled us into bumpy wagons and kept goin'. Many a sick Cherokee took their last breath in an army wagon bouncing down rough roads in the hot sun and was buried beside the road that evenin'—buried without a coffin in the clothes they was wearin' when they died. That's about all I remember of the stories I heard, Katie. Not much, is it, and not very happy stories, are they?"

27

"No ma'am. Those aren't happy stories," I said. I could feel my emotions beginning to bring tears to my eyes.

"But I have somethin' else you'll be interested in, Katie, since you like to read," she said. "I never did like to read history. I never did like dates and things. I'll be right back and then I'll tell you why I was expectin' you."

The old woman patted me on the knee, gave me a wonderfully warm maternal smile—a smile I needed. She stood with the help of her cane and walked slowly towards the rear of her little house. Just before she disappeared into her bedroom, she gave me a look over her shoulder—a look that made me feel a little awkward, as if she were trying to understand something deep inside me or make some decision concerning me. The old woman was just as sweet as she could be, but her penetrating looks were making me uneasy. I knew there was a mystery in this house and I guessed it had to do with the Cherokee. In a minute or two the old woman shuffled back with her cane in one hand and a large, tattered, old book held securely under her other arm— a very old book. She sat down next to me slightly out of breath holding the heavy volume fast with both hands in her lap. She gripped the book so tightly the knuckles of her gnarled old fingers had gone white, as if she was afraid the book would fly away. It took her a minute to catch her breath.

"I dreamed last night, Katie."

She paused again to catch her breath.

"I dreamed about this book right here in my lap, plain as day."

She smiled.

"I dreamed in color—fancy that. I don't usually dream in colors, but I did last night. The colors were vivid, like a rainbow or neon signs at night. I can close my eyes and see them. I can't tell you how lovely that dream was."

I couldn't imagine where she was going. I was transfixed by this old woman and her stories.

"This old book has been in our family since we came here in '38. My family has two things from the old days. We have this tea service and this book. They both came on the trail. There ain't much else in this house worth anything, 'cept me and my granddaughter."

She laughed and patted me on the knee again and continued without waiting for a response.

"I haven't thought about this book in years, Katie, but last night I dreamed about this very book. I don't dream much anymore, like I used to when I was younger. With all the medication doctors have me on, I sleep like I'm dead.

Last night I dreamed like a child. I don't even remember getting up to pee. For the first time in my life I dreamed about this book, this very book here in my lap, and the next day you show up asking about stories, stories from this book."

"Queer, isn't it?"

"Yes, ma'am. It is strange," I agreed, still wondering what the old woman would say next.

"Since you walked in that door, Katie, all this has been curious."

I didn't know what to do or say. My journalistic wit had evaporated. My mind had gone blank. My normal ability to asked pointed questions and get to the heart of a matter was gone. It was all I could do to listen. I decided I should be patient and learn.

"I guess you want to hear my dream?"

"Yes, ma'am," was all I was able to say.

"I dreamed I was a little girl walkin' barefoot on a dusty road, the Trail of Tears we been talkin' about, with my great-grandmother, her mother and other Cherokee folk. I see us in the old clothin' walkin' along and none of us with shoes—but that ain't really a problem, dear. I never did like shoes—still don't. I go barefoot most of the time. I only got shoes on now 'cause I knew you was comin'. There was a bright blue sky overhead—so blue it would hurt your eyes to look at it and the brilliant orange sun was a shinin' on the dark green grass growin' tall and lush beside the road."

"I remember a bright red cardinal feedin' under a tree—just as bright red as a fire engine and his mask black as night. My dream was vivid like a child's colorin' book. A tall, graceful woman, with coal black hair and a newborn on her back, was walkin' with us and she bent over and handed me this book, this very book in my lap. Her teeth were white as snow and straight as could be."

"She was beautiful, I can tell you—like an angel. I never saw a woman as pretty as she was. In the sunshine, her black hair glistened like a wet coal pile after a rain. She had kind eyes. Plain as day she told me to keep the book safe. I was to keep the book safe and give the book to the pregnant woman who tells stories, the woman said to me in my dream."

"Those were her exact words. In my dream she repeated that same sentence three times, 'give the book to the pregnant woman who tells stories' and she handed me the book—this book right here in my lap."

"That's it. The dream was over when she gave me this book. That's all I remember."

29

I was speechless.

Mrs. Allen tilted her head forward and looked at me over the tops of her glasses, "I reckon, Katie, you're the pregnant woman who tells stories I dreamed about last night, unless that's a pillow under your shirt."

The old woman laughed, patted my knee again and broke the tension. I was stunned. I couldn't speak. What was happening? I was dizzy. I felt sick to my stomach. I wasn't in control. What had I just heard? Things like this didn't happen in real life, did they? Was I living a dream or was this some convoluted Hollywood drama and I was really an actress on stage? Would I wake up in a minute? What was I doing in this old house in an out of the way corner of Oklahoma? How did I get here?

Silently, the old woman slowly pushed the old book into my lap under my unresisting hands. It was as if my hands and fingers and tongue were paralyzed.

"It was you I was told about in my dream, Katie. This book is meant for you. I don't have the story you came here lookin' for. I never did. You didn't come to Tahlequah to hear about a talkin' horse, an antique tea service or me walkin' barefoot. You didn't come here to listen to my stories. The story you're lookin' for is in this book."

The old woman put both her hands on top of mine as I held the old book.

"You were called, Katie. You were summoned. I'm supposed to give this book to you. If you decide to tell the book's story, be careful, my dear. It's goin' to be a story with many a twist and turn and you may not like events along the way or how it ends, but whatever you do, be true to the story, Katie. Don't sugar coat nothin'."

"Yes ma'am. I will. I promise."

"Tell the story like the woman said. Keep the book, Katie and tell its story. Tell it true. This book has been waitin' all these years for somebody who knows about readin' and writin' and grew up in Cherokee Country. It was waitin' in this house all these years on you, Katie. You grew up in Cherokee Country. This book wants to return home with you and complete the circle. It's been waitin' here all these years for you to take it back where it came from."

The old woman's far away mood suddenly changed to one much lighter as she slowly lifted the stained cotton tea cozy and poured us another cup of tea. She sipped her second cup and quietly looked at the floor. I was grateful she wasn't looking at me for a change. I was trying to sort out my confused thoughts. My mind was numb as I felt the weight of the book on my legs and wondered what mysteries I held in my lap. I was happy to have the tea cup to occupy my hands. The old woman wore a warm disarming smile as we sipped our tea. After a long time she finally broke the silence.

"It's an ugly old book, ain't it?" she said with a wry smile. "It was my great-grandmother's. She passed the tea service and this old book down to us. These two things have been in our family for a long time—ever' since we got here. I tried to read it a few times but the writin' is tiny and confusin' with all kinds of loops and whirls and all crowded together. I never seen writin' like that but I know there's a story in there—the story you're supposed to take back to Cherokee Country where it belongs—where it was written—where you grew up."

"We kept this old book in a wooden flour box that I think maybe came on the trail, too. To my knowledge, no one outside our family has seen this book—much less read it. You're the first, Katie. We still don't trust white folks much, and you can guess why. After my dream last night, I'm certain you're the person it was meant for. It's been waitin' on you. Words and writin' are your business, aren't they?"

I nodded. As I held my cup and saucer I looked down at the old book with the tattered corners lying in my lap. It was heavy. As the book lay there on my legs it felt alive, like a living thing. I felt as if it possessed a conscious mind and was trying even now to communicate with me on some obscure frequency, like a phone on vibrate. I felt as if I were in the wrong place and the old woman was mistaken. Surely the book was meant for someone else, for someone older, for someone more responsible with vast literary experience. I felt as if the old book was hazardous. I have never been afraid of ghosts, but the thought of the old woman's dream and knowing she had been expecting me made the hair on the back of my neck stand. When I was little, I was always afraid to watch horror films and now I was unexpectedly in the middle of something just as bizarre with no means of escape. I felt trapped.

"I don't really need to keep this book, ma'am. If you'll allow me, I'll have a copy made and return the original this afternoon. Would that be ok?"

"That would be fine, dear," she answered.

"I would feel better if you kept the original here and I had a copy," I said.

I wanted to get rid of the book, as if it were possessed and a photocopy would render the malevolent spirit within harmless.

"That would be perfectly ok, my dear."

31

We got up to leave and the old woman and her granddaughter thanked us for coming and listening to her stories. As they walked us to the door, the old woman looked tired and more bent and crooked than ever. Her energy had been drained by our visit and her storytelling. The hump on her poor old back seemed larger than when I arrived. She gently placed a quivering old hand on my arm.

"I'm tired, dear. I think I'll go take a nap after you leave. Before you go, I got one last thing to tell you."

"Yes, ma'am?" I said.

"I have no idea how this will turn out for you, Katie, but I'm sure the young woman in my dream is pleased you'll be tellin' her story. She brought you here. You'll do just fine. I'm sure of that. As you write, think about one thing for me, dear."

"I'll think about anything you want me to, Mrs. Allen, I promise."

The old woman looked into my eyes one last time and squeezed my arm. Her words, spoken almost in a whisper, seemed to echo from a great distance or from another era.

"Think about one thing as you tell the story. White folks back in Georgia need to answer this one question."

"When does the thief legally own that thing he stole?"

Chapter III

Katie's Dream - Return to Chattanooga

Chapter 3

Greg and I found a print shop, copied the journal and returned the original as fast as we could. I was relieved. I decided to walk around and decompress before I began to peruse my new treasure.

Tahlequah isn't an ordinary town as I first imagined. I noticed the unusual street names: Choctaw St., Chickasaw St., Keetoowah St., Shawnee St. and Cherokee Avenue. Greg and I took our time and looked at everything. We walked past the Cherokee Nation Courthouse on S. Muskogee Avenue. Across E. Keetoowah St. from the courthouse was the Cherokee Supreme Court Museum and the Cherokee Arts Center. I read every historical marker we passed. After two hours I was ready to go back to the room, relax and study the journal.

When we got back to the bed and breakfast, Greg ordered our favorite pizza, got himself comfortable on the king-size bed to watch a movie and let me do my thing. Greg is a TV person. He never reads. How he can get through college without reading I'll never know. My parents taught me to think for myself—to read and use my imagination. They told me watching television is like having someone do your imagining for you. The worst TV shows are those with canned laughter so you'll know what's funny and when to laugh—how silly and insulting. I want to think for myself and decide what's funny and what isn't. I like to write, be creative and use my own mind. I hardly ever watch TV.

Greg turned on the television, threw back the hand-stitched comforter and helped me prop on the feather pillows against the tall hand-carved antique headboard. I turned on the bedside lamp and picked up my copy of the old woman's book. What was in this old book that a white person hadn't seen in over a hundred and fifty years? I was excited. I felt my pulse quicken. What was I holding in my hand?

My copy of the journal was spiral bound. The interior was printed on high-quality 80-pound opaque text. The covers were copied on a high-quality color copier to give them the exact look of the original—both front and back. Except for the tattered corners, the trimmed final product was a perfect duplicate of the original—sturdy and easy to handle.

33

I examined the covers and began flipping through the pages reading an odd passage here and there. What did this old journal contain? The thick book was full of old-fashioned, handwritten text with just a few blank pages remaining at the very end. Whose life did I hold in my hands? Was I the first to read it? I wondered about the old woman, her stories, her colorful dream and how all that related to this document. I wondered how much of her stories were the invention of a lonely mind.

As I flipped through the pages, I tried to visualize where the journal was originally printed, who sold it, who bought it and who was the clerk who recorded the business entries? Who rescued the old ledger when it was finally discarded and how in the world did it end up in Oklahoma? I wanted answers. As I leaned back against the feather pillows, I knew the journal would take me to another world, a marvelous world of mystery, a world hidden for well over a century—a world awaiting my exploration.

I began to answer my questions systematically. The journal was a large re-purposed business ledger printed on foolscap and probably imported from England. The business ledger's opening date was January 1818. It recorded inventory, pricing, sales and receipts from an international shipping business in Savannah. The faint printed guide-lines were narrow—for economy I suppose. I could see a near-sighted overworked clerk hunched over his desk in a tall straight-back wooden chair almost two hundred years ago in a dockside Savannah warehouse. I can see him straining his eyes beside an oversized sash window recording bills of lading, shipping manifests, receipts and expenditures in a masculine hand so neat it looked as if it had been printed mechanically. I was amazed.

As I sat propped up in my comfortable king-size bed in Tahlequah, my imagination swirled with antebellum images of the unknown industrious clerk dipping his pen into his black inkwell. Outside his window tall ships would have been moored stem to stern as far as you could see with scurrying stevedores handling freight from around the world. If I had questions earlier, I had ten thousand now.

The unnamed clerk wrote symmetrically in perfect columns within the printed guidelines. After the book was repurposed, the subsequent journal writer began writing on the first available blank space on the inside front cover and wrote over, under, between and beside everything recorded by the clerk. The journal writer used small characters with almost no space between lines until no blank space whatsoever remained on the page. When the journal writer filled all the pages used by the clerk, the writer began filling the unused blank pages towards the end of the ledger—edge to edge, top to bottom—front and back.

Following the sequence of the journal writer's winding entries was a trick and would have been impossible without the dates of each entry. I laughed out loud when I saw how crowded the text was. Greg had to know what was so funny. I told him the journal writer reminded me of my grandmother's letters when. Every time my grandmother wrote me it was if she was using the last piece of paper she would ever be allowed. Her writing was small and the sentences jammed together. When my grandmother ran out of room on the front of her letters she would continue on the back. When she ran out of room on the back she turned the paper sideways and wrote in the margins until the paper was filled, edge to edge, top to bottom, on both sides in an impossible to follow sequence. I laughed out loud again. My grandmother made a point in every letter to use every square centimeter of space. I would always have to ask my mother to decipher my grandmother's letters. I suppose my frugal grandmother learned thriftiness from her parents who lived through the depression. All blank space must be filled—waste not, want not, I can hear her say. When I would visit with my grandmother she would follow me around turning off lights. I miss her terribly.

In like manner, the pages of the journal were crammed full of text, top to bottom, edge to edge, front and back. Whoever wrote this journal didn't waste paper—not one square inch. Blank space was at a premium.

The journal entries, unlike the business entries of the clerk, were in a compressed but flowing cursive feminine hand. The precise penmanship was more ornate than anything one sees today. The journal writer was neat and graceful. Her penmanship looked like modern professional calligraphy—like artwork. I began to think of more unanswered questions about the unknown person behind the pen.

I flipped back to the beginning. I noticed what appeared to be a transliterated word I suspected was Cherokee. Next to it, written neatly in English, was the name 'Cassie'. When I read the name Cassie, my baby kicked for the first time. I had felt my baby move but never kick like that. This day had suddenly become even more bizarre—if that were possible.

The business ledger, in the masculine hand, began in 1818. The first entry in the feminine hand was dated 1820 and written in English. It appears the journal writer was a Cherokee girl named Cassie. Throughout the journal I noticed occasional transliterated headings, but with the exception of those few transliterations, the journal was written entirely in English—excellent

35

English. I learned the writer was a young female, was classically educated with a stronger vocabulary than mine, had a friend named Ben and she possessed a keen interest in her political milieu.

I discovered from my first perusal the writer had been caught up in the Cherokee removal. Sadly, the journal entries ended abruptly without explanation in July, 1838. Why? As I lay propped against the pillows in Tahlequah, Oklahoma, I had an overpowering desire to learn everything about this young woman—every detail of her life. I felt as if I had been tasked to become a historical detective. I felt a pang of disappointment to think the end of her story would forever remain a mystery. How sad. How poignant to think someone would faithfully keep a journal for almost two decades and not finish. I wonder what happened? As I lay propped on my pillows, I felt an overpowering desire for a happy ending, but it was apparent I would never learn what happened to Cassie.

There was a huge amount of material in this journal, much more than I first thought. I skipped around and read odd passages here and there until long after midnight. Greg, full of pizza, had fallen sound asleep halfway through his movie. I suddenly realized I was tired—bone tired. My mind was tired. I fancied even my toes were tired. I was physically and mentally exhausted. It had been a long, arduous day. My emotions had been drained. I leaned back on the feather pillows without turning off the lamp, laid the open journal face down on my stomach, closed my eyes and fell into a deep sleep and dreamt about that mysterious place where they keep their Indians.

That night, in Tahlequah, Oklahoma, I first heard the voice in my dreams, or maybe it wasn't a dream. I'm still not sure. My dream was vivid.

In my dream, I was looking through an immense picture window at a bright daytime landscape. The sky was a rich bright blue with scattered inky black clouds. The clouds were as black as if someone were burning tires. Oddly, I saw myself walking alone down a wide unpaved country road. I watched myself stop at a bright green tree and listen to three beautiful bluebirds singing just for me. I could hear their song, and it seemed the birds followed my progress. The scene reminded me of the *Zip-a-Dee-Doo-Dah* sequence in the now politically incorrect *Song of the South*. I was indeed viewing 'a wonderful day'. The colors were intense.

I don't remember seeing another person in my dream, but I did hear a voice addressing me. I would remember that voice forty years from now. I would remember it if I heard it in the middle of a busy mall or a rowdy soccer match. It was a musical woman's voice and I knew instantly the friendly person behind the voice loved me.

As I walked that lovely country road, the voice said to me three times, 'Tell my story, tell my story, tell my story'.

When I heard the voice in my dream, I instantly sat bolt upright—wide awake—grasping the open journal still on my stomach. It was as if I was awake when I heard the voice—a voice so real I was certain the words I heard were spoken by someone in the room. I was frightened.

The light was still on. I jumped out of bed to check the room. The door was double locked with those secondary latches that make motel doors impossible to open from the outside even with a pass key. The window was permanently closed with big metal screws. No one was in the bathroom, shower, closet or under the bed. We were alone. Greg was snoring. The voice must have come to me in my dream—it must have. There was no other explanation. How could that be? Was I suffering some kind of nocturnal psychotic episode triggered by a weary overactive imagination?

I remembered the old woman saying the story was pursuing me. I shivered from a sudden childish fear of the dark and was afraid to turn off the bedside lamp. I needed to think and this thing with the journal, the old woman's dream, my baby kicking and now a voice invading my own colorful Disney-like dream was making me believe I was in some kind of sci-fi story or going crazy. Rod Serling could have used my day for an old *Twilight Zone* episode. The last time I remember looking at the clock it was after four. I didn't wake Greg. He wouldn't have been much comfort, and I probably couldn't have wakened him anyway. When I finally went back to sleep, I must have slept dreamlessly. I remember nothing.

I recall little about our visit with Greg's parents or the trip back to Chattanooga. I gathered plenty of material on the return journey for my university project, but I can't bring to mind the gist of one story from the homeward trip without referring to notes.

Since the day I returned from my summer trip I've been spending extraordinary amounts of time in the Chattanooga library on the third floor trying to understand the journal and its historical milieu. My journalism professor was on vacation when I returned. I couldn't wait to share my discovery with him.

If I wanted to understand this woman's life and her journal, I would need a crash course in Cherokee history. I had a lot on my plate.

The journal was written between 1820 and 1838. I searched my mind for what I knew of American history during those years. I drew a blank—a complete blank. I couldn't tell you one thing that happened during those eighteen years—nothing, nil, zero, zilch, nada. How could that be? How could an educated university student like me, about to receive her masters in journalism, be so ignorant of our American history?

As a personal research project, and to satisfy my own curiosity, I began asking friends, classmates, instructors and even casual acquaintances one simple question. I asked if they could tell me one event that occurred in American history between 1820 and 1838. I asked dozens and dozens of people my question—young and old.

No one I asked knew anything. Everyone was as ignorant as I was. One older man proudly said the battle of the Alamo was fought in 1836. The battle of the Alamo was fought in 1836, but at that time San Antonio and the Alamo were part of the northernmost province of Mexico and part of a Mexican civil war—a war between the Mexican government and rebellious white immigrants who had crossed into Mexico from the United States. It wasn't until February, 1845, that our Congress narrowly passed a bill that would annex the breakaway Mexican province, if the Texans agreed. They agreed. Understandably, Mexico has never come to terms with our unilaterally annexing their northernmost province. Who can blame them?

During my research I have come to realize nothing much remains of hundreds of years of Cherokee history around Chattanooga and north Georgia except a few scattered plaques and the memorials at Ross's Landing and Blythe's ferry. It's as if the Cherokee, their artifacts and their history were removed from my part of the world.

Greg and I go to the Riverbend Music Festival every year down by the Tennessee River in Chattanooga. We enjoy the food, listen to the bands and delight in the carefree carnival atmosphere. I adore the funnel cakes with all that delicious powdered sugar—yum. Riverbend is a unique music festival that takes place just yards from where thousands of Cherokee families were forcibly deported from their homeland.

Every year Greg and I get a wristband for Riverbend and never miss a night. Right there on the riverbank under and near the Highway 27 bridge is where the bands play. Ross's Landing was slightly upriver from Riverbend. There's nothing at the nearby site of Ross's Landing today to indicate the precise location of the old Cherokee trading post and village, other than a plaque or two and the memorial up on the hill between the river and the aquarium. There's not a thing to be seen from Riverbend.

John and Lewis Ross's trading post was of wooden construction and is long gone. Common photography wasn't in general use until after 1839 so there is no photographic record of the Cherokee Nation in and around Chattanooga. Since the construction of the Hales Bar dam in 1913, replaced by the Nickajack dam in 1967, and the completion of Chickamauga dam in January of 1940, the river level in Chattanooga is higher than in 1838.

In my research I found no extant drawings of Ross's Landing and pitifully few eyewitness accounts of Cherokee occupation or their removal. About all I could find were terse military reports, ration books and emigration rolls. I did read the Reverend Daniel Butrick's journal and found it somewhat useful. He lived and worked at the Brainerd Mission seven miles east of Ross's Landing on the other side of Missionary Ridge, where Brainerd Village is today. In his journal Reverend Butrick was primarily concerned with his parishioners.

The United States government referred to the removal of the Cherokee as emigration, the Cherokee problem or the Cherokee disturbance. Our government's convenient use of language back then reminds me how our government today euphemistically refers to the accidental killing of civilians in wartime as collateral damage.

Just up river and within walking distance of the Riverbend venue is the Market Street Bridge erected in 1930. The bridge has been graciously re-named the John Ross Bridge. The text of the two brass plaques placed at the ends of the bridge in 1930 are still there and reflect the mindset of the residents of Chattanooga when the bridge was constructed.

The 1930 plaque reads:

> "This Tablet marks the site of Ross's Landing--Here a Cherokee trading station was maintained by John and Lewis Ross during the early part of the 19th century. From this point, in 1813, General John Cocke led the East Tennessee troops through the Cherokee Nation to join General Andrew Jackson in the Creek war. Ross's Landing was designated as one of the three places of rendezvous for the removal of the Cherokee in February 1838. A ferry was operated at this place and around it grew up a flourishing village called Ross's Landing. On 14 November 1839 the name was changed to Chattanooga."

The military action of United States Army generals against Creek Indians was given center stage in this brief memorial. My curiosity was growing about our sanitized view of history—especially as it pertained to Cherokee history. Evidently, the death of thousands of Cherokee while under arrest by the United States military was considered collateral damage—therefore our government was not culpable and it wasn't worthy of mention.

I visited the new Cherokee memorial near the old Blythe Ferry. The seven raised stones record the 2,537 households from the 1835 Cherokee census. The memorial is impressive. When he was a little boy my grandfather crossed the river many times near here on the old Birchwood Ferry with his grandparents—the same crossing as the 1838 Blythe Ferry. The old Birchwood Ferry is gone—replaced by a modern bridge. Things change, don't they?

I appreciate the Passage memorial across the street from the Aquarium. The Cherokee memorial is located on the hill just above the area where Ross's Landing may have had their docking facilities for the big steamboats. The Passage is a permanent outdoor exhibit showing the seven Cherokee clans, a weeping wall, seven six-foot high disks recording the Cherokee story and a fourteen-foot high stainless-steel sculpture of Cherokee stickball players. It's a well thought out memorial.

I saw an aerial view of the Passage memorial and it struck me how minuscule it appears from the air, tiny and insignificant, disappearing between the rows of huge high-rise commercial buildings in the wide prosperous streets of our modern Chattanooga.

In 1835, Ross's Landing, on the Cherokee northern boundary, was a small Cherokee owned trading post and ferry with maybe two hundred full time residents—maybe not that many.

At that time, the Tennessee River was the northern and western boundary between the Cherokee Nation and the states of Tennessee, Alabama and Georgia. Before 1838, travelers going down from Nashville to Milledgeville or Savannah would have to pass through Cherokee Country and pay a toll to the ferry owner—a Cherokee. It was interesting to learn that these tolls created a small but prosperous Cherokee upper class.

By the spring of 1838, with the influx of the U.S. Army, government officials, Tennessee and Georgia militias, multitudes of contractors, hordes of squatters, ne'er-do-wells and scavengers and the incarceration of thousands of Cherokee in prison camps, the population in and around Ross's Landing would have swelled to as many as twenty thousand—probably more. Add horses, mules, donkeys, cows, oxen, dogs, chickens and hogs and it would have been a disorganized maze of camps and hastily constructed wooden structures—houses, barracks, forts, inns, stables, barns and corrals impossible for us to imagine in our modern world.

Before 1838 there were few permanent structures on the Cherokee side of the Tennessee River. In 1837 and 1838 temporary camps were erected as far as one could see in every direction preparing for the government ordered removal. Just forty miles up the road in Charleston, Tennessee, present day Cleveland, there was another large military operation rounding up and imprisoning the North Carolina Cherokee—another ten thousand souls, more or less.

In the spring of 1838, Ross's Landing would have been a chaotic madhouse generating a cacophony of competing sounds and unique odors. Morning and evening smoke from cooking fires would have filled the sky. It would have been an unforgettable sight. No one would see anything like it again until after1861 and the subsequent invasion of Federal armies.

Seven miles east of Ross's Landing was a long-established Christian mission to the Cherokee, opened in 1817 and visited by President James Madison, with fewer than a hundred Cherokee residents and staff. It was located where Brainerd Village and Eastgate are today. It was overseen by the *American Board of Commissioners for Foreign Missions*. Resident Cherokee youth were taught the English language and white European/American customs. Young Cherokee men were taught trades and farming. The girls were taught to be keepers of the home—to spin, cook and sew. The general government, the term widely used to describe what we refer to as the federal government, used Christian missionary societies as a government tool to teach Indians white language and customs and thus facilitate their absorption into white society and hasten their cultural demise.

Nothing remains of the Brainerd mission except their graveyard, which is open to the public and is still there if you care to visit. The graveyard is one of the few places in Chattanooga where the final resting place of any of the Cherokee who died during the removal are honored. You can find it located directly between the old Eastgate Mall and Brainerd Village. Look for the out-of-place square of mature trees in the midst of concrete and asphalt.

According to my research, the many hundreds who died in the camps around Ross's Landing and Charleston and the space in-between remain buried in unmarked graves—under buildings, under sports facilities, under roads and under farmland. In 1913, the new Hales Bar dam flooded many more native American gravesites. In 1915, government bulldozers pushed all remaining ancient Native American burial sites in that area into the Tennessee River to make way for Chattanooga's new Riverside Drive.

In 1830, the United States Congress, led by president Andrew Jackson, passed the Indian Removal Act authorizing the 'extinguishment' of all Indian land rights east of the Mississippi. U.S. Army General Winfield Scott accomplished that mandated removal in the first weeks of June of 1838. In October of 1838 the Christian mission at Brainerd closed and the remaining Cherokee were deported in the autumn of that year marking the end of Cherokee Country. By 1839 the Cherokee were gone, extinguished—the word the federal and state governments used in their documents.

In 1838 the deportation was enthusiastically welcomed by the state and federal government and the white populace at large. Georgia, Tennessee, Alabama and North Carolina opened up all of Cherokee Country to legal white settlement. Most of our present-day Smokey Mountain National Park was seized in 1838 from the Cherokee Nation—the result of the 1830 Indian Removal Act.

Soon afterward on 14 November 1839, the City of Chattanooga was incorporated on what had been Cherokee land. The Scenic City was built on what had been the year previous sovereign Cherokee soil.

I tried to visualize the location of the ferry and the steamboat docks and the center of Ross's Landing, but I found the task impossible. I couldn't find enough information. Greg and I parked as close as we could to where we thought the docks had been. I had my own crude hand drawn maps from my limited research and I tried to imagine the 1838 scene among the modern buildings and streets and the tidy lawns of the peaceful park on Riverside Drive beside the river. We drove up the river towards the UTC Scrappy Moore football practice field and past the Market Street and Walnut Street bridges. The old Walnut Street Bridge is a pedestrian bridge and tourist attraction now. My grandfather remembers as a small child riding over the Walnut Street Bridge with his grandmother in her old yellow Studebaker. What a memory.

Why don't we have more detailed accounts of the removal? Non-military records are scarce to non-existent. No one, military or civilian, cared to chronicle the deportation of the entire Cherokee Nation.

Two large Cherokee prison camps were located not far from Ross's Landing. Their exact locations are lost. From the top of the hill I looked down and tried to imagine those two crowded prison camps.

From what I've read, the Cherokee were packed together in open areas with scanty shelter, no sanitary facilities or provisions for cooking. They were supplied with a few tents and slept on the ground.

Where exactly did the Cherokee mothers cradle their babies while they waited their fate? Where were the docks where hundreds of families were herded under guard into the crowded, noisy steam vessels? I tried to visualize the overloaded steamboats as they powered down the dangerous river with hastily constructed, leaky wooden passenger barges lashed to their sides in early June of 1838.

Before the construction of the TVA dams on the Tennessee River, the water levels would have been lower at Ross's Landing. I pictured a young Cherokee mother, separated from her husband, struggling with a couple of terrified children as impatient white soldiers ordered her and her children down the hill into the frightening, smoking contraption at the water's edge to carry her and her babies to a land she knew nothing of. The young soldiers would have given their orders in a language the woman would not have understood and threatened her with violence if she disobeyed. I'm having difficulty imagining my government ordering the deporting of an entire nation for one reason—to possess their land.

Where were the Federal troops housed? Where were the Tennessee and Georgia Militia camped? Where were the several hundred Creeks imprisoned who were rounded up with the Cherokee? Where did the civilian contractors and wagon drivers eat and sleep and keep their thousands of draft animals? Who was housing, feeding and shoeing the thousands of horses and mules required? Who daily supplied the immense amounts of grain and fodder necessary? Who hauled the water?

Who carried off the mountains of manure? For those who were there, the sights, sounds and smells of Ross's Landing and the Cherokee removal would be unforgettable.

As I stood on the hill overlooking the river, I tried to envision the scene and explain it to Greg but my mind went blank. Everything I tried to call up into my imagination disappeared. I admit I cried uncontrollably. Greg thinks I'm taking the journal and my research too seriously and that I'm a bit crazy. He took me home early that night from Riverbend. He wasn't happy.

Chapter IV

The Second Journal

Chapter 4

I sent the old woman the information I discovered about her tea service. I enjoyed the research. I was quite surprised to learn her tea set was manufactured about 1790 in the Meissen factory in Germany. It's the oldest porcelain factory in Europe and still in business. The blue crossed swords with the asterisk on the bottom of the pieces indicated the set was manufactured between 1774-1815. I learned the Meissen company changes its markings periodically to signpost different time periods of manufacture. According to my amateur research, the old woman's tea set could be worth upwards of fifteen thousand dollars, maybe more, depending on the rarity and condition. I grinned to myself when I suggested she should have the set appraised and consider locking her door when they went for a barbecue.

A few days later I got a phone call. I had a premonition it was the old woman. I was right.

"I received your letter this morning. Thank you so much for the information on the tea service," she said. "I appreciate you taking the time to do that research for me."

"You're welcome, Mrs. Allen. It was really not much work at all. It was a pleasure for me to help you learn where the tea service came from."

"I would never have guessed after all these years you could find that information" she answered, "and thank you, dear, for the calligraphy display card. It looks so nice in my little china cabinet."

"You are most welcome," I answered. "It was no trouble. A friend did the calligraphy at no charge. It was the least I could do."

"Katie, your visit has renewed my interest in my family's history. Since your visit I've been searching every little nook and cranny in this old house. I've discovered things I haven't seen in fifty years. Just yesterday I found a small box I never remember seeing. In that old box I found a sheaf of yellowed papers—interesting papers. I suspect the papers may be another journal. They're written in a cursive hand much like the one you copied. Do you want a copy of these papers also, Katie?"

"Yes, please, please. I would love a copy," I answered quickly. "I'll send fifty dollars today, and you can overnight them to me and keep the difference. Will that work?"

She agreed. Two days later I received a FedEx envelope and ripped it open on my front steps. The old woman sent me the sixty-five page document copied and spiral bound just like the first journal—Cassie's journal.

The handwriting of this second journal was in a small cursive hand, almost identical to the first journal, although not quite as neat. There had been some water damage to the originals, but the copies were legible and apparently no text was missing. What a find. My hands quivered with excitement.

As I impatiently flipped through the pages there at my front door, I discovered it was indeed a personal journal similar to the first one and probably from the same time period. The hair on the back of my neck was standing. Was it possible this document was related to the first journal? If the two were connected, it could provide clues to the missing conclusion of Cassie's journal. Since the two documents were found in the same house, they must be associated in some way. They had to be. This was my lucky day. I should go buy a lottery ticket.

My research was paying dividends. The facts were coming together. I was learning tons of new information about our antebellum history and the Cherokee removal. Here I am doing investigative journalism a hundred and fifty years after the fact and loving it. Most of the staff on the third floor at the Chattanooga Library already know me by name.

Cassie's journal began in 1820 in a Cherokee community near New Echota not far south of where I was reared—near Calhoun, Georgia. Her journal ended abruptly on an obscure country road in Tennessee west of Ross's Landing in early July 1838.

The text in both the first and second journal were written in the first person—but not the same person. A Cherokee woman named Cassie wrote the first journal. I don't know the author of the second journal, but I'm sure I'll eventually find out. I am looking forward to every moment of my detective work. I'm amazed at the historical details I can uncover so many years after the fact.

The author of the second journal was deported in the same detachment with Cassie. Coincidentally, she was about Cassie's age and also pregnant. The author of this second journal completed the eight-hundred-mile journey arriving safely with her children at Park Hill where she delivered a healthy baby girl.

It appears this second journal writer had been associated with the Brainerd Mission in some kind of teaching capacity but, I could tell from the text, was not nearly as well-educated as Cassie. My guess is the author of the second journal would be the correct age to be the great-great grandmother of the old woman I visited in Tahlequah. This story is developing and becoming more fascinating every day.

Cassie's journal ended shortly after her detachment left Ross's Landing. The second journal, thankfully, chronicled the entire eight-hundred-mile trip recording detailed information about the writer's children and a small group of expecting women—recording sickness, deaths and births and the like. But why did Cassie's journal end so early in the journey? Why did she stop writing? Perhaps I would never know.

How difficult that eight-hundred-mile journey must have been for the pregnant women forced to walk. General Scott, overseeing the removal, ordered all able-bodied Cherokee to walk—walking would be good for them, he said in his orders.

It's impossible for me to visualize our young United States Army soldiers deporting the entire Cherokee Nation simply to allow white farmers to occupy their land and so we could enjoy Smokey Mountain National Park in October. How could this have happened? How could our government have permitted this? I discovered our government didn't permit the removal. They made it happen.

Now that I have the second journal, I want to know what happened. I want to know why. I want to know every detail. I want to know Cassie's story. Will I ever learn the truth or will this brave young woman's life lie hidden forever beneath an impenetrable historical shroud? I will never be the same after this research and I don't nearly have the pride in my country as before.

I don't suppose there's anything I can do to right an old wrong, but the big question for me is why didn't I know about this? I grew up in the middle of what used to be Cherokee Country and until recently I didn't know a thing about Cherokee history. The old woman was right. Our government's actions are long forgotten—erased as the old woman in Tahlequah said. That's certainly true in my case.

My government described the removal as emigration. The place where the Cherokee were held at Ross's Landing the government called a camp. Today we would call it a prisoner of war camp. The Cherokee weren't on a weekend camping holiday—they were under arrest by foreigners who couldn't speak their language.

Within a couple of weeks of that day in May, the entire Cherokee Nation was arrested. They were removed from their homes and escorted to three main deportation centers: Gadsden in Alabama, Ross's Landing and Charleston in Tennessee where they were confined in open fields under twenty-four-hour armed guard until deported.

My government provided no permanent shelters, latrines, cooking facilities, utensils, clean water or fuel for their prisoners. Cherokee families slept on the ground and were supplied by the army with meager rations. It wasn't unknown for Cherokee families to eat uncooked or partially cooked food while in detention.

The few doctors supplied by the government spoke a foreign language—English. That sounds strange, doesn't it? The Cherokee prison camps echo those I've read about in WWII. These prison camps I'm learning about weren't in Poland or Germany or some impossible-to-find Pacific island. The Cherokee were arrested and confined in the middle of our beautiful country and guarded by our own army. Some were held within a stone's throw of my university in Chattanooga.

Everyone I talk to knows something of the history of the famous local legend Scrappy Moore, the Battle of Chickamauga, the Confederate siege of Chattanooga and the Union charge up Missionary Ridge. Everyone knows about Robert E. Lee and Ulysses S. Grant. It seems no one, including myself, knows anything about Andrew Jackson, the 1830 Indian Removal Act and the Cherokee deportations of 1838. Why?

Learning more about the disappearance of the Cherokee from north Georgia has become an obsession for me. I was never aware I grew up in the middle of what had been sovereign Cherokee Country. When my grandfather was a small child he lived in Rossville, Georgia, named after the Cherokee chief John Ross. My grandfather said the Cherokee or their removal were never discussed in our family.

My great-great grandmother was born in 1892 in Lyrely, Georgia in Gordon County. She grew up almost within walking distance of New Echota, the old Cherokee capital. I'm guessing, according to my recent research, her grandparents probably came into what had been Cherokee Country very near the time of the removal. According to my grandfather, his mother and her family never talked about the Cherokee removal. Did they know about the removal? Had the memory of what happened in 1838 disappeared from her rural Georgia community and family by the late 1800s? Did her folks choose not to talk about how they acquired their farms? I suspect the latter.

Between May of 1838 and the spring of 1839, every Cherokee family was deported from what is now Gordon County where my relatives live. Overnight my part of the world changed from red to white.

I remember feeding the ducks in the pond in front of the old John Ross house in Rossville. I recently visited the beautifully preserved two-story log structure tucked up against the hill just behind the old Rossville Post Office near the intersection of McFarland Avenue and Chickamauga Avenue. I was surprised to learn the John Ross house was moved from its original location beside the main road to its present out of the way location. Someone wanted to make room for a drug store on the highway. How appropriate.

I don't ever remember being told why John Ross and his wife left their home or where they went. I don't think my parents or grandparents knew, to be honest. I suppose they thought John Ross and the rest of the Cherokee just disappeared one day. I didn't know until I began my research that John Ross, Chief of the Cherokee Nation, buried his wife on his journey west during their forced deportation outside the borders of the United States—a deportation necessary because the state of Georgia intended to seize all their property.

John Ross and his wife, Quatie, had six children. She died 1 February 1839 during their deportation. She was buried in the old city cemetery in Little Rock, Arkansas. Years later her remains were moved to the Mount Holly Cemetery at Twelfth Street and Broadway in Little Rock.

I am determined to learn more about Cherokee history. The additional journal the old woman sent will be quite a supplement to Cassie's journal. I'm excited. I have two journals and the second is complete. I should be able to piece their stories together. Perhaps, as the old woman said, the story has been pursuing me. Maybe the story has indeed found its way back home and chosen me to give it voice. I hope I'm up to the task.

The second journal is a factual treasure trove detailing the daily life of the Cherokee during their eight-hundred-mile deportation. The journal describes weather, landmarks, rations, camps, sickness, accidents, death, burials and estimated distance traveled each day, but little else.

I was especially moved when I read one of the pregnant women died in childbirth during the removal. The second journal gives the exact location where the poor woman died—directly opposite twin peaks of the ridgeline resembling the breasts of a woman, the right peak slightly taller than the left. The ridgeline paralleled the road they were traveling.

Could I find those twin peaks? They weren't far from Chattanooga. If I found them, would I find an old grave close beside the road? There's a good chance I have enough detail from the journals to identify their route, and I have the second journal's daily reckoning. I might get lucky.

My history professor was as excited as a little boy when I showed him the journals. He told me I may have a significant historical find. He said it was the most exciting new historical material he has seen concerning Chattanooga since he began teaching. He can't wait till I publish.

My history professor and a civil engineer friend of his studied topographical maps to determine the exact route of Cassie's detachment. They highlighted several locations that seemed to match the topography described in the journal where they thought the pregnant woman may have died. They told me not to be surprised if I found nothing conclusive, but it was obvious to us the writer of the journal had noted prominent landmarks so they could return, perhaps to erect a memorial. I was reminded that few Cherokee gravesites had ever been marked.

The second journal recorded the pregnant woman's death near a certain place but didn't mention a burial. I thought it would be logical she would be buried there, but I had no way of knowing. With patient detective work, I might find the Cherokee woman's grave but I was prepared to find her grave unmarked—to find nothing. Even if my search was fruitless I would have a nice outing in our beautiful Tennessee countryside and become more familiar with the topography of the route the Cherokee took westward.

The endless hills and valleys of Tennessee are confusing, even to professionals. On the other hand, my professor reminded me, the topography of Tennessee hasn't changed since 1838. If I were to accidentally find the two hills, they would appear to me from my car window exactly as described in the old journal.

I asked Greg if he wanted to help me scout for the spot where the woman died. There probably wasn't anything there, but the search would be fun. I wanted to get a feeling for the lay of the land west of Chattanooga even if I didn't find Cassie's actual trail. I want to have a sense of what the Cherokee detachments faced in their laborious westward trek. Greg didn't want to go. He had something else to do. I didn't really care. I was enjoying myself, my quest and the research. I didn't need his company.

The following day was the Fourth of July. I had told Greg the week before I was catching up on much needed work and he should make plans for himself for the Fourth if he wanted to celebrate. I knew he planned something without me, but I have no interest in partying these days. That will have to wait till after the baby. I have work to do. Greg can celebrate with his friends. I am determined to finish my degree and, in addition, I want to transcribe the two journals. I must be focused and I have no time to waste. The journals are haunting me. It would be more fun to find that spot beside the road by myself anyway. The fact that he didn't want to go told me something about Greg and our future, but that's another story.

The Fourth would be a good time for my adventure. The two hills and the grave were out there somewhere and only a short drive from Chattanooga. The weather would be perfect. Perhaps I would use my little Fourth of July outing and celebrate my personal independence as well as our country's independence. That thought gave me a pleasant feeling. Perhaps I should talk to Greg and tell him I want to re-evaluate our relationship. I smiled at that thought. That was a great use of language. Re-evaluate didn't sound nearly so bald as breaking-up—like using the word emigration instead of deportation or today's distasteful modern pejorative—ethnic cleansing. Using a euphemism to break up with Greg would be appropriate, if one were to think as our government does and did in 1838.

With luck, I might actually find the two hills and the burial site, though that wasn't likely. Some historians estimate between four and five thousand Cherokee died while under arrest—add to these the Choctaw, Chickasaw, Seminole and Creek deaths, each with their own Trail of Tears and I'm discovering we were responsible for many thousands of deaths.

On the Cherokee Trail of Tears there were upwards of twenty different groups deported on various routes—some deportation routes are traceable and some not. The records of the deportations are scanty at best and often nonexistent. There is no accurate record of the hundreds and hundreds of Cherokee burial sites along the various routes. Most of the Cherokee unfortunates were hastily buried beside the road in shallow unmarked graves by exhausted companions. After their arrival out west, even more Cherokee died in Oklahoma. I feel emotionally overwhelmed when I think of the many hundreds of unmarked roadside graves—and I'm looking for only one. I was indeed looking for a needle in a haystack.

Except for the TVA dams and reservoirs, our Tennessee topography has changed very little in the last thousand years, my professor said. I remember his smile as he made it clear he was green with envy at my discovery. I invited him to go, but he declined.

"No," he said, "this is your story. I want you to have the joy of discovery."

I took his advice. I decided to go alone—but then, after thinking about what the old woman in Tahlequah had said that day, perhaps I wasn't alone in this quest after all.

Chapter V

The Adventure Begins

Chapter 5

I left just after dawn the morning of the Fourth. I stopped at scenic locations along the way to stretch my legs and visualize the things I had been researching about the Cherokee deportations. I wanted to imagine what happened all those years ago.

It was educated guesswork figuring out how far Cassie's detachment traveled each day. There were no milestones or signage in those days on the Tennessee frontier. Cassie's detachment traveled, according to the journal, a maximum of ten miles a day—fewer in bad weather or in case of frequent accidents. Sections of the road, especially when negotiating hills and fording streams, would have slowed the detachment considerably. The second journal gave plenty of clues to the route. As I drove along, the Tennessee hills and valleys all looked the same. I kept my eye out for the distinctive ridgeline as I neared the area we had marked on my map as the most likely spot of the woman's death but, to be honest, I had prepared myself for disappointment.

Suddenly, plain as day there were the two hills on my left exactly as described in the journal. Could these two hills be the correct ones? They were right where they should be according to the daily reckoning taken from the journals. This had to be them. It must be. This was my lucky day. I should buy a lottery ticket. I giggled and thought how smart I was. I felt as if I knew something no one else in the world knew.

I pulled over and stared at the ridgeline recalling the journal's description of this very valley. In my imagination I transported myself back to that day in July all those years ago when the Cherokee came down this same road. In my imagination I watched a pregnant Cherokee woman, recently evicted from her ancestral home, struggle past my car with the help of her friends. Somewhere in front of me not too far from where I was parked she went into labor and died. Overcome by emotion, I laid my head and arms on the steering wheel and cried. I shivered and cried again. My mind's vision wasn't a make-believe Hollywood script. The story I was reliving wasn't creative writing. It was real.

It wouldn't be the last time I would shed tears for visions my overactive imagination conjured up in my mind.

I gathered myself and studied the two peaks. The hills were steep and wooded top to bottom with no structures or clearings. They were much too steep for agriculture and, without a doubt, looked precisely as they did when the Cherokee walked past them in 1838. As I studied the landscape before me and compared it with my research, I marveled that so little had changed after all these years. According to what I had learned, the landscape I was viewing was practically identical to how it appeared in 1838. My heart beat faster. Something was going to happen.

In front of me to my left were the two ridges just as described in the journal. Immediately up the road to my right was a magnificent three-story red brick house on top of a small hill. It had a long, shiny, black asphalt drive bordered with lovely ornamental cherry trees its entire length. Across the road from the house to the south was a huge soybean field. It was a picture postcard right off the cover of *Southern Living* magazine. I loved it. It was my dream home.

I made an executive decision and decided to enquire at the house. I probably wouldn't learn anything but it felt like the right thing to do. Because of the creek that ran for miles between the hills down the entire length of the valley, I could be pretty sure the road I was driving must be close, very close, to the original 1838 road. Where else could anyone build a road down this valley? The present road was the most logical way westward—especially if one was driving a horse-drawn wagon. Therefore, the spot where the woman died must be near, very near. It had to be.

As I approached the house I saw the long driveway was full of cars almost down to the road. I had to park way down the hill, and I was glad I had thought to bring a cane. I needed help to get my fat stomach up the hill. I have put on way too much weight since I got pregnant.

An elderly man with a big nose, bushy white eyebrows and shining china-blue eyes, opened the door with a smile. He introduced himself as Mr. Johnson, the owner of the farm.

"What can I do for you, young lady?" he asked politely. "You're the only person today who has rung our front doorbell. You must be a stranger in these parts."

I told him who I was and that I was writing a story about the Trail of Tears and the Indians that may have come through this valley.

53

We talked for a minute. I told him I would like to ask a couple of questions if he had time, or perhaps I could make an appointment and come back another day when he wasn't so busy.

"You come right in, young lady. You couldn't come on a better day. My daughter and granddaughter are here and they know more about the history of this place than anybody. They'll happily answer your questions. Come in and make yourself at home. Stay all day if you want. Heck, stay all week if you want to. We got more than a hundred folks here today and we all tell stories. Would you like to talk to my daughter and granddaughter?"

I thought what a wonderful grandfather this man must be.

"Sure, I would love to stay and speak to them if you don't mind. It would be a pleasure."

"Dear, stay with us all day if you wish and enjoy our festivities. You're welcome to eat with us later. We got enough for an army—two or three armies."

"I'm not hungry right now," I answered, "but I would gladly take a plate home to nibble on if you have left-overs."

"You take home all you want, young lady. If you'll follow me, I'll take you down and introduce you to my daughter and granddaughter. They're our family historians. Lately, my granddaughter has been especially interested in the history of this place before the war."

"Before World War II?" I asked.

He glanced over his shoulder and laughed out loud as he led me down the back stairs and out to the patio and pool deck where everyone was gathered.

"No, no, my dear. THE War. The Civil War. The War of Northern Aggression we call it around here."

I loved his hospitality and the holiday atmosphere and his interest in the past. I could tell I was in the right place. He led me down the back stairs and out into the huge crowd of happy people. He introduced me to his daughter, Ann, relaxing under one of the big orange umbrellas on the far side of the pool.

"I'm proud of Ann," Mr. Johnson said. "She made straight A's in school and graduated with honors from UT. Her daughter is eight and reads everything she can get her hands on. She stays here with us every summer. She makes straight A's, too. She's one smart girl. My daughter said they called her an autodidact at school. I asked if there was a cure. Ann, tell this lady what an autodidact is."

Mr. Johnson laughed heartily at his own joke.

"Oh Daddy," his daughter said, "autodidact just means that Cassie is self-taught, that's all. She's the kind of child who enjoys learning and doesn't have to be prodded to study and read. I'm sure this lady already knew what that word meant."

Mr. Johnson was beaming.

"I think my granddaughter is about the smartest kid in Tennessee—even smarter than her mother. Let me introduce you to Cassie," Mr. Johnson said proudly.

I must have had a strange look on my face. I drew back and felt as if I had been slapped.

"That's odd," I said.

The words slipped out. I had not intended to speak.

"What's odd about my daughter's name?" her mother said quickly, giving a sideways glance at her daughter and then looking back at me.

I didn't want to offend anyone. I felt as if I had put my foot in my mouth and I hadn't even been properly introduced.

"I'm sorry," I said immediately. "Please forgive me. I'm a bit surprised that your daughter's name is Cassie. I had no intention to appear rude. I'm transcribing an antebellum journal written by a Cherokee woman. That's why I'm here. That old journal led me here today. I feel a little embarrassed. Your daughter's name is coincidental to the journal's story. Would you like to hear my story about the journal?"

Cassie's mother patted me on the shoulder.

"We're not offended and yes, I would like to hear about that journal," Ann said sweetly, "but we have all day to hear that story. Cassie and I love history and stories. Our whole family loves stories. You're welcome to take as long as you like to explain anything you want, but what I want to know is why you think Cassie a strange name for my daughter. I must say that was unexpected."

"Well, of course Cassie isn't a strange name," I answered. "It's a lovely name. It's simply a coincidence your daughter is named Cassie—that's all."

Everyone was still looking at me as if I had two heads. I took a deep breath and began again, "May I tell you the story of how I came to be here today and that will explain the coincidence about the name?"

"Sure," they answered in unison.

I was nervous, but perhaps I was getting used to people looking at me in odd ways. I could tell they were kindhearted folks like the old woman in Oklahoma. I had no reason to be apprehensive.

"I want to know what's strange about my daughter's name?" Ann asked again.

I looked at the mother for a few moments. This wasn't going as smoothly as I had hoped. I didn't feel so brave and bold. I was thinking perhaps I shouldn't have stopped at this house after all. I felt uncomfortable and confused, but I knew everything would be alright when I began to tell the story.

I took another deep breath.

"I think I should start from the beginning," I said. "I'll tell you briefly about my trip to the Cherokee reservation in Oklahoma and the story of that trip will explain the coincidence about the name. Would that be alright?"

They nodded in agreement. I was feeling better. They were eager, good listeners and I knew immediately they were good people.

"I'm a journalist finishing my degree at UTC. My boyfriend and I were out west collecting stories about everyday Americana. Through an accident of language, we ended up talking to an old woman on the Cherokee Indian reservation in Tahlequah—the Cherokee capital. The old woman said her great-great-grandmother was a child on the Trail of Tears and I believe, from my research, she may have passed down this very valley. I think they must have walked right in front of this house, if I have read the old documents correctly."

"What old documents?" Cassie's mother Ann shot her words back to me in a quick staccato voice. Her eyes were burning—staring through me. If I had her attention before, I had it tenfold now.

I gulped and continued, "The old woman I met in Oklahoma gave me a journal written by a Cherokee woman. The journal entries began in 1820 and ended abruptly after the group was escorted out of Chattanooga from Ross's Landing and, perhaps, directly past this farm—that's in 1838, of course."

"Really?" said Cassie's mom still looking at me like I had two heads plus horns.

I didn't know what to say. My mouth was dry but I bravely continued, "The old woman who gave me the journal found another smaller, less significant diary that chronicled the entire trip of that detachment all the way from Ross's Landing until they arrived in Park Hill in Oklahoma territory."

Ann and her daughter Cassie sat silently waiting for me to continue with my story. With everyone staring at me, I felt like a goldfish in a bowl. I wished I had a drink of water.

"According to the text of the second journal, a woman died in childbirth very close to this house. I stopped here today because I recognized the physical location described in the journal where the mother and her baby died. They died beside the road across from a southern ridgeline with two peaks resembling a woman's breasts, the right slightly taller than the left, precisely like the ridgeline across the road from this house."

Ann and her daughter immediately turned to look at the two hills then back at me. They didn't make a sound.

I was gaining confidence, "Here's the important part—the coincidence I was talking about."

I couldn't help pausing for a bit of added drama before I continued, "The journal was written by a Cherokee woman named Cassie."

I paused again to see what effect that information would have on the mother and daughter. Both Ann and her daughter looked as if they had been slapped in the face. They didn't move, make a sound or blink. I don't think any of us were breathing. I didn't know why, but somehow I knew they knew more about this story. This was going to be a good story or a very quick and ugly one. I didn't know which. I hoped I hadn't offended them.

"That's a coincidence, isn't it?" Cassie's mother finally said quietly.

Cassie, Ann's little daughter, was still looking at me. I was uncomfortable and I knew I was missing something.

"Did I say something wrong. I hope I didn't offend you."

"My dear, you didn't offend us," Ann replied. "You didn't say anything wrong. You had no way of knowing, but there does happen to be a grave on our property down by the road that dates from before the war, but it's the grave of a pioneer woman and her baby. It's not Cherokee. My family has lived on this farm since 1809 and we would know things like that."

Ann took a breath and continued, "The historical society investigated and the results were conclusive. We've been told there may be a few unmarked Indian graves in this valley, but I'm afraid no Indians were buried near here. We appreciate you coming by. It's strange that the woman who wrote the journal was named Cassie, same as my daughter. That is a coincidence, I must say."

"I'm happy to share anything I know with you," I volunteered. "I've enjoyed reading the journal and learning Cherokee history. I grew up in northwest Georgia, but I never knew anything about the Cherokee deportation until recently. Cherokee history is new to me. I'm writing a book and gathering stories. I thought driving out this way would be a good outing.

Thank you so much for talking to me today. I hope I didn't take you away from your reunion."

"We appreciate you coming by, Katie," Ann said, "but Cassie and I do need to help mother with a couple of things just now. If you're not in a hurry, how about you hang out with us this afternoon, at least for a little while, and we can talk? Cassie and I will be back in a few minutes."

"I would like that very much," I answered.

"You picked a good day for collecting stories," Ann said lightly. "The only problem is, young lady, not many of the stories you'll hear today are going to be true. There'll be more tall tales told today than you can shake a stick at. Give us a few minutes to help Mother and we can talk again. If you hang around here, you can get all the stories you want and maybe some ice-cold watermelon, too?"

I was beginning to relax.

Ann continued, "There's always room for watermelon, right? And if some time in the future you want to come back and talk, you'll always be welcome here."

"That would be great," I answered.

I searched their faces to see if the invitation was genuine. It was.

"Would you mind if I record the conversations and take notes?" I asked.

"Not at all," Ann answered. "You record everything you want. Even though you're not a relative, Katie, you'll end up a celebrity, I'm sure. Most of us are UT students or grads, but Chattanooga is part of the University of Tennessee system so that makes you one of us or at least a first cousin. We play Chattanooga every year, even though they're not Division One. Well, I should say, your Mocs let us beat them every year. Chattanooga is our favorite cupcake team."

We all laughed.

I was enjoying the relaxing atmosphere. I was indeed in the right place.

"Yep," I answered, "Tennessee always gives us a thrashing, but we've got a good excuse now. I'll bet you don't know we changed our name from Moccasins to Mockingbirds?"

"No, I didn't know that," Ann responded. "I thought you were named the Moccasins after the Tennessee River's famous bend like the snake?"

I laughed.

"We used to be the Moccasins years ago but folks at the university didn't like a snake mascot so we became the Moccasins—a pair of leather shoes. That wasn't politically correct, so we became the Scrappy Moore Mocs with

58

Scrappy Moore riding the Chattanooga Choo-Choo with the big cow catcher out front."

"Folks didn't like that either," I continued, "so the university changed our name again. In 2007, we became the Power C. We're still called the Mocs except now Mocs is officially short for Mockingbirds—not Moccasins. UTC wanted to distance itself from anything to do with Indians, shoes, trains or snakes. A mockingbird isn't quite as dangerous as a water moccasin, is it? We're about as politically correct as we can get."

We all laughed again. I was enjoying my outing.

"A mockingbird isn't a power mascot like the Georgia Bulldogs or the LSU Tigers," I added, "but it is what it is, I guess. It seems only our UTC chorus fully identifies with our mockingbird mascot."

Ann continued to laugh and giggle.

"My word Katie, all that name-changin' sounds silly to me. Daddy says our football team lets your Mockingbirds have a good first half just to make them feel good, and then we pour it on after halftime. The Big Orange uses them to get ready for important SEC title games later in the season. Daddy says we're going to beat Alabama this year. I hope so."

Ann accompanied me to get my notebooks and introduced me around. She temporarily left me by the pool to help her mother and promised to return as soon as she was finished with her chores. I was indeed in story heaven. I couldn't help but wonder what twist of fate brought me down this road past this farm and persuaded me to pull into this particular driveway. This was going to be a most interesting day. I thought about Cassie's journal lying on the passenger seat of my car and remembered once again what the old woman in Tahlequah had said. I suspect she was right. When I left Chattanooga this morning, I wasn't entirely alone.

Chapter VI

The Reunion

Chapter 6

I was thoroughly enjoying my surprise Fourth of July outing and glad Greg didn't come. He would have been a boring nuisance at an event like this. I learned the Johnsons have had a family reunion on this farm every year since before the Civil War. I wonder if this might be the oldest annual family reunion in the United States?

The generous, well-planned holiday decorations of a patriotic family were everywhere. There were American flags, buntings and streamers around the entire house and even down the driveway to the elaborately decorated mailbox area. There was a huge display board against the garage with photographs of all the family members currently serving and a list with photographs of all the veterans, both living and deceased. My father has a Purple Heart. He instilled in me a keen sense of patriotism. Freedom isn't free he taught me. I always thank veterans for their service.

There must have been more than a hundred people at the reunion, judging by the cars—probably more. Folks were everywhere. There were a dozen families playing games on the manicured lawn. Some were relaxing, stretched out on blankets under the huge shade trees. Many were enjoying an enormous wrap-around patio and pool deck with colorful orange and white umbrellas shading all the tables. There was a lot of activity in the screened-in BBQ house and little knots of people everywhere chatting. It was a marvelous scene. I don't think I've ever seen so many kids running around except at a school yard recess.

The unconventional pool was high end, to say the least. I've never seen anything like it except in photographs. It had a shallow end and a large play pool and fountain for the smallest children, a spacious deep end where a water volleyball game was in progress and an out-of-the-way shaded conversation pool in the middle for older adults. The conversation pool would seat maybe twenty or thirty folks on the underwater ledge. It also had a tiki-hut bar at water level with half a dozen underwater bar stools that allowed swimmers to sit on the stools with their elbows on the bar with just their head and arms out of the water. The entire pool area had appropriate landscaping and greenery. It looked like something out of an exclusive Caribbean resort brochure. I could see myself there with friends and a nice Piña Colada just after sunset on a hot day. I wish I had brought my swimsuit, but no one wants to see a pregnant woman in a swimsuit, do they?

The pool deck, the barbecue house and its tables and the huge patio surrounded the multi-story, red brick home on three sides. It was obvious whoever designed the house, the gardens, the pool and the recreation area behind the house had planned to entertain large numbers. I decided to walk around, listen and get back on task. I was here for a reason.

The patio was beautifully tiled almost all the way around the house with a wide veranda. The patio joined the screened-in pavilion, with a huge state-of-the-art brick barbecue grill and smoker with screened-in table space for a small army. The tables were decorated in red, white and blue with matching centerpieces and everything had an American flag waving. The grill and smoker were tended by half a dozen laughing young men in their masculine themed aprons getting the BBQ feast ready. I wondered how many of them were single? They were cute. I had never seen a family reunion as big or well-organized as this one and certainly not one that had been going on for so many years continuously. The reunion would make a great story in itself, but I needed to remember why I had come. Maybe I would come next year and write about just the reunion.

As I walked around, I noticed about eight portable grills set up around the perimeter of the activity in addition to the big, permanent grill on the pool deck. I thought that was a lot of grills, even for this crowd, and I asked one of the guys tending one why so many.

"Ma'am," he said, "not only is this the Johnson reunion, but it's our annual family BBQ cook-off and ice cream competition. I compete every year for the best BBQ chicken and ribs. Everyone has their own secret sauce and method of cookin'. I don't mind tellin' you, I've won the blue ribbon two years runnin'. The secret is controlling the heat and cookin' time."

He grinned as he handed me a white plastic fork with a generous piece of BBQ chicken dipped in his special sauce.

"Try this ma'am. What do ya think? Good, huh?"

"It's very good, thank you," I answered.

"I only use seasoned hickory chips from mature trees, make my own sauce from scratch and I even grow my own peppers, onions, tomatoes and herbs," He added. "Only home-grown herbs—no store-bought stuff for me."

I couldn't help but like this guy, his smile and enthusiasm. This was a special reunion with special people. Those I had met so far made me think how wonderful it is to be a part of an extended family.

He was in a talkative mood and continued, "The serious ones of us don't share grills, and my wife don't share her ice cream recipes either. We want braggin' rights. Later this afternoon after we eat we'll have ten or fifteen big freezers of home-made ice cream and everyone votes on the best, so save room. This year my wife's doing cherry-vanilla with fresh cream we get straight from a Jersey farm, fresh cherries, real vanilla, not the fake stuff, and home-baked pecan pralines with sugar, honey and butter coating with a dash of malt she does herself. Yum, you'll like it, guaranteed."

I grinned. I had to move on. I couldn't listen to any more of his description of food. I loved everything about this place. I had forgotten myself again. I looked over my shoulder to the south. There were the two hills, just as I had read in the journal and had seen for the first time just an hour ago. Those majestic wooded hills have been standing for hundreds of years and look the same now as then. I shivered. I thought again of the Cherokee detachment who had passed down this road. They had looked at those exact same hills the same as I was looking now. No, I wasn't chasing a story, the story was definitely chasing me, like the old woman said. I shuddered again. I loved the story in the journal, but I didn't like the unpleasant sensation of being pursued by some macabre phantom inhabiting a hundred-fifty-year-old Indian woman's diary. I needed to lighten up.

I looked around. It wouldn't be long before the picnic's main meal would be served. The ladies were scurrying hither and thither making final preparations. Folks were laughing, chatting, sipping lemonade and sweet ice-tea and beginning to look forward to the call to eat. Kids were playing all over and splashing in the pool. Others relaxed in the bright orange deck chairs under the welcoming orange umbrellas with the big white T on each. Mr. Johnson was obviously a big Tennessee fan.

Who wouldn't love to be a part of this family, I mused to myself? As I looked around admiring everything I saw, I suddenly realized every person here, including me, was of European ancestry—mostly English I would guess—entirely white. We were white—all white—pure white. I wouldn't have noticed before, but I was planning a story about dispossessed Indians—

dispossessed by white folks and this farm was in the precise area where that seizure took place.

There were no Africans, Asians, Mexicans or Native Americans at the reunion. There were no Muslims, Hindus, Sikhs or anyone from India, Pakistan or Malaysia. There were no Chinese, Japanese, Koreans, Filipinos or Latinos. Everyone here, without exception, was Western European and spoke American English—with a southern accent, of course. In the past, the fact that everyone at a get-together was white would not have occasioned special notice to my mind, but that was before the journal—before I began my quest to understand my past and the people I grew up with in my northwest corner of Georgia.

Three hundred years ago the Johnson farm belonged to a prosperous non-European culture. Three hundred years ago the Cherokee Nation was happily raising their children in this valley, growing corn and vegetables and hunting in the forests filled with game. As I wandered around the Johnson reunion, it occurred to me that if I could be transported back in history to a Cherokee holiday, I would have witnessed a similar scene. There would have been no asphalt driveway full of cars and no swimming pool, but the joyous gathering of extended families with children running everywhere would have been the same.

The Cherokee and all the other tribes were unaware of the impending disaster coming from the east. The Johnsons, and the myriad of folks like them throughout Tennessee, were part of a European ethnic migration which had violently supplanted the original inhabitants. The Cherokee were gone and this entire area belonged to immigrants—immigrants who were enjoying their new homeland immensely as I was observing.

I sniffed the delicious aromas that filled the air and realized I was hungry. I had expected to get a little salad on the way back, but skipping this feast for a salad would be a travesty. I couldn't pass this up. If I eat here I won't be hungry for a week, and Mr. Johnson told me to take a plate home. I was looking forward to that. I was ravenous but I wouldn't be able to eat all I wanted. What a shame. After the baby comes, I'm going to pig-out every day for a month, and I don't care how much weight I gain. I'm so tired of not being able to eat a full meal. When I go to McDonalds these days, the only thing in my car that's super-sized is me.

As I wandered by the tables being prepared for the picnic, I saw all my favorite foods. There was homemade slaw, country style potato salad, bean salads and half a dozen other salads I couldn't name. I especially like those green congealed salads with pecans and the little marshmallows like my mother used to make for Thanksgiving. Someone had brought a big Greek salad which I love, but it seemed out of place. There were trays and barrels of ubiquitous southern fried chicken. There was barbecue chicken, barbecue ribs, green beans and real mashed potatoes with plenty of homemade gravy. There were huge bowls of butter beans, pinto beans, black-eyed peas, stacks of corn on the cob and both fried and boiled okra. There were bowls of collard and turnip greens cooked country style with big hunks of ham, big pans of cornbread that would be hot out of the oven with plenty of real butter, and all the pickles, relish, chow-chow and other condiments one could imagine. Yum, Yum, Yum.

Against the side of the house in the shade I saw three shiny new galvanized washtubs. I was curious. I found concealed under layers of big colorful beach towels a dozen huge watermelons covered in ice. Yum-yum-yum and double yum. There were the six big tables crowded with the desserts tucked into the four-car garage in the dark shade. They were the biggest temptation of all. Each table was covered with a big white bed sheet to keep away flies and naughty fingers.

One of the ladies guarding the dessert tables pulled up a corner to give me a look. Oh my word, there were peach, plum and blackberry cobblers and at dozen pecan pies. There were cakes—lemon, German chocolate, plain carrot cake with cream cheese icing with half chocolate, red velvet and a pecans decorating the top. There were coconut cakes and my Daddy's all-time favorite—plain yellow pound cake—the kind he loved with his coffee. There were brownies, big chocolate chip cookies the size of a dinner plate someone made for the kids, chocolate cream layered pies, a beautiful Cherry-O cheesecake made with fresh cherries, cupcakes galore, four or five old fashioned vanilla puddings and more desserts I couldn't name.

My personal all-time favorite is plain ole' homemade banana pudding, the kind my grandma makes from scratch. I love her banana pudding while it's still warm right after she puts it in the bowl with the big Nilla Vanilla Wafers. Maybe I would skip the ribs and just eat a big bowl of pudding or maybe a big piece of moist lemon cake with almond icing or maybe the homemade blackberry cobbler made with blackberries the family had picked right here on the farm and topped with a big dollop of homemade vanilla ice cream. This wasn't fair. It was good this happened only once a year.

I looked for someone to talk to. I needed to make the most of this opportunity and get my mind off food. Mr. Johnson walked by and asked if he could get me anything.

"No sir," I said, "but I would love to hear more of your stories. Since you're the host, I would love to hang around and listen and perhaps ask you a question or two, if you don't mind. I'll have a little barbecue later and then head home. I'll miss the fireworks but I don't want to drive home in the dark. Would that be ok?"

"My dear, stay as long as you wish. Stay a week. We have a big house and plenty of bedrooms, plus there are a couple of big RVs up by the woods with full hook-ups. You could stay there with all the other young people. Stay as long as you want and you'll get all the stories you want."

His old weathered face lit up with his typical big southern smile and he laughed. He reminded me of my own grandfather.

"You know, young lady, it isn't often an attractive young woman wants to spend the afternoon with me for any reason. I'm flattered."

One of the older boys shouted, "Hey Grandpa, you want another lemonade or somethin'?"

"No, Dustin. I'm good. I'm goin' to sit here in the shade and watch everyone havin' fun. I'm pooped. I been workin' for two weeks helpin' your grandma get this shindig ready. You don't know how hard these women have worked me. Your grandma got me up at four this mornin'. I told her once the kids were here, I wasn't doin' nothin' till all y'all leave. After I make my run to the dump, I'm finished."

I was enjoying listening to this exchange.

Mr. Johnson continued, "If she wants somethin' done she'll have to ask someone who ain't been drawin' social security for fifteen years."

"Ok, Grandpa," his grandson said. "If you need something, I'll get it for you. Just let me know. I tried to sneak us a cupcake but Grandma's guard hit me with her big wooden spoon."

"Grandpa, we're going huntin' again this fall, aren't we? Are you going to take us to your special valley again? I love that place. That's where me and daddy both killed our first deer. We never come back empty when we go with you, Grandpa."

"Sure, we'll go to my special valley, Dustin," his grandfather said. "I've already set aside the first week of deer season like we do ever' year. The women know they'll have to find somethin' else to do and that means an expensive shoppin' trip to Nashville, but it's worth it. There's nothin' in my

65

life I enjoy more than watchin' you boys bring back your own deer—especially your first."

Mr. Johnson leaned back in his chair and continued, "I got pictures of all of you boys with your first deer and it won't be long before I'll be puttin' a great-grandson's picture on that wall. If our family keeps growin', I'll need a warehouse to display all the photos. I was proud of my sons, but there's nothin' like standin' beside my grandson with his first deer and then watchin' him at the head of the table servin' venison he brought home himself. That's the way families should be. I want it to be that way when I'm gone and you have kids of your own."

"Don't you worry, Grandpa. When I'm grown I'll teach my kids to hunt. I can't wait to be with you and Dad in the woods and hear the leaves crunch under our boots."

I was listening and taking notes. My mind was going from the reunion to the journal and back again. This story was chasing me in ever-tightening circles. I was beginning to think I was brought here this day for a reason. It was as if everything I saw or heard was manipulated for my benefit by some unseen cinema director.

"We'll fill the freezer again this year for sure, won't we, Grandpa?" Dustin boasted.

"Yep, we always do," his grandfather answered. "Deer season is my favorite time of year. I like it better than Christmas. You takin' care of the rifle I gave you, Dustin?"

"Of course, Grandpa. There's not one speck of rust on that gun anywhere. I clean it every time we shoot. I'm the only kid in school with his name carved on his stock, and I'm the only kid with his own model 70 Winchester—that's for sure. It's one sweet rifle, Grandpa. Me and Daddy target practice most every weekend. My sights are dead on. I could pick a fly off a tomato down by the road."

His grandfather laughed as he replied, "I just about went broke buyin' you and your cousins deer rifles, but it's worth it. I want y'all to have the best and remember me when I'm gone. I got a picture on the wall of each of you boys in the woods with me with your first deer with the rifle I gave you. I wouldn't trade those pictures for this whole house."

"I know, Grandpa, I know. You told me that once already."

His grandfather continued repeating himself as if he hadn't heard. I was listening carefully.

"Family is everything, isn't it, Dustin? I wouldn't miss that week for the world," his grandfather said.

"I know Grandpa. I love your cookin'—'specially your breakfast. Your gravy's better than Momma's. She says everything tastes better when you're campin'."

Mr. Johnson stood up and put his arm around his grandson, "Come with me now, Dustin. I got somethin' I want to show you. I was goin' to wait till after we ate, but let's go now. We got plenty of time if we hurry. Go get your cousins and follow me up the hill."

"You want to come with us, young lady? Mr. Johnson asked me, "You might find this interestin'—maybe even write about it."

"Of course, I want to come. I would love to," I answered quickly.

This was one more marvelous thing I had stumbled into. I tagged along while Dustin's grandfather gathered the boys and led us up the hill behind the old log cabin and proudly showed us his new archery target. The target was cleverly tucked into the edge of the underbrush against the sides of three round bales stacked in a triangle. The target had the silhouette of a deer in some kind of durable substance that simulated the look and texture of actual deer hide. From fifty yards, it looked precisely like a proud buck in profile with his head turned looking straight at me. It looked alive—like it would bound away at any moment.

"Later on today I'll bring all you boys up for some bow practice," Dustin's grandfather said. "I bought a new compound bow this summer and I want to try out an antique Indian bow I bought from a dealer in Gadsden. The man said he's never seen one like it. He said it was over a hundred and fifty years old but would string and shoot like new. He said it's the best handmade bow he's ever seen—new or old. You boys want to try it?"

"I want to warn you boys," Mr. Johnson cautioned with a big smile, "it takes a man to string and draw that old bow. It's a harder draw than any bow I ever had."

"Sure, Grandpa. I want to shoot your old bow," Dustin volunteered. I'll bet I can draw it. I got a job this summer workin' on a big farm where they only do old-fashioned square bales like you and Daddy used to do."

"Puttin' up a few thousand square bales in Mr. Watson's big ole' barn is somethin', I can tell you. I'll bet he's the only farmer around here who still does square bales. I can string that bow. I could pretend I was an Indian. Maybe I'll hunt bow season this year."

I was curious. I wondered where this conversation would lead.

"May I have a look at that old bow before I leave, Mr. Johnson?" I asked.

"Sure, you can have a look at it, Katie. Let's go back down to the reunion before they send out a search party. I'll bring you up to the house before you leave and show you the old bow. I keep it in a display case over the mantel."

When we got back down the hill, I passed several cute, college-age men tossing a football. One was wearing a Florida State football jersey with the profile of their Seminole mascot with his two stripes of maroon war paint over his high cheekbones. Although I had seen that profile often, I studied it as if for the first time. I had never given a thought to the FSU mascot before. I had never even thought about the word. What was the meaning and purpose of a mascot? I wondered if I had thought of Indian mascots as not being real, like cartoon characters—like Bugs Bunny or Porky Pig. After reading about the Cherokee, I was becoming curious about Seminole history. Why did the Seminole leave Florida? What happened to them? Did the same thing happen to them as the Cherokee? Were the Seminole violently removed so Europeans could occupy their land? How would the Seminole feel about a white university using the image of one of their defeated warriors as a good luck charm for a sports team? I felt confused.

I had seen FSU play at home in Tallahassee this past year in their big stadium. It was an exciting game. I remember watching the Florida State University mascot dressed as the great Seminole Chief, Osceola. He was riding his handsome paint horse and carrying a dangerous looking spear as he galloped left and right rallying the student body in the stands in front of him. It was impressive.

During my Cherokee research I had learned United States Army General Thomas Jesup was frustrated in his many attempts to capture the elusive Osceola. Under pressure from Washington the exasperated Jesup came up with a plan. Jesup ordered his subordinates to ask Osceola for a white flag meeting during which Jesup ordered Osceola and his men to be captured. Jesup captured everyone—men, women and children. He rounded up everyone even though he had promised otherwise under the white flag truce.

Shortly after his arrest Osceola died alone under mysterious circumstances in a South Carolina prison. I can't imagine anyone choosing Chief Osceola as a mascot to bring a white university good luck. I'm learning a great deal about our history—history about which I and others seem to know almost nothing.

Osceola will have to wait. One thing at a time. I need to get back on track. I need to think about Cassie's journal and the Cherokee story.

From my amateur research, I have learned most folks know absolutely nothing about American history before the Civil War. I had never thought about it, but it's as if I was given the impression in school there was no one living on the North American continent when Europeans first arrived. I must have assumed Columbus discovered an unoccupied continent. It's as if no one lived here prior to the colonial period.

I'm surprised at what I'm learning. If I'm reading history correctly, the entire North American continent was populated coast to coast and north to south with hundreds of separate self-governing groups who had lived here for more than a thousand years before the Europeans arrived. The fact that our government, formed in 1776, celebrates Columbus Day as a national holiday told me how we think when it comes to Indians and their history.

I was surprised to learn I didn't know the answer to the simple question, 'Which is the oldest city in America?'

The answer in Jeopardy form: 'What is St. Augustine?'

I had been taught since primary school that St. Augustine is the oldest city in North America—founded in 1565 by the Spanish.

Nope. Not so. I was wrong—badly wrong.

When the Spanish founded St. Augustine, there were hundreds and hundreds of densely populated cities all over the North American continent from Canada to Mexico. There were long-established towns in North America from sea to shining sea in this new world, but since the inhabitants of these towns weren't white, didn't speak a European language, had no knowledge of gunpowder and didn't maintain a standing army and navy to fend off their European invaders, they were easily swept aside and ignored in our history books. Evidently, real history begins in western Europe.

I mentioned this to my father and he reminded me of a Johnny Cash song about the Seneca Indians. The Seneca's vast land holdings had been gobbled up by European immigrants. The powerless Seneca were forced into a tiny reservation in the Allegheny mountains in western New York. There they were guaranteed a permanent home by formal treaty by our federal government and by George Washington himself.

The United States decided we needed more of the Seneca's land. In 1965 we confiscated the Seneca's last ten thousand acres of arable land by right of eminent domain and built the Kinzua dam. The Seneca's objections fell on deaf ears. Per usual, our longstanding treaty with the Seneca was ignored. The Seneca were dispossessed once again. The unwanted dam and the ignored treaty got the attention of both Johnny Cash and Bob Dylan—but neither of them are generals or have a seat in congress. The dam was built.

I needed to get my mind back on track. I overheard a young man with a University of Tennessee T-shirt banter with his cousin from FSU.

"You've got a lot of nerve, Justin, wearing that pathetic FSU jersey up here. You been shoppin' at thrift stores? Jackson ran the Indians out of Tennessee a long time ago and we ain't ever goin' to let 'em back. The Volunteers are goin' to send you Florida boys packin' again this year. We don't have any use for Seminoles up here."

I couldn't believe what I had just heard.

His cousin from Tallahassee answered, "You Rocky Top rednecks better fear the spear when we come up, unless, of course, you turn yellow and forfeit like you might as well do."

The two boys were laughing at one another.

"We're goin' to send that old flea-bitten hound of yours runnin' for the hills with his tail between his legs, just like we did last year. When we're finished with the Big Orange, we'll drink fresh squeezed orange juice all the way home. Peyton Manning himself couldn't save you."

I loved the playful banter and the boys were cute. Too bad I was pregnant or I might have flirted a bit, but who's going to look at a fat pregnant girl like me?

"I don't understand why in the world you didn't go to Tennessee, Justin. You had a scholarship and everything. Why go to school way down in Florida? What's wrong with Knoxville?"

His cousin from FSU answered, "Well, if you were to see my girlfriend you would know why. She's got the prettiest auburn hair, big brown eyes and the cutest freckles you've ever seen. Her parents went to FSU. They're some kind of important alumni. Besides, it's warmer in the winter. I like playing golf and tennis and riding my motorcycle when it's snowing up here. You can't do that in Knoxville in January, can you?"

I left the boys and headed on down towards the pool. I noticed little Cassie was still sitting and reading where I had left her under her big orange umbrella. She was cute, dressed for the day in red, white and blue and her blond, almost-white, hair was pulled back in two braided pigtails tied with patriotic colored ribbons. Her brightly colored hair clips had little lights in them and flashed like exploding rockets as she held her book. She was adorable. I hope my baby turns out to be as cute as this little girl. As I watched,

70

a young pregnant woman sat down beside her. I was curious and joined them. Cassie introduced me to her cousin, Ashley.

"Nice to meet you, Katie," Ashley said. "Am I right? You're expecting, too?"

"Yep, I'm going on six months," I answered. "What would you have done if I had said I'm not pregnant?"

"Women know," Ashley said. "Your behind and your stomach don't match. I knew you were pregnant. If your behind and stomach were a match, I wouldn't have said anything."

We all three giggled.

"Do you mind if I join you?" I asked.

"Oh my, no. Two pregnant women should have plenty to talk about," Ashley said.

"Cassie, it's nice to see you again," Ashley said to her little cousin. "What-ya-been-doin'? You're so cute today. Bill and I miss coming down here to see you guys. We've been busy in Nashville. It's a long time since we've been down. So, what about Cassie? Tell me, tell me, tell me. Why isn't my little cousin joining the festivities?" Ashley asked. "You didn't come here to read, did you? This isn't a library. Everyone's havin' fun. You don't need to be readin'."

"Oh my, Ashley, are you having twins? You're so big," Cassie said as she looked up from her book. "You look too big for just one baby."

"Hush your mouth little girl. It better be just one baby. I don't know what I would do if it were twins," Ashley said.

"Ashley, Katie's a journalist from Chattanooga and writing stories about the Trail of Tears," Cassie said. "She's going to spend the afternoon with us asking questions. Paw-paw's going to tell her some stories, too. That'll be fun. I can't wait to hear his stories."

"When are you due?" I asked Ashley.

"I'm due next week on the tenth, but I would go now if I could. And, for your information, little Cassie, Bill and I know it's just one baby, thank goodness. It's going to be a boy and we're excited. I feel like I've been pregnant for two years. Maybe I'll pig out on cherry cheesecake, drink a bottle of castor oil and have the baby tonight. I'm so ready."

"I'm happy to see you, Ashley," Cassie said, changing the subject. "Isn't this reunion wonderful? I love celebrations and holidays and I'm glad you're here. I'm glad everyone is here. I love it when our family gets together."

"Yes, it is a wonderful day," Ashley answered.

They both paused and looked at the perfect sky and the wonderful family scene. My gaze was once again drawn southward to the two hills. It seems I couldn't get away from those two hills and pregnant women.

"There's not a cloud in the sky," Ashley said quietly. "We got a nice little breeze blowin' down the valley and this is a perfect day. It's a perfect picnic and reunion, isn't it?" Ashley said to no one in particular.

"Katie, you need to get some of Momma's lemonade," Cassie said. "She's got a secret recipe and everybody loves it."

"She makes it out of lemons she orders special from Florida. She won't tell anybody how she makes it. Nobody makes better lemonade in the whole world than Momma."

"I got somethin' I want to show you two," Ashley said taking her phone out of her purse. She put the screen close in front of both of us and began scrolling through photos.

"Bill and I were married right here on this very patio," Ashley said to me proudly. "You should've been here for the wedding, Katie. Cassie was the most beautiful flower girl in the whole world. I don't think Cassie has seen all my photos since then. I got every photo right here on my phone. Look at this first picture. You were so pretty, Cassie. There was only one girl at the wedding that day more beautiful than you."

Ashley giggled and paused for a moment to make sure Cassie and I understood she was talking about herself.

"Sure, I remember, Ashley. I loved your wedding and maw-maw's reception was fun. We had a great time, didn't we? Momma let me stay up late and dance with the grownups, remember? I even snuck some champagne. I like champagne better than beer. I hate beer, yuk. I don't see how anyone can drink that stinkin' stuff. I guess they need it to wash the tobacco juice out of their mouth—gross."

Cassie made a terrible face and we all three laughed out loud.

"The reception was fun. Our family always has fun," Cassie said with animation sitting up tall. "I think the funniest thing ever was when Bill jumped into the pool holdin' you in your wedding dress and you two danced in the water like it was the dance floor. Everyone laughed and laughed."

Ashley turned to me, "We've got the greatest family in the world, don't we Katie? We're lucky to have grown up in Tennessee. This is the greatest country on earth and we live in the best part of it, don't we Cassie?"

"What ya reading, Cassie, that's so important you don't want to talk to your relatives?"

"Oh, this is one of the library books I brought home for the summer," Cassie said holding the book up for us to see. "It tells about the people who lived here before the settlers came. There are things about Tennessee history I didn't know. Do you know much about Tennessee history, Ashley?"

"I know nothin' about history, Cassie," Ashley answered. "When I was in high school I was havin' too much fun teasin' boys, goin' to ball games and hangin' out with my friends. Daddy fussed because I didn't study, but my grades were good enough to get into UT. That's all I cared about."

Ashley lowered her voice and spoke in a conspiratorial tone, "Don't tell anyone, Cassie, but the only reason I went to college was to get my M.R.S. degree. I didn't care about schoolwork and I hate history, yuk."

"What's an M.R.S. degree?" Cassie asked.

Ashley and I both laughed out loud.

"My M.R.S. degree is my Mrs. William Benson degree, silly," Ashley said, still laughing. "It means I went to college to find a husband and not for an education. I wanted to be a Mrs.—I wanted to be married and raise a family. I wanted to find an ambitious man who would provide for me."

Ashley continued laughing, "I didn't want to marry some backwoods television watchin' redneck who couldn't read and didn't like to work. I went to college to find an intelligent, ambitious husband. I found him and he's a good man, too. I didn't want to live in a trailer, work night shift and do serious arithmetic every time I went to the grocery store. I married Bill when I was a sophomore and dropped out of school to have this baby. I'm proud of Bill and I'm happy as a pig in sunshine. He's finishin' up his law degree. He's goin' to be a real estate attorney. We plan on buyin' a place somewhere close by here. We want to live in the country. Bill loves to fish and hunt and wouldn't be happy in town. We want to teach our children to love the outdoors—to enjoy this beautiful country of ours. We want to have acreage, horses and a barn with woods right outside our back door. It's much nicer here than Nashville or living all bunched up in a crowded subdivision. Tennessee is a lovely place to raise children, isn't it? I wouldn't want to live anywhere else in the world. Nothin' could make us leave. Soldiers with guns couldn't run us away from this place."

Chapter VII

Another Dream

Chapter 7

Cassie's mother, coming up from behind, affectionately embraced both her daughter and Ashley.

"Isn't my little girl lovely? And she's smart too," Ann said, looking at Ashley and me.

"Yes, ma'am. Cassie's as cute as a button," Ashley replied.

Ann sat at our table beside her daughter.

"My Cassie loves to read. When I kiss her goodnight, I have to turn the light out or she'll read till dawn. Her teachers say she'll finish college before she's fifteen at the rate she's going. She wants to go to Vanderbilt and be a medical missionary. She has such a soft heart—softer than mine. She makes straight A's and she's the prettiest girl in school."

"Oh, Mom," Cassie had an embarrassed look and playfully pushed her mother's arm, "you tell everyone that."

Cassie's mom looked at us two adult pregnant women as if for the first time.

"My, my, I do remember what it's like to be twenty years old and as big as a cow. I think the only thing more uncomfortable than being big as a cow is bein' pregnant plus chasing a two-year-old around the house. You two young ladies do know where babies come from, don't you?"

We laughed.

"Katie," Ann said, "would you like to hear about my first pregnancy? I didn't tell you this earlier, but there's an interesting story about how I named my daughter Cassie. After listening to you tell us about the old woman in Oklahoma, I'm guessing you'll find my story interesting. You've got me thinking, I must say. You'll want to hear this."

Ann's face changed. She looked at me with that look I had seen when we first met.

"Do you know the story of my pregnancy, Ashley?"

"No, Aunt Ann. I don't think I ever heard that story. I would love to hear it."

"I got pregnant for the first time right here on this farm," Ann said and paused for a moment staring south over the trees with an expressionless face. "My fiancé came to spend Thanksgiving with me and my family here at the farm. Momma always fixes a big Thanksgiving dinner for all her kids and their families and we all sit around her big table. It's quite a tradition. We had a great time. I'm the youngest of four and I was the only one still living at home that year. My siblings and their families left that Thursday evening after the football games, and my honey and I had the rest of the weekend to ourselves. Those were days of roses and endless hours of romantic conversation. John is still romantic. Even now we sometimes talk for hours. We're best friends—soul mates really."

"You're a lucky woman," I said.

"He brings flowers, sends me love notes in the mail and leaves sticky notes around the house. Sometimes I'll find a note in a pocket or a sock or he'll put one in a book I'm reading. I found one yesterday in the freezer, of all places—on top of the chocolate peanut butter ice cream."

I was envious.

"Lately he's been leaving them in the sleeves of my clothes. I find them after he's gone to work when I get dressed. I love his notes and how I come across them at the oddest times. I love it when he brings flowers, opens doors, pulls out a chair or just touches me for no reason when he passes. I'll tell you a secret if you won't tell?"

Ann lowered her voice and looked around.

"When he's especially romantic, we'll go to a restaurant and share one entrée. He asks for one plate and one set of silverware and he'll feed me every bite. He lets me drink myself, but he feeds me. Oh my—is that romantic or what? I just sit there with my hands in my lap and he pays attention to me and nothing else—like I was a princess. I love it. I love to look around and watch the old folks watching us. I can't explain how much I love the attention."

Ann laughed a light, breezy laugh as she looked out over the landscape. I thought what a lucky woman she was.

She continued, "The old men don't get it and the old women are green with envy. My husband is the most romantic man in Tennessee, without a doubt."

"Daddy feeds Momma at home, too, when he thinks I'm not watching," Cassie said. "He likes to feed Momma. I sneak around and watch from the upstairs hallway when they think I'm asleep."

"Cassie," said Ann, as if she were scolding.

75

We all grinned and Ann laughed again in that fresh easy way I admired.

Ann continued, "The weather was warm that Thanksgiving weekend and a sweater was plenty, even in the evening. Friday afternoon my honey and I wandered up to the old cabin arm in arm while my parents were resting in the house. We were mad for each other. Our youthful hormones got the best of us."

Ann looked over our heads towards the ridgeline to the south and continued, "John and I were planning to wait till after the wedding, but we were alone and decided we couldn't delay. We made love right there on the dusty floor of that old log cabin. It was our first time. I wish we had waited, like you did, Ashley, but we didn't. It is what it is."

In unison we turned and looked up the hill at the old Johnson log cabin, long empty.

"That was a special day and the result of that special day was a special child," Ann said, as she kissed her daughter on the forehead. "John and I are blessed with this wonderful daughter and our lives could not have turned out better, could they dear? In case you're wondering, Katie, I've told Cassie the story of her conception many times and we've often wondered how many of our Johnson clan were conceived in that cabin. I guess we'll never know the answer to that one."

"That moment was special and when I tell you the rest of the story, you'll understand why I told Cassie. If you don't mind, please don't tell anyone this story. I'll tell those I want to know, ok?" Ann asked.

Cassie's mom continued to look up the hill at the old cabin and continued, "I knew the exact moment I conceived. I don't know how I knew, but that very night, after we made love, I had a dream that I remember as if it were yesterday."

I was the one staring now. I was suddenly paralyzed. I couldn't write. I couldn't talk. I could hardly breathe.

"My dream had intense colors," Ann said in a low voice. "I don't usually dream in color. I think I dream in black and white and I never remember my dreams. This dream was bright, dazzling like a movie, like the colors in *Wizard of Oz*. You remember how the *Wizard of Oz* begins in black and white and then goes to color? My dream was like that. I can close my eyes and see the colors even now."

I was so shocked hearing about Cassie's mother's dream, I stared at her with my mouth open like a surprised child.

76

Ann continued her story, "It was a beautiful happy dream—not frightening at all. It's as clear in my memory today as the night I dreamed it. I could sit down now and sketch every scene if I could draw."

"The sun was bright orange, the cabin a rich chocolate brown like a Hershey bar, the leaves and grass brilliant shades of springtime greens and the butterflies were dazzling, like neon signs at night. In my dream I walked up the path toward the cabin and felt a warmth. That's when I heard the voice."

Ann and I looked at one another and I shivered to my toes. This was weird. What had I gotten myself into? No one spoke for a few moments.

I whispered, "What happened next?"

Ann touched my arm and continued, "The voice was reassuring. It said, 'Your baby's name will be Cassandra'. And then the voice repeated that same exact sentence twice more—and that was all. In my dream, I was walking up the hill, but the voice was coming from behind me—from the direction of the old headstone on the other side of the house down by the road."

"That does sound spooky, doesn't it?" was all I could manage to say.

Ann looked into the distance remembering that day and smiled at no one in particular, "No, I must say the voice wasn't spooky at all. Although I knew where the voice was coming from, it didn't frighten me. I know it sounds a bit eerie now, but I'm not lying when I tell you the dream wasn't disturbing in the least—just the opposite. The voice brought comfort. It still does. It was the voice of a friend—a dear friend. I would recognize that voice today, no matter when or where I heard it."

"You heard voices?" I was barely able to get the words out.

"I didn't hear voices, plural," Ann said. "I heard just that one friendly voice, Katie. It was a dream, but the voice was alive—vibrant. The voice was real as if the person speaking was in the room with me. I can close my eyes and hear it now. I haven't heard a voice in my dreams before or since, at least not one I remember."

"I know exactly what you mean," I said to Ann.

Ann continued, "I haven't had a dream like that since Cassie was born, and I don't remember dreaming in color again either. The voice was warm but spoke with authority. I saw no figure but I felt a comfort. I knew if I were to meet the person with the voice, she and I would be best of friends."

Ann, with a pensive look, stared up the hill once again.

"I thought my dream was somehow connected to the cabin and the grave, but I have no idea how, and even that is a guess. It was as if some benevolent spirit wanted to bless my unborn child and the benediction began with this dream."

Ann smiled, "And, as you can see, I obeyed and named my child Cassandra. When I recounted my dream to Momma, she stared at me like you are now. Everyone thought I was silly when I told them I was going to name my baby Cassandra. They named their babies what they wanted, and I would name mine what I wanted. Nobody in our family on either side has that name, my mom argued. Momma said most folks name their first baby after a family member."

Ann laughed and continued, "I think Momma was disappointed I didn't name the baby after her. Even my husband, who's always on my side, revolted a bit, but he knew I was firm. He didn't care what we named our baby. Don't tell anyone, but I didn't want to name the baby after his mom. Gertrude wasn't a girl's name on my short list. If they had heard the voice I heard, they would have named their baby Cassandra, too."

Ann laughed again with her lovely light laugh. Cassie smiled. I was very glad I had come. I was where I should be today.

"Ann, would you mind if I asked you a few questions? Are you busy right now?" I asked.

"No, I'm not busy and of course you can ask. What do you want to know?"

"I would prefer our conversation to be just you and me. Would that be ok?" I asked.

"Sure, that would be fine," Ann answered.

"Would you two be offended if I took Ann away from you for a few minutes?" I asked Ashley and Cassie.

They both agreed that would be fine.

"Cassie," Ann said to her daughter, "why don't you take Ashley and go visit with your Aunt Peggy while Katie and I chat. She'll be ninety-five this year and she's the last of your grandfather's brothers and sisters. When I was in the hospital with you, she sent us both a bouquet of red roses—two dozen American Beauties. I'll bet you didn't know American Beauties don't have thorns. I thought that was so sweet."

"I would love to visit with Aunt Peggy, Momma," Cassie said.

Her mother continued, "I still have the card and some of the petals in your baby book. Remind her about the roses and how she used to take me for ice cream when I was your age. She may not be here next year, dear, and take her a cup of coffee. She likes her coffee scalding hot, but don't burn yourself. Put it in a to-go cup with a lid, Ok? If coffee's not boiling hot, it's not hot enough for her."

"I'll visit with Aunt Peggy, Momma. I promise. I've always liked her," Cassie said. "I'll get her to tell me the story about the roses and I'll get her coffee. I love to watch her make silly faces when she sips hot coffee. It looks like she's drinkin' poison or somethin'."

Cassie took her book and wandered towards the kitchen. Ashley went to sit with her husband and Ann and I walked out into the lawn to continue our conversation.

"Ann," I began, "I have something to tell you that happened in Oklahoma when I first found out about the journal and this story that brought me here today."

"Tell me. I'm all ears," Ann said as we walked along. I could tell she and I were becoming friends.

I told Ann about my interview with the old woman, her dream and how she heard a voice telling her to give me the journal. I told her how the old woman said the story was chasing me and not me chasing the story. I told her about the voice I heard that very night in my dream telling me to tell her story. I told Ann everything. She listened intently, and I could tell she and I were on the same page.

I continued, "This whole story from the time I went to Oklahoma until I arrived here today is so Twilight Zone, isn't it? Doesn't all this make you think? That's three of us now connected by dreams and voices. Wouldn't it be bizarre if it were the same voice—if this were all linked somehow? Maybe it's the same person contacting all three of us?"

We went back to the pool deck and I sat down in the shade of the big umbrella. My back was aching. I had a feeling of mental confusion I've never had when writing and investigating.

"You're right, Katie. This is strange. It's a bit creepy. Your story has really got me thinking," Ann said.

"I'll tell you something else, Ann," I added. "When you told me the voice instructed you to name your baby Cassandra, my baby kicked at that very instant—kicked really hard. That's twice now my baby kicked at a strange moment related to this story. Maybe this is all coincidence but it gets weirder and weirder, doesn't it? Maybe our babies know more about this story than we do."

Ann was looking at me again with her inquisitive sideways look, "Katie, I have no idea what's going on here with our dreams, the voices, the old woman's journal and the story you're writing, but I have a sneakin' suspicion all this is somehow connected like you said, and the old woman in Oklahoma was correct. This story is chasing you. I'm sure of it. How else could you have ended up here at this house on the only day of the year you could have possibly met me and my daughter and heard our story? Katie, I don't think your visit is a coincidence. You were led here."

Ann continued, "Out of all the houses in Tennessee where you could have ended up, it doesn't sound like you found this house by accident. You were guided here, weren't you?"

"All this does make me wonder," I said.

"Katie," Ann said, "I think you need to continue your quest no matter where it comes from or where it leads. That's my advice. I think the old woman is right. The story that has come into your possession needs to be told and I think you're the teller. You've been chosen. I also think you may have some answers I've been lookin' for myself. We shall see."

After Ann said that, we decided to get us a nice glass of cold lemonade and change the subject.

Chapter VIII

Cassie's Paw-Paw

Chapter 8

Cassie walked up to the old log cabin to get away from the noisy celebration and read. The old cabin was listed by the Tennessee Historical Commission and was on the National List of Historic Places with a beautiful brass plaque displayed on a stand just beside the front door. Cassie had recently learned her grandfather's farm had been acquired by their family in a federal land grant at the beginning of the nineteenth century. She also learned Martha and Abner Johnson, the third generation of Johnsons to live here, died just after the Civil War and were buried in the town's churchyard. Cassie often tried to imagine what life was like on this farm in the early 1800s—on the very spot where she was sitting.

The book she had brought home from school had piqued Cassie's interest in her family's history and the visit today by the journalist had increased that curiosity. She was also curious about the history of all of Tennessee before her ancestors moved here. Who had lived in Tennessee before her family was given the land grant?

Cassie's grandfather noticed her leaving and followed her up the hill, moving as fast as his arthritic hips would allow. Getting old wasn't for sissies, he mused. Pain and inconvenience were part of a farmer's life. He never worried about either. Pain was never an excuse for not putting in a day's work. His father had taught him, "Son, if you can put both feet on the floor in the morning, you can go to work."

If you were to ask Cassie's grandfather about his physical condition he would invariably reply, "I couldn't be better." He would never complain.

When her grandfather got up to the old cabin, he found Cassie sitting in the doorway reading.

"Honey, some of our relatives have driven a long way and would love to have your company. Some you haven't seen in years. Can't the book wait, sweetheart?"

Cassie looked up and smiled. Cassie knew her grandfather loved her. That was a given in this family. Her grandfather looked down at the old library book with the faded cover and could only make out a portion of the title, *...ail* *of Tears*, which, in any case, was of little interest. He had never been a reader and had never read a book in his life. He had quit school in the fifth grade to work with his father on the farm.

Like all the men in his family, in this entire valley for that matter, he would rather be outside working, hunting or fishing—anywhere other than inside a house. The house was for eating, sleeping, watching television and women's work. He was pretty much illiterate, but he wasn't embarrassed. He was worth several million dollars on paper, which was pretty good for a man who didn't finish the fifth grade. He smiled when he thought about that. They were always wanting to loan him money down at the bank.

"Paw-paw," Cassie asked, "did you ever read about the history of Tennessee? I've read some interesting things in this book—things I didn't know."

"No, sweetheart. I don't know much about history," her grandfather answered. "I quit school in the fifth grade and went to work with Daddy. I never was one for readin' and such. I leave that to your maw-maw."

Cassie watched her grandfather gaze around the expansive farm as he spoke, "Yep, I done pretty well for a man who didn't finish the fifth grade. I never did learn to read good, Cassie. Your grandmother, now she can read. She reads all the time. She's educated. She taught fifth grade."

Her grandfather laughed out loud, "Isn't that somethin', Cassie? I didn't finish the fifth grade, and your grandmother was in the fifth grade for over twenty years. I kid her about that."

"I think that's funny, Paw-paw," Cassie answered.

"Your grandmother's a good woman," her grandfather continued. "Anyone who can teach a room full of fifth grade boys is a saint, and I can tell you she's a saint. I don't do much readin', Cassie. If I want to know somethin', I ask her. If there's somethin' in the paper I want to know about, I ask her to read it. She's book smart like you."

"Paw-paw, why did you quit school? Was your father ill or something? Is that why you quit?" Cassie asked seriously.

"I had a good reason to quit, Cassie. Daddy needed help and he and Momma thought it was a good idea my brother and I quit when we did. I knew I was goin' to be a farmer and by the fifth grade I had enough schoolin'. My brother and I quit on the same day and we never regretted it. We loved working with Daddy and we made a profit ever' year. We've done real good."

"But why did you quit school, Paw-paw?"

82

"Well," her grandfather continued, looking at his little granddaughter sideways, "let's just say there was a little problem at school and that's all I can tell you, my dear. No use digging up old bones."

Cassie gave up and changed the subject.

"Paw-Paw, do you know anything about the grave down by the road? Why is there no name or date on the headstone? It just says Mother and Child."

Her grandfather sat down beside Cassie in the doorway to the old cabin and put his arm around his granddaughter.

"I was the one that found the grave first, Cassie," her grandfather answered. "We had a terrible wet spring that year. Clouds came down to the tree tops and it rained and rained—the sun hardly shined for days and days. Water gushed down the hills where we had never seen water run before. Our whole bottom was a lake where the big cornfield is. We replanted twice that year. We were so late plantin' we hardly had time for the corn to make before frost. It was an awful spring and we barely made a profit. It was the worst year ever for hay. I remember the hay rottin' in the field before we could rake it, and that winter we had to buy hay to get by."

Her grandfather continued after a long pause, "When the rains were over that spring, I found the skeleton in the wash right there behind that big white oak beside the road. I'll never forget that day. I've had nightmares my whole life 'bout seein' those bones."

"That would be scary, Paw-paw," Cassie said as she leaned against her grandfather's shoulder.

"It sure was. If I close my eyes, I can still see that skeleton plain as day."
He shivered.

"Daddy called the sheriff. The sheriff poked around and called Nashville. The forensic folk from UT came down and had a look."

Cassie was listening carefully.

Her grandfather continued, "They dug and poked and decided there was no foul play. I could've told them that. They finally told us they believed the bones to be those of a twenty-five or thirty-year-old female, and they discovered an additional tiny skeleton of a newborn. The woman and baby had been wrapped in a quilt and buried together in a shallow grave. They also found two gold rings."

Cassie remained quiet and listened to her grandfather.

"They told us the quilt and the rings were probably German, though they couldn't be sure. They concluded this was likely an unfortunate immigrant woman, probably German, who probably died in childbirth. In those days, the main road west went right past this farm. They guessed that the pioneers didn't have means to build a proper casket or time to dig a proper grave, which would explain why they wrapped the woman and baby in the quilt."

After a pause, her grandfather began again, "They told us the woman was young, had dark hair, was probably German and that's about it."

"Oh my, that's so sad, Paw-paw. That's so sad."

"Yes, it was," her grandfather agreed. "Momma wouldn't let me go near the grave. Anytime I go that way, even now, I walk way 'round. I don't even like to look over that way."

Cassie snuggled against her grandfather as he continued, "After the forensic folks left, Daddy re-covered the remains and put some big flat stones on top to keep it from washin' again. He made it look more like a proper grave like Momma wanted. The Society of Tennessee Volunteers paid for the gravestone. After they set a proper headstone it made Momma feel better. She said it wasn't right a pioneer woman and her baby should be left in an unmarked grave like animals. The society said it was an honor to place the headstone. Momma told Daddy to take care of the grave like it was one of our relatives and he did. Ever' year when we had decoration at the church in town, Daddy would take care of this grave too—just like it was family."

Her grandfather's voice took a brighter tone, "Those pioneers, like the woman and her baby buried under the tree, are the people who made our country what it is today. I remember they came the day before the fourth that year and put up the gravestone. They said they wanted it to be in place for the Independence Day celebrations."

"This is interesting, Paw-paw. Thank you for telling me," Cassie said.

Her grandfather smiled and patted his granddaughter's hand, "I remember watching them set the stone. Even as a boy, I knew puttin' up a headstone was proper. I remember Momma sayin' there was something terrible about bein' forgotten—an' not havin' a gravestone."

Cassie's grandfather, sensing the discussion had taken a depressing turn, changed the subject. He impulsively took a twenty-dollar bill from his wallet and held it up in front of Cassie. Cassie thought her grandfather sometimes behaved like an impulsive little boy. She loved him dearly.

"See this man right here," her grandfather's calloused finger pointed at the portrait on the twenty-dollar bill. "This is Andrew Jackson, seventh president of these United States, and he's from Tennessee. He was elected twice. Bet you didn't know that, did you? How's that for knowin' history?"

Cassie knew about Andrew Jackson, but she didn't interrupt her grandfather's speech. She loved it when he talked to her, and she loved the excitement in his eyes. She had never heard this story in so much detail. Her grandfather held the twenty-dollar bill up close to his face and inspected the image of Jackson carefully.

"There he is, right here on our twenty-dollar bill," he said pushing the bill out to arm's length and punching the portrait with his gnarled old finger as if he were playfully punching the real Andrew Jackson on the chest. Your great-great-great-great-grandfather, I think that's enough greats, once fed and watered Andrew Jackson and his Volunteers right here—right here on this very spot where we're sittin' now. Ain't that somethin'?"

Her grandfather sat up straighter and his voice was more animated. "Mr. Jackson sat right here where we're sittin', Cassie, in this same doorway on this same piece of old wood we're sittin' on. Mr. Jackson looked out over this same valley we're lookin' at."

Her grandfather paused and looked at his granddaughter, "I know something about history, don't I?"

"Yes, you do, Paw-paw. You know lots of things. I think you're smart," his granddaughter answered.

Her grandfather was grinning from ear to ear.

Although she had heard the story of Jackson's visit before and had read about it recently in her ancestor's journal, she wanted to encourage her grandfather. His marvelous rehearsal of family history was as if she was hearing it for the first time and she didn't want to interrupt.

Her grandfather continued proudly, "Mr. Jackson said, 'Abner, you got a beautiful place here, and this is what me and my boys are fighten' for. We whipped the British, and we gave the Indians what for. We found a wide-open country and we've made it ours. We're headed home today, Mr. Johnson, but you call on us anytime and we'll be right back in two shakes if you need us. We fought for ever' farm in this state and, I promise you, we won't give an inch, and you don't give an inch neither. Me and my boys won't let anyone stand in our way, or your way, of building this country and bringin' peace an' prosperity to our families. We discovered this country. We took it and it's rightfully ours. We'll defend it with the last drop of our blood. You can depend on us.' Ever' now and then I'll get your Maw-maw to read the old journal. I loved to hear about Mr. Jackson and his visit."

"Abner's wife, Martha, was a teacher, just like your Maw-maw," her grandfather continued. "Her journal's in a safe deposit box but we keep a copy

85

in the house and there's even a copy at the Hermitage. Bet you didn't know that either, did ya? I do know a little 'bout our history. Not bad for a man who don't read good and only went to the fifth grade."

Cassie's grandfather was on a roll and Cassie was enjoying every word.

"Daddy told us boys if we got land we don't need nothin' else. Ownin' land is the most important thing in this world. Daddy said there's four things to remember in life—never borrow money, work six days a week, pay cash for everything and buy land with all your extra money. He said 'they ain't makin' no more land—ain't never goin' to make more land, so the value of land will always go up'."

Her grandfather looked out over his farm and after a long pause continued, "I listened. Daddy was right. Ever' time I saved a little, I bought more land."

He smiled again as he looked with pride across the farm.

"Paw-paw, you do know a lot about history," Cassie said.

Her grandfather stood up and stretched his legs and sat back down beside her without a word. He put his arm around his granddaughter's shoulders again and continued looking over his farm.

"We're proud of Jackson and his Volunteers, Cassie. Everbody in Tennessee who owns an acre of land owes them men. Everbody in the whole United States owes a debt to Mr. Jackson, to tell the truth. He brought unity to this country more than any other president. Almost by himself he made America great."

"Paw-paw, I've been reading about our history. I'm learning a lot of things I didn't know. I love to hear you talk about those things."

He gave his granddaughter another squeeze.

"Our family came here to this farm in 1809. Bet you didn't know this farm used to be North Carolina land, did you? North Carolina was given this land but they gave it back to the government. You didn't know that, did you? I'm not just some dumb ole' farmer, am I?"

"I didn't know that, Paw-paw," Cassie answered with an appropriate amount of amazement in her voice.

"When North Carolina gave up this land," her grandfather continued, "we Volunteers turned it into the great state of Tennessee in no time at all. I may not read so good, but I remember things. I got a good memory."

Her grandfather grinned again and laughed out loud.

"Tennessee was too much for North Carolina then and you wait till this fall, Cassie. The Big Orange will take care of them Tar Heels again. We always do, don't we?"

"Yes, sir. Tennessee always has a good football team," Cassie answered.

"Tennessee boys have been winners from the beginning. After we take care of them Tar Heels, we'll go back down to Florida and take care of them Seminoles one more time, just like Andy Jackson did," her grandfather said.

Cassie changed the subject. She didn't like football.

"Didn't Indians live here before white people came?" his granddaughter asked.

"Oh, I guess they did," her grandfather said, "but nobody ever' talks about them. They left a long time ago. They was pretty much gone by the time our family came."

Her grandfather didn't like the difficult questions. He wanted to talk about Andrew Jackson.

"Jackson was a great general and Indian fighter. He's a great American hero. The pioneers loved him. Jackson even went down to Florida and fought Indians down there when Florida belonged to Spain. You didn't know that either, did you?"

"No, I didn't know that Paw-paw. Tell me more."

Cassie wanted to keep her grandfather talking.

Her grandfather, in an unusually talkative mood, obliged, "Jackson went down and whipped those hardheaded, trouble-makin' Seminoles a second time, yes-sir-ree-bob. If there was a job to do, Jackson and his Volunteers flew right into the thick of things. That's why we elected him twice. He wasn't scared of nothin'. He made this country great. Yep, he's the reason we have this farm."

"Why did the Indians leave? Where did they go? Do you know, Paw-paw?"

"I don't really know, Cassie. They mostly disappeared. Some went west, I think."

She was asking more questions than he had answers.

"To tell the truth, sweetheart, nobody cares about Indians," her grandfather answered. "Everbody around here was happy when they left. Indians weren't smart, Cassie, and they were lazy. They didn't know how to work the land like we do. They knew we were smarter than they were so they went somewhere so they could be happy. A pretty little girl like you don't need to be worryin' about history. History ain't important—at least history about Indians."

"Paw-paw, why would the Indians leave a beautiful place like this? That doesn't make sense to me. Where could they go that would be better than here? Why would they go somewhere else? How were they inferior to white people?"

Her grandfather was a kind man who never did anyone harm. He didn't have answers to his granddaughter's questions, and he didn't want to discuss a difficult subject on a happy day like his family reunion. He gave up.

"We're havin' a picnic, Cassie. This is a holiday. You don't need to be thinkin' about all that ole' dumb history. It don't mean nothin' now. Ask your teachers those questions. That's what school's for, dear. That book you're readin' don't have nothin' to do with us today. What's done is done. Today we're having a reunion."

He hugged his granddaughter tight with both arms. He dearly loved this beautiful child. He loved all his grandchildren. Cassie wasn't ready to end the conversation.

"I've been reading about the history of Tennessee, Paw-paw. They say the Indians didn't want to leave here. Is that true, Paw-paw?"

"Oh, my dear," her grandfather said as he stood and stretched his legs and back once again, "those were hard times. When you're older, stories like this won't interest you. What we did was right for back then. People did things then they wouldn't do now, but what they did wasn't wrong."

He was weary of answering hard questions and wanted to get back to the reunion. Her grandfather felt like he did when he was a kid trying to talk his way out of a corner with his mother who would always have more questions than he would have answers.

"There was no government out here then, Cassie," he continued. "People took care of themselves. Folks needed land and they took it 'cause they had to. They had to work hard to make a livin' in those days. There was no electricity, running water, telephones or cars. Can you imagine that? If somethin' needed to be done, they couldn't wait."

There was a hint of annoyance in his voice. Neither he nor his granddaughter noticed.

"Sweetheart," he continued with his patronizing tone as he sat back down beside his granddaughter, "we're good people here in Tennessee. We always been good people. Indians gladly left. They disappeared. They vanished, really. No one made them leave."

"What about all the Indians this book says Andrew Jackson killed?" Cassie asked quietly.

Her grandfather took a deep breath and took his granddaughter's hand, "Jackson didn't fight good Indians, sweetheart. He was a good man. He only fought bad Indians. Mr. Jackson always did right by the Indians. Indians are simple minded, Cassie. They weren't smart like you. They couldn't read. They couldn't learn like white folks—still can't, I hear. We did them a favor by lettin' them go where they could live in peace. Don't you worry about Indians, my dear. They ain't important—never was."

He paused a moment to catch his breath and continued, "It's not like they was white folks, Cassie. It ain't the same thing. It ain't the same thing at all. Come on, dear. Let's get back to the party before those cousins of yours eat everything in sight. Those boys eat like pigs at the trough, don't they?"

He wanted a big glass of ice tea after that long speech. He deserved it. His granddaughter had pinned him in a corner and he had probably never said that many words consecutively at one time in his life. His wife would have been proud of him. She told him he never talked enough. He took one last proud look at the portrait of Jackson, folded the bill in half and put it back into his wallet. His old legs were hurting again, and he needed to walk off the pain. They headed down the hill. It was time to eat.

As soon as they got back, Mr. Johnson's wife told her husband everything was ready, and he should ring the bell. The old bell, up by the cabin, had been on the farm since who knows when. It was tradition to ring it at mealtime for all family get-togethers. Mr. Johnson, sitting to rest his legs and hips, sent his son, John, to supervise the kids and the bell ringing that would commence the afternoon picnic.

Cassie liked her Uncle John. Every summer he took all his nieces and nephews on fishing trips on his big pontoon boat.

"Uncle John, do you know why Paw-paw quit school in the fifth grade?" Cassie asked her uncle as they walked up the hill.

Cassie's Uncle John, with a wry smile on his face, looked sideways at his niece.

"Why do you want to know, little girl?"

If Cassie had been a little older, she would have read more into his facial expression and sideways glance.

"I was talking to Paw-paw about this farm and Tennessee history and he said he didn't read much because he quit school in the fifth grade. I asked him why he quit school but he wouldn't tell. Do you know why Paw-paw and his brother quit school on the same day? I'm curious. Do you know?"

Her Uncle John laughed loud, "As a matter of fact, I do know. I also know why he didn't tell you."

He laughed out loud again.

"You're a smart girl, aren't you?"

"Yes sir, I always make good grades," she answered proudly.

Her Uncle John got down on one knee and held her by the shoulders and looked her in the face.

"If I tell you why your grandfather quit school, do you promise never to tell anyone, not one soul, not even your parents? Promise?"

"Yes, yes, I promise, I promise. Please, please. Why did he quit school?" Cassie asked, as she clapped her hands and hopped up and down in anticipation.

"If you tell your momma, she'll take a broomstick to me," her Uncle John said. "You can't ever tell, ok?"

Her Uncle John spoke sternly, but his eyes were sparkling.

"The only reason I'm tellin' you is you're about the only person who doesn't know that story. Just don't tell your momma I told you, ok?"

"I promise," Cassie answered quickly.

"Ok, I'll tell," her uncle said. "This is the story your grandfather's brother George told me. He's gone now, bless his heart. He was a good man and a hard worker, like your grandfather. He was a good husband and father. You can't tell anyone I told you, ok? You promise?"

"Uncle John," Cassie said with an impatient, mischievous grin, "you can trust me. I'll never tell—cross my heart and hope to die. How many times will you make me promise? Tell me, tell me."

Her Uncle John took Cassie's hand and told her the story as they continued their walk up to the cabin, "The story goes that your grandfather and his brother George were in the fifth grade in the old, red brick schoolhouse in town. Those two boys were always having fun and always looked out for one another. If you saw one, you saw the other. Because they were country boys and never did mind hard work, their momma made them wear bib overalls to school. That's all they ever wore. I guess you've noticed your grandpa still wears bib overalls. Daddy keeps a new pair he wears to church and funerals. He don't wear nothin' but bib overalls. Most of the kids in those days wore jeans or slacks and they made fun of Daddy and his brother and called them hillbillies. Those two got into many a fight over those overalls."

90

Her Uncle John laughed and continued, "One day during class your grandfather's brother showed a little red-headed girl next to him his 'thing'. You know what I mean by his thing?"

Cassie was embarrassed.

She nodded, looked at the ground and grinned, "Yes, sir, I know what that is. I've been around farms all my life."

Her Uncle John continued with a grin, "Well, the little red-headed girl told the teacher. The teacher scolded your grandfather's brother and told both boys to stay after school for punishment. I guess the teacher figured if one of the Johnson boys was guilty, they both must be guilty. My Uncle George never did say, but I suspect your grandfather was more involved in what the little red-headed girl saw than he ever admitted."

Her Uncle John laughed out loud, "The teacher said she was going to cane them both. Uncle George was a big boy, even in the fifth grade, and he decided he wasn't goin' back for punishment. When class was dismissed, my Uncle George picked up a brick-bat and threw it hard as he could from the doorway straight for the teacher's head. It barely missed her and buried up in the chalkboard and the two boys hightailed it for home."

Cassie's Uncle John laughed out loud once again, "And that, my dear, was graduation day for your Paw-paw and his brother. The boys told grandpa the truth and he never made them go back to school. From that day they helped on the farm. Grandma never said a word about them going back to school either. I guess she knew their school days were over. I never heard if she talked to the teacher or not."

"Now I know why Paw-paw wouldn't tell me. Thanks, Uncle John," Cassie said with a bright smile. "Thanks. I promise I won't tell anyone, but what is a brick-bat?"

"I don't really know, Cassie," her uncle answered. "Brick-bat is the term your grandfather and Uncle George used in their story. I always thought it was a broken piece of brick. Over the years I've heard older folks use that word now and again. Nobody uses that word nowadays, do they? You'll have to go look that up, I guess."

They arrived at the cabin and Cassie's Uncle John supervised the bell ringing and the kids ran back down for the traditional prayer before the big picnic began. Mr. Johnson, a lifetime member of the local Southern Baptist Church, led the traditional prayer.

"Everyone bow your heads and close your eyes. Let us pray. Thank you, Lord, for this beautiful day you've given us in your tender mercies. Thank you for our wonderful family gathered here once again this year. We're grateful for your bountiful gifts. Make us mindful of the needs of others. We thank you for all our children and our health. We're grateful for our homes and jobs and this beautiful country you've given us. Today, Lord, as we're all gathered together to celebrate our freedom, we ask you to watch over our soldiers defending our liberty in far-away places. Bless our many missionaries wherever they may be found. Bless our children and our children's children and may they always have a secure, happy home, free from oppression in the greatest country in the world.

Bless this good food and the hands that prepared it for the nourishment of our bodies, and may we continue in your service and always love others as we love ourselves. Bless us, O Lord, and these thy gifts we are about to receive through thy gracious bounty. In Jesus' name, Amen.

"Ok everyone, let's eat. I'm hungry."

After we had eaten I thanked Mr. Johnson for a lovely afternoon and all the stories. I told him I was headed back home to Chattanooga.

"Before you go, Katie, I'll tell my wife to fix you a big plate. We got plenty, don't we? I promised to show you that old bow. Follow me upstairs."

I followed him upstairs through the garage up to the living room. He took the bow from its display case over the mantelpiece. I know nothing about bows but it did appear old and, as I looked at it, I was struck by the small delicate carvings just over and below the handle. There were five feathers, maybe eagle feathers, in a curious running design. They were expertly carved into the hickory just above the handle and a buck's head carved in relief with the same fine artistic diligence below. Both carvings were exquisite, highly detailed and executed with perfect perspective. I had never seen woodcarving like it anywhere.

"Do you know the significance of these carvings, Mr. Johnson? Do you know who made them and where and when?"

"No, ma'am. The dealer didn't know either," Mr. Johnson answered. The dealer said this was an authentic Indian hunting bow and was maybe a hundred and fifty years old, maybe older. The folks at UT examined it and said it was genuine. They said it might be Choctaw, Creek or Chickasaw, but their best guess was Cherokee. It's beautiful, isn't it? I love bow huntin' and the minute I saw this bow I knew it belonged over my mantel."

As I listened to Mr. Johnson talk about the bow, I wondered what it was that I held in my hands. Where did this beautiful artifact come from? Who made it and why?

"The dealer said it's the best he's ever seen. It takes a stout man to string it and draw it back. He was proud of it, if you know what I mean. I don't usually buy things I don't need, but when I saw this I had to have it. I set my satchel down, but it was worth ever' penny."

As I continued to hold the bow, I felt an odd sensation—as if the old bow I held in my hands were alive—as if it were trying to communicate with me somehow. It was a spooky feeling. I felt goose bumps rise on my forearms. I wondered where the bow came from, who made it, who carved the handle and who used it. I wondered what stories this bow could tell. What piece of American history was I holding in my hands? I wondered who it was who first admired this bow and who hunted with it? I had the disappointing feeling I would never know the answers to those questions.

Chapter IX

Katie Visits New Echota

Chapter 9

As soon as I returned to Chattanooga after the reunion, I made an appointment with my journalism professor, just back from vacation. I needed advice. I showed him my notes, the two journals and recounted my story from the beginning, including Greg's offhand remark. I told him about our visit to Tahlequah, the coincidence of Cassie's name, the series of dreams and that my research was keeping me up every night till the wee hours. In my muddled excitement I tried to blurt out everything at once. I'm sure I sounded irrational but I did the best I could. When I breathlessly finished my hurried, disjointed recital, my professor leaned back in his desk chair and hooked his fingers behind his head. He smiled and stared at me for a minute.

"Young lady, you do have the gift, don't you?" he said.

"Thank you, sir," was all I could say.

"In all my years teaching," he continued, "I haven't had many students like you. You're a born storyteller—a born journalist. You are a writer. You have an inquisitive nature. You have passion and a desire to learn and communicate with others that can't be taught or acquired. It's in your blood. I'm privileged to have you as a student, Katie. I don't think you should be overly concerned about your confused emotions."

"Thank you, sir," I answered once again.

"You're not crazy. Not at all," he said seriously. "Whether you heard voices or not, I can't say. As far as I'm concerned, your mind is perfectly lucid and chomping at the bit to express itself. Writing is what you do—what you were born to do. If you want my opinion, you should embrace everything about this project, even if you have contradictory emotions. You're certainly not going daft."

"Thank you, sir. I was worried about that," I answered.

"I think your systematic mind is telling you it has a need to pursue this undertaking to its logical conclusion. Allow it to lead you," he advised. "My advice is that you should take as many weeks off as you can manage. Go somewhere without distraction and write, write, write. Allow your enthusiasm full rein. Let your passion infuse your work in a non-distracting atmosphere and you'll produce something we'll all be proud of. This is, I think, a special time in the development of this story and you need to concentrate. Go somewhere alone and work. Am I right?"

"Yes sir. I think you're correct," I answered quietly.

I took his advice to the letter and told Greg I would be working alone for a while. I found a little bed and breakfast on an out-of-the-way working farm near Rock Spring, in Walker County, about twenty-five miles south of Chattanooga. It was close to my grandfather's place and had a quiet little creek running through the property. There would be no traffic noise. I could write undisturbed day and night. The only thing I would hear would be owls and mourning doves and maybe a crowing rooster at dawn. Appropriately, I would be working smack in the middle of the last piece of land the State of Georgia took from the Cherokee. I wanted to get a feel for Cherokee Country—even if there were no Cherokee there now—even if it belonged to someone else.

The story was becoming surreal—bizarre. I've never believed in ghosts and goblins. My rational brain rebelled at the persistent uninvited imaginary visitors wandering in and out of my consciousness who seemed to want to take command of the direction of my life—demanding I join their adventure.

I rented my room at the bed and breakfast for four weeks and got a good deal. I brought my laptop, notebooks, a box of Cherokee history books, a small bag of comfortable clothes and five big packs of Oreos. I can't seem to write without Oreos. I planned to spend at least the next four weeks in journalistic hibernation curled up on the bed in my old cotton pajamas buried in Cherokee research, the journal and its transcription. I wanted to work hard and travel light. I intended to spend every waking hour reading and transcribing Cassie's journal and not much else. I wanted to see this project through to the end. When my tired brain needed rest, I planned to occasionally do some casual exploration of what used to be the Cherokee homeland. I wanted to do a good job. I wanted to be focused.

As I made my plans I couldn't help but think about the little girl named Cassie I had met at the Fourth of July reunion and the coincidence that she had the same name as the Indian woman who wrote the journal I was transcribing. I wondered what that connection was—if any. Maybe one day I would know more about that mysterious coincidence but, for right now, I needed to concentrate on the job at hand. Answers would come in time.

As a starting point, I decided to drive down to New Echota, the old Cherokee capital, and look around. I don't ever remember being there before.

I didn't expect to find much, but maybe I would find something that would give me a connection to Cassie, her culture and her people. I felt a little poking around where the journal was actually written would be an auspicious beginning. I wanted to see the actual place where Cassie lived and worked. I wanted to experience the soil where the journal was actually written. I wanted to look at the same landscape she looked at—the same hills—the same mountains—the same rivers. I wanted to see and hear the same birds. I wanted to see the clouds and feel the air. I wanted a taste of the same weather.

According to MapQuest, the old Cherokee capital was just south of Dalton, near Calhoun and Resaca, and only thirty-five miles south of my bed and breakfast. In the past I had driven by the meaningless roadside signs to New Echota a hundred times on the interstate but never visited. I suppose New Echota was to me and my parents like Ruby Falls and Rock City. I've seen them advertised on a thousand barns and billboards but, although we live in the area, my parents and I never visited. We never had an interest. Perhaps familiarity does breed contempt.

I remember the old woman in Oklahoma saying the story was chasing me. I remember her personification of the journal, as if it wanted to go back home, so I placed my copy of Cassie's journal on the passenger seat, face up, to ride with me to New Echota. I thought if I were going to the Cherokee capital to begin my work on Cassie's behalf, it would be a nice symbol to take the journal with me. I would take it back where it came from as if it were my companion assisting in my research—as if Cassie were actually sitting there beside me in the passenger seat. I must confess, as I drove south from Rock Spring, I glanced over occasionally at the book riding in the seat beside me. First, I imagined the original lying there instead of my copy. Then, without willing it, I imagined a young woman my age in the passenger seat anxiously looking out the window at the passing countryside with that original journal held securely in her lap—her hands squeezing the journal in anticipation until her knuckles had turned white. I could see by her features she was Cherokee. As my imaginary passenger watched the passing countryside I felt her rising emotion as we approached New Echota and the home she hadn't seen since that day in May long years ago. My imagination was much too vivid. As I visualized the woman sitting in my passenger seat, I lost control. My eyes were so full of tears I couldn't see to drive. I had to pull over. I put my head on my arms on the steering wheel and began sobbing in big heaving sobs with tears streaming. I was blubbering like a child. I guess the intense emotion and tension of the last couple of weeks had bubbled to the surface and required release.

When I finally gained control and blew my nose, I felt better. I looked over and there was the copy of the journal where I had placed it. My imaginary woman was gone. I was glad she disappeared.

For the next couple of hours, I drove around slowly getting a feel for the area and looking at nothing in particular. I headed down the Chatsworth highway and crossed the Oostanaula River towards the east. I didn't go too far and turned around and went back and turned right on the Craigtown Road and shortly turned left on Gee Rd. I was going in a big circle around New Eschota. I turned left onto Industrial Blvd. and then left on the Old Dalton Road and back left again onto the Chatsworth Road and under I-75. I completed the circle.

As I drove, I stopped at several convenience stores and asked about the Cherokee, but no one knew anything. 'No Cherokee around here', was the consistent answer to my question. I thought it interesting no one could tell me a thing about the Cherokee right in the heart of the old Cherokee Nation. They were as ignorant as I was and apathetic. How could that be? Evidently, the only remaining human memory of the Cherokee in this part of the world was the state park at New Echota. It seems when the Cherokee were rounded up and removed, everything that marked centuries of their national existence was destroyed—erased as the old woman in Oklahoma had said. The Cherokee had been deleted from the Georgia countryside and from local human memory. They had been vanished.

As I drove I found no sign of a Cherokee village or habitation. I didn't really expect to find anything. I saw no Cherokee historical markers other than the signs directing me to New Echota.

Around Chattanooga there are thousands upon thousands of signs, memorials, inscriptions, markers, plaques, statues, monuments, museums, tributes and the like to Civil War battles but nothing to speak of regarding the Cherokee who lived here for hundreds of years. I remember driving down the top of Missionary Ridge on scenic Crest Drive and enjoying that breathtaking view of Chattanooga below and Lookout Mountain, Signal Mountain and Moccasin Bend in the distance. It seemed like every other house on that road had two plaques and a cannon in the front yard. We seem to have a macabre pride concerning our cherished Civil War—a war between white people that we choose to remember and even re-enact. The war against the Cherokee has been forgotten. No one is interested in that war. No one re-enacts the Cherokee removal.

Before 1838, our United States government recognized where I had been driving all afternoon to be sovereign Cherokee Country and not governed by the state of Georgia or United States law. It was entirely Cherokee by longstanding treaty.

The area today is rural. As I circled around New Echota I saw picturesque, agricultural farmland dotted with homes, barns, outbuildings, fences, fields and livestock with the noisy I-75 running north and south through the middle. There was nothing in the countryside to indicate Indians had ever lived here. I saw a few folks of African origin but, almost without exception, every person I saw was white.

According to my research, the Georgia Militia, fortunate drawers and squatters who came into Cherokee Country in the spring of 1838 seized all Cherokee homes, property, assets, livestock and even ransacked Cherokee graves looking for silver, gold and valuable artifacts.

Within a few days after the deportation, nothing remained of the Cherokee Nation—not even their graveyards. I couldn't get the image out of my mind of someone digging up my deceased grandparents in order to steal my grandmother's rings or my grandfather's tie pin and coldly leaving behind their scattered remains.

During my drive I reflected on the scenic beauty of the area, but I didn't find one thing that would help me with Cassie's story or give me the beginning point I had hoped to find. I decided to end my quest by having a brief look around the old Cherokee capital at New Echota and then drive back to my bed and breakfast and get started on the transcription of the journal lying there in my front seat.

I was tired. It had been a long day, but when I arrived at the gates to the park at New Echota I could feel myself becoming invigorated as if an outside agency was supplying renewed energy. It was spooky but I was excited to see the old Cherokee capital and give my imagination free rein.

It was just after five. I was disappointed. I was too late to get in. Both staff and visitors were gone and mine the only car parked in front of the locked gate. I got out and leaned lazily over the hood resting my chin in my hands and watching the setting sun. I tried to imagine what this area looked like in 1838.

This part of Georgia marks the end of the Piedmont and the beginning of the mountainous region of the state and is quite charming. I especially love the stretch of road from here over past Sonoraville, Fairmont, Talking Rock and up through the narrow mountain roads to Ellijay. I remember my Sunday outings with my grandfather long ago. I remember stopping at a roadside vendor in Ellijay and buying fresh sorghum syrup in a shiny quart metal can with the paper label held on with a red rubber band. That was a warm, nostalgic memory and brought a smile to my face.

As I was leaning over the hood of my car watching the setting sun, I thought how today the State of Georgia proudly owns New Echota and operates it as a state park and tourist attraction. I have to pay the State of Georgia seven dollars to visit the old Cherokee capital. What a paradoxical turn of history—how ironic. In 1838, the State of Georgia took possession of New Echota. Somewhere near, perhaps where I was standing, several hundred Cherokee families were held prisoner for days and then marched north on foot by the Georgia Militia to Ross's Landing on the Tennessee River.

I don't understand why Georgia owns New Echota. Why wasn't it given back to the Cherokee? It was theirs, wasn't it? It wouldn't be the last time the actions of my white government would puzzle me. I looked around and wondered where the removal fort had been built. What did it look like? Where was the open ground where the Cherokee families were imprisoned—guarded night and day as if they were dangerous criminals. I closed my eyes. In the peaceful evening stillness, I imagined I could hear children crying in their mother's arms.

I heard the old woman in Oklahoma say, "When does the thief legally own that which he stole?"

As I mused about things long ago, I opened my eyes. A small yellow butterfly landed on the sleeve of my white blouse. I didn't move. It sat on my arm for quite a while gently moving its bright yellow wings. I imagined I was being welcomed to New Echota by a benevolent resident spirit who was blessing my quest to learn more about the Cherokee. After my welcome, the butterfly flew into the gathering gloom of the Georgia dusk and disappeared. I was alone.

In peaceful silence I watched the last crimson rays of the Georgia sun disappear behind the mountains. As the light began to fade, the tender twilight shadows crept from their hiding places embracing all of New Echota in their protecting arms. The long-abandoned Cherokee capital with no living residents other than myself lay still and silent before me. This evening, though only a temporary inhabitant, I felt honored.

In the gathering gloom New Echota seemed to quicken. I imagined tall, shadowy silhouettes slowly rise from the soil around me—their bowed heads rising from their chest to stand tall and proud as they reached their full height. They were appointed Cherokee sentinels—gaunt, wispy, majestic. The shadows around me grew. I beheld them—giant custodians of honor forever standing their sacred guard over the old Cherokee council houses protecting hallowed ground. I felt them welcome me to join them in their nightly vigil to preserve the dignity of the Cherokee Nation.

In the gathering darkness I suddenly heard what sounded like distant voices in chorus—soft harmonies that soon swelled into a gentle crescendo pouring their spectral lament over both me and New Echota. With soft, velvety words the chorus sang, "Tell our story."

I heard the voices sing their harmonies—one moment in sweet consonance and the next voices blended with an almost unpleasant, harsh dissidence. What was I hearing? Once again the voices grew louder—the sound surrounding me as if I were in the center of a sports stadium filled with singers and their song was meant only for me. For a second time I heard the sweetness followed by strange overtones of harmonic dissidence.

"Tell our story," they sang once again.

I looked around but saw nothing. I felt a rising panic. What was this? Then I heard the chorus singing a third time—or did I?

What? What? Did I really hear voices? Not again? I was confused. Something must be wrong. Was the sound I just heard an actual chorus of human voices—an ancient Cherokee lament sung for my benefit as I first thought? More likely it was my out of control imagination manipulating the sound of a speeding Covenant Transport eighteen-wheeler on nearby I-75 hauling eighty thousand pounds of freight towards its terminal just up the road in Chattanooga. Perhaps the sound I heard was explained by an invisible flock of noisy birds in the evening gloom heading to their roost? I couldn't trust my overactive mind. Surely I didn't hear a chorus of voices. That wasn't possible. I must be mistaken. It must have been my imagination.

I was unnerved—shaken. I was becoming weary of voices and dreams. Now I had a whole chorus of voices. Where would this end? Was I losing my mind? Was I unbalanced? Am I delusional—the victim of self-induced psychotic hypnosis? Was I becoming emotionally involved in a historical drama whose last act had begun right here under my feet in the spring of 1838? Maybe, because I'm pregnant, my hormones have become confused and I really am a little daft?

Suddenly I felt uncomfortable being alone and exposed. I wanted the familiar security of my car. I wanted to lock the doors and immediately drive away from New Echota straight to the safety of my room. I wanted to bolt my door and pull the cover over my head. I wanted to get away from the highway, eighteen-wheelers, voices and flocks of birds. I wanted to regain my sanity and rest my confused mind.

When I got back on the road I decided my mind had manufactured the voices out of the never-ending traffic noise on nearby I-75. That was the only rational explanation. Because of the journal and my research I knew my sense of injustice was overactive. I needed to come to terms with the truth that it was impossible for me to right old wrongs a hundred and fifty years after the fact. No one would ever be allowed to re-write the wretched end of the Cherokee—especially me. What was done was done. Nothing could be changed. The milk had been spilt. The genie couldn't be put back into the bottle. Pandora's box could never be shut. I need to write the story I was given and get on with the next project in my life—case closed.

Perhaps I should go back to traveling and gather happy stories about people who are alive—stories about children, their pets and their grandparents—helping nice people to become nicer. Perhaps I should forget this journal. Perhaps I should let sleeping dogs lie. I didn't believe I should forget the story but I was worried. I remember the old woman staring at me and saying the story was pursuing me. I knew the journal contained a great story, but I was feeling like a dog on a leash—tugged this way and that by the hand of some invisible master to who knows where. I felt like the journal had hijacked my life. I felt as if I were living some mysterious pre-determined stage play, written and directed by a nameless historical adjudicator intent on inhabiting my mind and body for some unknown end.

I needed to relax and quit thinking so much. I drove straight back to my room without stopping for anything. It was well past sundown when I arrived at my bed and breakfast. As I got out of my car, the oversized full moon, just rising over the nearby Peavine Ridge, was huge, yellow and beautiful as only a summertime moon can be when it first appears above the dark horizon. It lit up the landscape like daytime. It was a welcome omen and an auspicious ending to my long, confusing day. The vision of the rising moon made me feel better. I went inside and decided I didn't need to unwind. I went right to work transcribing the journal.

Chapter X

Katie Sets the Stage

Chapter 10

Since Greg's "that's where we keep our Indians" remark, I have thought of nothing but preparing Cassie's journal for publication. I'm almost finished. The editors asked me to write a foreword. This is it. What follows this foreword is a faithful transcription of Cassie's meticulously kept historical record begun about 1820 in the hills of northwest Georgia near New Echota—very near where I was reared. Her journal ended abruptly in 1838. Cassie's wish to tell her story has become a reality.

The Cherokee Nation once occupied most of what we now call Georgia, Tennessee, Alabama, North Carolina, South Carolina, Kentucky and some of Virginia. By 1820, Cassie's sprawling nation had been driven out of their network of coveted river valleys and squeezed into a tiny corner of non-arable mountainous land unwanted by whites where Georgia, Alabama, Tennessee and North Carolina intersect.

In her journal Cassie details her life from her girlhood until her deportation. She tells of her joys, heartaches, loves and loss. She talks of her family, the Cherokee Nation and the complicated politics during those last turbulent years. She tells us about her love for her handsome fiancé—son of a missionary to the Cherokee. She describes in detail how her land was seized and her people deported west of the Mississippi River—outside the borders of the United States to the end of the earth.

Who were the invaders speaking a strange language who seized the Cherokee Nation's land and deported her people at gunpoint? They were mostly English with a small number of Scots, Welsh, Irish, French, Germans and maybe a few East European and Scandinavian folk thrown in. All were white. I've learned a lot about my history and Cassie's story.

It was Cassie's lifelong wish that her story be told—that her journal be published. It seemed best to me and my editors to let you hear Cassie speak first person. We want this courageous woman to have her say. I want you to hear her brave voice—a voice denied for over a hundred and fifty years. This book is her story told in her words as it should be.

Cassie's Cherokee name was Walela. Her English-speaking friends called her Cassie. Until I accidentally wandered into the Cherokee Indian Reservation in Oklahoma, I never knew the area where I grew up in northwest Georgia was once an independent country—sovereign Cherokee Country—Cassie's home.

To my surprise, I learned the entirety of Walker County where I was reared was considered outside the legal jurisdiction of both Georgia and the United States before 1838. How strange. All of Walker County once belonged to Cassie's people—the Principal People, they called themselves.

According to my DNA test, my ancestors were all from the UK with a touch of German or French with the odd addition of five percent Scandinavian. Somewhere one of my female ancestors met a handsome young man from Denmark.

According to Cassie's journal, my white Georgia relatives from the UK, by force of arms, deported Cassie and her family outside the United States. To this day we happily occupy her land. Until recently I was unaware of this history—my history—Cassie's history.

The Cherokee are gone from northwest Georgia—long gone. Their villages gone, thousands of miles of crisscrossing hunting paths gone. Cherokee structures, barns, fields and houses gone. Their stories, culture, language and even their graves have vanished. Nothing remains—absolutely nothing. Even the authentic looking buildings at New Echota are modern re-creations—recently constructed by white descendants of the same people Georgia sent to burn the originals. Everything Cherokee was removed. Cassie's Cherokee Nation was bleached, using the modern term of irretrievable digital data removal. Cassie's people suffered what has become an irreversible vanishment.

I remember my grandfather taking us on long circuitous Sunday drives around northwest Georgia in his restored candy-apple red '63 Chevrolet Impala SS convertible. What a car. On Sunday afternoons, my parents, grandparents and I explored every highway and byway in that beautiful car and, at some time or other, picnicked on every roadside table. Not many of those tables are left from the old days.

My grandfather rebuilt the 327 engine himself. He insisted I learn to drive a stick shift. I spent many wonderful hours with my grandfather in vacant parking lots around Lafayette, Trion and Summerville learning to let the clutch out smoothly and then learning to shift just as smoothly into second with his fancy Hurst competition shifter and all without spinning the tires or stalling the engine. He says the car is mine after he's gone.

One of my grandfather's favorite Sunday outings was a drive south from Rossville where he had lived on Dry Valley Road before his father bought his farm in Rock Spring. Sometimes on Sunday we would leave Grandpa's house in Rock Spring and go the back way to Chickamauga. We always stopped at Crawfish Springs for a drink of cold water from the big stream that bubbled out from under that huge rock on the other side of the road from the old Gordon Lee Mansion. We would read the cast iron plaques, some grey—some blue, detailing local Civil War activity and the big battle that was fought in and around the sleepy town of Chickamauga.

We would continue our drive south through Walker County and sometimes go out the Cove Road through the historic Mountain Cove Farms, for many years a single working farm that filled the perfect triangle where Lookout and Pigeon mountains joined. My grandfather worked on that farm for a short time. He said his father used to occasionally coon hunt there in the early '50's. He said his father, my great-grandfather, would get permission to coon hunt from an old black man who lived in a shack up the first hollow on the right as you came into the Cove from Lafayette. My grandfather said his daddy told him the black man's old shack was as far back as you could go in your truck and then you had to get out and walk a ways. The old man was a descendant of African slaves freed on that very farm during the Civil War and the old man still lived in his family's old homeplace—originally slave quarters. Does anyone live there now?

Other times my grandfather would head his red Chevrolet east from Rock Spring and then south. As I write, I can see the rolling hills, the dark emerald green forests and the carpet of uninterrupted trees that climbed the mountain sides to the sky or so it seemed to me as a little girl.

We would drive through Lafayette and east through Naomi, Villanow and then down through Sugar Valley to Resaca. The road through Sugar Valley ran south through the hills from Armurchee beside the pristine Chattahoochee National Forest.

Sugar Valley—what a beautiful place name. When I was little I imagined small country grocery stores throughout Sugar Valley that sold nothing but five-pound bags of Dixie Crystal sugar. What a memory.

According to Cassie's journal, it was in this same picturesque Sugar Valley that young white Georgia boys arrested every Cherokee family at bayonet point and herded them into prison camps at nearby Calhoun,

Lafayette, New Eschota and other strategic locations. A few days after the round-up, every Cherokee family was marched north to Ross's Landing on the Tennessee River, present day Chattanooga. They were held at Ross's Landing and subsequently deported west. The Cherokee men, women and children arrested in Walker County and its surrounds would have been driven en masse up the valleys directly through Rossville where my grandfather had lived when he was a boy.

Other times on our outings my grandfather would drive us south on Highway 27 through Trion. When we went through Summerville he turned left and then immediately back right onto 114 into Gordon County towards my great-great-grandmother's home place in Lyerly—in a beautiful valley where my great-grandfather's mother and her siblings were raised on a working farm before WWI and where my relatives still live.

If we continued south past her old homeplace, we would go down towards Cedar Bluff and Lake Weiss and end up in Gadsden and Rainbow City just across the state line in Alabama.

Every acre we drove past on our Sunday outings had been sovereign Cherokee soil under sovereign Cherokee law. I don't understand why I never knew that. Maybe I was told and I forgot.

If my grandfather turned more towards the southeast on our Sunday drives, we would go towards Rome and Cedartown. We never went much past that because we had to be back to Rock Spring by dark and Sunday was bath night. We had to get ready for school. We would sometimes come back through Calhoun, Resaca, Dalton and then maybe cut back through Fairview by Lake Winnepesaukah from Ringgold, then down McFarland Avenue by the old John Ross house and through McFarland Gap and then past Happy Valley Farms. We would go around the ninety-degree Happy Valley curve, turn left onto Dry Valley Road and then back through Chickamauga, Shield's Crossroads, where my great-grandfather caught his car pool ride to Dupont for thirty years, and then back down 27 to Rock Spring. I love every inch of that country. I can call up this entire area in my mind at will—pretty much every turn in every road.

Even after reading Cassie's journal, I can't visualize what happened in the peaceful county of my youth. Hard as I try, I can't picture Georgia boys, my blood relatives, rounding up thousands of terrified children, parents and grandparents. I can't imagine my kinfolk seizing the Cherokee's every possession and herding them into prison camps and soon afterward deporting them eight hundred miles west—all sanctioned by our U.S. Congress. The Cherokee deportation was, and still is, quite legal.

My memories of Walker County and northwest Georgia are all happy memories—memories of enchanted, blissful high school days, afternoon band practice, Friday night football games, cruising John's Drive-in, family outings and riding our horses on the weekends through the endless maze of bridal paths in the enormous Chickamauga Battlefield—the largest military park in the United States.

Is Cassie's journal fiction? Are the graphic accounts I have been reading of the Cherokee being imprisoned at Fort Cumming, located not far from the old Lafayette High School on north Cherokee Street that my grandfather attended, a made-up story? Is the arrest of every Cherokee family and subsequent seizure of all Cherokee assets—every house, barn, smokehouse, pot, pan, hoe, plow, horse, mule and cow—all historical fiction?

According to my research on the morning of the twenty-fifth of May, 1838, young white Georgia soldiers arrested every Cherokee family. In less than three weeks after the arrests began, Georgia newspapers boasted the Cherokee had been extinguished as a nation. They had been vanished—eradicated—entirely removed. Georgia had been cleansed.

Soon after the removal white families of European descent occupied every acre of the land seized from the Cherokee. They registered their new deeds for their new farms at the new courthouses in Lafayette, Ringgold, and Dalton and the county seats of the other new counties.

When I began my research for Cassie's journal I was puzzled why I personally knew nothing of the history of the Cherokee removal. After transcribing Cassie's journal, I understand why I was never told.

Can you imagine a jovial grandfather with his white hair and big nose taking his wide-eyed grandchildren on his knee saying, "Let me tell you young'uns about the day we rounded up the Cherokee with our pretty bayonets glistening in the morning sun. What a glorious sight. You should've been there. Yep, we took everything they had. We sure did. We took their homes, cows and hogs. We took their barns and fields. We took every pot, pan and stick of furniture. We cleaned house, you might say. We even dug up their dead relatives looking for valuables. A new broom sweeps clean. Then we made those lazy, good-for-nothin' Indians walk barefoot to the other side of the Mississippi. Yep, we shoved them right outside the borders of our country. It was some sight to see. Our whole farm right here where we sit used to be Cherokee, and it'll be yours one day, I'm proud to say. We passed a law and got rid of them all."

No one could tell that story. The Cherokee removal was erased from the corporate consciousness of an entire nation. What we did in 1838 was swept under our big rug where it lies forgotten to this day.

Simon Wiesenthal, living in post WWII Austria, worked tirelessly hunting Nazi war criminals. After the war his Austrian neighbors opposed his work vehemently. Why? They wanted to forget. Austrians didn't want to be reminded of such horrible events. Simon Wiesenthal, however, didn't believe injustice could be swept under the rug and forgotten. He didn't believe they made rugs that big.

After transcribing Cassie's journal, I find a few histories, an odd granite memorial, a list of names carved in stone, a few small road signs and lame governmental apologies an inadequate response.

Compensation? Not in a million years, I'm told. You're not laying your white guilt on me. Everything we white folks did was legal, wasn't it? The Indian Removal Act of 1830 allowed for the legal deportation of all Indian tribes west of the Mississippi River—clearing the way for the unified growth of these wonderful and benevolent United States. The removal we read about in Cassie's journal was, and still is, perfectly lawful. In any case, it was for their own good, didn't Andrew Jackson say?

I must have supposed my grandfather's farm belonged to my relatives for long centuries. Didn't they always have title to our farm? I must have assumed European sailors in some distant millennia discovered a vacant continent waiting for benevolent European occupants—my relatives.

Cassie, an avid newspaper reader, included numerous quotes from Georgia newspapers in her journal. Those newspapers are extant and available today. Sadly, I was required to condense some quotes. Each time I deleted material from a newspaper article in the transcription, I would mark my deletion with an ellipsis. I would use three dots...for the deletion of a short idea or sentence and four dots....for a longer deletion. I wish I could have included the full text of the newspaper articles in every case, but my editors were afraid the modern reader, used to mindless television, would be bored and never finish Cassie's book and thus decrease profits. If it were up to me, I would include every word.

There are no Indian reservations in Georgia. There are no modern Cherokee farms with Cherokee families raising their families in Walker County or any county seized in 1838. There are no Cherokee towns in

Georgia. After reading Cassie's journal, you'll know why. Cassie's journal is one of the few surviving historical accounts of Cherokee history told from the other side—from the Cherokee perspective.

I am humbled to have had a small part in telling her story. I'll let her be creative. I shall be content to be her amanuensis. These are Cassie's words she wrote for you to read. I commend her to you. She is yours.

Chapter XI

1820 – Cassie's Gift

Chapter 11

18 February 1820

Today I received the best gift of my life—a journal. I wrote this evening until my fingers were sore. I am happy—more than happy.

I am Walela. I am eight years old. My name means hummingbird in Cherokee. My parents died soon after I was born. I live with elisi and edudu and my brother, Five Feathers. Elisi and edudu are my grandmother and grandfather. We live in Cherokee Country. Our community is at the southern end of the great mountains near New Echota, our Cherokee capital. It is the most beautiful place on earth. It is the land given us by the Great Spirit.

Mr. Lowry is my wonderful teacher. Today he gave me my special gift.

"Hello, Cassandra," Mr. Lowry said, still in his saddle.

"Bonjour, monsignor," I answered. I curtseyed properly as Mrs. Lowry taught me. I gave another curtsey to his son, Ben, who was also mounted.

"I'm doing well in my French studies, am I not, Mr. Lowry?"

"My dear Cassie, your French is splendid," Mr. Lowry said as he dismounted, "and your accent near perfect. You'll be speaking like a Frenchwoman before you know it."

"Thank you, sir," I answered.

"If you were a man, I could get you a job as a translator in Savannah," Mr. Lowry continued. "I'm pleased to have you in my school. I'll see you there tomorrow, will I not?"

"Yes sir, I'll be there," I answered.

Mr. Lowry handed me a small bundle of newspapers.

"I'll be there, sir. I can't wait. And thank you for the newspapers. I read them every day as I promised."

He handed me another package wrapped in a white cloth.

"Here are some walnut scones, Cassie. Eleanor baked them yesterday for you and your grandparents. Don't let Five Feathers gobble them all," Mr. Lowry said.

In one smooth athletic motion, Mr. Lowry's son, Ben, jumped from his saddle and landed in perfect balance beside me. Ben is my classmate, my best friend and handsome.

"Hello, Cassie. What ya doin'?" Ben said. "Don't go away. I'll be right back. I have to tie up the horses."

As Ben led their horses to be hitched, he gave me a big smile. I see Ben at school and some days when we don't go to school.

"Cassie, I adore your love of learning," Mr. Lowry said. "If everyone wanted to learn like you, this world would be a better place."

"Thank you, sir," I answered again.

"If I can pull the right strings," Mr. Lowry continued, "I'll get you into a college one day. Would you be brave enough to go north to a school for girls? Would you like that?"

"I would love that, and I would not be afraid, Mr. Lowry. I would be brave. I would. I would love to go to school. Can I do that please? Please? I promise to be courageous."

"If you keep learning at the rate you're going, it won't be long before you're ready. I can only teach you so much, Cassie," Mr. Lowry said. "It will be difficult for any school to refuse someone as gifted as you. When that day comes I have friends who will help us find you a place. I think we can count on that."

Young Ben returned from hitching the horses.

"Hello, Benjamin," I said. I curtseyed again to Ben, but it was a mock curtsey. I was teasing. I like to tease Ben. He gave me a playful push. When I tease Ben his face turns red.

"I brought something for you, Cassie—a special gift," Mr. Lowry said, "but I want to remind you to keep reading and learning and increase your vocabulary, young lady. Above all, increase your store of words."

"Yes, sir. I promise to learn new words. I love learning new words," I replied eagerly.

"Learning to communicate is the most important thing for any young person, even for a woman," Mr. Lowry continued. "If a person has a small vocabulary, they will have a small mind and think lesser things. You don't want be small-minded, do you?"

"Oh no, Mr. Lowry. Of course not. I want a big mind."

"A person with an extensive vocabulary can think big thoughts and roam the universe in their mind. One's imagination is fueled by words—each word an idea. The human mind is powerful and yours, young lady, is more powerful than most, plus you have a marvelous memory. Trust me, Cassie. Learn all the words you can and see if what I'm telling you isn't true."

"Give her the gift, Ben," Mr. Lowry said to his son.

Ben handed me a parcel wrapped in brown paper and bound with twine.

"You're going to like this, Cassie," Ben said. "Father got it just for you. I'm envious. Open it, Cassie. Open it. It's yours. Open it."

It was an old, strongly bound book with tattered corners. Two thirds of the pages were blank. It was bigger than my slate.

"Thank you, thank you, thank you, Mr. Lowry," I said, and I gave him an embrace.

"I've known you've been wanting to write, Cassie," Mr. Lowry said. "Now you can write all you want. When I came across this old book, I knew you would love it. I wouldn't be surprised if you could write in that big ole' thing for years. If you fill that one up, Eleanor and I promise we'll get you another. We want you to use your gift. I'm sorry it's so ugly. I wish I could afford a new one, but that's the best we could do right now."

"This is the best gift ever in my life," I said, almost in tears.

"Eleanor also sent a gift, Cassie," Mr. Lowry said. "When Eleanor saw this old book, she ordered your gift from Savannah. We both think you a special young lady."

Mr. Lowry pulled a small package wrapped in brown paper from his coat pocket. I unwrapped it immediately. It was a beautiful new pen. I will never have to use an awkward, dull turkey feather again. All I could do was hug his neck I was so emotional.

"Cassie, this is your journal and your pen—yours to keep," Mr. Lowry said. "Some folks write daily and some now and then. Some write for pleasure and some to remember what they did. Write anything you wish as often as you wish."

"I shall write, Mr. Lowry, I promise," I said. I could hardly contain myself. "I shall begin tonight."

"You can record daily activities, write prose, poetry or stories. You can write about what actually happened or you can use words to write the marvelous things you conjure in your imagination so we can see what only you have seen in your mind. Write whatever you please, but write, write, write," Mr. Lowry added.

"I promise I'll start this very day."

"May I give you some advice about writing, Cassie?" Mr. Lowry asked.

"You can always give me advice, sir," I answered.

"Cassie," Mr. Lowry said, "you and your nation occupy a special place in our hearts. First, write for pleasure. Above all, I want you to enjoy writing. Write from your heart. Express emotions. Write about things that give pleasure and things that make you sad. Write about things you love and things that make you angry. Let your new pen speak."

111

"Yes, sir, I promise I shall do that," I added quickly. I was so happy I felt like I would explode.

"Secondly, be yourself," Mr. Lowry advised. "Don't imitate the style you read in books or newspapers," Mr. Lowry advised. "Write like Cassie—not like me, or Ben or anyone else. Use words the way Cassie uses words. You can even invent words as long as they come from your mind. We've done that in school, haven't we?"

"Yes sir, we have. I love to make up words," I answered, and we both laughed.

"Thirdly," Mr. Lowry said, "write in English as we do in school. I wouldn't be surprised if one day your journal becomes a treasure for those who want to understand your culture. As you know, there's a dearth of literature by citizens of your nation. You're unique, young lady. You've been gifted. I want you to write."

"Fourth," Mr. Lowry said, "use our white calendar. White folks don't understand your lunar method of tracking the passage of time. I want white people to enjoy reading your journal. Lastly, if you, your grandparents or friends find anything in the newspapers interesting or disturbing—include those thoughts in your journal."

"I promise I shall do that, Mr. Lowry. I promise. I love to read newspapers," I said.

"You're intuitive, Cassie," Mr. Lowry continued. "You'll find these instructions easy. Tell your story. Tell your story from your Cherokee perspective. Only you can explain what you and your grandparents believe. Let your heart flow down your arm and through your pen onto the paper."

"I shall do that, sir. I can't wait. I'll do everything you say. I love my new journal and pen."

Mr. Lowry sat on a stone with his hands on his knees and laughed, with Ben at his side smiling.

"Mother and Father knew you would like your gift," Ben said.

"Cassie," Mr. Lowry added, "watching you with your new journal and pen is special. I haven't felt such gladness in a long time. I can't seem to stop myself from giving you advice. Forgive me."

"I love your advice, Mr. Lowry. Please continue."

"I'm almost finished, Cassie. Just remember writing isn't like mathematics. There is no wrong answer in writing. You can't write anything incorrectly if it comes honestly from your mind."

"Yes, sir. I promise. I promise I shall write," I said.

"Eleanor and I already know what white folks think. You write about anything you want to but it would be my wish that you write about your life—your Cherokee life."

"I would like that, sir. I love to write. I often listen to edudu and his friends when they talk on elisi's porch," I answered. "I had much rather listen to adult conversation than play games. Writing about what they say would be fun."

"Well, Cassie," Mr. Lowry said, "I'm looking forward to reading your writings one day. You have a gift. I've never had a student who learns as quickly as you. Writing is surely one of the things you were meant to do."

"Yes, sir. I love school. I think about writing every day. Writing will be easy. Sometimes I lie awake and write stories in my mind to help me sleep. I already read newspapers every day. Edudu's visitors talk about our nation—sometimes long after I go to bed. Now I can write about what they say. Thank you for the journal, the pen and the advice," I said. "I promise I won't try to write like someone else. You'll be proud of me, Mr. Lowry. I'll remember what you have told me. One day people will be proud of you and Mrs. Lowry, too."

19 February 1820

What a grand gift is my journal and pen. I know I shall be writing the rest of my life. What a lovely thought. What shall I write this evening? I can write about the moon hanging in the sky above the mountain and how it throws its soft light over my legs like a comfortable blanket. I can write about elisi's crackling fire keeping us warm on a cold winter's night. Who will read these words I write with my new pen? Will my children or grand-children read them? I feel a joy when I write, as if my body were packed full of jumbled up words begging to be allowed out to play through my mind. When I release them through the nib of my pen they promise to cavort and frolic on the paper while I sleep and entertain me on the morrow. What a lovely thought.

20 February 1820

I am by the fire again tonight. It is cozy inside our house. Whoever you are that may read this journal, I promise to think about you as I write. I share my fire, my words and my mind. Who might you be? Are you my child or grandchild? Are you an old friend or relative? Are you African, French, English or Spanish? Have years passed? Why do you read? How did you find my journal?

I promise, dear reader, to write from my heart. I promise to tell you the truth. I promise.

21 February 1820

Whoever you are, dear reader, we are friends. I pledge, when I see the first star appear, I will write as if you were here with me sharing a cup of tea and having a marvelous conversation. One day I shall sleep with my ancestors and you shall walk these pages. When you read you shall wake me from my comfortable bed beside my parents and I shall be transported to your side.

In winter we shall sit near to the fire and tell stories late into the night. In summer you and I shall sit on elisi's porch listening to the insects, frog and owl. We'll listen for whippoorwill's nightly call. We'll listen to all the creatures of the night performing just for us.

I wish you well, my new friend. To you I entrust my words, my heart and my soul recorded here in this book. I imagine us one summer night walking arm in arm under the tall pines with the moonlight dancing under our feet like scattered silver on the soft bed of pine straw as we whisper our deepest secrets.

Who knows what is on the other side. Who knows if in another time and place we shall laugh and talk and share. I would like that. I would like that very much. I look forward to your visit. I shall wait for a word from you that will waken me to things yet unknown. Edudu says things change. When that first star appears, remember it was upon that star I have pledged to write just for you. I wrote again tonight until the fire burned low and my fingers were tender. I wrote for you.

Chapter XII

1820 –Newspapers - Rabbit & Terrapin

Chapter 12

23 February 1820

While edudu whittles animal figures and pine basket centers and talks with Spinner on elisi's front porch, I read, think and write. I can't imagine anything better.

What shall I write in my new journal? Elisi asks me to read about food and cooking from the white newspapers. She loves to hear about different fabrics available for sale. Edudu raises hogs and we have a well-stocked smokehouse. We love bacon and ham. I found a recipe in the newspaper for preserving pork. Elisi and edudu want me to record it in my journal. On a cold winter's day there is nothing like the smell of sizzling bacon in our big black skillet. I love the smell of fish frying, but bacon is the best.

Copied from the *Georgia Journal* – 25 January 1820 – page 2

"Infallible recipe to preserve Bacon.—After pork is killed, and is become perfectly cool…commence the following process:--To one bushel of salt, add one pound of saltpeter, finely pounded; half pound of Cayenne pepper (red); half pound of ginger, both finely beaten and mixed together; and one gallon of vinegar; then apply the whole as follows—to one piece of pork or joint, on the flesh side, and with corn cobs, rub the skin, applying as much salt and vinegar as can be rubbed in—then turn it over and apply one table spoonful of saltpeter, with a tea spoon full of the pepper and ginger, (they being previously mixed together) over the joint with as much salt and vinegar as can be rubbed in, being very careful that the skin side is rubbed until it be perfectly porous, and thereby receive much salt and vinegar; after which, lay it away on boards for 8 or 10 days, and then hang it up, and keep log fires of green wood for the same space of time. Bacon thus saved, if properly attended to, according to the above direction, will keep twelve months, free from insects and moisture as it will then be perfectly cured. A Practical Farmer"

11 March 1820

Georgia requires their militia to ride regular slave patrols looking for runaways. The militia comes through often looking for escaped Africans.

Copied from the *Georgia Journal* – 7 March 1820 – page 3

"Stop the RUNAWAY…on the 27th of January last, a small negro man named Sam between the ages of twenty-five and thirty…a scar over one of his eyes; had on…a short black bearskin coat…he may endeavor to get to the Indian nation and pass for a free man…any person that will secure him in jail, or bring him to me shall be handsomely rewarded. Philip Stinchcomb."

19 March 1820

George Lowrey visited edudu today. He is an important leader in our nation and a friend of edudu. His Cherokee name is Agin'agi'li, Rising Fawn in English. His name calls up the most charming image and describes our country perfectly. We are one with the world around us. Everyone should learn to speak Cherokee, especially if they like descriptive and emotive poetry.

We Cherokee are given descriptive names taken from the world around us—like Red Bird, Dragging Canoe, Five Feathers, Calm Eagle, Corn Tassel and White Path. I am Hummingbird. Our names sound ordinary in English but are lilting and musical in Cherokee. English names are boring. Every other white man I meet is named John, Robert or William.

George Lowrey, Rising Fawn, spells his English name Lowrey, with an additional letter e, unlike my wonderful teacher whose name is Lowry. Mr. Lowry's name does not have an e. George Lowrey looks nothing like my teacher.

24 March 1820

Mr. Lowry, my teacher, cannot pronounce Cherokee names. He gives everyone in his school an English name to help us be civilized. I told edudu about Mr. Lowry helping us to be civilized and he laughed. Edudu laughed so much he finally went in the house and got his gun from above the mantel and walked into the woods without a further word. I could still hear his laughter echo as he disappeared up the hill with Spinner. He and Spinner go everywhere together. I think I heard Spinner laughing, too.

My teacher gave me the name Cassandra—from the Greek language in Europe. Cassandra is a woman in Greek myth. Greek myths are much like

Cherokee stories. Greeks told stories about the heavens, their gods, the earth, animals and their relationship with people.

Cassandra, a Greek princess from Troy, was blessed by Apollo with the gift of foreseeing the future. Mr. Lowry said I look like a Greek princess.

In the Greek story, Cassandra denied Apollo's romantic advances and he cursed her so no one would ever believe her prophesies. Mr. Lowry hopes, unlike Cassandra, people will read and believe my journal. I wonder if anyone will want to read my carefully written words? Years hence, will anyone want to know what a Cherokee girl thinks?

In school everyone calls me Cassie—never Cassandra. Sometimes edudu will call me Cassie instead of Walela. I like having two names and learning different languages.

4 April 1820

At the far end of our community, close to the river, is our seven-sided lodge for meetings and ceremonies. The seven sides represent our seven clans—Long Hair, Blue, Wolf, Wild Potato, Deer, Bird and Paint. My brother and I are Deer Clan, the clan of our mother. Mr. Lowry said the Jews had twelve tribes. We Cherokee have seven clans.

The men in Deer Clan are known to be fast runners and have great respect for animals. Our clan is recognized for delivering messages throughout our country quickly. My brother can run all day without resting. He loves ballplays. Whites can't run like my brother.

The members of our clan are like brothers and sisters and must not marry one another. When I marry, my husband must be from a different clan or a different country. We welcome people of all nations.

If a Cherokee woman marries a white man or African, the children are Cherokee. The children are not half Cherokee. If a woman marries a man who already has children, the children are considered the children of the current marriage. We would think it silly to say we have half a brother or we have part children. What an unhappy way to think—of half people and add-on children as if they are less important. All children of all marriages are fully Cherokee and fully welcomed into our community no matter what the marriage history of the parents.

We value intelligence and wisdom, both young and old, of the female as well as the male. On the whiteside men own everything and their wives own nothing. A husband in Georgia can legally sell his property and never tell his wife. We do the opposite.

When a Cherokee woman marries, she owns her home and the children belong to her. If her husband is bad, she can throw her husband's things out and send him back to where he came from before they married. The wife keeps her house, property and children and her decision will be defended by her family. Sometimes I hear elisi tell edudu if he doesn't continue to treat her well, she'll throw his things out. When she tells him that they laugh.

6 April 1820

Ben and I walked to the river and I showed him my special place on the riverbank where I come to think, read and write. It's a lovely place hidden by laurels. Ben loved it.

In the afternoon Mrs. Lowry gave us a cup of tea in a most beautiful tea service. She is a charming woman. After tea, Ben and I sat on the front porch with Mr. and Mrs. Lowry and had a most interesting conversation. Ben had been reading a book about animals, birds and insects and found it curious how different groups of animals, birds or insects have different names.

"What do you call a group of fish, Cassie?" Ben asked.

"That's easy. They're a school," I answered quickly.

"Your turn, Cassie," Ben said. "Ask me a question about animal groups and see if I know the answer."

"How about whales?" I asked. "What do you call a group of whales?"

"That's too easy," Ben said. "Whales in a group are a pod."

"May I play your game?" Mr. Lowry asked.

"Of course, Father," Ben answered. "Please do. You and Mother can both join. It'll be fun."

"Cassie, let's see how smart you are," Ben's father said. "What do you call a group of bees?"

"Everyone knows that, Mr. Lowry. Bees are in a hive."

"What do you call a grouping of cows?" I asked.

Ben laughed, "That's about the easiest of all. Cows together are a herd."

"May I have a turn?" Mrs. Lowry asked.

"Of course, Mother. We would love for you to play," Ben said.

"Very well," Ben's mother said, "what do you call a collection of geese?"

"Geese together are called a gaggle," Ben answered.

"What do you call a bunch of quail?" Mrs. Lowry asked quickly.

"Mother, that's easy. Everyone knows it's a covey of quail."

"My turn," I said. "What do you call a bunch of hogs?"

"Well, there won't be any hogs around here if they keep getting into our vegetables," Mr. Lowry said. "A group of annoying, stupid, rooting wild pigs that are always getting into my garden and ought to be shot are called a passel."

We all laughed. Mr. Lowry was always chasing the wild pigs out of his vegetable garden.

Mr. Lowry asked the next question, "What is a group of salmon called? I read about that recently."

"I read about that too, Father," Ben answered. "A bunch of salmon aren't called a school. They're called a run."

"Very good, son," Mr. Lowry said. "Very good. I thought you would miss that one. We must be reading the same books. One more before I lose my turn. What do you call a group of beavers?"

"That's simple, Mr. Lowry," I answered, "Everyone knows when you find beavers together they're called a family."

I continued my turn.

I said, "I found a most fascinating reference recently about buzzards. Does anyone know what to call a group of buzzards?"

"Would that be a flight or a flock?" Ben asked.

"No," I answered. "They're not a flock or a flight."

"I know the answer, Cassie," Mr. Lowry said. "The reference for a grouping of buzzards is most curious, I must say. I read about that years ago and I've never forgotten. What buzzards eat makes them a bit sinister. Buzzards grouped together are called a wake."

"Very good, Wilbur—and very appropriate," Mrs. Lowry answered with a grin. "Let's see if you know this one. What do you call a group of camels? We don't have camels in this country, do we?"

Mr. Lowry chuckled.

"Why Eleanor, you know I know the answer to that one," Mr. Lowry said. "A group of camels is a caravan. That was too easy. You'll have to put your thinking cap on to stump me."

We all laughed with Mr. Lowry.

I asked my next question quickly, "What do you call a group of coyotes?"

No one could answer.

"Coyotes in a group are called a band," I said proudly. I was reading about them recently in the newspaper. Farmers don't like coyotes—especially bands of coyotes."

"Very good, Cassie," said Mrs. Lowry. "May I have one more turn before I go inside to get my work done?"

"Of course, Mrs. Lowry," I said.

Mrs. Lowry asked, "This may be a hard one. What do you call a bunch of ducks when they're swimming on a lake? Does everyone give up?"

None of us could answer.

"Ducks swimming on a lake are called a raft. I knew I would stump you with that one," Mrs. Lowry said. "I have enjoyed our animal quiz and if you will pardon me, I need to go inside now. You three please continue. This has been fun."

After Mrs. Lowry went inside, Mr. Lowry said, "I'm going to do two at once. What do you call a bunch of wasps and a bunch of flies?"

"Father, that's the easiest one today. It's a wasp nest and flies always swarm," Ben said.

"I knew that was too easy, but I can't think of any more. Do either of you two youngsters know any more?" Mr. Lowry asked.

I answered, "Well, I know it is a colony of ants and a cloud of grasshoppers."

"Very good, Cassie," Ben said. "I didn't know about the cloud of grasshoppers."

I asked, "Well, everyone should know this one but what do you call a group of possums?"

"Cassie, everyone knows that. It's a grin of possums," Ben said and we all laughed together. I was having a good time playing our guessing game.

I asked again, "What do you call a group of owls?"

"Ah, Cassie. You are smart but so am I," Mr. Lowry said, as he clapped his hands. "It's a parliament of owls. And, of course, along those same lines, it's a congress of crows."

"Very good, Mr. Lowry. I didn't think you would get that one about the owls," I said.

"I'll take my last turn," Mr. Lowry said. "I'm having fun but I have some work I must get to today. What do you call a bunch of wild dogs?"

I answered, "Wild dogs are a pack. That was easy. Before you go, Mr. Lowry, let me ask you one more. What do you call a bunch of baby chickens?

Mr. Lowry answered, "I know it's a brood of hens and I think little chicks are called a peep. That does it for me. I don't know any more."

"I've had a wonderful time, Mr. Lowry," I said, "I loved our little game. Please let's do this again sometime."

18 April 1820

Ben rode over today and we went down and spent the afternoon at my spot beside the river. I love our long conversations listening to the water go by. We often talk about books we have been reading and lands far away.

29 April 1820

Mr. Lowry loaned me *The Swiss Family Robinson*. It's an English translation of a book originally in German by Johann David Wyss. He also loaned me the story of *Rip Van Winkle* by Washington Irving. My favorite stories will always be the fairy tales and animal stories like edudu tells on our front porch.

27 June 1820

Copied from the *Georgia Journal* – 20 June 1820 – page 1

"TWENTY DOLLARS REWARD. –Ranaway from the subscriber living in Oglethorpe county, three miles northwest of Bowling Green, a likely negro man named JESSEE, 22 years of age, five feet ten or eleven inches high; had on when he went away, a patched green pair of pantaloons, a cotton shirt, an old wool hat and bare footed, dark complected—he has a wife at Mrs. Jewels, he is very apt to be lurking about there. Ranaway on the same day from the subscriber a negro girl named CHARITY, 16 or 17 years of age, well made, dark complected, about five feet high, had on when she went away, a white cambric dress, had on her head a red bandanner handkerchief, bare footed—very likely to be lurking about Ofphy Hills' as he owns her mother. The above reward will be given to any person that will deliver said negros…or give information, so…I can get them, or ten dollars reward for the delivery of either of them, and all reasonable expenses paid. They went away on the 29th of May. Spencer Hand. June 4"

I would run away to see my wife or mother. I hope Jesse and Charity are never returned. White masters horsewhip their slaves when they are returned after running away.

28 June 1820

Copied from the *Georgia Journal* – 20 June 1820 – page 3

"And a hunting we will go. Thirty-three persons in N.H. determined to hunt for one week. They divided into two parties, and commenced the pursuit of game on Monday the 15th ult.

121

continuing until Saturday evening.—The following is the number and description of animals killed: 43 Foxes, 10 Hedgehogs, 2791 Squirrels, 18 Crows, 44 Woodchucks, 148 Woodpeckers, 6 Hawks, 20 Blue Jays, 14 Blackbirds, 9 Threshers and 4 Polecats for a total of 3107 animals and birds."

When I read this to edudu, he sat, looked down at the ground, and shook his head sadly.

"Walela, this is why game is becoming scarce. White men shoot everything that moves. Killing animals is sport to them. They don't understand how precious animals are. Killing animals is not for amusement. They have forgotten they themselves are connected to the earth. We hunt to survive and when we harvest an animal we ask forgiveness, which is right. Whites in the forest behave like naughty boys."

"The English are a strange bunch," I answered.

"You can tell from that article that not one of those men had a rifle," edudu said.

"How can you tell they didn't have rifles, edudu?" I asked.

"They didn't kill any deer, bear or elk. They were using smoothbore guns accurate only at very short range. These men were using smoothbores loaded with pellets. At short range, the pellets come out in a pattern as big as a wash tub. They'll easily kill small animals, like a squirrel or bird. It's hard to miss a poor little squirrel with one of those scatter guns. The white men didn't eat all that game, Walela. I've never known of anyone who ate a polecat and why would anyone who knows anything about the forest shoot a woodpecker who eats the insects that destroy trees? Why would anyone shoot a beautiful hawk? Bad things would come to me if I killed woodpeckers and hawks."

"I understand, edudu. This newspaper article disturbed me," I said.

"Mark my words," edudu continued, "one day when the English have taken all our land there will be no game. Whites will bring a great evil upon their heads. What will these men do with three thousand dead squirrels? I can't imagine someone boasting about what these men have done. It was a bad day for our earth when the English came to our shores."

22 July 1820

Copied from the *Georgia Journal* – 18 July 1820 – page 2

"The drawing of the Land Lottery will commence on the eighteenth of August."

Whites seize our land and give it away. Soon we will not have enough land to plant corn.

22 August 1820

Whites continue to take over all Indian lands. I shudder from fear when I think of the words they use about us and the Seminole.

Copied from the *Southern Recorder* – 15 August 1820 – page 3

"The Floridas....The country is divided into East and West Florida...the present population, excluding Indians does not exceed 12,000....Pensacola is the capital of West Florida and is situated on the west side of Pensacola bay....The Indians principally reside in the neighborhood of Aplachia bay, are called Seminoles, and as their name imports, are principally runaways from the Creeks, and other nations to the north of Florida. They are a horrible band associating with runaway negros and live by plunder....In 1763 Florida was ceded to England in exchange for Havana, and while in their possession was divided into West and East Florida. During the American war in 1781 both the Floridas were captured by the Spaniards, and it has remained in quiet possession of Spain, until the late war, when Pensacola was entered by Andrew Jackson. In 1818 war broke out between the United States and the Seminole Indians; the latter being protected by the Spaniards, Gen. Jackson pursued them to the Spanish ports, St. Marks, Pensacola, &c, which he captured, and transported the Spanish governor to Havana....Since that period the United States have acquired the Floridas by treaty, but which has not yet been ratified by the Spanish government.(New York Daily Advertiser)"

Copied from the *Georgia Journal* – 15 August 1820 – page 1

"TEN dollars reward for the delivery of my negro man WILL. He is about 35 years old, an African, yellow complected, 5 feet 2 or 3 inches high, thumb on the right hand crooked, had on white homespun shirt & pantaloons, and wool hat; he has a wife at Mr. Lewis Wimberley's in Jones, where he may probably be found. WM. D. Wright. Baldwin, 10 above Milledgeville, July 28"

13 October 1820

People come often to hear edudu's stories, especially when we have a ballplay. I think edudu knows every Cherokee story ever told. I never tire of his stories. Edudu has the ability to make me think he is telling his story just for me even if many are listening. I love to watch his eyes, his gestures, his facial expressions and listen to his musical voice as he makes his stories come alive.

Today, because we are having a ballplay, the crowd that came to elisi's house wanted edudu to tell us the story of Rabbit and Terrapin. As usual when edudu tells his stories, he sat in his straight-back wooden chair on the front porch with Spinner at his feet and people gathered around.

"I know that story well," Edudu said. "Years and years ago, when I was quite young, I talked to one of Terrapin's relatives whose edudu was at the finish line of that great race on that very day. I heard his story first hand. I know exactly what happened."

Edudu leaned forward and began his story with a flourish of his arms. "Rabbit is a fast but boastful and arrogant fellow. He is always reminding everyone how quick he is. Rabbit is proud of his feet. When Rabbit runs in a straight line, he cannot be beaten. Rabbit can outrun everyone. He can even outrace Deer for short distances."

Edudu paused and put his hands on his hips. He leaned his face far forward almost to the edge of the porch, looked around at everyone and continued, "But Rabbit is not always wise, and Rabbit can be annoying when he boasts again and again about his superior speed. Rabbit loves to brag. He had become tiresome to the other animals.

Terrapin, on the other hand, is slow, brave and dependable. Terrapin is the kind that will finish every project he begins. Terrapin never boasts. If terrapin says he will do something, you can count it done."

"This day, because Terrapin was weary of listening to Rabbit's boasts, he devised a plan. He challenged Rabbit and his fast feet to a special race that would teach Rabbit a lesson to end his annoying boasts—and make Rabbit a better person. Rabbit accepted Terrapin's challenge."

Edudu laughed and slapped his thighs. Everyone laughed with him and Spinner barked his agreement.

"The crafty Terrapin asked his friends and family to help with his scheme. They would teach Rabbit a lesson he would never forget."

"The day came for the race," edudu continued. "Terrapin and Rabbit agreed to race across four ridges. The first one to cross the finish line on the crest of the fourth ridge would be the victor. Rabbit, as usual, was arrogant and sure of himself. Because Terrapin was slow, Rabbit graciously allowed Terrapin to get to the top of the first ridge as a head start. Rabbit, irritating everyone as usual, said he would rest on the soft green grass and wouldn't begin to race until Terrapin crossed the top of the first hill. It's only fair I give the slowest animal in the forest a head start, Rabbit said with a smirk. Until I see Terrapin at the top of the first ridge, I'll take my rest on this lovely soft bed of green grass, Rabbit said."

"So," edudu continued, "all the animals gathered to watch and the race began just that way. The confident Rabbit, lying on his soft patch of green grass beside the start line, watched Terrapin begin the race. Terrapin, with his stubby legs and heavy body, struggled to carry his home through the high grass and weeds. Rabbit, lying lazily on the grass, watched Terrapin finally reach the top of the first ridge."

Edudu leaned forward once again and lowered his voice.

"Rabbit knew he could easily catch slow Terrapin and win the race. This race would be effortless, Rabbit thought. Rabbit watched Terrapin as he labored up the hill and finally disappeared across the top of the first ridge. Rabbit walked casually to the top of the first ridge but was greatly surprised to see Terrapin already beginning to disappear down the far side of the second ridge. How did Terrapin get to the second ridge so fast?"

Edudu's voice was louder. He raised up from his seat and put on a puzzled face and made motions with his arms, "What was happening? How could Terrapin be so far ahead and so much faster than Rabbit? Rabbit couldn't understand how Terrapin could have already gone over the top of the second ridge. Rabbit knew he must hurry. Still confident he would win, Rabbit began jumping faster to catch up. When boastful Rabbit got to the top of the second ridge, he saw Terrapin beginning to go over the top of the third ridge. This was a fast Terrapin, the foolish Rabbit thought."

"Rabbit began to panic. 'I'm behind. I must run fast—very fast—as fast as I can', Rabbit said to himself. So that's what Rabbit did," edudu said. "Rabbit began running, jumping and hopping as fast as he possibly could through the grass until he was almost exhausted. When he got to the top of the third ridge, so exhausted he could hardly run, Rabbit saw Terrapin climbing up the fourth hill and approaching the finish line. Rabbit tried to run even faster but, despite his best effort, he wasn't in time to win the race. Terrapin crossed the finish line first."

Edudu leaned back and laughed and slapped his thighs with both hands and Spinner barked his approval with a long howl.

"Just a few moments after Terrapin crossed the finish line, Rabbit fell to the ground in exhaustion and cried mi, mi, mi, mi, mi as rabbits do to this day when they're too tired to run any longer," edudu said.

"How did Terrapin win the race, edudu?" I asked, as if I had never heard the story.

"Walela," edudu said with a big smile as he leaned back in his chair, "Everyone in the forest knows how wise and dependable Terrapin is. Terrapin finishes any task he begins. Terrapin had many friends and family who wanted to help with his plan. All Terrapins look alike, don't they? Terrapin posted his look-alike friends at the tops of the hills in the tall grass waiting for the signal to join the race. When Rabbit came across the hill it appeared as if Terrapin was about to cross the next ridge when it was really his friend who had been hiding in the tall grass and waiting. Rabbit thought Terrapin was ahead, but it was Terrapin's look-alike friends who were deceiving Rabbit. The real Terrapin was concealed near the finish line so when he won the race and the animals asked questions, they wouldn't be suspicious."

"And that's not all of the story," edudu added with another laugh. "Even today, when young men go to a ballplay, someone will boil a soup of rabbit hamstrings. They pour it across the path the opposing ballplayers must travel to arrive at the competition."

Edudu laughed heartily and everyone in the audience laughed.

"When the players cross the line of hamstring soup they become tired like foolish Rabbit and unable to run fast. I must confess on many occasions in my youth I poured hamstring soup across the path of my competitors."

21 October 1820 The Harvest Moon – Du ni nv di

Last night Bear Paws caused a disturbance. He was drunk. Bear Paws smells nasty when drinking whiskey. When he comes to our house after he has been drinking whiskey and tries to hug me, the odor of his mouth is disgusting. I hate the stupid way he behaves. He frightens me. The last time Bear Paws came to our house drinking he was so drunk he had soiled himself.

Whites often sell whiskey to our men. Edudu, elisi and I hate whiskey. Mr. Lowry dislikes whiskey, too, but no one can stop whites from selling it in our country. Bear Paws and his friends cause trouble every time they drink the white man's whiskey. Sometimes, if he doesn't have anything to trade, Bear Paws will steal in order to have something to trade for whiskey. Edudu says whites give our men whiskey in order to steal their money and intentionally destroy our communities. Edudu says the whites have an evil purpose in selling whiskey to our young men.

Mr. Lowry says many white men have also been ruined by whiskey. Bear Paws is a good hunter, like my brother, and almost as good at ballplay, but whiskey makes him dull, slow, stupid and forgetful. Once when he was drunk he fell into the fire. He lay in the fire and didn't know the flesh of his arm was burning. He has a terrible scar.

Bear Paws will not remember last night's disturbance. Elisi says there is not one good thing about whiskey as do Mr. and Mrs. Lowry. Why the English make it, drink it and sell it, I will never know. Why would anyone pay to make themselves stupid, unpleasant, sick, nasty and wake up with no money?

The English consider themselves superior, yet they sell whiskey and destroy our families. One day, edudu says, Bear Paws will find the strength to stop. Bear Paws is a good man—a very good man. He is a good fisherman and brings us fish when he doesn't buy whiskey. I love to go with Bear Paws fishing when he doesn't drink.

16 October 1820

General Jackson has constructed a new military road through Alabama and Mississippi to New Orleans. Edudu thinks new roads through our country will be a disaster for our nation. He says roads invite more whites. He says the white military will use the roads to destroy the Creeks, Choctaw, Chickasaw and us Cherokee.

Copied from the *Georgia Journal* – 10 October 1820 – Page 3

> "The military road is completed from this place (Florence, Alabama) to New Orleans...it has been opened under the immediate direction of General Jackson...Houses of entertainment have been erected at short stages to render every comfort to the traveler. This road runs through a delightful and romantic country and eventually must become the great thoroughfare of the southern states...the day is not far distant when a line of stages will be established from Nashville to New Orleans which must necessarily render the military road the most important of any on the continent."

Edudu has been to the great river often. The delightful and romantic road the whites have completed runs through the Creek, Choctaw and Chickasaw nations. Edudu says those lands are delightful and that's why whites covet them. Whites don't want to use our land. They want to possess it. They want to take it from us. Everywhere the English go, they build wide roads for heavy wagons and for their army. They love to fight. One day, edudu says, our nation will disappear down one of those long roads.

127

3 November 1820

I love the autumn and our festivals. Today we are celebrating a Cherokee boy becoming a man—a provider and protector. Everyone is in their best.

I love to listen to old friends greet one another and talk about old times. A big black kettle steams and the smell wafts over everything. Smiles are everywhere. I love to see families when they are re-united. Children run around, under and through everywhere. Edudu will tell stories until late in the evening. It is a happy day for Five Feathers, elisi and edudu and my community. Now that my brother is becoming a man, edudu will take my brother on his first hunting trip as an adult. We are proud of Five Feathers. If my mother's brothers were alive, they would teach him to be a man and take him on his first hunt. My mother and father and my mother's two brothers died in the same week when I was a baby. Edudu says the English brought sickness, but I shall not think of those things. Today is a day of great joy in our community. It is a day to remember good things. Families are reunited and life is good. I am happy for my brother.

Chapter XIII

1820 - Deerslayer

Chapter 13

8 November 1820 - Month of the Trading Moon – Nu da de qua

Five Feathers is preparing for his first hunt as an adult. Until now he has been considered a child. How wonderful it will be to watch my brother return with his first deer. He will leave as a child and return as a man. We are farmers, but we respect our hunting traditions and love the old ways of the forest. We understand our world and find joy being part of it. We are of the earth.

On my brother's return he will assume adult responsibility in supplying sustenance and security. Everyone is proud. Elisi, our grandmother, says he already carries himself like a chief. Perhaps he will be chief. I think so. Elisi says our father would have been a chief had he lived. Elisi says my brother is tall, powerful and handsome like his father.

12 November 1820

Five Feathers and edudu have been preparing for his first hunt for over a year. Edudu has been helping my brother make his 44bow. Edudu told me the story of my brother's new hunting bow and his first hunt as an adult.

"How do you like your new bow, Five Feathers?" edudu asked.

"I love my new bow, edudu," my brother answered.

"It is a good bow," edudu said. "It's the best of bows. It's right to bring down your first deer with a bow and even better with a bow you crafted with your own hands. That's the right way—in harmony with the forest. Guns are noisy, smelly and kill easily with no skill."

"You're right, edudu," my brother said. "Even bad hunters can kill with a gun. A bow is the proper instrument for the forest."

Edudu answered, "Yours is the best bow I've ever seen, Five Feathers. It's better than mine."

Edudu, looking down the length of my brother's new bow, let his fingers glide gently down its length, feeling the flowing texture of the perfectly polished wood. He examined the sheen of the velvety grain of the seasoned hickory and noted its straightness.

"Your bow is alive, Five Feathers. It lives. It was living wood when a tree, and it continues to live. When you are an old man, this wood will remember. It will be as alive for you then as today."

Two years ago my brother and edudu cut the top out of a perfect hickory sapling—the part with no knots or big limbs that grows straight towards the sun. Then came the gentle skinning of the bark and patient drying making certain the bow continued perfectly straight at every stage. Later, after the wood seasoned, edudu carefully selected flint pieces to precisely shape the limbs to give strength, flexibility and beauty.

English traders brought iron axes, knives, plows and guns. Our old ways have almost disappeared, but edudu still knows flint.

My brother and edudu carefully honed the hickory. They flattened the limbs in the right places for maximum efficiency, flexibility and power.

I know little about crafting bows, but perhaps I shall learn. It has been a pleasure to watch Five Feathers and edudu work together. The bow is quite an achievement. More than a few men came to inspect the progress. Everyone wanted to try Five Feathers' new bow, but edudu would not allow anyone to draw it until after my brother's first deer. He told them they could shoot their guns or make their own bow.

"You shall harvest your first deer in the same valley where my father killed his first deer and I killed mine," edudu said. "It is the same valley where your mother's brothers and your father brought down their first deer. When you find your deer there, all will be in balance. Your father and my father shall greet us there and rejoice with us when you bring down your deer."

"I look forward to that day, edudu," my brother answered.

"Your first deer will give our ancestors joy and their joy will overflow. Because you have upheld our traditions, your family will never forsake you. I will be honored to watch you bring your first deer and feed your people. It will be the proudest moment of my life."

As we sat on the porch in the autumn dusk, I listened to edudu as he spoke to my brother about the hunt.

"I remember the pride I felt that day when I carried in my first deer," edudu said. "My mother's brothers were proud. My edudu and elisi were proud. My mother's brothers supported me on my first hunt. When I returned I was a man."

I was watching my brother. I knew he would remember every word spoken to him this evening.

"You will see the same looks of approval from the men and women of our community when you return with your deer," edudu said. "I remember the smaller boys' envy. I remember the honor of being accepted as a provider. You will remember your moment. There is no greater fulfillment for a man than to care for his family and community."

Edudu and my brother sat quietly on the porch looking into the forest. At last edudu spoke.

"Many are too old to hunt. When I was a child they were strong men. They laughed at the foolish deer who thought he could escape. When they became too old to follow the deer and the turkey, I became a man and brought them life. We shall depend on you, Five Feathers. The deer will not laugh at you. The deer will fear you. This was our way and it shall be your way. One day children yet unborn will sustain your life in your grey years. The young care for the old."

"I will do that, edudu," my brother answered proudly.

Edudu leaned over and scratched Spinner's ears.

"There is one thing more we must do," edudu said. "You must pass the test of manhood as I and as your mother's brothers did. After that test, we will go through the days of fasting and offerings. Are you ready for the test, Five Feathers?"

"Yes, I am ready, edudu. When shall I be required to pass this test? I have never heard of this in our traditions."

"No, you have never been told," edudu answered. "Young men are not allowed to know until the day of their test. Tonight you will be tried as I, your mother's brothers and your father were before you. Are you afraid?"

"I am ready. I am not afraid. How could I be afraid with you to guide me?" my brother replied.

"That is a good answer," edudu said. "Tonight you shall be tested. I shall take you deep into the forest far from home for your test."

Early that afternoon two Cherokee males, one old and one young, walked deep into the forest and began to climb the eastern slope of the tall mountain. When the pair arrived at a rocky ledge selected by edudu, my brother's test was explained.

"Here on this rock ledge you will sit with your eyes covered until morning. You may not leave your place. You may not cry out for any reason. You may not sleep. You may not have any weapon. If attacked, you must defend yourself with bare hands."

"I will do as you say, edudu. I will obey," my brother replied.

"When you feel the warmth of the morning sun on your face it will be the first day of your manhood. You will have become a man and may remove the covering from your eyes and return home," edudu said affectionately. "Are you afraid?"

"I am not afraid, edudu," my brother answered. "You taught me to never fear the forest or anything in it. I have no fear of the creatures who roam the darkness. I do not fear owl, fox or raccoon. I do not fear possum with her babies in her pouch. I am not afraid of the yellow eyes of bobcat or the scream of mountain lion."

Edudu listened proudly.

"You taught me to understand every forest creature. Animals fear me, edudu. I have no fear when I see with my eyes in the daytime or when I see with my ears and my nose at night."

"That is a good answer—a very good answer," edudu said. "After your trial you may never tell another young man until the day of his test—as I have done with you. Are you ready?"

"Yes, I will do as you say," my brother answered. "I will sit on this ledge until the sun warms my face. I will listen to the sleeping forest, but I will not sleep."

Edudu covered my brother's eyes as he received final instructions.

"Be patient, Five Feathers," edudu instructed. "The morning will come as mornings always have come. This night will be no longer than the night years ago when I sat alone and blindfolded as you sit now. Tomorrow you will be a man and we will go for your deer."

Five Feathers heard edudu's footsteps as he walked down the mountain slope.

My brother was alone.

Five Feathers' active mind would think of many strange things and invent even more before the morning sun kissed his face, allowing his return.

My brother sat in his place listening to the sleeping forest. The fox and raccoon are mischievous but harmless. There is no harm in the noisy owl. Bobcat, mountain lion and bear hate the smell of a man. They will never come near.

It was a long night under the brilliant stars Five Feathers was not allowed to see. The damp night air chilled his limbs as the invisible mist curled upwards from the valley below towards the summit of the purple mountain. Five Feathers had spent many nights in the forest and had never been afraid to be alone. He knew the forest to be his friend both day and night.

After many hours Five Feathers heard the songbirds begin their morning melodies. He heard the loud mockingbird sing from the top of a nearby tree and the soft cooing of the doves. It wouldn't be long before he would feel the gentle sun caress his face, welcoming him to the new day and the new chapter of his life—giving him permission to leave the mountainside. This day would be the dawn of new adventures and his longed-for manhood.

At last he felt the warm morning sun gently kiss his face. He removed the covering from his eyes.

To Five Feathers' surprise, just on the other side of the clearing and hardly a stone's throw from where he had kept his patient vigil, edudu was sitting against a tree trunk watching.

"Edudu, I didn't hear you arrive? Your footsteps are quiet this morning," my brother said. "You came up the mountain like the fox. I heard no sound."

"I did not come up the mountain this morning because I did not go down last night," edudu answered. "I did not leave you. Your vigil was my vigil. Your night was my night. Your watch was my watch. You did not know, but I was with you."

"So, edudu, I was never alone even when I felt no one was near?"

"You were not alone, Five Feathers. Dark days will come when your eyes cannot understand the world around you. You have learned that a man must see with more than his eyes. Even when all is dark and you can't see, you must remember you are never alone. I and your nation will be with you. Let us return home."

After Five Feathers' night in the forest, Calm Eagle, edudu's Cherokee name, called my brother to begin to prepare for the hunt five days before their departure.

"I need to talk to you, unisi, about your hunt," edudu said. "We must keep our rituals. Our preparations to go into the forest to hunt are as important as anything we will do. They are as important as making your bow. The rituals of our fathers guide the making of your bow, our preparation to hunt and the killing of the game and bringing it back to share."

Five Feathers and edudu prepared the next four days for the hunt in proper Cherokee fashion, observing every ritual and fast. Just before they went to bed that last evening, edudu handed Five Feathers the bow they had made together.

"Look at your bow, Five Feathers. What do you see?"

My brother examined the bow carefully. Just above the hand grip he saw skilled carving that had not been there before. Carved into the hickory were five eagle feathers in a graceful and clever design. He loved it. Just below the handle was an equally artistic carving of a bust of a big male deer and his proud antlers.

"Edudu, the feathers are beautiful. It's my name and I love the deer and his antlers. The deer is my clan. I love what you have done with my bow and my name. This is a wonderful surprise. Thank you."

"You and your sister are Deer Clan, Ani'-Kawi', Deer People," edudu said. "This carving is for you to carry with you the rest of your life. Even though we have become farmers, hunting is our way and will always be our way. This is our country to hunt. Every path belongs to you. The forest has been given us to care for—we must care for it for from the earth comes our life. One day, Five Feathers, you will give this bow to your sister's son or to your own son. This bow is yours. It will always be yours."

"I love my bow, edudu," my brother answered. "I love being with you in the forest. I can't imagine anything more wonderful than being in the forest with you—and hunting. We were born to hunt. Truly the land doesn't belong to us. We belong to the land."

"That is a good answer, Five Feathers," edudu replied. "This land doesn't belong to us. I will teach you the old ways—the good ways that bring balance. We will not slaughter with the gun. Having a farm, a barn and a smokehouse and plenty in the winter is good, but we must never forget who we are. We must always have respect for the forest and the animals. We must never be negligent with that which we have been entrusted."

"I wouldn't want to live anywhere but here in Cherokee Country and be with you," my brother answered.

They slept.

They would rise long before sunrise to begin their long-awaited journey to complete the young man's test and his first hunt.

They would find great delight in the fresh, clean air of the hills and mountains. They would enjoy each moment of the long, patient hours required for a successful hunt. Our men are proud of their skills. We hunt for sustenance and never for sport or the pleasure of watching an animal die.

If we hunted like white men, our forest would soon disappear. We harvest from our forest only that which we need to survive. Nothing from our hunt is wasted or discarded. We are one with the land, the animals, the forest, the sky and the mountains. We maintain the balance—we are the Principle People. The land doesn't belong to us—we belong to the land.

The two hunters were far along the trail when the first happy fingers of dawn gently crept over the eastern mountains to softly lighten the sky above their heads. They walked quietly throughout the day enjoying the woods and the wildlife they occasionally disturbed.

Curious squirrels peeked from the safety of their broad tree trunks at the two single-minded hunters who interrupted their morning's play. The two rarely spoke on their outward journey. The silent hours in tandem were as comforting to the pair as lively conversation is to some. The camaraderie of these two, one old and one young, was as rich as the land they traversed. It was as if their souls were connected by invisible cords of a mutually shared existence.

There are misty winter days in our country when the clouds descend and it would be difficult to see our barn just down the hill, but this autumn day had dawned so clear it would hurt your eyes to look through the leafless limbs at the deep blue cloudless sky. The two men breathed the pure crisp air that gave energy to the purposeful travelers as food does to the hungry. It was as if the forest, having cast off its verdant summer garments, had invited the hunters to breathe the pure clean air of autumn on a tall mountain peak and view their tomorrow being prepared for them somewhere far beyond the mountains—at a distance only visible on these clear days.

Although they had seen signs of game all along their path, there would be no hunting until they reached their chosen valley—the valley. It was important Five Feathers harvest his first deer in the valley where edudu and his mother's brothers and his father had killed their first deer.

Late that evening they arrived at their destination. Edudu felt a rising excitement as they topped the last ridge and the familiar valley extended before him—inviting him to come forward and renew the bond of their long friendship. The enchanting scene was precisely as he remembered. Edudu recognized individual trees, paths, boulders and streams as his mind flooded with nostalgic memories of glorious hunts with men he would never forget— men who had taught him to live. He was pleased to bring Five Feathers to his valley. Edudu pointed to spots here and there and described to Five Feathers how at each location he, his father and his brothers had harvested their first deer as men.

The two hunters surveyed the valley carefully until nightfall searching for the deer runs to identify the perfect spot to position themselves for the hunt the following morning. They must not leave their smell anywhere near the deer's favorite paths. Deer can see well and have excellent hearing, but their nose is perhaps superior to any animal of the forest. A deer can detect a human at a great distance and they have an instinctive fear of the human smell—and rightly so.

They saw fresh signs on a well-worn path leading down to the boulder-strewn stream flowing through the quiet floor of the valley—a stream full of stones worn flat and smooth by eons of time. The comforting smell of decades of decaying vegetation in the silent dampness was the only smell the deer would be allowed.

The deer had left recent droppings and rubbings beside the path which indicated a well-used route to their favorite morning water source. Deer would not be skittish if the two hunters were careful to hide downwind of the unsuspecting animals. The pair carefully chose their spot where they would prepare themselves on this promising path. A thirsty deer would be drawn irresistibly to quench his morning thirst in the cool water of the gently flowing stream. All they had to do was make certain they were carefully concealed and wait quietly in a well-chosen place for an hour or two. Waiting silently was not always an easy task for an active hunter, but it must be done. Patience, of all the virtues, is perhaps our greatest asset. Edudu thinks the patience of our nation will be tested to the limit in coming years—and not by deer.

An appropriately large tree, close beside the run, was chosen by Five Feathers. All was prepared for the morning. The two had been fasting as required. They had obeyed each of our cherished customs for harvesting the forest's bounty. They lay together, side by side, in peaceful dreamless sleep throughout the night.

At last, the time had come.

Long before they could tell a black thread from a white, the two hunters had arranged themselves beside the trail—carefully obscured from the sharp eyes and ears of the vigilant deer and downwind of his expected path. As they waited, the blushing autumn dawn crept over the distant mountains creating long welcoming shadows. The sunrise stretched across their hazy valley like a lazy man rising from his bed. Little by little the sun turned the invisible clouds high above them into soft, gentle ridges of pink cotton—barely visible to the two hunters. If their preparations had been adequate, in a short time the young Cherokee boy would for the first time draw his bow in earnest—and leave his boyhood behind.

He was in his chosen perch ten feet off the ground snuggled against the dark green mossy bark in the first big fork of a gnarled white oak and just a few feet off the path they had determined the deer must surely take to slake his morning thirst in the clear, cold stream below. It was a perfect location to surprise their quarry.

The sun's first rays were finally beginning to light the tops of the tallest trees on the distant western mountains when Five Feathers heard the deer's quiet footfalls. With the greatest care, Five Feathers peeked around the trunk of the tree from high above the trail. There were six does daintily mincing down the path in search of water. It wasn't a doe Five Feathers wanted today—even a big doe. The female deer were smaller than the male and would produce offspring. It was never wise to kill a doe. The females would be allowed to live. The six does walked almost directly under Five Feathers unaware of the sudden death that lurked above. The doe doesn't have the fear and intensity of sense of the proud buck. Five Feathers let them pass unmolested. He wanted the unseen buck yet obscured in the shadows who must be somewhere on the path above—the big deer he knew must surely follow the does. The wary buck, though still concealed in the half light of dawn, would be drawn to the water on the same path as the female deer. The big deer's thirst must be quenched. He must have water.

The graceful brown does with their little white tails and careless manner passed unaware of the young Cherokee man balanced above them in the old white oak tree. Then, quietly and with great caution as they knew he would, came the noble buck. The suspicious deer, antlers held high, walked down the trail in the smoky haze of early dawn following the six females in his care—pausing every few steps, as was his custom, to listen and scan the forest and sniff for danger.

Five Feathers, hardly breathing and nestled in the high fork of the white oak, watched the buck's timorous approach. The big male deer and the young Cherokee man were now engaged in a deadly struggle as old as the earth itself. The wary male deer would take a few careful steps and pause once again with his nose elevated high sniffing for the least trace of hidden menace—listening constantly for any unusual noise that would warn him of a concealed threat and mortal danger. If the young man, hidden in the fork of the old tree, were to make the slightest sound in the morning silence, the deer's keen ears would hear and the magnificent animal would instantly bolt out of the valley and disappear into the trackless mountain never to be seen again. My brother hardly breathed.

The deer and the Cherokee, although ancient of adversaries, shared a mutual reverence. Young Cherokee men have been harvesting deer for centuries. The primordial contest is one in which the opponents have a common deference—a reciprocal respect that commenced with time itself. Some days the crafty buck anticipates the danger and escapes. Other days the buck will be carried back to the village on the shoulder of a proud hunter. This morning Five Feathers was hoping to be the victor. He had made every preparation and taken every precaution. This would be his day.

Edudu, farther from the path, was also perfectly concealed and quiet. Edudu would not draw his own bow this day. On this trip, only one deer would be killed and only one deer would be carried back to the village. Only one man would receive the adulation of his peers. It would be Five Feathers' deer, tracked and killed by Five Feathers' own hand, that would be carried on Five Feathers' own shoulders into the Cherokee community. The old man, his mentor, would support and defer—as it should be.

The splendid white-tailed buck took a long time to come abreast the tree where Five Feathers was concealed. The buck, with his magnificent rack, had survived past encounters with hunters because he was never careless. Five Feathers was not the first human who had attempted to take the life of the cautious deer.

The big buck made his way warily down the worn path towards Five Feathers, drawn irresistibly by the clear cold water he must have. His small black hooves seemed to test the very soil for danger with every careful step. My brother waited, his blood running hot, his heart pounding as the big deer approached with agonizing slowness. Would he ever arrive? The hammering in the young man's head felt like the wild beating drums at a festival—ever louder. The wait was maddening. Surely the deer would sense the danger. Could the big deer not hear the mad thumping of a human heart coming from the fork of the old white oak? If the deer heard anything, even the smallest sound, he would turn and fly.

My brother is never hasty, as he has been taught. He is patient, like edudu. He will make a steady man and perhaps be a chief one day. He will make a great chief—everyone says.

Five Feathers spoke to his own mind as he had been taught and practiced.

"Now is the time. Slowly. Carefully. Place the arrow silently. Not a sound. Not a sound. Draw the bow slowly, slowly, slowly, carefully, silently, carefully—Wait, Wait, Wait. Steady, Smooth, Make No Sound. Breathe—breathe in quietly. Wait, wait, WAIT. Exhale quietly. Make not a sound—not a whisper of a sound. Hold the arrow still—perfectly still. Hold with strength. Hold steady. Hold still. No wavering. Hold steady. Hold steady. Wait. Wait. Draw. Wait for the moment. Draw. Draw. Hold. Wait for the deer—Wait—Hold—WAIT—WAIT—WAIT—WAIT—WAIT—RELEASE."

The truest arrow in Five Feathers' quiver was on its way.

"Edudu," the boy shouted the instant his arrow left the bow. Five Feathers saw the flint head bury into the deer's side.

"Edudu—Edudu," he shouted again.

The terrified deer, with the burning pain in his side and his worst fears realized, bolted up the hill through the forest underbrush away from the danger that had surprised him and the voice of the dreaded monster shouting from the limbs overhead. The huge body of the buck was soaring between the tree trunks, flying like the wind over the carpet of dry brown leaves—almost faster than the eye could follow as he escaped his pursuers.

In his panic, the buck's small, sure hooves were hardly touching the forest floor as he fled from the unseen danger that had somehow escaped detection. The frightened animal, darting this way and that to avoid trees and underbrush, was doing his best to outrace the pain in his side. He flew between the leafless trees effortlessly brushing aside the small, limber branches as if they were nothing. The deer's instinct was to fly—to fly fast and far without pause. In only a moment the deer was out of sight.

Bow in hand, in one single, graceful leap, without bothering to climb down, the lithe Five Feathers jumped to the path below from his hiding place landing perfectly in balance. Edudu appeared instantly at his side and without a word exchanged between them they pursued the deer. They ran, but they didn't sprint mindlessly. They knew if Five Feathers' arrow didn't immediately sever an important artery, the chase could take hours. They must pace themselves to conserve strength. They must not lose the deer's trail. To lose the deer's trail would be to dishonor the deer himself.

Though both men had been perfectly still for well over an hour in the cold predawn, they were now instantly breathing deeply and stretching their muscles with the welcome excitement of the moment. Their keen eyes scanning the forest floor before them, missing no sign of the deer's path of escape. The two hunters, still without a word, followed the wounded deer using all their senses. It could be a long chase. They must not lose the trail.

The deer ran hard and fast in a mad panic to escape the unseen enemy which must surely be close behind. Flight is the deer's only defense and this majestic animal was sailing like the wind, bounding high over fallen tree trunks and boulders in his path. In the briefest of moments he had crossed the ridgeline out of the valley and was out of the sight and hearing of the hunters.

My brother and edudu pursued. They ran through the hardwood forest with the effortless pace and stamina of long years of practice—a pace they could maintain all day if pressed—and had done on many occasions.

My brother followed the deer's path by observing the telltale droplets of blood on the carpet of dead leaves, broken twigs and disturbed leaves. The deer would run as fast as he could to put as much distance as possible between pursued and pursuer. The buck was strong and running fast. The blood droplets were far apart.

Even a mortally wounded deer can run miles before his collapse. When exhausted, he would conceal himself in dense underbrush, hoping to escape detection and recover strength. The two hunters must be patient but must not delay—they must not lose the trail. They must not hesitate or the deer would die unobserved—obscured in some hidden cluster of brambles and the hunt would end as a dreadful waste and dishonor to both deer and hunter. To respect the forest, their nation and the wounded deer, they must not fail. They must be vigilant as they tracked the deer. They must be alert and run and keep running even when they thought their lungs would burst. The telltale drops of blood, still quite far apart on the dry leaf bed, told the hunters the deer was running fast—continuing to run as if uninjured.

As the morning sun continued its slow rise into the autumn sky, the two hunters ran on and on and on without a word. Five Feathers expertly followed the nearly invisible trail on the leaf bed. Their deer skin moccasins hardly made a sound in the autumnal carpet. With each succeeding footfall their skilled eyes found the precise spot to place their feet in order to avoid the unseen dangers concealed under the thick layer of dead leaves and at the same time dodging the low limbs, vines and underbrush that rushed and slashed and pulled as they flew past.

As they ran, the sun rose above the mountain tops. The misty valley gradually filled with the first rays of sunlight. In the long shadows of morning, the two Cherokee men ran on without pause following the deer's trail. They would, as they had many times before, chase the deer for many hours if required.

The hunters were moving fast. Edudu, following Five Feathers, was avoiding the whipping low hanging limbs and the vicious green saw briars my brother pushed to the side. As one runs in the forest away from well-traveled trails, the saw briars are difficult to see. Their pointed, metal-like thorns are small, sharp, cruel knives that can penetrate leather and lacerate the careless. They dodged the dense underbrush, leaped over the fallen tree trunks and avoided hidden stones. They leapt over concealed cavities in the forest floor full of leaves where the stump of an old tree had rotted away—some as deep as a man is tall that could snap a careless man's leg in a moment. All the while their eyes were scanning the leaf bed before them to follow the telltale path of blood and disturbed leaves without which all would be in vain. The young Cherokee man was still in the lead. This was his hunt. Our edudu would follow. The morning sun, now shining brightly in their faces, gave them renewed strength. They had been running without pause since daybreak yet they were not winded.

As the dry brown leaves crunched under every footfall, the drops of blood began appearing more closely together. The deer, losing strength, was at last slowing. They continued to follow carefully and quietly. The signs on the path said the deer was not far ahead. They climbed the side of the ridge. They topped the next rise quietly, making no sound whatsoever—not wanting to spook their quarry if he had paused to rest. There, in a laurel thicket about a bow's shot away, they saw the proud antlers of the big ten-point buck as he knelt on the ground resting. Even from a distance, they could hear the huge animal's labored breathing as he lay exhausted. The majestic buck could run no more. The big deer had collapsed to the ground, exsanguinated, hoping to avoid detection in the laurels, regain his strength and somehow escape the pain in his side and his relentless pursuers.

My brother knew what to do next without instruction. He had seen many deer wounded, tracked, killed and hung. He had been taught well. He cautiously removed his knife from its scabbard and quietly walked to the deer. He cut its throat rehearsing the traditional Cherokee prayer for forgiveness for taking the life of a forest creature—a creature created by the Great Spirit—a creature giving the entirety of its existence for the necessary sustenance of the Principle People and thus participating in the ordained cycle of life. Today, the young Cherokee man was the victor and the magnificent deer the vanquished. The world was in balance. The deer had fulfilled his existence.

Edudu nodded approval. They must be grateful. Evil follows those who kill without gratitude—who kill for pleasure.

When the deer stopped moving, Five Feathers cut out the hamstrings, leaving them on the leaves beside the deer. They would cut off the tip of the tongue and offer it in the fire later. All must be done according to tradition.

The hunt was successful. The two men were thankful. We are always grateful for the gifts of the sky, the land, the water and the forest—all gracious life-giving gifts given by the Great Spirit. As the two hunters rested under the bright morning sun, all was in balance.

Then came the quiet joy of success as the deer was patiently hoisted from a limb of an old white oak tree. This was a large animal and it had been an unusually long chase. It would be a heavy burden to carry home, but the two would share the labor, and there was no urgency in their return. It would be a pleasant journey. They would rest often and take all the time required. This was a day of joy for Five Feathers, edudu, our community and our nation. A day long-awaited by both men. The balance of the earth was maintained, Cherokee customs had been carefully observed, Five Feathers was a man, and all was approved in the presence of the unseen Cherokee ancestors according to custom. Edudu was the proudest of men.

The men continued their work in silence. The adoring relationship between the two was one in which they had learned to communicate without words. Theirs was a perfect human bond—two lives in total harmony.

Both men would share the burden of carrying the deer home, but only Five Feathers would have the honor of carrying the deer into the village. It was a wonderful conclusion to a flawless day. They would let the deer drain and then tie it in the leather carry sling. Five Feathers' entrance into the community would be the happiest of moments in my brother's life—the day we had waited on for years and the moment he would remember the rest of his life.

Edudu spoke, "I have no greater joy than to see the son of my daughter become a man and harvest his first deer and return home in triumph. I will remember every moment of this day with you. You have done well, Five Feathers. I am proud."

Suddenly, there was a disturbance in the underbrush above them. From behind a large boulder on the crest of the adjacent ridge came two noisy, unkempt white men running and stumbling down the slope with long guns at the ready. As they made their way clumsily down the hill towards the two resting Cherokee they shouted that edudu and Five Feathers were not to move. As the white men ran, they were accusing the two Cherokee men of trespassing and poaching. A hard thing to do, edudu thought, since this was Cherokee Country by treaty—by many treaties.

"No one gave you permission to hunt our land. You two are god-damned poachers—god-damned Indian poachers. What the hell are you doing sneaking around our farm? We told y'all to stay away. This is private property now," one white man shouted as he came near.

The Cherokee hunters quietly stood their ground staring at the approaching intruders.

"You god-damned Indians keep traipsing through our land. We ought to kill you where you stand. You reckon they understand English, John?" one white man said.

"They might not understand English," his companion answered, "but they understand powder and lead, I reckon. Keep your gun on 'em, Bill. Don't take your eye off 'em for a moment. You can't trust these god-damned sneaky Indians."

The two white men, completely out of breath from their short run down the hill, were shaking with rage, fear and the excitement of the moment. They were cowards, edudu thought. These nervous men could accidentally pull their triggers at any moment. Edudu was calm, thinking quickly and looking

142

from man to man planning what to do. Both white men were armed with loaded smoothbore long guns and knives. They had by now approached to point-blank range. It was impossible for edudu and Five Feathers to escape and, with only their unstrung bows and skinning knives, they had no defense. It was a dangerous situation. They dare not turn and run. Without guns, the two Cherokee men were at the mercy of the two angry white men.

The enraged white man continued, "What in the hell are you god-damned savages doin' slipping around my farm? You're goin' to have to learn respect. This is private property—my property and you're trespassin'. That's my buck you got hanging there. You two get the hell back where you came from, you lazy bastards, and stay off my property."

Edudu did not panic. He knew exactly where they were and that they were many miles inside the legal borders of Cherokee Country. This land had been guaranteed to the Cherokee nation twenty times by twenty different authorities in twenty different treaties in recent years. Even the greedy government of Georgia would grudgingly admit the two Cherokee hunters were well within Cherokee Country. The Cherokee had been plagued by the increasing numbers of white squatters who had no respect whatsoever for Cherokee boundaries. There was nothing to be done about the steady encroachment of white families seeking free land within the Cherokee Nation. Edudu thought to himself that if he had a rifle he would kill them both and cover their bones so they would never be found but, at the moment, survival was his only concern. He had one task. He must get the boy home safely—even if it cost his life.

Agreements with the Cherokee meant nothing to squatters, who believed unoccupied Cherokee land had been abandoned. Whites, like these two squatters, were defended by their fellow white soldiers of the militia. These men would build their cabins where they wished. Agreements with Indians were consistently ignored. The squatters knew the Cherokee had no standing in white courts any more than Africans. The squatters believed in the force of law but only as it applied to whites. Today, at this moment, the only thing that mattered to the old Cherokee man was to get Five Feathers home unharmed.

If they were to retrace the white men's steps back over the ridge, they would find a newly constructed cabin under a big shade tree near ten acres of newly cleared bottomland. There would be a lean-to shed, a mule, wagon, vegetable garden, smoke house, pig pen, chicken coop and a milk cow. They had seen it many times.

As far as Five Feather's edudu was concerned, the white squatters were welcome to return to their new cabin unmolested. All edudu wanted was to preserve the life of his beloved. He must act instantly to defuse the evil intentions and confused fear of these cowardly men. In their white arrogance, they were capable of killing without compunction—even accidentally. He must act instantly.

Five Feathers, though now considered an adult, was confused by the unfamiliar mortal threat before him. We haven't had a red chief in many years. Though we are peaceful, we continue to value honor and courage. Few of us have the fighting skills we possessed a hundred years ago.

These two white men had invaded their sacred valley, their hunt and their lives. They had ruined Five Feather's special day—a day planned for years. The emotions of anger that flooded the young man's heart were unbearable. My brother was about to make an error in judgment that would cost both their lives. My brother was about to respond in kind.

Edudu understood if my brother were to respond violently the white men would shoot them both, cover them with leaves and leave their bodies to rot. Before my brother could make his ill-fated decision to retaliate, edudu grabbed his right wrist with all his strength, making it impossible for Five Feathers to use his bow or knife with one hand. With the strong fingers of his left hand, edudu held Five Feather's wrist and whispered calming words into the young man's ear. He told my brother to look at the men's feet and slowly back out of their sight. He was to say nothing, not a word, and make no sudden movements. Edudu, with his iron grip on my brother's wrist, pushed my brother backwards and partially behind him. In case one of the men fired his weapon, edudu's body would shield the young man from the first shot. Five Feathers might escape the second.

"Do as I do immediately. Get behind me. Stay in step," edudu warned. "Look only at the ground in front of the men. Do not look into their face— not a glance."

He squeezed my brother's wrist even harder.

"Do not turn your back on these men until we are out of sight. Do not look them in the eye. Obey me now. Do everything I say. Stay behind me."

The painful pressure on my brother's wrist kept his mind fixed on edudu's warning. Calm Eagle, edudu's Cherokee name, knew the white men would not likely shoot if he and Five Feathers kept their faces towards the men and backed away slowly giving no challenge. Edudu understood that bold eye contact with the cowards would communicate defiance and might provoke the jumpy white men.

"Stay the hell away like you been told. If I catch you around here again, I'll shoot you on sight. I'm tired of you sneakin' around stealin' everything we got."

The man shouting shoved the muzzle of his smooth bore straight towards edudu's chest. The white man's gun was so close there was no chance of a miss. The two white men, now almost within an arm's length of the two Cherokee, were still recovering from their run down the slope.

Edudu was angry, but controlled, and thought to himself, "If I were here alone, I would die on this spot and end my life in honor."

It wasn't to be a moment of honor. Five Feathers and edudu slowly backed away from the men, bending their upper body in mock reverence, not looking the white men in the face. Edudu continued to hold my brother with a rock-hard grip. To save their lives they would have to abandon their packs, provisions, personal items and the coveted deer hanging from the white oak limb. The white men might shoot them in the back if they turned, ran, protested or hesitated. The only course of action to preserve their lives was to slowly shrink backwards out of range—like cowering dogs with their tails between their legs.

This wasn't the first time white men had stolen edudu's game. Unskilled white hunters routinely followed Cherokee men and robbed them of their game at the end of a successful hunt. Edudu knew these men in front of him were inexperienced in both hunting and fighting. They were no more than animals themselves, intent on satisfying their animal instincts.

A bad situation turned suddenly worse. Before they had taken five steps backwards, one white man ran forward with his rifle at the ready, reaching for the boy's bow with his free hand. He pressed his smoothbore into edudu's chest with his right hand and with his left ripped the precious bow and quiver from Five Feathers' back. Each of the fifteen arrows in Five Feathers' quiver the young man could describe in detail. The young man's world collapsed. Edudu could feel Five Feathers' disappointment.

When the Cherokee pair had backed completely out of sight of the white men, edudu paused to make certain there were no sounds of being followed. Edudu, now standing tall, turned and held the heartbroken Five Feathers by the shoulders. He held him in a firm grip and scanned his face a long time before he spoke. My brother's back straightened and he returned our edudu's gaze.

"My dear Five Feathers, you are indeed a man," edudu said proudly. "You were tested in the forest all night. We offered our prayers and you killed your first deer according to tradition. You kept faith with our ancestors—we maintained balance. You killed your first deer but just now you accomplished your greatest deed. You shall bring home something of much greater worth than a deer."

Five Feathers stood taller.

"You bring to us honor," edudu said. "Unlike the carcass of the big deer that will be gone in a few days, the honor you have earned this day can never be taken from you. Your name will be known. Today, on your first day of becoming a man, you have faced death fearlessly. You touched your enemy in battle and never once turned your back."

Edudu continued proudly, "You were in the forest alone—and grew into a man. You killed your first deer—and grew into a bigger man. Today you touched your enemy. You never once turned your back—even with a loaded gun pointing at your face. Songs will be sung in your honor. Today you became both deerslayer and warrior. In battle, you faced guns with only your knife and bow and did not flee. I am the proudest edudu in all of our land. When we enter our village, you will bring something of much greater worth than a deer that will be consumed and disappear. The honor you bring will last forever."

After edudu's speech, hardly another word was spoken as the two men began their return journey. There was nothing to say. Two men have never been more in tune with their life and love and themselves than those two were that day.

That next evening edudu told their story to the community assembled. Never could a Cherokee man have been prouder than to see the admiration and knowing glances the old men gave my brother. Every person there had experienced multiple loss from white greed.

Five Feathers was a deerslayer and warrior—a warrior who had touched the enemy and never once turned his back. I overheard the story recounted many times.

That evening my brother vowed he would never again allow a white man to steal his deer. The next time white men would attempt to rob him, he would be ready. It would not be my brother who would be dispossessed. The next time he would bring home the deer and the white man would die. I believed him, but his words filled me with sadness to the depths of my soul. I feel sorrow for our young men and the daily humiliation they endure. We do not understand the greed of the English. They intend to take everything we have or ever will have.

Chapter XIV

1821 - Fourth Lottery – Spain Sells Florida

Chapter 14

9 January 1821 - Month of the Cold Moon – Du no lv ta ni

We found Bear Paws on our porch this morning. He was filthy with a dreadful odor. His flesh was cold. He was hardly breathing. He appeared dead. We brought him in to the fire. When Bear Paws awakened, he said he had come to tell us that he had decided to never drink whiskey again. He asked if we would help.

He told us his story.

"Yesterday I wakened under chestnut trees. I had no idea where I was. Hogs were rooting around me. When I tried to lift my head, I couldn't move. I was paralyzed. I thought I was dying and would be eaten by hogs and no one would ever know. All day long I lay paralyzed with the hogs coming and going around me. It was horrible. I was sick. The hogs were not good company. I went to sleep and when I woke the second time I felt worse. My head was hurting terribly and still I could not move. As I lay under the chestnut trees looking at the sky, I thought of my mother, my mother's brothers and friends like you who are happy and never drink whiskey. I thought about hunting, fishing and ballplays with Five Feathers. My life has not been good. I think only of myself. I made bad choices. I don't want to drink whiskey, Calm Eagle. I never want to drink whiskey again. I almost died surrounded by hogs. I want to be like you and your wife Ravenwolf and Five Feathers."

"Drink this," elisi said, giving Bear Paws hickory milk. "It will help you stop shaking. Stay here today and we will care for you. Have something warm to eat and good to drink. You must eat."

Bear Paws drank.

"The hickory milk is good," Bear Paws said. "I will not stay here today, Ravenwolf. I came to tell you that when I was under those chestnut trees I could see my life clearly. I would not want my mother to know I was eaten by pigs. I want to live again."

"I have tried to stop drinking whiskey but white men are everywhere selling whiskey. I have tried to resist but I can't do this alone. I need help. Will you help me?"

"We will help," edudu said. "Come here often. Come every day and we will help you resist white men."

Bear Paws' face and arms were dirty, red and scratched. His eyes were swollen as if he had been fighting. His arms had ugly wounds and scabs. His unwashed clothes smelled of pig manure. His hands shook so he could hardly hold his cup of hickory milk.

"My dear Bear Paws," Elisi said, "you never need permission to sleep by our fire. Stay away from white men. They sell whiskey in order to rob you and your friends. They do not think it wrong to steal your money. If you see whites don't greet them. Come straight here and talk to me."

Elisi put her arm around Bear Paws' shoulder, "There isn't one good thing to say about whiskey, Bear Paws—not one good thing."

"You are right. There is nothing good about whiskey—nothing," Bear Paws answered quietly with his head down."

"Your decision to stop drinking is powerful, like a single corn seed," edudu said. "If you plant that seed on a fish head and give it water, the sun will turn it into a tall plant to feed your family. Your decision will grow. Whiskey leads to death. We can't live your life, but we can help. Today is the only day that matters. We'll worry about tomorrow when the sun comes up tomorrow."

"Thank you, Calm Eagle. Thank you, Walela. Tell Five Feathers I am ready to hunt. I want to live again. I have forgotten what it's like to hunt and fish and go to ballplays. I want to remember that joy."

Elisi embraced Bear Paws.

"Bear Paws, when you were a tiny child you played under our porch with Five Feathers. You were happy. Everyone loved you. Everyone still loves you. White man's whiskey has stolen your smile, but I see happiness growing in from the little seed you planted this morning."

"Come see us again in the morning," Edudu said, "and we shall pour more water on your little seed of corn. We'll go to the river and get us a fish."

For the first time Bear Paws smiled, "I would like that. I would like to go fishing with you tomorrow."

"When you think about whiskey," edudu said, "remember those of us who would give our lives for you."

Bear Paws paused and hung his head. We listened to the logs crackle in the fireplace.

"My friend, I know you would give everything for me," Bear Paws said. "When I was lying among the hogs, I thought of you and your good wife."

While we sat before the fire, Bear Paws said something I shall remember.

"Calm Eagle, you make me want to be a better man."

Elisi gave Bear Paws two skillet cakes and he left. I have a good feeling Bear Paws will never drink whiskey again.

17 January 1821

We have a new boy in school, Saloli—squirrel in English. He is six years old, smart and beginning to learn English. He runs around like a busy squirrel. Some older children asked Mr. Lowry to tell Saloli not to come back to school because of his ugly language in English.

Mr. Lowry asked me to talk to Saloli. I discovered his parents worked for white traders. He was learning English from rough, uneducated men. It will take time but I promised Mr. Lowry I would teach this beautiful little boy to speak properly and avoid ugly words. In Cherokee I explained to Saloli he could not attend school if he used bad English words. He didn't know the English words were bad.

I would love to be a teacher one day like Mr. Lowry. I love teaching children and helping them learn. I was thrilled to see the eagerness in Saloli's eyes. I was born to be a teacher.

19 January 1821

I read every newspaper Mr. Lowry gives me. I sometimes read aloud in school. While learning new words and reading from the newspapers, I learn about the white government.

Mr. Lowry says the more words I understand, the bigger, deeper and wider thoughts I can think. If I know few words, I will be like a carpenter who can only build crude structures because he had few tools.

19 January 1821

Copied from the *Georgia Journal* - 9 January 1821 – page 1

"Population of Milledgeville – Whites - 4,606. Blacks 4,005."

There are almost as many Africans in the Georgia capital as whites. Africans often come to Cherokee Country to escape bondage. I would run away if I were a slave. I would risk the horrible beating they receive when caught. Whites tell us we are stealing when the runaways come and we don't tell the authorities. They say we should return a runaway the same as we would a runaway horse. Slaves are property—chattel. How can I compare a man or a woman to a milk cow? Sadly, a few rich Cherokee own slaves.

16 February 1821

Mr. Lowry gave me two books of poetry. I read both as soon as I got home. He said, because I am Cherokee, I have a colorful understanding of the world and a rich command of words in three languages, not counting Latin and Greek. He said poetry helps capture emotion and convey a person's deepest thoughts. There are no mistakes in the creation of poetry he says. There is no wrong poem.

Poetry is art. Mr. Lowry says my poem is my personal artwork. I like that idea. Poetry isn't like mathematics where there is only one right answer. Drawing and poetry can never be wrong.

Mr. Lowry wants me to draw with words. I like drawing, poetry and writing. I love creating with words. It is an inconceivable joy to think I have the power to cause ideas to appear inside of another person's mind. What a marvelous privilege—to paint pictures with words that will enable others to see with their heart.

What is a Word?
Tree, flower, cloud, corn, elisi, deer, hawk,
Love, joy, compassion, delight,
Words are knowing,
Words fill my mind,
Words satisfy my heart,
Words bring happiness, rest, comfort, knowledge,
Words transport,
Words lift,
Words heal,
I love words,
Words bring color, grace, light, love, passion,
Words paint the sky,
Words fill my mind,
On the wings of words,
I explore the universe and beyond,
I love words,
I am made of words,
I give my words to you.

Mr. Lowry loved my poem and asked me to read it in class. He asked everyone to write poetry. Everyone's story is worth telling and everyone's poetry is worth reciting. Everyone has ideas no one else has or ever will have. Mr. Lowry wants us to learn words and allow our mind to use them freely. I feel good when I think about school. Mr. Lowry is a good man—and getting gooder. Ben taught me that silly word.

23 March 1821 - The Windy Moon – A nu yi
>   Copied from the *Georgia Journal* - 6 march 1821-page 2
>   The Florida Treaty Ratified – The Senate yesterday gave its consent…to the ratification of the Treaty between the United States and Spain, concluded in the City of Washington on the 22nd day of February, 1819. It is understood that the votes against the treaty did not exceed four or five in number. The completion of this long-suspended transaction has afforded us great satisfaction. We facilitate our readers generally that Florida is not attached to the territory of the Union.

Spain has sold the Florida territory to the United States for five million dollars. On 10 March 1821, the United States president, James Monroe, appointed Andrew Jackson to be Florida's first territorial governor.

Mr. Lowry said Spain claimed Florida as a possession in 1512, twenty-one years after Columbus first arrived. We lived here for hundreds of years. How can nations from across an ocean justify taking our land? Are we meaningless to European governments?

Spain ceded Florida to England in 1763 in exchange for Cuba and then after the American Revolution England returned Florida back to Spain in 1784. Florida has changed hands again. This back and forth ownership is confusing.

In 1818, Andrew Jackson invaded Spanish Florida in order to remove the Seminoles from the southern borders of the United States and at the same time powerfully demonstrate that Spain did not have the resources to militarily defend their Florida territory.

Seminoles, Creeks and Africans had fled to Spanish Florida to escape oppression from the United States. Andrew Jackson, Florida's new white governor, will eagerly hunt them as he did in the past. One day, perhaps, someone will hunt Andrew Jackson.

1 June 1821

Good news. Saloli is learning English properly. He no longer uses bad language. He has a beautiful smile. I have been helping him learn to read English. We read newspaper headlines and I'm teaching him the sound of each English letter. He learns quickly. His Cherokee is improving also. Saloli speaks Cherokee almost as well as an adult. I am teaching him to love words. I wish every Cherokee child could learn to read both Cherokee and English.

9 June 1821

Copied from the *Georgia Journal*-5 June 1821 page 2

"...And be it further enacted, that the territory acquired aforesaid (from the Creeks and Cherokee), shall be disposed of and distributed, in the following manner, to wit: After the surveying is completed and the returns made thereof, his Excellency the Governor, shall cause tickets to be made out, whereby all the numbers of lots in the different districts intended to be drawn for, shall be presented, which tickets shall be put into a wheel and constitute prizes. The following shall be the description and qualification of persons entitled to give their names for a draw or draws, under this act: Every male white person 18 years of age and upwards, being a citizen of the United States three years..."

For the fourth time, Georgia is giving away huge tracts of our land in a whites-only lottery.

Georgia's map is expanding—our map is shrinking. Georgia added five new counties from land taken from us: Dooly, Monroe, Fayette, Houston, and Henry. Mr. Lowry is embarrassed. White Europeans alone have privileges in the Americas as in Europe. Indians and niggers, as they call us, are inconsequential. Mr. Lowry says that is not what is written in their Book. The English have developed two standards—one for the Cherokee and Africans and a different one for themselves. "Do unto others as you would have them do unto you" must be for whites only.

30 December 1821

Mr. Lowry gave me a bundle of newspapers yesterday. The following issue of the *Georgia Journal* was published on 25 December, the day whites exchange gifts to celebrate the unselfish gift of their God to all of humanity.

Copied from the *Georgia Journal* - Page 2 – 25 December 1821

"Measures have been adopted to procure a further extinguishment of Indian title to lands within the limits of this state. We trust they will be attended with success."

Georgia wants all our land as a Christmas gift. When I showed Mr. Lowry this article, he stared at the newspaper in his hands for a long time. Finally, all he could say was, "I'm sorry Cassie. I'm sorry. I wish it wasn't so. I would do anything if this wasn't so."

He said nothing more. There was nothing to say.

Chapter XV

1822 - Two Wolves

Chapter 15

4 February 1822 - Month of the Bony Moon – Ka ga li

My cousin and I were throwing stones at an old white cloth we had hung on a bush. We were pretending the cloth was a white man. Edudu was watching. He called us to the porch to tell us a story. Edudu has a wonderful way of teaching with stories. I always feel older after I listen to edudu.

Every day edudu sits in his wooden chair on the side of the little front porch towards the woods that leads down to the river—the side with the warm sun in the morning and the cool shade in the afternoon. Some days he will sit all day whittling—making us beautiful things. Some days he will sit quietly and look into the forest. Some days when I am near he will call me to sit with him while he tells me a story.

As my cousin and I came up on the porch, Spinner's big brown eyes followed us. Sitting cross-legged on the worn boards of elisi's porch, we made ourselves comfortable at edudu's feet.

"I have a story for you," edudu said. "I saw you throwing stones at your white man. I heard your words. You were cruel, weren't you?"

"Yes, edudu. We were. We hate the English," I said in reply. My cousin and I didn't think we had done anything wrong. What could be wrong with throwing stones at white men? The whites hate us.

Edudu continued, "You girls know there are good and bad people? All whites are not bad—all are not good. Would you throw stones at Ben or Mr. Lowry or Ben's mother?"

"No, edudu. We would not throw stones at them. That would be a terrible thing," I answered.

"There are good Cherokee men, but there are some who might hurt you," edudu said to us patiently.

We listened respectfully as everyone does when edudu tells stories.

"It is true," edudu continued, "whites have taken much of our land and perhaps, one day, may take it all. Whites do not like us. They alone have privileges. There is nothing we can do about that. If you two girls had a few bad blackberries in your basket, would you throw all your blackberries away? If elisi finds a bad egg, does she throw all her eggs to the pigs?"

154

"No, edudu, elisi would never do that."

"What is true with eggs and blackberries is true of people," edudu said. "All English are not bad and all Cherokee are not good. It is true whites have made it difficult for us and other tribes. Even if all our land is taken from us, we must not become haters. There is something much worse than bad things happening to good people."

Edudu has a way that captures the attention of his listeners when he is telling a story. When he is talking his words tug me towards him. I feel as if I want to preserve everything he says in my heart forever. I don't want to let a single word escape.

Edudu continued, "Good people learn to live with bad things. A storm blows away our roof, but we can fix our roof. You lie ill for days, but you will recover. You injure your hand, but your hand will heal as if you were never injured."

"Yes, edudu," we said.

"You pick blackberries and get chiggers, but chigger bites go away," edudu said.

"We understand, edudu," we answered. "We hate chiggers. We understand bad things will happen. We will never be bad. We want to be good, like you."

Edudu stroked our hair and smiled. Nothing bad could ever happen to us when edudu is near.

"There is something worse than losing the roof of our house, injuring your hand or a chigger bite," edudu said. "Hate in our hearts is an enemy more dangerous than white men. Would you girls keep a pet rattlesnake in your house?"

We giggled.

"No, edudu. No one would have a pet rattlesnake. That's silly. A rattlesnake would bite us."

We laughed together with edudu. Keeping a pet rattlesnake was a big joke.

"You wouldn't bring a rattlesnake into your home," edudu continued "and likewise you can't bring hate into your heart. Both will wound you. Neither can be your pet. Can you imagine a pet rattlesnake here beside me instead of Spinner?"

"Oh no, Edudu. That would be horrible. We don't want a rattlesnake on our porch."

"Hatred should be feared more than white men, rattlesnakes or death itself," edudu said. "You can't keep hate in your heart any more than you can keep pet rattlesnakes under your bed."

I love the way edudu paints pictures with words when he tells stories—words that sound like music. I can see edudu's stories and feel them in my heart. I watch edudu's face and how he moves his arms. Edudu tells his stories with every part of himself. Even Spinner listens. Edudu says Spinner is wise because he listens to everyone and talks very little. Edudu says it's a mark of wisdom to listen more than talk.

"You know, dear ones," edudu continued, "we are here because Mother Earth and Father Sky made this world and everyone in it, both Cherokee and white. You, my dear children, will become a nuisance if you hate."

"We don't want to become a nuisance, edudu. We don't want to hate," we answered quickly.

Edudu leaned over close to us until his nose was almost touching our faces.

He whispered his words, "Children, it is a horrible thing to mistreat Mother Earth and Father Sky's people, even white people."

Edudu paused, sat up straight in his chair and looked at us.

"Do you hate your cousin Red Bird because he is different? Do you hate him because he was born deaf?"

"No, edudu. We don't hate Red Bird. We love our cousin. He is a good man. He is kind," we answered.

"Just because someone is different, we don't hate them," edudu continued. "You do not hate Africans because of their dark skin and curly hair."

"We love Africans, edudu. They are gentle and caring. They tell stories like you do."

Edudu nodded.

"Africans belong to Mother Earth and Father Sky just as we do—just as whites belong."

Edudu paused. For a few moments we watched the squirrels chasing one another on the white oak in front of the porch.

"Cherokee, Africans and whites are all the children of Mother Earth and Father Sky. We all live under the same blue sky. When I saw you two girls throwing stones, I knew it was time you learned about the two wolves."

When he said that, he gathered us up into his arms and held us—one on each knee. We put our arms around his neck and laughed and gave him kisses.

I have never felt more secure than with edudu—especially listening to his wonderful stories.

I remember everything about that day edudu told us about the two wolves. I remember the cool winter breeze blowing through the tall pines that were stretching their green arms up into the blue sky as if they were trying to touch the sun's face as he passed. I see the carpet of leaves and pine needles in the semi-light of the forest around our house. I remember the soft fluffy clouds hanging like great balls of cotton and the strong brown hands of edudu as he stroked our hair and held us against his chest. I see Spinner beside edudu's chair with his chin on his paws and his brown eyes following our every movement. Occasionally I watch him raise his ears to listen more carefully.

I hear edudu's soothing voice. His words poured over us, covering us with a peacefulness I can't describe. Edudu's words went inside me and made me bigger, brighter and stronger. His words filled me with magical pictures that live.

"It is time you girls learned about the two wolves," edudu said. "There are two wolves living inside each of you two girls. There are two wolves living inside of me. There are two wolves living inside of everyone, including whites and Africans. Your two wolves will live inside of you the rest of your life."

We began to understand what we were hearing was of great importance.

"One wolf is good—the other bad. One wolf adores you. The other despises you," edudu said. "Both wolves want your attention. The wolves constantly struggle with one another. One wolf is hateful, envious, cruel, ugly, selfish, spiteful, deceptive and a liar."

I shivered when edudu described the bad wolf. I felt a terror I had never felt before.

"One of your wolves will get stronger and the other will get weaker," edudu said. "The bad wolf inside you never tells the truth. He wants to destroy everything good in you. The bad wolf has no sun, moon or stars. His world is cold and dark. His heart is a dark empty shell. He wants to take you to his barren land where nothing grows. He has no mother or father. He wants to bend you to become like him. He has contempt for everything good. Bear Paws knows about the bad wolf. Bear Paws can tell you about his struggle with the two wolves."

"Yes, we know about Bear Paws, edudu," we said.

"Your other wolf is kind, generous, sweet, affectionate, tender, patient, trustworthy and always tells the truth," edudu said.

I was glad to hear about the good wolf. I felt stronger to hear about the good wolf. I didn't like to learn about the bad wolf. I knew there must be a good wolf.

"Your good wolf loves everyone and everything—especially you. The good wolf is your faithful servant who wishes you well," edudu said to us gently.

My cousin and I listened with wide eyes. I knew no one would ever care for us as edudu did. We loved the truth we were hearing about ourselves and our world.

"Both of your wolves want to be petted—even the bad wolf. One wolf will become stronger and the other weaker. You must choose the one you wish to be powerful. The bad wolf will tell you lies, for that's what he is—a liar. He will tell you a lie but make it sound like truth in order to lead you down a devious path to your destruction. He will teach you to lie to yourself, which is the worst lie of all. It would be terrible to lie to yourself, wouldn't it?"

"Yes, edudu. We always tell the truth. It is a terrible thing to lie."

Edudu smiled and nodded.

"I have good news. Don't be afraid. Your good wolf is honest and always tells the truth. He will teach you to be brave and valiant instead of a nuisance, as you were earlier. The good wolf will never deceive you. You must choose which wolf you will believe."

We listened patiently. I imagined I could hear the bad wolf prowling about in the shadows of the forest. The thought of him wanting to destroy me was frightening.

"My dear girls, do not fear," edudu said. "You have the ability to make one wolf stronger and the other weaker. You have the power to protect yourself from the bad wolf. You, and only you, have that power. You didn't know that, did you?"

"No, edudu. We didn't know about the wolves," we answered.

"You must choose which wolf will become strong and which will become weak," edudu said.

We were captivated. We had never heard anything like this. We were spellbound.

"Do not believe your bad wolf when he asks you to hate. What if someone told you to sit on a yellow jacket's nest in the ground or keep fish in your bed? What if someone told you to put skunks under your house for good luck? Would you believe those things?"

We laughed and laughed. Edudu laughed with us.

"No one would believe those things, edudu. We would never sit on a yellow jacket's nest or keep skunks under our house. How foolish that would be."

"You are right, dear children," edudu said. "Those are lies. Skunks do not bring good luck and yellow jackets sting everyone who disturbs their home. There are other lies just as silly yet some people choose to believe them."

"I am warning you girls. Day and night your two wolves will ask you to choose between the two. Choose you must. I cannot make your choice. Elisi cannot make your choice. You must choose which wolf will become strong and you must choose which wolf will become weak."

Edudu paused and petted both of us.

"As you grow into women, you will sometimes find yourself confused. You will not always know for certain which wolf is lying and which is telling the truth. I will not always be beside you to help you make the correct decision. Elisi is teaching you to make good cornbread and to care for chickens. One day you will cook cornbread without her and care for your chickens without her help. Likewise, as you grow you must choose which wolf becomes strong. I saw the wolves struggle inside of you two girls when you were throwing stones."

As we sat quietly at edudu's feet, he looked at us for a long time. I could hardly wait for him to continue. Spinner was as anxious to hear the rest of the story as we were. I wonder if there are two wolves inside of Spinner?

Edudu continued his story, "Your struggle will never end, but don't be afraid. Remember, my dear children. You will decide which wolf becomes strong."

He paused again for a long time looking into our eyes with the most beautiful image of affection. I felt safe but I wanted to know the end of the story. I wanted to know which wolf would prevail. I wanted to know which would become strong inside of me. How could I know such a thing?

"Edudu, which wolf will win? Which will grow? Which will become strong? How can we know the answer?"

"My darling children, you have asked the question I wanted you to ask. You have asked the question Mother Earth and Father Sky want you to ask. You have asked the most important question of all. I know the answer to your question."

"Which wolf will win?" We both anxiously asked at the same time. "Which wolf will win, edudu? Which will be strong? Tell us, edudu. Tell us."

Edudu smiled.

"The wolf you feed will be strong," edudu said. "The wolf you don't feed will wither."

I shall never forget the look in edudu's eyes.

"It is your choice which wolf you feed," he said. "The wolves are like our moon. The wolf you feed will grow. He will shine more brightly every night. When your moon is full you can safely walk in the forest as if it were day, can you not? The wolf you ignore will wane. He will become smaller and smaller until he almost disappears."

Edudu gently nodded as he gave us his advice.

"Feed the good wolf and you shall live long and well and your path shall always be full of light. Today, when you girls were throwing stones, you were feeding your bad wolf. You were listening to his hate. He was teaching you to be disgusting like him. Choose to feed your good wolf and be happy all your days."

I made the decision that day to feed my good wolf and never believe a lie. It was a decision I promised myself I would always keep.

"Edudu, why do the English come? Why do they take our land? Why do they hate us? We don't hate them." I asked. "Why don't they stay on the whiteside and leave us alone? I do not understand."

"I do not know," edudu answered. "The land across the sea must be a cold and dark land. When the English arrived here their hearts were already full of selfishness. They did not learn to be ugly here. The good wolf must have become feeble in their land long ago, but do not trouble yourself with them, my dear. Your happiness does not depend on whites—or upon anyone. Your happiness does not come from your elisi or your edudu. One day we will be gone. Your happiness is your decision."

Edudu continued with his wise advice, "You cannot live your life and someone else's also. Feed your own good wolf and you shall be happy and you shall make me happy, too. Feed your good wolf and he will become strong and you will be strong and happy and live long and well."

Chapter XVI

1822 – Ellemander J. Warbington

Chapter 16

26 February 1822 - Month of the Bony Moon – Ka ga li
Copied from the *Georgia Journal* - 19 February 1822 - Page 1

"Florida-A bill is now before congress, providing for the government of East and West Florida, under the name of the territory of Florida. The executive power to be vested in a governor…appointed by the president for three years. The legislature, to be composed of the governor and thirteen discreet and fit persons--the latter to be appointed, annually, by the President….The laws of the United States are declared to prevail in the territory from the passage of the act."

The Seminoles, Creeks and Africans have nowhere to flee. I fear they will drown in the white flood that will surely come upon them.

3 March 1822
Copied from the *Georgia Journal* - 26 February 1822 - Page 3

"Thirty Dollars Reward-Runaway from the subscriber, living in Burke county, Georgia, near Walker's bridge, Brier creek, sometime in November or December last, his negro fellow named EMANUEL, about 25 years of age, 5 feet 8 or 9 inches high, has lost one of his eye teeth, and is of yellowish complexion. He was purchased from a gentleman living in Madison, Morgan county, where he has a wife, and for which he will probably aim. The above reward and all expenses will be paid to any person who may apprehend and deliver him to me, or lodge him in any safe jail, so that I may obtain him again. Amos Wiggin"

How can Amos Wiggin legally keep a man from his wife? Whites insist they are highly civilized. I don't think so.

I wonder how Emanuel's wife felt when he was sold? I would risk a beating for my love. What is his wife's name? Do they have children? Does she cry at night in her loneliness?

A White Killing Frost

How ironic the young man's name is Emanuel which means "God with us" in Hebrew.

3 May 1822

Copied from the *Georgia Journal* – 16 April 1822 – page 3

"Now in Baldwin County Jail, as a runaway, a man about 5 feet 1 inch high, black straight hair, long before, says his name is Emanuel Sanders, a scar from his nostril on his right side, to his mouth on his upper lip, and one about an inch long on the right side of his face, also a scar over his right eyebrow, a scar under his nose near his left eye, has on white pantaloons filled in with wool, striped swansdown vest, stripes around him, white cotton shirt. Attempted to pass in this place as a free man, speaks English, Spanish and Indian in a broken manner. F. Sanford. Jailor April 15"

21 May 1822

Copied from the *Georgia Journal* - 14 May 1822 – page 3

"...Mr. Gilmer submitted the following: 'for the purpose of holding treaties with the Cherokee and Creek tribes of Indians for the extinguishment of the Indian title to all the lands within the state of Georgia pursuant to the fourth section of the first article of the agreement and cession concluded between the United States and the state of Georgia on 24th April, 1802, the sum of $30,000.00'."

23 June 1822

Ben and I spent the day together. We read poetry. Ben loaned me Gulliver's Travels by Johnathan Swift and the Decline and Fall of the Roman Empire by Edward Gibbon, Volume One. I am most interested in Gibbon. The modern spread of western European culture and military power across an ocean seems to imitate growth of Roman dominance.

12 August 1822

Copied from the *Georgia Journal* – 6 August 1822 – page 2

"A conspiracy of the Negros has been lately detected at Charleston, S.C.—We at first hoped it was a trifling matter; but the following extract...shows the alarming extent of the danger:

"Twenty negros were executed this morning for the crime of

being engaged in an attempt at insurrection. Eight have been previously and, nineteen are now under sentence. Four or five are condemned to be transported, and sixty or seventy are in jail, yet waiting their trial. It was a most merciful interposition of the goodness of God, that this scheme was discovered just before it was to be carried into execution...We know the negros of Charleston are excessively indulged by their masters..."

The whites believe their god intervened on behalf of the Americans and exposed the African's plan. Americans must think Africans godless.

30 December 1822 - The Month of the Snow Moon – V s gi ga

I walked over to visit Ben. When I arrived, Mr. Lowry and a friend were on the front porch enjoying a conversation on an unusually warm winter's day. I heard their animated discussion long before I reached the house.

As I walked up their wide porch steps, Mr. Lowry and his guest stood to welcome me.

"Hello, Cassie," Mr. Lowry said. "How nice to see you this lovely December afternoon. Ben's gone hunting. His mother told him to be home before dark, but you're welcome to visit with us if you want to wait till he returns?"

"I would love to visit with you until Ben returns," I said.

"Excellent," Mr. Lowry said with a smile. "Cassie, I want you to meet my dear friend, Mr. Ellemander J. Warbington. He's a Moravian missionary from Spring Place over on the Federal Road. He's checking on us Presbyterians to see what kind of winter we're having and catch up on all the latest."

"A pleasure to meet you, Mr. Ellemander J. Warbington," I said. I pronounced every syllable of his name carefully and curtseyed properly.

"A pleasure to make your acquaintance, Cassie," Mr. Warbington said in return, and bowed politely.

I have never seen a man so tall and slender as Mr. Warbington.

"Cassie, would you like to join our conversation or wait inside with Eleanor?" Mr. Lowry asked. "We're discussing history, I'm afraid. A young lady like you might find our discussion rather dry, but you're welcome to join us. Eleanor sat with us for a short while but excused herself to get things done in the house. To be honest, I think she went inside to get away from two tiresome men who read too much."

"I would love to listen out here with you two, if you don't mind. I do not find history dull in the least," I answered.

"Cassie," Mr. Lowry added, "you don't have to call our guest by that long name of his. We call him Els for short. I've known Els for years. I loved his name the first time I heard it. I think it the most magnificent name I've ever heard, don't you?"

Mr. Lowry chuckled and continued, "The name Wilbur Lowry is quite insipid when compared to the grandiloquent Mr. Ellemander J. Warbington, don't you agree?"

"I like your name, Mr. Lowry," I answered. "I don't think your name lackluster at all. And I do like your name, Mr. Warbington. It is a magnificent name. I've never heard one like it but, to be perfectly honest, Mr. Ellemander J. Warbington, you must forgive me. I cannot agree with Mr. Lowry. I must confess there is another name I know that is considerably more grand."

"My dear young lady," Mr. Warbington said with a big grin, "and what is the grandest of all? What superlative appellation receives the laurels from your gracious hand and stands as the exalted sobriquet above all others?"

Mr. Warbington couldn't contain his laughter.

"I must know. Do tell young lady. Do tell. I'm all ears," said Mr. Warbington amidst his laughter.

As Mr. Warbington asked me to tell the name, he bowed sweeping his long arms before him as if we were dancers in a palatial ballroom. I couldn't help but smile and join in the humor of the moment. His was a wonderfully gracious gesture.

"Why, Mr. Ellemander J. Warbington—," I hesitated and smiled at both men before I answered, "the grandest name of all is Ben, of course."

Mr. Lowry and Mr. Warbington laughed so loud Mrs. Lowry poked her head out the door to see what was happening.

"Hello, Cassie," Mrs. Lowry said. "I didn't know you were here. May I bring you something? Would you like to come inside or are you going to listen to these two monotonous, tiresome men droning on and on endlessly about history and politics?"

I answered politely, "Nice to see you, Mrs. Lowry. Thank you for the offer but, if you don't mind, I'll stay out here and listen for a while. I find these discussions interesting. You won't be offended if I stay out here, will you, Mrs. Lowry?"

"Of course I won't be offended, dear," Mrs. Lowry answered sweetly. "You stay out here as long as you want. When these dusty old men bore you, come inside and the two of us will have us a nice cup of tea and a hot buttered scone and we shall discuss more interesting things."

Mrs. Lowry went back inside and Mr. Lowry brought me a chair.

"Thank you, my dear Cassie, for that information about the most magnificent name of all," Mr. Warbington said, still laughing. "I've been fond of young Ben since he was a babe in arms, but I'm guessing you have quite a different view of that intelligent young man, and his name, than I have?"

Mr. Warbington gave me a knowing smile and another polite bow.

"My mother named me after her grandfather who she adored," Mr. Warbington added. "My middle name is just plain ole' Joseph after my father. Now I know by expert authority that I have an almost magnificent name—at least in these parts. However, I'm flattered to be so high as number two in your list."

Mr. Lowry interrupted, "This young lady, Mr. Warbington, is perhaps the most astute student I have ever taught. She is bright, intelligent and quick with logic, reasoning and wit. Language is her forte. She has a stronger vocabulary than I, which you will soon discover. She must know the meaning of every word she reads or hears, no matter what the language. She is a word sponge. I wish I had been given her desire to learn when I was a lad. Most of the time it's not me teaching her but she teaching me."

I love Mr. Lowry's compliments. It gives me a nice feeling inside and he is correct. I do love words and language. I try to learn new words in more than one language every day.

"I thank you for inviting me to join your discussion," I answered. "You know how much I like history, Mr. Lowry. I have learned a great deal about our world through reading history. I love to study the past. Studying history, as you have taught me, is the key to understanding human motivations in any era—especially in our modern times."

Both Mr. Lowry and Mr. Warbington nodded in agreement.

"Governments change," I continued, "but people are today as they always have been. Human behavior hasn't changed since history began. I would love to stay here and listen. If you don't mind, may I ask questions like we do in school?"

"Of course, Cassie," said Mr. Lowry. "With Els' permission, I declare this porch an official classroom and I elect Els headmaster."

"I like that, Wilbur," Mr. Warbington said. "I'll be a good headmaster. I promise not to discipline you too severely for your inattention."

We laughed together once again. I was enjoying the intellectual atmosphere.

"Before you walked up, Cassie," Mr. Warbington began, "Wilbur and I were examining the flow of history leading to the current political situation in

Cherokee Country—a rapidly deteriorating situation, if you want my opinion."

"My heart is with your nation," Mr. Warbington continued. "I agree with Eleanor and Wilbur. The Cherokee are under increasing pressure from a growing malevolent power. I know it may not seem like it to you and your people, Cassie, but there are some on the whiteside who wish your nation well—a meagre few, I'm afraid. Few have the courage to stand against their peers. When push comes to shove, we white folks tend to take the easy road."

"It's a hard thing to hold a position that requires one to bear the ridicule of one's neighbors," Mr. Lowry interjected. "Do you remember, Cassie, when the young teacher from Nazareth was tried before the Roman governor? Do you remember what became of his closest friends when he was hauled into court?"

"I have heard you read that story often, Mr. Lowry. His friends abandoned him because they were afraid of the authorities."

"Yes, indeed," Mr. Lowry continued, "that's exactly what happened. I think that's what's happening in Georgia. People are afraid to voice their opinions about injustice for fear of retribution."

Mr. Warbington continued, "Wilbur and I are discussing the implications of events of the last fifty years with the United States and especially Georgia, and how those events conspire against your nation. What is happening isn't much different than what happened long ago in Palestine and recently in the French Revolution. Good people, with feet of clay, are afraid.

Specifically, Wilbur and I find the addition of the new states interesting as it affects the future of the various Indian tribes—especially the Cherokee. I think, Cassie, if we analyze our past, we can foresee a bit of the future, don't you think? With applied wisdom from history, we can avoid the worst mistakes of our progenitors and take prophylactic action to prevent the social ills that plague mankind."

Mr. Lowry interjected, "Cassie, just before you arrived, Mr. Warbington and I were talking about the formation and addition of the new frontier states. For example, before 1776, the State of Virginia included enormous tracts of land that extended across the mountains to their west—what we call Kentucky today. Virginia, the most prosperous and densely populated of the English colonies, found those western lands too cumbersome to govern after independence."

I was listening carefully. I had read this history before, but I loved the way Mr. Lowry and his guest were tying historical events together.

Mr. Lowry continued, "Virginia ceded their western land to our new general government in Washington City and asked nothing in return—an interesting political decision, as it turned out. Shortly afterward, Kentucky was organized out of Virginia's ceded western territory and admitted to the union as the fifteenth state. That was thirty years ago and political events have moved rapidly since."

"Pardon me, Wilbur," Mr. Warbington interjected. "Keep in mind, peace wasn't signed between the rebellious colonies and the British until 1783. That was only thirty-nine years ago. Seems longer, doesn't it? Although England granted their colonies independence, the Crown did not cede its westernmost holdings, forts and assets in the Treaty of Paris. Most folks don't know that."

"I like the direction of your thinking, Els. Please continue," Mr. Lowry said.

"Well, thank you, sir. I shall continue," Mr. Warbington said with a little bow in his seat. "The British and the new United States government granted one another perpetual navigation rights to the Mississippi River. The British wanted to maintain influence beyond the United States' western frontier and limit the influence of France, England's arch enemy who at that time owned all the land west of the Mississippi—land Napoleon had acquired from Spain. Some say those British addendums to the peace of 1783 were the primary cause of the War of 1812 which, as you know, gave General Jackson occasion for his military fame and launched his political career. Fortunately for General Jackson's future success, he didn't get word that the War of 1812 had ended until several weeks after the battle of New Orleans."

I was paying attention to every word Mr. Warbington was saying.

Mr. Warbington asked, "Cassie, I don't know where your inquisitive nature came from but I wish I could give a healthy dose of it to my students. Your interest in education and love of language will serve you well. I can't imagine a young lady like you having such a desire to learn. Mr. Lowry is a lucky man to have you as a student. I'm privileged to have met you. You're probably the only girl in all the South who would choose of her own free will to sit with two stuffy old men and listen to a dry historical discussion like ours."

I smiled, stood, and gave a little curtsy in return.

"Well, thank you, Mr. Warbington," I answered. "I love compliments, especially from adults. I had much rather converse with adults than play children's games. This kind of discussion has always been of interest."

I continued, "A few minutes ago, Mr. Warbington, you used the word prophylactic. I guessed its meaning, but I've never heard that word before or seen it in print. What does it mean?"

Mr. Warbington answered, "Good question, young lady. Prophylactic is a simple compound word coming from two Greek words. It means to guard. The preposition, pro, means towards and the last part is to guard. After the invention of the printing press, progressive French and English authors coined many new words using Greek and Latin compounds. Language is most interesting, isn't it?"

Mr. Lowry interrupted, "Well, if you two philologists will allow me to direct our conversation back to history and the formation of the states, I want to follow the previous line of discussion about the state of Virginia ceding its western lands. Georgia, imitating Virginia, ceded its vast western lands to the general government in 1802 but, unlike Virginia, Georgia wanted something in return. Georgia wanted money and assistance to remove all Indians from its chartered boundaries. Virginia gave away their western land with no compensation whatsoever, but Georgia made a deal—a lucrative deal, as it turned out. In 1802, Thomas Jefferson agreed with Georgia, and the Compact of 1802 was signed—a horrible political decision for the Creek and Cherokee."

"Interesting turn of events, wasn't it?" Mr. Warbington interjected.

Mr. Lowry continued, "Yes, sir. It was. Out of the land ceded by Georgia in the compact of 1802, congress admitted Mississippi to the Union in 1817. That same year congress created the Alabama territory and Alabama became a state in 1819. Since then, Cassie, the vast Indian nations on our North American continent have been gobbled up by this voracious monster we call the United States. The Cherokee Nation has survived, but barely. Your nation is a shrinking island in a sea of white. Tennessee and North Carolina lie to the north. The Florida Territory, Georgia and Alabama border Cherokee Country to the south and west. The Principle People are being squeezed, aren't they?"

Mr. Warbington interjected, "The last few years have been a disaster for Indians everywhere. Indians have lost most of their holdings east of the Mississippi by the political design of whites. Since the Louisiana Purchase, the Indians west of the Mississippi are increasingly threatened."

Listen to this," Mr. Warbington said. "On 10 December 1817, Mississippi was admitted to the union. On 14 December 1819, Alabama became a state. In 1818, Kentucky annexed more land lying to their west making the state of Kentucky much larger. The additional land acquired by Kentucky was ostensibly purchased from the Chickasaw."

"What are you thinking, Cassie?" Mr. Warbington asked. He could see my puzzled expression.

I was confused.

"I have learned a lot from Mr. Lowry and by reading histories and reading many different newspapers," I said. "I often talk to edudu about these things. Whites take what they want, when they want. They say they purchased land from us when, in practice, they intimidated, threatened and bribed. Edudu doesn't believe Kentucky purchased their land from the Chickasaw just as the Cherokee land in Tennessee wasn't fairly purchased. Threats, intimidation and violence are the tools whites use to acquire land. Whites are like men who swindle children out of their inheritance and later boast of their deeds. We cannot defend our borders. We are not a nation of lawyers, soldiers and surveyors. We do not have a powerful standing army. You are correct, Mr. Warbington. We are surrounded."

The two men nodded. I knew they had listened.

Mr. Lowry continued, "It's Veni, Vidi, Vici isn't it? The white governments imitate Julius Caesar and the Romans. They came, they saw and they conquered. Victori Spolia, is it not, Mr. Warbington? The Cherokee cannot stand against European governments working together to dispossess an entire continent. They intend to turn the map of the North American continent from red to white. It's that simple."

Mr. Warbington silently nodded in agreement.

"With the admission of Alabama and Mississippi as new frontier states," Mr. Lowry added, "and Florida as a territory, the Cherokee are surrounded. Whites intend to own every acre of land between the Atlantic and the Mississippi River—if they can't purchase it, they'll take it by force of arms. The Creeks are almost gone from Georgia and Alabama. The Cherokee are the only Indians left with any land to speak of. Cherokee leadership has made many agreements with white governments but, I must say, I don't trust the fidelity of white politicians."

I thought Mr. Lowry should let me make him a Cherokee talking stick to use in his class and on the front porch.

I interjected quietly, "Edudu says no one can stop the white killing frost that is coming. The *Georgia Journal* reported not long ago that two thousand immigrants came into New York in one week alone. It seems all of Europe has heard about the free land available in the New World, but I am bewildered why so many want to leave their homeland? They must hate it there."

Mr. Lowry asked, "Tell us your thinking, Cassie. Els and I want to know what it is you're pondering."

"We Cherokee have lived here for hundreds of years," I continued slowly as I organized my thoughts. "It is inconceivable to us that we shall not continue to do so. The world changes, Mr. Lowry, but we Cherokee are not changing. We are a happy people. We have everything we desire. Why would we want to change and become miserable like the whites? If we were unhappy, like the whites, we would leave our country and go somewhere else, but we are happy here. We have our houses, barns, fields and farms. We grow our crops and raise our families. We have our own country. We have strong communities. We have plenty to eat and we don't worry about who owns what. We don't mind sharing. We take care of our own. We are not a divisive bellicose people controlled by lawyers and judges. Whites have an overweening need for exclusive ownership at the expense of everyone else, including their own kind. Whites appear to us as grasping, self-seeking and insatiable."

"Els, that is a sad commentary, isn't it?" Mr. Lowry said. "I have encouraged Cassie to write a journal. I asked her to write anything she wished, but I asked her to write about the interaction of the Cherokee and white culture and what her people think. She is a thinker, isn't she? I gave Cassie a list of interesting events that happened just this year in the United States for her to mull upon. I wanted her to get the feeling of how fast our world is changing in these new United States and in Europe. I want her to write what her community thinks about those changes and how they view their future. Would you like to hear that list, Els?"

"Yes indeed, sir," said Mr. Warbington. "Please share with me."

"Here's the list," Mr. Lowry said.

"In February of this present year, 1822, Boston was incorporated as a city. In May, Congress combined East and West Florida into one territory. On June 9th, Charles Graham was granted a patent for false teeth. I would like to see those teeth, wouldn't you? That must be some invention. In September of this year, the brilliant Frenchman, Jean-Francois Champollion, deciphered the Rosetta Stone—a most amazing and helpful feat in the study of ancient languages. I intend to learn more about his discovery. I would like to know the details of his discovery. On December 12, only a few weeks ago, Mexico was officially recognized as a sovereign nation by our United States. Things change, don't they, Els? Our world is in flux. Spain's influence is waning in the New World and English-speaking North America is waxing—a rising giant."

"Please continue," Mr. Warbington said. "This is most interesting."

"The point is," Mr. Lowry continued, "not one of these events, and hundreds of others like them, are of the least interest to Cassie's nation. The Cherokee don't read white newspapers, they generally do not speak English and they have no interest in white politics. The Cherokee have no interest in Mexico, Paris, London, Madrid, Washington City, or even Milledgeville. It's of no importance to the Cherokee that the United States recognizes Mexico as a nation or that Boston has become a city. Sadly, the opposite is true. The United States has no interest in the Cherokee—none."

We sat silently listening and Mr. Warbington added, "The Cherokee are being squeezed, but maybe, just maybe, what happened October past will end that. I hope so. As you know, Chief John Ross and fifty-four other tribal leaders wrote and signed an open letter to the State of Georgia and the general government after important treaty negotiations. The Cherokee leaders hope these negotiations will finally end the incessant illegal encroachments on Cherokee land by the state of Georgia. Perhaps, at long last, the Cherokee have a treaty Milledgeville will honor and international borders which will be respected."

Mr. Warbington continued with a sad tone, "The general government and Georgia agreed the continued seizing of Cherokee land would end with current 1822 boundaries. Chief Ross, and his fellows, worked long and hard for this agreement. I want this treaty to be the last, but white governments have broken every treaty in the past. That's a sad thought, isn't it? The United States government has demonstrated it cannot keep promises—not one. It's sad to think our United States cannot be trusted."

"Will this be a landmark agreement or will the United States break its word again?" Mr. Warbington asked. "I don't see how they can break their promises now, but they have broken every promise in the past. We shall see. We shall see."

Mr. Lowry chuckled under his breath and smiled.

"The white governments make piecrust promises, Eleanor says."

"And what, pray tell, is a piecrust promise?" Mr. Warbington asked, looking sideways at Mr. Lowry. "How could your good wife possibly compare government promises to the crust of a pie?"

Mr. Lowry laughed out loud.

"Well, Jonathan Swift popularized the phrase long ago, but my good wife, who has on occasion accused me of making piecrust promises, says our government makes piecrust promises with the Cherokee and all the other Indian nations. She says a piecrust promise is "easily made and easily broken". I think she's right. Our government talks out of both sides of its mouth. As far as concerns the Indian tribes, white governments have no integrity whatsoever."

"That would be humorous, Wilbur, if it wasn't so very true," Mr. Warbington said quietly.

Mr. Lowry continued, "And what is worse, I'm afraid, Andrew Jackson will one day have a greater say in the Cherokee future. Rumor has it Jackson will stand for president in '24—in just two years. He has a good chance of success. Everyone knows Ole' Hickory's reputation. Jackson's election would be a black day for the Cherokee."

"I've read Jackson's speeches," Mr. Warbington said. "Would you like to hear the kind of thing he would say—the kind of arguments Jackson would make for white ownership of land? My mother's people are all from Tennessee. I'm an expert when it comes to Jackson and friends.

"Yes, please," Mr. Lowry and I said at the same time.

"Ok, here's my imitation Jackson speech," Mr. Warbington said. "This isn't the political position I hold. This is Andrew Jackson's thinking. Don't be angry with me. I don't believe these things," Mr. Warbington said with a smile—wagging his finger towards both of us.

He began:

'Our country needs a decisive hand', Andrew Jackson would say. 'You missionaries can't expect the government to go around with a law book in one hand and a Bible in the other. I've been criticized but I took care of business. Do-gooders can't protect themselves or anyone from the merciless savages. We have a manifest destiny. We own the future. Whites run the governments of every state. Whites control all commerce. Whites own all the land. We operate every port and sail every ship. White armies and navies control the world. This is a white country and I'm proud to have had a part in building it. We don't need to consult anyone about our future."

"I know what Jackson would say, don't I?" Mr. Warbington said, "Jackson would continue by saying:

'I don't have time to listen to a flock of chicken-livered, do-good lawyers with tall hats resting on empty heads. I'm for action—not talk. I've stared down the barrel of a loaded gun on more than one occasion. Never once did I run. Me and my men take care of business. My Volunteers aren't afraid of the Spanish, French, British or Indians. They would follow me to hell and back and I assure you we would return victorious.'

'This continent is ours. We own everything above it, on it and under it according to long established law. We surveyed it. We work it. We live on it. We plow it. We harvest the crops. We haven't taken anything from anyone. We have occupied and developed abandoned land. This is our God-given land. It was taken away from the savages who didn't know what to do with it. Our occupation has been legal—sanctioned by every government. It's our destiny.'

"I want you to know," Mr. Warbington continued, "these folks I'm quoting can only think in terms of extinguishment of legal rights—real or imagined. The white culture that came from Europe wants one thing. They want to own land with an uninterrupted title—fee simple."

Mr. Lowry nodded his head. He and I remained silent.

Mr. Warbington continued, "Jackson would tell us:

'An Indian nation within our borders is absurd. Indians have less value than niggers. Can you imagine a negro nation within our borders? Of course not. An Indian nation within our borders is just as absurd. When elected I'll remove the lazy, good-for-nothin' Indians entirely. It will be in their best interest. There's plenty of room out west.'

'We know what the Indians need better than they do. For their safety, they must be removed. Under my administration they will be benevolently transported outside our borders. We are a kind-hearted people. We know what's best for that benighted race.'

"Basically, Els," Mr. Lowry said, "you're saying Jackson is a white know-it-all demigod?"

"Yes, Wilbur, I'm afraid you're right. That thinking doesn't bode well for the tribes within the borders of the United States. Let me finish Jackson's speech. I've thought a lot about this over the last year or two. Jackson's supporters, like Lewis Cass, governor of the Michigan Territory, are cut from the same bolt of cloth. White governments have worked for the eradication of the Indian nations since they first set foot in North America. Jackson would continue:"

'I promise the good folks in Georgia I will keep Jefferson's 1802 promise. We'll do in Georgia what we've done in Tennessee, Kentucky and Alabama. There's plenty of open land on the other side of the Mississippi.'

'When elected, I'll remove the lot, by force if necessary. I won't hesitate to repeat Horseshoe Bend if they're foolish

173

enough to resist. Removal is for their own good and the good of mankind. Removal will be the final solution to our Indian problem.'

When Mr. Warbington finished, we sat speechless in the darkening December afternoon. Our shared melancholy was tangible. The mid-winter sun, hanging low above the distant mountains, seemed to echo the chilling words of Andrew Jackson and the icy sound of his final solution. There was not a cloud to be seen in the cold December twilight. The first twinkling winter stars of dusk warned of a bitter chill that would descend as we slept. At dawn everything would be covered by a white killing frost.

Chapter XVII

1823 – Edudu Speaks - Right of Discovery

Chapter 17

11 April 1823 - The Flower Moon – Ka wa ni

My happiest day would be in a library filled with books. Mr. Lowry loans me books. I sometimes borrow books from his friends, but it would be glorious to read uninterrupted in a proper library filled with more books than I could possibly read.

Copied from the *Southern Recorder* - 1 April 1823 – page 3

"There are in Paris 5 libraries daily open to the public containing together 1,072,000 volumes and 80,000 manuscripts—any decent person is admitted gratis, and accommodations are supplied for reading, consulting or writing."

26 April 1823

"Walela, would you please read from the white newspaper. I want to hear what the whites say," edudu asked one evening.

We sat on the porch with Spinner between us in the gloaming. I love to translate newspapers into Cherokee for edudu and his friends. I have learned a great deal about the English language, whites and Georgia politics. I love learning languages. Learning is a wonderful game.

When I read edudu listens carefully. When what I read makes him angry he sometimes stands in front of the porch and looks up into the sky with his arms crossed as if he were looking at the moon or watching a buzzard. I asked him why he stood like that. He said he can think better when standing and looking up. Edudu makes me laugh.

The first article I read:

Copied from the *Georgia Journal* - 4 March 1823 - page 2

"Gen. Glascock, one of the Commissioners appointed on the part of our state, to treat with the Cherokee Nation…returned home on Tuesday last. We learn…an indisposition strongly prevails among the Cherokee generally to make any further cession of their lands: but this…proceeds from the influence of a few…who would monopolize themselves to the injury of the tribe, and to the exclusion of our claims--Our Commissioners flatter themselves, however, that at the convention in August they will be enabled to do away with the false impressions which have been made on the minds of our Red Brethren and thereby effect the object of their mission."

"The white man says we are his red brothers," edudu said. "They use words they do not mean. They have lied since they landed on our shores. They believe us uncivilized and heathen, yet they call us brothers. They feign friendship only to acquire more land. We will not give more. We should have never given them land. One day, Walela, we won't have enough land left to dig a hole for my coffin. Read more please."

Copied from the *Georgia Journal* - 11 March 1823 - Page 3

"The results of the late attempts to hold a Treaty with the Cherokee Indians, has been truly unfortunate. And from the disposition manifested by that nation there is but little hope that the meeting in August next will be more successful. The Commissioners…procured a large supply of provisions and had tents built. Some few did attend, but so scrupulously did they observe the orders in Council, which had been previously passed, that, although the weather was very inclement, they would not touch a ration or venture inside a tent. We could wish that civilized society should always present such examples of obedience to the laws of the land. A deputation of Commissioners waited on Hicks, the Principle Chief and remonstrated with him on the course that had been pursued by the nation. He heard them through their story very patiently and dryly asked: "Will you give us two dollars an acre for our land?" Being answered in the negative he answered, "Very well, we know it's value and can keep it--as for the claims your people have against us, we do not regard them. We can pay them without selling our land, whenever they are properly presented."

"My dear Walela,' edudu said laughing, "whites think themselves unfortunate when they don't own everything. I am proud our people obeyed Chief Hicks and didn't take government rations or sleep in government tents."

I read another article in which Mr. Ware, senator from Georgia, expresses anger towards his general government because they have not granted Georgia's request to be reimbursed for military service when Georgia fought against us and the Creeks. He said ugly things. Edudu is right. He tells lies.

Copied from the *Georgia Journal* - 18 March 1823 - page 2

Congress - In the Senate- Mr. Ware, of Georgia, delivered the
following remarks...on the Militia claims....Considering
Georgia, then, as a member of the Union she was entitled to the
support...of the general government whenever her rights or
sovereignty were invaded...It should...be recollected that at the
period of time which gave birth to the claim under consideration
the frontiers of Georgia, nearly four hundred miles in extent,
were bordered by a race of people whose...predominant passion
was war, and who readily embraced every opportunity to satiate
a jealous and revengeful disposition with the blood of the
innocent. Against those savages, who were numerous and
warlike, the state, with a thin population and limited resources,
had to defend herself. At a time when neither sex or infancy
afforded security against unprovoked massacre and slaughter,
when the most harassing hostilities were carried on against the
unprotected frontier settlements of Georgia, under practices of
Indian barbarity and warfare, calculated to arouse all the feelings
of hatred and vengeance, and the utmost abhorrence and
detestation against the authors and perpetrators of such
cruelty...He informs the President...the Creeks and the Cherokee
are unfriendly and hostile, that murders and other wrongs have
been committed by them...that already blood had been spilt in
every direction and that such was the havoc and carnage making
by them, that retaliation by open war became the only resort.

"How can men be allowed to print such lies?" edudu asked. "The Georgia
senator lies in order to get more money from his government. He is self-
serving. He never mentioned the wrongs whites committed against us."

"Please read more, Walela."

"Edudu, a white judge says white Europeans have the right to occupy our
land because they have been given the right of discovery. Whites divided the
world among themselves as directed by the Christian Pope in Rome. It is a
law among white European nations."

I read:

On 28 February 1823, Chief Justice John Marshall of the white
Supreme Court delivered a landmark ruling that the Right of
Discovery superseded any Indian right of occupancy in all
disputes concerning land ownership."

Quoted from the judge's ruling:

"The United States ... maintain, as all others have maintained, that discovery gave an exclusive right to extinguish the Indian title of occupancy, either by purchase or by conquest....The power now possessed by the government of the United States to grant lands, resided, while we were colonies, in the crown, or its grantees."

"Mr. Lowry gave me another quote from the Catholic Pope about the Right of Discovery. Their Pope believes Christians have been given the exclusive right, by their god, to rule the world."

"Romanus Pontifex, January 8, 1455 - ...we bestow suitable favors and special graces on those Catholic kings and princes, ... athletes and intrepid champions of the Christian faith...to invade, search out, capture, vanquish, and subdue all Saracens and pagans whatsoever, and other enemies of Christ wheresoever placed, and... to reduce their persons to perpetual slavery, and to apply and appropriate... possessions, and goods..."

"What is this Right of Discovery, Walela?" edudu asked. "What does the white judge mean? How can this white chief who lives across the sea give away land he has never seen?"

"Mr. Lowry says the Christian governments of Europe claim possession of the entire world by the right of their religion. They believe themselves superior. Even people far from England in the huge continent of India are under English rule."

Edudu spoke after a long silence, "Walela, the whites were lost when they came here. They thought this was India—a remarkable mistake for people who believe themselves superior."

"Europeans gave the world to themselves. The white judge affirmed that truth in this newspaper," I answered.

Edudu laughed again, but it was a sad laugh.

"Whites have strange ideas, Walela. They think themselves privileged above all peoples in the world. They think they know what is best for everyone. They force everyone to become white. They believe their way is the only way."

Edudu silently gazed into the forest for a long while without speaking. I knew he was thinking melancholy thoughts.

"Walela, whites live with whites. There it ends."

"I think you're right, edudu," I said. "According to the judge, we can only sell our land to white governments. We have been disenfranchised."

"Disenfranchised—what does that mean?" edudu asked. "I think I know, but tell me anyway."

"It means they have everything and we have nothing," I answered.

I was sitting beside edudu as he continued looking into the forest—leaning forward with his hands braced on his knees.

"Whites are like the Blue-Jay," edudu said. "They are loud and arrogant. They steal the eggs of other birds and devour their young. I wish they had stayed in their place."

Edudu and I are one in mind and spirit. We talk every day. Men often come to edudu for advice and I listen. We can talk, but we also know how to sit for hours without speaking. This evening edudu and I said nothing for a long time. He and I listened to the quiet sounds of the afternoon forest. Edudu says a person who talks all the time has something broken inside their head.

We watched the lengthening shadows as the sun slowly set behind the purple mountain. We listened to the myriads of invisible musicians as they began to tune their instruments for our evening serenade—a summertime lullaby performed by our private orchestra. We sat in silence as the long shadows embraced elisi's little house in welcoming darkness.

Edudu continued to stare into the gathering night as if he could see beyond our shadowy perimeter. He absently stroked Spinner's head. Our big mountain to the west began to disappear in the gathering gloom.

"Darkness has come upon us, Walela. I have little hope. There is nothing to be done to save us," edudu said after the long silence.

As edudu spoke he continued to stare into the dark forest without looking left or right. Spinner jumped up into his lap nuzzling his wet nose under edudu's brown hand. Edudu smiled.

I remained silent. Edudu says one can learn the depth of another's wisdom by how much time a person sits quietly listening to others and listening to their own mind. If a person talks too much, it's a sign their wisdom has leaked away and their head is empty.

"This is not something I say to others, but I say it to you. You know whites, Walela. You are clever—wise beyond your years. We talk every day. We have no secrets. You go to the white school and talk to white men. You read white newspapers and white books. Your mind is deep and strong. You can bear the knowledge I share—you shall write of this in your book tomorrow."

"Why have you no hope, edudu?" I asked. "We have been here a thousand years. Why do you say such things? Our memories are long. I have believed our nation will be here for many more years. Why would we leave this beautiful land in which we live? We are strong and have many villages. We have agreements with the whites that assure us we can keep our borders. I do not understand. Why would you go hunting if you believe you will come home empty? You always have hope, edudu. Why do you speak tonight as if we have no future? If we walk with no hope, where shall we be?"

Edudu turned and looked at me for a long time. He gently touched my face and let his fingertips slowly trace the length of my arm to my hands and then held my hands softly.

"My hair is white, Walela. My eyes and ears have gotten old. I cannot see the dogwoods because of the morning fog in my eyes that never goes away. The happy little birds who used to wake me with their cheerful songs have all gone silent. Long before the rooster wakens, I must rise to please my protesting bones who believe I sleep on a bed of stones. I am old, Walela."

"Once I was powerful like your brother. I could see Squirrel hiding at the top of a tree. I laughed when Deer tried to run from me. When I looked at Bear he would hide his face. Now, when Buck sees me he walks away laughing."

"I have been in this land a long time, Walela," edudu continued. "I have learned many things. Long ago whites asked to trade. We agreed. We traded furs for axes, pots and knives. We welcomed their goods and they taught us much. They asked permission to build dwellings for shelter. We agreed. We traded furs for guns and then more furs for more guns. They built more shelters."

As I waited quietly for edudu to continue I heard the first whippoorwill calling.

"More traders came with the axe, adz, drawing knife and surveyor's tools. They asked permission to bring their women. We welcomed them and their little ones. We didn't know they came to stay forever. The whites multiplied. We complained they were destroying our game and occupying our land without permission but they laughed from inside their big forts with their long guns. They said our land had become their land according to their law which was the only law. Too late we realized our folly. We gathered our families to escape their wrath. They followed. They took more land. We gathered our children and moved once again."

Edudu's words were woeful but I knew in my heart he was right. He was saying things I don't want to think upon. I could see the logical conclusion of his thoughts.

"Walela, whites love war. They brought war with them across the waters. They have a passion for fighting. They made war against us again and again.

They fought the Spanish and the French. When those wars weren't enough, they fought their own fathers. Whites love war. The whites defeated the Spanish, French and forced their father's soldiers, dressed like red birds, to sail back across the ocean from whence they came. Strangely, even more whites came from their English homeland and took more land from us—from the Creeks, Seminoles, Choctaw and Chickasaw. The English are the same wherever they go. They want all the land. They want everything they see."

"We moved our homes and children again," edudu continued sadly. "Now you read to me that they demand we move once again far across the great river. One day they will push the Principle People off the western edge of the earth. When we fall into nothingness they will rejoice. The English care only for themselves, Walela. They call us savages and unfortunate. They do not want us near."

As edudu talked I heard the whippoorwill repeat his mournful call reflecting edudu's melancholy. I heard the hoot owl in the growing darkness. I heard the insects begin their songs, but this evening as I listened to edudu's words there was no pleasure in their music.

"In my youth," edudu said, "our country was filled with running, shouting children by the rivers—more children than could be counted. Not so now. Whites have taken all the river land that grows the best corn."

"They forced us away from our rivers into the mountains. It is hard to grow corn in the mountains. White hunters kill everything that moves. They spread a pall of death over our people. Your mother and father died in this very house from disease the whites brought among us. The English have taken our past, they are taking our now and you read to me they plan to steal our future. They have seized everything between the sea and the mountains, but everything isn't enough. They want more—always more. They want to reach into our tomorrow and steal the light from our children's eyes."

In the dim twilight, we watched the last of the purple fingers of color retreat above our black mountain silhouette. The pale streaks of violet faded until we were surrounded by darkness. We watched the stars awakened to adorn our overhead tapestry. The nocturnal hymn of the caroling insects, normally joyous to my heart, had become a requiem. I had never heard edudu talk in such gloomy tones. I knew he was right but I hope for something better. I want to marry and have children—Cherokee children. Will the whites allow me to love my children or must I become white to be loved?

"I remember Overhill," edudu continued quietly. "I remember our beautiful rivers—the Little Tennessee, Hiwassee and Tellico. Life was good. I can see our happy towns—Tuskegee, Toque, Tanasi, Chota, Citico,

Chilowee, Great Tellico and many others. Those were pleasant, happy towns. Our children had plenty to eat when we lived beside our rivers. Then white men came. They loved our rivers."

"Tell me more, edudu," I asked softly.

"I wish I could tell you good things, Walela, but those towns are no more. They're all gone—destroyed. They destroyed our corn, beans and squash. They burned our homes. They killed women and children. I buried my mother and father in the Overhill. I alone survived. They chased us. We escaped across our big river to New Echota."

Edudu laughed.

"Why do you laugh, edudu. What do you laugh about?"

"The English are strange. After they destroyed our nation, they named their home Tennessee after our people—as if it were an honor. They have no feeling for the dispossessed. They honor no one but themselves. Now the English want the little we have left. They want it all—they would have more. They want our fields, rivers and mountains. They want everything. They want our tomorrow."

Edudu continued in a voice I had never heard.

"The English are buzzards. They flap and fuss and hop among the bones of their decaying prey with glazed eyes. They push and shove one another gobbling everything they see until their belly is too fat to fly. They will clean our bones and leave them bleaching in the sun. They never have enough.

When Jackson destroyed the Creeks, I knew our days were few. We should have killed Jackson and died with the Red Sticks. Tecumseh was right. It would have been better to die with the Red Sticks than have my flesh removed a little at a time. Soon, when the whites have more men and wagons, they will build roads and forts and take what little we have. No matter what they promise, they cannot be trusted. One day a white family will live in this house and work elisi's corn. This will be, my dear Walela. This will be."

I was too sad to speak. In my entire life I had never felt as sad as I did listening to edudu share our history.

"One day we will disappear into Father Sky and Mother Earth, never to be seen again. My white head shall vanish," edudu said.

I sat close to edudu in the twilight with my arm tucked around him and my head snuggled on his shoulder as he spoke softly. He stroked my hair. I was unable to speak.

"Before they came here they fought great wars," edudu continued softly. "Whites will multiply and fight among themselves once again. It is their way. They are wolves. Their eyes burn red in the night as they seek to consume their own. Their next war will be ugly because there are a great many more of them than their last war."

I suddenly felt a strange emotion as if were eavesdropping. I felt as if I were listening to edudu converse with our gathered ancestors—as if they were sharing thoughts not meant for my ears.

"But there are good whites like Mr. and Mrs. Lowry. What about them, edudu?" I asked.

"My dear Walela, You are my great joy. Since the day your little fingers pulled my nose like a toy, I have lived every day of my life for you, but I am old and will soon fade away. Were I younger, perhaps I could protect you. Nothing can be done now to save our nation. Whites are too powerful. You and your brother must find a way to survive. We Cherokee are givers. We are happy and share. We welcome white and African. Whites are unhappy and love only themselves. They believe if they take our land they will be satisfied. They have taken everything from the sea to the mountains. They will soon take everything from the mountains to the Great River. One day they will cross the Great River and take everything there. Their appetite is never-ending."

"Perhaps the Great Spirit is testing both whites and Cherokee," edudu said. "Perhaps we have failed the test or perhaps it is the whites who have failed. Perhaps a new day will come when the Great Spirit may fill the forest once again with the deer, the beaver and the bear and the Principle People shall be renewed. Perhaps the Great Spirit will one day right all wrongs. If that day comes, Walela, it shall be the whites who will be found lacking. I am tired. I long for that day of renewal as a bridegroom longs for his bride. That day will come, but not before I rest with our ancestors."

As the little fire in front of our little house was dying, the last charred sticks fell into the bed of glowing coals sending bright, crackling sparks towards the tops of the trees like busy fireflies with their tiny torches disappearing into the black canopy high overhead.

Our village was at rest.

We were being serenaded from all sides by our nightly chorus—this night in a minor key. A lonely dog barked once in the distance. Spinner raised his ears. An owl sounded his solitary call from a nearby tree. I once again heard the song of a whippoorwill ring out of the gloom by the river echoing edudu's mournful words. Edudu's hair shined white and red in the final glow of the fire—both soon to fade.

"Walela, that last morning we will wake and open our door. The icy ground will crunch under our feet. In the night everything green will have died—covered by a white killing frost."

The sun had set behind our western mountain. The fired had died. We were surrounded by blackness. It was time for sleep. Edudu rose. His form barely visible by the dim light of glimmering stars. With no further word he touched my face and went inside. Our home lay quietly in the forest's soft arms. As I followed edudu into our house, I heard the final echoing voice of the whippoorwill bid me goodnight. I shivered.

Chapter XVIII

1823 - 1824 – Ben's Future

Chapter 18

3 July 1823-Month of the ripe corn moon – Gu ye quo ni

Copied from the *Southern Recorder* – 24 June 1823 – page 3

"...the Florida Indians will meet Commissioners on the part of the U. States...on the 5th September next, with the view of concluding a treaty of amity and limits. Some satisfactory arrangement is expected to be made with the Indian tribes who wander over that territory, by which they will be located within prescribed bounds, sufficient for their purpose, and which will assure to white settlers greater security against the intrusion or hostility of the savages."

Mrs. Lowry apologized that her fellow citizens think me an animal.

1 May 1824 - The Planting Moon – A na a gv ti

Ben and I discussed the news about our nation. What will happen?

Copied from the *Georgia Journal* - 20 April 1824 - page 2

"...The Cherokee Nation have now come to a decisive and unalterable conclusion, not to cede away any more lands. The limits reserved for them by the treaty of 1819 is not more than sufficient for their comfort and convenience, taking into consideration the great body of mountains and poor lands which can never be settled. It is a gratifying truth that the Cherokee are rapidly increasing in population; therefore, it is an incumbent duty on the nation to preserve unimpaired the rights of posterity to the lands of their ancestors. We have told you of the decisive and unalterable disposition of the nation in regard to their lands. John Ross, Geo. Lowrey, Major Ridge, Elijah Hicks, A true copy--January 28, 1824."

3 May 1824

We discussed the following letter that was in the newspaper with our Cherokee letter. Everyone is concerned. The missionaries are talking about the desire of Georgia and the United States to extinguish our nation.

Copied from the *Georgia Journal* April 20, 1824 - page 2

United States Department of War - 30 January 1824

"Gentlemen--The president has received your letter of the 19th inst and after giving to it...mature consideration...he has directed me to communicate to you the following answer."

"By the compact with Georgia the U. States are bound to extinguish...the Indian title to lands within the state as soon as it can be done peaceably, and on reasonable conditions, and the Legislature and Executive of Georgia, now press for the fulfillment of that...This government is anxious to fulfill the agreement....With a view to this object...You must be sensible that it will be impossible for you to remain...in your present situation, as a distinct society, or nation within the limits of Georgia, or of any other State. Such a community is incompatible with our system, and must yield to it. This truth is too striking and obvious not to be seen by you surrounded as you are by the people of several states, you must either cease to be a distinct community, and become at no distant period, a part of the state within whose limits you are, or remove beyond the limits of any state. For the United States to fulfill the compact with Georgia, the title which you hold to lands, as a distinct community, must be extinguished, and the state, objects to the extinguishment of it, by vesting in you, or in any of you, in lieu thereof the right of individual ownership...I have the honor John C. Calhoun"

Copied from the *Georgia Journal* – same newspaper, same page
The Cherokee response to John C. Calhoun's letter.

"Sir—We have received your letter of the 30th ult. containing the answer which the president directed you to communicate to us...in this answer we discover new propositions for the extinguishment of Cherokee title to lands, for the benefit of Georgia...the Cherokee Nation are sensible, that the United States are bound by its compact with Georgia to extinguish...the Indian title to lands within the limits claimed by the state as soon as can be done *peaceably,* and on *reasonable* conditions, and are also sensible that this compact is no more than a conditional one, and without the free and voluntary consent of the Cherokee Nation, can never be complied with on the part of the United

States;..." the Cherokees have come to a *decisive* and *unalterable* conclusion *never* to *cede away* any more lands." And as the extinguishment of Cherokee title to lands, can never be obtained, on conditions, which will accord with the import of the compact between the United States and Georgia...the government should adopt some other means to satisfy Georgia...the United States have by treaties, solemnly guaranteed to secure to the Cherokee forever, their title to lands, which have been reserved by them. Therefore the state of Georgia can have no reasonable plea against the Cherokee..." JOHN ROSS, GEO. LOWREY, MAJOR RIDGE, ELIJAH HICKS

Copied from the *Georgia Journal* – same newspaper

Governor Troup's response to the Cherokee letter.

"Sir I have received this day your letter of the 17th Inst. Be pleased to present to the President my acknowledgements for the attention he has given to the requisition of Georgia...to adopt any measure in his power, which may tend to the fulfillment of the convention with the state of Georgia, with the least possible delay...In your effort to open negotiations with the Cherokee Delegation for the extinguishment of claims, you are met by a flat negative to two fair and liberal propositions. The 1st to purchase for valuable consideration in money. The 2nd to accommodate them with equivalent Territory...beyond the Mississippi—It has been made known to me for some time before, that a Council has been formed...to enable the Chiefs to present themselves before the President with a boldness bordering on effrontery...with an emphatic No!...not the spontaneous offspring of Indian feeling and sentiment, but a word put in his mouth, by white men, who are nourished and protected by the power of the U. States—...From the day of the signature of the articles of agreement and cession, this word ceased to be available to the Indian...On that day the fee simple passed from the rightful proprietors to Georgia, and Georgia after a lapse of twenty years...are now told in answer to their just and reasonable demand, that this compact is only conditional, depending on its fulfillment on the will and pleasure of the Indians..." G.M. Troup

8 May 1824

"Did you read the April newspaper Ben gave you, Cassie?" Mr. Lowry asked.

"Yes, sir. Ben and I talked about it at length. It was disturbing—very disturbing," I answered.

"It was disquieting, Cassie. I'm sure you've heard Ben's point of view?"

"Yes, sir. Ben is angry. He wants to do something, but he doesn't know what to do."

Ben interrupted, "Yes, Father. I'm angry. I want to help. If I were a lawyer I could do something for the Cherokee. Cassie thinks it would be a good idea too."

"You have a good heart son," Ben's father said kindly. "Your mother and I feel the same way."

22 May 1824

Ben has decided to become a lawyer. He shared with me his decisive conversation with his parents.

"Father, I've made my decision. I want to do something noble for the Cherokee. I want to dedicate my life to the service of others the way you and Mother have done."

"Good for you, son. Your mother and I will help any way we can."

"Thank you, Father. Cassie and I believe a white lawyer who understands the Cherokee culture would be helpful, Father. Do you and Mother think law would be a good profession for me or should I become a missionary like you, or perhaps medicine should be my career? Those are careers of service to one's fellow man. The Cherokee need doctors. Would I make a good physician?"

"Son, your mother and I want you to use your God-given intellect in the way your passion leads you. We can't tell you what to do. Our passions are not your passions. What you choose doesn't matter as long as it's an honest decision. Solomon's advice remains unequivocal, 'Whatsoever thy hand findeth to do, do it with all thy might.' Whatever you choose to do, Ben, give it your best and you'll be blessed. If you choose to be a farmer—be a good one. If you want to be a lawyer—be a good lawyer."

"Yes, sir. I promise to do that. I will do my best."

"Son, the final choice is your decision alone. Only you know your heart. Only you know what will satisfy your life's desires. Become a missionary if that's what you want, if that's your passion, but unless you are certain being a missionary is all you will ever want, it shouldn't be your choice."

"I've always had the greatest respect for your vocation, Father."

"Thank you, son," his father answered. "Since I was your age, I've never wanted to do anything else but be a missionary. Perhaps that might not be the way you feel. Ministering to the sick is another welcome vocation for a young man. The Cherokee need physicians, but I've never heard you express a desire to practice medicine. To choose a career as a physician, one must have a strong passion."

"No, sir," Ben answered. "I must say I have never thought much about a career in medicine. I've been drawn to the legal profession for some reason."

"Since the day you were born your mother and I have tried to teach you to love and respect your fellow man. Living here in a missionary environment you're positioned to understand the Cherokee, their culture and their political problems. Among white people, we have a unique perspective."

"Yes, sir. I understand. I have a great respect for the Cherokee and what I'm reading in the newspapers makes me angry. I want to do something. I wish I could do something now," Ben answered.

"Son, you have a kind heart and have a strong sense of justice," his mother said. "I'm very proud of you at this moment."

"It makes me angry, Mother, that people want to take the Cherokee land from them. That isn't right," Ben said.

"Son," his mother said, "that rising anger can be frustration or fuel great achievement. Many great things have been accomplished because of the properly channeled anger of good men and women. Righteous indignation is divine. As long as you're angry at the right things at the right time, you'll be fine."

"Your mother's right, Ben," his father said. "If your anger leads into an honorable law career, that would be good, but you must choose for yourself. As your parents, we can give advice, but we can't make your decision."

"Remember, son," his mother said. "if you choose law, you must eschew the singular pursuit of wealth in favor of defending morality within the law— not an easy task. Human laws are the product of flawed mankind and thus themselves flawed. Men have used the cloak of legal precedent for personal enrichment since the beginning of civilization. I suspect the legal profession is the best of all careers for the dishonest—all the more reason to be an honest lawyer."

Ben stood.

With both hands on his hips he answered proudly, "In my case, Mother, I don't think you have to worry about that. You and Father have taught me well by both word and example. You can trust me there. I won't let you down. I would never be dishonest."

Ben's parents knew life's pressures would be different when their son found himself in the world.

"We trust you, son," his father said. "You're well educated and hardworking. You have a great start in life. You understand language, reason and logic. You have a systematic mind, plus you're highly skilled in language arts, especially Latin. I have no doubt you'll make a good lawyer, if that's where your heart leads you."

"I'll be a good lawyer. I know I will," Ben said proudly once again.

"I believe you, son. I admire your wish to do something noble for the Cherokee. As for myself, I've wanted to be a missionary since I was a boy. I don't see that same passion for missionary work in you, which is perfectly fine. To my knowledge, not one Cherokee man I've ever heard of has been professionally trained as a lawyer. The Cherokee leadership are wise, experienced, skillful men, but they aren't expert in white law. Except for a few men like Chief Ross and a handful of others, they know little about law, government or the legal profession. There would be plenty of honorable work for a lawyer in the Cherokee Nation, but be aware, it would not be lucrative. As a lawyer for the Cherokee you would make enemies—strong enemies. The entire white population of Georgia would view you as a traitor. Even though I'm a missionary, I'm often viewed by whites as a turncoat and without exception my fellow men believe my work to be wasted."

"I know, Father," Ben answered, "but I wouldn't be working just for the money. I want to do what's right."

His father suddenly laughed heartily, "Forgive me, son. I wasn't laughing at you. I was thinking of the Cherokee and their marvelous understanding of sharing for the common good. I was laughing at myself. To this day I have a hard time understanding the Cherokee right to pick fruit off my fruit trees without asking, but that's the Cherokee way. We must bend to their ways when in their country. When in Rome, do as the Romans do, correct? To be honest, Ben, I've found the Cherokee's broad concept of community refreshing and surprisingly biblical. The biggest crime of our white culture is our demand that the Cherokee become like us, as if our white European society were the sole paradigm of human existence. We invade their land and demand they become like us. We whites are a proud people."

"Yes, sir," Ben answered. "Cassie and I have talked about that. The Cherokee really don't want to become white and probably never will."

Ben's father laughed again, "I am so sorry, son. I'm not laughing at you. I can't help but think about Cherokee men walking through my orchard at harvest time eating my fruit without permission as if the trees belonged to them. Actually, Ben, that Cherokee custom mirrors Jewish law. In Israel, the poor could eat off of a roadside fruit tree to satisfy immediate hunger, but they couldn't fill a basket and take it to market. They could eat one apple in passing but couldn't take fruit home. That's exactly how the Cherokee think. The Cherokee understand how important it is to share. I find that a most interesting parallel. There are some, like Reverend Buttrick, who think the Cherokee may be connected to the ten lost tribes of Israel."

"I have heard that, sir," Ben said.

Ben's father laughed again, "I came here to teach the Cherokee, but it is they who have taught me. I'm reminded of Robert Burns' poem, *To a Louse*. Burns was right, Ben, 'O would some power the gift give us, to see ourselves as others see us.' To see our voracious, selfish whit culture as we really are would be a divine gift indeed. I wish I could recite his poem in the vernacular, but you'll have to manage with my poor English rendition."

Ben's mother interrupted, "It would be tragic for Cherokee customs to disappear. I wish you well in your decision to become a lawyer, son, and work for the Cherokee. The biggest crime of our white society in regard to the Cherokee is the white demand that the Cherokee become like them—become white. I agree with your father. He and I have loved the Cherokee and their culture since the day we arrived, and, of course, your friendship with Cassie will be good for you in that regard. She's as smart as you are, if not smarter."

"I agree with your mother," Ben's father said. "The Cherokee need help. They could use the assistance of a hardworking white lawyer. Georgia is expanding. Unbelievably, Milledgeville is our fourth capital in our short history. It's hard to imagine things changing that quickly. Savannah was the first capital, then Augusta, then Louisville and now Milledgeville. Sadly, Georgia's westward expansion has been at the expense of the Creek and Cherokee. I wish whites could figure out a long-term lease of Cherokee land, but they don't want that. They want fee simple ownership. They want it all."

Ben answered, "Yes, sir. Cassie and I were talking about that. The Cherokee live in community and share. The English culture wants all land held in private ownership and every man for himself. Cassie believes that's where the central conflict is. I do, too, sir."

191

"This is definitely a clash of cultures and Cassie's right, I'm afraid," Ben's father said. "I see no end to Georgia's desire to occupy the entirety of the Cherokee homeland. The Cherokee need help. Therefore, the short answer to your question is your mother and I will support you implicitly if you decide on law."

"Thank you, sir," Ben answered. "I appreciate you taking the time to talk to me about this."

"Ben, you've been patiently listening and I've said too much, but let me conclude with this," his father said.

"Things change, son. No matter how hard we strive for continuity, things change. Change can't be prevented. Your mother and I wish you to be part of a change in this world for good. One person armed with determination can sometimes do more than an army. Do you remember the story of David and Goliath?"

"Yes sir, I remember that story, Father."

"One young man armed with fortitude and confidence can accomplish great things. You can do great things with Him on your side, Ben. No one gave David a chance, did they?"

"No sir, they didn't," Ben said.

"Things change. You never know what a single righteous decision will accomplish. If you choose to support the Cherokee, you'll have chosen a parallel path to David. You understand that, don't you? You understand the Goliath you'll be up against?"

"Yes sir, but that's ok. I'll do what I can."

"Good for you, son," his father said. "There's been an active debate in the legislature about Georgia's Indian problem—as they call it. Georgia is full of immigrants who know nothing about the Indian culture. Are you familiar with the popular song I've been hearing about the Cherokee, Ben?"

"Yes sir," Ben answered. "It's not a nice song at all."

"I can't sing but the lyrics go like this," his father said:

> *All I ask in this creation,*
> *Is a pretty little wife and a big plantation,*
> *Way up yonder in the Cherokee Nation.*

"The song's popularity reflects the pervasive mind-set of white Georgians and their poor respect for the Cherokee. Whites believe Cherokee land is theirs regardless of past agreements. Shall I continue?"

"Yes, Father," Ben answered respectfully. "I value your insight. Maybe next year I could go to law school? What do you think?" said Ben, anxiously looking back and forth between his mother and father, waiting for their answer.

"You've mentioned your interest in law on more than one occasion," his father answered. "We've noticed your developing sense of justice. I don't think a young man as quick as you will have any problem finding a place in a good law school. You could skip law school and be apprenticed straightaway, but if you want to be at the top of your profession, law school is imperative."

"Yes, sir," Ben said. "I would prefer a law school over a simple apprenticeship."

"Good for you, son," his father said. "In the meantime, continue to discuss current political developments. Defend your intellectual positions verbally and in writing. Use unencumbered reason as you develop your arguments, but remember to debate with folks who hold both sides of any position. If you only debate with people you oppose, you'll never fully understand your own position."

"Yes, sir, I have learned how important that is," Ben answered.

"Most important is to debate dispassionately," his father continued. "When I began debating, I often allowed my emotions to influence my arguments. Displaying childish impatience in a debate is a signpost of immaturity. I learned that when I felt myself becoming impatient in a debate, I knew I didn't understand the issue. Impatience must be kept on a short leash—a short leash indeed. It's not wrong to be angry. God is sometimes described as angry, but God's anger is always directed at the right things, at the right time and in the appropriate measure. Righteous indignation is to be admired, but out of place in an honest debate. If you want to be a good lawyer, you must learn to control your anger. Emotional anger that lashes out with poorly reasoned arguments will cause you embarrassment. I know that first-hand."

"Yes, sir," Ben answered.

"It's important to present facts in a logical, dispassionate sequence," his father continued. "Practice crafting a logical, rational argument in a didactic and systematic manner devoid of emotion."

His father laughed, "Ask your mother how often she has caught me in an inconsistency. I've been guilty of a failure to think logically with your mother more often than I like to admit and my good wife has never been afraid to point out my inconsistencies as a husband or a father."

Ben's mother and father laughed. Eleanor put her arms around her husband's neck and gave a him an affectionate kiss on the cheek. They are a loving couple and I think they may love each other as much as elisi and edudu.

"Ben, you have a quick mind and sharp memory," his father continued. "If you wish, we can hone your debating skills right here at home. It would give you a head start. We could take the Cherokee right to own land as our first point of debate. One night your mother and I will take the position that the Cherokee do not have the right to possess land within the chartered limits of Georgia. We'll debate for an hour, and the next night we'll exchange positions with you and Cassie and see what new ideas we can uncover. How does that sound?"

"I would love that, Father," Ben said. "Cassie would love that, too. That would be fun, wouldn't it?"

"It would be entertaining and instructive," his father said. "We'll use newspapers as a fact reference. Your task will be to find the central flaw in your opponent's chain of logic—on both sides of the argument. That's the key to successful debating and in the courtroom, I might add."

"I like that idea, Father. It would be fun. Let's do it," Ben said."

"Your mother and I will be looking forward to it, also," his father answered. "I like Aristotle's quote, 'It's the mark of an educated mind to entertain a thought without accepting it'. Argue your adversary's viewpoint to find holes in his reasoning. Perhaps, with due diligence, you'll find to your chagrin you were the one holding the flawed position."

Ben was smiling. He was thinking of standing before a group of men and crafting an argument none could gainsay. He couldn't wait to go to law school.

His father continued, "For example, the Cherokee are not considered citizens in Georgia. They're not allowed to vote, which makes them politically meaningless. The white government has no mechanism to insure justice to politically meaningless aliens—which is what the Cherokee are. It was not many years ago there was a cash bounty on Indians, and you know what that meant. Throughout the eastern seaboard, from Massachusetts down to the southern states, white governments paid cash bounties for dead Indians. We're a proud race with a short memory, aren't we?"

"Yes, sir. We are," Ben said.

"Can you imagine hunting Indians as if they were game?" his father asked? "Well, it happened in every state in our union before the revolution and some say even afterward. We whites, in our high position of assumed privilege, tend to forget our indiscretions quickly."

Ben's father handed him a document.

"Ben, I set this argument on paper a few weeks ago. Read this speech. How would you respond to this man's logic? I took all these ideas from the newspaper. How would you craft your rebuttal? Study this and later this week we'll have our debate."

Ben read as requested:

"According to the 1802 agreement, the land the Cherokee occupy now legally belongs to the state of Georgia—end of argument. The Cherokee possess no land and have no legal rights to such. Georgia is the only original colony who has not rid itself of its Indian problem. Law and history are on our side. Are we not allowed to do exactly as New York, Massachusetts and Delaware have done and rid ourselves of Indian occupation without outside interference? The only difference is that now we have a general government.

Indian violence has been commonplace since Georgia's founding and will continue. Our only protection is complete Cherokee removal. I cannot understand anyone's hesitancy in this regard. For decades, we've given Indians every Christian benevolence, yet they obstinately prefer their wild ways. They have proven unteachable and unchangeable. These untamable savages do not possess white intelligence or its potential and never will.

Whites are superior. Indians must make way for a higher culture. All attempts by past governments to aid Indian advancement were a waste of public resources. Indians must be persuaded, or forced if need be, to give up all claim to land. They must be removed beyond the borders of the United States. We demand the general government keep their 1802 promise to extinguish the Cherokee title to land within our chartered limits.

Cherokee Country is ours legally. Georgians are progressive. Indians are backward. We build houses, barns and plant wholesome communities. They are illiterate—incapable of advancement. Because of their dearth of intelligence, they continually suffer the indignities of wind, weather and famine without thought of their future."

Our white culture has a God-given destiny to occupy this land. Can you imagine your sons and daughters marrying into that lazy race? Only one solution presents itself. The Cherokee must be removed per the Compact of 1802. Legally, they must go. It's the law.

General Jackson knows how to deal with savages. Georgia is not a territory, province, region or district. We are a sovereign free state. England is a state. France is a state and Virginia is a state. Spain is a state and according to the articles of confederation Georgia is a state. We are self-governing. We are part of a federal union but we are not a puppet of northern politicians who have forgotten their recent past when as a colony they violently removed the Indians living within their borders. They did not consult their sister colonies and we will not allow them to tell us how to take care of our own business with Indians.

The final solution is removal. That is an honorable and liberal arrangement. We've had enough talk. The irredeemable must go for their own good. We will do what's best for the Indians. We are a benevolent people."

Next debater. Ben continued to read:

"We heard wise words. Since the founding of Savannah, Georgians have brought prosperity to an undeveloped wilderness. We tamed a vacant land that was lying idle waiting for compassionate occupants.

Savannah is an international seaport. By our hand it has become a great center of foreign and domestic commerce.

We claim this land by both Right of Discovery and Right of Conquest. Georgia, through its charter, has the legal right to own and occupy the entirety of land that lies within our chartered limits. That's the law. The unhappy heathen savages who sided with the British in the glorious War of the Revolution must be removed just as they were previously removed by our twelve sister states. As Henry Clay said, the world wouldn't notice if they vanished completely. We should hasten their vanishment from our chartered boundaries for our mutual benefit."

Next debater:

"What is Georgia's future? I see great seaports taking Georgia's commerce to the world. I see grand inland cities. I see wide thoroughfares connecting the remote portions of our prosperous country to our neighboring states and seaports. I see canals and bridges. I see spreading plantations with myriads of slaves producing a cornucopia of plenty. We'll ship timber, cotton, tobacco, corn, livestock and a multitude of manufactured goods around the world bringing never before seen prosperity to our shores. We cannot be denied. Our success is ordained. The backward, uncivilized Cherokee cannot be allowed to stand in the way of such progress. They must be removed.

We will not allow a few misguided do-gooders to halt our magnificent progress. Our destiny is guided by the hand of God himself.

Imagine, my friends, the tallest and most graceful merchant ship ever built docked in Savannah harbor. See her pure lines and majestic masts. Imagine that elegant ship rigged and ready standing in the harbor. Imagine the paint fresh, canvas new, rigging strong and the crew eager. Imagine that ship idle month after month rotting at its moorings for lack of use. Such would be a travesty, would it not?

In outrage, the citizens of Savannah would commandeer that ship and put it to work for the common good as they should. And neither will we allow lazy savages to hold hostage huge tracts of fertile land that lie fallow within our chartered limits. God gave us this land. The Compact of 1802 assures us unencumbered legal title. The law is on our side. When we remove the Cherokee, we are not taking anything from anyone. We are occupying ours by right.

Many thousands of acres of fertile farmland lie waiting for eager yeomen to bring never before seen prosperity. Zealous farmers will own a piece of land on which to raise their family and fulfill our forefathers' vision. We Georgians cannot do less than the Tennesseans. Let us not behave like bleary eyed old men who cry easily. Let's take control of the land we were eternally meant to occupy and immediately rid ourselves of hindrance. Let's free our land from the bonds of that pathetic, lethargic race."

Last speaker from the newspaper articles:

"The Cherokee are not white. They do not deserve white privilege. They are savages. They are no more than intelligent animals. Their continued existence within our chartered limits is an affront and has no defense. They must be removed. Every man in this assembly has said that very thing and I'm going to say it out loud for the record.

This land is ours. Indians are lazy and never will be good or good for anything. They are inferior, like the Africans. Those who feel sorrow for Indians are misguided. Such misplaced sentiment is a delaying tactic promulgated by the uninformed who would likewise feel sorry for lazy vagabonds in the street. I agree with the righteous words of Henry Clay, 'If the Indians disappeared entirely, they would not be missed'. Their complete removal is our final solution—and the sooner the better."

"You read well, son. Think about what we have talked about. Your life's vocation must be your decision and your decision alone. Your mother and I won't make the choice for you. Whatever you choose as a career, your mother and I will support. You can count on us to stand behind you."

"Yes sir, I promise I'll be considering my future, but I'm determined law will be my calling," Ben answered proudly, standing tall and thinking about his future.

Chapter XIX

1824 - The Green Corn Festival – Edudu's Stories

Chapter 19

13 June 1824 - The Green Corn Moon – De ha lu yi

My most special place in the world, outside of elisi's house, is my large flat stone on the river's edge. It is obscured by thick green laurels and open to the entire vista of the river. It's where I read, think, write and dream. I watch the water go by, hear the songbirds, see the animals come to the far shore and smell the bewitching fragrances. Ben likes the river too, but I think he would prefer to catch fish, but we will not be fishing today.

Ben and I had a wonderful picnic in my special place. In long conversations, I have felt our hearts entwining, and Ben feels the same. We will be together forever. I will bear him a dozen beautiful children. Elisi said she has long known Ben is my only love.

As we were walking to my place hand in hand, Ben said, "Cassie, I have good and bad news—news that makes me happy and sad—but you'll think it mostly good news, I hope. I've been talking with my parents and I may be going to law school. In fact, I'm sure of it. My parents asked me to think about what I want to do to earn my living, and I'm seriously considering law. My father suggested a Connecticut law school. It's a great distance but Father says it's the best. I will miss you terribly. Maybe you could go, too?"

"This isn't bad news at all, Ben," I answered. "We've talked about this and I agree. I think you were meant for a career in law. You'll be back from Connecticut before you know it and we'll be together again here talking like old friends. I love you, Ben. I believe you need to go to school to launch your career, don't you? You shouldn't delay. I shall wait for you."

"I haven't made the final decision, Cassie. You make it sound like I'm leaving tomorrow."

Ben and I, laughing and talking as always, spread our picnic. I have never felt so alive and carefree as when I'm with him. I brought a bit of cornbread, roasted venison and some shelled nuts. There are not many fresh fruits in our village yet, but they will come soon.

"Ben, I love how we never keep secrets. We'll be friends forever like your parents. We are the most fortunate of people, are we not?"

"I agree, Cassie," Ben answered. "I have the best parents in the world. My goal as a father is to be friends with my children—just like I have with my father. I don't want to be my children's master. I want to be my children's friend."

Ben brought his face close to mine, "Cassie, everyone needs a confidant and you're mine. I trust you with my most intimate thoughts—only you. I'll never keep secrets from you."

"That's probably the most wonderful thing you've ever said to me, Ben. We Cherokee are not embarrassed to share our secrets. Your mother says white men mostly treat their wives and children like servants—yet whites consider themselves the most civilized."

"You're right, Cassie. Cherokee men do have greater respect for women, plus the Cherokee matrilineal family builds strong community. I love your extended family."

"You are right," I answered, and I laughed. "Elisi inherited her house from her mother and one day it will be mine—not my brother's house. It would have been my mother's if she had lived. When elisi and edudu married, edudu came to live with her. I read of a new law in Georgia that says a white man can sell his property without his wife's permission and is not required to give her a portion or even inform her of the sale."

"Cassie," Ben said seriously, "I don't understand how folks can call the Cherokee savages. I guess a hundred years ago conflicts between Indians and whites over land disputes promoted irrational fears, but if white people could live in Cherokee Country, they would see a strong community that would be the envy of any society in the world. I love your people, Cassie. I love living here, and I love my mother and father's work."

As Ben and I held one another, we listened to the gentle waters just beside us and watched the peaceful silvery clouds drift slowly overhead in the soft azure sky.

"I love our country, Ben," I said finally. "You're right. If whites lived here and understood our language, the forest would come alive for them—they would understand the birds, animals and fish and how we all relate to one another in community. They could comprehend our world—even the weather and the way we keep time would make more sense to them. If they walked our old paths, paths as old as our nation itself, they would understand. Edudu says we didn't build roads or use wagons in the old days. We walked everywhere. Even though my people traveled on foot, we knew every tribe between Florida and Canada and from the ocean to the great river. We still know every animal, bird and path even though we're farmers. Our world was in balance."

Ben and I lay quietly watching the unhurried clouds, high in the blue sky, slide silently past our valley floating to their unknown destination on the other side of the mountains.

"Our men can travel for moons and still know where they are," I said, "but things have changed since the English came. We have wide roads through our country—roads built to make it easy for soldiers, wagons and big guns. The English demanded we allow roads for our own good. It's not for our good we have roads—it's for their good. Roads bring soldiers and squatters. Edudu says our destruction will come along the white roads. I think he is right."

"Cassie, let's make this a happy day. Let's think about good, upright wholesome things—things you love. Talk to me of noble things—would you please?"

"I was going in a dark direction, wasn't I?" I answered. "Do you suppose I read too many white newspapers?"

"Forget the newspapers, Cassie, and tell me what you love about your country. Tell me about the good things right here where you live."

"What a grand idea. What do I love, Ben? Oh my, I love many things. I love my family. I love the faces of children when they gather around edudu to hear his stories. I love endless hours making pine baskets with elisi. I love feeding elisi's chickens. I like to watch them scratch and peck as I toss their feed. I listen as they greet me and cluck politely to be fed. I know each by name. When I go into their little house and gently take the hen's warm eggs, I call her name and tell her thank you and not to worry. I enjoy shutting them in their little chicken house for the night when they come home to roost. I'm so glad to live here. We are a happy people, aren't we, Ben? I wouldn't want to live anywhere else."

"Keep going, Cassie," Ben said. "I want to hear more good things."

"I love the springtime. I love the trees when they wake from their winter's sleep and dress themselves in their new clothing. Their new leaves have a special color found only then when they burst from the buds and each one spreads its beautiful green face to the sun. It's like the forest is born all over again every spring, isn't it? I adore the dogwoods and redbuds that explode with color and dress the hem of the forest. Edudu never cuts a dogwood or a redbud."

"Keep going," Ben said.

"I also love that first cool day of autumn after a hot summer when the trees change their clothes and dress gaily with the colors of the rainbow to prepare for their autumn festival before they sleep. I love that first chilly morning when I get out of bed and hurry to stand with my back to elisi's fire."

"Keep going, Cassie. I want to hear more," Ben asked. "This is beautiful. You should write this in your journal."

"Perhaps I shall. I love to write. I love the Green Corn Festival. I love those first ears of delicious tender corn and all the other fresh vegetables after a long cold winter. I love the fresh breads. I love corn—rich and sweet off the cob. I love cornbread. During the Green Corn Festival, I love stories, traditions, dances and happy children. I love how our families enjoy seeing their relatives. I love seeing my friends and relatives I haven't seen since last year. I always look forward to our reunion during the festival. It's quite a holiday. I love the melons and the fresh breads. I love the roasted venison. I love to watch my brother's ballplay. Do you want me to continue, Ben?"

"Please, please do. I should take notes," Ben said, as we lazily reclined beside the river. Side by side we lay looking up at the lazy clouds.

"I love the fruits and nuts that the forest gives. Nothing tastes like the sweet orange persimmons when they're ripe, but if they're not ripe your tongue will shrivel. I love the talvladi. The English call them muscadines or scuppernongs. Whites have strange names for things, don't they? I love to find the talvladi vines climbing high into the trees and the fresh fruit that has been lying on the ground waiting for me—fruit so sweet it tastes like the bees brought them from a honeycomb. No one goes hungry in the summer and autumn in Cherokee Country. The generous forest gives more than we can eat. We pick it up and avoid the bears. The bears love the same things we do and they eat to prepare for their long winter rest. I've spent many wonderful days with elisi and edudu in the forest gathering its bounty."

"Keep going, Cassie. I'm loving this. Keep talking," Ben said. "Tell me about the things you love. This is special."

"Did you know," I said with a bit of seriousness in my voice, "no fruit, nut or berry that comes from a tree, bush or vine is poisonous if it tastes sweet?"

"No, I didn't know that," Ben replied. "Keep going. I'm loving this."

"If the fruit tastes sweet, edudu said, it is good. If the fruit is not sweet, it might make you sick. Did you know that? Nothing sweet in the forest can be poisonous."

Ben nodded for me to continue.

"The forest is good to us, Ben. I love hickory nuts, walnuts, persimmons, muscadines, huckleberries, blackberries and tili. Whites call the tili chestnuts. When the chestnuts fall, the squirrels, deer, possoms, turkeys, coons, wild pigs, rabbits and bears rejoice—the whole forest rejoices. The majestic chestnut trees fill our forest. We and the animals feast when the chestnuts drop. The forest provides more chestnuts than we could possibly eat. Chestnuts, walnuts and hickory nuts keep all winter. Elisi makes many foods and breads from them."

"What's your favorite, Cassie? What do you like the best?"

"My favorite, at the moment, is the talvladi vines that climb high into the trees. I love to sit under a spreading vine and eat till I can eat no more. Every year elisi and I gather bags and bags of the muscadines. We eat them fresh. We squeeze them for a lovely drink or elisi will cook them into a delicious pie or cake. I also love it when edudu and Five Feathers find a bee tree. I love honey with elisi's bread."

"You may think me silly, Ben, but one of my favorites when I was a little girl was to find a honeysuckle vine in full bloom. We would pick the bloom and bite off the tip end, the part that joined the vine, and suck out the nectar. There really isn't much nectar in the honeysuckle bloom—just the faintest hint of sweetness, but the children love doing it. Do you think that silly?"

"Of course not," Ben answered. "I don't think that silly—in fact, I think it precious."

Ben and I continued side by side on my big rock. I rehearsed the good things in my country. Perhaps I should stop reading the English newspapers. I think from this day forward, every time I go to my special place, I shall begin thinking about good things.

I continued my rehearsal as we lay watching the magnificent clouds drift by, "I love the ganugala—blackberries. The sweet blackberries are plentiful, but the diganawali are terrible. I hate chiggers. Chiggers must have been put here by the Great Spirit to punish us for some horrendous past crime. Chiggers burrow under my skin and itch for days. They're maddening. I hate them worse than mosquitoes. Why the Great Spirit made mosquitoes, chiggers and poison ivy, I don't know."

We laughed so hard we cried thinking how we disliked mosquitoes, chiggers and poison ivy.

"I hate them too, Cassie, but I dislike poison ivy most. I had a poison ivy rash all over my face when I was little. It was even in my eyes. After that Father taught me to spot those three leaf devils a mile away. Father and I often walk around our place in the summertime with a hoe and axe and cut all the poison ivy vines and plants we find. When we get back we wash with plenty of lye soap. I despise poison ivy."

"I know, Ben," I said. "Our people know to avoid poison ivy. We cut the vines to stop them from spreading in the forest, too. But we were talking about good things. I should not have mentioned the chiggers or poison ivy, should I?"

"I'm guilty, Cassie," Ben said. "Go back to good things."

"I love blueberries," I said. "Huckleberries, the whites call them. I love your mother's blueberry pies made with wheat flour. When I think about the fruits and nuts in our forest, I have no favorite. I suppose my favorite is the one I am enjoying at the moment."

"Ben, the English want our land because it's the most fruitful land in the world. Whites are amazed at the abundance found here. They must not think us fit to possess it. I don't understand them. This is the land given to us. Your father told us about your Adam and Eve. The whites lost their paradise and can't go back. Now they want ours."

"Just good things, Cassie. Let's talk of good things. No talk of injustice today," Ben said smiling.

"I've been reading too many newspapers," I said laughing. "Well, the most wonderful thought of all is my future with you. Being with you is even better than living here. I want to be close to you day and night. I wish I could borrow the songs of the birds to sing my love for you. If you took me away, I would miss our country, but I love you far more. I have been happy here with edudu and elisi. As a woman, I will only be happy with you—wherever you are."

Ben and I said nothing for a long time as we listened to the river and the wind sing their duet, wishing us well.

"One day we'll be together, Cassie," Ben said quietly. "We must be patient. It will be a while, but that day will come."

"I know it will," I said. "It will be just as you imagine—as I imagine."

"I love it here," Ben said. "The reason I like it so much is you. If it wasn't for you, I would want to go elsewhere. I love Cherokee Country. I love Mother's pies and cakes she makes from the gifts of the forest. But, Cassie, I'm not sure how I could practice law here? If you and I are together we'll have to be where I can work. That will mean living on the whiteside—maybe not in Georgia but somewhere on the whiteside—maybe in Washington City. I want to be where Indians are respected. Our children would be outcasts in Georgia."

"I'm willing to wait," I answered. "With you, each day is more beautiful than the one before. One of the things I like about you, Ben, is you never interrupt when we talk. I love the way you look into my eyes when I'm speaking. I've never communicated to another's soul as I do with you. Your mother believes we were meant for one another—so does elisi. Through all my talk about the fruits of the forest, you didn't say a word. You let me finish my entire thought."

"Why would I ever want to interrupt the most beautiful woman in the world?" Ben said. "Your voice is like music but you're correct. I've noticed we white folks interrupt often. My parents think the Cherokee talking stick one of the greatest inventions of human history. I love how only the person holding the talking stick is allowed to speak. I've never seen meetings as orderly as the Cherokee councils. With customs like that, I wonder how we can say the Cherokee are not civilized?"

We lay quietly together. We talked about different things. We ate our little picnic and discussed the future and tried to avoid the problems we have with white settlers. It doesn't matter what Ben and I talk about, our conversations always conclude with a discussion about our future.

Finally, there in our special place, we said out loud what we had believed for a long time. We confessed our mutual love. In that moment on my big flat rock beside the river we became adults with our future certain. We left our childhood behind.

"Ben, Cherokee men have begun to notice me. Several have spoken to edudu and elisi about a future marriage, but they tell them to come back next year. Don't worry, Ben. I'm yours. I'll wait all my life, if I must. I'm yours and only yours—now and forever. I want to belong to you."

"I know you'll wait," Ben said, holding me tight. "I never worry about you. I know you're mine."

"That's true," I said. "I'm finding pleasure in becoming a woman. I love the attention, but edudu, elisi and my friends know I have chosen you—I'm not embarrassed to tell everyone. Elisi says you are special and worth the wait. She likes you, Ben, and thinks you handsome. All the girls think you're handsome."

Ben leaned back and put both of his hands behind his head and stared up at the passing clouds and grinned.

"I'm glad they think me handsome but you can be sure I'll always love you. I knew you were mine—and will be mine forever. I love you."

The moment he said he loved me, I threw my arms around him.

"Ben, I love you. I loved you when I first saw your smile in your father's schoolroom. Anything you want I shall give. I will bear your children. I will care for you. You are my man. You will never have to win my love. You have it—now and forever."

As he held me against his chest, I could feel his heart beating against my face.

"Ben, I feel our spirits intertwined like dozens of honeysuckle vines twisting upward so interwoven with one another they're incapable of being separated—like the Gordian Knot. We'll be together. You are my man—my best friend. You are my soul, Ben Lowry. I was meant to be yours from the day I was born. There never will be another."

I felt him breathe deeply as he held me. I'll always remember his response.

"What a lovely thing to say, Cassie. I believe that, too. I have loved you since you were a cute Cherokee girl in my father's schoolroom. You're constantly in my thoughts—every day. I want the same things you want. I'll never be ashamed of you. I promise to fulfill your dreams. We'll have a good life together. You'll never want for anything, ever—I promise."

"I know that, Ben. I know you don't lie. You don't know how to lie."

When Ben spoke his words of love and promise, the sky vanished, the river disappeared, the birdsong ceased. Everything was absorbed into the single vision of my love—into a vision of Ben—a vision filling my now and my forever. My soul overflowed as he kissed me as a man would kiss a woman. I shivered from head to toe.

With that kiss, our relationship passed a milestone. Two childhood friends left their playthings and embarked upon the road to maturity—becoming adults and lovers as partners. From that moment, we were destined to build a life together.

I kissed Ben again with my arms around his neck giving him all my love as he held me. He breathed gently into my hair. His smell filled my soul. I will give everything I will ever possess to this wonderful man.

"Cassie, I love everything about you. I love your eyes, ears, hands, nose, mouth, hair, feet, fingers and toes. I love your mind, the smell of your hair, the sparkle in your eyes. I love your toes. You may think me silly, but you have the most beautiful feet. Every part of you blends into a magnificent whole. All of your parts are so nicely put together. I want all of those parts, Cassie. I'll never have a friend like you. You are the only woman for me today, tomorrow and the rest of my life."

His kiss was the seal of our commitment. It was more enduring than any golden ring.

"Cassie, I swear, I've never felt emotions like this. I'm glad I've finally told you how I feel. You make me want to tell you everything—to break open my chest and expose my deepest secrets. I want to tell you everything about myself—even things I'm ashamed of. Does that sound silly?"

"Of course not," I answered. "I know exactly what you mean. I feel the same. When you are near, I want to take my heart out and give it to you for safe keeping."

Ben pulled me close and whispered, "Cassie, I want you for my wife. I want to provide for you. I want you to be the mother of my children and I want them all to look like you. I want to make you happy. That's what I want. I want to make you happy. More than anything, I want to fill your life with joy. I want to give you things."

When Ben said those things, it made me want to somehow slip inside of him so we could become one forever. I knew it wasn't time, but I wanted him. I wanted him to prove his passion—to show me his devotion. I wanted every ounce of him in that moment. As I laid my head on his chest, I felt his heart, his gentle breathing into my hair as the mellow water beside us played romantic music for two lovers who heard nothing but the voice of their beloved. I have never felt more alive.

Ben whispered, "Cassie, as long as this river flows and birds sing I shall love you. I'll remember this day and what you mean to me."

Tears of joy came. I was the happiest of women.

We heard leaves crunching on the path above. A young Cherokee fisherman had come to find a likely spot. The spell was broken. With sheepish adolescent grins, we suddenly descended from our new-found romantic heights back into the innocence of childhood. As we walked home up the hill from the river, we were oblivious of anything except one another—we were different than when we had walked down the hill. We had moved on. We had grown. Our lives would never be the same.

The inoffensive intruder had no idea what had taken place behind the laurels. Our future was secure even though we had not joined ourselves physically or exchanged rings like the English.

We giggled and whispered like school children. After that day, we were different and it became important we touch one another at every opportunity.

I have never felt the comfort, assurance and safety in the care of my edudu and elisi as I feel with Ben. Ben will keep me safe—of that I'm sure. Elisi says the way I feel is the way it should be. Parents can provide some things, but they can't complete a child's soul. There comes a time, edudu says, when the little bird's nest becomes too small.

Ben is the air I breathe, the water I drink and the sun that lights my way. I wish my mother and father could be here. I wish I could whisper to my mother of my love for Ben. I smiled all the way home, walking as close to Ben as I could. Life is good.

The unwelcome fisherman found his favorite spot. He will not remember the lovers. He wanted to catch a fish. I have found something more valuable than a fish.

14 June 1824

"Ben and I had a wonderful day yesterday. I wrote a little poem to express my emotions. Would you like to see it, Mrs. Lowry?" I said.

"Of course I would, my dear."

"I would like to read it to you," I said. "I think poetry is more powerful when recited, don't you?"

"You're right, my dear," Mrs. Lowry answered. "Poetry is at its best when spoken. Poetry is music written with words. If it's not recited out loud, it loses its music. Reading poetry silently is like hanging an empty pot on the hearth, but let that pot simmer with stew and it fills the house with its joy. The ancients recited their stories and poetry out loud. It's the only way. Please read."

Ben is...
My clear flowing river,
My solid rock,
My safe place,
From storm and strife,
Ben is my sun, moon, stars,
My dawn, my sunset,
I love his smile, eyes, hair,
His breath, hands, arms,
His fingers,
His toes,
I dream of days unending,
In his strong arms,
To share mind and body,
Our future one,
Ordained,
To cherish,

Inseparable,
Never ending,
Until we two disappear,
Into the oneness of eternal devotion.

When I finished reading, Mrs. Lowry gave me a big hug.

"I want you to keep writing, Cassie. That was lovely. You know you just wrote a poem that no one in the universe except you could have written, don't you?"

"Yes, ma'am, and I enjoyed writing it," I answered.

"Whatever you do, please keep writing," Mrs. Lowry added. "I like prose but there is something about poetry that goes deeper into human emotions than prose. Keep writing, Cassie. Keep writing."

25 June 1824 - The Green Corn Moon

Tomorrow begins our Green Corn Festival—our most important festival. It maintains balance and connection with our ancestors. Families are re-united, we have fun, we eat, we dance, we tell stories, we pray, we are cleansed, we forgive and we play games. It is our grand reunion. We forgive debts, grudges, crimes and betrayal. It's a time of renewed purity, commitment and healing.

We have the stomp dance, the feather dance and the buffalo dance. Elisi's porch will be crowded late into the night with people listening to edudu's storytelling. Spinner will inspect everyone and give his approval.

Because we were having an important ballplay, Five Feathers asked edudu to tell the story of the contest between the animals and birds.

"Tell us about the animals and the birds and their famous ballplay," the young men asked.

"I love that story," edudu answered. "Spinner, should I tell the story of the ballplay between the animals and the birds? Would you like to hear that story?"

Spinner sat up and barked his agreement. The porch and the ground in front of our porch was crowded in anticipation of edudu's story.

"I love that story and Spinner agrees," edudu answered the young men.

"That was some ballplay between the birds and the animals that day long ago," edudu began. "No one thought the birds could win. I talked to some old birds whose ancestors were at that ballplay on that very day. They told me the entire story. I have the facts. You shall hear exactly what happened all those years ago when the birds challenged the animals to a grand ballplay."

209

I love to watch people watching edudu as he begins his stories. I think it's almost as much fun to watch the people as it is to listen to the story.

"The animals were excellent at ballplay," edudu said as he began his story. "No one could remember the last time the animals had lost. The animals, weary of playing only among themselves, invited the birds to a great competition. The birds reluctantly accepted. Both groups met at the ballplay ground on the assigned day. Word went throughout the forest. There were crowds and crowds of both animals and birds gathered for the ball dance. Everyone enjoyed the festivities. Nothing like this had been seen in a great many years. The birds danced in the tree tops. The animals danced on the grassy bank beside the river. It was a great day—a great day indeed—the greatest of days."

Every eye was upon edudu as he spoke. No one made a sound.

"Bear was captain of the animal team. On the way to the ballplay Bear would pick up heavy logs and smash them to the ground to demonstrate what he would do to any opponent who would dare to take the ball from him. Terrapin was boasting he would crush any bird who would get in his way attempting to snatch the ball from him. Terrapins, the ones who can talk, are much larger than terrapins today, as you know. Their shells are so hard they can resist any blow delivered by a stick, stone, beak or weapon. Terrapin boasted he would stand and fall on any bird that got in his way. They will never take the ball from me. I'll crush them if they try, Terrapin boasted. Deer boasted he was the fastest of all the animals and no bird could catch him to take the ball. He was swifter than the fowls of the air. He could run under and through the forest, unlike the birds who had to fly over the trees. Not even Eagle, the bird's captain, could take the ball from Deer."

Edudu paused and looked around at the eager faces and continued.

"The birds' captain was Eagle. He is majestic and regal. With his powerful wings and strong talons he can carry great weights over long distances. Eagles never tire. The birds also had Hawk and other powerful birds on their team, but they were still afraid of the animals. The birds needed a resourceful plan if they were to have even a small chance to win. No one believed the birds could possibly defeat the powerful animals—not even the birds themselves."

"After the ball dance the birds were in the tops of the tallest trees preening their feathers getting ready for the ballplay when two tiny animals no bigger than field mice climbed slowly to the treetops and asked politely to talk to Eagle. Their request was granted."

"The tiny animals asked Eagle if they could play on the side of the birds. We want to join your team in the ballplay today, the two tiny animals requested."

"Eagle, majestic and powerful, looked down at the two tiny animals with great admiration. Big Eagle leaned his head down near the two little creatures and smiled. Eagle was impressed with their boldness and bravery."

"You are brave but you are animals and little animals at that, Eagle said. You are tiny, have fur and four legs and you crawl on the soil. You should be playing ball with the animals. You are not birds. You don't have wings, feathers or a beak. You don't lay eggs. You are powerless against the big animals."

"The tiny animals listened to the Eagle with great respect."

"You two could not take the ball from Rabbit—much less from Deer, Terrapin or Bear, said Eagle. Why do you want to play with the birds? great Eagle asked."

"Eagle politely leaned down his beautiful white head even closer to the two little animals to hear their small reply. The two little animals answered in their tiny voices."

Edudu was using his arms and facial expressions to help communicate his story—sometimes leaning forward or standing—sometimes almost shouting. As I surveyed his audience I could see every face turned to edudu, intent upon absorbing his every word. Each person carried along by edudu's expert storytelling. It was a wonderful moment. I love our Green Corn Festival.

"We did ask the animals, the two little creatures squeaked, but they laughed and wouldn't let us join them. They said we could watch. We want to participate therefore we humbly ask to play with the birds."

Edudu paused and looked around. I watched as he made eye contact with everyone.

"Eagle felt a great compassion for the two furry creatures. Eagle had great respect for their boldness. Eagle reasoned their tiny heart must be a great deal bigger than their little bodies. Anyone with so much courage should be allowed to join our ballplay, Eagle said. Courage does not always come in big packages. I warn you that you may suffer great harm in the ballplay, but because of your greatness of heart, I have decided you will be allowed to play on our team. However, we must equip you like a bird. We must be fair to the animals."

"Thank you, Eagle, the two little creatures said."

"You two must have wings if you compete with us birds, Eagle said."

211

Edudu leaned forward and his voice took on a more energetic tone to communicate the drama.

"There was a long consultation with Hawk and the other birds. Someone remembered the drum they used earlier in the ballplay dance. They decided to take a portion of the dried skin of the drum and use pieces of cane and stretch the skin of the drum into the shape of wings. They could attach the little wings to one small animal's powerful front legs and then the valiant creature could fly like the rest of the birds. The birds went to work quickly and that's exactly what they did. They fastened the cane and the new wings made from the dried skin of the drum to the front legs of the little creature and that is how there came to be Bat, Tla'meha. They threw the ball to him. He seized the ball and dodged this way and that more rapidly than lightening. He kept the ball in the air no matter what the other birds tried. Not one bird, no matter how swiftly they flew, turned, dipped or dived, could take the ball from Tla'meha. He could change course and avoid his pursuers more abruptly than any creature with wings."

Edudu paused once again, looked around and took a drink of water. Everyone was anxiously waiting for him to continue.

Edudu leaned forward and asked, "And do you know what happened next?"

Edudu's audience was enthralled with his story. They were waiting in anticipation for edudu to continue as if this were the first time they had heard of the great ballplay between the birds and the animals.

"The birds saw that Bat would be one of their best players," edudu continued. "They wanted to make more wings for the other furry animal, but they had used up all the leather from the drum. What could they do? Two wise old owls noticed the other brave little animal had plenty of loose skin around his legs. The two wise old birds took hold of each side of the little animal's fur and stretched and stretched and stretched. After a sufficient time they pulled the skin out from his front and hind legs and that was how we came to have Flying Squirrel. The birds threw the ball to Flying Squirrel. He jumped, sailed and caught the ball. He glided across the clearing to the next tree far above the ground and kept the ball safe."

Edudu laughed, clapped his hands and slapped his thighs.

"This was going to be some ballplay," edudu said. "Perhaps the birds had a chance after all. The birds couldn't take the ball from Flying Squirrel either and now you know how the two teams prepared for the ballplay. When both teams were ready, the great ballplay began. Flying Squirrel caught the ball first and carried it high into a tree. He sailed across a clearing and gave the ball to other birds. One of the birds dropped the ball to the ground. Big Bear almost picked it up but quick Martin swooped down and threw the ball to Bat who dodged and darted this way and that."

Edudu stood. He demonstrating how the ball play progressed with wide sweeping motions of his arms. Everyone was excited.

"The animals were surprised. Bat, showing the animals his quick skillful maneuvers, dodged this way and that way and avoided every thrust, kick and swing from the frantic animals. Bat dodged and flitted. Bat finally threw the ball between the posts and won the game for the birds. It was the greatest ballplay victory ever for the birds. Bat won the game but Martin saved the day for the birds. As a reward for his quick thinking and for saving their ballplay, Martin and his family were given gourds for a home, which they have to this day. We love to have Martin near. He promised to eat all the mosquitoes— every one."

Edudu slapped both his thighs with the flat of his hands and laughed and laughed.

"And that's how the birds won the first ballplay against the animals."

Everyone voiced their approval and thanked edudu for his story. Edudu promised they could come again later to hear more stories.

When everyone crowded around, Five Feathers showed them his ballplay stick. Attached to the top were the wings of Bat and Tema, Flying Squirrel. With these attached to his ballplay stick, our Five Feathers calls on the agility of both Bat and Flying Squirrel when he competes in a ballplay. It isn't the power of Bear or the speed of Deer that wins. Victory comes from the quickness of Bat and Tree Squirrel, Five Feathers reminded us.

30 June 1824

During the Green Corn Festival, the men in training for ballplay are forbidden to eat the flesh of rabbits. Rabbits are quick but confused when running from an enemy. When Rabbit is frightened he runs erratically or even in circles and is easily caught. Rabbit has great speed but often cannot escape his pursuer. Ballplayers don't want to run in circles mindlessly, like Rabbit, so they avoid eating rabbits before a ballplay.

After we give respect to our ancestors and fast, we will feast with the most delicious foods of the year. We will rinse our bodies in the river and pray. We cleanse impurities and bad deeds from our life. Edudu leads this ceremony. Edudu knows our traditions. He knows how to keep the balance.

The third day edudu will lead the most important dance. He will lead the many dancers in front of our seven-sided council house at New Echota around our open area with one dancer behind the other. He will have a gourd, with small stones inside, to make a loud rhythmic sound so the dancers can stay in step. He will lead the large number of dancers and zigzag. Everyone will be in step, one behind the other, a beautiful sight. I always thrill when I see the dancers. It is the happiest of times. Our corn is beginning to ripen and there will be plenty. Life is good in Cherokee Country. No one will go to sleep hungry.

I love the bread elisi makes from the new corn during the festival. It is better than any other time of the year.

Our festival will last four or five days. Many will come from surrounding villages and some from far away. During this festival I think we are still the Principle People. They have nothing like this festival in the whiteside. Every year we have a wonderful reunion of our families for the sake of our nation— it is my favorite time.

Chapter XX

1824 – Presidential Election - Law School

Chapter 20

23 July 1824 - Month of the Ripe Corn Moon – Gu ye quo ni

I love long afternoons with Ben and his parents. We have the most interesting conversations. They are interested in the upcoming presidential election.

"Father, who will be our next president and how will he view the Cherokee?" Ben asked his father.

"I don't know if I can answer that question, son, but I'll try," his father answered. "First, most of us missionaries prefer Adams over Crawford, Jackson or Clay. Adams' position concerning Indians is better plus he's opposed to slavery. I favor his experience. However, three popular southerners are running against him which muddies the water, doesn't it? With four men on the ballot it's going to be a complicated election."

"What about Andrew Jackson, Father?" Ben asked. "Does he have a chance?"

"General Jackson is a different kettle of fish—that's for sure," Ben's father answered. "His victory at New Orleans, his success in the Indian wars, his invasion of Spanish Florida and our recent acquisition of Florida have made him look as if he alone is responsible for America's triumphs. If Andrew Jackson, Indian fighter, is elected, it will be a black day for all the tribes. No, son, we don't want Jackson—not at all."

"Yes, sir, I understand," Ben answered, "but Henry Clay wouldn't be any better, would he? Mr. Clay said it would be beneficial if the Indians should disappear completely."

"From the Cherokee perspective, any white man would be a poor choice, including Clay," Mr. Lowry answered. "Crawford, because he's from Georgia, wants the Cherokee removed immediately. Crawford has been a judge, Senator, Secretary of the Treasury, minister to France during the war of 1812 and Secretary of War. When Vice President Clinton died in 1812, Crawford was elected president of the Senate and vice president pro tempore until 1813. He's an important man in Washington City. Unfortunately, I've heard he's confined to his bed with a severe stroke. I don't think he can win, but he will split the vote, even from his sickbed."

215

"Well, Father," Ben continued, "who do you think will be president? What's your opinion? You sound unsure?"

"My colleagues and I think it's between Adams and Jackson. Adams, from Massachusetts, will carry the northern states, but he's running against three southerners—all from slave states, of course. All four are popular. This may be the most problematic election ever for our electoral college."

I interrupted, "What is this electoral college, Mr. Lowry? I thought a college was like the University of Georgia?"

Mr. Lowry and Ben laughed.

"Forgive me, Cassie. That's a good question—a very good question. The Latin word collegium simply means partnership or association. In English, the word college is used to describe an association of like-minded folks. I used the word colleague a moment ago. It comes from the same root. As usual, you keep us on our toes. You ask better questions than our Ben," Mr. Lowry said with a grin.

"Thank you, sir," I answered and I pushed Ben playfully.

Mr. Lowry continued, "The electoral college is a unique political mechanism to ensure fairness. In all United States elections, save the presidential election, the man who gets the most votes wins. The election for the chief executive is different. Electing a new president requires two elections."

"In the first election, the voters in each individual state decide who they want for president by popular vote. Then, in a second election about a month later, representatives of each state vote for president—our chief executive. This second election determines the president. The president is not elected by popular vote. In that second election, Cassie, each state is allowed the number of electors equal to their seats in congress and each elector has one vote for president. Understanding how electors are allotted to each state is the key to understanding the electoral college."

"I have never heard of this, Mr. Lowry," I said.

"I understand, Cassie. The electoral college is confusing, even to Americans, but it's important. The number of electors in each state is equal to the number of representatives that state has in both the House and Senate."

"How am I doing so far, Cassie? Do you understand?" Mr. Lowry asked.

"Yes, sir, your explanation is clear," I replied. "I understand perfectly."

"Let's continue with this example," Mr. Lowry said. "Georgia has seven seats in the House of Representatives and two seats in the Senate for a total of nine seats in Congress. Therefore, Georgia is allowed nine electors. Georgia can cast nine votes for president in that second election in the electoral college. You can be sure that every one of the electors from Georgia will vote for Crawford since he's from Georgia."

"Connecticut has six seats in the house and two in the Senate. Therefore, Connecticut has eight electors. Vermont has two Senators and five house seats for a total of seven electors. The huge state of Virginia has twenty-two house seats but, like all the states, only two Senate seats for a total of twenty-four electors and so it goes for all twenty-four states."

"I think I'm following you, Mr. Lowry. This is interesting," I said.

"Excellent, Cassie. I'm rather enjoying this," Mr. Lowry continued. "Since I'm an educator, I think it important to explain systematically. In the second election in December, each elector casts one vote for president and one for vice president. The electors will vote for the man who won the popular vote in their state."

"Here's another example," Mr. Lowry said without pause. "Let's say in Vermont the popular vote goes for John Quincy Adams. Remember, this is the first popular vote election where every citizen of the state is allowed a vote. If Adams receives the most popular votes in Vermont, then Vermont's seven electors will be required to vote for Adams in the second election—in the electoral college election in December. If Georgia votes for Crawford in the general election in November, then Georgia's nine electors will be required to vote for Crawford in the electoral college in December. Are you following me so far, Cassie?"

"Yes, sir. This is interesting. Your explanation is clear," I answered.

"Well," Mr. Lowry continued, "the twenty-four states have a total of 261 representatives in congress. Therefore, there will be 261 electors voting for president when they meet in the electoral college—in that second election a month after the general election."

I answered, "I understand about the two elections and how the electors are chosen, but why have two elections in the first place. Why not have just one election by popular vote?"

"Good question," Mr. Lowry said. "We have two elections so the president can be chosen by the states."

"I don't understand, Mr. Lowry," I asked. "What is unfair about having one election and allowing everyone to vote? Why would one election by popular vote be unfair. A popular vote seems fair and less complicated."

"My word, Cassie," Mr. Lowry said with a sigh, "you do keep me on my toes and tax my brain. If Ben and I hadn't been talking about this just yesterday, I couldn't explain this. Let's see if I can present this logically. The United States began as a collection of thirteen diverse British colonies. Each

217

was a different size and all were self-governing under the oversight of the Crown. Each of the thirteen colonies had their own charter. There was no common government. There was no congress. When those thirteen colonies decided to become independent they immediately turned into thirteen separate political states. Each newly independent colony viewed itself as an independent country—an autonomous political state. The United States is a collection of thirteen little countries who chose to band together for the common good and yet retain their individual freedoms. Some states are large and some small. Some, like Rhode Island, are tiny yet they wanted to maintain their identity and not be swallowed up by the bigger states. When the thirteen little countries decided to band together, they wanted to maintain their original identity and influence. They didn't want to become one homogenous big country. How am I doing, Cassie?"

Ben interrupted, "Father, that's the best explanation of the origin of the United States I've ever heard. You're brilliant."

"I don't know about brilliant, son," his father answered. "I'm a teacher and doing my best to explain a complicated subject one step at a time—that's all I'm trying to do. The best bricklayer in the world lays one brick at a time."

"You're doing a good job, Mr. Lowry," I said. "Keep going. I'm interested."

Mr. Lowry continued, "Well, the little states didn't want to be marginalized by the big states. The small states, like Rhode Island, Vermont and Connecticut wanted the same rights as the big states like New York, Pennsylvania and Virginia. We won't talk about it now, but that's why each state, large or small, has two Senators and why the Senate has more power than the House. Having two Senators gave the small states a large measure of political power. As you know, the final say on all laws is voted on in the Senate."

"When the Constitution was being hammered out, the small states knew a popular vote for the chief executive would be unfair to them because of their small populations. If the presidential election were decided by a national popular vote of all thirteen states lumped together, the densely populated states, like New York, Pennsylvania and Virginia, would forever control the executive branch. If the president were to be elected by popular vote, the smaller states like Rhode Island, Vermont, Delaware and Connecticut would become meaningless. States' rights are central to the Constitution, Cassie—still are, as a matter of fact. I guess you know that from reading the endless talk about nullification—but that's another story. Tiny Rhode Island has the same rights as Virginia or New York. The smaller states wanted constitutional protection from domination by the larger states. This protection came in the form of a compromise election. The compromise between the big and small states was to elect their chief executive by a secondary electoral election and not by popular vote. In other words, the states elect the president—not popular vote. That idea is key to understanding the presidential election. Simply put, the second election gives the smaller states more say in who is elected president."

"Oh my, Mr. Lowry. I think I have the idea," I said. "When you explain it that way it seems quite simple."

"Well," Mr. Lowry continued, "I don't know if I would call it simple. There's one more important thing to understand. According to the Constitution, the winner in the electoral college must win with a majority—not just a plurality. Majority means at least fifty-one percent of the votes. Plurality means one more than the others and could be less than fifty-one percent. If I eat more than half the pie, I've eaten the majority. A majority, more than half the votes, must be achieved in the electoral college to become president—a plurality won't do."

"Yes sir, and if you ate more than half of the pie you would be sick, wouldn't you?" I said, and we all laughed.

"Yes, Cassie, I would be sick. As good as Eleanor's pies are, I should never eat a majority of her pie, should I? One piece of her good pie is sufficient unless it's rhubarb. I'm sure I could eat a majority of Eleanor's rhubarb pie. I do like rhubarb pies. Remember, in our discussion a majority would be more than half of the total votes of the electoral college—not more than half of the popular vote. That can be confusing."

Mr. Lowry continued and we listened carefully, "The word plurality in election nomenclature means 'more than'. Let's say Eleanor makes a lovely apple pie and cuts it into eight equal pieces. If you have two pieces of Eleanor's pie on your plate and I have one piece, you have a plurality. You have more pie than I have. If you have two pieces of apple pie you have a plurality but do you have a majority of the pie?"

"No, sir," I answered. "Two pieces of pie is not a majority. It would require five pieces of Mrs. Lowry's pie to be a majority."

"Exactly, Cassie. It's that simple. In all the elections in all the states, the winner only needs one more vote than his opponent to win. In the electoral college, however, the winner must have a majority—more than fifty percent. To be president, the winner must have most of the pie—most of the votes. In the electoral college the winner must have more than half and not just a plurality. The framers of the constitution wanted to make certain the presidency would be elected by more than fifty percent of the vote. If a candidate has thirty or forty percent of the vote in the electoral college, he is not the winner and that might happen this year with four men running. Obviously, if all four received the same number of electoral votes they would each get twenty-five percent, wouldn't they?"

"Why does your Constitution require over fifty percent of the vote in the electoral college, Mr. Lowry?" I asked. "What was their reasoning? Other elections allow their candidates to be elected without a majority. What's the difference?"

"Good question once again," Mr. Lowry said. "I tried to explain that earlier but let me try again."

"If a citizen of Georgia should seek to be governor of Georgia and wins his election, he will govern Georgians and only Georgians. The presidency is different. The man running for president might be from Virginia, but he has to govern the people from all the other states. Many are suspicious of the motives of politicians who aren't from their state—and with good reason. The men who wrote the Constitution didn't want a man doing the job of president who didn't represent more than half the states. The president is tasked to represent all states—not some states. You can see it would be difficult for the president to govern if he didn't receive a majority of the electoral votes."

"Yes, sir, I understand that now and it makes sense to me," I answered.

"There are four candidates in this year's election," Mr. Lowry added. "They may split the vote and no one receive the required fifty-one percent.

I asked, "What happens then? What happens if no candidate receives a majority in the electoral college? Would you keep the old president or would the United States have another election?"

"Another excellent question, Cassie," Mr. Lowry said. "You always think logically. You're a most sensible girl, I must say. Here's the caveat. If no candidate receives a majority in the electoral college, there must be a third election."

"A third election?" I asked. "This is getting complicated, Mr. Lowry."

"You're right, Cassie. It does get complicated," Mr. Lowry answered. "The electoral college votes one time and one time only. If a presidential candidate doesn't get a majority in the vote by the electoral college, the top three men with the most votes are then voted on by the full House of Representatives to determine who will become president. The entire House of Representatives will elect the president from the top three candidates in that third election. The framers of the constitution wanted to make certain their president would be elected by a majority of the states—thus the third and deciding election would go to the house where all the states are represented. Does this help at all with your confusion?"

"Yes, sir, I understand," I answered. "I wonder how many understand your electoral college. After your explanation, I see the extra power granted to the smaller states by the electoral college. That seems wise."

"One last thing, Cassie," Mr. Lowry added. "As you now know, the winner of this autumn's electoral college must have more than half the pie. Therefore, the winning candidate must have at least 131 votes in the electoral college to become president. That's simple, isn't it?"

"Yes sir, I understand the electoral college now," I said.

"We'll talk about all this after election day and this will be easier to understand when we look at the results."

"I would like that, Mr. Lowry," I said. "Sometimes I wonder how any of your politicians can be honest? It seems your government is an endless series of compromises and no one is happy."

6 August 1824 - The Fruit Moon – Ga lo nii

Ben's parents have secured a place for Ben in a good law school. The news was a surprise. The term lasts fourteen moons—fourteen months. I will miss his smile, a smile brighter than the morning sun. Ben is fulfilling his dream and doing the right thing. When Ben is happy, I am happy.

We Cherokee need a lawyer like Ben. He will be a good lawyer—a very good lawyer. He will have our best interest at heart.

We have no legal standing in white courts. Men from the whiteside rob our barns, smokehouses and corn cribs—sometimes in daylight. They steal our livestock and squat on our land with impunity. We don't have anyone to stand up for us in white courts. Henry Clay famously said we are "essentially inferior and not an improvable breed," and "on our way to extinction".

This morning as a surprise, Ben's mother cooked his favorite breakfast of thick-cut bacon, poached eggs with soft yellows, steaming flour biscuits made with lard and buttermilk, white gravy made with bacon drippings, grits swimming with butter and his mother's special blackberry jam and all washed down with sweet milk.

Ben and his father, as they finished, poured a little sorghum syrup over soft butter and mixed the two into a marvelous paste. They ate that wonderful mixture on fluffy buttered biscuits. Sorghum syrup is definitely Ben's favorite. I think it is mine too. I like sorghum syrup better than honey.

As they sopped up the last of the sorghum on the last bite of biscuit, Ben's mother said, "Wilbur, eat this last biscuit. It's too good to give to the pigs. Don't let it go begging."

Mr. Lowry leaned back in his chair, looked up at his wife and patted his full stomach, "My dear Eleanor, I can't eat one more bite—not one bite. I'm full as a tick on a lazy dog, but if it would make you happy, I'll put some jam on that biscuit and rub it on. That's the best I can do for you. I'm sure I couldn't eat it."

Everyone laughed. With that answer Ben's mother could be certain there were left-overs because the men she loved were full and not because her cooking wasn't tasty.

"Eleanor," Ben's father said, "I can't eat that last biscuit but I'm going to tell you the truth. I think that was the best breakfast of my life. It was your best breakfast ever."

Eleanor made a face. She shook a big wooden spoon at her husband. "Wilbur, exaggeration isn't much different than a lie. You know what the good Book says about liars. You counsel Ben to tell the truth. How about you take your own advice and tell me the truth about my cooking."

Wilbur, still sitting at the table, suddenly wore a serious expression. He looked up at his wife who was still holding the wooden spoon. In mock humility he said, "Eleanor, you're standing there with that spoon in your hand as if it were your scepter and you were a queen. I submit to your Majesty. You're correct. I'm at fault. Please forgive your humble servant. You're right and I'm wrong. I confess. I need to be honest even when I'm talking about your cooking. Therefore, queen of my heart, I pledge I shall never exaggerate ever again about your cooking."

"The honest truth is," Mr. Lowry continued, "your cooking gets better every day. Your breakfast this morning was without a doubt the best breakfast I've ever eaten in my life and I would say that under threat of beheading."

They laughed again.

After Ben and his father helped his mother clear the table, Ben's father began, "Son, this breakfast was a surprise for you. We've been talking about law school for over a year. If you're ready to make a decision, your mother and I are ready to assist. Are you ready to commit to law school or would you prefer to wait and maybe go a different direction with your life? Your mother and I want to know what you really want to do? Whatever you choose is fine with us. We don't want to unduly influence you one way or the other. The decision is yours alone."

Ben's father patiently waited for his answer. He is like Cherokee men that way.

"Sir, I know we've been talking about law school," Ben answered, "but do we have the money? Law school would be expensive, wouldn't it? I've saved only a little. You and Mother don't have much. Wouldn't school be impossible?"

His father patted his son on the shoulder affectionately. "Son, your mother and I have been saving in anticipation of this very day. We couldn't do better than invest in you and your education. What do you think, Ben? Once you are established as a lawyer, could you repay your debt and care for us when your mother and I are too old to work?"

It was a special moment.

"Father, I'll do it. I'll go. I want to go. Yes, of course I want to go if I can. I would love to go to law school."

Ben threw his arms around his mother and father in an emotional childlike embrace as he continued to burst with his emotive response.

"I'll be the best son and lawyer you can imagine. You can count on me, Father. I'll take care of you and Mother—of course I will. I promise I'll take care of you just like you took care of Mother's parents. You and Mother will live in a nice house. Mother will wear new dresses and you'll have servants. Mother will never have to cook again. You'll never have to shoe your own horses, either. I'll take care of you. You'll be proud of me."

"Son," his mother answered, "we don't need a big house. I don't need servants. We want to help you with your education like all good parents should. We want you to be happy doing something you love. Your father and I have taught you as much as we can. It's time we turn you over to someone smarter. If you're going to reach your potential, you need instruction beyond that which your father and I can supply. We need to take advantage of this moment, don't you think?"

"Yes ma'am, I'm ready," Ben said enthusiastically. "I would love to take the next step."

"Your mother and I thought you might say that son," Ben's father said. "This breakfast was your mother's idea. I received a letter yesterday from Professor James Gould with *The Litchfield Law School*. Per my request, he's holding a place for you in his next class. He's waiting for my return letter. What do you think? Should we confirm or wait? Professor Gould says there are other young men from Georgia accepted next term. If you choose to go you'll have good company. Do you want to stay with us another year or go to Connecticut and read law?"

223

Ben was speechless. His father chuckled to himself to see his son's reaction.

Finally, as his mother and father waited, Ben found his voice, "You and Mother are the best parents in the whole world."

They embraced once again. His mother had tears in her eyes. Ben didn't often see his mother this emotional.

"Yes, I want to go to law school," Ben said. "I do want to go. I'll be the best lawyer in Georgia. I'll stand up for the Cherokee, Father, just like you have. I promise. I'll learn to do all the things you and I have talked about."

Ben was talking so quickly he sounded like a sputtering kettle. His youthful exuberance thrilled his mother, but her heart had an unexpected downturn. When Ben went to law school she would not be able to wash his clothes, prepare his meals or kiss him goodnight. For a moment the young man who stood as tall as his father disappeared and Ben's mother could only see a little boy tugging on her skirt-tails. She saw him sitting at the table as he did years earlier with little feet that didn't reach the floor. Emotions rose in Eleanor's breast that could not be denied. Tears came to her eyes. With one look at his wife Mr. Lowry understood. He gave her a long embrace before he continued.

"Good choice, son," Ben's father said. "The Litchfield School is the second oldest in our nation. It was founded in 1774 by Tapping Reeve. You couldn't do better. I'm impressed with the achievements of their students. Litchfield is quite a distance from here, but it's the best. It has a strong fourteen-month vocational curriculum. Mr. Gould tells me the school has produced successful lawyers, politicians, judges and members of congress working throughout all twenty-four of these United States. According to my friends who know, it's the place for a young man who wants a head start in his legal career. You could apprentice in Milledgeville and bypass law school, but I'm told you'll begin your career with a head start if you go to law school. Can you keep your nose to the grindstone and finish what you start? Fourteen months is a long time."

"I want to go to law school, Father. I do. I'll finish what I start. I promise," Ben said proudly.

A tentative departure date was set. Ben was going to read law in Connecticut. He couldn't wait. I am proud of Ben but, along with Mrs. Lowry, I felt as if my heart would break.

8 August 1824

"My parents believe Cherokee, Africans and whites are all equally human," Ben said to me, "and so do I, Cassie. Many don't believe that. For the life of me, I don't understand why. I'm not sure what I'll be able to accomplish as a white lawyer on behalf of the Cherokee, but I can do good if I'm patient. At least I can help my father and his fellow missionaries. I can do that. Cassie, I respect my parents and share their beliefs about the rights of the Cherokee, the Creek and others—even Africans."

"Your parents are a tiny minority," I answered. "Our nation is being stolen from us little by little—day by day. You have a soft heart. I admire your sense of justice. Most missionaries teach we must become like the whites, but your parents aren't like that. The proof is your parents have encouraged our relationship. I hope you'll never be ashamed of me. I would never be ashamed to be associated with you or your parents."

"If white folks lived among the Cherokee, like I do," Ben said, "they wouldn't be afraid of you and your people. Perhaps, with time, things will change. I hope so."

"I remember you from the first morning in your father's schoolroom. You have always loved us. We need men like you. People like you may make all the difference. Your father said there is nothing more honorable than giving one's life to support the vulnerable. You're going to do good work. I know you are."

"Yes, I hate injustice," Ben answered. "Especially what I've seen here. The white culture puts great stock in Rule of Law. Therefore, a white lawyer for the Cherokee would be a noble profession. I could make a difference with patience—perhaps a lifetime of patience would be required. I won't be popular or make a lot of money, but I don't care. Father never cared about reputation or the accumulation of wealth. I want to do what's right. Father didn't choose to be fashionable and neither will I."

"Cassie, future Cherokee battles will be won and lost in white courtrooms. The Indian nations are at the mercy of the white legal system. If European land lust isn't controlled there will be trouble. I want to help, if I can. I don't want to see you dispossessed."

12 August 1824

I saw Ben every day after that morning. We talked of his future plans and the grand things he would accomplish in Milledgeville and Washington City. We talked about law school. Sometimes he seemed more excited about the journey to Connecticut than attending school. I am so happy for him, but I will miss him every moment of every day. At night I miss him as if he were already gone. I cannot wait until we're old enough to marry. I want to feel his arms around me and know I will be secure. I want to belong to him. I will not be complete until we are together. Only then will my emptiness be filled.

14 August 1824

"Cassie, Father and I decided the journey to Connecticut will be easier if I go by coaster," Ben said this morning. "I can sail from Savannah right up the coast to New London rather than go overland by stage. That would be a much more comfortable journey and more interesting, don't you think? It won't be any more expensive than traveling by stage and I've always wanted to go to sea. Traveling by ship will be interesting, don't you think?"

I was as excited as he was.

"The sea will be so much better than the stage," I answered. "I have never even seen the sea, but I love to read about the ships and the sailors' adventures. That will be interesting. I envy your journey. Edudu said when he was a child he heard many stories of the Cherokee who lived close to the sea before the whites forced us inland."

"Father has arranged for me to stay with friends in Milledgeville and Savannah on the first leg of the journey. I'll be traveling with four boys from Georgia who are also going to law school. Mother thinks that's a good idea. She wants to make certain I eat properly and my shirt is clean."

"I'm not worried about you, Ben, not one bit," I answered. "You can take care of yourself. I know that. You won't forget me, will you? I'm thinking of all the lonely days I will not hear your beautiful voice in my ears and see your handsome face. I miss you already."

"Oh, Cassie, you're silly. How could I forget you? You're my best friend. I'll write reams and reams. I'll share everything. I want you to write, too. You will write, won't you? I'll write you a letter every day. I will. I promise," Ben said.

"Of course I'll write. You're silly too," I answered. "Your mother told me your father thinks her daft. She told him she couldn't help thinking of you sitting on the side of a lonely bed in some shabby room wearing dirty clothes with nothing to eat and no one to care for you. Ben, do remember in your mother's heart you're still a little boy. Even though you are as tall as your father, your mother sees you as a child. She misses that little boy. I know exactly how she feels. I miss you already. We embraced and not another word was spoken that day about Ben's departure.

17 August 1824

Elisi wants to make certain I can teach my granddaughters to make pine baskets.

"Walela, teach me to make a pine basket."

"I'm ready, elisi. Where do we start?"

"Let's start from the beginning," elisi said. "Teach me how to make a basket as if I knew nothing—as if I was a little girl. One day I won't be here and you must teach what I have taught you. I learned from my elisi. Our people have been making pine baskets since the beginning of time. Your daughters' baskets will be better than mine. You are smart, Walela. You see things I can't see, but I always enjoy making even simple baskets. I love working with you. It calms my mind."

"Walela, some baskets are for daily use and some we want to look nice. I'll let you do the complicated baskets. We can trade them for new laying hens. I hate to feed these old chickens. It's a waste when they're not laying properly. We're not nearly getting as many eggs as we should."

"I'm ready to begin, elisi," I answered.

"Let's pretend I don't know anything about making baskets," elisi said. "Start from the beginning. Teach me."

"First, we gather the pine needles," I said. "Long, clean ones that have recently fallen are best. I love to go where the old pine trees grow tall and close together and the carpet of new needles is thick and dry."

"Very good, Walela. What's next?"

"We bring as many needles home as we can carry. I lay the needles on a large, flat surface with all the needles pointing the same way. I'm careful not to break them. I use hot water to clean them. I pour off the water when they cool and let the needles dry."

Elisi nodded her approval and I continued.

"Once they are clean and dry I make sure they're lying straight. We throw away all bent, crooked or broken needles. After they dry, I carefully tie them into neat bundles the size of my wrist for storage. We stack all the bunches together and make sure Five Feathers and edudu do not use them for a bed."

I continued, "When I'm ready to make a basket, I get as many bundles as I need and soak just the cap end in hot water. When the caps are soft, I pull them off with the bone tool edudu made for us. I stack the needles carefully laying them all the same way and allow them to dry."

"Well done, Walela," elisi said. "You have a good memory. Go on."

"Once the caps are removed and the needles dry, we're ready to make a basket. I separate fifteen or so needles from a bundle and wrap sinew around

227

and around to secure the cap end of the needles. I thread the sinew between the needles snugly until the needles are firmly held together in a perfectly little round rope. This is the beginning of a pine needle rope we will make longer and longer that we will coil around and around and build our basket from the bottom up. We'll coil the rope around in different shapes to form the basket we want. Some baskets will be round, some oblong and some rectangular. If we have a centerpiece for the bottom of the basket, we won't need to bend the pine needle rope as much as when we first begin. I prefer to make a basket with a large centerpiece in the bottom. Edudu will whittle us any shape or size centerpiece we want. A symmetrical centerpiece makes the basket easier to begin and build. Edudu makes small holes around the edges of the centerpiece to make it easy to secure our rope of pine needles with the sinew at the beginning."

I love to watch edudu whittling on the front porch with Spinner. He sits for hours carving wooden things for our home and centers for our pine baskets. Sometimes I see edudu whittling a human figure, an animal or a centerpiece, but other times I have no idea what he is whittling. No matter how many times I ask edudu what he is carving out of the wood, he always replies, "shavings".

I continued with my rehearsal, "As we extend the coil of pine needles, I use the hollow bone tool edudu made for us to continually gauge the diameter of the rope. The coil should be continuous with the same diameter and shape with the same number of pine needles as we make the rope longer and longer and longer. The rope must be a symmetrical continuous coil in order to have a basket pleasing to the eye."

"Excellent, Walela," elisi said. "The hollow bone tool is useful, isn't it? After you have been making baskets for a long time, you'll be able to make all your coils exactly the same by feel, but the bone tool is useful."

Elisi sat back and nodded her approval and I continued.

"We let the pine needles bend the way they want to bend. The coils of needles can't be forced. If I bend the rope too sharply, it will break the needles and the basket will be ugly. When we build a rope of pine needles, we can make the coil as long as we wish. We can make the basket as large as we wish by extending the coil. We make the coil rope longer by adding new needles to the very end of the first coil and securing the additional needles at regular intervals with sinew."

Elisi interrupted, "To tell the truth, Walela, I begin my baskets with an idea of what I want but I let the basket shape itself. Pine baskets seem to have a mind of their own. I am sure you know what I mean."

"Yes, I know exactly what you mean," I said. "I remember one basket I made that ended up with three sides instead of four as I intended. It was lovely, but I didn't plan it that way. I named it Trinity. I love the way you name your baskets. It's a wonderful tradition."

Elisi said quietly, "My mother and her elisi named all their baskets. I spend so much time on them it's like they become my children. Tell me more."

I continued, "As we add needles to the end of the coil, the rope coil of pine needles gets longer and longer. We bend it around in circles and use the sinew to hold one coil to the next as we build the sides of the basket higher and higher. We can make the sides vertical or we can make the basket in a bowl shape depending on how we secure the sinew. If we want an unusual pattern, it requires some unusual bending and if we want different colors, it requires dying the needles. Most of the time, I make the baskets with natural color. Sometimes, when I'm making a lid for the basket, I will dye it a color."

"Walela, you amaze me," elisi said. "You are a smart young woman. That's exactly how I was taught to make baskets. You are a wonderful teacher with a marvelous memory. Let's make a pine basket today. In a few weeks, when we finish ten or fifteen, we'll send your edudu to Ross's Landing to trade them for cloth, thread and laying hens. I like the thread to bind the needles instead of sinew. It's much easier to work with."

Elisi and I often work late into the night. We sit by our fire that never goes out making baskets, often without a word passing between us.

Chapter XXI

1824 – Bookends

Chapter 21

18 August 1824 - The Fruit Moon - Ga lo nii

Ben came on his saddle horse early this morning so I could share breakfast with him and his parents before he leaves for law school. It was hardly daylight. When I ride double, I wrap my arms around his middle, bury my nose in his shirt and smell his masculine aroma. I would ride behind him every day if I could. On the way we had an unexpected adventure. We laugh about it now, but we weren't laughing then.

As we rode back to his house, Ben's horse was walking along quietly—head down. Ben and I were talking about the interesting things about to happen in his life. We weren't in any hurry. As we came around a bend, we could see the welcoming smoke above the trees from Mrs. Lowry's chimney. We were almost there. She was preparing an extra special breakfast and I couldn't wait. Just at that moment Ben and I saw what looked like a large dog standing motionless in the middle of the road looking at us. Ben stopped his horse and we looked carefully. It wasn't a big black dog. It was a chubby, fuzzy, black bear cub. We stared at the little bear and he stared back. The little bear was adorable, but we know where you see a bear cub his mother is close by. Ben kept his horse still and he whispered for me to be quiet as we surveyed the surrounding woods and especially the area behind us. We were only a stone's throw from the cub. We continued perfectly still on Ben's horse as the curious little bear sat up on his haunches in the middle of the road and watched us watching him. The cub didn't move and we didn't move.

Suddenly, we heard a noise in the underbrush to our left and there, twenty yards into the woods and much closer to us than the first bear, was another cub—just as cute as the first. Ben's horse heard the noise and I could feel her bow-up. Her neck arched, her nostrils dilated and her ears were standing straight up and close together—rotating left and right listening to every sound. She was nervous. This second cub wasn't frightened either and it was watching us watch him. Immediately there was a clatter to our right and I was surprised to see a third cub in the edge of the woods on the other side. It was a humorous moment—at least it is now. We were surrounded by bear cubs and we both thought the same thing at the same moment. When we saw the third cub, Ben swiveled in the saddle and looked at me and in unison we whispered, "The mother bear is close. We need to get out of here—now."

Ben whispered in a commanding voice, "Hang on tight. I have no desire to let momma bear ride with you on the back-end of my mare. We need out of here now—and I mean now. I'm going to start my old mare walking towards that bear cub in the road in front of us and about the third step she takes I'm goin' to call on her for everything she's worth. You be ready. It's goin' to be a wild ride. We'll gallop past that cub in the road as fast as my old mare can go. If that little bear doesn't move, we'll jump him. I don't know where that momma bear is, but she's watchin' and it's time we were gone. It's going to be fast and rough, and I don't know what this mare will do when she gets to the cub. She may jump sideways, but I'm not goin' to let her stop so hang on. Be prepared for anything. It would be really bad if you fell off— but I don't have to tell you that."

Ben grinned and kissed me and I held on. I felt remarkably alive. I could feel every part of my body tingling at one time. I did as Ben said. I put my arms around his waist and held him with all my strength. I'm sure I bruised his ribs. He clicked his tongue and gave his mare rein. She began walking forward with her ears standing straight up and quickly turning this way and that—her ears were swiveling like two little weather vanes in a storm. She was almost prancing sideways she was so nervous. She wanted to get away from this place as much as we did. After the mare was moving forward in a walk, Ben gave her full rein and called on her with a shout, kicked his heels into her sides and we were at full gallop in four quick strides. Ben was leaning over his mare's neck holding the reins with both fists buried in her mane. I was sitting behind Ben's saddle holding to his middle for dear life. Ben's hat blew off, but we weren't about to retrieve it. The mare went a bit sideways as we passed the frightened cub, but we were galloping so fast she never left the roadway. The poor little bear ran for the woods in terror almost as fast as Ben's mare was running.

We never did see the momma bear. When we got to the house I slid off, still shaking, breathless and exhilarated beyond words. I could feel my face flushed and warm. Ben jumped down and we embraced right there behind the house. As we hugged one another, we began to laugh. Our mad gallop to escape the bears was one of the most memorable moments in my life. Ben's eyes were shining.

"That was some ride, Cassie. Are you alright?" Ben asked smiling.

"I'm good, Ben. In fact, I've never been better. Could we do that again?"

"Not today, Cassie," Ben answered laughing. "We've had enough for one day. I hope my mare didn't hurt herself. I'm starving. Breakfast should be ready. You help Mother and I'll put the horse up."

Ben didn't let me go from our embrace. Even though his mother or father could have come out the back at any moment, Ben and I kissed the most passionate kiss ever. I thanked the bears.

As I went inside, I was still quivering with the thrill of the ride and Ben's kiss.

"Mrs. Lowry, you'll never guess what we saw around the bend from your house," I said.

I told her about our encounter with the three bear cubs and our mad race home.

"Cassie, you're teasing me, aren't you?" she said with a little laugh. "We haven't seen bears around here this year. You're joshing, aren't you? You didn't see three bear cubs, did you? There aren't any bears around here and certainly not in the middle of our road."

When Ben came in he confirmed my story. Ben's father, sitting in the chimney corner, was watching his wife's response but didn't say a word. Ben's mother laughed at us again.

"You two are teasing me, aren't you?" Ben's mother said again. "You two are having fun with me, aren't you? We haven't seen any bear signs all year. You two go wash up and quit pulling my leg. I know you didn't see three bear cubs. You can't fool me."

Ben gave his mother a big hug and looked her in the eye with both hands on her shoulders, "Mother, whatever you say, but you and Father should pay attention around here for a day or two. If I was Father, I would keep a good eye on the smoke-house. It would be bad if we lost our hams."

Ben's mother looked at him sideways for a moment and said, "Very well, bear or no bear, it's time to eat."

No one wanted to argue with Mrs. Lowry with a wonderful breakfast ready to put on the table.

I love Mrs. Lowry's buttermilk biscuits and her white gravy made with sweet milk, flour and bacon drippings. I love smoked ham, hot steaming grits with butter and eggs fried just right.

Mr. Lowry mixes butter and sorghum syrup to put on the last of the biscuits. What a glorious mixture. I like sorghum better than honey. When I think about Mr. Lowry's heaven I'm sure Mrs. Lowry's breakfasts must be the kind of food served there.

One of their missionary friends has two Jerseys and brings them milk. I love to put a spoon or two of the cream in my tea or coffee. I like coffee even better than tea. Mr. Lowry does, too. When Ben and I are married, I want a Jersey—maybe two or three. I love the milk, cream and butter.

I'm going to miss Ben and our rides while he's gone. I might even miss the bears.

22 August 1824

Ben will be gone for fourteen months. The world is cold. The birds have forgotten their songs. The moon has forgotten to greet me.

23 August 1824

Ben shared his mother's final advice. I think his parents have learned from us. Their wisdom is that of elisi and edudu.

Under the big chestnut tree behind their house Ben's father set up two waist high cross sections cut from a big hickory for chopping blocks. Ben uses them for splitting the small wood his mother needs for cooking in her fireplace. They're seasoned so hard Ben's axe bounces off them. Those stumps will last forever. Hickory is even harder than oak. Persimmon is hard too, but persimmon trees don't grow nearly as big as hickory. I love persimmons in the autumn. We never cut a persimmon.

We love the hickory nuts. We cut hickory trees to make tools but never for firewood. We carefully conserve our trees and animals. Our hunters harvest what we need for food and no more.

I was reading a book of Greek fables. One story is about a man who had a goose that would occasionally lay a golden egg. The man killed his goose expecting to find many golden eggs inside. The foolish man should not have killed his goose any more than we should cut down our productive nut trees for firewood or kill a doe for food, or worse—kill a doe for pleasure as whites do.

Sometimes Ben and I spend hours talking while he splits wood for his mother. Summer and winter Ben's mother uses cooking wood, split as small as my little finger, to control the fire under the pots, kettles and skillets she uses.

It's fun to watch Ben work. He will sometimes see how small he can split the short logs that have a clean straight grain with no knots.

Ben said his mother surprised him while he was splitting kindling. He turned and she was sitting on the hickory stump behind him.

"Hello Mother. You startled me. I didn't know you were there."

233

"I was watching you, son. It's a lovely morning, isn't it? I want you to know I appreciate your hard work. You make cooking easy when you split my wood short and neat. Thank you."

"You're welcome, Mother," Ben said. "I don't really call this work. It's a small price to pay for your good cookin'. I'll swap a few hours out here for your bacon, eggs, biscuits and gravy any day, but can I help you with something, Mother?"

His mother, without a word, gave him a big hug.

"Son, I need to talk to you, if you don't mind me being your mother. Please allow me to worry a little. I know you're pretty much a grown man. You can take care of yourself. I was looking at you yesterday and I think you stand taller than your father. I reckon you're six feet or more. You've grown like a weed these last few years. You're not a child any longer, Ben. You're as capable as any. I love you dearly, but I can't help wanting to give you some motherly advice before you leave."

His mother continued without waiting for an answer and asked sweetly, "Ben, I need to ask you a question. May I?"

"Of course you can, Mother. You can ask me anything you wish, you know that."

Ben blushed. He was embarrassed by the unusual request for permission to speak from his mother. Ben said his parents have always treated him like an adult and a friend.

"Please, son, may I give you some advice?" his mother said. "Will you allow me to share my heart? I thought out here in the fresh air in the shade would be a grand place."

"Oh Mother, of course you can say anything you wish," Ben replied. "You don't have to ask for permission."

He gave her a big kiss and bear hug. Sitting side by side on the two chopping blocks made a perfect venue for Ben's final motherly advice before his departure.

"Ben," his mother began, "I've lain awake for the last week rehearsing this moment. I told Cassie we were going to have this talk. I have a great affection for her, Ben. I think you two are good for one another. I wouldn't be surprised if you don't marry her one of these days. I doubt you could do better. As much as I love Cassie, it's not your relationship with her I want to talk about."

Ben, still embarrassed, sat on the hickory stump and waited for his mother to continue.

"Ben, you've been raised well. I've done the best I can and Wilbur's done right by you. He's been a good father. Ben, when you return from Connecticut you won't be my little boy, not that you're little now, but you know what I mean. When you return you're going to be your own man making your own decisions. This talk we're having now is the last talk I'll ever have with my little boy."

His mother patted his knee affectionately.

"Please don't be offended if I think of you today as my little boy, Ben. Allow me one last indulgence. When I woke this morning I had a nostalgic parade of visions of my little boy. I remembered you as a baby when you threw up in our bed twice in one night. I remember that first little red hat and how you used to insist you wear it even when you slept. I remember the first time you helped your father bring in firewood. I can still see that little boy with blond curls and two little sticks of firewood in his arms as proud as could be for helping his father. We would go walking and you would always explore. You were fearless. Your father and I had the dickins of a time keeping up with you. You worried me silly. You wanted to explore everything and everywhere. You could disappear in an instant. I was always afraid you were going to fall into the river or get on a snake."

Ben felt the emotion of the moment and saw his mother's eyes rimmed with tears. He knew this was a time when he needed to let his mother speak.

"Here we are today," his mother said, as she wiped her eyes on the tail of her apron. "You're tall, handsome and smart. You're still a little boy in some ways. You're like your father. You're both just grown-up boys. You're going to go far, Ben. You'll be successful at whatever you choose in life. If you will allow me, I want to give you one last piece of advice and I have one last gift for you. May I give you my advice now, Ben?" his mother asked again.

"Of course you can, Mother," Ben answered.

"I knew this day was coming and I've dreaded it," his mother said. "In other ways I've rejoiced. Not every parent is as fortunate as I am to have such an intelligent and obedient son. I guess I should have written this speech and let you take it with you, but I think you'll remember."

His mother laughed a nice easy laugh and Ben laughed with her.

"Son, my mother and I had a talk much like this one as I was preparing to leave home. The first thing she said that day was, 'Eleanor, I was born at night, but it wasn't last night.' I remember us laughing together at that statement. My mother understood how naïve young women like me could be. My mother wanted to warn me about the dangers I was going to face outside the home. Her advice may be the main reason I chose Wilbur as my husband.

I wanted a good man to be the father of my children. Son, I say to you the same thing my mother said. I may have been born at night, but it wasn't last night. May I give you my advice?"

"Of course you can, Mother," Ben replied. Ben felt his face turning red once again. He had never experienced anything like this with his mother. He was embarrassed.

"Son, I trust you but when children are far from parental authority they sometimes do things they would never do at home. Son, this advice I'm giving you is like icing on your cake or the top rung in the ladder of your ethical education. After this, it's all up to you."

Ben, unable to speak, waited patiently for his mother to continue.

"When you leave tomorrow you'll begin your adult life without your parents near. I wish I could keep you a few more years, but it's time. Can you imagine how it would be if I were allowed to keep you? That wouldn't be right, would it?"

Ben was unable to respond. Ben's mother continued quietly, "Beginning tomorrow you'll carry adult responsibilities and consequently bear adult punishment. Children live in a protected cocoon. After tomorrow your father and I won't be able to protect you. There comes a time when the young birds must leave the nest. This is your time."

Ben's mother suddenly threw her head back and laughed out loud, and even though Ben didn't know the reason, he began laughing with her.

"I just had a vision of three or four fully grown big crows crowded together in a tiny nest squawking madly to be fed with that awful sound crows make. I can see them waiting with their black heads thrown back and their long beaks open wide—not realizing they had wings to fly. That would be humorous, wouldn't it?"

"Yes, ma'am," Ben answered, and they both laughed again.

"You're leaving my nest, Ben, but you can come back as often as you wish. You can always count on my cooking—well—as long as you keep the wood split."

With that, his mother brushed another tear from her cheek with the corner of her apron and gave her son another kiss on his forehead.

"Son, do you remember when we went to the big stone mountain last year? The mountain was spectacular, wasn't it? When you get back from law school, I want to go back and spend a few days and explore. It was one of the most beautiful places I've ever been in my life. I think I'd rather go there than Savannah or Charleston, to tell the truth. The mountain is one big round rock, isn't it? Surveyors told your father it rises almost seven hundred feet and is about five miles around. We could see it long before we arrived. It was huge, wasn't it?"

"Yes, ma'am. I remember. That was a lovely trip and I would love to go back anytime you want to. I've never seen anything like it," Ben said.

"Do you remember the Indians?" his mother asked. "They were camped all around. I think they were mostly Creek and Cherokee. It's their favorite meeting place, I understand. Anyone can find it. Your father says the mountain is considered a geological anomaly. It's made of quartz but not in layers like other mountains. Your father said he's never heard of a mountain formed like that anywhere in the world."

Ben listened patiently and was still a little embarrassed at his mother's formality of speech.

"Ben," his mother said pensively, not looking at her son's face, "I always thought the big stone mountain looked like a mixing bowl turned upside down on some giant woman's kitchen table. Do you remember the view from the top? I was astonished. I could see for miles and miles in every direction. It seemed as if God had covered the entire world in an endless carpet of trees—forests that went on and on forever. That view was one of the most beautiful things I've ever seen."

Ben's mother continued, as she stared into the distance remembering her trip, "Do you remember our hike up the mountain? On the top, right in the middle, was a flat spot where Indians were standing on a tall pile of stones looking this way and that. They stayed up there all day. I was never sure for what purpose. I remember we admired the view for while and came back down for lunch. Do you remember?" his mother asked.

"Of course I remember, Mother. I was so pleased Father took us. I'll never forget that trip."

His mother turned suddenly and looked Ben in the eye and held his gaze without blinking.

"Do you remember your father's warning as we hiked up the mountain? The Indians also warned us. Even Cassie's grandfather warned us before we left. He especially warned you. He knows how adventuresome you are. Do you remember?

"Yes, ma'am," Ben replied, a little nervously. "That was one of the most interesting things, Mother. One corner of the mountain has a gentle incline anyone can use to get to the top, but most of the mountain is rounded and completely inaccessible from the ground. Cassie's grandfather said the mountain is dangerous because its sides are not sheer but shaped like a round loaf of bread. The sides become imperceptibly steeper as a person walks from the top toward the nonexistent cliffside. I was surprised how Cassie's grandfather insisted in no uncertain terms that I not try to look over the side of the mountain."

"That's right," his mother said, "the mountain is deceptive—dangerously deceptive. The Cherokee say many have fallen to their death over the years trying to look over the side of the mountain. Foolishly, those men were looking for something which didn't exist—there was no cliff to look over. The imprudent, both white and Indian, have ignored good advice and fallen to their death. They should have listened to those of us who weren't born last night."

"Yes, ma'am," was all Ben could answer. His throat was dry.

"The day we visited we heeded the warnings. We stood on the top and enjoyed the spectacular view and went back down the way we came up. We took Cassie's grandfather's advice and chose the safe path. There are some things one can't risk in life."

His mother put her hands on Ben's knees and stared into his eyes.

"Sometimes you must take advice. There are some things you can't afford to find out for yourself, son. Some lessons are much too dangerous to learn the hard way."

His mother looked away and stared up at the white clouds floating in the crisp blue sky. She let her words sink deep into her son's mind. The air was perfect for sitting outside.

"The summertime clouds are beautiful, aren't they, Ben," his mother mused—still not looking at her son. "I've always loved the moderate weather here in Cherokee Country. The winters aren't too cold and the summers are lovely in the mountains, aren't they?"

With her gaze fixed on the clouds, she said in a soft voice, as if reflecting to herself. Her words caught Ben by surprise.

"If you had been on top of the stone mountain alone would you have ignored advice and tried to look over the edge?"

She slowly turned her face from the clouds and looked straight into his eyes once again. Ben lowered his eyes.

"I wonder, Ben, if you had been alone, would you have listened to advice or searched for the cliff edge?"

"No, ma'am, I wouldn't have tried to look over the edge," Ben responded. "You know I would obey you and Father—even if you weren't there."

Ben felt a quiver inside his chest as if he had told a lie. He knew he wasn't lying, but he also knew he had gone places and done things in the private thoughts of his mind against his parents' advice. The thought he might disobey his parents and look over the edge worried him.

His mother leaned and whispered with her face just a hand's breath from his, "Son, the mountain is innocuous on one hand and deadly on the other. Such is life. After today we won't be with you as you make your life's decisions. You'll be on your mountain alone. Some lessons in life are too dangerous to learn the hard way. Unbridled curiosity isn't from above. After you leave home, your friends may invite you to cross forbidden fences. After today, when your father and I aren't there, you'll have to rely on stored wisdom. We want the best for you today, tomorrow and long after your father and I have gone to our reward. What is true today will be true when you're an old man with grandchildren of your own."

His mother touched his shoulder and spoke in a normal voice, "Only a fool wants to experience everything for himself and ignore advice."

Ben was soaking in his mother's words.

"Son, never be tempted to see how close you can get to the edge."

"Yes, Ma'am," was all Ben could manage.

"For fourteen months you'll be in the company of unsupervised young men. Like little birds who fly from the nest for the first time, you'll want to test your wings. You must find out who you are. You'll want to suck the marrow out of life. There's nothing wrong with that, but remember—unbridled curiosity isn't from above. If it isn't from above, we know where it's from, don't we?

"Yes ma'am. Just because I'm away from home doesn't mean right and wrong have been altered."

"Exactly, Ben," his mother continued. "Turn a deaf ear to those who say, 'Let's look over the edge. Nothing bad will happen if we take a little peek. Your mother and father will never know. Let's have some fun? I won't tell your parents if you won't tell. Join me, Ben. No one will ever know.'

Ben's throat was dry. He couldn't have said a word if he wanted to. His mother's speech was unlike anything he had heard in his life. He felt as if he had been chewing cotton.

His mother sensed his tension. She patted his knee and gave him another kiss on his forehead.

"In a few weeks when you're in school far from home your friends will tempt you. They'll invite you to accompany them to the edge of your moral mountain. Be the same person then as you are now, Ben. Listen to stored wisdom. Never allow peers to bully you into stupid actions just because you're afraid of rejection. You'll never regret choosing the safe part of the mountaintop. Life should be enjoyed from the high ground, but there are forbidden pleasures. They're forbidden because they lead to death. They're called pleasures because they give a momentary pleasure, but it's a pleasure that leads to death. Never believe something is right because it feels good. When you're an old man you'll never regret good decisions. Live on the top where the best views are found. Don't let so-called friends lead you in a search for the nonexistent edge that leads to death."

His mother looked up once again at the beautiful clouds floating by in the hot August sky.

"Every night I pray to the Lord I might live long enough to hold my grandchildren—your children, Ben."

His mother paused again and looked her son in the eye.

"I want my grandchildren to have a good father. Experimentation with the forbidden destroys—like the use of tobacco or ardent spirits—you know about that. We've seen whiskey ruin white men and Cherokee alike, haven't we? I detest whiskey and I despise those who sell it. You know the story of Bear Paws? Unethical whites knew exactly what they were doing when they tempted Bear Paws and his friends."

His mother leaned over into his face once again with her hand on his knee, "Ben, if you walked slowly and carefully, would it be safe to look over the edge of the big stone mountain?"

His mother, looking deep into her son's eyes, waited for his answer.

Ben swallowed and swallowed again until he could speak.

"No, ma'am. No matter how slow and carefully a person places their feet, there is no edge and once a person slips they're gone."

"That's correct," his mother answered. "Live at the top and resist the forbidden. You'll discover the danger of some temptations only when you've gone too close. Unbridled curiosity is not from above. That's my advice. You have the good Book we gave you. Read it. Guard your heart. If you listen to us, life will only get better. You'll finish on the top of the mountain and leave the best of legacies for my grandchildren. You'll have good company on that mountain. Wilbur and I will be there. Your grandparents are there now."

Ben's mother leaned over and they embraced once again, and once again she kissed him on the forehead as she had done since he was a baby.

"Ben, I have one last thing to share with you," his mother said.

From the pocket of her apron, his mother handed him two strings of braided homespun cord.

"Ben, these are yours. Maybe you could use them to bookmark your Bible. These were the ties on the old apron I used to prepare your breakfast

240

this morning. I cut them off just before I walked out to talk to you. Son, you're no longer tied to my apron strings. These are yours now. You're no longer a child. You're a grown man. Remember who you are. Remember my advice. Keep these with you. Remember that from before you were born your father and I have always wanted the best for you."

Ben's mother was unable to continue. She held her son and buried her face against his shoulder. Ben felt her tears.

"I know I must let you go, but I wish you were a little boy again."

Ben's mother related to me the entire conversation. I agree with her advice. Edudu has been to the big stone mountain many times.

The day of Ben's departure was the saddest day of my life. Ben brought me to their house before daylight to share their last quick breakfast before Ben and his father left in the carryall for Milledgeville. Ben and I said little. It was a bittersweet parting. He held me for a moment then he and his father stuffed their provisions under the seat and they were ready.

"I promise I shall write often, as often as I can—I promise," Ben said.

"I shall miss you every day and every night. The day you return will be the happiest day of my life," I said.

After our brief goodbyes, Ben and his father headed down the road on Ben's great adventure. His mother and I held each other and continued waving long after Mr. Lowry's old carryall was out of sight. Ben will be gone for over a year. I have never experienced an emotion like this parting. I hope I never do again.

7 September 1824

Ben's first Letter - Savannah – 2 September 1824

My Dear Cassie,

The trip to Milledgeville with Father was lovely. I have met the other four boys who are traveling with me to Connecticut to law school. They're friendly and I'm sure we'll get along famously. We're looking forward to the sea journey. I have never been so excited. I can hardly sleep. On the journey to Milledgeville, Father gave me his advice. I shall share it with you. Along with my mother's advice, it's like the moral bookends on my life. On the first part of the journey Father and I talked of the beauty of Cherokee Country and Father's continuing work and the school. We discussed Greek, Latin, the Bible, history and politics—both ancient and modern. Finally, just before we arrived in Milledgeville, Father gave me his final word of advice. I want to share that with you.

"Son, the modern medical profession relies on Greek for their nomenclature and the legal profession uses Latin. Were you aware of that?"

"Yes, sir. Why is that, Father? I answered.

"You already know but allow me to rehearse. Rome established a strict legal system wherever their armies went. A Roman's legal rights were sacrosanct—protected by an extensive judicial system. We Europeans adopted the Roman legal system and thus we use Latin for our legal nomenclature. The words civil, citizen and civilized come from Latin. To be civilized means one has placed themselves under a body of regulating laws for the common good. You know, of course, the Romans controlled most of western Europe and even England."

"Oh, yes sir. I've read Gibbon, sir," I answered. "I have a good idea of how the Romans organized their government."

"Very good, son," Father continued. "The Romans concentrated on law. They had a highly developed legal system. The Greeks, who predate the Roman Empire by centuries, were curious about the physical world. We've adopted Greek in the nomenclature of medicine and science to a large part."

Father continued looking straight over the top of the horse's ears down the road and continued, "It's good you know so much Latin, Ben. You won't have any trouble with the vocabulary of law."

I could see a tear in Father's eye as he began to give his final advice.

"Your mother told me about her talk with you about the stone mountain. Your mother is wise. Do you want to hear my advice, son?"

I grinned thinking about Mother's advice and responded immediately, "Yes, sir. I would very much like your advice. I shall need it, Father."

Father's horse ambled along pulling the little carryall at a steady walking pace. Father and I swayed in unison on the high seat as the big wheels slowly trundled over the uneven roadway.

"You and I have split a lot of firewood, haven't we, son? In cold weather we would put a big backlog in the fireplace to last all evening, and then we split the smaller sticks and put them in front to make hot coals and throw out heat."

"Yes, sir," I answered. "I've carried many a backlog for you, sir."

"I appreciate your hard work, son," Father said. "You're a good young man. If you remember, when we have a nice red oak with a straight grain, we can split it with one smooth blow of an axe, right? Red oak is my favorite and I love the smell. The older oaks sometimes have a gnarled, twisted grain and we're required to use a hammer and wedge if we need to split them. We usually cut the logs with a twisted grain shorter to make them easier to split.

Remember that? Remember how hard it is to split poplar? We never did burn much poplar, did we?

"No, sir," I answered. "Poplar's impossible to split and worthless for burning. It pops and sparks all over the place."

Father laughed.

"Poplar is no good. I don't like it for lumber and I don't want one for shade either. I like the chestnut. Do you remember when we were splitting the long straight chestnut logs for rails? We chose the straightest trunks with the fewest limbs. We didn't want knots. We used steel wedges along with our big wooden persimmon wedges. Remember how patiently we worked to split those rails? You can't split a long log with one mighty blow, can you? Splitting fence rails requires time and patience—a wedge here and a wedge there—tap-tapping here and tap-taping there until the job is done. If you get in a hurry and hit a wedge too hard before it's in far enough, it'll jump and hit you between the eyes, won't it?"

As I was listening, I was already beginning to think of my parents' advice as moral bookends that would hold me upright through future temptations. It's a good analogy. It's good to think of my parents' ethics and morals supporting my character throughout my life.

"The sharp end of the wedge," Father continued, "has to go ever so slowly. We lightly tap-tap-tap the wedge into the log. After enough patient, soft tapping, we finally split the log with a big blow or two then cut any stringers with our axe."

"The log will easily split with patience, but not if you try to drive the wedge prematurely. When you were softly tap-tap-tapping the thin end of the wedge into the log, the wedge was hardly moving, right?"

"Yes, sir. It was hardly going into the wood at all. We've spent many long days splitting firewood and fence rails. I understand what you're describing perfectly, Father," I answered.

"Was it a waste of time and energy when we were barely striking the wedge with our hammer?"

"No, sir. It was not a waste of time. A soft tapping of the wedge is required to get the wedge deep enough to apply the final big blow that splits the log."

"That's right, son," Father continued. "With enough soft tapping for long enough, anyone can split a log with a twisted grain. You break down the resistance of a mighty oak with many small taps of the hammer. The thin end cannot split open the log but it opens the way for the thick end of the wedge. I can split the most difficult log in the world if you give me a hammer and wedge and allow me enough time. Son, beware the thin end of the evil wedge.

Never allow the thin end of evil to enter into your life. You can't toy with temptation. You can't play with fire."

Father stopped his old horse right in the middle of the road and looked me in the eye, "Son, beware the thin end of the wedge. Just like your mother told you, one of these days you're going to be around folk of dubious character. It could be next week—it could be next year or ten years from now. You'll not recognize these folks as dangerous. In fact, you may think of them as friends. They'll influence you using the same method we use to split the logs. They'll use friendship to slip the thin end of their immoral ways into your life to slowly change your views about right and wrong. Was Bear Paws hooked with only one drink?"

"No, sir," I answered. "Bear Paws took his first drink and kept drinking. Over time his drinking became uncontrolled."

"That's right, son," Father said. "Bear Paws made a choice over time. Neither Bear Paws or anyone else would begin with that nasty stuff if they knew the end of that path. Someone asked Bear Paws to take a drink of a harmless fluid that would make him feel good. That's the thin end of the wedge. That person who offered Bear Paws his first drink of alcohol will have a heavy price to pay one day. We humans don't seem to be afraid of death when it comes in small packages. Son, your friends will entice you, little by little, until they drive their wedge of temptation deep into your soul. They'll insert the thin end of their godless reasoning in an attempt to fracture your integrity. No one splits a log with one blow, and evil friends cannot destroy integrity in one blow either. You must be vigilant or you will not feel their tap-tap-tapping over time. You must guard your heart. If you allow the wedge to go deeper into your character, one day someone will ask you to do something you would have never considered earlier in life—and you'll do something you'll regret. After I leave you in Milledgeville, your mother and I will not be near to warn you of danger. You must recognize temptation and avoid it. From this day forward, you're in charge. You know the book you need to read every morning, don't you?"

"Yes, sir, I do," I answered proudly. "I read it every morning just like you and Mother do to reinforce your teaching."

Father stopped the horse in the middle of the road once again, "Keep reading, son. Read daily and guard the wellspring of your life. Your mother told me about her talk with you and her gift. I loved that. She's a wise woman. I have an additional gift for you."

While the horse was stopped Father took two short pieces of leather from his pocket, "Son, this morning before you rose, I cut a short piece of leather off the end of the reins of my old bridle—the one I've had since you were born. I tied the two pieces together. They're yours. From this day you hold the reins. Your mother and I have brought you this far. Our task is complete. We can take you no farther. I hand the reins to you. Ask our advice any time, but from this day forward you're a man. Keep these little bits of leather handy. From this moment on it's your job to recognize the thin end of the dangerous wedge. You hold the reins of your life."

The leather was quite a gift to go with mother's apron strings. Father's big dun was standing quietly in his harness totally unaware of the philosophical conversation in the carryall behind him. I watched the patient horse drive a yellow horsefly from his flank with an accurate swish of its long tail. The uncomplaining horse stood waiting—understanding nothing of wedges, temptation, wood or leather.

"Son," Father continued, "all men aren't good. Remember your raisin'. Don't allow a person of careless morals to tap-tap-tap a fissure into your character. Evil loves company. Evil men want to corrupt the innocent—like you. It gives them a sense of security and justifies their ways to themselves. It's as if corrupting your innocence vindicates their behavior. Evil people want everyone to become like them."

When Father finished, I was filled with determination. I committed myself to never allow anyone to divert me from the path I had learned at home. When we arrived at our destination, Father leaned back and retrieved a small package from under the oilcloth.

"Son, when I left home my parents gave me a new King James Bible. I read it every day. You have the one your mother and I gave you. Let it be the overarching guide of your life. You'll never go wrong reading that book. Your mother and I begin each day with the Lord. I can honestly say I have read my Bible every day since I met your mother."

And with that, Father handed me a thin package, "Unwrap it now, son and turn to the passage marked."

I opened the little package and inside was a small familiar volume of Shakespeare's Hamlet. I dutifully turned to the passage marked.

"Son," Father said, "you're about to leave your home and the safety you've enjoyed since birth. From this day our work as parents will be tested. Your mother and I have lived before you as well as we know how. Take this little volume and leave it on your table with the good Book—in full view. I'm giving you this to help you remember who you are."

And with this, Father quoted the passage from Hamlet by Polonius to his son, Laertes.

"This, above all, to thine own self be true, and it must follow, as the night the day, thou canst not then be false to any man. Farewell, my blessing season this in thee."

Tears came into my eyes and, without referring to the open page in front of me, I quoted back to Father the parting words of Laertes.

"Most humbly do I take my leave, my lord."

12 September 1824

6 September 1824 - Milledgeville

My Dear Cassie,

I can't wait to board the coaster in the morning and begin my great adventure and get back to you. I miss you terribly. I understand now why so many never leave home. I had intended to continue my studies on the trip, but everything is happening much too fast and is much too interesting to spend time reading. I am already friends with the four boys going with me to Litchfield. We'll have a grand time. Write soon. I'll post a letter immediately upon our arrival.

I can't wait to finish school and get back and go to work in Milledgeville on behalf of you and your people.

I'm missing you more than you can possibly know.

Your Ben Forever, xoxo

26 September 1824

Ben has arrived in Litchfield. I was shaking so much it took me forever to open his letter.

Saturday - 22 September 1824 – Litchfield, Connecticut

My Dear Cassie,

I loved the sea journey to New London. I had one thought the entire trip—that you should have been with me to share the voyage. One day we shall make that trip. You would love the journey. There is so much to see. I marveled how so few sailors could harness the wind and manage the little ship with cargo holds filled and the decks stacked with bales of cotton, timber, tobacco and huge hogsheads. It was incredible. I can understand the hold the sea has upon some men. If I were to decide not to become a lawyer, I would be a sea captain and sail around the world. I would visit the capitals of every nation. How grand that would be with you at my side.

246

I arrived in Litchfield this Saturday evening and was met by Mr. Gould. He showed me to my lodgings which I found small, spartan, but satisfactory. A country boy reared in the bucolic mountains of Cherokee Country needs little diversion beyond books and education. I could tell immediately Mr. Gould and I will get along famously. He is most kind and on first meeting discernably intelligent, like my father.

Our studies begin Monday morning early. I'm sure I'll have a dreadful time composing myself for sleep. I'm thinking of you and can't wait to receive a letter in return.

Impatiently yours, Your Ben Forever xoxo

19 November 1824

Ben's life is simple. His accommodations are spare and he has dedicated himself to study. He writes every week. I share his letters with his mother. Ben knows, as an only child, his mother and father will need his support in their declining years. No one works harder at his studies than Ben. He is a good man—a very good man. How slowly will the days pass before I see him once again.

Chapter XXII

1825 – Creeks Removed

Chapter 22

10 January 1825 - Month of the Cold Moon – Du no lv ta ni

My Dearest Ben,

I'm thinking about you so far away on your birthday. Do good work and you will soon be back here where you belong and I shall see your handsome face. I am impatient for your return. Wish you were here.

In the first light of dawn I woke to deep snow and shivering cold. I immediately thought of you. I have never seen snow so deep. As far as I can see into the forest and down toward the river the glistening snow is perfectly smooth—untrammeled by man or beast. There is not a footprint to be seen anywhere. Wish you were here.

As I marveled at the landscape before me, the bright sun peeked his rosy face over the hills into my window to welcome me to his glorious morning. He cast his dazzling sunbeams through the snow laden limbs of the forest revealing a carefully laid glistening blanket covering the entire earth. It was as if I alone was privileged to be present to observe a majestic jeweled landscape greater than any royal court. Wish you were here.

The snowy carpet has covered our world in a perfect fairy-tale panorama as if I were viewing a grand illustration drawn for children from the pages of Hans Christian Anderson. The birds and animals remain snuggled in their winter beds. They share my wonderment at the marvelous morning snowscape. All is silent. Wish you were here.

When I rose this morning, the silvery landscape made me think that during the night some marvelous magician covered all of earth's inequities with a welcomed incorruptible innocence. In one enchanted night he wrapped the entire world in perfect joy. Wish you were here.

I watched the tall stately trees, gifted with brilliant snow-covered limbs, bow to one another, proudly displaying to their neighbors their sparkling new winter garments. They posed in timeless gowns of sparkling diamonds—each flashing with a million facets in the bright morning sun. I watched as they paid homage to their creator in grateful modesty. The silent night's magician had spread before each stately tree a soft thick carpet so the trees would preserve their glittering white slippers and hose as they danced in the silvery light of dawn. Wish you were here.

Although the sun has risen, it's quiet—unusually quiet—as quiet as midnight. There is not a sound to be heard save the gentle crackle of the quiet fire behind me. There is not a cloud anywhere to be seen in the pale winter sky nor a breath of wind. For today, for this one day, the earth and everything in it has paused to consider what might have been. Even the songbirds have forgotten to share their morning melodies. From the lofty fastness of their cozy nests they marvel at the winter landscape spread below. This morning provides its own eternal music. It needs no serenade. Wish you were here.

The rough brown earth of yesterday has been cleansed and pressed and grandly presented for me alone to enjoy. This impossible task was accomplished in one night by our divine enchanter. Wish you were here.

The glistening icicles, hung for our pleasure by our heavenly glassmaker, suspend from the eaves like fiery gems in the morning sun, brilliantly adorning the corners of our home—now become a mighty castle. There is a purity in the air. The cold, the peace, the silence bestow an indescribable wholesome innocence—as if, at least for one day, the vestments of corruption have disappeared and our world has been clothed in perfect serenity. It is as if the pure mercy of God bestowed this flawless gift to me alone—a perfect morning given by heaven itself. Wish you were here.

Elisi and edudu are enjoying the wondrous morning as we breakfast in front of our cheery fire. As I write, I smell bacon sizzling. What a beautiful land this is. It is the most beautiful of all lands. I can't imagine living anywhere but here. I want this day to last forever. This winter's day I'm thinking of you with every stroke of my pen. The one deficiency of this glorious day is your absence. Hurry home.

Sending you all my love forever, Cassie xoxo
Wish you were here.

11 January 1825

The snow is melting. It will soon be gone. Perhaps it will come again this year or maybe next. Were it my choice, I would have snow more often. Edudu and elisi do not like to get out in the snow. Although he doesn't like the snow, he says it will make the corn grow taller and greener this year. Yesterday I walked in the snow through the meadows and woods to enjoy the winter scenes. I felt like my footprints spoiled the work of a great artist. It was the most beautiful landscape I have ever seen in my life.

16 January 1825

Mr. Lowry wants me to write of our relationship with the whiteside. He gives me newspapers, the *Georgia Journal, Federal Union, Southern Recorder* and others from places like Charleston, Nashville or Washington City.

This following letter was on the front page of the *Southern Recorder*. I observe war is centrally important to whites. They devote an entire portion of government to war and give war its very own secretary.

> "...The organization of the Indian Department has been much improved in the course of the year; the beneficial effects...already apparent...by improving the condition of the various tribes...Already 32 schools have been established in the Indian nations, and, for the most part are well conducted...and cannot fail to effect a beneficial change in this condition of this unhappy race."

I read this to edudu.

"Walela," edudu said, "whites believe they alone experience happiness. They must think us a woeful race indeed if they say such things about us. They must think our only wish is to become white."

"Why do they believe us unhappy, edudu. I don't understand. We are happy. We're always happy. We love where we live and how we live. We don't want to go elsewhere or change anything about our life and we don't want to become white."

"Walela, whites are proud. Their lives are filled with things and with an unquenchable desire to acquire wealth. They are self-righteous because they know how to make things. They believe knowing how to make things makes them superior. The believe discovering things about this world is the equivalent of wisdom. They don't understand how anyone who isn't white can be happy."

Edudu laughed.

"Why do you laugh, edudu?"

"I laugh at the whites. They must believe themselves the only people of worth. They are an unhappy people from an unhappy land. The land they left must be a gloomy land indeed.

21 January 1825

I would love to cross the ocean in thirty-eight days. I would love to see London, Paris and Madrid with Ben. One day he and I will cross that ocean.

Copied from the *Southern Recorder* – 18 January 1825

"Charleston - January 7…the ship Sarah & Caroline arrived here yesterday in 38 days from Liverpool.

24 January 1825

I found these two opposing newspaper articles. This makes clear the value whites put upon their stock—their property.

Copied from the *Southern Recorder* – 18 January 1825 – page 4

"10 Dollars Reward. Runaway from the subscriber, living in Sandersville, on the 8th November last, a negro fellow SAM, 22 years of age, about 5 feet 8 or 9 inches high, remarkably stout built and well formed, dark complection, has worked some at the Blacksmith's trade, and plays well on the fife. Any person who will deliver said negro to me, or lodge him in any jail, shall receive the above reward and all reasonable expenses paid. WM. HARGROVE. December 10"

Copied from the *Southern Recorder* – 25 January 1825 – page 3

"50 Dollars Reward. Stolen out of the stable of the subscriber at Easley's Cowpens, Walton county, on the night of the 7th instant, A Bay Gelding about 16 hands high, shod all round, 8 years old, his two hind feet white about halfway to the hock joint, and white snip on his nose and part of his face, trots and paces, handsomely nicked, and is a fine looking horse; works very nicely in harness; and has some marks of them—he was raised by Matthew Carswell, of Wilkinson county. I will give a reasonable reward for the horse, or information so I can get him,

251

and the above reward for the conviction of the thief. THOMAS W. HARRIS.

26 January 1825

My Dearest Ben,

Today a new girl named Virginia came to Mr. Lowry's school. She is sweet and smart and likes to be called Ginger. Today is her birthday. I shall make her a pine basket and fill it with good things. Ginger has a wonderful way with animals much like edudu. I'll ask edudu to carve a center for her basket in the shape of an animal. Perhaps Ginger and I can make a pine basket together.

19 February 1825

The white president, James Monroe, thinks we should be removed. Copied from the *Georgia Journal* - 15 February 1825, page 2

"...the removal of the Indian tribes from the lands which they now occupy within the limits of the several states and territories, to the country lying westward...is of very high importance to our Union, and may be accomplished on conditions and in a manner to promote the interest and happiness of those tribes..."

"For the removal of the tribes within the limits of the state of Georgia, the motive has been peculiarly strong, arising from the compact with the state, whereby the United States are bound to extinguish the Indian title to lands within it...In fulfillment of this compact, I have thought the United States should act with generous spirit...the removal of the tribes from the territory which they now occupy...would accomplish the object for Georgia under a well digested plan for their government and civilization which should be agreeable to themselves would not only shield them from impending ruin but promote their welfare and happiness...in their present state it is impossible to incorporate them, in such masses, in any form whatever, into our system...it will be difficult, if not impossible, to control their degradation and extermination will be inevitable."

"...the removal proposed is not only practicable, but that the advantages attending to it, to the Indians, may be made so apparent to them that all the tribes, even those opposed, may be induced to accede...to...make them a civilized people, is an object of very high importance...by the establishment of such a government over these tribes, by their consent, we become, in reality, their benefactors...There will be no more war...Accepting such a government their movement will be in harmony with us and its good effect be felt throughout the whole extent of our territory, to the Pacific."

A speech delivered to congress on 27 January 1825.

If we are exterminated, it will be they who are the exterminators. I wish they would go away. I wish they had never come. President Monroe speaks of our impending ruin. If we are ruined, it will be by white hands. They don't want to share. They want everything.

I look at my arms, hands and feet and wonder what it is about me that is so detestable in white eyes? Do I have an evil shape or horrible odor? Is something wrong with my hair, eyes or skin? Do I appear to them as a malicious fiend? They want to become our benefactor. They choose to benefit us by making us disappear from their presence. We've lived happily before they came. We can be happy without the benefits they provide. I don't think they are benefactors. They believe only they have a right to exist freely and prosper. Perhaps one day they shall reap what they sow.

Copied from the *Georgia Journal* - 15 February 1825

"...resolved...the committee on Indian affairs be instructed to enquire into the expediency of making an appropriation for the extinguishment of the Indian title to land lying in the state of Georgia..."

"The president...has connected the performance of the obligations of the United States to Georgia, with the great plan of collecting all the Indians in our Western territory, for the purpose of civilizing them."

When edudu heard this, he said something ugly.

"Is there no justice, Walela? Do the powerful go unpunished forever?"

"Mr. Lowry said the whites behave like the Romans," I answered. "They view everything as Victori Spolia. They believe they have the right to dominate and be privileged above all others because they are stronger."

Edudu laughed cynically.

"Whites are like men who steal from children and boast about their theft," edudu said, and went inside.

The Creeks have a treaty with the general government and thus with all the states—even Georgia. The Creeks have had many treaties, as we have.

Governor Troup believes the general government does not understand Georgia's need for land.

Governor Troup threatened the Creeks with war if they did not agree to Georgia's terms—convincing some to sign the treaty. The missionaries say that both the negotiations and treaty with the Creek are a sham. Georgia wants to make their seizure of Indian land appear legal. Mr. Lowry says it's what strong countries do, divide et impera—divide and rule. The Romans conquered and subjected everyone and all according to law.

Copied from the *Georgia Journal* - 15 February 1825

"We invite the attention of the people of Georgia to the message of Mr. Monroe...It is based on principle which will be approved by philanthropists everywhere...Hence it is contended...that the discharge of these obligations (the compact of 1802)...should be made a separate and distinct matter, claiming the FIRST and undivided attention of the general government."

Ben is gone. The proud Creek Nation is being removed. I am surrounded by those who covet my homeland and demand my removal. Only my future with Ben gives me reason to continue—to have hope.

25 February 1825

I long for Ben's return. Perhaps we are wasting time negotiating with the whites. Some say we should remove peacefully while we can. Elisi and edudu are too old to leave the only home they have ever known. I don't understand how they can force us to leave. I will never leave elisi and edudu. I yearn for my mother's comfort. When I walk by their graves, I wonder what they looked like. How would it have been if they had lived? What would they look like now? How would I be different?

27 February 1825

While Ben has been in law school, political events in Georgia have moved fast. Governor Troup, a supporter of Andrew Jackson, is a proponent of the removal of all Indians—not just the Creek.

Older men say the worst thing we ever did was allow whites to build roads. Allowing roads gives permission to invade, edudu says.

Troup's cousin, William M'Intosh, a Creek chief, signed the treaty to give away all Creek land and in return received a large sum of money. We say it was a bribe. The treaty said Georgia purchased Creek land. Immediately upon signing the treaty the Georgia Militia forced the remaining Creeks to remove—even the ones who didn't want to give away their house and farm and go out west.

Where will they go? What will their women do? Where will their children play? Where will they grow corn? Why couldn't they live on their ancestral land? Edudu thinks we, too, will be forced to leave. All Creek land will be given away by lottery—to whites only. Civilization and soil belong to whites. Whites make all laws to serve themselves. Whites are the trouble makers. They shall arrange we inherit nothing but the wind.

According to edudu, the Creeks do not recognize William M'Intosh, the governor's cousin, as their legal representative in the new treaty. There will be trouble. Governor Troup's corruption is obvious, even to whites.

However, what Troup did is considered legal within Georgia. Georgia has what it wants—a piece of paper with signatures which gives them the right to dispossess by force. William M'Intosh is rich. Troup and his political friends are happy. The Creeks homeless. If the whites want something, they make a law to get it—exactly as the Romans did.

Horseshoe Bend severely weakened the Creek Nation and now the Creeks are helpless. Edudu understands. He said it would be better to die honorably defending one's nation than have our flesh slowly flayed from our bones. Edudu said not one Cherokee would have participated in that war if they knew that all the white promises were false. Edudu said he should have fought for the Creek rather than against them.

The missionaries say the treaty of Indian Springs will be rescinded, but edudu says it's too late. Creek land has been surveyed and the lottery is in place.

Ben does not like the way Milledgeville justifies all their actions. Over a million acres of Creek land have been transferred to Georgia ownership. One day, edudu says, the English will come for our land.

8 May 1825

The Creek chief sold his nation for personal gain and now William M'Intosh is dead—murdered. Edudu said it was an execution. He said he would have killed him himself for signing away all the Creek land without the tribe's permission. Whites don't understand. Our land doesn't belong to us—we belong to the land. Where will we be without our land?

Copied from the *Southern Recorder* – 31 May 1825 - page 3

"...The bill for disposing of the lately acquired territory (from the Creeks) by lottery, it is expected will pass the House of Representatives...in the course of the week..."

This is an excerpt of a letter by Governor Troup.

Copied from the *Southern Recorder* - 14 June 1825 – page 1

"The crime of M'Intosh...is...in the wise and magnanimous conduct which...produced the Treaty of the 12 of February, and which, in making a concession of their whole country, satisfied the just claims of Georgia; reconciled the state to the Federal Government and made happy...the Creeks..." G.M. Troup

"Walela, we never needed lawyers and courthouses," edudu said. "Whites fuss with everyone. Every Cherokee family enjoys our land as far as our eyes can see. We are one. Whites can't see past their fence. We have no need of fences. Georgia has no just claim over our land. How could people from across the ocean have a claim on our land? How could that possibly be legal? I don't think it was magnanimous of the Creek chief to give away all his people's land, as the Georgia governor said. How can invaders, who can't speak our language, ever have a just claim?

22 June 1825

Alabama is removing all Indians. The Creeks, Choctaw and Chickasaw will, in their turn, be extinguished. To extinguish our right to land is the same as taking our life. Soon, we Cherokee will be alone. Hurry home, Ben.

Andrew Jackson and his Volunteers boast they have rid themselves of savages. Maybe it is they who are the wild and untamed ones. Maybe our leaders can find a solution in Washington City. Maybe Ben, with his law degree, can help. Maybe the designs Georgia has upon our land will be defeated or at least deflected.

24 June 1825

I love how Ben thinks of me even when he is far away.

My Dear Cassie,

I miss you terribly. I wish you here. You would love the school and my friends. You and I could explore the surrounding lovely landscapes together.

I shall benefit greatly from the constant intellectual atmosphere and uninterrupted hours of study. I love everything here except your absence and the impossible distance between us.

I study night and day. Perhaps, if I work harder, I can emulate the work ethic of the Grimm brothers and speed my return. I have avoided frivolity. My main recreation is correspondence with you and my sketch book. I read the Scriptures in the morning. Gibbon's Decline and Fall is my companion in the late hours. I use his exact prose as a tonic to settle my busy mind. His scholarly texts and I are old friends I have known since childhood.

I cannot express my excitement about the school and my future. As Father correctly assessed, I am advantaged by my knowledge of Latin. Law uses Latin almost exclusively for its technical nomenclature. I find it sad to think of the death of the Latin language yet Latin lives in our law—in our civilization. Roman law, the mortar of their empire, to this day pervades Europe and has flowed across the ocean to America centuries after Rome's glory days. Quite remarkable, don't you think?

I cannot wait to tell you everything. I cannot wait until my time here is complete and I return to you. I am bursting with impatience. I must see you. Until that day, I shall long each waking moment to be in your welcome presence and bask in the radiance of your glow, Your loving Ben, xoxo

Mr. Lowry shared with me some of the Latin words Ben will use in law. Bona Fide—something in good faith, Caveat Emptor—let the buyer beware, De Facto—in fact, Flagrante Delecto—caught in the act, Corpus Delecti—it must be proven a crime has been committed, Per Diem—per day, Pro Bono—for the public good and usually means a fee will not be charged, Sine qua non—without which it cannot be, Non-Sequitur—it does not necessarily follow, Quid Pro Quo—a favor granted and expected in return—you scratch my back and I'll scratch yours. The politicians in Milledgeville understand that last one. Mr. Lowry talks about victori spolia. I suspect whites also perfectly understand that phrase.

I enjoy Latin. Ben and I are like two peas in a pod. I miss his face and the sound of his voice. I shall burst asunder if I don't see him soon.

18 June 1825

My Dear Ben,

I have included a newspaper clipping. Do good work and hurry home. This article is worrisome. You are needed. If whites find it so easy to take the entire Creek Nation, they will take ours. We need an advocate—an advocate like you. Hurry home.

Copied from the *Southern Recorder* – 14 June 1825 - page 2

"Be it enacted by the Senate and House of Representatives of the State of Georgia…that the territory acquired of the Creek Nation of Indians…shall be divided…after surveying…the governor shall cause tickets to be made…which tickets shall be put into a wheel and constitute prizes…"

I love the way your passion grows. I can feel your developing maturity. I cannot wait to see our future unfold.

With all my love, Cassie xoxo

Although he hasn't proposed marriage, I want more than anything to be Ben's wife, bear him a dozen children and see our grandchildren grow into successful productive adults. I want each child to look like my beloved, have his eyes and be as clever as he is. We will have our own school and fill our home with books.

19 June 1825

I remember the first time I saw Ben. The joy springing from his eyes pierced my soul. I knew, even as a child, I would love him forever. My love has grown. I wish he were here.

19 August 1825

Mr. Lowry believes this article reflects white thinking throughout Georgia.

Copied from the *Southern Recorder* - 9 August 1825 - page 1

"Was it unbecoming in him (Governor Troup) to ask…the removal of the Indians and the possession of our public lands— lands which were ours, before the union, by conquest, and since, by purchase--for which we had fought and for which we had paid. Who believes that it was treasonable…to say that our negros should not be wrested from us…? What is dearer to us than *property*?…Is he blameworthy for his indefatigable efforts to obtain the possession of the land, and to effect as early a settlement as possible?...The lands on the border states have been acquired and the consequence is, the Indians have been thrown in upon us...presenting the odious alternative, to be acknowledged an independent nation, in our very bosom, or to be incorporated in colour, and identified in privilege, with the Georgians...this glaring outrage is...forced upon us under the hypocritical cant of Christian benevolence...Can the United States seriously entertain...Georgia will submit to this? Do they believe our people will consent to mix with that unfortunate race?...that they ought to remain in the very heart of the state, a sovereign and independent nation, a sanctuary for villainy and a harbor for renegade outlaws and refugee slaves?" Atticus

Do I smell bad? Does my Cherokee visage hurt their eyes? Does my voice grate? Why do they call me names? Why do they forbid our children to play with theirs? Why hate us so?

12 September 1825

My Dear Cassie,

I love the endless hours I am allowed for reading here in Connecticut. I have few chores here but I miss the routine of home. I miss Mother's cooking most of all. Other than that, and the fact that I can't be with you, I am perfectly happy spending long hours preparing for my career. Do not worry. As Father says, "Yesterday was the best day of his life and today is already better".

I remember your grandfather's advice about complaints and complainers. I do not complain and I avoid keeping company with anyone who does. I understand his advice clearly now. We have two students who complain about everything. They darken the day when they enter the room. I miss you and can't wait to see your face. Loving you always, Ben xoxo

11 October 1825

It would be great fun to ride on a steamboat. I want to see it travel up river against the current.

From the *Southern Recorder* – 27 September 1825 - page 2

"Steamboats on the Ocmulgee and Oconee...a steamboat and four tow boats, will run constantly from Savannah to Macon and Milledgeville, stopping at the intermediate landings for the reception and delivery of Produce and Merchandize on Freight. The steamboat is now ready...starting on her first trip from Savannah on the fifteenth day of October next...they will be prepared to receive cotton...direct without the delay of landing and reloading in Darien...John T. Lamar Macon – G. B. Lamar – Savannah."

12 November 1825
Copied from the *Georgia Journal* – 8 November 1825 – Page 2

"One thing is certain—the contract with the state of Georgia must be fulfilled. The Indians must be removed, 'peaceably if they can—forcibly if they must,"...it only requires energy on the part of the government...A very high obligation is imposed upon the Federal Government to relieve the Southern States of their Indian population. In this respect the North and South are upon a very unequal footing—the Northern States...exterminated their Indians before they became partie to the Federal Constitution...Not so in the south...Georgia, Alabama, Mississippi and Louisiana are covered by an Indian population which contribute nothing to the wealth of the states, and subtract from their strength by the necessity of watching them. The Federal government alone can put these states on an equal footing with those in the North, and it is the duty of the Government to do so. We would enquire if these gentlemen had forgotten the manner in which the Indians were got rid of in the Northern States?...we would beg them to refresh their memories by reading...from their own histories...'The government increased the premium for Indian scalps and captives to one hundred pounds...This encouraged John Lovewell to raise a company of volunteers to go out upon and Indian hunting'....After reading this...we would ask which is the most humane—to remove Indians from Georgia by treaty to a country west of the Mississippi...or exterminate them under a law..."

Whites view us as an invasive species of insufferable varmints. They wish for our immediate removal—extinguishment is the word they use in their official documents. I wonder how it will feel to be exterminated?

Chapter XXIII

1826 - The Sketch Book

Chapter 23

2 June 1826 - The Green Corn Moon – De ha lu yi

Mr. Lowry brought a magnificent letter. Ben is coming home. I'm giddy with excitement. Hurry home Ben.

18 June 1826

Words cannot express the simple joy I experienced sitting with Ben on elisi's porch and listening to his voice—a joy so long denied. He would ask a question, but I would fail to answer—as if I didn't hear him speak. He laughed at my inattention.

"Ben, you are taller and more handsome than I remember."

"I don't know about that, Cassie, but I know you're lovelier than I remember and I don't see how that's possible since you were the most beautiful woman in the world when I left."

We laughed at one another. I was excited to be looking at Ben—to hear his voice and touch him.

"Tell me about school. Tell me about your friends. Tell me what you learned. I want to know everything. Start from the beginning and leave nothing out."

"Cassie, I've written you so many letters you already know everything. I wrote you more letters on more sheets of paper than I wrote assignments. I wrote you a book, didn't I?" Ben replied.

"And I kept every letter," I said smiling.

"Well, there's one thing you don't know," Ben continued. "Please forgive my boasting. I graduated first in my class. I wanted to tell you that in person. I'm proud of that, but I'm not sure it was such a grand accomplishment. I had a distinct advantage. When I arrived I was far ahead in vocabulary. My language skills were superior, thanks to my parents. I was ahead in both Latin and Greek. I studied more than most of the others, too. For the most part, my classmates didn't know how to study and manage time effectively and they couldn't read nearly as fast as I read."

"You underestimate yourself, Ben, but that's the kind of answer I would expect. Everyone is proud of what you've done. We never doubted your success. Even edudu, elisi and their friends are as proud of you as if you were a Cherokee boy. Your father is right. Language skills are the single most important thing a parent can teach their child—except for teaching morality, of course. Your mother told me she began teaching you to read about the same time you learned to walk. I wish I had started that early. You have the best parents, Ben. They've been good to you and our people and have never asked anything in return. Their unselfishness has made an impression around here. I have a marvelous education because of your parents."

"I give my parents the credit for my success, Cassie," Ben said. "Without them, I would have ended up a farmer. What a thought. Here's something else I haven't told you. I received a commendation from the State of Connecticut for graduating first in my class. That commendation included a job offer in Hartford. I had no idea how easy it is for a trained lawyer to get a job. Each of my fellow students had multiple job offers upon graduation. Governments all over the United States were seeking to hire my classmates. North Carolina, Virginia, Maryland and South Carolina also offered me a job. There aren't nearly enough trained lawyers in the United States. Our developing legal system is different than England, France or Germany. I'm excited to be a part of that growth. I'm going to enjoy the legal profession, Cassie."

I was loving listening to Ben's voice. I didn't want to interrupt and my wish was that he would never stop talking to me.

"I turned down all those jobs, and you know why. I want to work here in Georgia. I want to do something good for the Cherokee and be close to you. I couldn't bear to be away from you one more day. During the entire trip home, I had one overriding thought. I wanted to see you—to see your face and hear your voice. It's hard to explain. I wanted to be with you, my parents and your people. I want to be here—nowhere else. Those were lucrative jobs I was offered, but I like to think my soul is not for sale. I want to imitate my parents. Money will never be first in my life. There are adventures enough right here where I can see you whenever I want."

I laughed and leaned against Ben's shoulder.

"Your parents don't have a selfish bone in their body, do they, Ben? Their generosity has rubbed off on you. Whatever happens, you and I will find happiness. You're my best friend. I'll wait for you another fourteen months or fourteen years. I'll wait for you forever. I'm so glad you are home and you can go to work doing what you've been trained to do."

19 June 1826

Ben rode over to see me and left a special gift.

"I can't stay long, Cassie. Mother's preparing a special meal and sent me to ask if you would eat with us and spend the afternoon? We would love to have you."

"Of course I'll come. I would love to," I answered.

"Great, I knew you would," Ben replied. "I have a special gift for you. I was a little embarrassed to give you this in my parents' presence. I suppose I didn't want them to see it or at least see me give it to you. It's something unique just for you. I know it sounds juvenile, but I wanted this to be between us."

Ben took a small folio from his saddlebag.

"You probably don't remember," Ben said, "but a few days before I left for school, we were down by the river in your special place and I recited a list of things I liked about you—things I love about you, actually. It was a long list. Do you remember? We had a great time that day. We talked about everything."

"Of course, I remember," I answered. "I know what you like. You like our friendship, our common love of words, language and learning. We like many of the same foods. You love our long conversations—that sort of thing? Right?"

"You don't remember, do you?" Ben said with a big grin. "You've forgotten, you silly girl. On my way here, I wondered if you would remember. While I was in Connecticut, when I was exceptionally lonely and needed a break from my studies, I would sketch in charcoal to clear my mind. The inspiration for those sketches often came from that single afternoon when we had the picnic on your big rock by the river. I have often rehearsed the list of things I liked about you that day. Do you remember? As I would sketch, I would challenge my memory to call up the finest details of your body—of specific parts of your body I have committed to memory. I sketched in detail the things about you from that day."

"I recall now," I said. "I remember that day. You are so sweet to remember."

Ben was excited as he explained and handed me the sketch book.

"I've never forgotten that list I recited to you that day, Cassie. Look here. The more I thought about you, the more I wanted to sketch. I had to sketch. It was the only way I could feel close to you. I had the most horrible sensation in my chest being away from you week after week—unable to talk to you. The only thing that allowed me to conquer my loneliness was the thought I was doing right by being in school and sketching that list. Drawing the things I love about you became an ongoing project. When I was so impossibly far from you, drawing became the tonic to ease my mind and give relief. When I felt that dreadful pressure building in my chest, the charcoal sketches brought you near. In my mind I was able to touch you."

When I saw Ben's sketch book I was astonished. He had sketched parts of my body from memory in simple line drawings with uncanny precision and perfect perspective and shading. I never knew he possessed this remarkable skill—and all from memory. The first drawing was of my nose and nothing else. The second was my eyes alone—no other part of my face. The third was a profile of one of my feet and so on. There were three dozen beautiful charcoal sketches of different parts of my body in different poses. Each drawing was in perfect detail and all from that single day. I was amazed. Of all the romantic things Ben has done, this is the most special.

The last image was sketched from quite a distance behind. In the drawing I was sitting on my rock with my knees pulled up to my chest. My chin was resting on my arms as I pensively stared out over the river. My hair hung in a single long braid down my back.

I was unable to speak.

"Cassie, these sketches are yours," Ben said. "They're my gift to you. They're a permanent marker of my affection. Now that I have you to look at, I don't need them. Besides, I have them in my mind. I could draw you from memory a hundred years from now. I'll never forget you, Cassie. Come on. Let's go home. I'm hungry."

19 June 1826

I'm so happy Ben is home. I guess absence does make the heart grow fonder because I love him more than before he left. When he was gone, it was as if a part of me was missing. When the English are lonely, they say to their loved one, "I miss you", but the French say, "you are missing from me".

Ben was very much missing from me and I understood when he tried to describe the painful ache in his chest. My longing for Ben sometimes felt as if an unrelieved weight was crushing my body. It was a darkness that filled my insides. It was an internal physical torment that grew daily. My loneliness was an unfulfilled yearning enlarged by time, as if my life was being squeezed from me simply because of the absence of my love.

20 June 1826

From the moment Ben returned, he has been a nuisance. He follows his mother around like a puppy dog. He does chores before she asks. Mrs. Lowry said he took out the ashes five times yesterday and went to the spring when water wasn't needed. He does all the feeding for his father and his mother has mounds of kindling. There is no place like one's home surrounded by loved ones. I would not want to be away from elisi for fourteen months. I fully understand.

21 June 1826

This is an editorial about the latest treaty with the Creeks.

Copied from the *Georgia Journal* – June 13 1826 – page 1

"The Indians, by the late treaty, will be restricted to a district…so narrow that they must steal, beg, or starve for they will not work…the cattle, hogs…of the border Alabamians will be laid under heavy contributions to support these idle vagabonds. How much more humane would it have been…to have removed the Indians over the Mississippi where they could have lived in their wild roving manner."

Georgia has stolen a million acres from the Creek Nation and they brazenly accuse the Creeks of being thieves. It would be humane for whites to leave us alone. How could it be humane to remove us across the Mississippi?

20 June 1826

Ben and I had a long, wonderful day together. We walked in silence and other times laughed about old memories. We're always discussing the future. Being in Ben's presence gives the most pleasant sensation—a sense of peace—as if the next moment and every day thereafter will be better.

We walked to the river holding hands, talking and laughing.

"I must tell you, Cassie, I missed Mother's cooking every day I was away but it wasn't my mother's cooking I longed for most of all. It was you I missed more than anything when I was in Connecticut," Ben said.

I thought my heart would beat out of my chest at Ben's words. I playfully jumped into his arms, threw my arms around his neck and he cradled me like a child. That was fun.

"Ben, you can tell me things like that anytime," I said playfully as he held me like an infant. "The way you express your longing is most romantic. I remember the first time we were together after you got home. You told me you wanted to hold me and kiss me every day you were away. We have matured, haven't we? We're not the same children we were before you left—our relationship has grown."

"I want to make you happy, Cassie," Ben said, as he put me down. "That's what I think about. After I get a job I'll save so we can set up housekeeping. We'll be together. I promise you that. I want to make you the happiest woman in the world."

He tenderly touched my arms and hair as we stood in the warm sunlight at the opening to my place by the river. I watched his eyes glowing with his love. He held me and buried his face in my hair and inhaled deeply. It made me shiver.

He held me at arm's length and stared at me.

"Cassie, when I was away I can't describe the horrible feeling I had not being able to see you. When I walked into town with my classmates I would do my best to catch a glimpse of a woman who looked like you. Even the smallest resemblance to you would have been a vision that would have momentarily satisfied my heart. In all the time I was away I never saw such a woman."

"I would imagine myself holding you. I would imagine the texture of your skin and, as you can see in the sketch book, I remembered what you looked like—every part of you, but for the life of me, no matter how hard I tried, I couldn't imagine your fragrance or the smell of your hair. I knew you smelled refreshing and alive, but I couldn't remember your scent. Isn't that strange? I remembered everything else about you. I remembered the musical quality of your voice and every detail of the shape of your hands and feet, but I couldn't remember your fragrance. I could remember the smell of my mother's cornbread, but not the smell of your hair."

Ben, holding me gently by my shoulders, paused for a long time staring into my eyes.

"Cassie, I want to inhale the scent of your body every time I'm with you so I'll never forget again. I want to remember everything about you. I want to experience everything about you. When I hold you, your fragrance is like a field of brilliant wild flowers in the morning sun."

Ben buried his face in my hair once again. I heard him inhale and I collapsed into his arms, "Ben, you are more romantic than ever. I love the way you smell, too. I always have."

I put my arms around his neck and whispered, "You know what I imagine about you?"

"Tell me, Cassie. I would love to know. Tell me."

"Don't think me silly, but I remember the freshness of your breath, your white teeth, your playfulness and the sunlight reflecting off your hair. I love your hands and arms. I love the soft melody of your voice, but my favorite memory of all is when you hold me tight and I lay my head on your chest and feel your heart beating. That's my favorite memory. That's the thing I think of before I sleep. When you hold me that way, it's as if we are one. Feeling your beating heart is my favorite memory of all."

As we sat looking out over the river I said, "Ben, I have read how men and women express their love in literature and I have seen love in my community. Now I am experiencing romance with you. I yearn to be with my beloved. I want to know my beloved feels the same."

Later, when I tried to describe my love for Ben to elisi, her face beamed.

"My dear, Walela," elisi said, "I have long known of your love for Ben. You wear his love like an ornament. A woman cannot conceal her love for her man. A man completes a woman's soul. A woman's feeling of fulfillment is one of life's great joys. Your desire for your beloved will grow. The love between a man and a woman is like a tree. As it grows over the years, the branches spread and the roots go deep. The tree becomes tall and strong to resist storms. Ben completes the joy of your youth as nothing can. Your edudu and I had that love when young, but our love has grown. Our love has matured into a magnificent tree that provides refreshing shade with roots strong and deep—roots so deep no tempest can harm us."

Elisi caressed my hair as she spoke softly of her love for edudu.

"I cannot tell you precisely how your love will grow, but it will grow. No two trees are exactly the same. Each day with your love will be happier than the last—that I know. I am glad for you, Walela. Your Ben is a good man and will be a good husband. Come to me and tell me what is in your heart, child— anytime day or night. Nothing gives me more pleasure than to know you have a man to love—a man to make you complete."

Elisi continued, "Times will come when you will need to talk. I'm here to listen. Your edudu and I have weathered many storms. Our love is strong and deep. My grey hair is earned, my dear Walela. I can help you understand those days when your heart is confused and doesn't agree with your head."

Elisi held me close and I recalled the security I felt as a little girl. I will love Ben with the same love I have seen between elisi and edudu. I will fill his life with devotion. Our roots will grow deep.

22 June 1826

Another grand day with Ben. The birds sang to us under a magnificent sky. The sun held us in his arms. I wouldn't want to live anywhere else than here in our country. I wouldn't want to love anyone other than Ben.

We walked.

Ben's arm was tight around my waist.

"Cassie, when I look at you, I remember a story my father told me long ago. Would you like to hear that old story?"

"I love your father's stories. I have great respect for his wisdom."

I listened.

"Father and I were on our saddle horses riding to a preaching engagement," Ben said. "We rode the trail side by side. I remember our horses were walking easy and slow with their heads down. It was a beautiful sunny day. As we rode along Father told me a story I didn't understand—well, I didn't understand it until I came back from Connecticut. Now I understand him perfectly."

"I'll explain. Father's story goes like this. In the Mishnas and the Gemaras, the Jewish commentaries on the Hebrew scriptures, the rabbis warn their students of the dangers of women. 'Never look directly into the eyes of a woman,' the old rabbis cautioned. 'A woman can seduce the unwary soul' the rabbis warned. 'Under no circumstances risk looking into her eyes', they said."

"I remember Father paused as if the story were finished," Ben continued. "I was curious and, as my father planned, I asked why the rabbis warned their students against looking into a woman's eyes. 'What could be dangerous about a woman's eyes', I asked my father?"

"I remember my father chuckled before he replied, 'Son, that's a good question, a good question indeed. I'll tell you the answer. A woman's eyes are her greatest weapon and her greatest asset. A woman's eyes are dangerous because she captures men with her eyes. A woman's eyes are the windows to her soul—her inner being. Her eyes are the broad avenue that allows travel from her soul to yours, from her heart to yours, from her mind to yours. Once you look into her eyes and travel that road, you're never the same. The rabbis were correct, son. I was a changed man after I looked into your mother's eyes. If there was a moment when I can say I fell in love with your mother, it was that first time I allowed myself to gaze into her beautiful blue eyes as she stared back into mine. I remember my father telling me after I met your mother, 'Son, you've been smitten.' He was right. Remember that, Ben. That's how your mother won me—with her eyes. Beware of a woman's eyes.' I remember Father chuckling to himself as he reflected on the story he had just told me."

"What a wonderful story, Ben," I answered. "Your father is a wise man."

"Well, Cassie, Father said one last thing that day, 'Ben, the eyes of women have captured more men than all the armies of all the world put together'. Since I've met you, Cassie, I understand Father's story perfectly. Your eyes have made me a lifelong prisoner and never has a man been more pleased with his incarceration. In your eyes, I see the most wonderful things. I see the future. Did you know that, Cassie? Did you know your eyes reveal more to me than a crystal ball to a gypsy?"

"I didn't know that," I answered. "What can you divine from my eyes at this moment, young Ben Lowry? What do you see in the crystal ball of my eyes?"

"My dear Cassie, I see us walking along loving one another many years hence. That's what I see," Ben replied.

"Ben, your eyes are the prettiest eyes in the world. I see the same vision as you," I told him.

"Ben, I have something to show you. I brought your sketch book with me today. Look on the last page. I read something while you were away that made me think of you—made me think of us. I copied it into your sketch book. I want to share that memory. Turn to the last page."

I handed him the book.

"While you were away," I said, "I read a Robert Burns poem. It made me think of you. I copied it for us today—for us to remember. Please read it to me, Ben."

Ben glanced at the page of the book and gave me a kiss on the forehead.

"Cassie, this poem is one of my favorites, too. It's simple, but it expresses my love for you precisely. We should read more poetry together. Do you want me to read it in the vernacular or in plain English?"

"Oh no, Ben," I answered. "I can't understand the Scots vernacular. Read it in plain English, please."

Ben put his arm around me, "I agree. I prefer English, although the Scots vernacular, when done correctly, is marvelous when you get used to it. You're right, Cassie. There's something about reading poetry aloud that brings the meaning home, doesn't it? The words, when spoken aloud, go straight to the heart, don't you think? Poetry must be spoken to be understood correctly. Thank you so much for sharing this, Cassie. This is special."

O my love's like a red, red rose, That's newly sprung in June.
O my love's like a melody, That's sweetly played in tune.
As fair are thou, my bonnie lass, So deep in love am I.
And I will love thee still, my dear, Till all the seas run dry.
Till all the seas run dry, my dear, and the rocks melt with the sun.

I will love thee still, my dear, while the sands of life shall run.
And fare thee well, my only love, and fare thee well a while.
And I will come again, my love, Though it were ten thousand
miles.
Robert Burns

23 June 1826

With each passing day Ben becomes more anxious about Georgia's bar examination. The sooner he passes the bar and goes to work, the sooner he will save enough for marriage and the sooner he will accomplish something noble for our nation. I wouldn't tell him, but I would be happy if he could stay in New Echota but I know that can't be. There is nothing here for a young man like Ben and he would be miserable working on a farm.

I loved it yesterday when Ben told me he remembered our first kiss. I want him to show me his love. 'Show me' love is so much better than 'tell me' love.

Ben and I are beginning to discuss the more intimate things between lovers. Ben says white people don't often openly discuss the coming together of a man and a woman.

"With our people, Ben, both the husband and wife are important. A Cherokee woman can express her opinion in meetings, business and in her marriage. There is nothing shameful about discussing intimacy or about a woman initiating a conversation about intimacy. A Cherokee woman is not a second-class citizen. She can throw her husband out of her house if he's bad to her, and it's not shameful."

Ben laughed, "I've heard of that. To be honest, I think that's something white men don't like. It's not that way with us whites. In Georgia, the husband owns everything. All property is inherited through the male and only males can vote. Once a white woman marries, she is stuck with her husband for good or ill. If her husband treats her poorly, it's a cultural shame for her to leave. She has no options."

"From what I've seen," I answered, "white men treat their women more like slaves than lovers. It's not like that in our nation. I remember one day I was with elisi. She and I watched elisi's sister throw her husband's things out—right out on the front porch. She threw everything out of the house that belonged to him. When her husband came home, he had no choice but to gather his belongings and leave. Elisi said it served him right for what he had done. He was not happy about being thrown out, but he had to honor her decision. He was required to go back where he came from before the marriage and leave the children with his wife. A Cherokee woman's community will always support her. In our nation, the house and everything in it belongs to the woman. Cherokee children belong to the mother if the couple separates. Would you allow me to own our home, Ben?"

"My dear Cassie, you can own anything you wish as long as you're with me. You can even own me if you want to. I'll happily belong to you," Ben said.

"I agree," I said laughing. "I wouldn't care if you owned everything as long as I can be with you."

"Cassie, As far as you and I are concerned I think it's important a man be prepared for marriage. Before a man marries, he should have a good job, a furnished home and be able to support his wife. I don't know how long it will take, but I'm guessing in four or five years I should have enough saved for us to marry. I don't think a man should ask a woman to marry him unless he is prepared to provide for her properly. Don't you think that's the right thing to do?"

"Ben, I'll wait as long as it takes. I know we're still too young to marry and we can't make promises, but I promise I'll wait and I'll never marry another. I'll wait for you as long as I live."

Ben and I didn't say more about our marriage, but he knows I'm his.

24 June 1826

Mr. Lowry says one day my journal might help whites understand us. We Cherokee haven't written much, but that is changing. I think about reading, writing and education every day. I'm disappointed there are no Cherokee history books written by our chiefs two hundred years ago. There is a detailed history of the empire of Rome and even a history of the Greeks who predate the Romans. They wrote history, poetry, stories and myths—even books about science and mathematics. They wrote about everything around them. I think the *Iliad* and the *Odyssey* are amazing. I'm learning classical Greek, but I love those books in English. Edudu tells many wonderful Cherokee stories that remind me of the Greeks. I should write them.

Edward Gibbon's *Decline and Fall of the Roman Empire* is interesting. Gibbon said the Germans have no written history for hundreds of years of their existence because they did not write books. I wish we Cherokee had learned to read and write long ago. This passage from Gibbon is disturbing.

Copied from Gibbon's *Decline and Fall of the Roman Empire* –
Ninth Chapter

"The Germans, in the age of Tacitus, were unacquainted with the use of letters; and the use of letters is the principal circumstance that distinguishes a civilized people from a herd of savages, incapable of knowledge or reflection...let us...calculate the immense distance between the man of learning and the illiterate peasant. The former, by reading and reflection, multiplies his own experience...whilst the latter, rooted to a single spot, and confined to a few years of existence, surpasses, but very little his fellow-laborer, the ox...The same...will be found between nations...without some species of writing, no people has ever preserved the faithful annals of their history, ever made any considerable progress in the abstract sciences, or ever possessed...the useful and agreeable arts of life. Of these arts, the Germans were wretchedly destitute. They passed their lives in a state of ignorance and poverty..."

I wish my ancestors had left us a written history, but I think it is a mistake to believe human joy comes only from literacy. We Cherokee are not kin to animals because we didn't have a written history like England or France. Human happiness comes from loving families—from mothers and fathers loving their children. We have strong families. We have been and are now a happy people, but I would love to know the details of our history—where we came from—who our leaders were—what they did. Although the Romans were highly literate and civilized, they were not the happiest of people—far from it.

I shall help educate my people and I shall write. Many of us can read and write English. Every day more are learning to read our Cherokee syllabary. I hope we'll have our own newspaper.

Because one powerful culture dominates other weaker cultures around them, it doesn't mean they are righteousness. The Romans weren't righteous just because they were powerful.

I would like to go to a college, but a Cherokee woman will never be allowed such an education. I shall be satisfied to learn from Mr. Lowry. He taught me many wonderful things like how the Arabs invented our number characters. They used simple angles to count from one to nine. They wrote the number one with a stroke and one angle, the number two with two angles, the number three has three angles and so forth to nine. The number seven has a stroke across the middle of the upright to give the simple line character seven angles. Arabic numerals are much easier to understand and use than the cumbersome Roman numerals. I am amazed. We live in an exciting time of learning and advancement. I wish I could go to a big library and read all day. I wish I were a man so I could go to college. Maybe one day women will be allowed to do such things.

26 June 1826

I am officially Mr. Lowry's assistant and permitted to teach the children and the girls. Ben and I could teach every Cherokee child to read and write if we were given the opportunity. Since our nation adopted Sequoya's syllabary last year, we have an official written language that many are learning. I'm proud to be Cherokee.

1 July 1826

Ben and I talked today about his career plans.

"Cassie," Ben said, "Father and I are going to Milledgeville next week to find a placement for me in a law firm."

"This is an exciting time in your life. I'm going to miss you when you go to Milledgeville."

"Don't worry, Cassie," Ben answered. "Everything will be good for us. Milledgeville isn't far. Things will work out—you'll see. I know one thing. I'm the luckiest man in the world to have the most beautiful woman in the world care about me. I can't wait to get to work and do all the things we've talked about. I'll write often and I'll be up here visiting you so often you won't even know I've been gone."

Chapter XXIV

1826 - For Sale: Houses, Horses, Humans

Chapter 24

18 July 1826 - The Ripe Corn Moon – Gu ye quo ni

Ben and his father are back from Milledgeville. They met with quite a few lawyers looking for placement. It won't be long before Ben will make a decision about his future.

23 July 1826

In every newspaper I read advertisements for the return of runaways and of Africans for sale. I feel ashamed I can't help. In every Georgia newspaper humans are bought and sold—as chattel—as property. I wonder about the hundreds of thousands of stories behind the advertisements. I have been reading Gibbon and I wonder how the Romans who kept slaves and the Americans who keep slaves differ?

Copied from the *Georgia Journal* - 18 July 1826 – page 4

> "On the first Tuesday of August next will be sold at the courthouse in Madison, Morgan county, between the usual hours of sale the following property, to wit: Three Negros, Sarah, a woman about 30 years old, Mariah about two years old, the other an infant--name not known. Levied on as the property of Caleb Early to satisfy fi-fas in favor of Frizell M. Hardwick. Levy made and returned by a constable. Four negros, Big Mary, about 22 years old, Little Mary 15, John 4 and Robbin about 2 years old levied on as the property of Jubal E. Watts to satisfy two fi-fas."

I had a lovely tea with Mr. and Mrs. Lowry. Ben had gone hunting. I shared my feelings about Africans being bought and sold.

"Wilbur and I feel the same way you do," Mrs. Lowry said. "Unlike most whites, we believe the Cherokee, Africans and whites are equal—equal in every way. We believe all races are the same before our good Lord."

Mrs. Lowry gave a little laugh and continued, "You have reminded me, Cassie, how fortunate I was to have met my wonderful husband. Wilbur's genuine egalitarianism attracted me at our first meeting. His high standards exactly reflected mine—and still do. Our beliefs have changed the direction of our lives. We aren't conventional—far from it. Ours is a minority view—a small minority, I'm afraid."

Mrs. Lowry continued with a frown, "When Wilbur and I hear Indians referred to as savages and Africans as niggers, we understand those terms are used to maintain class status. Ethnic slurs are as old as the earth—used to raise one group, class or culture by lowering another. The British call the Portuguese Dagos, the French Frogs, the Irish Micks and Shylock is a word they use for Jews. These terms are intended to be insulting and lower an entire culture and thus elevate the English. The truth is, the English want to be the privileged."

"Yes, ma'am. I fully understand that," I answered. "From my reading, I understand every culture has a certain level of xenophobia."

"Good word, Cassie, and sadly true," Mrs. Lowry said. "As you know, albus is the Latin word for white and niger is simply the Latin word for black. The word niger in itself is innocuous, but it has become a strong pejorative in the United States. When whites use the word nigger it reminds everyone that Africans not only have a dark skin color, but that they belong to the lowest slave class. Because of the Africans' unique physiognomy, dark skin color and forced illiteracy, it allows the white mind to justify the continued abuse of Africans. Whites have come to believe their use of Africans as slave labor to be normal. The truth is the privileged don't want to do menial tasks. They want inexpensive servants to do the hardest tasks. I understand that, believe me. Cooking in the summer isn't easy and I've never particularly enjoyed wash day."

Mr. Lowry added, "I understand why people want slave labor but I wish it wasn't so, Cassie. Eleanor and I are in a minority in Georgia and the United States. The pervading view of Africans makes it impossible for me to be successful in business in the South. Even in the non-slave states of the north, whites believe Africans inferior—as well as Indians, of course. They may verbalize their distaste for slavery and espouse equality, but in practice they are complete segregationists. No matter what they say, whites in the north don't want their children associating with the lower-class Africans or Indians. White families in the non-slave states don't want their children associating with negros of any kind—even if they're free.

Eleanor continued, "Whites don't dare allow the belief that Africans are fully human. Cassie, I saw that same advertisement you saw in the newspaper. I wondered where Sarah came from. Who would purchase her? Was she married? Is the child Mariah and the unnamed infant hers? Does Sarah have enough to eat? Will she ever wear nice clothes? I wonder how often Sarah cries herself to sleep?"

No one spoke for a few moments as each of us thought of Sarah who had suddenly escaped from the newspaper and become a real person.

Finally, Mrs. Lowry broke the silence.

"In the last census there were almost two million men, women and children in bondage here in the United States alone. Imagine that, Cassie. That's two hundred hundred thousand unfortunate souls who find themselves enslaved in a foreign country—our country—far from their homeland. They'll never see their native soil. Their children and their children's children are destined to remain in never-ending captivity. I can't bear to think of Sarah's misery multiplied by two million, and those numbers don't reflect the Africans sold into bondage in the Caribbean, Brazil and other countries."

Mr. Lowry interjected, "I'm grateful for men like William Wilberforce and Thomas Clarkson. I would God would raise up men like them here in the United States. Too many here worship at the altar of mammon and have forsaken their Creator and care nothing for Sarah."

"Have you read about William Wilberforce, Cassie?" Mrs. Lowry asked.

"Yes, ma'am," I answered, "I know Mr. Wilberforce is persona non grata here in the United States, especially in the South. No public discussion of abolition is allowed in Georgia."

"You have a good heart, Cassie," Mrs. Lowry said, "as does the rest of your nation—or at least most of them. When I read the newspaper, I also wondered what will happen to little Mariah? Will she ever be free? Will she be allowed to marry and have children and live with her husband or will the father of her babies be sold to the highest bidder? Since you're reading Gibbon, you'll know we humans haven't changed much since Roman times. They had a strong class system controlled by the privileged that continued for centuries. The privileged manage to keep their advantage in every society, don't they?"

"Yes, ma'am. You're right. I wonder what the future holds for us Cherokee? How long will we be allowed to live free? Whites are a proud, powerful race. They seize our land and make laws to justify everything they do. They're like children who change the rules of their schoolyard games as it suits them. They don't want us to own land any more than they want Africans to own land. I am afraid for our future, Mrs. Lowry. I wonder where white privilege will end? I wonder how long it will be before we'll be evicted."

Mrs. Lowry rose and gave me a strong loving embrace, "Sometimes, my dear Cassie, there are no words to express one's fears. Sometimes an embrace is the only way to say I love you to someone you care about—to quell the besieging demons.

She poured another cup of tea.

"There is something else I've noticed," I said. "We Cherokee know people by name, no matter their heritage, culture or origin. We give them a name and respect. I've noticed whites use skin color or the actual mathematical ratio of blood kin to identify people. Whites are never happy to know only a person's name—heritage must be expressed if they are not white."

Mrs. Lowry asked, "What do you mean, dear? Would you explain? This is an interesting point."

"Yes, ma'am. I've noticed whites, even those who profess Christianity, must mention the race of a person in any casual conversation if that person isn't completely white. If a person is part African, Cherokee or any other non-white combination, no matter how slight, it must be mentioned—as if an injustice would occur if a person's non-white status wasn't communicated. Whites only use a person's name without racial qualification when they're all white."

"Could you illustrate that, Cassie?' Mrs. Lowry asked.

"Yes, ma'am. They say things like, 'Oh, you know, the nigger who works at the blacksmith's shop, or, 'you know, the Indian who raises pigs', or 'you know, the half-breed who works for Mr. Smith'. If the same people in that conversation had been all white instead of Indian, African or mixed, they would have been given a name and spoken of as, 'You know, George who works at the blacksmith's' or 'You know, William who has the pig farm' or 'you know, Carl who works for Mr. Smith'."

"You're right, Cassie," Mrs. Lowry said with a sour look on her face. "We hear it even among the missionaries. The fact that the Cherokee refer to everyone by name and never by race is one of the most humbling things about your nation. Wilbur and I have seen the most pious folks offended to see a white man with a Cherokee woman—much less a white man with an African woman or a quadroon. We whites apply racial names to indicate anyone who isn't pure white. I fear, Cassie, these people have never taken their scriptures seriously. But Cassie, there is something else I despise even more—if that's possible."

"What could be worse, Mrs. Lowry?" I asked.

Mrs. Lowry continued with a dark expression, "Wilbur and I have also noticed the words whites use to identify mixed race children. Just as you have said, they can't simply use a child's name in conversation. They call the child a half-breed, mulatto, half-caste, mixed-breed, mestizo, quadroon and the worst word of all—mongrel. Those racial designations follow the poor child all their life. I recently heard someone refer to an infant in a mother's arms as a mongrel—as if the child's parents were stray dogs. I'm ashamed and I have no explanation. I can only say that Wilbur and I have chosen to never participate in such—but peer pressure, even among missionaries, is enormous. I wonder if I could stand for what I believe if I were under constant pressure? I wonder if I would buckle under the constant pressure of my peers? I am thankful skin color is of no issue to the Cherokee. I share your fears, Cassie. Where will unfettered white dominance lead us? I wonder what we whites are laying up in store? I'm afraid, dear, most folks don't believe their Scriptures. They're more afraid of their neighbors than God—that's the root of the problem, isn't it. Folks are afraid to oppose their neighbors. The pressure of one's peers can be overwhelming—especially when it means harming one's children."

"Thank you for sharing that, Mrs. Lowry. I agree with you. I think there are a lot of whites who go along with the crowd. The problem is they are teaching their children to go along with the crowd also."

"My dear Cassie, continue your path. Never compromise. You and I can't do much about the darkness, but you can be a light here in your corner of the world—one small candle can light the darkest room. You can love and you can write. Please continue to write. Let your beautiful light shine in your life and through your pen."

It had been an emotional conversation. Mrs. Lowry put her hands over her face and began to weep silently. I couldn't help but weep with her. Mr. Lowry didn't say a word but sat beside his wife and held her as she cried. All three of us were thinking about what we had been discussing.

At last, Mrs. Lowry regained her composure.

"You and your people have meant a great deal to us and we promise to do our best to serve the needs of your nation as long as God gives us strength. Wilbur and I will never leave you, Cassie. I promise. We shall never leave you."

25 July 1826

Since Ben returned from Connecticut, we've seen one another every day. I love having him back. We are enjoying one another and becoming better friends with each passing day. I have especially enjoyed watching him around his mother. He cannot get enough of her hugs and cooking but with every conversation he mentions his desire to quickly begin his career.

If Ben is to help our nation, he has no time to spare. He must pass the bar and find a job. It will take time for him to gain skill and influence. The Creek Nation is practically gone and we are increasingly isolated. We need help soon if help is to come at all. Ben isn't sure what he can do, but at least he can learn, and who knows what good he may accomplish.

Ben and I talked about his work as a lawyer on the whiteside. He knows when he goes to work he must be circumspect. If whites were to believe Ben gave assistance to the Cherokee in any way, his career would be ruined.

27 July 1826

"Cassie," Ben said, "Mother was telling me about your conversation concerning the continued bondage of Africans. When I was in Connecticut I learned Africans, even to this day, continue to be smuggled into the United States. Southern agriculture requires cheap labor and they don't care a fig about international law. Also, northern folk are selling their slaves south for big profits. I witnessed as much white prejudice against the negros in the north as here.

"I know, Ben," I said. "That's a terrible thought. Even a few wealthy Cherokee own slaves, but most of us dislike slavery. Most of us think of blacks equally human and wouldn't think ill of any Indian who marries an African. I wanted to ask you a question, Ben. In the newspaper, it often says a slave is sold because of a fi-fa. What is a fi-fa precisely?"

"Good question, Cassie. Fi-fa is an abbreviation for fieri-facias. It's the Roman legal term meaning you shall make it happen. Here in our country it's the legal authority behind a court judgment. The fi-fa law provides the judge with the legal right to force repayment of a legal debt. If the court forces someone to pay a debt, they send the sheriff to seize enough property to be sold at auction to cover the outstanding debt. Since slaves are quite valuable and easy to transport, the sheriff takes them first. It's a lot easier for the sheriff to seize a slave than for him to carry off a houseful of furniture or a stubborn mule. Not a very nice thought, is it?"

"No, it's not a nice thought. Thank you, Ben. I thought the word meant something like that."

Ben continued, "Well, Cassie, fi-fas are bad but worse are breeder farms. Since the foreign slave trade was made illegal, breeder farms have increased. These farms, in Virginia, Kentucky, Maryland, and other places, force

African women to have sex with select males—like a horse breeder would use a prize stud. As soon as the young African girl has a baby, they force her to get pregnant again—as if she were a brood mare. They sell the children down the river to slave traders—down the Ohio, Tennessee, and Mississippi to labor-intensive plantations."

"Ben, that's horrible. I have heard of the farms but I didn't know they were so prevalent."

"I know, Cassie. There's no law against the breeder farms and no one talks about them. When I was in law school, I heard it proposed the United States should annex Cuba to provide an endless source of domestic slaves in order to by-pass the international ban."

I was speechless. I wondered what it is in us that allows us to be so cruel to our fellow man. I suppose we humans will justify most anything to have servants to do our chores.

"Perhaps," Ben said, "if we can achieve some justice for the Cherokee, we can also successfully defend the African's rights to life, liberty and the pursuit of happiness like it reads in our Declaration of Independence. They should have the same rights as whites. That would be a wonderful day, wouldn't it? I doubt it will be in my lifetime, but it's my dream."

"Cassie, I remember on a trip to Savannah watching Father stop briefly to observe a young African woman in an alley. The woman and her daughter were sitting in the shade beside a white's-only establishment. They were smiling and laughing and paying no attention to us watching from the street. The two adored one another. I remember thinking, 'they're human as I am human. They love as I love'. I remember thinking that I was watching a moment of pure innocence. How could I or anyone buy and sell such love, much less intentionally sever it for monetary gain?

"On that same day Father took me to the slave auction in Ellis Square. He wanted me to see and feel the emotion of the moment. He told me to watch their faces as they wait to be put on the auction block. I watched a young mother with small children clinging to her skirt-tails. She wore an expression of confused fear as she watched her husband being sold. I can still hear the auctioneer's call—as dispassionate as if he were selling cattle. As we left, we saw that same woman and child I had seen earlier that day in the alley being prepared for auction by her European masters. I've never forgotten that day or those faces."

I answered quizzically, "What do you mean, European masters, Ben? Slave owners don't live in Europe, do they? I thought all the slave owners lived right here in Georgia?"

Ben laughed, "You're precious, Cassie. I didn't make that clear, did I? I was emphasizing that all slave owners in Georgia are recently descended from European immigrants—almost entirely English and all white. There are no negro populations in Europe. The island of Haiti has the only negro government in the world. Whites won't talk about it. The French granted suffrage to landed negros in Hispaniola in 1790 when they abolished slavery entirely. Southern slave owners don't want anyone talking about that. Slave owners in Georgia call themselves Americans to distinguish themselves politically from the British. American is a term of civil convenience. The Spanish refer to all of us, British and American alike, as Anglos—to the Spanish there is no difference between the white Americans and the English."

Ben continued, "English motives are confusing, even to me. That's why Father believes the study of history important. Times change but people never change. Did you know the name America is a marker of European political domination of this continent? The fact that some call you a Native American is, in itself, a symbol of white supremacy. You didn't know that did you?"

I was confused, "I don't understand. We don't call ourselves Americans. We are Cherokee—Tsalagi—we are not Americans in any sense of the word. What do you mean?"

"Well, here's the story, Cassie. Americus Vespucci, an Italian sailor, wrote about his explorations of South America in 1502 and 1504. His writings were widely published throughout Europe. In those days little was known about the lands Christopher Columbus had discovered. Vespucci, unlike Columbus, correctly understood the land he had explored was not part of Asia but a huge intervening land mass between Europe and Asia. The Italian sailor, Americus Vespucci, is the first man to call your continent the Novus Mundus or New World. He knew Columbus hadn't discovered the back way to India and he knew your people were not Indians."

I answered, "How interesting. I didn't know that. Tell me more."

Ben continued, "It is interesting, isn't it? Studying history is important. In the early 1500's, your new continent was known only as Novus Mundus by cartographers, the New World, for lack of a proper name. Those were exciting times, Cassie. People were curious, insatiably curious, just like you are. The printing press had just been invented and the enlightenment was upon western Europe."

"I'm listening, Ben. Tell me more," I said with eagerness.

"Well, the story goes," Ben continued, "a famous German cartographer was making a huge map of the entire world for public display. He didn't want folks to think he was ignorant by using the name New World. The German cartographer had read Americus Vespucci's writings so he invented a name for this huge land mass by changing Vespucci's forename to the feminine. Folks in those days thought of continents in the feminine like we do ships. Ships are always a she, aren't they? So, on this cartographer's famous new map in Germany, he called your continent where we stand today, North America. So, this land you live in soon became America and its residents were called Americans. All this is because of an Italian explorer and a German cartographer who didn't want to appear foolish in public. Cartographers everywhere copied the German mapmaker's new name and that's where the name America came from, Cassie. White European governments legally assumed ownership of all the land they discovered here even before they arrived. They assumed complete political and cultural hegemony on this continent. When someone calls you a Native American they're using a white European term given by white Europeans for the benefit of white Europeans. Calling you a Native American is not any different than calling you an Indian and is another way to establish class status. Both European appellations are equally inaccurate. That's why I always speak of you and your nation as Cherokee—never Native American, aborigines or indigenous, which is equally prejudicial."

"I understand. Edudu is right. We have been invaded. I prefer to be called Cherokee for that is what I am. Let them call us what they will—they're going to anyway, aren't they? There's nothing we can do about it."

29 July 1826

Conversations with Mr. and Mrs. Lowry and Ben's stories about Africans and slavery have left an indelible imprint on my mind.

More than anything, I want to be at Ben's side in his quest to help the Africans and us Cherokee. Whatever happens, I want to do the right thing. I want to be with Ben.

In Georgia, as in all slave states, it is illegal to teach a slave to read and write, even by their own family members. Whites deny education to Africans to prevent the spread of anti-slavery sentiment through literature. Whites know the power of the written word. Southern governments are terrified of an organized African rebellion. There are almost as many Africans as whites in many rural areas with large plantations. An organized revolt by literate Africans could not be stopped.

Georgia doesn't want us to have a newspaper, either. They don't like it that we are becoming literate since we adopted Sequoyah's syllabary. Perhaps I can't do much but I can learn and I can teach others of my people to read and perhaps one day teach Africans. Perhaps Mrs. Lowry is right and my one small light can illuminate an entire room and dispel the darkness.

1 August 1826

Ben's ambitious project to help us preserve our heritage will require an infinite amount of letter writing.

Mr. Lowry said to Ben, "Your mother, Cassie and I will help you, son, whenever you get your job and get settled. Let us know what to do. We're here to help. We're at your service. We can't do a great deal, but we can do something and perhaps over time we can do something beneficial."

Ben didn't know what to say when he heard his father say this and we could see the emotion on his face.

"I will do all I can, Father. A battle is coming. Our dreams for the future integrity and perhaps even the survival of the Cherokee Nation rest on working within the white legal system. I will do my best to be their champion, sir. We can accomplish something. Our long journey begins with a single step."

"You know the old Chinese saying about planting trees, don't you?" Ben's father asked. "The Chinese say the best time to plant a tree is twenty years ago. The second-best time is now."

3 August 1826

I am proud. Our people have begun to set up our nation with a constitution, laws and law enforcement. Next year we may ratify our own constitution. Whites don't want a remnant of the Cherokee Nation in the south. In every newspaper someone writes that we Cherokee must go. They want us removed. We are in danger of being washed away by a flood—a flood, not of muddy water, but of white immigrants who want to take the very last thing we possess—our land."

Chapter XXV

1826 – Ben Meets Zach

Chapter 25

6 August 1826 - End of the Fruit Moon - Ga lo nii

"Cassie, the third law firm Father and I visited was the one I chose and they chose me, too. They were looking for a law school graduate. After our second interview they asked me to go to work and I accepted. It was all that quick. I'm sure it's the right choice and Father agrees. Isn't that wonderful?"

"I am proud of you, Ben. You're going to make a great lawyer. I'm going to miss you in Milledgeville, but I know you're doing what you want to do—what you were meant to do. This is the fulfillment of your dreams—of our dreams, and Milledgeville isn't so far from here, is it?"

"You're sweet, Cassie. I'll miss you, too, and no, Milledgeville isn't far. I'll visit and write so often you'll hardly know I'm gone. Father and I found a respectable boarding house within walking distance of the law firm. Would you to ride down with us when Father takes me back? I would love for you to come with us. We'll have fun on the trip and I could show you around town. Won't you ride down with us?"

"I would love to. What an adventure. I know a lot about Milledgeville from reading the Georgia Journal but I've never seen a big town. The farthest from home I've ever been is Ross's Landing and the Agency. Are you sure it's alright with your father if I come?"

"Father would love you to ride with us, Cassie. You can keep him company on the way back. You'll love Milledgeville. There are dozens and dozens of shops with people coming and going all day and into the night. I'm going to love it there. There's lots to see, but I want to take you to the book shops and printers. You won't believe all the books. Father and I visited a couple, but we didn't stay long. I'm sure I'll spend all my extra money in the book shops. We can spend all afternoon looking at books if we want to. Do come, Cassie. We'll have so much fun."

In his excitement, Ben had forgotten he would be in Milledgeville and I would be in New Echota and we would be separated once again. He was suddenly embarrassed about telling me how much he was going to enjoy Milledgeville without me.

"Oh, Cassie, I'm so sorry. Don't look so sad. I didn't mean it to sound like I would be happy when we're apart. I'll miss you every day I'm away. I'll be coming back regularly and I'll write often. I promise I'll write. I don't want you to think I'm happy about leaving you. I'm just happy about beginning my work—that's all."

Ben took both of my hands to make sure I wasn't offended.

"Ben, let's walk down by the river. It's a lovely day and I can't sit still. I need to walk. May I share something with you?"

"Sure, Cassie, you can tell me anything, you know that," Ben said.

"Ben, I will miss you. I'll miss you every day you're gone, but I want you to know I'm proud of you. I'm proud of your new job. I'm glad you're going to work in a profession you love. I would never take that from you. I'm not offended you will enjoy Milledgeville when you're away from me. I know very well you can't stay in New Echota the rest of your life. There's nothing here for a young man like you and I know you don't want to be a farmer. If you're going to help your father and us Cherokee, you must leave New Echota. I'll think of you every day. My heart is with you. You are doing the right thing. You have chosen the right path, Ben. I believe in you and I believe in your decision to help the Cherokee when and where you can. You must believe that, too."

When we reached the privacy of my special place, he kissed me by the river behind the tall laurels.

"Ben, I'm not embarrassed to tell you that when I see you smile it's like the sunshine breaking through dark clouds. I wake every day thinking about you. Your kiss is my last thought before I sleep. You are my sun, my day, my night and the air I breathe. I wanted to tell you that and you may kiss me anytime you want to. In fact, I wish you would kiss me more often. I like that very much."

After I said that, Ben looked at me silently. I could tell we were both thinking the same wonderful thoughts. We smiled at one another and without a word we kissed again.

"Kissing you more often, you wonderful woman, is something I certainly won't have any problem with. I plan on kissing you the rest of my life, if you don't mind."

He kissed me once again as we sat in my special place—our special place by the river. We watched the leaves float past on the placid surface of the river. A big tree limb came slowly by. A fish jumped just beside us.

"Ben, while you were at school, your mother and I talked often about you—about us. Your mother fully approves of our relationship even though

I'm not white. She's looking forward to grandchildren. She thinks we will have the most beautiful children in the world. I do too. Your mother is special, Ben. I love her dearly. I'm blessed to have found both you and your parents in my life. You're a fortunate man. You picked your parents well. I want to name our first little girl Eleanor."

Ben took both of my hands.

"Well, you and Mother feel free to talk about me behind my back, don't you? So, you and my mother think our children will be beautiful?

Ben laughed and laughed.

"Cassie, I think my mother's right. Maybe she knows more than we know. Our children will be beautiful but, before we get married we have to make preparations—a lot of preparations. I must save a substantial sum to set up housekeeping, or would you rather live in poverty?"

After a long conversation we reluctantly began our walk back home. After a few moments silence Ben laughed out loud once again.

"What are you laughing at now, Ben?" I asked.

"Cassie, I was thinking about you and my mother talking about me while I was gone. I can't conceal anything from my mother, not that I have tried to hide my love for you. Mother's right. I can't see anyone but you as the mother of my children. When I was away, I thought about you every day. You are, and will be, the only woman for me. I know that for sure and it feels good to say it out loud. I'm not surprised my parents know about my love for you, although I haven't told them in so many words. My parents have never thought of folks as white, black or Cherokee. I have never one time in my life heard my mother or father use an ugly name for anyone. My parents have always had good thoughts about you, Cassie. The color of a person's skin is of no consequence to them. Something like that wouldn't enter their mind. I believe the same thing they do. It's what's on the inside that counts."

"Ben, your mother says men don't talk about emotional things the way women do. I think she's right. Your father and I discuss things in school but he never talks about his emotions. I'm glad you and I share everything. Edudu and elisi know how I feel about you. I don't have any secrets from them either."

"Cassie, to communicate one's deepest feelings as you and I are able to do makes us the luckiest of people, don't you think? I'm so glad we found one another. Maybe I've learned to share my heart with you. I hope so. Like I've told you before, there's something about you and our relationship that makes me want to open up my chest and expose everything I am—everything both good and bad. I can't keep a secret from you. I don't want to keep anything from you."

"I think we will have the most wonderful marriage," I said. "Elisi thinks you'll be a worthy husband and good father. The only thing my family cares about is that you love me and our children. They wouldn't care if you were English, Spanish, French or African. If you treat me right, they will love you. They think like you and your parents. It's what's inside that's important."

"Cassie, every night when I say my prayers I thank God I met you. You are the best thing that has ever happened to me or will ever happen. I mean that. I brought you a gift. It's in my saddle bag. I was so excited when I got here I forgot it. Let's go now and get it. Before I give you your gift, Cassie, you'll have to guess what it is."

"It's a book," I answered quickly.

"You peeked," Ben said laughing.

"No, I didn't."

He handed me the gift wrapped in plain brown paper.

"You guessed it," Ben said. "I told you I can't keep secrets from you, can I? I hope you like it, Cassie. My father would think I wasted my money, but I knew you would love it. It's a popular novel on both sides of the Atlantic, I understand."

It was a copy of *Pride and Prejudice* by Jane Austin. I jumped into Ben's arms and he cradled me like a child.

"You are the best friend ever, Ben, I love you, I love you, I love you," and I kissed him as he held me.

"I read about this book in the newspaper," I said. "I know I'll love it. Your father never gives me novels to read."

I gave him another kiss.

"I knew you would like it," Ben said, as he put me back down. "It's about a bookish country gentleman and his wife in England. Her task in life is to find prosperous husbands for her five daughters. It seems, Cassie, I can't get away from young women looking for husbands, can I?"

We laughed.

"I haven't read it, Cassie. I thought I would wait until you're finished and then we can discuss it. I know the kind of books my father loans you. I thought you would enjoy something a little lighter. I don't think every book should be exclusively for the immediate improvement of one's mind. Who knows, Cassie, you may even write your own novel one day. You could do that, couldn't you?"

"You know, Ben, I think I could," I answered. "Maybe I'll do just that. A romantic historical novel about a young white man who falls in love with a beautiful Cherokee princess. They live happily ever after and have fifteen children and fifty grandchildren. That would be fun, wouldn't it?"

10 August 1826

The sad morning of Ben's return to Milledgeville dawned dark and dreary. Low scudding rain clouds covered the sky. It would be a warm but nasty day. The occasional blustery wind was bringing intermittent rain showers.

Mr. Lowry planned for us to stay the night with his friends on the Hightower Road. We were leaving early to make certain we wouldn't be required to travel on the Sabbath. Mr. Lowry never travels or works on a Sunday.

I was helping Mr. Lowry make final adjustments to the harness. Ben was checking to make sure our things were properly secured and covered under the oilcloth in the bed of the little carryall. Ben's mother was sitting on the top step of the porch. She brushed away wisps of her greying hair blown across her emotionless face by the gusting wind. As she watched her son, her hands dropped into her lap and she twisted her apron nervously just as she had done earlier in the house betraying the deep emotions she was trying desperately to conceal. I could only imagine her feelings as her little boy prepared to leave home for good.

"I'm excited about our trip, Ben, and your new job, but I feel for your mother. I'm not sure you know how much she's going to miss you. Give her plenty of hugs before you leave. I saw her wringing her hands in her apron just now. She didn't know I was watching. Remember, you're her only son and leaving her nest. My heart would be breaking if my only son were leaving."

When the moment came, Ben did give his mother plenty of hugs. This parting was different than when Ben left for law school. This time Ben would leave never to return. He was leaving the nest for good. He was beginning his adult career—never to reside with his parents again. I asked Five Feathers to come over every day to help Mrs. Lowry with the chores while we were away, but Five Feathers' help would be no consolation for the ache Ben's mother would feel in her heart for a very long time.

Mr. Lowry flicked the reins. Gunsmoke started us down the hill. I felt sorry for the poor horse. First, I felt sorry for Mrs. Lowry and now I felt sorry for Gunsmoke. I guess it was my day to feel for others.

"It is going to be a long trip for Gunsmoke, Ben," I said. "Milledgeville is a long way for your poor horse to pull us and this heavy wagon."

Ben put his arm around me and pulled me tight.

"You have a tender heart, Cassie. You needn't worry. Father loves his old gelding. This little carryall is light as a feather for Gunsmoke. He's an especially strong horse and Father will make sure he doesn't work him too hard. Father will let him rest every mile or two. He always gives his horse a well-deserved rest at the top of a hill after a long pull. Father has a soft heart for his animals just like you do. Gunsmoke's one of the family. Father will never trade him. He's easy to catch, great in the traces, a wonderfully obedient saddle horse and Father taught him to ground tie. We don't do any farming, but he's broke to plow and he's the easiest horse ever to shoe. I just wish he wasn't so short-coupled."

"What does short-coupled mean?" I asked.

"Well," Ben answered, "short-coupled means Gunsmoke has a shorter back than normal. The distance between his front and back legs is less than most horses. Because he has a short back and long legs, his back hooves sometimes go all the way forward and bump the front hooves. If you'll listen, you can sometimes hear the shoe of his back-hoof give a loud clank when it hits his front shoe. The farrier, which is always me, must be extra careful. If I leave the heel of the front shoe sticking out just the least little bit, he can stomp off his front shoe with his back foot. I've seen Gunsmoke going along at a nice clip and stomp off a front shoe and leave it right in the hoofprint with all six nails sticking straight up. But I think you should worry more about the rain than Gunsmoke. Look at those low clouds."

"What if it rains? What will we do then?" I asked.

"If it rains, we'll sit close together and cover up with an oilcloth. I won't mind sittin' close to you. In fact, I've been praying for rain," Ben said with a grin.

We laughed together and I said quietly into his ear, "I think I shall pray for rain, too."

Ben laughed again.

"Father thinks of everything, Cassie. He has two big oilskins tied tight with grommets around our things in the back. Nothing can get wet back there, no matter how hard it rains. He has two more oilskins to cover us on the seat in case of rain—one for Father and one for you and me to share. Our feet might get a little damp, but that's all. We won't get soaked and our things will stay dry."

The first two days traveling were pleasant. Ben, his father and I loved the novelty of our journey and we were constantly in good spirits. Even though Gunsmoke did all the work he seemed to enjoy his outing as much as we did. Ben and I groomed him evening and morning and talked about many different things as we watched him patiently eat his grain and fodder. Gunsmoke is gentle and willing when handled. When I talk to him he picks up his ears and looks at me with his big brown eyes most intelligently. I imagine he understands. I'm sure edudu could talk to him.

On that first morning we passed an orchard and picked apples off the ground for everyone—Gunsmoke included. I laughed at Mr. Lowry who would only take apples that had fallen to the ground. He said it was stealing if we took them off the tree. Ben cut the apples into little pieces for me and I fed Gunsmoke from my open hand. I took great pleasure in watching him softly nibble the apple wedge ever so carefully, tickling my hand with his whiskered lips. He loved his treat. I think I heard Gunsmoke say thank you when we finished. I marvel at the trusting nature of animals—especially horses who are so much more powerful than their masters. I wish people were as dependable and innocent as Gunsmoke.

What fun to spend four days in a row with Ben. I hope I will be allowed to make the journey with him again. I want to see every shop on every street in town. I've read so many newspaper advertisements over the years, I think I know Milledgeville as well as I do New Echota. Secretly, edudu gave me money for a surprise for elisi. Her only interest in Milledgeville is cloth—like woolens, linen, cotton and other fabrics. Elisi is an excellent seamstress—especially in leather. Edudu wanted me to bring her a bolt of cloth and thread.

I want to visit a shop that advertised a newly arrived shipment of writing paper and used books. It would be fun if elisi, edudu and I could go together, but they won't leave home. I can't get them to walk to the river with me, much less travel to Milledgeville.

13 August 1826

As scheduled, we arrived late Saturday afternoon at the Branswell's just as we were entering the whiteside on the Hightower Road. The Branswells were dear friends of Mr. Lowry's mother and father. They and their six children were expecting us. Mr. Lowry knew they would be keeping the Sabbath. Mr. Lowry never works or travels on the Sabbath. He does his best to arrange it so he won't chop kindling or fetch water. Mr. Lowry does his Sunday chores on Saturday.

We had a wonderful visit with the Branswells and slept soundly in their comfortable home. I was allowed to peruse their many books—what an unexpected pleasure.

15 August 1826

We rose before dawn the morning after the Sabbath and arrived in Milledgeville in the early afternoon. I found the activity incredible. Do whites ever rest? Everywhere I looked I saw finely dressed people, carriages, wagons, horses and Africans.

There were tall buildings everywhere—some old, some new and some under construction. Whites love to build. It's no wonder they think us lazy. Ben asked his father to drive by the Capitol building on Greene Street before going to his boarding house. The city, its people and its buildings filled me with astonishment.

As I sat between Mr. Lowry and Ben in the carryall looking over this grand city and the magnificent capitol building where important men from all over Georgia gather to make laws, I realized my tiny rural nation could never resist these industrious people. I understood how they could think us backward and an obstruction to their very lives. Nothing would be denied the society who could build such a city in so short a time. Ben said Savannah was bigger with even more people and Charleston bigger still. Our magnificent council buildings at Crawfish Springs and New Echota suddenly became crude, insignificant structures. We can no more stop white expansion than I could hold a runaway horse. I wish whites were as kind as they are industrious. I think the problem is they equate industry and knowledge with worth. It's a terrible feeling to be thought of as worthless.

Mr. Lowry stopped in the street in front of Ben's boarding house. The proprietor hurried out before we could get down from the carryall.

"I'm sorry, sir. Indians use the back entrance with the niggers. A servant can assist you but only through the back entrance. Indians must stay with the niggers. I'm sure you appreciate we do our best to keep a reputable establishment."

"Yes sir," Mr. Lowry answered politely. We'll go around back."

These people I had seen walking, riding and doing their business all over Milledgeville as we arrived are the same ones who write the articles in the *Georgia Journal* about uncivilized savages. These are the very people who believe me incapable of advancement and doomed to extinguishment—the people who want me removed. How foolish to have come. I understand perfectly how Africans must feel. Now I understand why edudu and elisi never travel to the whiteside where every sideways glance is meant to put us in our place.

"I'm sorry," Mr. Lowry said quietly. "Eleanor and I have been secluded in New Echota far too long. We've forgotten how white folks behave. I apologize. I wouldn't have you embarrassed for the world."

We delivered Ben's things to his room from the back entrance. As we were mounting the carryall, the proprietor once again approached and spoke politely to Ben, not caring I was sitting next to him and would hear his every word.

"Sir, we're pleased you've chosen our establishment. It's a pleasure to have our own resident attorney. I promise, sir, you can count on us night and day. My door is always open to a gentleman like you."

The proprietor cleared his throat and continued in a more subdued tone, but I heard every word.

"Sir, we appreciate your business, but if you'll pardon me sayin'—in the future it would be better if you didn't bring Indians. We run a reputable establishment. Indians are not welcome anywhere, sir—for good reason. It wouldn't do if folk saw Indians hanging about—even in the back. Folks don't trust Indians."

Ben and his father said nothing. Their faces wore no expression. There was nothing to say. I gave Ben the money edudu had given me and told him what I wanted for elisi. Ben apologized again. After Ben and I said our goodbyes, I asked Mr. Lowry to begin the homeward journey immediately. I didn't want to stay another moment.

22 August 1826
Ben's first letter from Milledgeville
Huff's Boarding House - 16 August 1826
My Dear Cassie,

I am missing you terribly and can't wait to see your face again. Even though you weren't welcome in Milledgeville, I appreciate you coming down with me. I remain embarrassed by your reception. I wish there was something I could do. Perhaps in the future things will change. I will work for such.

Your company made the trip down so much more enjoyable. I loved every moment with you. I hope the day comes soon when white folks won't be so rude and maybe we can take a more pleasant trip together—perhaps an excursion to the big stone mountain?

I have been assigned a desk by a very adequate window. The owner's son, Zach, also a lawyer about my age, is in charge of my orientation. Zach is excited to have me with the firm—his father's firm. He said it was his idea to hire a man from law school.

Zach and I will complement one another, I believe. He needs help applying himself and I need assistance adjusting socially in this strange town. I've been sheltered and have a lot to learn about the world. Father said I have two ears and one mouth for a reason. I should listen twice as much as I talk. I shall take his advice.

I'm tired this evening—exhausted. I hardly slept the last two nights. I can't express my excitement as I begin my career. I can't wait till you and I can spend more time together and I shall communicate everything. I promise I'll tell you every detail of every day. I'm missing you. You are indeed missing from me, as the French say. Visit with Mother as often as you can and cheer her heart in my absence.

Missing you more than you can know, Ben xoxo

4 September 1826

Milledgeville - 27 August 1826 - Huff's Boarding House
My Dear Cassie,

This short note is to remind you how much I'm missing you. I think of you especially as I compose myself for sleep.

My new friend Zach doesn't like the practice of law. His main interests are clothes, food, wine, parties and the daughters of his father's clients. I miss you. I shall use my education and do my best to help Father and the Cherokee. I'm determined to work diligently on your behalf and learn as much about the legal profession as I can. I'll tell you more about Zach and the law firm on my return. You're missing from me. Can't wait to see you.

Yours always and forever, Ben xoxo

12 September 1826

Ben came home today and we talked and talked and then talked more. Actually, he talked and I listened. He was like an excited little boy. His excitement reminded me of when he came home from law school. He told me all about his job, his new friend and his assignments.

"Zach is a character, Cassie," Ben said. "He's fun and already depending on me for legal advice. Zach is not like any of the men in law school."

Ben related in detail many conversations with Zach.

Milledgeville – September 1826

"Ben," Zach said, "being a lawyer is easier than working and a lot more profitable. I don't really like the work but I love easy money. I studied just hard enough to pass the bar and prevent Father from putting me into some boring mercantile business or managing a farm. Can you imagine workin' on a farm for a living? Farming, ugh, what a terrible thought. Growing cotton and managing niggers is not for me. My forte is working with business people. Because of Father, I've been introduced to most every family of consequence in Georgia and our referral business is growing. Imagine that. Even Father admits I'm becoming an expert in public relations, but I need an assistant who can help me put together a smart legal argument for my clients when they need it—and that person is you. I need someone to spend time in the boring law books on my behalf. We'll make a good team, don't you think?"

As instructed, Ben listened more than he talked.

Zach continued without a pause, "My father includes me in most of his important interviews. He says learning how to handle rich folks is my main education now. I'm good at it. The key to wealth is the ability to understand the wealthy, Ben. It's that simple. Money is found in the company of gentlemen and in politics. We hired you to help me with the legal part of my work."

Zach continued, "Father says a successful law firm depends on who you know. Father and I know everyone in Georgia who has influence. We know who has money and who doesn't. Our business is understanding money, power, prestige and, of course, electing our friends to office. There is nothing so lucrative, my father says, as having your friend in the legislature. That's the quickest way to wealth. If someone we don't know gets elected, it's my job to make them our friend."

Zach continued as if giving a lecture, "Ben, maneuvering legislators and judges is the key. If the judge doesn't like you, you're skint. If the judge owes you a favor, it doesn't matter how well your opponent argues. You see my point? It's the way the world works, but we still need to be top notch lawyers and that's why we hired you. We want to be a step ahead. If you want to make money, the judges need to be in your pocket—that's what father says. The closer you are to judges, the better off you are. I do a lot of social work, you might say, with judges and their families. I listen and I provide, if you know what I mean. I'm always willing to go out of my way for a judge or member of the legislature. Quid pro quo, Ben, quid pro quo—that's our motto. That's the most important thing I've learned. Quid pro quo. I'll do the back scratching and you take care of the lawyering and we'll make money—a lot of money."

26 September 1826

Ben has returned home. I'm glad he is visiting his parents often.

"Cassie," Ben said, "I laughed and laughed at Zach's confession that he loves money but doesn't like to work. Zach is happy allowing me to do much of his legal work. I've learned one thing, Zach's father has done well practicing law, but they made more in land speculation and the slave trade— Zach says his father knows how to be in the right place at the right time. Zach's father picks up a lot of slaves at bargain prices because of his client base. When a man dies, they sell his slaves along with the estate and Zach's father often gets first choice."

"Are you going to be involved with the slave trade, Ben?" I asked incredulously? I couldn't believe what I was hearing.

"No—of course not. I'll never do that. I'll never own a slave. Zach's father does all that on the side—that's not part of the law firm. Thankfully, I'll have nothing to do with anything like that. My work is all legal, above board and honorable. The firm's big interest is land. Zach's father was on the good side of the Yazoo land fraud, and because they were seen to be honest, they have acquired a sterling reputation. Zach's father has a front row seat for land speculation in Georgia and beyond. As we knew, I'm learning firsthand that unrestrained land speculation is the main reason there is political pressure on the Cherokee. People are looking for land and driving the prices up—and they want Indian land."

As I listened, Ben went on and on about his job and Zach like a child with a new toy. In some ways, Ben is a still a little boy and naïve. It doesn't sound like Zach is naïve at all.

Ben continued, "Zach is trusted when it comes to deal making, especially with large tracts of agricultural land. Zach tells me all kinds of stories about past deals. Now that I'm in the firm, Zach plans to use my legal knowledge to help them make even more money. It's strange being around someone with so much ambition. Father taught me the love of money will pierce one through with many sorrows. He calls it the pursuit of filthy lucre. I think Father is right, Cassie. I love my work and I enjoy being with Zach and the others, but they're not like my father and his friends. I'm determined to work honorably and maintain integrity—and gather wealth the proper way—by steady, honest work—day by day, little by little. I'll work as hard as anyone, maybe harder, but I don't want to work simply to acquire riches. I want my motto to be an honest day's work for an honest day's pay. You can trust me. I'll never fall in love with money."

"You're right about money, Ben," I said. "For the most part, we Cherokee have never pursued wealth. I think that's one of the reasons the whiteside grows and we don't. Whites want more and we're happy with what we have. One of the reasons your father has been welcomed here is everyone knows he's not here at our expense. It's known your father and mother don't covet our possessions or our land. It sounds to me like Zach trusts no one but himself. I don't know if I like the sound of that, but I'm sure Zach will help your career. Be careful, Ben. Remember who you are. Remember your mother's advice."

"I'll be careful, Cassie," Ben answered with conviction. "I know who I am. I won't forget that. I love the research, the courts and the debates. I love the intellectual pleasure of crafting a logical, systematic argument based on fact. I love the sober judgment required to put together a case where justice prevails. Father taught me to pursue a conclusion based upon fact and not one held up by guesswork or theories."

"You know, Cassie, you and I both are good at mathematics and we have excellent recall. Zach's father says I have an outstanding legal mind. He wished his son was like me when it comes to intellectual pursuits. Zach's father knows the ability to make money is a unique skill necessary to the firm. That's Zach's skill—not legal research. I think the thing I love most about the legal profession is the ability to use my mental powers to the fullest—not a blind pursuit of wealth."

Ben laughed and continued, "Zach will never be a great lawyer—maybe not even a good lawyer. It's humorous to see his eyes light up at the mention of barbecues, hunting, receptions, and outings. You ought to hear him, Cassie. He sounds like a man reciting poetry when he talks of bourbon, leather and French perfume and how he loves spending other people's money. I know Zach's life is not the life for us. You can trust me. I'll be careful. So far Zach and I make a good team. I like him. He's a fun person—easy to get along with. I'll let him get richer and I'll get smarter. I won't fall into the same trap with the greedy. I thought it humorous when Zach confessed that when he was a child he learned to manipulate anyone in authority—even his parents. I was the opposite. I've never wanted to manipulate anyone, least of all my parents. I still don't."

"Tell me more about Zach, I asked. "What does he look like? Is he handsome, short, tall, fair or dark? Tell me."

"Well, Cassie, I suppose he's handsome, but how would I know that? Women think he's handsome—that's for sure. All I can tell you is, he isn't ugly. He has dark hair, brown eyes, a big dimple in the center of his chin and a boyish smile. He's always happy. I like that part. He never complains. He's as tall as I am, has flawless manners and is always perfectly dressed. When I met him the first time, I noticed his clothes straightaway. There's never a spot, stain or crease on anything of his. Cassie, I can't imagine how much money Zach spends on clothes. He wears more clothes in a week than I've owned in my lifetime. I've never seen a man more concerned with appearance, but I must confess, his dress does communicate success to his clients. He's confident and never afraid to meet people and does seem to have a power over others."

"I know exactly what you mean," I said and gave Ben a big grin. "When you look at me, I feel your confidence. I feel your power and I like it. Your power over me has nothing to do with the way you are dressed. Your power comes straight from your soul. It's who you are. You make me want to listen to you—to be with you and I'm sure Zach knows that, too. You didn't know that, did you? And, to top it off, you have the most beautiful cornflower blue eyes. When you look at me, it's as if you're looking into my soul. You have a manly appearance but a boyish innocence—a good combination. People trust you, Ben. Along with your confidence, I'm sure that's why they hired you. Your parents taught you confidence. That's like us Cherokee. We teach our children to behave like adults. Discipline is never a problem with us. Your father learned quickly we never use corporal punishment like whites. Cherokee parents won't stand for anyone striking their children."

I continued and Ben listened.

"Zach sounds selfish—like he would take advantage of anyone including his parents—including you—maybe especially you. Be careful, Ben. The way you described him it sounds like Zach loves himself and only himself. Be careful he doesn't rub off on you. Remember your parents' advice. Zach doesn't sound like he has any love of community."

"I'll remember, Cassie. You don't have to worry. I'm my own man—I know who I am. Zach won't rub off on me. I'm perfectly aware of his shortcomings and my strengths."

"Ben, it sounds like you and Zach make quite a pair," I said finally. "I'm sure you two are making a name for yourself in Milledgeville, but remember me and remember your parents. Even when you're away from home and no one is watching, remember who you are, Ben. Remember who you are."

Chapter XXVI

1826 – Zach's Warning

Chapter 26

19 November 1826 - The Trading Moon - Nv-da-de-qua

Copied from the *Southern Recorder* – 31 October 1826 – page 4

Valuable Land and Negros for Sale,

The subscriber, being very desirous to close his farming business with a view to turning his attention to the mercantile business, offers for sale, nearly all his land, negros, stock and every other article that pertains to the farming business...I will sell with this land 15 to 18 Negros....all on credit of 1,2,3,4 and 5 years, the purchaser satisfactorily securing the amount of the purchase money. I would prefer selling them together but would sell them separately if preferred by persons wishing to purchase...any communication addressed to...Shady Grove, Greene County, Georgia will be promptly attended to. He also offers for sale for CASH or on a short credit Ten or Twelve Very Likely Negros, among which are two fellows, two women, a boy ten or twelve, and the balance boys and girls of smaller descriptions; which Negros have been left with the subscriber by a friend, for sale, and will be sold at very low prices—Persons wishing to purchase negros of the description mentioned, would do well to call and see them, as they are uncommonly likely and valuable. REUBEN THORNTON, Fork of the Oconee and Apalatchie rivers, Greene County, August 8

I wish I could buy those children and raise them myself. I would teach them to read and write. We would have the most magnificent school. Maybe Ben and I can do that when we are married and live on the other side of the Mississippi and take care of as many as we can buy.

Edudu says things change, but I wish they would change more quickly for us and for the Africans—change for the better.

Copied from the *Southern Recorder* – 31 October 1826 - Page 4

25 Dollars Reward...Ran away from the subscriber on the night of the 19th instant a very bright mulatto fellow named CHARLES; he is about 20 years old, about 5 feet 10 inches high,

one of his upper fore-teeth out, some freckles and a few moles on his face, dark hair and a timid countenance, well dressed, carried off a shot gun—he expects to pass for a white man, and I am of the opinion is conveyed off by one—He will endeavor to get to East Florida or Alabama, Any person securing said fellow in any safe Jail or delivering him to me in Monroe County, Geo, seven miles east of Forsyth, shall receive the above reward, with liberal expenses. Joseph Reese.

Whites think it a terrible thing when an African or Indian is mistaken for a white person and criminal when they pretend to be white. That puzzles me. Why does that bother them so? What is it about white skin that is so precious? I hope Charles gets safely to Florida and has a wonderful life. I hope he escapes the soldiers who have been sent to Florida to hunt runaways.

November 1826 Milledgeville

Ben was looking forward to his Tuesday afternoon meeting with Zach. It wasn't Ben's first visit to Zach's father's sumptuous hotel, but it was the first time to have a meal prepared by their new French chef everyone was talking about. He wanted to try the dish prepared with the French sauce mayonnaise. Everyone was raving that the lobster mayonnaise was the best dish they had ever eaten.

This would be a welcome change from the plain table-fare in Ben's boring run-of-the-mill boarding house. He was weary of beans, cornbread and boiled cabbage—day after day. Zach told him his father, just returned from England, had eaten at Delmonico's in Manhattan and was so impressed he persuaded their chef to come with him to Milledgeville to oversee both his hotel kitchen and his domestic staff. Zach said his father might open another hotel in Savannah specializing in French cuisine. Ben was looking forward to the meal and learning more about Elizabeth.

Ben had heard all about Elizabeth and was anxious to meet her formally. Zach had painted her as exceptionally attractive and a most ambitious business woman.

"Glad you could join me, Ben," Zach said, greeting Ben on the three broad steps leading up to the private dining room and bar area on the left of the foyer—the room reserved for the hotel's special guests.

As Zach escorted him to their reserved spot, Ben scanned the well-decorated private room and bar. Mr. Mitchell had spared no expense. The combination of the vibrant colors, the exquisite leather, the detailed workmanship of the carved wooden panels, the bright chandeliers hanging

300

from high ceilings and the strategically-placed gilt mirrors gave a visual impact of highest luxury. It wasn't a terribly large room, but it contained a marvelous labyrinth of private cubicles and polished mahogany tables with pink marble flooring. It was the perfect setting for a morning coffee, a private dinner, a leisurely brandy and cigar or an undisturbed, unobserved business meeting. Every well-to-do businessman in Georgia knew of this room.

"What would you like to drink?" Zach asked.

"Whatever you're having will be fine, my friend. I've never been much of a drinker. I don't know one drink from another."

Zach made a motion to the tall African servant standing in the shadows.

"Well, I don't suppose there's anything wrong with someone who doesn't drink, but for me, I like to relax and have some fun in the evening and to tell the truth, I'm always suspicious of a teetotaler."

Zach changed the subject, "Ben, before I forget, I want to tell you how pleased my father and I are with your work. You've added everything we were looking for. Hiring you turned out a better decision than we imagined."

Ben didn't know what to say and nodded in return.

"I knew you were the man for the job from the beginning," Zach continued. "We're going to do some good work and make money, too. That won't be bad, will it?"

"I've never been afraid of hard work and I appreciate being paid for it," Ben answered. "Like I told you that first day, I want to earn my wages—every penny. I'll give a fair day's work for a fair day's pay."

"That's the spirit, Ben. Good for you, young man," Zach said with a patronizing chuckle. "That's exactly the kind of attitude we expected from you with your background. We love that protestant work ethic around here."

The servant quickly returned with their drinks. Ben wasn't used to such service. The tall negro, dressed in black with white gloves, moved about the room without making an audible sound. Ben's drink glass, handed to him on a silver tray, sparkled in the light from the brilliant chandeliers, the reflected light of various mirrors and the welcome flames of the oversized fireplace.

"Ben," Zach said, when they had their drinks in hand, "this is the best sipping whiskey there is. Since you don't know anything about alcohol, let me teach you how to enjoy it. First, take the smallest taste and don't swallow. Then breathe slowly over your tongue. You'll get the full flavor of the whiskey that way. After you taste this, you'll never be happy with anything else, I promise you. Everything else will taste like nasty snake oil."

Zach raised his glass and said, "A toast to you, Elizabeth and myself and our future—to us and our success."

"To us," echoed Ben.

They clinked their glasses and Ben sipped. As Ben breathed in as instructed, his mouth seemed to explode with new sensations. Even though Zach assured him this whiskey was the best, Ben still thought it tasted more like medicine—not something anyone would enjoy. He guessed it was probably an aged corn whiskey, from what he had heard. It would be potent but, after he swallowed, he was surprised at the remarkable sensation the whiskey delivered. It left a strong but agreeable feeling all the way from his mouth to his empty stomach. Zach was right. He had never tasted anything like this in his life. He felt the glowing sensation continue even after it reached the bottom.

Ben returned the toast, "To our friendship—may it last forever."

Zach and Ben sipped again. Ben leaned back, relaxed and began to take his father's advice and listen more than he talked. Zach, on the other hand, didn't mind talking. Zach was a talker—even when he wasn't drinking.

"Elizabeth will be here shortly, Ben. Before she gets here, let me tell you a few things about her you should know. First, you'll like Elizabeth. All men do. In my opinion, she's the most attractive woman in Milledgeville—maybe in all of Georgia. She's one of a kind, for sure. She's a unique lady."

"Tell me about her," Ben asked. "How's she different from other women?"

Zach took another sip, "Well, I've known Elizabeth since we were children. Our parents were travel companions. Our families traveled to Europe every other year or so. Elizabeth and I weren't born into poverty. Our parents still love to travel together."

Zach laughed, "Ben, I want to be frank with you. There is no need to hide anything. Elizabeth and I have been business associates for years—since childhood really. We learned what can be done with money early. Neither Elizabeth nor I have siblings and we were both spoiled rotten—still are as a matter of fact. For years now, she and I have had our own business interests, investments and bank accounts with full approval of our parents. We were groomed to understand business, handle money and be wealthy. We decided, if things work out, that our duet might become a trio with the right person. She and I have been looking for someone like you. We chose you as the addition to my father's firm with a view to becoming a future partner. Therefore, you need to know about Elizabeth—about us. I don't want you to get off on the wrong foot with her or misunderstand. She isn't what she seems."

Ben wanted to hear more about Elizabeth. He sipped and answered, "I'm ready to listen, Zach. I'm enjoying this drink and I'm all ears. Tell me about Elizabeth. Tell me more about your plans. This is interesting."

Zach continued, "When we were little, Elizabeth and I learned we could get away with anything if we were moderately careful. I guess you can say we learned to play our parents—to play all adults really—from an early age. Elizabeth and I make a good team. We've always been on the same page. We learned to get what we wanted when we wanted it. Our parents, like most well-to-do parents I suppose, wanted to avoid problems with their children. They gave us great latitude as long as we didn't cause trouble. They didn't want us to interfere with their lives. We learned that early."

Zach laughed again with an easy laugh that made Ben feel comfortable, but Ben reflected he had never played his parents and wasn't sure what Zach meant. It didn't sound like something to be proud of.

"When we were young," Zach continued, "Elizabeth and I learned to stay out of our parents' way and have our fun. It became a formula we've carried into adulthood. I'm amazed how lazy adults can become when they have a surplus of money and assign the care of their children to servants. Our parents wanted a problem-free life and Elizabeth and I wanted to grow up fast. We got what we wanted. This is my point. The byproduct of our youth is we learned we needed money to be happy."

Zach paused and leaned over towards Ben and shook his cigar towards Ben's face to emphasize his point.

"Now that we're adults, we like to spend money. We learned our continued happiness requires a liberal income—that's what Elizabeth and I work for. Acquiring wealth is a game to us. It's the game."

Zach looked at Ben and shook his cigar towards him once again.

"It's the only game. Our parents discovered their life ran more smoothly when Elizabeth and I were supplied with liberal buying power and allowed to conduct our own affairs with a minimum of supervision. We became experts at getting our own way. The point for you is, Ben—the skills Elizabeth and I learned as children we use now as adults."

"Do you play chess, Ben?" Zach asked.

"Yes, Father taught me to play when I was small and we played often. It's a fascinating game. Do you play, Zach?"

"Yes, I'm intrigued with the game myself," Zach continued, leaning back in his big chair and examining Ben carefully.

"One day we'll have to see just how much strategy there is in that country boy mind of yours, Ben," Zach said. "I'll put you to the test before long. One evening after work we'll have us a good chess game. You can learn a lot about a person by playing chess with them. Have you ever heard of Francois Philador?"

"No, I don't think so," Ben said. "Father and I have read some about chess strategy and I know a few openings, but I'm not familiar with that name. The Spanish opening is the only opening I remember."

Zach waved his cigar again towards Ben, "Philador was a French chess prodigy. He has an oft quoted saying about chess, 'Les pions sont l'ame du jeu'--'Pawns are the soul of chess'. Elizabeth and I play occasionally and she usually wins. She wins because she is always willing to sacrifice her assets— to sacrifice pawns or any other piece. She loves to open up the board and attack. She's vicious on the chessboard."

Zach paused, took another long sip of whiskey and observed Ben again.

"She's a fearless competitor on the chessboard and likewise in business— remember that, Ben," Zach said. "To Elizabeth, life is one big chess game. People are the pieces and wealth the ultimate prize. There are things Elizabeth and I want and we're willing to play the game—to manipulate the board—to sacrifice pawns to get the big prize. We're looking for checkmate and we don't care how we get it. We're willing to play any kind of gambit to defeat our opponent. We're going to take care of our future and make it secure. If we don't, who will? I promise you, with Elizabeth on your side of the board, you'll win the game every time."

Zach laughed and Ben laughed with him. Perhaps it was the alcohol that Ben wasn't used to or the sumptuous surroundings or Ben's willingness to please but Ben felt an undercurrent of uneasiness in Zach's speech.

"Well, I hope Elizabeth doesn't think of me as a pawn to be sacrificed. That wouldn't be good, would it?" Ben answered.

"My word no, Ben," Zach said. "Let me suggest you think of yourself as an intrepid knight carefully selected by his queen to lead a courageous charge, capture the enemy fastness and secure vast amounts of gold to be given into the royal treasury."

Zach continued with another chuckle, "Don't misunderstand me, Ben. A couple of years ago, Elizabeth and I decided we needed a man like you—a chivalrous knight, if you will. My father needed a new man at the firm and you were our choice to fill both positions. You're going to work for my father and, if you want to, you can work for Elizabeth and me at the same time. I think it would be more accurate to say you'll partner with us. The three of us will work together. We'll be a team. We'll play the big game together. We've been watching you since you went to work for my father and we've decided to make you privy to our business. Who knows, you might want to be a full partner one day and cash in as we have. If you want to be rich, really rich, all you need to do is listen to us. We're experts—and don't worry about being sacrificed in the big game. I can assure you Elizabeth wouldn't treat you in such a cavalier fashion."

Ben didn't know what to say. He wasn't sure he was understanding everything Zach had been talking about, but he did understand Zach's ambition for money and power. That was clear. Zach and Elizabeth sounded as if they could, and would, accomplish their plans. This was interesting.

"All this is fascinating, Zach," Ben answered. "I appreciate you taking the time to fill me in and I'm looking forward to meeting Elizabeth. With your introduction, she is even more intriguing than before. Is this job I've been selected for secondary to the one I have at the law firm? I'm confused. I thought I was hired to work for your father? I thought you and I both worked for your father?"

Zach laughed out loud and continued. His face had become slightly red from the whiskey.

"I understand the confusion, Ben. There's no conflict. Your first priority is with Father. You'll represent Father's clients and help him make a lot of money. However, with my father's full knowledge and blessing, Elizabeth and I have a secondary job for you. We're always looking for ways to make more money—a lot of money. Elizabeth and I, and Father too, wanted a young, handsome intelligent man like you, who was good with people, who could represent the firm and could run for a state-wide office—and maybe eventually an office in Washington City—the House or Senate. We want to begin with representation here in the Georgia legislature."

Ben sat back, sipped his drink and listened to this exuberant lawyer continue to share his grand plans. He had certainly chosen to work for a progressive law firm. That was clear. Everything Zach said was interesting.

"On the surface," Zach continued, "Elizabeth and I may appear normal, but we have a hidden agenda. We want to travel the world and bask in the golden sun of unlimited wealth. You'll discover Elizabeth to be determined. She gets what she wants. She always gets what she wants."

Zach paused to sip his drink and smoke his cigar.

"Well, Zach," Ben replied cautiously, "you know I couldn't agree to anything that would violate your father's trust. I certainly couldn't participate in anything illegal. I wouldn't do that. I don't want to be prudish, but I want to be aboveboard. I want to be honest. I'll never go behind your father's back."

Zach signaled for another drink and laughed again and waved at Ben with the hand holding his expensive Cuban cigar.

"I understand, Ben. Don't be silly. Elizabeth and I aren't going to do anything illegal or even dubious. Nothing we do is shady. Father wouldn't allow it. Father knows everything Elizabeth and I are involved in—well, almost everything, and he approves. We're honest folks, at least as far as the letter of the law is concerned, but it's a big interesting world out there with plenty of opportunities for the ambitious who are willing to use all the tools available. Father has ambitions, but Elizabeth and I have ambitions that go far beyond the walls of a stuffy old family law firm."

Ben liked what he was hearing. He liked the privileges that came with his job. He could get used to this. His future looked brighter than ever.

Zach paused for a long while and puffed his cigar, blowing the silvery smoke casually towards the ornate ceiling.

"Ben," Zach said lazily, still looking at the ceiling, "you wouldn't mind living in the nicest house in town, extended trips to Europe, a wardrobe full of French fashions for your wife, plenty of servants and everyone tipping their hat when your big coach and four passed? You wouldn't mind hiring the best tutors for your children, would you? What's wrong with that? That's what we have in mind for you—if you, my friend, are willing. We're thinking of your best interest, Ben."

Zach continued without giving Ben the chance to answer and Ben was content to listen. He had always wanted to tour Europe.

"Ben, I understand Elizabeth and you should, too. She isn't complicated. If you're agreeable the three of us are going to work together, but here's the warning about Elizabeth—this is why I invited you here today. This is what I've been trying to tell you. I guess I talk too much but that's alright. I like to talk. I'm relaxed when I talk. Here's my point about Elizabeth."

Zach paused, took a sip of his whiskey and a lingering puff of his cigar. He leaned back again in the leather padded armchair and watched his silvery cigar smoke slowly rise.

"Elizabeth is business—all business," Zach said quietly. "Elizabeth loves Elizabeth. All she cares about is her security. Elizabeth will never be in love with anyone but Elizabeth. If she were to marry, it would be for money—certainly not for love. Elizabeth uses men, Ben. Beware. You've been warned. I've seen men sucked into her web, consumed and discarded. Elizabeth loves Elizabeth and she'll never allow a rival—certainly not you. She's the master of the pawn sacrifice—and to her, men are pawns."

"You make her sound cold-hearted, Zach," Ben answered. "Why would I even want to work with a person like her if what you say is true?"

Zach paused for a moment and swirled the clear liquid in his expensive glass, watching it go around, and continued deliberately.

"That's a good question. That's exactly what I wanted to talk to you about. You'll want to work with Elizabeth because Elizabeth is a brilliant business partner you can trust. Elizabeth will help us make a lot of money. You can depend on her implicitly in business—just not in matters of the heart. I'm not sure she has a heart, Ben."

Zach laughed, broke into a big smile, leaned over and slapped Ben's shoulder. Zach was enjoying the whiskey and the conversation—as was Ben.

"Don't get me wrong, Ben. I like Elizabeth. She and I are best friends. We trust one another. I would do anything for her. I trust her with my life but not my heart. She's not the kind of woman I want to be the mother of my children, if you know what I mean. The only man she would be happy with is a groveling drudge—a menial to do her bidding. She will always be queen on her personal chess board and there will be no rival—no king or even a prince—only servants and a queen."

Zach continued and Ben listened, "Life is a game and we keep score with money. As long as you're aware of Elizabeth's greed and accompanying cold heart, you'll be fine, Ben. That's all I'm saying. I wanted to tell you this today to protect you."

"What makes you think I need protection from a woman?"

"Ben, Ben. You are naïve. She is beautiful, charming and tempting. I'm afraid, my friend, you'll forget my warning the moment you meet her. You mustn't think her capable of love. Never allow yourself to think you could make her happy. If you fall for her, she'll use you up. I tell you that from personal experience. I learned that lesson when I was a boy and I've never fallen for her again."

Ben didn't know what to say and responded lamely, "Well, Zach, it sounds like you don't really want me to meet her. You make her sound dangerous—like someone I should be afraid of. Why would I want to do business with an icy, cold-hearted woman like her?"

Zach paused, smiled, leaned forward towards Ben and looked him in the eye for a few moments to cement his words.

"I laid it on thick, didn't I?" Zach said, leaning back again. "It's simple. We'll work with her because she'll help us make a great deal of money. She has the best business mind in the state. We need her skills. You need her. I need her. My father needs her. As a business partner, Elizabeth is much more perceptive than I am. I absolutely want you to meet her. That's why I hired you. That's why Elizabeth hired you. Elizabeth and I need a man like you."

Zach paused for a moment and shook his glass, hand and all, towards Ben's face as if he were shaking his finger in a warning.

"We chose you, Ben. We chose you because of your country boy innocence and good looks. You're smart and people trust you. You have a way with people. A man like you was the missing piece in our plan. You were the valiant knight missing from our chess board. Now that you're here, we intend to send you into the fray—right onto the floor of the Georgia House. It took us a couple of years to find the right person, but you're our man. Remember, to Elizabeth everyone is a servant. Trust her in business—never in love. That's my warning, Ben. That's what I wanted to tell you this afternoon."

"Well," Ben replied, "You paint her as the most egotistical, selfish woman I've ever heard of, but I hear what you're saying. You're telling me she's a good business woman and I should be careful. I have ambitions of my own. I don't think I want to accumulate as much as you two, but I would like to acquire some security for my later years. You and Elizabeth come from a different background, Zach. We have different values."

Ben laughed and continued, "Zach, my parents taught me, 'do unto others as you would have them do unto you'. It sounds like you and Elizabeth believe you should take it away before they know it's missing."

"You're humorous, Ben, and witty and not far from the truth. I'll be frank. Elizabeth and I will use anything and anyone to get what we want—as long as we don't go to jail. We use the law to our benefit, but there is another side to Elizabeth. She can be fun. There's nothing wrong with you spending an afternoon with her. I hope you two have many, but I know better than to fall for her and you better not fall for her either. That's all I'm trying to tell you. She broke my heart a long time ago. I learned my lesson. If you allow her to steal your heart, she'll tromp it under her feet. You'll curse the day you met her and remember every word of this conversation."

The tall negro servant refreshed their drinks once again. Ben marveled how he moved through the room without making a sound. Both young men, now slightly red-faced, were beginning to feel the effects of the strong whiskey.

"Ben," Zach said as he swirled his drink, "the most beautiful woman you've ever seen will walk up those stairs in a few minutes and everything I've tried to tell you will disappear like a morning mist. When you look at her and her fragrance fills your head, you'll behave irrationally—mark my words,

Ben. I've seen it over and over, but I don't think you been listenin'," Zach said slightly slurring his words.

Ben made the decision to be wary of this mercenary woman who cared for no man. He already had the love of his life in Cassie. He could be sure he wouldn't fall for the woman Zach had described. He was too smart for that.

Ben, unused to the effect of liquor, noted Zach's warnings were actually having the opposite of their intended effect. Although he hadn't met her formally, he had begun thinking of Elizabeth as the ultimate challenge—the grand prize rather than a selfish woman to be avoided. What if he could win her heart? What a trophy she would be, but he was thinking nonsense. He was yet to meet Elizabeth. He mustn't forget Cassie.

Zach continued, "The three of us will be about business and nothing else. That's my point in this whole conversation. Remember that and you'll be fine. I never trust a woman and I trust a woman with money even less."

Zach laughed so hard at his own remark he spilled half his drink on his father's expensive floor. Ben laughed, too. It was impossible not to like Zach. The tall negro suddenly appeared with a towel and cleaned up Zach's mess.

On schedule, Elizabeth walked up the three stairs from the foyer to the private dining room. The two finely dressed young men stood. She was dressed in white linen with ruffles, a pale green satin bow in the back with open shoulders and just the proper amount of exposed white bust. She completed the ensemble with a light green hat tilted to the side, a neat satin bow under her chin, a matching wrap, purse and shoes. She might have just stepped off a fashionable Paris street.

She curtseyed and Zach introduced her formally and the three sat close together.

"My word, Ben," Elizabeth said in a low husky voice looking straight into his eyes, "You are handsome. I think you're even more handsome than Zach, and you definitely have the most beautiful eyes I have ever seen in all my born days. It's a pleasure to make your acquaintance, Ben Lowry."

As Zach had known, Ben was not at all prepared for this meeting. He was completely undone by Elizabeth's opening remarks and was only able to mumble a near-incoherent reply, "A pleasure to make your acquaintance. I'm at your service, ma'am."

When Elizabeth spoke, everything Zach had told Ben disappeared from his mind. Ben immediately thought she was the most beautiful creature imaginable. He hoped the conversation wouldn't turn serious. With the alcohol, Ben was quite unable to think clearly.

Elizabeth, sitting between the two young men, said, "Sadly, as much as I would love to spend the afternoon with you two handsome men, this meeting will be brief. I wanted to come by and meet our new partner. Alas, I must presently join my parents, but I wanted to meet Ben—and I'm not disappointed—no, not disappointed in the least."

Ben didn't remember much of the brief conversation. He had never seen a woman wearing clothing with such power and this was his first encounter with French perfume. Sitting next to Elizabeth made him think he was in the middle of his father's apple orchard in full bloom. Ben had, in the first few moments of meeting Elizabeth, forgotten every warning about spider webs and chess boards. His head was spinning.

After a few moments of small talk, Elizabeth stood and extended her hand to Zach, "I wish I could stay, but I promised my parents I would dine with them. I assured Father I wouldn't be a minute late. I'm enjoying your father's new chef, Zach. I've never eaten cuisine like this before outside of France. I think the food is better here than when we were in Paris, to tell you the truth. All Milledgeville is in a fuss over him. You better be careful or my father will steal him away. You know how my father loves his food."

Elizabeth, facing Ben, gave him her hand and moved close—almost touching.

"It's been a pleasure to meet you, Ben Lowry," she said in a low voice. "I've been looking forward to this introduction and I'm not disappointed. You are handsome," she said, never taking her eyes from his. "You'll have to bring me to dinner here one night, Ben Lowry—just the two of us so we can get to know one another properly. I would like that. I want to know all about you. Will you bring me here, Ben? I would love to have dinner with you. I want to know every little thing about you—every little thing. Would you, please?" she begged.

Ben stuttered his reply in a voice much too loud.

"Of course, I would love to take you to dinner, Elizabeth. It would be a pleasure. I would be honored, I'm sure."

Elizabeth, continuing to hold her hand in Ben's, continued to look straight into Ben's eyes without blinking and asked immediately, "Would this Friday evening about seven o'clock be good for you? We'll have a nice bottle of wine and a wonderful meal. I want to know everything about you from the day you were born. After our meal you can drive me home. I would like that. That would be a good evening, wouldn't it? Would you drive me home afterward?"

Ben was captivated, stunned—unable to think or respond intelligently. If Ben had been observant, he would have noticed Zach's big grin. There was nothing anyone could have said to warn Ben of the danger resident in Elizabeth's feminine charms.

"My father keeps a table reserved in the dining room. We'll have a cozy meal, a nice bottle of French wine and you can tell me all about yourself, Ben. I'm dying to hear all about you. Zach has made me most curious."

At that moment, Elizabeth's parents entered the foyer. Elizabeth gave the young men a polite curtsey and Ben took the white gloved hand she offered once again in parting.

As he held her hand, she squeezed his fingers, stared into his eyes for a moment longer than necessary, "Ben, I can't tell you how much I'm looking forward to Friday and us getting to know one another. I find you an unusually attractive young man. I truly do."

She walked down the three stairs to the foyer to join her parents. She didn't look back. Her fragrance lingered.

8 December 1826

Ben told me about Zach and Elizabeth and their plans for him and the legislature. He believes they will help his law career and his ability to do something for the Cherokee. Ben said they are intelligent, understand business and come from well-to-do families. Ben says Zach and Elizabeth were both born with a silver spoon in their mouth and can't go past a mirror without checking to see if they are put together properly. After my trip to Milledgeville, I find it much easier to imagine such things. Although I was never inside Zach's father's hotel, I did see the façade.

I love Ben's boyish innocence. I don't want him to change. It would never occur to my gullible Ben that a beautiful woman would be deceptive. I am not jealous but I warned him. Ben may be a good lawyer, but he has a lot to learn about the unseen world of avaricious white men. I hope he remembers his parents' advice.

Milledgeville December 1826

"Ben, what did you think of your dinner with Elizabeth Friday?" Zach asked, "How did that go? I heard you two had a nice meal and you saw her home afterward. She's an engaging woman, isn't she? Did you survive her charms? Did you fall in love with her or did you take my advice and guard your heart?"

Zach laughed heartily and slapped Ben on the back.

"She is beautiful, Zach, I'll grant you that," Ben said, joining Zach in his laughter. "You were right to warn me. Yes, I enjoyed the evening with Elizabeth. I enjoyed it greatly, but I'm sure I was poor company. I felt awkward the entire time. For years my mother tried to teach me social etiquette, but I'm afraid I was an inattentive student. I'm afraid I allowed Elizabeth to do most of the talking—and that was fine with me. I'm sure she thinks me a boring farm boy with no conversation skills. I've never been in the company of a sophisticated woman like her, Zach. She's nothing like my mother. Without your warning, I'm sure I would have fallen for her right there at the table and turned into a blubbering puddle of jam."

Zach laughed again.

"I warned you about her, didn't I?

"You were right, Zach. I'm unprepared for Elizabeth. I see your wisdom. She's the most charming woman I could imagine. It's hard for me to believe her charm is entirely assumed."

Still laughing, Zach interrupted, "Remember, Ben, she's interested in money, large amounts of money, and she'll use you to get it. Elizabeth and I are in search of talent. That's why you were chosen. You'll make a good politician because everyone will think you trustworthy. That's what we want. Elizabeth is like a cat with a mouse. When she's finished playing with her captive she'll devour her plaything and search for another. Enjoy her fashions, perfume and coquetry, but don't fall for her. She'll break your heart. If you want a shrewd calculating business partner, Elizabeth is your woman. She's the most selfish person I know, but the best business partner you could possibly have."

"Elizabeth, what do you think about our boy?" Zach asked. "Can we groom him to task? Will he make a successful politician we can control? That's what I want to know."

"He'll do fine. He's nice-looking, able and malleable and incredibly naïve—just what we needed. He'll make the perfect hand-crafted politician. He's so green he thinks everyone is honest. We have the right man, Zach. Eventually he'll figure out how the world works, but by then we'll have him so confused he won't know up from down. By the time he figures things out, we'll have put so much money in his pockets, he'll eat out of our hands. He'll be entirely dependent upon us. It'll be nice to finally have our own personal politician—and besides, I like him. He's handsome. It's been a long time since I had my own plaything. He'll be amusing."

Elizabeth laughed unusually loud.

"With Ben, I can have my cake and eat it too. Won't that be fun? Did you see how he melted like a schoolboy when I flirted with him? You should have seen him at dinner. He drooled like a fawning dog the entire meal. It was humorous. We couldn't have picked a better man. If there's one thing I know how to do, it's wrap men like him around my finger, don't I? If he eventually balks, we'll find us another just as good or better. There are plenty more where he came from, but I think he's going to work out just fine.

Chapter XXVII

1827 - Ben Passes the Bar – An Afternoon with Zach

Chapter 27

2 January 1827

The sky is clear. It is bitterly cold. The ground is frozen solid—like a rock. It's the coldest I remember. It has been cold for days. The animals can walk across the river. The only time I'm warm is in bed under thick covers. Edudu and I must break ice and carry water several times a day for the chickens and hogs. Edudu says it's the coldest he ever remembers. I wish we had a beautiful blanket of snow instead of this constant biting cold with the punishing north wind blowing down off the mountains. I'm glad we have a cozy house, plenty of wood and a well-stocked smokehouse. We sit by the fire most of the day. My face is warm and my back cold. These are good days to read. Elisi and I have made many pine baskets to trade at Ross's Landing. I'll be so glad to see the dogwoods blooming and feel my toes warm again.

4 January 1827

English laws make our life difficult. I won't be surprised if one day they make it illegal for me to be a Cherokee.

> (604) An Act to prevent the Testimony of Indians being received in courts of Justice.
>
> Be it enacted by the Senate and the House of Representatives of the State of Georgia, in General Assembly met, and it is hereby enacted by the authority of the same, that from and after the passage of this act, no Indian, and no descendant of an Indian, not understanding the English language, shall be deemed a competent witness in any court of justice created by the Constitution and laws of this State. IRBY HUDSON-Speaker of the House of Representatives, THOMAS STOCKS- President of the Senate.
>
> Assented to, December 26th, 1826 G.M. TROUP, Governor.

11 January 1827 - The Cold Moon - Un ol v ta ni

Our chief and edudu's friend, Pathkiller, died 7 January at his home in 'Di'ga-duhun'yi, Turkey Town, one of our largest towns by the Coosa River.

Pathkiller became principle chief in 1811. Edudu loved him. He was a good man. We shall miss him. William Hicks has been appointed chief. This is a bad time. We have many troubles.

29 January 1827

Bad news upon bad news. Pathkiller died and William Hicks became chief. Two weeks after his appointment William Hicks died. Who will be chief now? Sadness follows upon sadness.

30 January 1827

Shall we survive? Whites insist our agreements with them be written on paper and signed with ceremony which makes the agreements unbreakable— a forever contract. Whites make promises and break them soon afterward. Then they ask us to make another forever agreement.

1 February 1827

Today after I read the newspaper to edudu he stared into the forest without speaking a word. The news is not good for us. Without a single word to me, he went into the woods with Spinner and his gun and they didn't come back till long after the moon was shining. After he returned, I saw him talking with my brother on the porch. I could not hear their words, but I know their thinking. I have been thinking the same things, but I don't want to say them. I don't want to believe those things. Georgia can't wait to take possession of our land. As edudu talked to Five Feathers, out of the darkness I heard the call of a single owl. He called once again and was silent. I went to my bed.

2 February 1827

Copied from the *Georgia Journal* - 16th January 1827

"The surveyors…employed on the lands lying between the new treaty line and the Georgia boundary have been arrested in their progress by the Indians. Here is another impediment to the occupation of the country this year. It is excessively provoking for there is no time to be lost...the lottery will be late going into operation...this impertinent interference with the affairs of the people of Georgia will meet with severe retribution."

Have the English forgotten where they came from and whose land they survey? Have they forgotten they promised we could live here forever? Edudu says they are invaders. We are the true owners of our country. It is our land. We are the Principal People.

4 February 1827
> Copied from the *Georgia Journal* - 27 January 1827
>> "NOTICE: Will be sold at the house of Sarah Waites, in Gwinnett county, on the second Wednesday of March next all the Negros of the estate of Esther Waites, dec'd. consisting of one negro woman and her children--sold for the benefit of the heirs and creditors of said estate. Terms made known on the day."

Whites have taken most of our country, but at least we are free. In every newspaper I read of Africans for sale as if they were a bushel of corn or a yard of cloth. Whites refer to Africans as their stock—chattel. Edudu says when a person tells a lie for long enough they will begin to believe their own words.

Mr. Lowry teaches from his Book every Sunday when the white missionaries gather in fine clothes. He teaches us that we should use his Book as a guide for living. It is the book whites brought with them from across the ocean.

17 March 1827
> Copied from *The Athenian* - March 9th 1827
>> "The claims of Georgia on the General Government for services rendered by the militia in the years '92, '93 and '94 have at last been allowed by the House of Representatives....The amount is $129,375.62. One great cause of dissatisfaction with the General Government will be removed. There then will remain no main subject of contention but the extinguishment of the Indian title to the Cherokee Territory within the limits of this state."

I extinguish my candle. My room goes dark. I lie under my warm quilts thinking before I sleep. The whites want to extinguish my nation. They want me to vanish into obscurity never to be seen again.

21 March 1827
> Ben asked his father to share this letter with me.
> Huff's Boarding House - 16 March 1827

My Dear Father,

The enclosed article from *The Athenian* represents the political mood in Milledgeville. The news is not good. Georgia has seized all Creek land in the pine barrens. They want to complete that seizure by occupying the Cherokee land in the north. I do not know why they want the worthless pine barrens, but they do. I have discovered in Milledgeville an irrational hatred of all Indians. Until I moved here I had no idea how deep that sentiment runs. The thought of Indians having title to land drives them mad. I remember when my landlord told us to never bring Cassie to the boarding house again. I think perhaps the entire white population of Georgia feels that way. I often hear things about Indians which are patently untrue, and I have begun to suspect the authorities spread malicious rumors intending to bend the mind of the populace to their rapacious ways.

The General Government has revoked the tainted Treaty of Indian Springs but it's too late for any good to come of the reversal. All Creek property and assets in Georgia have been confiscated—nothing can be done. Creek removal is fait accompli. The Creek have no advocate and cannot oppose the militia. Georgia is too far from Washington City for there to be any teeth in opposing directives from the War Department. My fear is, Father, Georgia will continue to survey new counties, ever squeezing the Cherokee until they are extinguished as have been the Creeks. Georgia insists the general government honor the Compact of 1802. I am afraid, Father. I have no confidence in our government to act justly. What will you and Mother do if the Cherokee are also evicted? No matter what might happen, you can depend on me. I shall continue to be, Your loving son, Ben xoox

2 April 1827

Ben was nervous about his bar examination, but he need not have worried. He is smarter than his father, but I wouldn't tell him that. For two weeks before the examination Ben studied late into the night and then rose early to read and re-read every law book in the firm's library.

I love his energy. I am impatient for our union. Some days I take his letters to my special place and imagine past conversations. I need him like I need water, air and sunshine. He is my true special place.

Today I watched a pair of river otters at play. I think I have never seen anything as singularly lovely. Sometimes I watch a mother with her kits. Just across the river they have a slide and play as if they were human children. I cannot imagine a creature that enjoys its existence more than river otters. I hear them chirp and grunt. I imagine I hear them laughing. They swim by my rock most every day and greet me as they pass. They notice everything. Their big brown eyes watch my every movement. I told edudu I didn't want anyone trapping them for their fur. What a horror to kill these lovely creatures. Edudu says the otters are fewer than when he was a boy. He said we would go the way of the otters. What a loss it would be if there were no river otters.

12 April 1827

I love how Ben shares his deepest thoughts with me in his letters.

Huff's Boarding House - 9 April 1827

My Dear Cassie,

Grand news. I passed my examination with an excellent score. I'm much relieved. The night before I slept only an hour. I could not compose myself for sleep. I lay rehearsing things I had read. I shall sleep now. I am a lawyer in the State of Georgia. Our dreams are coming true, aren't they?

The next chapter of my life has begun. I wonder what life has in store for us—for my parents and for the Cherokee? I promise to work hard for our future and for your nation.

Zach invited me to celebrate my success with him and friends in his father's hotel. Zach's father owns property in Milledgeville, Savannah, Charleston and is buying more all the time. Mr. Mitchell uses his hotel to impress his clients. Maybe Zach gets his ability to use people honestly from his father.

The private dining room has its own bartender. It has private access to rooms above and the stables out back. Guests are served by unobtrusive, perfectly trained and immaculately dressed Africans. Mr. Mitchell insists on the best of everything. Zach's father says we reap according to how we sow. A good farmer must be liberal with his seed if he wants an abundant harvest. Father says the same.

It's never a waste to spend money on one's clients, Zach says—mimicking his father. Life is easy when you're rich. Having experienced both, I prefer the way the Cherokee go about their carefree life in community. I love the simple uncomplicated life in your country. I can't wait to see you again and rest my soul in your arms.

Yours Always, Ben xoox

Milledgeville – May 1827

"Elizabeth was visiting Mother yesterday and was asking about you, Ben," Zach said with a grin.

Their usual waiter silently served their drinks. Ben had noticed he would never make eye contact with the guests which seemed to be typical of slave staff.

"She's interested in you, young man. That's for sure. She asked me all sorts of personal questions about you."

Zach changed the subject.

"Elizabeth rode over with her father. He's lookin' to add to his domestic staff. He heard my father bought a hundred niggers at the Charleston slave market last week at a bargain price before they even went to auction. Father says they're the best stock he's seen in years. Father seems to be in the right place at the right time. He'll make a pretty profit, I imagine. Father knows a bargain when he sees one, especially when it comes to niggers. He's not a professional trader, but he knows slaves."

Ben didn't know what to say and was afraid to say anything in reply.

"You want to go with me and have a look, Ben? I always have an eye out for a good lookin' mulatto woman, but you have to be quick and get there before Father's overseers. Nothing wrong with having a little fun, is there?"

Since he had come to Milledgeville Ben heard talk like this often, but he still didn't like it. Sometimes it was hard to ignore, but if he wanted to keep his job he could not openly oppose slavery.

Zach looked sideways at Ben.

"Father's going to keep the best for the hotel and his friends."

Zach slouched back in his chair and puffed his cigar. He was relaxed and talkative. Zach talked and Ben listened.

"He never keeps field hands or women with children. He says there's a couple of excellent blacksmiths in the bunch and if he can find a good manager, he'll get a livery up and running in Macon and give it to me. I can make a tidy little profit, I'm sure. Since the Creeks left, that area is growing like crazy. Life is good, isn't it, Ben? There is more and more land available every day and opportunities everywhere but we have to strike while the iron is hot, don't we?"

Ben's view of Africans and their place in the world was different from Zach's. Ben could never voice his parents' abolitionist views with Zach or anyone in Milledgeville—to do so would be to destroy his career. Zach continued to lean back and took another sip of whiskey and gave Ben another sideways glance.

"Father's smart when it comes to slaves. He says pickaninnys are nothin' but trouble. He sells the women with children first, even if he takes a loss."

"Have you and your parents ever owned slaves, Ben?" Zach asked.

Ben answered trying to be neutral, "No, we've never owned slaves. My mother and Father are missionaries and have strong views about slavery."

Zach laughed and looked at Ben again, tossed down the rest of his drink and motioned to the waiter in the corner.

"Well, I guess some folks think of slaves as people, but if you ever hear them talkin' among themselves you'll know they're not exactly what we would call human. They sound like a bunch of monkeys jabbering about a banana. I can't understand a word they say."

The waiter delivered Zach's drink on a polished silver tray. Zach took a big sip. Ben knew he had to be very careful. He mustn't let out an unguarded comment.

"You should get yourself a slave, Ben, at least for show, if you know what I mean. It would let Father's clients know you're with us here in Georgia. You could do with a good servant, couldn't you? Talk to Father. He knows how to pick the ones who won't run. Father says you got to be smart when buyin' slaves or you can waste your money. He makes a lot of money by just keepin' his ear to the ground. He's getting this lot ready for sale now—feeding and clothing them—makin' them look good. You got to spend money to make money. Isn't that right, Ben?"

Ben made a face. Zach noticed and laughed.

"What a face, Ben. You need to be careful with your body language as well as your words. I don't care what you or your parents believe, but you don't want anyone to think you're an abolitionist, do you? If people thought you were opposed to slavery, they'd run you out of town on a rail. I promise you, Ben, you wouldn't look good in tar and feathers. If Father thought you were a nigger-lover you would be gone. You'd be farming somewhere in the backwoods if you're lucky. Once you're branded an abolitionist, you're done for in the south. You would never get anywhere, especially in politics—not here in Georgia, Ben."

Ben answered in a low voice, "Yes, I know you're right, Zach. I agree. I'll take your advice. I promise. I'll watch what I say. I like working for your father. I won't rock the boat."

"Good for you, Ben. Every plantation owner in Georgia has a fortune tied up in niggers. Our economy would collapse without slaves. We have to have slaves to function, don't we? If we didn't have niggers who do you think would pick the cotton?"

Ben noticed the tall waiter in the corner, although almost invisible in the shadows, was watching and listening to their conversation.

"I don't know what the abolitionists are so concerned about anyway. Niggers ain't the same as white folks. The truth is, Ben, we treat slaves right well here in Georgia—right well indeed. Father spends a lot of money on his slaves—all responsible folks do. Everybody takes care of their stock. We have to take care of our niggers, don't we? Father puts new clothes on them, pays for their boarding and doctorin' and he's getting them all new shoes—why, I couldn't believe Father's bill for nigger shoes alone. Takin' care of slaves is expensive, if you do it right—and Father does everything right. He's feeding them like they're white folks and calling the doctor in at the first sign of sickness. My father is good to his niggers. I can testify to that. He treats them like family—sometimes better than family. He treats them better than they would treat themselves. They surely don't have any reason to complain now, do they?"

Ben said in a low voice, "I saw a man horse-whipping a slave the other day in public. It was a terrible scene. I didn't like it."

Zach turned and stared at Ben for a moment and leaned back in his chair again with his hands behind his head.

"Ben, ever' now and then a nigger gets uppity and he'll have to be whipped. If you don't whip them in public what good is a whippin'? Niggers ain't got no money, Ben. You can't fine 'em like you can white folks. You can't take nothin' from them cause they ain't got nothin'. The threat of fines and jail time works for white folks but it don't work for niggers. They had rather be in jail than work. The threat of a good horse-whippin' is the only thing they understand. Ever' now and then niggers need to see what it's like— to hear the lash bite into a stupid nigger's back—that's the only thing they understand. Father says it's good to give one of his slaves a good whippin' so they know their place—just not too often. We can't have them gettin' uppity, can we? First thing you know they'd be thinkin' they have the same rights as white folks. Can you imagine living in a town full of free niggers? Who would want that?"

Ben was watching the tall waiter in the corner. Zach was talking away. He finished his drink and signaled for another and laughed. Ben was anxious for Zach to change the subject.

"Father won't keep slaves that have to be whipped. When he buys young niggers, he looks in their face and makes them look at him. Father says he can see in their eyes if they're a runner. He won't keep a runner—not one day."

Ben was speechless. He had never heard anything like this in his life. He understood he couldn't say a word, public or private, in argument against slavery. He wouldn't rock the boat. He wanted to keep his job. He would do exactly as Zach had instructed. No one could succeed in Georgia, or anywhere in the South, who was publicly opposed to slavery—and it was true that they needed someone to pick the cotton and do the hard work.

Zach, well lubricated with whiskey and never at a loss for words, continued to taunt Ben to see if he could bait him into compromising his position.

"One more thing, Ben. I don't want to ever hear you refer to a nigger as a person. Remember that. Niggers ain't never a person or a man. A nigger is always a fellow or a boy. Niggers ain't men. They ain't like us. If you start calling them men, it might give them the idea you think they're equal in some way. If you do that, first thing you know we'll have a bunch of god-damned Yankees down here talkin' up some modern French claptrap about equality. We'll put a stop to talk like that and right now. That won't work here in Georgia, and it especially won't work if you run for office, but don't you worry, Ben. I'm here to keep you straight. I'll keep your foot out of your mouth."

Ben was glad to be feeling the dulling effects of the alcohol. He was happy to listen. He certainly didn't want to enter into an intellectual conversation with anyone about slavery. Ben wanted to work. He wanted to work in Milledgeville. He wasn't interested in some egalitarian philosophical debate about the demerits of forced servitude. He would listen, enjoy the whiskey and not talk and avoid all discussion of slavery in the future. He would make certain he could not be baited into a discussion that could ruin his career.

"Ask Father's servants here in the hotel if they're not well taken care of?" Zach continued. "I had rather be one of Father's niggers than a farmer. Yes sir, Father takes care of his niggers. He can send his slaves to town with money in their pocket to do his business and they come back."

Ben knew better than to comment on Zach's observations. If his mother and father had heard Zach's discourse they would have opposed him in no uncertain terms, but then, his parents' job didn't hinge on their social views. Ben said nothing. What could he say? He certainly didn't want to quarrel. He dare not bite the hand that was feeding him.

Zach, weary of teasing Ben, changed the subject.

"Elizabeth asked about you, Ben. I told her you were looking forward to seeing her again. Are you looking forward to seeing her? I told her you were. She has her eye on you, my friend. The word is she thinks you're especially handsome."

Zach chuckled and changed the subject once again.

"How do you like these whiskey glasses, Ben? They're beautiful, aren't they?"

"I've never seen anything like these before," Ben admitted, as he examined the glass carefully, turning it slowly before his face in his long slender fingers, happy that Zach had changed the subject away from slavery.

The facets of the expensive glass in Ben's hand caught the glow from the chandelier refracting the light into fascinating hues and shades.

"Without a doubt, this is the most beautiful glassware I've ever seen," Ben said, continuing to stare at the glass. "I love the design, Zach, but isn't this glass unusually heavy? Why so heavy? Where did they come from?"

Ben wasn't interested in glassware. He wanted to hear more about Elizabeth and was wondering what she had said about him.

"Tell me more about Elizabeth. She is an exquisite woman, just as you said, Zach. I've never met anyone like her."

"This glassware is beautiful," Zach said, completely ignoring Ben's remark.

Neither young man was thinking about crystal glassware.

"My father heard it called flint glass," Zach continued, staring at the glass in his hand. "It's striking, isn't it? Father was in Ireland last year and was so impressed when he saw this Waterford Crystal he ordered a supply for the house. We had so many compliments Father replaced all our glassware in the hotel with Waterford. Father should have taken a job as salesman with the company. I can't tell you how many of Father's friends have ordered Waterford for their homes. Maybe I'll do a little sales work myself. One of the ingredients in this glass is lead. You didn't know they put lead in their glass, did you? That's why they're so heavy. Aren't they beautiful? Some folks call this lead crystal. You should see the fancy wine glasses. The stemware is the loveliest I've ever seen in my life—even more attractive than the glassware I saw in Paris. The French tend towards plain stemware, from what I've seen."

Zach laughed, sat more upright and looked at Ben again.

"We don't have anything like that here in Georgia, do we? All we have here is timber, cotton, slaves, cornbread and Indians."

Ben didn't laugh.

"Oh—I forgot," Zach added. "We do have our share of pretty girls. I think Georgia girls are as pretty as I've seen anywhere—maybe the prettiest—prettier than the French girls, I think. I do like pretty girls, don't you Ben. And the prettiest Georgia girl of them all is asking about you."

That last statement got Ben's attention. Zach laughed again and Ben couldn't help but smile and nod in return. They continued to talk about glassware and think about beautiful women.

"My mother would love these glasses," Ben said, "but she would never use them—a pity. My parents do everything as inexpensively as they can. They never spend money, if they can help it. Maybe when they move down here, I'll buy Mother some glassware she will actually use. Life would be different for my parents down here. They are frugal way up in Cherokee Country. Father could do quite well with a school here. Although my father's ideals are noble, I think he's wasting his time teaching the Cherokee—to tell the truth."

Zach was leaning back in the big upholstered chair sipping his whiskey, smoking his cigar and watching the clouds of silvery smoke curl towards the ornate ceiling—storing Ben's comments carefully for future use.

"The Cherokee are never going to change," Ben said. "They're set in their ways. They don't want to be like us and I can't blame them. I rather enjoyed my time with the Cherokee."

Zach observed Ben as he began talking about his youth in Cherokee Country. He could hear the animation creep into Ben's voice.

"I understand their simple lifestyle and their distrust of whites," Ben added. "The thing about the Cherokee I like the best is their contentment—they're always happy. They're not struggling to achieve happiness—or achieve anything. They have a carefree existence inside of a strong community. That is attractive, I must say. Their view of corporate ownership of land gives everyone identity and place. They always feel important—part of a greater society. What whites label as laziness, I would call serenity. I like their poised outlook, to tell the truth. They're not lazy at all."

As Ben mused about his life in Cherokee Country, Zach was thinking that responsibility for community was something he cared nothing about.

Ben continued, "To tell the truth, my memories of Cherokee Country are special. I love wandering the woods listening to the music of the wind in the pines. There's nothing like drinking cold water coming out from under a big rock on the side of a mountain on a hot summer's day. There's nothing as clean and pure as the forest. There's nothing as comfortable as lying on a soft bed of pine needles on a lazy spring day, a bed softer than my bed at home, and finding shapes in the lazy clouds. There's nothing like an afternoon by the river fishing and eating fish that were swimming just a few moments ago. I can understand why the Cherokee wouldn't want to abandon their lifestyle to look at the back end of a stubborn mule all day."

Zach took a big puff of his expensive cigar and watched the smoke curl towards the ceiling.

"Well, Ben, I like the woods and I like huntin', but that's about all. I like a good rifle and shootin' animals. That's a sport I can go for. I love sittin' on the side of a hill in the mornin' and seein' how many squirrels I can pick off. Those little devils are hard to hit, aren't they? I killed thirty-five squirrels one morning last year. Father said he and two friends killed a hundred and fifty one morning with their scatter guns."

Ben recovered his thoughts, remembering where he was and who he was talking to and paused a moment. He ignored Zach's remarks about hunting.

"My father could be down here and have all the paying students he wanted from families who understand the importance of a good education," Ben said, avoiding any discussion of hunting. "Father hasn't earned anything from teaching Indians, although everyone respects his noble intentions. I respect him immensely. Father is a good man—the best of men, and I know why he wants to teach, but there's no money in it and never will be. Mother and Father need to look out for their future. I appreciate the advice you and Elizabeth have given me. I feel better about my future and the future of my parents. I'm already beginning to save. Man does not live by bread alone, but he sure does need bread to live, doesn't he?"

"Ben, I couldn't have said it better myself. But enough about that. I don't want to talk about abstract morality or the natural beauty of the rural Georgia countryside or the drawbacks of watching the south end of a north bound mule. I want to know, my friend, what you think of this whiskey in this beautiful glass as we sit in this wonderful hotel? Pretty smooth, isn't it?"

Zach had a big smile on his red face. The effect of a considerable amount of alcohol had softened his thoughts.

"I'm not interested in philosophical discussions about anything today—certainly not Indians, slaves or religion," Zach added.

It had been a long day. Drinking on an empty stomach, the whiskey had tempered both young men.

"It's the best whiskey I've tasted, by far. Where did you get it?" asked Ben.

Zach paused, thinking about what he was going to say. Zach's interest wasn't glassware, sipping whiskey, the Cherokee, hunting or Ben's father. Zach and Elizabeth had a clear agenda for Ben's future.

"Ben," said Zach, "I got this whiskey from a friend of mine who's just come from the Hermitage—that's in Nashville, you know. This whiskey comes from Andy Jackson's special stock—his own private still and he sent this down himself. It's the best white whiskey you'll ever drink, I'll wager. I'll bet you didn't know Jackson has a famous nigger who runs the best still in Tennessee. Jackson keeps him busy, I hear. You can bet he'll never sell that ole' slave. He makes Jackson more money than a dozen field hands. The ole' timers, the Scots-Irish, called this stuff we're drinking the water of life. The story is that ole' slave of Jackson's learned whiskey makin' long ago from the ole' Scots. He knows more about makin' good whiskey than anybody in the whole south. I've heard Jackson won't let anyone talk to him he's so jealous. He keeps him shut up at the back of his place with a big slave that does nothing but guard his ole' nigger. Jackson's afraid they'll steal his recipe or bribe him into runnin' away and makin' whiskey for someone else."

Zach held up his glass, laughed again and continued in his planned speech and, because of the alcohol, repeated himself frequently.

"This is the best Tennessee sour mash you have ever tasted, ain't it?" Zach said, staring at the liquid in his glass. "I ain't never tasted better myself. There's none like it. The only thing as good as this whiskey is the glass I'm drinking it from and my present company. Ben, Jackson himself, with his compliments, sent this whiskey to you through my father's firm."

Zach had Ben's full attention.

"That's right," Zach said, leaning over almost in Ben's face to emphasize his point—eyes slightly out of focus—holding his glass up as if making a toast. "I've been waitin' to tell you that. Jackson himself sent this whiskey to the newest and most promising young lawyer in the south. That's you, Ben Lowry, in case you don't know. You're already gettin' a reputation as far away as Tennessee. What do you think about that? Ole' Hickory himself has taken notice of you, young man, all the way from Nashville. He thinks there's good things in store for you. Jackson knows you're goin' to be gettin' into Georgia politics. He wants you on his side."

Zach's nose had a red tip exactly as if someone had just squeezed it.

"Ben," said Zach, "It's time you begin thinking about your future. Elizabeth and I have talked. You need to think about your expectations just as Elizabeth and I have. We want the best for you. We'll always look out for your best interest. You can count on us and you can trust Andy Jackson, too."

Zach, the tip of his nose beginning to glow, continued, "True, you are young, but there'll come a time when you'll get older and you'll want to take it easy. We have to make hay while the sun shines, don't we? Of course we do. Well—your sun is shining, Ben—it's shinin' bright. If you don't think about yourself now, you'll end up working hard when you're an old man, your parents will have nothing and you'll end up livin' on charity. You don't want that, do you?"

Ben continued to sip Andrew Jackson's whiskey and study Zach's face. He liked what he was hearing and he wasn't worried in the least about his future or ending up on charity.

"You can have a prosperous future, Ben, and not just as an advocate. You can have a life of plenty, and I mean plenty, and retire by the time you're forty, if you're smart. You wouldn't mind living in the best house in town, taking a couple of trips to Europe every year, a houseful of servants for your wife and giving your children the best of everything, would you? Maybe smoking Cuban cigars and drinking the best whiskey every evening served by a well-trained staff? Maybe you'll even have your own hotel like Father's one day. It's within your reach—well within your reach, young man. You need to think about the things you want. My preference is sparkling wine and beautiful women."

Zach began laughing loudly. Ben noticed the tip of Zach's nose was now bright red.

"My father recognized your potential and wrote Ole' Hickory about you," Zach continued without a pause. "Everyone needs help in this world. Ole' Hickory needs help, I need help, Father needs help and you'll need help, too. Political help is what I'm talkin' about. We need to help each other to find the end of the rainbow. Quid pro Quo, Ben, Quid pro Quo—the three most important words in our profession and in politics. Learn them well and you'll be successful. With my father and Andrew Jackson on your side, you can do anything you want in Georgia. Elizabeth and I think you're the right man in the right place at the right time, Ben. We saw your potential."

The whiskey, as usual, was proving an excellent conversational lubricant. Ben, as he usually did with Zach, listened. Ben's father had told him that people always believed a man of few words to be wise.

"Ben, you can have the sun, moon and stars with a little help from your friends. You might even get a woman like Elizabeth in the bargain. You wouldn't mind having her on your arm, would you? I'll guarantee, if you go to Washington City, Elizabeth will be on your arm. She wouldn't miss seein' that town for the world. If you take Elizabeth to Washington City, she would do anything for you, Ben—she would make a pact with the devil. That would be the grand prize, wouldn't it?"

Zach laughed out loud and Ben couldn't help joining. This was turning into a most relaxing afternoon. Zach painted a wonderful scene, even if it was fanciful. Ben could see himself with Elizabeth on his arm walking into a formal dining room, chandeliers sparkling and every eye on Elizabeth as they were seated next to the host. Ben could smell her expensive perfume.

Ben didn't have Zach's confidence or his overweening desire for wealth. His success in politics was yet to be seen. He wouldn't rule that out, but he knew success isn't achieved by whiskey fueled boasting and cigar smoke. Talk is cheap, his father cautioned. Wealth is gained by hard work, little by little, over time. He would let Zach worry about politics. He would work daily on becoming a better lawyer and let his future take care of itself.

Ben leaned back, puffed his expensive cigar and pleasantly considered Zach's imagined limelight. Ben was uncomfortable but not afraid. He could take care of himself. The excellent whiskey was loosening his tongue also. He should have remembered his mother's advice about the stone mountain, but for some reason, he didn't think his mother's advice applied in this situation or in regard to Elizabeth. The situations his mother warned him about weren't parallel.

"I must confess, I do like your lead crystal and sour mash whiskey," Ben said. "I like women in silk and lace, French perfume, moonlight nights and I do like Elizabeth. Oh my yes, I do like her. I like to look at her, talk to her and smell her. I like to think about her. Have I gone too far, Zach? I could get used to all this," Ben said, knowing he was saying things that would have been better left unsaid.

Zach, grinning from ear to ear, gave a circular motion with his hand and cigar for Ben to keep talking.

Ben obliged.

"What I like best is the fact that the next president of the United States is taking an interest in us way down here in Georgia. I think that's amazing. Don't you, Zach? It's flattering, but it seems incredible Andrew Jackson thinks I could be useful. Were you serious when you said Elizabeth would be on my arm in Washington? Did you mean that? Did she tell you that? Does she believe I can get elected to congress?"

Zach laughed.

"You mean when we get elected to congress, my handsome friend," Zach said, with a big smile and another wave of his cigar.

"This is going to be a partnership. It isn't just you. Elizabeth and I are on your bandwagon. Include us in your plans, if you please. We needed you to help us get the things we want and we'll help you get the things you want. Quid pro Quo. We're scratching your back now, Ben, but when you get elected we'll expect you to scratch ours, if you know what I mean. You won't have to worry about what to say or do when you're elected. We'll take care of that for you. We'll get you elected and we'll guide your every word and every decision. Don't worry about a thing"

Zach continued without waiting for Ben to speak.

"The three of us will be a team, Ben. And yes, I talked to Elizabeth. It wouldn't surprise me if I saw you in Washington City with her on your arm. That's her dream. In fact, I would bet on that eventuality. What a lucky man you are. We want to get to Washington City where the big prize is. Fortunes are so ripe there they fall off the tree into your hand. A few years in congress and the three of us will never have to worry about money again. Why, even Jackson himself will be askin' us for favors. We'll probably loan money to the government."

Ben and Zach laughed uproariously at Zach's optimism. Ben continued to chuckle.

"I propose a toast to the three brightest stars in Andrew Jackson's southern sky—Elizabeth, Zach and me."

Zach loved Ben's toast. They clinked glasses. Life was good for these two young lawyers.

There were many pleasurable perquisites in Ben's new life. Although his job required long hours, his off time with Zach was stimulating. He had never had a friend like Zach who was introducing him to a social life he had never experienced. His father had warned him of the long-term implications of routine decisions. Ben knew, in the back of his mind, he was approaching the fine line between enjoying the marrow of life and drowning in the pursuit of an epicurean lifestyle.

Zach took another big taste of the very good sipping whiskey.

"Ben, you'll qualify for the Georgia House on your next birthday. That's a cinch. Then it'll be the United States House or the Georgia Senate when you're twenty-five? Which do you prefer? The House of Representatives in Washington or the Georgia Senate in Milledgeville?"

Zach didn't wait for Ben's response.

329

We'll skip the Georgia Senate, if you don't mind. Then, when you're thirty, we'll get you a United States Senate appointment. Then the biggest prize of all. If you've been a very good boy and scratched enough backs, the presidency of the United States could be yours, and why not?"

Ben couldn't believe what he just heard.

"It's lookin' like Jackson will support you all the way. In fact, I'm sure of it. I have that straight from his secretary and you know Jackson's personal integrity, don't you? My father and I are going to support Jackson whole hog and, of course, you will too—that's a given. What do you think, Ben? The future I just described can be a reality if you'll get on board. It's that easy," said Zach, staring into Ben's slightly glazed eyes.

Zach waited for Ben's response. Zach, the consummate salesman, knew when to persuade and when to be silent and wait for an answer from his mark. Ben could not conceive of anyone wanting to use him for personal gain. Ben was incapable of thinking in such a devious manner.

Ben, still staring through the hotel walls towards an imaginary future, said, "I would love that, Zach. I believe I can. I think you're right. Things are changing fast and only the forward-thinking will survive. I know that."

"I love your vision, Ben. When you've been appointed to the US Senate, and that can be in less than ten years, you'll have friends in every state, not just in Georgia. Then you can push your private agenda. You can influence congress. A Senator is a king, Ben. As a United States Senator, you can help or hurt whomever. You'll have presidents comin' to you—ambassadors knockin' at your door. That's our goal. Father, Elizabeth and I want our own Senator. Father is building the influence needed to secure that appointment. You didn't know that, did you? Now you know. You're going places, Ben Lowry. You've been chosen. You're being groomed. You're going places you never dreamed of, my friend—high places—very high places—and takin' all of us with you."

Ben smiled thinking about Zach's statement.

"That would be something, wouldn't it? Think of all the good I could do for folks if I was a Senator."

"Ben, you need to get something straight from the start. Folks are in politics to feather their nest. Do you think my father and I spend all this time and money because of our altruistic love of our fellow man? That's hogwash. We're in this for ourselves. Everyone's in this for themselves. Let the common man work his forty acres from can to can't, but our intention is wealth. We're goin' to let folks work for us. We're not fools."

Zach laughed uproariously and Ben couldn't help but join although he knew his father would not have agreed or laughed. It was impossible not to like Zach and his easy friendly manner.

Zach became more serious.

"Ben, someone will be a Senator from Georgia and twelve years from now someone will be elected president and it might as well be you."

Zach paused, cigar in one hand and drink in the other and leaned over in Ben's face with a serious expression, "I been thinkin', Ben. I've chosen my goal in life. You're goin' to be the first person I've shared this with."

Zach put his drink on the little table and his cigar in the ash tray and leaned back and relaxed for a moment with his hands locked together behind his head.

"When you've been elected United States Senator, but for sure when you're president, I want to be appointed ambassador to France. I never told anybody that. I want to live in Paris. Being ambassador to France will be the crowning achievement of my career. You'll do that for me, won't you Ben? I want to spend four years in Paris—eight if you get re-elected. I love Paris. Oh, my yes, do I have fond memories of Paris. Will you get me posted as ambassador to Paris? When you're Senator will you do that for me, Ben?"

Zach picked up his drink and cigar.

Ben, a little tipsy, laughed out loud and even the negro servant in the corner had to stifle a snicker when he heard Zach's request.

"Zach, you would be a perfect ambassador. You already dress like a French dandy and you have about the same view of wine, food and personal morality as the French. I think you and the French ladies would get along nicely. You'll be my first appointment—on my first day in office. My first nomination will be Zach Mitchell, United States Ambassador to France."

Ben and Zach couldn't stop laughing.

Ben suddenly remembered how, when he was little and first learning to read, his father would tease him with a childish use of language. His father would say, 'Life is good, Ben—and gettin' gooder'.

Ben laughed again to think of that.

"But, Ben," Zach emphasized, using his cigar as wand when their laughing subsided, "you can't get on the wrong ship and get to the right port. Do you understand? You don't want a bad political reputation early in your career. You must listen. You must say and do what we tell you. Don't you ever say anything in public Elizabeth and I haven't told you to say."

"I promise, Zach. I'll make sure we get to the right port," Ben agreed. Zach continued.

"You can't put a foot wrong for the next few years, but don't worry about that. When you're talkin' to folks you don't know, never say anything specifically until you find out what they want. Always speak in generalities and you'll be fine. Promise them the world in generalities and never tell them what you really believe. Never, ever tell anyone, including me, what you really believe. I'm not interested in stuff like that. Tell them what they want to hear. That's how to get elected. It's my job to keep your mind on the right path. Going to Washington City is the easiest thing you'll ever do, if you listen to me and Elizabeth. We know. Remember, we chose you because we want our own man in the legislature."

"Ben, some may accuse you of loyalty to savages because of your father, even though you've never said anything like that to me. I don't care one way or the other, but be careful what you say. Elizabeth wouldn't like it if you were spineless. Be firm. Have backbone, Ben. Listen to Elizabeth. You must uphold the law when it comes to Indians," Zach said.

Ben winced. Zach continued.

"When you're in company, say the right things, even if you don't believe them. I don't care what you think personally about the Cherokee or niggers or a Chinaman for that matter. Keep your mouth shut about the Cherokee. Keep your mouth shut about niggers. Let the do-gooders cry about injustice in their worthless pamphlets—nobody reads them anyway. We want to make money. Every landowner in Georgia wants to make money. If you make money for folks, they'll make sure you're elected again. When you're a Senator, you can say and do anything, but not now."

"Ben," said Zach, as he motioned to the tall negro waiting patiently in the corner, "give that boy your glass. You need a re-fill. I can't talk to you with an empty glass. No one likes to drink alone, do they? Andrew Jackson has been generous to you with his whiskey and I'm going to be generous with his whiskey, too."

The two red-faced young men were oblivious of everything but the present conversation. The tall, well-dressed negro servant was used to serving boastful young white men who drank too much. He had a good position and he didn't mind being called boy even though his hair was turning grey. Life was good for the old African servant in this hotel.

"Jackson will be our next president, Ben. We've already put an Ole Hickory Pole in front of our business. Jackson's party will win every seat in Georgia and he never forgets a friend—or an enemy. Crawford is forgotten—long gone. Jackson is Georgia's man now. People love military men with backbone and their physical courage, especially when they possess little of that commodity themselves. We haven't had a president with the mettle of Jackson since Washington. Folks love a fight and a fighter."

Zach laughed much too loud. Ben was curious at what.

"Ben, folks love to watch a fight even if they're not fighters themselves. They'll vote for anybody who fights. If folks are too chicken to fight, they'll watch a dog fight or watch roosters fight. Yep, you can count on it. Jackson's goin' to be our next president."

Ben was happy to listen to Zach drone on about politics. He was enjoying the effects of the potent alcohol and wishing the afternoon wouldn't end. Zach continued giving Ben advice. He was repeating the same advice he had given a few minutes earlier but Ben listened patiently—or at least tried to listen. He wouldn't remember much on the morrow. He didn't care. He was enjoying the afternoon and he had never felt better.

Ben thought how warm his face felt. Had they thrown extra logs on the fire? It was awfully warm for May.

"Jackson is unifying the country like never before," Zach said. "He knows we need an all-white English speaking country. That means the Indians must go—all of 'em. No French or Spanish will be allowed here either. Hell, we don't even want the British. We want their money but we've had enough of them. Be wise, Ben, and we'll retire before we're forty and have everything we dreamed of."

Later, as Ben walked to his boarding house, he thought of the evening's conversation. His head was spinning not only from the whiskey, but from the most unusual conversation of his life. He had never expected this when he went to law school. Life was exciting but a disturbing darkness lurked at the edges of his mind. He sensed a prowling discomfort in the shadows he didn't like. He decided the uneasiness wasn't anything to worry about. It was pleasant to drink whiskey and abandon all care—to think of Elizabeth and imagine the glorious things that might be—both in Milledgeville and in the nation's capital. He would love to walk up Pennsylvania Avenue with Elizabeth on his arm.

With Zach's help, Ben reasoned, he could do things for those who couldn't help themselves—as he had originally planned. Zach was right about a lot of things, but Ben didn't like the way his conscience felt when Zach used words like savage and nigger. He wouldn't think about that now. He would deal with that later. After all, he was free, white and twenty-one and Elizabeth was interested in him.

Ben couldn't help but think about his time in Cherokee Country. He couldn't forget the beauty of Cassie and her people. When he thought of

Cassie, his thoughts were comfortable and relaxing. His mind was at ease with no hint of peripheral guilt. Except for his own home with his parents, he had never felt more fulfilled than when he was with Cassie. She brought peace to his life. Thoughts of her dispelled the lurking demons that had gathered when he was listening to Zach. Ben resolved to think of her more often—to write her more often—to remember their time together. In his better moments he thought Cassie more desirable in her rustic simplicity than Elizabeth in all her expensive Paris fashions, sophisticated urban coquetry and French perfume.

Ben loved his parents' honest work in Cherokee Country. They cared about injustice—always had. He was glad his parents had taught him to honor all men. Life, he had learned, is a compromise. No one, not even a king, gets their way all the time.

Ben thought of Cassie. He looked up at the stars brilliantly shining above the darkened street outside his boarding house. True, injustice does exist, but tonight all is well. Everyone is safely in their bed. He felt a lasting euphoria after the evening's conversation with Zach. He could have drank whiskey with Zach and talked all night if he didn't have to get up early for work.

As he mounted the stairs, he thought his future to be as bright as the stars above. It was a silly, worn metaphor but he could accomplish good things for the Cherokee if he were a Senator—and then there was the added thought of Elizabeth—Elizabeth on his arm in Washington City. His thoughts seemed to stray back to her—her eyes, the way she touched him and her fragrance. Everything about her lingered and drew him irresistibly.

As Ben lay in his bed, he couldn't stop himself from thinking of Elizabeth preparing herself for her bed. The way she looked at him when they were together seemed to invite him into the private corners of her life.

Ben slept fitfully, dreaming of a seductive woman just out of his reach— beckoning him to follow—tempting, laughing, inviting, mocking. In uneasy dreams, he smelled the fleeting fragrance of French perfumes, tasted champagne and repeatedly caught a glimpse of an elusive woman—laughing just beyond his sight—teasing, tormenting, tantalizing. It wasn't like Ben to toss and turn so.

Chapter XXVIII

1827 – The Approaching Storm

Chapter 28

6 June 1827 - Month of the Green Corn Moon – De ha lu yi

I keep Ben's letters in a box under my bed. They are a never-ending source of happiness.

Huff's Boarding House – Milledgeville 2 June 1827

My Dear Cassie,

I can't wait to share with you all that has happened. I think of you every evening as I walk to my room. I look at the sky and am comforted that you are not so very far from me looking at the same evening sky and thinking of me. I recall when we were children we would watch the first stars as they peeked from behind some distant curtain to welcome us to their nightly reign. I miss you. I miss those soft summer evenings, long conversations. I miss the smell of your hair.

Zach and I are making plans. Zach thinks I'll be a good Georgia legislator and in time be elected to the United States House and possibly get an appointment to the U.S. Senate. The Senate may be a bit fanciful, but it's fun to think about. Zach is certain the Georgia House is within our reach. After work we go to his father's hotel and discuss many different topics. I enjoy talking to Zach, but I had much rather be with you. It is usual that Zach is talking and I am listening, but I don't mind. I have a lot to learn. Our conversations would be ever so much more interesting with you there. You are missing from me.

I'm exceedingly tired this evening. I shall close. Every night, as I compose myself for sleep, my last thought is of you. I'll visit soon. I can't wait to hold you once again. I can feel your heart beating against my chest. Until I see your marvelous face and we once again view the stars together,

I'm Yours Always, Ben xoxo

Sometimes, when I'm especially lonely, I'll take Ben's letters from their box and think how the paper in my hands was touching his hands. Most of his letters I have memorized. Hurry—hurry, our wedding day.

13 June 1827

Ben was a good student and he's becoming a better lawyer, stronger friend and perfect lover. He continues to read everything and talk to everyone who has anything to do with government and law. He knows every book in their library as if each were his best friend. I adore his mind and can't wait for his touch, his arms, his kiss and especially our long conversations. I love his sweet voice.

At least once a month Ben makes the hundred and fifty mile trip from Milledgeville if he can get a stage connection. The stage is exhausting and dirty, but fast. If he visited every other day, it wouldn't be too often.

19 June 1827

Ben is visiting his parents. I am overjoyed but I heard Ben and his father discussing political affairs in Milledgeville that made me tremble. Dreadful things are being planned by the whiteside.

"I have important news, Father. Let's go out on the porch. There's a storm brewing, but it will be a while before it gets here, and I want to enjoy the breeze, don't you, Mother? The cool air will be refreshing after this stifling heat."

We sat in the plain, straight-backed wooden chairs Ben and his father had crafted themselves. Ben had warned me his news would be disturbing.

"Father, I'm sorry, but I bring bad news—the worst of news. I've heard the Compact of 1802 is to be activated. Governor Troup began the complete removal of all Indians with the Creek Nation and now Governor Forsyth wants to do the same with the Cherokee. Governor Forsyth is demanding the general government keep their word and adhere to the terms of the compact."

I could hear the strain in Ben's voice. Ben, like his father and mother, has a tender heart. If possible, my love for him grew.

Ben continued and we listened.

"In 1802, as you know, Georgia traded their western land for one thing— assistance in the removal of all Indians from their chartered boundaries. Georgia is now insisting the general government keep that bargain."

As Ben talked, I watched Inky black clouds building far to the southwest over our distant mountains. After a long hot day, the freshening wind was delightfully cool as it gently wafted along the length of the front porch.

Occasional blustery gusts stirred tiny circling billows of dust in the soil Mrs. Lowry swept clean and smooth every morning. I love thunderstorms. I love the rumble of distant rolling thunder, the gusting wind, the lashing rain and the crash of lightning. I love to hear the thunder as it rolls away into far distant lands, but best of all is the deliciously cool wind the storms bring after a hot summer's day. Since I read Washington Irving's story, the sound of rolling thunder conjures up an image of an old bearded man watching little people bowling nine pins in a mysterious mountain hollow.

We heard the distant boom warning us of the storm's approach. I thought of Ben's news and the storm coming upon our nation."

"What?" his father blurted in response. "Did I hear you correctly, son. I thought that agreement permanently dormant. We never thought they would implement that foolish, foolish pact. You're telling me, son, Georgia will insist upon the removal of the Cherokee despite subsequent treaties?"

"Yes, sir. That's exactly what I'm saying. From what I'm hearing, all treaties made with the Cherokee since 1802 have been faithless. The treaties were a ruse, Father—a stalling tactic to pacify the Cherokee until assets could be gathered for their removal. There's no other way to view the government's actions. Jefferson and all presidents since have intended to implement the compact no matter what Indian agents signed or promised. The government was hoping the Indians would leave of their own accord or be forced out by settlers. The compact supersedes everything—including treaties. That's what I'm hearing. I'm sorry to bring this news, Father, but I thought you would want to know. I feel terrible about these things."

"Son," Ben's father asked, with his voice hardly above a whisper, "How did you learn this?"

Mrs. Lowry, no longer listening to the conversation, sat quietly next to her husband with her arm around his back, concerned only about soothing her husband's battered emotions. She understood her husband's work depended on the good will of the government of Georgia. She gently massaged his tense shoulder muscles as she looked into the face of the man she loved more dearly than life itself, wishing she could somehow soften the dreadful news he was hearing.

Ben's news was difficult. I didn't want to interject anything into Ben's narrative or ask a question. This conversation was between Ben and his father. Mr. Lowry, hands on his knees, stared into the distance digesting his son's news.

"I've always thought Jefferson honorable—a man who believed in equality. I've thought better of our young country. I hoped, after we separated from England, we would raise the standard of integrity here in the New World. From what you're sayin', son, our leaders have proven themselves as rapacious as the nation from which we were born."

"Good man or no, Father, I am not to judge. Jefferson's government believed in the equality of white men. The truth is, the United States Government, since it's conception, has believed in the advancement of the European races only. Georgia's renewed interest in the Compact explains the arrogance of Governor Forsyth towards Cherokee issues."

Ben continued to speak as his father stared into the forest beyond the cleared land around the Lowry's home. The top limbs of the trees were beginning to sway gently as the first gusts of cool wind swept down from the distant mountainsides. We were beginning to enjoy cooler temperatures after a hot sultry day.

There was another rumble of distant thunder. The storm was closer. Two tears silently rolled down Mr. Lowry's tanned cheeks onto the homespun shirt Mrs. Lowry had made herself. Mrs. Lowry dried his tears. Neither spoke. There was nothing to say.

The four of us sat quietly for a very long time enjoying the cooler breeze. Breaking the silence, Ben continued sharing what he had learned.

"Father, even before the War of 1812, the general government was concerned with the possibility of foreign aggression coming up from the Gulf of Mexico. New Orleans is far from the populated Atlantic coast by both land and sea and therefore difficult to defend. The general government wanted Georgia's western lands for the creation of two new buffer states, Alabama and Mississippi, to be populated by white settlers to defend our southern coast. Jefferson foresaw those four coastal states, Louisiana, Mississippi, Alabama and Georgia, organizing strong militias to deter invasion. He reasoned this four-state military shield would give the rest of the states time to deploy a defending army in case of invasion."

"Secondly, Father, the general government is afraid the Cherokee might side with a foreign power as happened in the Revolutionary War. They believe the removal of the Cherokee is necessary for national security. The same is true of the Creek, Choctaw and Chickasaw. If Jackson is elected, we can be certain he will consummate this plan. The Cherokee removal is set in stone, Father. Under no circumstances will the War Department allow the Cherokee Nation to exist within our nation. The government has instructed the War Department to remove every Indian nation east of the Mississippi outside the borders of the United States for national security. All Indian land east of the Mississippi will be summarily seized, Indians removed and all vacated Indian lands settled as quickly as possible by whites. It's to be a clean sweep."

Mr. Lowry, hands still on his knees, was rocking slowly back and forth listening to his son's news that forecast the doom of his life's work.

Ben continued in subdued tones.

"There's an additional problem—a big problem, Father. I'm afraid the ratification of the Cherokee constitution will trigger their removal. The Cherokee leadership believe if they have a national constitution they will legitimize politically the continued existence of the Cherokee Nation within their present boundaries and avoid removal. From what I'm hearing in Milledgeville, the Cherokee constitution will have the opposite effect. Georgia politicians view the Cherokee intention to ratify a constitution as a threat—a big threat. The talk is, the Cherokee constitution is a violation of the sovereignty of both Georgia and the Union. Frankly, Father, I don't see what can be done to stem the tide."

The dark clouds of the fast approaching storm suddenly obscured the hot afternoon sun bringing the promise of relief from the sweltering summer heat. As the wind gusts increased, the birds stopped their singing. I listened to the distant rumbles of thunder becoming increasingly louder. I imagined the sounds of the approaching storm to be my ancestors listening to Ben's words and expressing their displeasure. Soon the first drops of rain would begin to fall and the refreshing thunderstorm would be upon us.

Ben continued.

"Georgia ceded its western land to the general government for four things, Father. First, the general government promised more than a million dollars in gold."

"Second, they promised to pay the entire cost of the extinguishment. Extinguishment is the word they use."

"Third, Jefferson promised the general government would never interfere in Georgia's internal affairs. In other words, Jefferson gave the state of Georgia carte blanche in their dealings with Indians. Therefore, all treaties subsequent to 1802 were a deception. Our government has pretended to be working for a Cherokee homeland. Government agents accept proposals from Indian delegations when all the while the general government is planning their removal. I understand the Indians' outrage at our perfidy. We're seizing their land just like the story of Naboth's Vineyard and I fear the conclusion of the matter will be much the same."

"Fourth, the general government will supply the money and troops required for the extinguishment within Georgia's chartered boundaries. The removal will cost Georgia nothing. Georgia will survey all Cherokee land, complete the lotteries and send settlers. Georgia will become all white. I can only surmise the final removal will begin soon after the surveying is complete—certainly within the next decade—maybe sooner. The writing is on the wall, Father."

Ben's father answered in an almost inaudible whisper, "Yes, son, the general government must keep their promise to their fellow white citizens, I suppose, and break all promises to the Indian nations. I'm not surprised."

Ben was finished sharing his news. No one spoke for a long while. We were waiting on Mr. Lowry's response. The wind increased. The storm was near. When Ben's father began speaking his words were whispered—hardly audible in the freshening wind.

"It's ironic that Georgia, who said the Cherokee were incapable of civilization, will now remove them precisely because of their advancing civilization. Who would have thought a Cherokee constitution would be the straw that broke the camel's back? One day, Ben, if the Scriptures can be trusted, the pendulum will swing. Naboth will be justified. Thank you for sharing this difficult news."

"It was a traumatic message, Father. I'm sorry to be the bearer of bad news."

The flashes of lightening were coming closer. The storm clouds would be on top of us soon. We continued together on the front porch reveling in the pleasure of the cool blustery wind of the approaching summer storm and suffering with the thoughts of my nation's future. Without warning, a few large raindrops fell on the dry ground in front of the porch. Each raindrop exploded on the surface of the bone dry soil in a little cloud of red dust.

"The general government's plan," Ben added, "is to call up militias and mobilize the United States army, complete with artillery units, when the time for removal comes."

Helplessly, Ben observed his father's tears. He had never before seen his father display emotion like this in his life. Ben didn't know how to end the conversation. His father buried his face in his big calloused hands and Ben hoped his father wouldn't continue to cry. We knew this news meant the end to his father's life's work—of everything Ben's father and mother had lived for.

Abruptly, a noisy spattering of cold rain began to fall in huge drops, and in another moment it was falling in blinding sheets. The full force of the storm's gusting wind, brilliant lightening and pouring rain was upon us. In spite of the horrible news Ben was sharing, I was enjoying every moment of the storm. We were surrounded by lightning strikes in rapid succession. The uninterrupted rolling claps of thunder reverberated through the distant hills and echoed off faraway mountains. Water began to flow in streams off the wooden shingles Ben and his father had cut and placed themselves. None of us wanted to forsake the refreshing coolness of the porch and go inside to the stuffy interior. We put our backs against the wall of the porch to experience the pleasure of the cool air as long as we could before being driven inside by the driving rain. As I watched the rain and the wind gusts in the trees I wondered how it could be possible that life would not continue as it had for centuries here in Cherokee Country.

As I held Ben, I could feel his tension. Ben's father responded almost in a whisper.

"The white race is never satisfied. They always want more. 'I would have more' is the American dream. The white race doesn't know and doesn't care where the boundary lies between what they own and the property of others. I always hoped compassion would prevail and the Cherokee would be allowed to stay on their own land. Sometimes I wish I could be extinguished with the Cherokee."

The lightening was crashing everywhere now. It was time to go inside but no one minded the blowing rain after so many muggy days.

"Father, I hope their sins aren't visited upon their children—or upon my grandchildren. One day soon, Father, New Echota will be a white town without a single Cherokee family."

Rivers of muddy red water began to run through the yard in front of the house—the yard Mrs. Lowry swept clean every morning in her daily ritual. The bright orange and red streams of water rushed down the hill towards the woods and river beyond. We stood on either side of Mr. Lowry and held each other for a few moments longer.

Mr. Lowry stood.

"Let's go inside before we get struck by lightning," he said softly. "I want to lie down. I'm sorry for the uncontrolled display of emotion, Eleanor. Please forgive me."

As we entered their home, Mrs. Lowry shed a single tear that fell on her dry wooden floor leaving a perfectly round dark stain as the rain lashed against the small curtained windows and the gusting blasts whistled down the narrow chimney with a supernatural howl.

Chapter XXIX

1827 - Cassie's Happy Thoughts

Chapter 29

8 July 1827 - The Ripe Corn Moon – Gu ye quo ni

We use the moon to tell time and whites use the sun. I can tell the day of the month by the moon, but I can't tell one day from the next by looking at the sun. I know how to use the white calendar but I prefer moon time.

The ripe corn moon is a happy time for us—the happiest of times. I love the celebrations, food, gatherings, stories, friends, dances and the warm summer weather. I love the excitement of the festival but most important is the renewal of friendships. There is no life without relationships. I love our community and the balance it brings to our lives.

9 July 1827

Soon our leaders will meet in New Echota to ratify our constitution and we will have achieved everything demanded by whites—we will be fully civilized. We have a written language, we are planning our own newspaper, we live in houses, we farm, keep livestock, build barns and raise crops for sustenance—we even wear clothing and hats like whites. When edudu was a boy, not one Cherokee man wore a hat or white men's clothing. We dress like whites now. In a few days we will have a national constitution, legislative body, judicial system, law enforcement and established international borders. We lack, however, a powerful army to defend our borders. Perhaps we will not be invaded. Perhaps white politicians will respect our civilization.

10 July 1827

Ben is learning. He says his firm leads all others in land transactions. Because of the Yazoo land fraud, speculators and lawyers are careful to go by the letter of the law. Everyone needs Ben's expertise. No one wants to be cheated and no one wants to go to jail for malfeasance, especially Ben.

12 July 1827

When Ben comes home, he is as vivacious and innocent as a child—as when we first met.

I want the day to come when I can hold him every night and wake to find his strong arms around me. My heart is bursting to have him near. I wish I could be with him in Milledgeville. I try not to think about that. My heart is with him every moment of every day. I wonder if in that higher realm our love will be vouchsafed by the Great Spirit and we shall retain the memories we have made in this existence?

Ben is saving for marriage. I will be a good wife. He says he thinks of me only as the woman of his desires—not as a white or Cherokee woman. I love to hear him say he needs me. Ben is a good man.

He must save a great deal before we marry. I will wait forever and beyond.

24 July 1827

19 July 1827 - Huff's Boarding House,

My Dearest Cassie,

I am missing you. I am missing you, my dear. You are my best friend—my confidant. I love the way you and I share our deepest secrets. I feel as if I can tell you anything. I have never had a friend with whom I could share my most intimate thoughts—I certainly can't share them with anyone down here. I don't know what I would do without your friendship. When I'm writing, I pretend you are across the desk listening to my thoughts as I pen each word.

Zach and I are becoming friends. Zach is the owner's son. I enjoy being in his company and our conversations. He is teaching me a great deal about his father's business and life among the influential landowners here in Georgia, but our time together is nothing compared with time spent with you.

He is bold, straightforward and supremely confident—unlike anyone I have ever met. Sometimes his confidence appears as arrogance, but I suppose being self-assured comes with wealth and privilege. Zach wants me to run for political office—with the help of the firm. He plainly said he wants to ride my coat tails to power and wealth.

Zach and I go to his father's hotel most days after work to relax, discuss the day's events, his political plans and the latest news.

Zach thinks my isolated upbringing makes me a perfect political candidate for the Georgia legislature. He says I have few personal liabilities and my educational background will surpass those of any contender.

I must close for now. I'm missing you and hope to see you soon—very soon,

    Your Loving Ben, xoxo

25 July 1827

Zach thinks he can ride Ben's coat tails. What a marvelous image. I had a vision of Ben madly running down main street in Milledgeville with a tiny man desperately holding his coat tails with the little man's tiny feet flying in the breeze. I'm glad Ben has a friend in Milledgeville. I'm glad I'm Ben's best friend in the entire world.

Milledgeville July 1827

Zach and Ben walked together to the hotel after work saying little to one another. They went straight to their reserved table. Zach was served his first drink and lit his first cigar. As soon as it was drawing well he tossed down his first whiskey and turned to Ben.

"That's good whiskey, isn't it? This is my favorite moment of the day— to walk in here after a long day's work and without a word have the waiter bring my drink and cigar—to take that first puff and taste that first drink. Life is good, isn't it, Ben?"

Ben nodded in agreement and sipped. This was also his favorite moment of the day but he preferred to be allowed to sit quietly and relax until the alcohol began to work its magic. Ben would be patient. Zach could prattle on all he wanted.

"I love coming here after a hard day's work," Ben said. "I suppose the emotional satisfaction of knowing that I've done everything I was supposed to do today allows me to fully relax with no nagging guilt. When I've worked hard I have self-respect. I like that feeling. And I like sitting here—just sitting here doing nothing and thinking about the first thing that comes into my mind."

Zach listened to Ben and looked at him sideways with a steady, incredulous gaze. He laughed.

"Ben, Ben—you amaze me. I try to avoid work and you're forever tryin' to find more. Well, that's why we hired you. You're honest and you like to work. The only reason I work is to get out of future work."

Ben sipped his drink and listened. Zach waved his cigar to make a point as if he were speaking to a group of men and continued as if lecturing.

"I need a lot of money tucked away so I won't have to work. That's my motivation. We have slaves and servants to do the work. Let them work. I am definitely not that kind of man. Money and power are my goals. Pleasure, for now, is a distant third. Later, my friend, after we've achieved adequate quantities of wealth, we'll devote ourselves entirely to pleasure, but for now, Ben, we have to work hard to get there, don't we? I don't mind working. In fact, I enjoy what we do. We must make hay while the sun shines, don't we?"

Zach, already on his second drink, leaned back in his comfortable upholstered chair in his father's luxurious hotel and looked up at the ornate ceiling.

"Ben, I like to think I understand how to use the greed of others to accumulate wealth for myself. Father's smart and he taught me to be smart. If you'll trust me, Ben, we can make a lot of money."

As was his custom when he was with Zach in the hotel, Ben sipped his drink and listened. Zach's world view was diametrically opposite that of Ben's parents. Zach's long-term plans for self-enrichment in order to live out a privileged life in the pursuit of pleasure made it sound as if pleasure were the be-all and end-all of human existence. Ben grinned, thinking how Zach repeated himself in a never-ending rehearsal of his desire for accumulating wealth as if he had no memory of previous conversations. Ben didn't mind the repetition. Zach was fun to listen to and Ben enjoyed the pleasure of not having to think after a long day studying law. He was more than ready to allow Zach to take him away from the daily stress. He noticed that although Zach was only on his second drink, his cheeks were already turning pink.

"As you know, we hired you for two reasons," Zach said. "First, we wanted a smart young lawyer. You fit that bill perfectly. Second, in addition to your legal skills, we wanted our own man in the legislature—a man both we and our clients could depend on to carry out our agenda. You, Ben Lowry, are also that someone. You are electable. If everything works out, we can easily plan your political career for the next ten years—probably longer."

"And how would you plan my political future for an entire decade, Zach?" Ben asked. "Do you have a crystal ball? Don't you think that a bit ambitious?"

"We've talked about this before, haven't we?" Zach said. "Politics isn't complicated. It's just arithmetic, money and time. That's all. It's arithmetic, money and time. You'll qualify for the Georgia House when you're twenty, the United States House when you're twenty-five and the United States Senate when you're thirty—that's ten years. My father and I think we have a good chance between now and then of gettin' all three—quite on schedule. We'll have to grease a lot of palms, but we have ten years to apply liberal amounts of grease—and it'll be money well spent. A man can clear a lot of new ground in ten years, can't he? Our ultimate goal is to have our man in the Senate."

"Zach," Ben said, "there's many a slip twixt the cup and the lip. A lot can happen in ten years."

"Ben, Ben, Ben," Zach countered with humor, shaking his head in mock criticism, "listen to me, young man. This is so easy it'll be like shootin' ducks on a pond. Remember, it's just arithmetic, money and time. There are 213 seats in the House of Representatives in Washington City, but every bill must go to the Senate before it goes to the president's desk. Did you know that?"

Ben laughed. "Of course, I knew that."

"Well, Ben, there are 24 states and two Senators from each state for a total of 48 Senators. In the Senate, every state is equal—Rhode Island and New York have two Senators each, don't they? Power is concentrated in the smaller Senate and watered down in the larger house. Not only that, but Senators serve six-year terms. Two or three consecutive terms in the Senate will generate a life-time of political power, Ben, and political power is our goal. Political power generates money. Being a senator is better than having your own private gold mine and in ten years we want you to be our Senator. With you in the Senate, everyone will know my father has influence in Washington City. With me helping, we might as well have your official stationary printed now."

The dark-skinned African waiter, quite invisible as he waited comfortably in his quiet corner within earshot, observed and listened to the two young men, anticipating their every need. He smiled to hear the arrogant talk about a Senate appointment. It was quite usual, he thought to himself, to hear young whiskey-drinking white men make big plans and pretentious claims.

"If you want power and money," Zach repeated, "you must have a Senate seat. In some ways, the Senate is more powerful than the president. You must be elected to the house, but Senators are appointed by their legislatures. Getting a Senate appointment is the most difficult political office of all. When you reach the age of qualification, we'll have the people in place to get that appointment. It's then that Father and I will call in all favors. That's when we'll find the pot of gold. Businessmen will promise their soul, plus their first-born, to a sitting Senator. Except for the presidency, the Senate is the pinnacle of power. Would you like to be known as "Senator Ben Lowry", from Georgia? That does have a ring, doesn't it?"

Ben continued to quietly sip his drink and smiled at Zach's outlandish political fantasies. Ben chuckled to himself. He thought how, if his cautious mother were here, she would warn Zach not to count his chickens before they're hatched.

"Senators pass all laws, approve treaties and confirm appointments," Zach droned on. "The House of Representatives is a bunch of fuss and feathers schoolboys compared to the Senate. There are no term limits for a Senator. A multi-term Senator is almost as powerful as the president. Father wants a Senator in his pocket. We won't deceive you, Ben. That's our purpose in choosing you. That's the reason we court influential political families. We don't want to be rich, Ben, we want to be really rich."

Ben listened patiently, giving Zach a long thoughtful look as he considered what Zach had just said. He sipped from the glass the servant in the corner never allowed to become empty and wondered how much, if any, of Zach's political fantasies would actually come to pass.

"Ben, you're learning. When you first came here, you were shy. It's nice to see you coming out of your shell. Folks are impressed by your expertise and your quick wit and the women think you're handsome. We like the easy, country boy way you have with people. To be honest, I like the new sophisticated Ben who knows what he wants and is willing to take it. We'll go far, Ben. We'll go far and that's a promise."

Zach laughed and Ben noticed the tip of Zach's nose had become quite red and shiny and matched the pink of his cheeks.

19 July 1827

Ben is home. What a happy day. Ben came as soon as he could after he arrived and we walked down to our favorite spot.

As we walked hand in hand to the river, I enjoyed Ben's conversation and the pleasantness of him being near me—touching me.

"Ben, I remember when I would have to kiss you first. Now you kiss me—I love that. I love your kisses and your willingness to touch and be touched. I know you want to wait till we're married before we're intimate, but I want you to know I'm yours. I love you and respect your parents' morals. I'll wait if you want to. I want what you want."

"Cassie, you're the sweetest girl in the world. Of course I want to kiss you and you're right about me wanting to wait. I think it's important to honor my parents. I want to do as they did. That's the right thing, Cassie."

I changed the subject.

"Ben, I'm excited about your decision to run for political office. I think the legislature is the place for you if you're going to do anything for us or the poor Africans. Somehow, I knew you would run for office. I'm sure it's the right thing."

"I think you're right, Cassie. Father and mother are excited, too. This is a good year for a young man to get into politics in Georgia. Things are changing with new faces everywhere. I'm looking forward to the challenge.

"I think about things I read in the white newspapers, "I replied. "They never say anything good about us in the newspapers. I never see an article defending our rights. Every week edudu tells me of some new squatter who has moved in around us. They build a cabin and put up fences. Every week someone we know has a cow or pig stolen. Whites do as they please. All the militia cares about are slave patrols and drinking whiskey."

"Cassie, who knows what can be accomplished if I am able to get into the legislature. Maybe I'll be able to help. Maybe I'll have influence—maybe not. I could never be elected if I openly support Indians. Just the fact that my father is a missionary is a liability, but to be honest, Andrew Jackson and his new political party worries me the most. He's been building a nation-wide power base. Zach told me all about that. The South is growing exponentially. Slave labor has become the heart of major agricultural growth, but manufacturing is growing, too. Southern landowners are shipping agricultural products to foreign markets around the world. Every year thousands and thousands of acres of virgin woodland are cleared to plant cash crops. Things are changing, Cassie. What bothers me is much of this prosperity is accomplished on the backs of men and women of bondage. I wonder when this injustice will end?"

I could see the image in Ben's mind was painful to him. Ben has a soft heart. He will make a good politician. He will be forced to compromise, but I'm sure he will do good things for us when he can.

"Agriculture is booming and slavery cannot be opposed in the South— too many are being enriched. Slavery will end one day but not soon—perhaps not in our life-time. I don't like to talk about it or think about it."

"I know, Ben. Newspapers talk of nothing but the coming election. Georgia wants Jackson. They're impressed by his reputation fighting against the Creeks and Seminoles. Georgians believe Jackson will side with them against us and they're probably right."

"The election next year will be interesting, Cassie. It's hard to vote an incumbent out. After the hard-fought election of '24, I'm certain there will be a lot of mudslinging between Jackson and Adams."

"What's mudslinging, Ben? I don't understand."

Ben laughed out loud.

"Politicians don't actually throw mud, Cassie. I didn't mean that. It's a figure of speech. I'm sure you knew that. They throw dirty untrue words meant to discredit their opponent. You'll read all kinds of untrue things in the newspapers—patently false. You've read the newspapers more than I have and if you think about it you know all about political mudslinging against the Cherokee. The newspaper says terrible things about your people.

Andrew Jackson accuses Adams and Calhoun of a corrupt bargain that cheated Jackson out of the election of '24. He's still angry about that. Jackson will win Georgia for sure. He'll get every electoral vote."

"Ben, I am curious. What was the corrupt bargain Andrew Jackson is so angry about?"

Ben laughed, "In the last presidential election of '24, four men ran for president—Andrew Jackson, John Quincy Adams, Henry Clay and William Crawford. None of the four received a majority in the electoral college. We talked about that. According to the twelfth amendment, the president must be elected by a majority of electoral college—one man must receive more than half of the total votes to be president. A plurality is not enough. He has to have more than half the pie—remember?"

"Of course, I remember, Ben. The newspapers were full of it for months and now they're all writing about it again."

"If no candidate receives a majority of the electoral college, the House of Representatives elects the president. Well, that's what happened in '24. Jackson was the winner in the vote in the electoral college but he didn't get a majority. He didn't get more than fifty-percent of the electoral votes. Therefore, the election went to the House of Representatives. The top three in the electoral college were voted on in the House for the presidency. John Quincy Adams won with Henry Clay's help. Henry Clay was Speaker of the House. That cooperation between John Quincy Adams and Henry Clay made Jackson furious and furious isn't a strong enough word. He was hopping mad. He's still not over it."

"Henry Clay persuaded all his supporters in the House of Representatives to vote for Adams instead of Jackson. Then, after Adams became president, Adams appointed Clay as Secretary of State. It's what we call quid pro quo. You scratch my back and I'll scratch yours. The deal was never admitted to in public, but everyone knows that's what happened. Jackson called it a corrupt bargain. Jackson has been running for president since then—since he lost in '24. He's like a man possessed."

"It seems to me everything in white politics is a backroom compromise, Ben. I wonder how any white politician can be honest?"

Ben replied with a serious sideways look, "I know what you mean, Cassie. A compromise is like building a tabletop out of boards and puttin' in the middle board last. If the middle board is a bit too wide, which side do you plane for a fit? A compromise is taking a little bit off each side of the board to make it fit into the smaller space rather than shaving it all off one side. In a compromise, both sides give—and some would say that makes everyone unhappy. That's how politics works, Cassie. That's what I will be required to do in Milledgeville when I'm elected. I'll have to compromise if I want to accomplish anything good for the Cherokee. I'll never be able to oppose the government openly, but I'll be honest, Cassie. I promise you—I'll be honest. When I'm elected, I'll tell the truth. I will not lie in order to please folks or to get re-elected or to line someone's pockets."

I love to listen to Ben talk, but I don't care much for white politics. I hope Ben can protect his integrity when he makes compromises.

"Cassie, things are changing in the United States. Up and down the Atlantic seaboard folks are pouring into this country from Europe, and every immigrant is anxious to go to work and acquire land. Georgia has more acreage controlled by Indians than any other state. Georgia is the place to go if you're free, white and twenty-one and want to get ahead."

"I know, Ben. I hear stories all the time about squatters, not to mention the lotteries. I see no end. I think you're right. I read of a law passed in Georgia, mimicking a Virginia law, that says a newborn child can only be listed as white or black—not as Indian. The only two choices on the birth certificate are white or black. As far as the South is concerned, we Cherokee have ceased to exist. It's white or nothing if you want to succeed. According to white law, a Cherokee can never be considered a citizen. We don't exist. We can't vote or take a white man to court. We have no rights and, of course, neither do Africans."

"I will never understand, Cassie."

"We're aliens in our own country. Sometimes in the evening edudu and I talk and I wonder what kind of people whites really are to be so heartless. The truth is, Ben, white Europeans are invaders. That's what edudu says. They steal everything and call it legal. I cannot imagine a greater injustice than to go to another country and take the people's land away from them."

We paused for a long time before either spoke.

"Ben, let's talk of something brighter. We can't carry the weight of every injustice. We must make the best of what we have as we do every day. Can we talk about happy things? Can we talk about things that give hope? Can I share my happy thoughts with you, Ben?"

"Of course you can, Cassie," Ben said and kissed my forehead as we sat in our private spot by the river.

"Tell me your happy thoughts. I want to hear good things. I'm like you, Cassie, I'm weary of politics and bad news. I have days when I refuse to read the newspapers because of so much bad news."

"Ben, my happy thought is that I know you love me."

"That's my happy thought, too," Ben said smiling.

"I think about that all the time, especially when you're not here," I replied. "I want you to continue to tell me of your love. I want, above everything in this world, to be your friend, confidant and lover. I want to share your dreams—dreams of us in a house full of children. My happy thought will not be too long in coming, I can tell. I will be ready whether today or a year from now or twenty years from now. My happy thought is you—anywhere in the world with you. You, Ben Lowry, are my happy thought, whether you are by my side or in Milledgeville."

Ben smiled and kissed me and said nothing. I could tell he was thinking about what I had said. I felt so warm and comforted inside to have told him those things.

"I know you want me, Ben, and I want you. I can't wait for the day we are joined. I know you want to consummate our relationship like your mother and father did. It would be wonderful if we could begin that relationship soon, very soon, but I'm perfectly happy with your decision to wait."

Ben held me a long time without speaking. I could feel his powerful body as he held me and I allowed myself to be enfolded in his love and security. Sometimes, when I think of him and his handsome face and powerful muscles, I shiver thinking of my great desire for him.

As he was holding me he finally answered.

"I know, Cassie, and I feel the same way. I want things to be right when we set up housekeeping. I wouldn't want to begin our life together on the wrong foot. The best things in life come with patience. I want to have a nice place where our babies won't be called half-breeds. I must first save, but I promise our dreams will happen. We'll figure out where we can live, be happy and raise our children free from white ridicule."

Ben left later that day for Milledgeville. I missed him even before I watched him disappear down that long lonely road.

7 August 1827

My greatest delight is when his mother hands me a letter from Ben. Ben said the custom of including the letters xoxo at the bottom of his letters originated in Europe. His mother's relatives in Germany were using xoxo to end their correspondence long before they immigrated to the United States. The x represents a kiss and the o is a hug—written together they are kisses and hugs sent to one's beloved. Ben says his mother has always ended her letters to him with xoxo. I think it a marvelous tradition. From this moment on, I shall end every letter I send with xoxo.

19 August 1827

The feelings Ben and I have for each other are natural, like breathing in and breathing out. Our passion fills my waking thoughts. Even when he isn't here, I feel his presence—enfolding me—protecting me. I close my eyes and feel him breathing on my neck, his arms around me and his body pressing against mine. I love him with all my heart and soul and mind and strength.

Chapter XXX

1827 - Zach Plans Ben's Career

Chapter 30

9 December 1827 - The Snow Moon – Vs gi yi

In his frequent letters Ben shares his discussions with Zach, their work and their political plans. I love his letters.

Milledgeville – December 1827

"Ben, if you want a career in politics next year, now is the time to act. We can't hesitate. This comin' year we'll elect a new president. Everybody's goin' to vote."

Ben and Zach were sharing their usual drink in their usual spot. Ben stretched his legs out in front of him crossed at the ankles and watched the flames in the fireplace through half open eyelids, resting his mind from hours of intense concentration.

Zach continued his encouragement.

"If you want a political career, this is the year and now is the time to begin. Do you want to be a sixty-year-old lawyer burning the midnight oil? If you procrastinate, you'll miss this political cycle and waste two years. Time, tide and politics wait for no man. Elizabeth and I want to encourage you to continue on to the prize."

Zach didn't wait for Ben's response.

"Ben, you're handsome, but I'm more handsome. You're well-dressed, but I'm the best dressed man in Georgia. You're smart, but I'm smarter. You're wise, but I'm wiser. You're goin' to be rich, if you'll listen to me, and you need to listen to me. I'll take care of your future."

Zach and Ben laughed. Ben, perfectly happy to sit quietly and listen to Zach, sipped his drink and grinned at Zach's flattering description of himself.

"I know how the world works," Zach continued. "Times are changing and you need to put both feet in the stirrups, hold the mane and ride. This is December and we have less than eleven months to get you elected. If you want to make a lovely wine, you can't begin a month before you drink it, can you? And we can't wait till summer to begin electioneering. It takes time to persuade and it takes time to discredit your opponents. We need to establish your base while we cut the legs from under your competition. Elizabeth and I know how to do that. You have the two best people in the state as your staff. What do you say?"

Although Ben was relaxing, he had listened carefully to everything Zach said.

"Zach, you're right. I know you're right," Ben said. "I'm a novice. No one knows me and it'll take time to establish my name in politics. I think you're right. I say let's go to work and make sure of my election. I'm all in."

"Good attitude, Ben. You can trust us. That's a promise."

"Ok, Ben," Zach raised his glass, "a toast to the brightest, and one day most powerful politician in Georgia, with my help of course, and a commitment to cross the finish line first."

The young men clinked glasses, drank their toast and laughed together as they began to plan the political campaign they would be involved in for the coming year.

"Good for you, Ben. Elizabeth and I believe you're the right man, in the right place, at the right time. With money behind us, you're a cinch. Elizabeth and I have plans for you—big plans—first the House and then the Senate. With a little luck and Jackson's help, it could even be all the way to the White House. We might as well think big, hadn't we?"

Ben grinned, "Don't you think you should help me get elected here in Georgia before we plan to move into the White House?"

Zach's optimistic mood was so contagious Ben could feel his political dream. He was beginning to believe Zach himself.

"You don't think me too confident, do you, Ben? Jackson almost made it to the White House in '24. He'll certainly make it in '28 and you're a far better man than he is. With hard work, you'll have as good a chance as anyone. If he can do it, you can do it—with our help, of course. There is no reason not to be optimistic, is there? In politics, anything can happen—nothin' ventured, nothin' gained. Ben, the prize we're really after is a Georgia Senate appointment. What marvelous stories we'll tell our grandchildren."

Zach took a taste of his excellent sippin' whiskey.

"Money runs the world, and politics is run by money, Ben. You know that. I know that. Every politician in the world knows that. Altruism and politics have nothing in common. Morality and politics are not bedfellows—not in this world. Politics revolve around money, money and more money. People go to church to do nice things for others and to salve their conscience. Rich folks get into politics to pass laws to get richer. You can have anything you want in this world, including a Senate seat, if you have enough money. My father and his friends are planning on spending a lot of money on you.

Father wants his own hand-picked man in the Senate. Of course, he'll expect you to take care of him and his business when you succeed. Quid pro quo, Right? You're a smart man Ben. When we get you in the legislature, you'll know better than to bite the hand that feeds you."

Ben listened to Zach discourse eloquently on the path to success and thought how easy it was to run for office and have someone else manage the campaign. Ben enjoyed thinking about the power and prestige of elected office and was perfectly willing to let Zach do all the work.

"It's money and backroom agreements that make people rich," Zach continued without a pause. "Go to church for morality but go into politics for wealth. Honesty never won an election. You can't deposit morality in the bank, can you? You told me yourself your father is as poor as a church mouse. A lawyer can be rich. A lawyer turned politician can be very rich. Elizabeth and I intend to be very, very rich. We'll see to it you have everything you ever dreamed of, Ben. You'll make a lot of money and we'll make even more. You'll have so much you'll never have to work. You'll be a man of position, privilege and leisure. You'll be the head and let others be the tail."

Zach motioned to their servant to fill their glasses once again.

Ben's new job in Milledgeville was his first taste of class privilege and it was pleasant. It was a wonderful change not to have to work hard at menial tasks on a daily basis.

His father and mother did all of their own chores, cut all their own wood, cooked all their own food and washed their own clothes. Here in Milledgeville Ben's new friends were all slave owners and business people who never did their own chores. Ben's father would have been suspicious of Zach, and rightly so, but Ben's father wasn't here. Ben, in his rustic country boy naiveté, was recognized by Zach and Elizabeth for what he was—low hanging fruit to be plucked and consumed.

Ben listened patiently as Zach continued.

"Elizabeth and I know what to promise to whom. We know about their hidden past. We know when to intimidate and how to pet a wounded ego. Ben, you don't want to end up a two-bit lawyer, do you?"

Zach laughed out loud, "Ben, I just can't see you with a complaining wife and a houseful of barefoot kids and not a servant in sight."

Zach was right. Ben certainly didn't want to end up unhappily married with insufficient means to support his family.

Zach continued his alcohol-fueled speech.

"Time and tide wait for no man, Ben. Mark my words. You'll go to the top and you can trust us every step of the way. Another toast, Ben. To our

355

success and friendship on the final leg of our journey into the vast political realms of the uncharted worlds of the rich and famous where we shall forever reside."

Zach and Ben held up their expensive crystal glasses containing the best Tennessee sour mash and once again toasted their success. Ben had no desire to run for office alone. He knew he needed Zach and Elizabeth, and he understood politics was the perfect career for a smart lawyer—and the career path that would best help his father and the Cherokee. When he was younger he had dreamed of helping Africans but since he had been in Milledgeville and had been in the company of the upper classes he had found himself rethinking his view of slavery.

Ben's first year at Mr. Mitchell's law firm had flown by and Ben was getting comfortable in his role as the firm's number one real estate and research lawyer. Times were moving fast and the prospect of the next ten years in the Georgia political scene was exciting. He could fulfill his dreams and accomplish at least some of the more noble goals he and his father had discussed. Ben could see himself as an influential politician. It was a pleasant vision. He would do some good and, of course, enjoy the privileges of success.

After this conversation, Ben and Zach had frequent meetings planning the details for Ben's election to the Georgia House in the autumn of '28—a presidential election year. Ben wanted to be in the forefront of progressive political thinking and do good things for the citizens he represented.

Ben liked Zach. He liked the banter and fun that seemed to follow Zach and Elizabeth. He couldn't stop thinking about Elizabeth. He had never been around people so full of life and energy—and so interesting. For years Cassie had been his only love and the center of his attention, but she was a long way off in New Echota and he found himself thinking of her less often.

Ben's regular meetings with Zach and Elizabeth were always business but perhaps, before too long, he would have an opportunity to be alone with her. Perhaps she would develop an interest in him. That was a good thought. She was a desirable woman and most of the time he thought her unapproachable. Surely a beautiful, sophisticated, modern woman like Elizabeth would never be interested in a lowly country boy like him. She could have any man she wanted. There were lots of handsome, wealthy men around. She could have her pick. Ben couldn't imagine Elizabeth would ever be interested in him and yet—and yet she had given some veiled indications.

Ben trusted Zach and he fancied Elizabeth as someone he might trust and be with—at least he could dream—like being elected to the White House—it would probably never happen but it was a pleasant thought. Being with Elizabeth was a fantasy. He knew in his heart what Zach said about her selfishness was probably true, but what if Elizabeth did learn to care for him? It was possible Elizabeth could choose him. He could never be seen in public with Cassie, but he could daydream about walking down main street with Elizabeth. He could see the two of them living in a fine house with servants and a dozen children. He could see Elizabeth on his arm in Washington City. He could be seen anywhere with Elizabeth. He loved that flight of fancy. It never once occurred to him that the pleasant daydream of a life with Elizabeth could turn into a nightmare.

"Ben, we got a lot accomplished this afternoon. I'm ready to have some fun. I know a couple of Southern Belles who have indicated strongly they want to explore privately, with the two of us, the vagaries of international politics along with a late-night dissertation concerning expensive imported wine, aged Cuban leaf and tasty French cuisine that I've specially ordered to be brought up for the occasion. What do you say? Ready for some adventure? I promise we'll have a great time."

Zach had teased Ben often with such escapades, but Ben always refused. Ben intended to wait on his union with Cassie. Zach didn't unduly make fun of Ben about his refusals. Zach knew perfectly well Elizabeth would twist Ben into any shape she wished when the time came. He would leave Elizabeth to take care of Ben's social education. Zach didn't want to move too fast and ruin their investment. Elizabeth would make the right decisions.

It had been ingrained in Ben by his parents that he should wait until marriage to consummate his wedding vows. For the time being he had determined he would delay, no matter how much Zach should entice him to violate his conscience. Ben wanted to save himself for marriage. He wanted Cassie. Ben was prepared to resist Zach's straightforward temptations, but he had no idea of the irresistible pleasures Elizabeth would offer. He would have done well to remember his father's warnings about the thin end of the wedge.

Ben responded with a grin, "Zach, I appreciate the honor of the invitation for this evening and I know it would be fun. I'm sure those are two intelligent girls and the conversation would be grand, but I think I'll go home. I'm tired. I've a lot of work to do tonight and I don't feel like discussing international politics, even if she is pretty. You're the tireless one, Zach. You go have fun and maybe I'll join you next time."

Zach gave Ben a playful push.

"You don't know what you're missing, my friend, but someone needs to work around here. I'll play and you work. I like that arrangement. Keep it up, Ben."

On slightly unsteady feet, Ben left the hotel for the short walk to his room. As he observed an especially beautiful evening sky, his thoughts strayed to Elizabeth. He imagined he could smell her perfume and feel the lingering touch of her slender hand on his thigh. He had noticed an ache in his chest when he thought of Elizabeth—an ache which was occurring more frequently. It would have been better for Ben if he had thought of Cassie or written her or his parents a letter.

Ben's protestant work ethic, instilled by his hardworking parents, was transferred to the world of law and thus into success and money. Zach's father was more than pleased with Ben. In only months, Ben was generously gifted as a new junior partner in Zach's father's firm. He began his practice specializing in land, land acquisition and litigation concerning such and as a legal research expert. Everyone was surprised how quickly Ben's skills developed and how rapidly he had established a broad clientele. Ben's clients always came back. Ben was a good lawyer and was learning how to spot a bargain in the midst of another's misfortune.

Georgia upheld the individual's right to own property and to leave their real property to heirs. A man's land was sacrosanct in the western world. It was curious, thought Ben, that in the Cherokee culture land was owned corporately. There was no fee simple in Cherokee Country—no deeds or personal ownership and there lay, as his father believed, the central problem with Cassie's people. The Cherokee understanding of the word community, and by extension the ownership of land, was the leading cause of the clash with the invading white culture. Whites wanted private individual ownership. Europeans coveted the ability of individuals to amass great wealth at the expense of everyone else. The Cherokee practiced corporate ownership and the sharing of wealth and maintaining strong family ties within the community. The dichotomy was most interesting to Ben.

Ben had learned nothing in law is black and white. He had learned, when needed, to turn a simple legal problem into shades of grey and watch his opponent founder. It's our job as lawyers, his professors had said, to represent our client's best interest. We must convince the judge and jury that our client's shade of grey has a solid basis in legal precedent. If any dispute comes to litigation it means the issue isn't black or white, or it would have never been litigated in the first place. We represent our client, not a religious moral code. There are no morals in law. The law itself is moral. The law is always moral.

Winning in a courtroom has to do with interpreting law in combination with precedent on behalf of one's client. The lazy lawyer always loses.

Our lawmakers represent society as a whole. Therefore, if a law is on the books, it is the consensus and therefore moral. Ben was taught that it wasn't preachers and theologians who understood right and wrong. Right and wrong were the sole right of our legislators. Ben's father would never agree that all laws are moral, but Ben's father wasn't a lawyer, wasn't in the legislature and did not sit as a judge. Ben's father had no legal standing.

Ben understood the entire western legal system is built on Rule of Law—straight out of the courtrooms of Rome. Established law is the only way to determine right and wrong and govern society—not religion. All Western efforts to develop a political theocracy had failed miserably. Western civilization was based on the Rule of Law. Thus, the lawyer who wins in court is assured he has the moral high ground in his society. It must be so, he was taught. Even in a monarchy or oligarchy, Rule of Law was of paramount importance for the smooth function of society. Without Rule of Law there was anarchy.

If the Indians are removed by legal means, such removal becomes, as a matter of course, morally right. The law is always morally correct. From the moment Ben began to practice law, he began to see another star guiding his conscience, other than the polar star of his parents. Ben had learned the Sunday morals his father espoused from the pulpit did not hold true in the courtroom.

He had learned that when the authorities pronounced judgment on right and wrong there were always mitigating circumstances, especially in this world of state, federal and international law. In law, it's the legislature who set the position of the polar star. Societal probity wasn't fixed by ancient eastern religious texts. The legislature set the direction for the true north of society's moral compass.

His mother and father had one idea of morality and businessmen another. Ben discovered the lawyer's personal conscience, like his sidearm, must be checked at the courtroom door. Laws must be obeyed. Without the Rule of Law, society would collapse. Judges and courts are obliged to uphold the law on the books. Otherwise, society would descend into chaos.

Laws came from Milledgeville and Washington—not from the pages of an outdated religious text. The simple life of a ten-year-old country boy raised by missionary parents had morphed, for Ben, into the complex adult society of bewildering shades of grey—a confusing landscape of mists and fogs—a legal world that required a smart lawyer to lead his client to success through the shadowy gloom.

Ben was becoming a different man after fourteen months in law school and his time at the firm. He felt liberated. He could feel the influence of the progressive authors he had read who applauded the freedom of an enlightened intellect. Although he knew he had changed his world view, he continued to respect his father's firmly held beliefs. For the time being, Ben chose to live comfortably in two worlds and ignore the widening chasm. Ben preferred to allow his two world views to co-exist as if there were no clash. It was as if his life had two compartments—like saddlebags on his horse. On one side was the world view he received from his parents and the other contained the law library—and men like John Locke. What could be more outdated than five-thousand-year-old morals carved in stone? Real life contained those who swindle, lie, cheat, steal and kill. There were men who would do whatever they could at the expense of others to improve their lot. We need law and law enforcement. The law existed to protect the real community—not his father's imaginary Sunday dream world. Preachers could protect no one.

He would carefully avoid discussing such with his parents. He knew they would never be part of the progressive scientific democratic spirit fostered recently by the Jacksonian party. He didn't like the Jacksonian view of Indians and Indian removal, but he did like Jackson's ability to get things done. The United States was prospering as never before. Jackson, although sometimes pigheaded, Ben thought privately, wasn't afraid to lead from the front. He had to give him that. Ben had to admit Jackson would make a good president. Ben would have to tread a fine line between his parents' morals, his personal political views and the best interest of the Cherokee. Ben's future would be complicated.

26 December 1827

William Hicks has been appointed interim chief. John Ross is secondary chief. Elijah Hicks has been appointed president of the National Committee. Our leaders have a lot of work to do in these troubled times in Cherokee Country. I wish them well.

I haven't had a letter from Ben in several days.

Chapter XXXI

1828 – Zach, Ben and Elizabeth

Chapter 31

10 January 1828 - The Cold Moon – Du no lv ta ni..

I am invited to Ben's twenty-first birthday celebration this afternoon. What fun. Ben wants to be a lawmaker in Georgia. When elected, he can tell us the truth about Milledgeville. Ben's friend, Zach, says his election is certain. The wealthy befriend politicians to protect their investments—they're not all his friends. Ben can't believe every good thing people say about him, but he can believe me when I tell him I love him.

11 January 1828

Ben left for Milledgeville at dawn. His mother and I, arm in arm, waved him goodbye until he was out of sight. I wish I could live with him in Milledgeville, but that wouldn't be good for us right now—for him. Whites don't like me and it would make Ben look bad.

13 January 1828

Hurrah! We have a printing press in New Echota. I can't express my joy. We have a mailing list and soon the first issue of our Cherokee Phoenix will be published. We will be the first Indian nation to have our own newspaper. Mr. Lowry says the printing press is the most important single development of the Western World. Our newspaper will help us establish national credibility. Well-chosen words, he says, can motivate heroic deeds. I certainly hope so in our case. Our newspaper will make a huge difference in our ability to communicate. Perhaps Georgia will let us stay.

January – Milledgeville 1828

Ben shivered in the January cold as he and Zach walked quickly to the hotel.

"I wish your father would keep the office warmer. I'm frozen. It's cold, Zach. I hope they have a good fire at the hotel. My hands are like ice. I've been cold all day—chilled to the bone."

"Father always keeps a nice fire at the hotel," Zach said. "Don't be a wimp, Ben. If Father kept the office as warm as you like it, everyone would be asleep. We'll have a drink by the fire and you'll be fine. Since you just had a birthday and you're free, white and twenty-one, the world's your oyster— it's time we made our move, don't you think?"

Ben laughed, "It seems like just yesterday I was a boy at home with my parents. My biggest worry was taking out the ashes and chopping Mother's kindling."

Zach gave Ben a big slap on the back, "Well, speed it up, Ben—walk faster. Let's get to the hotel, have a drink, get warm and plan your election campaign. I'm ready for a drink," Zach said.

"That's all right by me, Zach. You're the schemer. I'm just a country boy lawyer."

"You're a country boy all right—but you're about the smartest country boy I've ever met."

"I don't know about that."

"Ben, I don't understand how anyone can enjoy books the way you do. You'll read anything. You keep doing my legal work, Ben, and I'll take care of things that distract you with this election. That's a good exchange—a proper division of labor, isn't it?"

Ben grinned, "Zach, I don't know a thing about politics and I hate rubbing elbows with strangers. That's the onerous part of this thing for me. If you and Elizabeth want me to run for office and will take care of as much of that as you can, I'll happily do your law work."

They entered the hotel and turned left up the three wide stairs straight to Zach's reserved table by the big fireplace in the corner with the long, polished mahogany inlaid mantelpiece. Ben loved Zach's father's hotel and their private space and their relaxing time after work. On this dreary January afternoon, the fire was most welcome. The servant took their coats and immediately served their drinks. A young, strong African, well dressed like all the staff, brought in a huge hickory backlog. As they watched, he scooped some of the cold ashes, pulled the hottest coals forward and placed the seasoned backlog against the firebrick in the back. The wood had been kept in the dry since summer and Ben could hear it begin to crackle almost immediately. The boy immediately returned with another armload of seasoned wood he put on top of the hot coals in front of the backlog. In just a moment the wood was bursting into flame and in two moments it was beginning to roar up the chimney.

Zach, as usual, was leaning on the end of the mantelpiece, drink in hand, puffing on his favorite Cuban cigar. Zach drank the same special whiskey from his private stock sent from the Hermitage and Andrew Jackson's personal still. Ben was getting used to the luxury and the service. He was learning to enjoy the advantages of privilege—of white privilege. He was glad he had been born white. It was nice to be waited on hand and foot.

Zach placed his drink on the mantelpiece and cigar in an ashtray and turned his back to the freshening fire, lifted his coat tails and rubbed his back and posterior.

"It doesn't get better than this does it, Ben?" Zach said with pleasure.

"This is good—very good," Ben agreed.

"I think this is the first time I've been warm all day. I'm glad I'm not the one who has to cut all this wood."

Zach grinned, "For a country boy, you are a wimp, Ben. I've seen little girls who have more gumption than you. If you can get your mind off the temperature and your personal discomfort, let's talk about your future—our future. We've got a lot of planning to do to get you elected this year."

"That's fine with me," Ben answered. "You talk about anything you want. I'm going to drink, relax and enjoy this fire."

Zach retrieved his drink and cigar, turned his back away from the fire and continued to lean against the mantel. With a wave of his cigar, he began speaking.

"Your election is certain, Ben, but one never knows with elections. We've already done a lot of work and I don't want to waste all the time we've got invested in you. I've learned to dot the i's and cross the t's when it comes to gettin' a man elected. There are a lot of new folks on the rolls and new business people. Lots of folks we don't know moving into town. I wouldn't be surprised if some folks don't vote half a dozen times. Things like that can't be helped. If anybody votes two or three times, we want them to vote for you—not your opponent. Nothing wrong with that, if they don't get caught."

Zach and Ben laughed.

Zach rotated before the fire once again to warm the other side.

"Ben, we've got to get your name out there starting now. I can get anyone elected I want, if I have time. We've got plenty of time, if we get busy now. If we do this right, we'll have bigger fish to fry in the years to come. The Georgia House will be easy, but the big prize is the United States Senate. That will take time. That's why we're starting now with you at your age—that's why we hired you. Elizabeth and I are sowing the seeds for your future success. You see that, don't you?"

363

Ben was listening carefully. As usual, he was enjoying his drink and the pleasant fire after a long day of intense study and research at the law firm. Since he was a boy, Ben's father advised him to listen more than talk, and he didn't mind relaxing and listening to Zach ramble.

"First, we'll solidify Father's friends. That'll be easy and they'll influence others. Elizabeth and I are working now to secure the support of the wealthiest. We'll plan a series of breakfasts, dinners, socials and the like that will crescendo to election day. In the last couple of weeks before the fall election, we'll see to it that every important person in Georgia shakes your hand. We'll connect your name with good things—like barbecues and civic achievement. We'll be your behind-the-scenes power brokers. We'll tell folks you'll take care of them after you're elected."

Zach raised his glass.

"This plan will work. We'll find someone to scratch the rich folks' back and they'll scratch yours on election day. Quid pro quo, Ben. The most important three words in English—quid pro quo."

Zach laughed and Ben couldn't help but join. Zach's energy, easy manner and ever-present smile made his company pleasant even if he did constantly repeat himself.

"Zach, you make this sound easy, but nothing is that easy."

"You're right, but I'm way ahead of the game. This first election isn't difficult, but it does require a brain put together like mine, doesn't it? On your own, Ben, you couldn't get elected to a backwoods city council. You need me—you know that, don't you?"

Zach, already a bit tipsy, laughed so hard at his comments he spilled his drink. Ben laughed too and chuckled to himself as he watched the colorfully-dressed Zach standing beside the fire waving his arms as if he were on stage. Zach continued to make his points with hand gestures, drink in one hand and big cigar in the other. Ben grinned to himself watching Zach, dressed as if he were going to an embassy ball, standing on the white marble inlaid hearth with one elbow leaning on the end of the long polished mahogany mantelpiece and a polished boot on the brass fender. Zach reminded Ben of one of his mother's colorful banty roosters—arrogantly strutting around the barnyard sporting his brightly colored tail feathers for all to see, crowing to everyone about their great abilities and picking a fight with anyone who disagreed. That made Ben laugh out loud at Zach's expense. He couldn't help glancing down at Zach's shiny new boots to see if he had spurs coming out the side like a rooster.

Ben knew Zach's boasts weren't empty. Zach knew how to influence people. Zach didn't mind work, as long as it was work he enjoyed, like arranging smoky backroom deals that put money in his pocket. Zach loved giving people what they wanted and getting things in return. Zach had described himself precisely—a power broker.

Ben continued sipping his Tennessee sour-mash. The whiskey gave his face and stomach a pleasant glow and warmed him all the way to his toes. This was the way to relax after a long day.

Ben didn't mind the idea of doing a portion of Zach's legal homework. He had never considered books, reading, research and study as work. He loved every moment in the library. Reading and study were pleasures—an avocation, not simply a vocation—something he would gladly do without pay and had done since a child. Ben generally disliked socials which meant less study time and a cloudy head the next day from the ever-present alcohol. He was amazed how it seemed everyone consumed alcohol and those who didn't were considered a stick-in-the-mud. Zach was doing him a favor by allowing him to help with Zach's legal responsibilities. Yes indeed, Ben thought, he and Zach did make a pair. He suddenly corrected himself and thought of Elizabeth and was reminded it was a trio—not a pair.

Zach turned to face the fire and warmed his other side. With his back to Ben, Zach continued, "We'll need money for a variety of things to get you elected, but raisin' money is easy. Gettin' a man to tell his friends he's supporting you—now that's the hard part. When I'm trying to win a man's support, I ask myself what's the one thing this man wants above all else? When I know the answer to that question, I've got him—hook, line and sinker."

Zach lowered his voice and turned to face Ben, "What is it a man wants and is afraid to get for himself? When you know that about a man, he's in your pocket. It takes time to learn a man's secrets, but I have folks who work for me who can find out anything.

Ben was listening and enjoying the fire and had learned not to be surprised at anything Zach might say.

"Men motivated by money are the easiest to catch," Zach continued, "but there are other things we can exchange for support. There are a lot of things men want besides money."

Ben, staring at his beautiful crystal glass and the pure liquid, was beginning to feel its calming effects and thinking he had never felt better in his life. Ben, his feet still cold, stretched out his boots towards the fire to warm the bottoms.

"I've seen that myself," Ben said. "My parents were never motivated by money, never. You could offer Father a basket full of money and it wouldn't influence him. He's the most incorruptible man imaginable. Even now, my parents aren't motivated by money. I didn't know much about the world until I came to work here. I've also learned everyone isn't as honest as Father. Many a churchgoer, I have discovered, will stab their neighbor in the back over money. You're right, Zach. Greedy people will do most anything to get what they want."

Zach, with both sides well warmed, sat beside Ben in the warm high-backed upholstered leather chair, sipped his whiskey and blew clouds of silvery cigar smoke towards the fireplace—watched the smoke catch the draft and be sucked up the flu.

"Ben, you're a quick study. I knew you would make a good politician the day I met you."

As usual, at this time of the afternoon, Zach's cheeks and the tip of his nose were beginning to redden.

"Well, there's money, but there's also power," Zach lectured on. "Some folks don't care about money but would love to be on the city council or be mayor or be a judge or even an important contractor. Other folks thrive on orderin' others about—they would love to be sheriff. People who want power are a bit more difficult to figure out. Jackson, for example, wants power. He wants to make executive decisions—be the one in the lead. Jackson hates to follow. Money is secondary to him."

Ben twirled his drink in his fingers, slumped down in his big upholstered chair and watched the fire through the cut glass as it diffused the flames into various colors.

Zach continued, "Some want money, some power and some pleasure. Some men dream about a pretty woman their wife doesn't know about. Those are the stupidest, of course. Once you supply their need, you have them over a barrel, don't you? You have both them and their pocketbook. Those folks will never feel comfortable about doing anything to make you angry, once you know their dirty secret. They'll be afraid of you, and you can trust me, Ben, I know plenty of women who will help us with that sort of thing—for money, of course."

Zach laughed again, "Understanding politics is easy, isn't it, Ben? I know how to do this, don't I?"

Zach motioned to the tall, immaculately dressed, greying African waiter in the shadows to have their drinks freshened and continued, "Ben, I got this all planned out. About six weeks before the election, we'll have a rapid-fire series of socials, events and balls culminating in a huge event in Milledgeville the day before the election. We'll invite the whole town. We'll cozy up to everyone. I feel a little embarrassed at how easy this is. They ought to just go ahead and give you your seat. By the time of the election, people will think anyone a fool if they don't vote for you."

"It's a done deal," Zach said. Holding on to the mantelpiece to steady his legs, he raised his glass high above his head for a tribute.

"Here's a toast to the smartest, handsomest, and soon-to-be richest legislator in the state of Georgia—Ben Lowry. You know I stretched the truth a bit about you being the handsomest, don't you, but then I'm getting used to tellin' folks things about you that aren't exactly true."

The two young men laughed with one another. Ben loved the moment. He always loved listening to Zach ramble on about different things even if he was sometimes monotonously pedantic. He and Zach were becoming good friends.

At that moment Elizabeth and her parents walked into the foyer. Zach and Ben stepped quickly down the three wide steps to greet them.

"Good evening Mr. and Mrs. Cooper. What a pleasure to see you this cold January afternoon," Zach said. "And a good evening to you too, Miss Elizabeth. Would y'all care to join us for a glass of wine before your meal and warm in front of our perfectly marvelous fire? We would love to have you join us. You could relax with us before your dinner."

"No son," Elizabeth's father said. "Caroline and I are going to our table. We're tired and we expect guests shortly. Elizabeth may wish to join you. She's always full of energy. Would you like to join the boys, Elizabeth?"

Mr. Cooper's daughter lowered her eyes with respect for her parents, "Yes sir, I would like that if you and Mother would be content without my presence for a while. I would like that indeed."

Since Elizabeth was a little girl, she had learned to handle her rich parents—manipulate might be a better word. Her parents loved their daughter dearly and provided their princess with everything possible for her happiness. Elizabeth, in return, never created problems for her parents. In her parents' eyes, she was the perfect daughter. The practical result was she could do anything she wanted within reason and, with her handsome allowance, she could do a lot.

"Go, my dear girl. Enjoy your evening. Stay with Zach and his friend as long as you wish. Your mother and I are going to our table. I need to sit down and have a drink. Join us when you're ready, dear."

Zach took Elizabeth's arm and escorted her to the warm upholstered leather chairs in front of the welcoming fire, "And what would my dear Bethy have to drink this afternoon, may I ask?"

Elizabeth's eyes sparkled even more than usual as she sat between the two finely-dressed, attentive young men.

"Zach, I have all the time in the world for you two handsome men, and I have no desire to hobnob with my parents' stuffy guests."

"Hello, Elizabeth," Ben said as he kissed the back of Elizabeth's extended hand, never taking his eyes from her face. "You can have anything you desire this evening, my dear, up to and including my very soul."

The three laughed together at Ben's words. They seemed to get along perfectly—always on the same page.

Zach asked again, "And what does our Bethy want to drink this evening? Your wish is my command."

"I'm like Father this afternoon. I need a drink to warm my frozen toes. I'll have a double bourbon and water if you don't mind."

Ben's eyebrows raised. He had never seen a woman drinking straight whiskey—and certainly not a double. The usual feminine choice was a sickeningly sweet mint julep, a sherry or a dainty glass of white wine.

Ben learned something new and delightful about Elizabeth at every meeting. There was something overpoweringly attractive about a beautiful woman who threw caution to the wind and drank bourbon in public. He liked her carefree attitude. He laughed to himself as he imagined her joining the men and smoking a big cigar with her whiskey. Elizabeth, in her element as the center of attention between two young men, made herself comfortable.

"You look most lovely this evening, Elizabeth," said Ben with a polite little bow as he sat beside her. "I'm sure you are once again, as rumored, the most charming woman in Milledgeville and Zach and I the most honored of men—graced by your presence. We are at your service."

Ben meant it. Elizabeth was a striking woman who knew how to dress. With her near unlimited clothing budget and her father's business connections overseas, especially in France, there wasn't a young woman in Georgia better turned out. With the addition of her expert coquetry, an art form she practiced daily, she was the most desirable woman a young man could imagine.

Elizabeth smiled at Ben as he moved to sit as close to her as he dared.

"Why Ben Lowry, I do think you're flirting with me. Are you flirting with me? Mother always says the best compliment a girl can have is a flirtatious beau, and I do agree. Mother told me a girl of modesty and breeding will flirt back to gain the upper hand and thus defend her virtue with both beauty and wit. I think that's what Mother meant to say, don't you? I love a battle of wits with a handsome young man, and you, Mr. Ben Lowry, are exceptionally well-armed. I'm sure I would never have to defend my virtue in the presence of such a gallant man as yourself. You would always defend my honor, wouldn't you, Ben? You would never take advantage of my virtuous feminine innocence, would you? Could I depend on you to defend my dignity as a chivalrous southern gentleman should?"

Elizabeth, her eyes sparkling with amusement, gave Ben the most flirtatious smile she could manage and accomplished perfectly that which she intended.

Zach, understanding exactly what Elizabeth was doing, looked sideways at the exchange, chuckled to himself and took a sip of his drink. He knew Elizabeth's ulterior motives when it came to men—pecuniary motives that coincided with his—motives that had brought Zach and Elizabeth together years earlier and made them two of the richest young people in Georgia society.

Ben flushed. He thought Elizabeth exceptionally attractive and she had only grown more captivating with every meeting. He had been alone with Elizabeth only that one time at dinner and found her enchanting. Her perfume turned the room into a springtime orchard in full bloom. Ben was having trouble thinking clearly and even remembering why he was there. The unwanted thought came into his mind that Cassie never smelled like that. Now was not the time to think of Cassie. He didn't want to think of Cassie. He wanted to think about Elizabeth. He needed to concentrate on the beautiful, fascinating woman beside him.

Elizabeth politely asked, "I understand you made your final decision to run for office. Is that true?"

"Yes, ma'am. I did," Ben answered. "Zach will manage my campaign. He says my chances of election are excellent. I can do good things for the people of Georgia and I understand you'll assist. I'm looking forward to that, too. I'm sure we'll be successful."

Ben was feeling more confident after several drinks. It was a wonderful thing to be well thought of. Life couldn't be better than this.

"Spoken like a true politician, Ben," Elizabeth said as she leaned backward and looked at Ben with playful eyes and unsuccessfully restrained a laugh as she covered her mouth with her white gloved hand.

She continued mischievously, "So, you plan great things for the good people of Georgia, do you? Your legislative career will be filled with noble ideas and wonderful deeds of chivalry as you, their prince valiant, perform an endless series of altruistic actions for your constituents? Am I right?"

Elizabeth was in a lighthearted mood and couldn't restrain another laugh, "My dear Mr. Lowry, with that attitude you'll go far in politics, I assure you. For a moment, you almost had me convinced you were telling the truth."

Her infectious laughter had all three laughing together like old friends. Ben had to concentrate with all his strength to process what she was saying and make an intelligent reply. Elizabeth continued with her light breezy attitude and a wave of her hand.

"You're not just another handsome lawyer, are you, Ben Lowry? You're ambitious, talented and determined. I like that. As for me, I have ambition but not so much talent, I'm afraid. I'm certain, my handsome philanthropic friend, you'll be elected to high office and history will record you as being responsible for countless charitable deeds. You'll be known throughout Georgia as the grand purveyor of compassion."

Ben couldn't help but be attracted to this beautiful witty woman who enjoyed life to the fullest and wasn't afraid to poke fun at societies' most cherished institutions—and even at her friends. He loved her openness. He loved the way she combined clever speech with body motions to communicate her interest in him. He always felt he had her full attention when she was near—as if she were truly interested in him—attentive to his every word. He knew she was flirting, perhaps even toying with him, but he didn't care. All he wanted was for her interest, genuine or feigned, to continue. He didn't want this moment to end.

Elizabeth continued with a grin.

"It occurred to me since I am free, white and twenty-one, that an aspiring politician like you might consider helping little ole' me achieve my personal goals in life? Would you, Ben Lowry, in your quest for benevolent public office, consider assisting me in exchange for my political support? In return, I promise to show you every gratitude imaginable. I would be eternally grateful for your assistance. Would you be so kind, Ben? I promise you'll never regret your decision to lend me a hand."

They all three laughed again a bit louder this time. Ben couldn't wait to spend more time with this amusing woman whose bright green eyes shone like stars in the night sky and made his blood flow hot at the mention of her name. He had never met anyone like her. Not even Cassie had made him feel the way he felt at this moment, but then, when he was in New Echota he never drank whiskey. Ben, despite what he had been taught by his parents, did his best to believe he could control whiskey and manage his mind through the alcohol-induced fog. Ben knew there were important differences between Cassie and Elizabeth. When he was with Elizabeth he chose not to think of those differences.

Ben had never met a woman with a quick mind like Elizabeth—well—none except Cassie. He would think about Cassie later.

When the laughter subsided, Zach continued with obvious amusement.

"And, my noble-minded friend, I don't wonder if your newfound goodness will result in the great accumulation of personal wealth—both for yourself and your associates. Quid pro quo, Ben, Quid pro quo. Don't forget that's what we're all about. From now on your motto is quid pro quo. Everything we do is for our future."

"Ben," Elizabeth interrupted, "I was wondering if you and Zach might need the advice of an erudite woman who knows the ins and outs of Georgia high society in places other than smelly taverns? The three of us might form an entertaining and profitable relationship, don't you think? You young men know I have access to parlors you two could never enter. I've been bored lately. I'm interested in a challenge."

With this little speech, she allowed her head to tilt backwards as she gave another teasing laugh that communicated her interest in the two young men. She knew very well she was the center of attention. Ben, if he had been thinking clearly, would have noticed with each of Elizabeth's actions his interest in her was growing. Ben wasn't thinking clearly. Between Zach, the dulling effect of the alcohol and the seductive charms of Elizabeth, Ben was disarmed—helpless as a newborn.

Elizabeth accidentally touched Ben's trousers just above the knee. He hoped she didn't see the resulting shiver. She saw. Elizabeth had plans for Ben. Elizabeth believed this rustic specimen might be more exciting than others she had conquered recently. He was certainly a healthy breed, tall and well groomed—very healthy, in fact. Time would tell, she thought to herself.

The tall African waiter, never making the least noise, refreshed their drinks, quietly observing the exchange between the three young people.

"I don't think we need to take this under further advisement, do you?" Zach said. "I pronounce our partnership in Ben's election a done deal. Let's the three of us drink to our corporate success. I propose a toast to the most prosperous triumvirate in the history of Georgia and to the second-most handsomest lawyer and his upcoming election. May he soon be crowned king of Georgia and live forever."

They laughed, clinked their glasses and drank. All three believed the words of the toast would be fulfilled and Ben would be elected to the Georgia House—the beginning of an influential and profitable political career.

Ben was watching Elizabeth to see how she reacted when she sipped the strong liquor. Her facial expression didn't change. Her eyes and mind were as clear as when she entered the room. She might as well have been sipping lemonade. That told him something.

"Elizabeth and I have been putting our heads together, Ben," Zach said. "Would you like the three of us to begin meeting every Tuesday afternoon for a regular planning session here in this room? You'll benefit from the intellect of the most sought-after belle in town and gain access to clandestine feminine enclaves of information. How about we meet right here every Tuesday until the election and work on our plans?"

Ben and Elizabeth agreed. Zach stood on unsteady feet and, with a red face and a silly grin, raised his glass once again, "Another toast then. To many a Tuesday spent in the delight of one another's company and to our acquisition of a cornucopia of pleasure and wealth gifted by the singular political success of one Ben Lowry—future king of Georgia."

They laughed even more loudly, touched glasses and decided two in the afternoon each Tuesday would be the perfect time. They could have a few drinks, plot and scheme for an hour or two and dine afterward. Elizabeth swallowed the rest of her bourbon in one gulp, stood and extended her hand to Ben, "Would you young men pardon me? I must be a good daughter and join my parents and their insufferable guests. I'm looking forward to seeing you more often—much more often, Ben. You and I will certainly become the best of friends. I'm sure of it."

Elizabeth stood and excused herself. Ben's eyes followed her graceful form as she left the private dining area and stepped down the three wide steps into the foyer, turning left to join her parents. She didn't look back—not once. She never looked back, he noticed. He had never met a woman with more self-confidence and poise. She had the most beautiful facial features and figure he had ever seen and before she was out of sight he was already wishing to see her again. Ben wondered if he would ever have the courage to call her Bethy as Zach did? He wondered why she never looked back?

Chapter XXXII

1828 - Ben and Elizabeth

Chapter 32

17 January 1828 - Month of the Cold Moon- Du no lv ta ni

I love Ben's long letters. I love how he shares the daily details of his life. His letters are windows into his life—a glimpse into his soul. I read every one and imagine myself there with him.

He and Zach meet each Tuesday preparing for his November election to the Georgia House. I am thrilled. He will be successful and accomplish great things both as a lawyer and politician and for the Cherokee. I wait impatiently every day for his letters.

January 1828 - Milledgeville

Ben made himself comfortable in Zach's private corner beside the big fireplace. If it wasn't for his inherent frugality, instilled by his thrifty parents, and the fact that Huff's Boarding House was just around the corner from his office, Ben would have moved his lodgings to the hotel months ago. He would love to spend every evening here and have a comfortable, quiet place to do all his light reading. He could have an evening drink and cigar in comfort instead of rubbing elbows with the coarse, uneducated men at Huff's. Well, maybe if he were to be elected he might move, but moving would be an unnecessary expense—no sense throwing that much money away. Zach's father had given him free use of the private dining room, smoking room and library so sleeping at Huff's would work for now. He would save his money for a rainy day and use his room in the boarding house for a dormitory.

Ben loved his career as a lawyer but was thinking more about his political campaign and his Tuesday session with Zach and Elizabeth—especially about Elizabeth. He had to admit to himself he was much more interested in politics because of Elizabeth and her interest. Since their first meeting, he often thought of her lovely face, cute upturned nose and her eyes—how she smiled with her eyes—and encouraged him to run for office. He hadn't forgotten the accidental touch of her hand on his thigh at their last meeting. The memory of that touch gave him the shivers—even now. He knew she was flirting and it probably didn't mean anything, but he loved every exciting moment when she was around. He was looking forward to more.

Elizabeth, arriving late, walked into the hotel foyer alone—without Zach. Ben chuckled to himself when thinking about the strict time-keeping among businessmen in Milledgeville. He loved the Cherokee casual approach to appointments he had grown up with and appreciated. White folks, he had learned in Milledgeville, are conscious of the passage of time almost to the minute. They divide their day into the smallest of segments. 'Time is money' he's often told.

Among the Cherokee, who have no timepieces, there is no such awareness. The Cherokee are never in a rush to accomplish anything, and Ben liked that—he liked that a lot. In Milledgeville he felt pushed and shoved as if every hour of the day were a matter of increasing urgency—as if during every day he was required to run a race from the time he rose until the time he walked out the door of the law office.

Among the Cherokee, no one would be upset if a man was a day or two late for a meeting. Tardiness was expected. How different we white people are, Ben thought, and how unnecessarily we put ourselves under time pressure. That couldn't be healthy. He smiled as he felt for his expensive gold pocket watch on his new gold chain and laughed at himself as he rose to meet Elizabeth.

Ben met Elizabeth at the top of the three wide steps to the private dining room. She gave Ben a bright smile, extended her hand and Ben escorted her back to their cozy spot by the fireplace. He noticed her eyes never left his face and she walked as close to him as possible. He had never met a woman like this. He loved the way she looked up at him. It made him feel important. He couldn't describe the emotion he felt knowing Elizabeth was interested in him. Ben found it impossible to believe that Elizabeth's interest in him was a charade.

Their regular servant, the tall, slender, well-trained negro, politely asked their pleasure in perfect English. If Ben had closed his eyes, he would have never known by his speech the servant was African—there was no accent and no indication he was illiterate as most Africans were. Previously, Ben thought he had detected a bit of a French accent and had heard him speak fluent Spanish to a visitor on more than one occasion. He wondered where Zach's father had found this 'boy' who moved about soundlessly, spoke multiple languages and waited on them with impeccable manners. Ben noticed one of the African's incisors was missing and a neat pie shaped notch was cut from the top of his right ear. This wasn't the time to think about it, not with a beautiful woman beside him, but those disfigurements were put there by slave owners to easily identify a runaway. He mustn't think about such things. He must concentrate on the beautiful woman in front of him and give her his full attention. Ben's mind deferred to Elizabeth.

"What would you like to drink, my dear? Our usual?"

"Oh no," she responded. "Don't you think we should have something special today? I think this afternoon a nice glass of white wine would be in order, don't you, Ben? When we were in Bordeaux last year, I enjoyed their lovely Chardonnay, but perhaps a German Riesling would be nice? What do you think? And when we've finished here with our business, we might take a little ride into the country if it's not too cool, and later we could have a romantic dinner here at the hotel. Do you know how to be romantic, Ben? I think you do."

With that speech, Elizabeth squeezed Ben's arm and he couldn't help blushing like a schoolboy. She laughed easily at his shyness. Ben loved her soft musical voice and the way she teased him. He understood she was flirting, and flirting was exactly what he wanted—what he needed. He craved the feminine attention she was giving.

Ben ordered two glasses of their best German Riesling.

"Zach left for Savannah early this morning," Elizabeth said. "He wanted me to give you his apologizes for not being here. He didn't have time to let you know. He told me to tell you he would be gone the rest of the week and maybe next. He thought you and I should get together and talk about our plans and continue to get to know one another. I think that's a good idea, don't you? We do have a lot to talk about, don't we, Ben? I'm one of those people who must know everything about a person I'm interested in."

Her eyes sparkled as she spoke. Ben gulped. He knew he appeared clumsy to the refined Elizabeth who seemed to be in full control of every situation. She and Zach were never ruffled or uncomfortable and he envied that. He wanted to be like them. He wanted to have their confidence. All too often he felt as if his emotions were uncontrolled and easily read by others. Elizabeth couldn't have more poise if she were a veteran actress playing a part on the stage of a crowded theatre. Zach and Elizabeth were never frustrated—never irritated. He liked people with self-assurance. He wanted to develop that same discipline over his life and emotions. He promised himself he would work on that. His rustic upbringing in Cherokee Country led to his shyness in the unfamiliar social circles of Milledgeville. He hated the idea of appearing socially awkward. He was embarrassed by every faux pas and the smiles they raised among Milledgeville's upper class who noticed his every lapse of etiquette.

The silent, white-gloved waiter brought the polished silver tray with their wine in the sparkling crystal glasses on finely woven Irish linen.

Elizabeth raised her glass, "To the success of my friend Ben and his certain election,"

They drank the toast. Her eyes never left his. He knew she was studying him—looking inside of him. Ben knew his body language made him an open book. His mother had told him he was a bad liar and she was right. He was a complete failure at deception and, like most folks with a good heart, could never attribute dark motives to others. He had never practiced concealing his emotions with his wonderful open parents and was used to telling the truth. Ben's upbringing made him trusting and gullible. His mother had counseled him he should tell the truth in any situation. The truth, she said, was never out of season and always the most valuable currency.

Ben believed Elizabeth and Zach, and all people for that matter, were basically like his parents—were trustworthy and would have his best interest in mind. Ben had little worldly experience and had never in his life been betrayed.

It would never occur to Ben that Zach and Elizabeth could possibly be pseudo friends. It wasn't possible for Ben's naïve mind to believe anyone would pretend friendship and discard that friend when their purpose was accomplished. No one would do such a thing, would they?

When he looked at Elizabeth sitting beside him, he felt as if he were in the warm sunshine of the first day of spring and she was the sun. It was a most pleasant feeling. He wanted that feeling to continue. He felt his emotions stirring with a pleasure swelling from deep inside—a pleasure he had only experienced with Cassie. He knew it wasn't the best thing, but he was beginning to think of Elizabeth at the most inopportune times. He thought again of Zach's warning. Surely this beautiful woman sitting beside him was not as callous as Zach had portrayed. Surely some of her flirtations were genuine.

Elizabeth had long been a shrewd business woman in a man's world and knew exactly what she was doing around men. She always operated with a single goal in mind—personal enrichment. Zach understood Elizabeth's mind completely. He was just like her. They were two peas in a pod. He knew her for the clever business person she was and had no problem enjoying her friendship despite that knowledge.

As adolescents, Elizabeth and Zach learned to cooperate to gain wealth. They learned relationships with the opposite sex were for sport—never to be taken seriously. Any serious love relationship, much less marriage, would only detract and delay their plans. Life was about using any means available to acquire wealth. Hedonistic pleasures were simply a perquisite—an occasional by-product of those who sought self-gratification. They considered permanent relationships and unconditional loyalty counterproductive—interfering with their long-term goals and a waste of energy.

Ben was the opposite. His mother and father were unselfish—magnanimous. Their transparent generosity was the reason the Cherokee permitted Ben's parents to work in Cherokee Country. The council had complete trust in Wilbur and Eleanor Lowry and trusted them with their children. Ben had seen his mother on more than one occasion give a hungry Indian, a complete stranger, the last morsel in their house.

Elizabeth was sitting as close to Ben as their upholstered chairs would allow. She smelled of Paris—of sunshine and springtime. Her bare arms and perfectly done hair were more than Ben could manage—his heart raced. Sitting next to her, he found himself sometimes forgetting to breathe normally and more than once caught himself staring at her generously exposed bosom.

The waiter refreshed their wine.

"Where shall we begin?" Elizabeth said. "Zach and I will help you get elected any way we can. How can I personally assist? Tell me what you and Zach have been planning."

Ben didn't know what to say and only managed to stutter, "I don't really know, Elizabeth. I've never run for office before. I'm an absolute novice. Other than talking to my clients about my candidacy, I don't know what to do or what to say. What do you suggest? You and Zach have plenty of ideas. You've done this before."

Elizabeth leaned her shoulder against his as if to warm herself and continued in a low, controlled voice, "Ben, I know a lot of important people. We'll convince them you're the person to assist their business. You'll help them make money. That's it in a nutshell. Quid pro quo. They help us and we promise to help them. You're the perfect man to be in politics. I trusted you the moment I met you and I must confess my heart fluttered a bit. You're handsome. Oh my, yes—very handsome. First impressions are important in politics—perhaps the most important thing. You should appear handsome to the women, innocuous to their husbands and wise to everyone. Zach and I hired you because of your trustworthy appearance. You have a rare gift, Ben—and of course your innate intelligence and advanced education are a bonus. You have an honest face. The fact that you're an uncomplicated country boy is in your favor. When someone talks to you they are immediately struck by your command of language which communicates wisdom. You have a friendly manner that puts folks at ease. They like being around you. No one would ever dream that you would be devious or a liar."

Elizabeth, with her easy girlish manner, touched his arm allowing her hand to linger a moment longer than proper.

"Oh my yes, Ben, I trusted you the first time I saw you and I have a lot of ideas how I can help your career. I love your ambition. You certainly have the assets a man in politics needs. Zach and I will insure you have a successful career all the way to a Senate appointment. You know that, don't you? Right now, Ben, you're the number one interest in my life. If you succeed—I will succeed. What could be better than that? I would dearly love my new best friend to be a Senator from Georgia."

She laughed as her blond curls bounced on her bare shoulders. Ben was defenseless. Elizabeth knew exactly what she was doing. Young men were so easy, she thought.

Elizabeth wanted Ben to be successful and she wanted to guide that success. She wanted control—complete control of her own personal politician. If her plans worked, she would be enriched—incredibly enriched. If their schemes failed she would move on to Ben's replacement. She always had a backup plan. She never kept all her eggs in one basket. Ben wasn't the only young man in Georgia interested in politics. He just happened to be the one at the moment most likely to make a success of his political career—with her help, of course. Plus, Ben would be amusing. Ben wasn't much of a romantic challenge, but there was the distinct possibility he would go far with her amorous coaching. Ben would be fun to teach.

Elizabeth continued, "You'll be elected to the Georgia house this autumn. After a few years building your brand, we'll skip the Georgia Senate and go up to the U.S. House. If we work hard and play our cards right, the U.S. Senate could be ours the first year you qualify. What do you think? Zach and I believe it's within our grasp—your grasp, and that's why you were chosen. Zach and I think you're the man."

She laughed again. Ben's mind raced through the ten years Elizabeth had just described and visualized himself appointed by the Georgia legislature to the Senate. He would have his own desk in Washington City and Milledgeville. The business world would be lined up outside his door. That was exactly the kind of thing he had wanted when he became a lawyer—to have influence with lawmakers in order to have political influence on behalf of the Cherokee. He had never dreamed such personal success possible—not in so short a time. Elizabeth's dream for him was almost believable. Perhaps, with the help of Zach and Elizabeth, it might happen.

"I suppose that might be a possibility," Ben replied. 'We'll do good things for our fellow Georgians and we'll have fun doing it. I'm like Zach there. I had much rather do this than be a farmer."

Ben was looking into Elizabeth's eyes and would have done well to remember his father's warnings. This would have been a good moment to think of Cassie, too, but she was a long way from Ben's mind and didn't wear French perfume or the latest French fashions, in any case. Elizabeth's green eyes and perfume had him spellbound. When Elizabeth spoke, he felt mesmerized—hypnotized. He must remember to breathe.

"May I make a suggestion?" Elizabeth asked.

"Of course, you may suggest anything," Ben replied.

Ben didn't know it, but he would be doing everything Elizabeth would ever ask from this moment forward.

Elizabeth's voice took on a serious business tone, "Our initial plan is simple. We target men who control large groups of white men, since only white men vote. Slaves and Indians count for nothing. We ignore them. They're meaningless. White women are important only as a secondary influence, but in general we ignore them, too. When the traditional methods of gaining influence don't work, Zach and I sometimes reach men through their wives and daughters. I can assure you, Zach knows how to gain the confidence of a woman—even an older woman. It's amazing how silly older women can become when a handsome young man like Zach pays them attention. He finds women of all ages a challenge—especially the more experienced. He loves the game and plays it very well, I might add."

Elizabeth, with a cute pout as if she were confused, paused for a moment and looked into Ben's eyes as she lightly placed her hand innocently on his thigh as if unaware of her actions, "Do you like women, Ben? Do you like me? Do you find me attractive?"

Ben, suddenly flustered and unable to speak at such an odd question coming out of the blue, could only mutter in reply. All he could think of was Elizabeth's hand touching his trousers. The room had, for all purposes, disappeared into a swirling sensual mist of Elizabeth's creation. He had to use every ounce of his inner determination to speak intelligently. He didn't want to babble to this intelligent beautiful woman who was asking him questions.

He took a deep breath, "Yes, Elizabeth, I like women. I do. You know I do and I like you very much. I always have. I've never met anyone like you."

Elizabeth kept her white gloved hand on Ben's thigh for a few moments longer before she returned it to her lap.

Ben's blood was racing. He felt confused—unable to think. The room was spinning. Surely everyone in the hotel could hear his heart beating.

Elizabeth dispassionately observed what was happening to Ben. She understood healthy young men and what went on in their minds when they were around her. She had learned from Zach. To her, young men were a game, a means to an end, never an end in themselves. She loved to play the game, but it wasn't a game she wanted to take home. She despised clingy men. She had learned most men would give anything to be alone with her, and she was perfectly willing to trade if the result was clearly in her favor. She would make an exchange if it meant she could gain control of a man—especially his assets. A man without assets, no matter how attractive, was worthless. Personal wealth was the only thing that mattered. Ben, although he presently had little monetary worth, was a clear means to a lucrative end if her plans worked out—a very lucrative end. Ben would be her avenue into the male halls of power—her horse in the big race.

It amused her to think of men as if she were training animals. Few women were willing to do what she did, but few women had her ambitions and few would reap the extraordinary rewards. She wanted financial security accompanied by an inexhaustible supply of entertainment along the way. Perhaps this handsome, naïve young man would help her achieve both. She would soon find out. If not, she would move on. She always had handsome candidates in mind.

"Well, Ben, that's exactly what we'll do. We'll make two lists. One list of men on our side. We'll monitor them and keep them hooked, but that list is easy. We won't lose a one of those to your opponents. The critical list will be the influential men who don't now support you. You and I will concentrate on those men and Zach will concentrate on their wives and daughters."

She laughed out loud.

Ben didn't know what to say and answered, "I'm not sure I'm up to that, Elizabeth. I really don't want to be deceptive. Do you think I can actually plan to influence folks I have never met?"

Ben had one glass of wine too many and was finding it impossible to think about election strategy. All he could think about was this beautiful creature beside him who was toying with him unmercifully.

Elizabeth laughed out loud again and once again gave Ben's thigh another lingering touch as if to accent her point. She leaned against his shoulder.

"Ben, do you know how to be polite to a woman and pay her attention? Can you listen without appearing bored? Of course, you know those things. That's all you do to gain influence over a woman. You have excellent social skills. Everyone likes you. I like you a lot—probably too much. All you have to do to be elected is be yourself. Zach and I will coach you on the actual political issues. You thought you were going to talk to men all the time, didn't you? You have a lot to learn about politics, Ben. The people in power don't really care about what you believe. They want to know if you can help them when they need help—help making money. That's all they care about. That's how you get elected."

Ben still didn't know what to say, "I'll do the best I can. I'll promise to help people."

"Ben, if you learn to pay a woman attention she'll think you're as cute as a puppy dog. Pay attention to a woman properly and she'll tell her husband to vote for you. You don't have to be romantic or overtly flirt with her. Simply give her attention. Don't look away when she's talking to you and never interrupt. Listen to every word she says. Occasionally tell her how intelligent she is and ask simple questions. If she asks you a question, preface your answer with, 'that's a good question'. Under no circumstances look at a clock or watch. Tell her how impressed you are with her thinking. If someone interrupts your conversation, continue to listen to her. Keep your eyes on her and give her your full attention until she's finished talking. If you do that, you'll be the only man in her life who does. Without trying, you might have some unexpected pleasure along the way. That would be alright, wouldn't it? You do like women, don't you?"

Elizabeth continued in a voice that Ben found hypnotic, mesmerizing—a voice that transported him to a place of unending pleasure.

"I can do that," Ben replied.

Elizabeth was smiling and enjoying the conversation and knew exactly what she was doing with Ben and his emotions.

She continued, "There are women who would happily spend an afternoon with you and never let their husbands know, if you pay them attention. Remember, Ben, I have access to the women's parlors. I hear things that would never be spoken in mixed company. I often hear things I wasn't meant to hear and I can read between the lines. I think I would make a good spy, don't you? I have friends who tell me things. In politics, information is of greater value than money. Zach and I have quite a circle of folks who simply gather information."

Ben finally collected his wits enough to answer.

"Elizabeth, you would make an excellent spy. You have the temperament for it, I do believe. Sometimes I wonder if you know what I'm thinking."

She smiled and nodded in agreement and continued her instruction.

"I'll do the same with the men as you do with women. Men are easy—easier than women. I listen and laugh. I ask them about their work. I praise their intelligence and business acumen and tell them they're handsome. In a few minutes they're unable to escape—unwilling to escape. Men are easy."

Ben's head wasn't clear. All he wanted was for Elizabeth to continue talking to him—to continue looking at him. The waiter filled their crystal glasses once again.

"Now, don't think ill of me," Elizabeth said, "but I know how men think. I know how their minds work and I know when their mind doesn't work, if you know what I mean. I'm a business woman in a man's world. I have to know these things. You wouldn't hold it against me if I were to ask someone for a favor at the most opportune moment as a matter of business, would you? You would do the same, wouldn't you? I understand business. I have something men want and why wouldn't I use my most valuable asset? A smart girl can have her cake and eat it too, if you know what I mean. My power over men will not last forever. I need to make hay while the sun shines, don't I, Ben? One day I'll be wrinkled and plain and my poor neck will sag like a turkey gobbler and I'll be as grey as a goose. One day, Ben, you'll be bald, fat and ugly. Now, while we're young and healthy, is the time for us to act, isn't it?

Ben smiled to himself as he looked at this beautiful woman who could be so marvelously candid—who wasn't afraid to broach any subject. He had never met a woman so straightforward. He admired that trait. She was intelligent, cultured, finely dressed and the most ambitious woman he had ever met. She was at this moment the sole object of his desire. He wanted her no matter what the risk. This beautiful woman knew exactly what she wanted and wasn't afraid to strive for it. She appeared innocent yet she could drink bourbon and water and never flinch. He liked that about her. He knew she would help him get elected and achieve his career goals. He was certain of that now. He knew he could trust her to accomplish what she said she could do. He was in good hands with Elizabeth and Zach.

Ben knew exactly how a young man felt around an attractive young woman. Elizabeth's frank talk excited him. He was vulnerable, but he didn't care. He loved where he was at this moment with Elizabeth at his side and her hand on his thigh, and he didn't care what she did. All he cared about was that this moment of intense pleasure in Elizabeth's company wouldn't end. He would gladly throw caution to the wind.

Elizabeth was watching Ben carefully. She laughed to herself that young men were so predictable. She loved to have fun occasionally with strong young men and it was time she had some fun with this handsome young lawyer with his powerful tanned hands, athletic physique and full lips. It was time to spring the trap—set the hook. It was time to put the next stage of their plans for Ben and his future into action if she wanted to go to Washington City on the arm of a successful politician.

Perhaps, Elizabeth thought to herself, this handsome young man would become an ongoing project or maybe it would be a fling for today. She didn't care. She wanted Ben today, now—at this moment. One never knew what untold adventures would come one's way on the morrow and provide unexpected diversions. Today she needed to consolidate gains and continue to work to secure her future with this up-and-coming young politician. What she was about to encourage in Ben would, of course, give her pleasure but it might also be her ticket to the United States Senate. If he did become a Senator, she would be on his arm—no one else. She would see to that. It was time to act to ensure that future just in case Ben's political aspirations were to come true. If Ben didn't get an appointment to the Senate, she would find someone else who would. It was a wonderful thing, she thought, when the principles of business and necessity for pleasure coincided—a wonderful thing indeed.

"Ben, I don't think you know, but Zach and I have permanently reserved a suite here in the hotel for business purposes—for out-of-town clients and such. We keep the suite prepared at all times for our guests and clients for whom confidentiality is a requirement. The suite has a private entrance, twenty-four-hour private butler, private bath, full bar and restaurant service and a discrete back entrance to the stables in the rear. One can be most inconspicuous here in Zach's father's hotel. In the business of politics, it's important to be prudent on occasion, don't you think, Ben? All of the staff associated with our suite and this private dining room were selected with the utmost care. They never remember what they have seen or heard. That's important, isn't it?"

It was time. She had never been more charming. Ben was incapable of resistance.

She continued, "I decorated the entire suite myself. It has the best of everything. We have a private balcony with an exquisite view. I have some interesting French prints I brought back from Paris. You'll be impressed. I've never seen anything like them. If I remember correctly, you just had a birthday, didn't you? I have a special gift upstairs I've been saving for you. I was waiting for a special occasion, and I think today is the day. It will be your belated birthday gift. You'll love it. I know you will. I brought it from Paris, too, just for you."

Elizabeth stood and extended her hand to the flushed young man whose heart was pounding.

In the sweetest of voices she said, "If you'll accompany me to our room, you can admire my decorating handiwork. We'll have a look at those French prints and you can receive your gift. Let's go now, shall we? It's cold but we keep our room cozy. I ordered a nice fire just in case you and I were to have a little extra time this afternoon. I promise you'll be more comfortable there than in this stuffy old room with no privacy. You don't have any urgent appointments this afternoon, do you?"

She was standing close to Ben by the end of her little speech. Ben's chest was on fire as she pressed herself against his coat. Her perfectly manicured hands were resting on his forearms. With her head thrown back, she looked directly up into the tall young man's cornflower blue eyes.

Ben stammered, "Of course I don't have any appointments and I would love to see the suite. I'm sure it's lovely. It would be a pleasure."

Ben almost choked as he spoke.

Elizabeth smiled to herself. This was a handsome man but they had a lot of work to do if they wanted to get this naïve country boy a Senate appointment. She and Zach had long planned on having their own personal politician. Nothing could be more lucrative than their own Senator. Ben fit the bill.

As the two left the room, the white-gloved, greying African waiter with the missing front tooth silently collected the empty crystal wine glasses. The romantic interchange between the young white couple had provoked fond memories of an attractive young woman he had known years ago who had looked up at him as this woman had looked at Ben. Tray in hand, he leaned against the mahogany mantlepiece and enjoyed the warmth of the fire for a moment and smiled as he let his mind wander back to the romantic days of his youth. His eyes followed the handsome white couple. With only eyes for one another, they walked up the wide, carpeted circular staircase arm-in-arm to Elizabeth's private suite. As they mounted the stairs, she pulled her body tight against his and allowed her head to rest against his shoulder. She could feel the coiled tension and power in the muscular young man.

As the couple disappeared up the stairs the old man smiled once again and returned the silver tray and the crystal glasses to the kitchen.

The wintery afternoon sun was hanging low in the southern sky, dimly lighting the frigid January landscape of the Georgia capital city. With no promise of warmth, its icy, dull-orange rays flickered across the modern city skyline onto a frosty winter scene. For just a moment, the weak sunlight reflected brightly off the polished balcony windows of a third-floor suite in a sumptuous Milledgeville hotel.

Chapter XXXIII

1828 - The Phoenix

Chapter 33

10 January 1828
  Ben's birthday today. I wish he were here. Rained all day.

11 January 1828
  Copied from the *Georgia Journal* – 7 January 1828 – page 3
  "...We now have six mails per week from Milledgeville to Augusta...a stage goes once a week from this place to Tallahassee. There is also a stage going once a week, from this place to Athens. The facilities of communication between the seat of government, and various parts of the state are thus rendered very great..."

9 February 1828 - Month of the Bony Moon Ka ga li
  Georgia opposes our new constitution. We have become civilized as they demanded but Mr. Lumpkin, his committee and the State of Georgia want us extinguished according to the 1802 compact. They say we are the cause of our own demise. If we suffer injury, it will be at the hands of Milledgeville.

Copied from the *Georgia Journal* – 4 February 1828 – Page 2-3
  "House of Representatives, Mr. Lumpkin, from the committee on Indian Affairs...Cherokee Indians have organized an independent system of government with a view to a permanent location in the States...The committee has seen their constitution...no doubt can be entertained of their determination to locate permanently in their current abode. They declare...their present boundaries shall forever remain unalterably the same and that the sovereignty and jurisdiction of their Government shall extend over this country which they occupy...The committee are of the opinion that good faith and justice require of this Government promptly to discountenance the formation of such Government, so far as it may,...assume a permanent jurisdiction over the soil, or in any way alter the tenure that they

386

have heretofore held their land; because an idea of this kind must prove fallacious and injurious to the best interests of the Indians themselves...the sooner they are assured this cannot be permitted, the better it will be for them; and they will the more readily ...join their brethren in the west...To arrest the idea of a permanent location of the Cherokee Indians within the limits of the State of Georgia, the motive is peculiarly strong, arising from the compact with that state, whereby the United States are bound to extinguish the Indian title to the lands within it,...With a view to the fulfillment of this contract...your committee would earnestly recommend that a generous and liberal provision be made to accomplish that object, as the best course, which can be pursued by the United States, to prevent conflicts, which may disturb the harmony of our citizens, and prevent the degradation and ruin of the Indians.

When I finished reading edudu said nothing. No matter what we do, whites want the general government to extinguish us. Mr. and Mrs. Lowry are greatly disappointed. Perhaps with our constitution and newspaper we can persuade enough whites we are worthy to exist—in our own country.

21 February 1828 - Thursday

Wonderful news. We have our own Cherokee newspaper printed here in New Echota on our own printing press. Our dream is a reality. The first edition was printed today. A new and happy sun is rising. The lead type for our Cherokee syllabary was cast in Boston but we had to wait for our paper from Knoxville—but the wait was worth it. We finally have our own functioning newspaper. I am more excited than I can put in words.

Our newspaper will be printed in Cherokee and English. It is important for our nation to communicate in both languages. This newspaper will help us become fully literate and we can share our nation's story with newspaper editors far and wide. I am as excited as a little girl at a festival.

I can quote our newspaper in my journal. It would be a dream come true to start a school in New Echota to teach our language and English.

24 February 1828

In the first issue of the Phoenix, is a copy of our Constitution ratified last summer.

Copied from the *Cherokee Phoenix*

21 February 1828 - page one--first edition

"CONSTITUTION OF THE CHEROKEE NATION: Formed by a convention of delegates from the several Districts, at New Echota, July 1827. We, the Representatives of the people of the Cherokee Nation in Convention assembled, in order to establish justice, ensure tranquility, promote our common welfare, and secure to ourselves and our posterity the blessings of liberty; acknowledging with humility and gratitude the goodness of the sovereign Ruler of the Universe in offering us an opportunity so favorable to the design, and imploring his aid and direction in its accomplishment, do ordain and establish this constitution for the government of the Cherokee Nation."

Article One: Sec. 1. The boundaries of this nation embracing the lands solemnly guarantied and reserved forever to the Cherokee Nation by the Treaties concluded with the United States; are as follows and shall forever hereafter remain unalterably the same--to wit--..."

Article one continues with a detailed description of the boundaries of our Nation. Surely with this paper and the hard work of our men like John Ross and other leaders, we shall survive. We must establish our borders to prevent whites from continuing to annex our land.

I love the story of our Sequoyah, a silversmith, who invented the characters of our language. We are the first Indian nation to have a written language and a newspaper. In 1821, just seven years ago, our Nation officially adopted Sequoya's syllabary. We do not have an alphabet like western languages based on Greek and Latin. We have eighty-six characters which represent syllables and not individual sounds, as in the English alphabet. What a magnificent accomplishment Sequoya accomplished all alone.

Mr. Boudinott is our editor. While at Cornwall, Connecticut, a Congregationalist foreign mission school, he met and later married his beautiful Harriet. She and I have become fast friends. Harriet is a special woman. I love her and her charming intelligent children. I hope I can be as good a wife to Ben as Harriet is to Elias. It is wonderful to have our newspaper and the Boudinott family here in New Echota.

Elias and Harriet remind me of edudu and elisi. Elisi loves my edudu as much as the day they married. Whenever he is gone, elisi awaits his return impatiently. When he is away she tells me she misses his face. I laugh when she says that, but I know what she means. I miss him, too. I like to watch elisi welcome him home. I am fortunate to live in a home overflowing with love. I want Ben and me to be just like them. I always miss Ben's beautiful face.

25 February 1828

Our editor, Mr. Boudinott, is fluent in Cherokee and English. As our newspaper's circulation grows, we will exchange newspapers with editors throughout the United States. Perhaps our story will be told in their newspapers as well as our own. Mr. Lowry suggested I be allowed to assist on the newspaper. Perhaps there is hope for us in our beautiful mountains. Now that we have the newspaper, I have renewed hope for our country.

28 February 1828

Grand news. I am allowed to assist the newspaper as an unpaid apprentice. Ben thinks working on the newspaper is a wonderful thing for me—the best of things. Ben and his family always see the good in people.

Now that our nation has a national voice, surely the political landscape will change. I will work hard to that end. With the publication of our newspaper, it will be possible for people all over the United States to understand what Georgia is doing to us.

There will be a great deal of work organizing, writing, editing, setting type, printing and publishing and Elias can't do everything. Helping will be fun and rewarding—like helping Mr. Lowry in school.

"Mr. and Mrs. Lowry assured me you're the perfect person to help with the newspaper," Elias said. "They care about you, Walela, and Mr. Lowry is right. There aren't many fluent at such a high level in both Cherokee and English and can edit both. It would be a pleasure to welcome you to our newspaper staff, but I have one problem."

I answered quickly, "What is the problem. I don't have a problem at all working on the Phoenix."

"Harriet and I will be paid enough to live on," Elias said, "but the newspaper has nothing left to pay volunteers. We need volunteers and it will be a shame you won't get paid for your work, but that's the way it is for now. Do you still want to work even though you won't be paid?"

"I care nothing about wages," I told him. "I would love the opportunity to assist you and I will be perfectly happy to volunteer with no pay. Count on me. I'll do anything you need done. I was born to write and I will enjoy any work you ask me to do in the newspaper office. I am proud to serve."

"Well then, Cassie, it's settled. We'll work most days except the Sabbath. The deadline days will be incredibly busy. You can help me proofread the Cherokee galleys—English too, when we need you. We want a professional newspaper with no typographical errors—a newspaper of the highest quality.

We want the Phoenix to look and read like the best English language newspapers and it will, with your help. Thank you for volunteering. This is a labor of love for all of us."

Later that day I sat with Harriet watching her children play. She was telling me about the prejudice she and Elias faced when they married.

"Today is a wonderful day, isn't it, Cassie?" Harriet said. "Elias and I are so happy with the newspaper and I'm glad you're helping."

"It is the best of days. I'm giddy with excitement," I answered.

"I love being here in New Echota with you—and the others, of course," Harriet said. "I wouldn't want to live anywhere else. Elias and I have a wonderful life here, but it wasn't so when we first married. White prejudice again Indians in the north was horrible."

Harriet and I became friends the moment she arrived. I love her children and enjoy helping her with them since she has no local relatives. She does miss her mother. I miss mine, too.

"I was the baby of my family," Harriet continued, "the youngest of fourteen. When I announced my engagement to Elias, most every white person in town and maybe the whole state was angry. The Congregationalists felt it their Christian duty to educate the heathen, but it became obvious they didn't consider a converted Cherokee man their equal in any way. Even after the conversion of Cherokee men to Christianity, the Christian faithful continued to refer to them as savages. I still don't understand."

"How can anyone understand that sort of thing," I said.

Harriet sat silently for a long while staring into the trees across her tidy front yard. I allowed her time to think. I knew her memories were traumatic. I have many similar memories—memories I keep hidden.

"White folks believe the teachings of Christ are for everyone—as long as the new converts are not included in white society," Harriet said. "To the Congregationalists, a non-white person cannot be allowed into their society. "Love thy neighbor" in Connecticut means love your white neighbor. Do unto others as you would have them do unto you in Connecticut means do unto white people as you would have them do unto you. I experienced this firsthand. When I was a girl, I was taught we should imitate Christ and treat all people with his unselfish love—but I know now in Connecticut those words were meant for white ears only. They believe the Great Commission— that they should go into all the world and spread the good news, but they don't want the converted heathen to mix with their children. That's what I experienced first-hand. I'm not spreading hearsay."

I have heard many stories like Harriet's. The Cherokee are all too familiar with white-only Christianity. Most white families, even missionary families, would never allow a Cherokee man to marry their daughter, or worse, an African to marry into their family. Socially, whites consider Indians and Africans anathema. They believe we must be kept separate.

Harriet continued, "I know what would have happened if the story of the good Samaritan had taken place in Connecticut. If the injured man lying beside the road had been an Indian or an African, the good folks of my congregation would have walked by, just like the priest and Levite passed the wounded Samaritan without helping."

"Cassie, I'm so glad to be away from that bigotry. I don't even like to talk about it."

Harriet paused and we sat quietly together for quite a while watching her little children play in front of the porch.

"When I announced Elias and I were to be married," Harriet continued in a pensive voice, "I saw what they believed written on their faces."

I understood Harriet's every word. There isn't one Cherokee man or woman who doesn't understand exactly what she has experienced.

"It was fine for Christian folk to teach the heathen to earn their living," she continued, "but they allowed the converted heathen in their homes only as servants—not as equals. I've chosen to forgive them, Cassie, and let what dwells in their hearts be their problem. They'll have to stand before the bar that last day and answer for their actions before the righteous judge of all men. Their judgment has nothing to do with me. I trust Him not to make a mistake or accidentally get it wrong. He has all the information. His judgment will be perfectly just. I will not let untoward thoughts of others ruin my life. I will not return evil for evil or keep a record of wrongs. I pray for them every day."

I laughed a melancholy little laugh and nodded in agreement. I thought of the tale of two wolves and how important it is to feed one's good wolf.

"Harriet, you are correct," I said. "Most whites don't believe we possess a soul, even if we have professed Christ. What happened to you in Connecticut I have seen a thousand times here. Whites, without thinking about it, maintain a strict racial purity. I think that's the central reason they insist upon our removal. They don't want their children playing with our children. They don't want our men to marry their daughters."

"I understand that kind of thinking, Harriet, and I am sorry to hear your story. I'm thankful that in my case, Mr. and Mrs. Lowry are perfectly happy to allow a Cherokee woman to marry their son. I love them for that, but Mr. and Mrs. Lowry are most unusual. They love me as if they were my own mother and father. Somehow, they learned not to see people as white, Cherokee or African. They see everyone as human and equally in need of acceptance. They learned to see a person's worth regardless of race, ethnic background or current religion. There aren't many like them, Harriet. In fact, they're the only ones I've ever met who practice what they preach. Perhaps things will change. I hope so. Edudu is always saying things will change. If the whites remove us, nothing will change. We will be forgotten and Cherokee Country will become all white. Their exclusive society will continue—a complete, all-white privileged society.

Harriet gave me a hug.

"Cassie, I'm so happy for you. You are fortunate to have Ben's parents in your life. I wish my family had been like them. I'm happy now with Elias. I'm happy down here. We have a lot of friends and the children are happy. I would never go back and attempt to live with their ridiculous equal but separate views. I can only imagine how they would treat our children if we were in Connecticut. Elias and I were even shamed in the newspaper."

"What?", I answered back incredulously. "They wrote bad things about you in the newspaper?"

"Oh yes, Cassie," Harriet answered. "Their hatred was blatant. When we announced our engagement my friends in the choir wore black armbands as if I were dead. They believed my decision to marry Elias a mortal sin. They believed I had betrayed them. To them my marriage to a Cherokee was the same as renouncing Christ. I'm glad that's behind me. Elias and I have moved on. We've chosen not to harbor ill will."

Harriet paused for a moment, stared into my face with her hand on my arm and continued, "My own brother, Stephen, burned me and Elias in effigy on the village green in front of a crowd. Even the missionary society responsible for Elias' conversion opposed us. They were embarrassed and needed to defend themselves before their peers, I suppose."

As Harriet silently stared into the woods, I could feel the pain in her soul. I felt the pain of the dismissal of our entire race by whites. I observed Harriet's children playing peacefully in front of us. I was glad her children would not have to be reared in such an ugly environment. I hope my children can be free. I hope my children will not be called half-breeds.

Harriet looked up at me with a crooked smile.

"Because of my engagement to Elias, they closed the mission school. They were unprepared for the logical consequences of their teaching. After the announcement of my engagement to Elias, they decided to fulfill the great commission in distant lands only. I can still quote the newspaper article from memory.

> "The foreign mission school proclaims our unequivocal disapprobation of such connections...and the conduct of those who have been engaged in or accessory to this transaction, as criminal; as offering an insult to the known feelings of the Christian community."

Harriet hardly spoke above a whisper.

"Our Christian leaders promised the Cherokee the privileges of a civilized life. The cultural success of whites was given as the example of what happens when folks convert to Christianity. Elias accepted Christ, spoke perfect English and became a scholar but it wasn't enough—not nearly enough. When he fell in love with a white girl he was threatened with death. We had many death threats. I was happy to leave. I'll never go back."

Harriet paused again and looked around at the beautiful scenic panorama that surrounded her beautifully kept little home.

"Cassie, I'll be buried right here—right here in Cherokee Country where I'm accepted. This is home. This is where no one judges my worth based on the pigments in my skin or sneer at the facial features of my children."

"You're welcome here," I told her. "You are most welcome here and always will be. I'm so glad you're here, Harriet," I told her.

"This is home now, Cassie. I'll never leave. I'm sharing this with you but I let this thing go long ago. I've talked about these things with you here today but I don't think about them normally. I have chosen higher things to occupy my mind. However, I'm afraid what's happening to the Cherokee is history repeating itself. It's the same wickedness I experienced in Connecticut. It's a malevolence straight out of the abyss."

I felt perfect empathy with Harriet. I was glad she was with us in New Echota and my friend.

"A year before Elias and I married, Major Ridge and Sarah Northrop married. They, too, had a terrible time with their friends and relatives. They were written about in the newspaper just like we were by a man named Isaiah Bunce. I'll never forget that name—Isaiah Bunce. He wrote, 'The girl ought to be publicly whipped, the Indian hung, and the mother drowned'."

"I find human behavior astonishing sometimes, don't you, Cassie? It seems to me if a Christian chooses to be unforgiving, that person has chosen to say that Jesus' sacrifice was ill-advised. I choose to forgive. I will not join them. I will not return evil for evil. There will be a judgment day. That gives me peace. That judge won't make mistakes."

Harriet and I agreed with one another that, after this day, we would never talk about these things ever again. We have chosen to forgive and feed the good wolf and let the bad wolf go hungry.

3 March 1828

I, along with others, have begun work at the Phoenix. Elias is capable.

I was born to write. I love printing and newspapers. Like edudu says, 'I'm happy as a pig in sunshine'. I'm overjoyed to be an apprentice exercising my talents. It is a joy to write in multiple languages and translate. I even like the physical job of producing the newspaper. Spending hours proofing galleys is a pleasure I can't explain. There is great satisfaction making the type match. I find pleasure in making the leading and margins perfect. I love how we cooperate to correct the spelling, grammar and punctuation. Ben and I will make good partners in a print shop and school. One day we might have a second Cherokee newspaper.

4 March 1828

Ben has been working for his firm and in the legislature doing what he can for his father and for us. Ben's parents and I have been writing letters and gathering contacts and information. We are working to educate our people.

12 March 1828

I celebrated our first issue of the Phoenix with Mr. and Mrs. Lowry. Mrs. Lowry opened a topic of conversation I was anxious to continue.

"I'm happy for you, Cassie. Whites say Cherokee are unable to adjust, or achieve a high level of civilization. They can't say that now, can they?"

"Oh my, no," I answered. "We've done everything asked of us to be allowed to co-exist—we are fully civilized. They wanted us to become farmers. We are farmers. Our men never used to wear hats, edudu told me, and now almost every Cherokee man wears a hat and clothing like white men. Many of us have learned to read and write both Cherokee and English. Many have become Christians. We have our own newspaper, a written constitution, law enforcement, judges, a judicial system and international borders."

"Wilbur and I have been here going on ten years and we've seen marvelous improvements. We are so proud of you and your people, Cassie."

"Thank you, Mrs. Lowry. We're proud, too. Our country is divided into districts. We have a representative government similar to the United States. What more in the way of civilization could they ask for?"

Mrs. Lowry frowned.

"From what I'm reading, Cassie, those in power have a white vision of the future. Georgia views the Cherokee organization as a serious threat. I hope I'm wrong, but I don't think so.

"Ben thinks Andrew Jackson will be elected this year," I answered. "He doesn't think this election will have the same problem with the electoral college as last time. I don't know what Jackson's election will mean, but he has never been a friend to the Cherokee or any Indian tribe."

Mrs. Lowry refilled our cups and put another turnover on my saucer.

"We know Andrew Jackson, Cassie. It's my guess, based on what he's done in Tennessee, Alabama and Florida, he'll continue to be the enemy of all Indians. His party doesn't want a co-existing civilization for any Indian nation—especially not for the Cherokee. In everything I read, they want to remove all Indian nations to the western territories outside the borders of the United States—and the sooner the better. I'm embarrassed to be white. I'm afraid I'm pessimistic about your future—our future, too, but maybe the Phoenix can change enough public opinion to save you. I hope so."

17 March 1828

Mrs. Lowry is humorous. She wishes she was tall like me. She cannot reach things stored high in her kitchen. Ben made her a sturdy little four-legged stool—like a milking stool. Ben is handy like his father. I like to work with my hands, too. I enjoy making pine baskets.

Mrs. Lowry told me, while helping in her house, that I carry myself with grace. I love the way she says nice things. She is envious of my facial features. I have always thought Cherokee more handsome than whites, except for Ben, of course. Ben is the most attractive man in the world. He says my skin is velvet, my eyes sparkle like stars, I have the grace of a swan and my hair is like silk from China. Ben said his father was right to name me after a Greek goddess. I miss Ben's compliments, even if he exaggerates. It seems all I care about is what he thinks. I haven't stopped smiling since I read his letter. I wish every woman had a man who loved her as Ben loves me.

20 March 1828

Copied from the *Cherokee Phoenix* – Page 3

"...a motion was made in the House of Representatives, by Mr. Wilde, a member from Georgia, to take measures to ascertain, what white persons have assisted the Cherokees in forming the late constitution...It has been customary of late to charge the missionaries with the crime of assisting the Indians, and unbecomingly interfering in political affairs...Our object, when we commenced to pen this article, was to correct the mistake, under which some may labor, and to declare once for all, that no white man has had anything to do in framing our constitution and all the public acts of the nation...We hope this practice of imputing the acts of Indians to white men will be done away."

Whites think if we write anything intelligent in our newspaper it must have been written by white men. They think we are eternally stupid and incapable. They'll be asking the missionaries to leave Cherokee Country next. They detest everything about our country and loath anyone who works for our improvement. Many whites consider Mr. and Mrs. Lowry traitors.

30 March 1828

I want to ride a steamboat. It is amazing how they go easily up river against the current. Edudu is right. Things change. Who could have imagined we would see noisy steamboats huffing and puffing up and down our peaceful rivers. I'm going to ask Ben to take me for a ride on a steamboat.

Copied from the *Georgia Journal* – 27 March 1828 – page 1

The steamboat company's packet boat CAROLINA, Captain Wray, having undergone a thorough repair, including a new boiler...will ply...once a week, between this place and Savannah, leaving August every Saturday morning at 9 o'clock, and Savannah every Tuesday afternoon at 4 o'clock. No care or expense has been spared to render her a first-rate passage boat; her accommodations are spacious, comfortable and elegant in every respect; and from the long practical experience of Capt. Wray, on the Savannah River, passengers may always feel assured of a safe and expeditious, passage, together with excellent fare. For freight or passage, apply at the Steam Boat's Company Office, on the wharf, or to the Captain on board.
R. Wood Agent.

Chapter XXXIV

1828 – Ben and Zach Make Plans

Chapter 34

28 May 1828 – Month of the Planting Moon – A na a gv ti

Copied from the *Georgia Journal* – Page 4

Mr. Woods - Indian Immigration

"...I will now Mr. Chairman, examine into the situation of the country which the Indians now possess within the limits of the several States; and into the advantages which they enjoy in their present homes. The Indian lands lying within our borders is that portion of their original possessions which they have never sold or transferred to us, or any other Government. We are told by one of our sovereign States..."It belongs to her and that she must and will have it: that we are bound, at all hazards, and without regard to terms to procure it."...Sir, the same argument may be urged, or rather the same language may be used by all the other States, within the limits of which there is any Indian territory. It was by virtue of the same sovereign right, that the Pope, in the name of St. Peter, gave to Spain all the countries which Columbus discovered. It is the right which power gives..."

Our nation and our people were given away by the Roman Catholic Pope—by the 'right of discovery'. How can one man on the other side of the world give away our country—a country he has never seen?

June 1828 - Milledgeville

"Ben, it's Friday and you've been burning the midnight oil but I've arranged a spur of the moment event. Election day will soon be upon us. This is late notice, but your attendance is necessary. The host is one of Father's important clients, a personal friend of Jackson and the single largest landowner in our county. Whether you feel like it or not, it's a no-miss affair, sorry."

Zach slapped Ben's tired back.

"Besides, my friend, Elizabeth would be terribly disappointed if you didn't come. She's looking forward to seeing you this evening. You wouldn't want her to pout, would you?"

"Zach, you're something else," Ben answered back. "Where do you get your energy? Don't you ever get weary? I've worked into the wee hours every night this week doing my work and half of yours. I don't know if the thought of seeing Elizabeth is enough to give me strength. I'm dog tired. All I want to do is flop across my bed, clothes and all, and sleep for two days. I'm exhausted."

Zach laughed.

"Zach," Ben continued, "you have the endurance to go late into the evening no matter how much sleep you lose. Well, if you insist, let's go have a drink and a bite to eat and perhaps I'll rejuvenate. You're right. I need to go if I want to win this election. I'm willing to do whatever it takes. Time and tide wait for no man."

Ben and Zach walked the short distance to the hotel and went straight to their corner by the big fireplace, but this warm June afternoon there was no fire. By the time the two young men had finished their drinks and the hors d'oeuvres prepared by their French chef, Ben was magically on his way to recovery.

Ben loved the hotel. He was becoming used to superior meals, expensive wines and impeccable service. Full board was included at his boarding house, but of late Ben had been eating his evening meals at the hotel. The French cuisine was worth it. His boarding house fare was plain at the best of times. Since his first meeting with Elizabeth, the good whiskey, Elizabeth's scent and the hotel had become intertwined. He loved everything about the hotel including the beautiful intriguing woman which had become such an important part of his life in Milledgeville. Life was good since he had begun working in Milledgeville and met Zach.

"Our plan for you this evening is simple," Zach instructed. "Everyone you'll meet tonight is wealthy and a potential supporter. Pay attention. Listen when people talk. Look them in the eye. At the appropriate time during every conversation, promise them they can come to you with their problems day or night. Promise you'll see they get what they need no matter what it is. Tell them all you want in return is their public support and their vote. Simple, isn't it? Quid pro quo—always quid pro quo, Ben. Never forget that. Those are the only three words a politician needs to remember."

Zach continued without allowing Ben time to respond.

"After every conversation ask permission to leave their presence. There's nothing as ingratiating as requesting a person's permission to leave their company. Every little bit helps. Elizabeth and I will provide you with special targets. We'll direct you to the most important men and women. Don't worry about anything. We'll tell you what to do. The rest of this year we'll plan socials, meetings, breakfasts, dinners, and barbecues right up to election day. We're going to do the work, provide the money and all you have to do is show up. You'll be elected, Ben. There's not a chance of your opponent winning, if we follow our plan."

Ben was tired but Zach appeared tireless. Even during their comfortable carriage ride with his efficient well-dressed African driver Zach continued to instruct and encourage his protégé.

"Elizabeth and I will coach you all evening, so don't worry."

Ben changed the subject, "What will Elizabeth be doing this evening?"

"Glad you asked, Ben. Of course you'll see her. She's goin' to keep an eye on you all evening. She's an expert at events like this. This is her showcase. To tell the truth, she'll probably get you more votes from important people than I will. She'll find the important men who have an eye for a pretty woman. When she's finished flirting they would vote for the devil himself if she asked. No man is safe from her charms."

Ben was thinking how true Zach's statement was. He had never seen a woman more desirable. She was perfect. Ben found it remarkable that she was interested in him—a plain country boy without social skills.

"Elizabeth and I are also experts in discretion. That's a must in our business. We know how to get people's attention and also how to avoid it."

Ben looked sideways at Zach and marveled at his openness about his almost nonexistent morals and careless attitude. Zach was so different from his parents and their friends.

"How in the world did you and Elizabeth learn all this? How did you come up with this clandestine circle of 'friends' that you can trust in dubious circumstances to supply you with information? You two are amazing," Ben said with admiration.

"Elizabeth and I learned years ago how to tactfully manage our parents, our servants and our business associates. I guess you could say over the years we've put together a team—a group of individuals who work for us and for the wealthiest. They're slaves mostly, but there are others—folks you wouldn't suspect who don't mind extra money now and then just for keepin' their ears open. We're motivated, Ben. That's our secret. We're motivated like no one you've ever seen. We want to be rich. We want to be so rich we'll never have to work and we won't have to worry about anyone taking our wealth—even the government."

Zach leaned back in the open carriage with his hands behind his head, legs crossed and his boots resting on the seat opposite. He stared up into the clear June sky recalling some of those successful moments.

"Ben, over the years we've put together a covert group of trusted employees—social detectives you might say. We pay for information that's useless to most folks, but we know how to turn information into money—sometimes a lot of money."

"We're incredibly generous when it comes to acquiring information, Ben. Money can buy anything. We reward those who do good work for us, but they know there's a severe penalty for betrayal. We've learned we never have problems as long as we hire folks who are like us. Our associates must value money above everything. We learned we get what we pay for. You can't skimp when it comes to the hired help—especially when buying prudence. I don't think you want me to tell you much more than that. I may not have completely satisfied your curiosity, but let's leave it there. The less you know about that side of our business, the better. All you need to know is everything we do is legal and above board, but who knows what you might say one night to the wrong person when you've had a little too much to drink."

Zach continued to look upwards at the clear evening sky and laughed. Ben didn't want to know more than he knew now and that was perfectly alright. He would let Zach and Elizabeth handle the murkier side of his election. That was their business and they were good at it and, as long as it was legal, that was all he cared about. He was responsible for himself and no one else. Zach's father paid him each month and he earned every penny with honest work. He couldn't and wouldn't worry about the morality of others. That was none of his business.

Their carriage rolled up the long perfectly smooth gravel drive lined with mature oaks and arrived at the entrance to the magnificent white columned plantation house with its broad white marble steps. They were met by perfectly dressed servants who assisted them down and opened doors. Ben was always impressed when he visited a well to do home like this. There was a good life to be had here in Georgia for anyone willing to work hard. This was a magnificent house with extensive gardens manicured to perfection. Inside they met Elizabeth. Ben's weariness instantly melted away. They were immediately served their first drink. Suddenly Ben felt like he could go till midnight. Maybe Zach's company was good for him.

It was a well-attended event. Ben recognized a number of important Milledgeville folk. The purpose, for Zach and Elizabeth, was to showcase Ben. Because the plantation owner was a client, Zach had been allowed to add a few important names to the invitation list. The election was still months away, but there was no time to lose, Zach said, and nothing should be left to chance. Everyone at this event would be useful to Ben's election and to Zach's father's firm.

Elizabeth chatted with Ben and Zach and assumed her charming professional self. Ben thought her even more irresistible than the last time they had met, if that was possible. She could have any man she wanted and she knew it.

As they conversed, sipped champagne and assessed the crowd, Elizabeth moved close to Ben and spoke quietly, "Men are so predictable, Ben. I notice how they look at me. I can tell from across the room what they're thinking. It doesn't require special skill to read their mind, if one has the right assets."

She laughed out loud and tossed her hair in a most disarming manner.

"If I want to influence a man, I pay him a little attention and the trap is laid. I play hard to get at the beginning. I always play hard to get. It works every time. First thing you know, he's following me around the room like a puppy dog. Once he begins following me, I capture him with an easy laugh, a warm smile, a toss of my head and then finally he looks into my eyes. I touch his arm, move in closer and the trap snaps shut. It happens every time—without fail."

She moved in close to Ben, "It's easier than shootin' fish in a barrel," she said, looking up into Ben's eyes.

Ben loved her infectious laugh and easy smile. He loved the way she made him feel. He had never felt that way around any woman except maybe Cassie, but Cassie was a long way from Milledgeville and Cassie never wore the clothing or perfume like Elizabeth.

Elizabeth was right about her assessment of men and their desires. That's exactly how she had captured him months ago. Ben had become aware of an almost permanent and uncomfortable ache in his chest that could only be relieved by Elizabeth's physical presence. He was thinking about her more and more every day.

"I do the same as Elizabeth," Zach said, with a casual laugh, "except in reverse. I get information from Elizabeth and her scouts. Elizabeth is privy to the private conversations and gossip of all the women. She tells me who among the women will be vulnerable to my influence. I have to tell you, Ben, this job can be pleasurable at times—a lot of fun. I do love mixing business

401

with pleasure. Elizabeth and I knew, as soon as we met you, we could take you far in politics. Your popularity is growing and it's our goal to take care of you—for our mutual benefit, of course. You can trust us, Ben. We'll always take care of you. Our advice is, don't think too much about our methods. Just like the old proverb, 'don't look a gift horse in the mouth'."

Zach and Elizabeth laughed together once more and Ben joined them. Ben was beginning to enjoy himself. He couldn't imagine two better friends. The champagne was taking effect.

The trio separated and began to promote Ben's cause among Georgia's wealthy and influential. Ben knew he needed to mingle with the guests but it seemed he couldn't take his eyes of Elizabeth. He didn't want to talk to the important men and women. He wanted to talk to Elizabeth.

Zach gave Elizabeth the names of men to 'work on' when she had the opportunity. Elizabeth and Zach circulated, listened and promoted Ben.

They wouldn't close every deal this evening, but they would lay the groundwork for later in the year. It was amazing how easy it was to gain influence with a little personal information and bold promises. Zach and Elizabeth had a file on every person of importance in Georgia and some beyond—especially in Washington City. They knew their favorite wine, if they liked to hunt or fish, if they gambled on horse races or cards or if they were happy at home. They often gathered household gossip from the slave staff. They knew if important men were neglecting their wives, which might be information of greater worth. Zach and Elizabeth's extensive network of scouts, men and women, both white and negro, gave them an insurmountable lead on Ben's benighted competition.

Elizabeth's ultimate goal was to go to Washington City as a Senator's wife. She and Zach had chosen Ben believing he might be the man. She knew she could bend him any way she chose at any time. He was putty in her hands as were several other up and coming young men in the Georgia political arena. Elizabeth wasn't one to put all her eggs in one basket. Ben's career wasn't the only one Elizabeth was watching and promoting. Whoever would win the Senate appointment was the man Elizabeth would assist. Time would tell which man would win and receive, at least temporarily, Elizabeth as the grand prize.

As Elizabeth strolled around the beautiful home and gardens, she marveled how dull were most people's lives. She felt pity for those with no ambition who never went anywhere, did anything and whose days were filled with the constant tedium of running a home and childrearing. It would never occur to Elizabeth that loving a man, raising children and filling a home with happiness could be fulfilling. To Elizabeth, children were a bother, keeping a home a nuisance and having a husband related to being in prison. She was only interested in that which gave a broad financial advantage and freedom. She had no idea how selfish she was. She never would.

As Ben made ready for his bed after a tiring evening, he smiled at the memories. The social had been a great success and so would be the election. He knew that now. He could trust Zach and Elizabeth. Ben fell asleep the moment his head touched the pillow. He slept dreamlessly.

Ben looked forward to the Tuesday planning sessions. To tell the truth, Tuesday and its marvelous afternoon with Elizabeth and Zach had become the highlight of his week. Occasionally Zach would be away on business and leave the afternoon free for him and Elizabeth. Ben was never suspicious when Zach didn't show. It would never occur to Ben that anyone, especially Zach and Elizabeth, would actually make plans to take advantage of him.

When Zach was absent, Elizabeth and Ben would discuss upcoming events, the important men and women yet to be 'persuaded' and how they could 'gift' them into their camp.

"The most important single principle in politics is this," Elizabeth instructed, "a gift obligates. If you give someone a nice gift, it's their natural response to feel obliged to give you a gift in return. This isn't a mystery, is it? If you want to receive, you must give. That's in the Bible, isn't it, Ben—'Give and you shall receive'? It's true in the Bible and it's the first principle of politics, too. After all, politicians are human—well, most of them, anyway."

Elizabeth and Ben both laughed—a loud carefree laugh. Elizabeth allowed her hand to innocently touch Ben's chest and move down his shirt.

"Give and you shall receive, Ben. Give and you shall receive. You do know the importance of giving when necessary, don't you?"

Ben quivered uncontrollably. He knew exactly what she was doing but was powerless to quell his body's intense response.

Elizabeth smiled.

"In politics, when one person gives, the other person cannot help but want to return the favor. Everyone knows how that works. You know very well as a lawyer, don't you? It's called quid pro quo, isn't it?"

Her finger touched the outside of his trouser leg by his knee and lingered as she made her point. The spot burned as if on fire. She was almost staring into his eyes as she continued.

"You see how the act of giving works, don't you? I give to you and you automatically want to give to me. It's human nature. You can't help wanting to do something nice for me. One day, Ben Lowry, I may think of something quite special I want. Then it will be my turn to receive and I'll expect you to give. We'll have a good time, Ben—you and I. I give to you and you give to me in an ever-widening benevolent circle. I'm looking forward to our mutually shared gifts. I love to give, Ben. I do love to give. We'll have fun, Ben. Oh my yes, we'll have fun."

Elizabeth threw her head back and laughed. Ben knew what she said to be true. He would give her gifts. He wanted to give her gifts. He wanted to give her gifts at that very moment. He couldn't wait to give to her. He didn't realize it yet, but he would give her anything including his future.

Ben trembled. She was right. The things Zach and Elizabeth had done for him made him feel obligated. Although they had never asked for anything in return, he knew if they did ask, he would happily give without hesitation.

Tuesdays, Ben's favorite day, often found him and Elizabeth sharing a bottle of wine and a romantic meal in her private suite after their meeting. Ben's letters to Cassie were becoming less frequent. He never wrote Cassie or his parents on a Tuesday.

Zach knew Elizabeth was 'paying attention' to Ben and fully approved. He understood her motives. Elizabeth and Zach were on the same page. Zach knew Elizabeth didn't love Ben and never would. She would never love anyone other than herself. Ben was a tool—their entrance into politics. Zach and Elizabeth had no rules when it came to relationships. A long-term relationship for love's sake would never occur to either. They fed off the adventures they shared as they worked towards their monetary goals. Influencing people was fun, a game within the big game. They were professionals and did their homework, spending hours comparing notes and choosing the perfect strategy. Between Zach's law firm and Elizabeth's spy network, there wasn't much they didn't know about anyone of consequence in Georgia and beyond. They would never be givers. They were takers—users.

The people they dealt with were chess pieces and moving them about life's complicated board provided constant amusement. Elizabeth thrived on the complexities of influencing others the way some enjoy puzzles or intricate mathematics. She loved risks and her relationship with Zach, Ben and a dozen other men, some young and some not so young, was one of treading near the edge. To her, Ben was a passing challenge, a simple means to an end with an occasional bonus. Elizabeth's relationship with any man was nothing more than the physical satisfaction of pleasure on demand with no strings attached. Those were her rules and an inviolate principle from which she never varied.

Chapter XXXV

1828 – Ben Elected to Georgia House

Chapter 35

13 October 1828 - The Trading Moon - Nu da de qua

Ben made a surprise visit. He took me to his parents' home for the afternoon. We had a wonderful time. I loved the gifts he brought.

"Father, for you, sir, a box of books. They're not new, but they're the ones you wanted and a few extra I thought you would enjoy. One I bought specially."

Ben handed his father an unwrapped volume he had held behind his back. It was Robert Southey's *Life of Wesley*.

His father took one look at the book and embraced Ben, "Thank you, son. I've been wanting to read this. I don't agree with everything the Methodists teach, but I admire their character. The Wesley brothers worked long and hard for the Lord in Georgia, along with Whitfield, and they continue to have a strong influence with both Creek and Cherokee. I'm sure I can learn from them. Thank you for such a thoughtful gift."

"Mother, here's your gift. I must confess Father helped me select it. Open it, please."

Ben's mother had tears in her eyes even before she opened her gift. Unlike his father's gifts, his mother's present was wrapped in beautiful shiny silver paper and tied with a bright red ribbon. When she unwrapped her gift she could only stare down at the colorful new blue tailored dress and bonnet lying in her lap, along with matching handbag and scarf.

She was speechless.

After she gathered her thoughts she finally said, "Oh, Ben, I don't know what to say. I'm not used to gifts like these. I've never had anything like this."

Ben received another long embrace as his mother wiped the tears from her cheeks.

"Thank you so much, son," his mother said through her emotion. "I don't think I've ever seen a lovelier dress—not in all my born days. It's the most beautiful thing I've ever seen. I am so blessed, son."

As his mother looked up into her son's eyes, I witnessed an exchange of love between two who loved one another with every fiber of their being.

Finally, after another pause, his mother said, as she stared down at the beautiful garment in her lap, "You know, son, this dress is going to cost you dearly? This dress will be the beginning of a never-ending expense for you. Perhaps, you should have bought me books instead. You're welcome to take this back if you think it will be too expensive."

"Pray tell, my dear Mother, will this dress cost me more than it already has? I paid cash and it was worth every penny."

His mother answered with an innocent look, "Now that I have this beautiful dress you must take me to Savannah, Charleston and maybe Richmond, too. Where could I wear this around here? Wouldn't I look foolish wearing this to go fishing or to feed the chickens? I think a trip is in order, don't you, son?"

She smiled and laughed and everyone joined her. It was a wonderful moment.

"Mother, I see your wisdom. I see how this gown will cost me a small fortune, but you, my dear Mother, are worth it. There's nothing too good for my mother. If you'll be patient, I'll take you, Father and Cassie to London, Paris and maybe Madrid—perhaps as early as next year. In the meantime I suppose we'll have to begin with a trip to Savannah. How would that be, Mother? I can see this dress is gettin' more expensive every moment, isn't it? And if we go to Paris I'll have to buy a gown or two while we're there, won't I? It wouldn't do for you to wear the same dress every day."

Ben's mother embraced him again and we continued to laugh at Mrs. Lowry's humor.

Then Ben handed me my gift.

"It's not a ball gown, Cassie, but I promise I'll get you a most beautiful gown when we take Mother to Paris."

My small gift was also wrapped in pretty paper with a red ribbon. Inside were two bright silver bracelets with a clever geometric design.

"But that's not all I have for you, Cassie. I have another gift."

From behind his back, Ben handed me an unwrapped copy of Grimms' Fairy Tales translated by Edward Taylor. I was thrilled. I love fairy tales and stories—edudu loves them too and he will insist I read this to him. I would much prefer a book over a gift of clothing.

"This book is early, but I bought it especially for your birthday. Nothing is too good for you, Cassie," Ben said.

For the third time, Ben received an affectionate embrace.

"Ben, you are the most thoughtful man in the world. You couldn't have given me better gifts," I said. "I'll read these to edudu and elisi and maybe my brother, too. Just holding this book in my hand makes me want to write stories of my own and I shall."

Afterward, Ben and I, hand in hand, walked and talked about everything—his job, Zach and Elizabeth, his political aspirations—about the Cherokee and our desire to stay in our homeland. We had a perfect afternoon together.

"Ben, what a wonderful day this has been and what thoughtful gifts. Up here we have a different view of life than folks in Milledgeville, don't we? I love the bracelets and the book. At this moment I understand the whites desire to always have more. I would love to have more jewelry and more books. I feel that desire growing. I'm starting to sound like a white woman, am I not?"

"I like you just the way you are. Don't ever change," Ben said.

He kissed me right there in the middle of the lane.

"Cassie, I've thought a great deal since I went to work in Milledgeville. You're right. White folks want more. The Cherokee are satisfied with what they have. There's the difference. The growing white economy is putting pressure on the Cherokee. It's simple. Georgia wants more land—specifically Cherokee land."

"I know, Ben. It seems we have a never-ending stream of whites coming through Cherokee country. Squatters are everywhere."

"Business is booming, Cassie, and Cotton is king. The price of everything is going up—land, commodities and slaves. People are spending a lot of money on things in order to get more things. You should see Milledgeville during harvest. The cotton gins run night and day and cotton bales line the streets waiting shipment downriver to Savannah. You're right, Cassie. Lots of people are making lots of money and buying lots of things. Everyone wants more—more books, more jewelry, more clothing, more slaves, bigger houses and especially more land. Everyone wants land. They want Cherokee land."

We walked and I listened as Ben continued.

"I've thought a lot about those things," Ben continued. " I wonder what the future holds for the Cherokee. Merchants are selling virgin timber all over the world cut from confiscated Creek and Cherokee land. We'll never see virgin forests like this again. I feel sorry for the trees. Isn't that strange to feel sorry for trees? No one replants the cleared land. The trees didn't grow overnight, did they? I've read that every forest in Ireland was clear-cut hundreds of years ago and most of England's old forests are gone. I wonder where this unquenchable desire will end. Europe is denuded and our beautiful land will be next. Your grandfather told me the land around here teemed with buffalo, elk, catamounts and wolves before the whites came. They're all gone now. I fear there will come a time when every place will be like Milledgeville. All that will be left will be a few skinny squirrels and birds."

"I've seen what the white squatters do, Ben," I answered. "They cut everything that grows and shoot everything that moves. They clear land and burn everything cut—even in the summertime. When they deplete the soil, they clear more land and cut more forest. One day there will be no forest."

"I know, Cassie, "Ben answered.

"That's the problem in Georgia—in the whole United States really. Everyone in Europe knows we have land for the taking. They don't know it already belongs to someone else. I guess they believe only white people have a right to own land."

We sat together for a while without speaking. Ben held me and I leaned my head on his shoulder.

"Things are changing, Cassie. Georgia attracts people with money and energy. Milledgeville has been transformed from a dirty little town into the envy of the South. It's become a charming town with a busy social life. I'm enjoying the city, but there's not a day goes by I don't wish you were there with me. I'm a country boy at heart, Cassie. I'm a fish out of water down there. Maybe one day folk's attitude towards the Indians will change and you'll be welcome. I miss you every day we're apart."

I was happy listening to Ben as we strolled along walking aimlessly down the worn paths around his parents' home.

"My nostalgic boyhood days come to mind often when I'm in Milledgeville, Cassie. I daydream of Father's schoolroom and your long shiny braids. You were distracting, you know. I always loved your hair. I still do. I miss those days. I miss you every day I'm away, Cassie. Your grandfather is right. Things change."

Ben held me and kissed my forehead. We sat on a large lichen covered rock in the autumn sunshine and held one another silently for a long time. Ben's words didn't give me a lot of hope for the future of our country.

"Cassie, I remember the first day I saw you. You were a timid little girl who hardly spoke a word, but I could tell from your eyes you were smart. I knew that first day we would become friends. We've had many wonderful days together, haven't we?"

"Our future together is about all I think about these days, Ben."

We were silent again for a long while as we casually walked along enjoying the peaceful countryside around us and reflecting on the changes in our lives and in my country.

Ben finally broke the silence.

"Cassie, we're not children in Father's schoolyard any longer. All that is past. We need to think about our adult lives. One day I would love to live with you in a big house with lots of children and servants. Would you like that?"

Before I could answer he continued. He was excited thinking about our life and our future and the delights of city life. I loved his thinking, even if I wasn't welcome in white society but I know we will find happiness somewhere.

"You know, Cassie, Savannah is Georgia's second city now. Milledgeville is growing. They're building everywhere. I've been told the best architects are in Milledgeville building original homes, cantilevered porticos and lovely sculpted gardens—creating new styles not seen anywhere else. I guess there's a lot of money in Milledgeville."

"I love it there, Cassie, but I miss you. I love everything about the law profession, politics and the social life, but I wish you were there with me. Before you think ill of me, I want you to know that after I save enough in a few years for us to set up housekeeping we can move somewhere, maybe up north, or even go to the western territory with the Cherokee and other tribes. It would be a tough life out there, but we would be together. That's what I want one day after I've saved enough."

As we walked along, I looked at Ben carefully. He was over-dressed. He had a new horse and expensive tooled tack. Life is good for Ben in Milledgeville but I hope he never changes. I hope he doesn't get used to the good life he's building in an all-white town where I'll never be allowed to live.

"Ben, all I ever think about is being with you—of us being together. I know it will never be in Georgia—perhaps nowhere in the South. We could go west. There will be legal work there. The Choctaw, Chickasaw and others are being removed. We could live with any of those nations. A good lawyer like you who understands Indians could find work anywhere. We would be happy. You could have a law practice. We would have a nice home, a little farm with horses, hogs, chickens and a couple of Jerseys. The girls and I could sell eggs, milk and butter. You could work in town. We could train our boys and have a school. Maybe we could have a newspaper. We could read every evening with our children. We could have shelves and shelves of books. I would make you the happiest of men."

I didn't say more. I didn't want to press him. I knew it would be impossible for Ben to work in Milledgeville if we were married. Ben hasn't thought through all the difficulties of our marriage. We have plenty of time to save for our life together in a place where our children will be respected. I must be patient. I must give him time to think.

Ben and I talked the rest of the day, walking the paths near his parents' home. I enjoy remembering the sweet things he says. I love telling Ben's story as well as my own. He will do good things in the legislature, both for us and for himself.

Since Ben went to law school, he has been the right man in the right place at the right time. He is handsome, intuitive and tells me he has far more social invitations than he can accept. He marvels at Zach's extensive social calendar and stamina. Ben can't keep up with him. Ben said he would not have to buy food, drink or pay for lodgings if he were to accept all of his invitations to balls, barbecues, weddings and such.

Ben said he sometimes does things his parents wouldn't approve of. He assured me everything he does is legal and done to insure the financial future for his parents and our marriage. He wants to further his career while he has the opportunity—to make hay while the sun shines.

Ben left at dawn on the fourteenth, my birthday. I cried. He will be back and I will hold him again. I will weep again when he leaves. I long for the day when he never leaves.

October 30 1828

John Ross is our new chief after Pathkiller. John Ross has been a good leader for many years. Pathkiller believed John Ross would make a good chief. John Ross is wiser than his years. Edudu believes he is capable.

Today is Ben's election day. Zach thinks both Ben and General Jackson will be elected. We will see. No one likes Jackson but it really doesn't matter to us. The whiteside will choose who they will and do what they want.

1 November 1828

Ben assured me I can be confident about our future together. His legal work is going well. He is saving money. I need not worry. He is working every day so we can be together. His mother says that since Ben went to work he helps them regularly with their expenses. He is a good son but his visits are becoming less frequent. I understand. The stage is dusty and tiring. I wouldn't want to make that trip in a jarring, jerky, dirty old stagecoach. Ben is busy.

3 November 1828

Ben is proud of his growing knowledge of buying and selling of land. Land, he says, is the prime form of barter and will increase in value with time. He says men will make more wagons, ships, saddles and bricks, but no one is making more land. We have all the land we will ever have. Fee simple land ownership gives the owner the legal right to use land, store waste, use the fruits and pass land on to heirs without government interference. If a fee simple landowner dies intestate, the property descends to heirs—never the government. We Cherokee do not own land individually like the English. Our nation owns the land and we Cherokee use it, with permission. I like the Cherokee way. Ben says the whites don't understand us and don't like our method of corporate ownership and culture.

4 November 1828

If Ben is elected, he wants to buy a house in Milledgeville for his parents. His father could have a successful school in Milledgeville. Wealthy folks want their children tutored by a man with his father's background. Ben thinks it would be a good idea to begin a law school in conjunction with his father's school. Ben always loved working with his father. Maybe we could start a school for girls and young women, also? What a marvelous idea. Maybe one day. It's a marvelous dream.

Milledgeville - November 1828

Ben loved Cassie, but he reasoned a friendship with Elizabeth would be advantageous. He would one day marry Cassie but, like the law, life contains grey areas. He had physical needs and Cassie was far away. Besides, it wasn't the right time to marry—especially to an Indian woman. He must consider his career first. Zach cautioned him to allow plenty of time for sowing wild oats before any consideration of marriage.

After he had acquired adequate wealth, he could figure things out with Cassie. He could find a place to work where a mixed couple could live in peace—maybe in the west. There wouldn't be much of a living for a lawyer among the western Indians, but at least his children would be treated normally. He thought the white fascination with racial purity and the white abhorrence of even the smallest ratio of mixed blood strange. Growing up in Cherokee Country allowed Ben to notice the odd way white folks had in conversation of always mentioning a person's race if other than white. Ben had heard often phrases like, 'You know, the woman whose grandmother is an Indian' or 'you can tell by lookin' at them there must have been a nigger in the woodpile'. Ben had heard it all and thought the racial arrogance of whites curious—ridiculous—as if whites were superior to all others. Ben had been reared by good parents. He loved the Cherokee culture. He appreciated how, for the most part, they accepted Africans as equals with no hesitation. With the Cherokee there was no silly measurement of race, physiognomy or skin tone as a gauge of human worth. Never in Cherokee Country was the percentage of blood purity a qualifier to begin every conversation.

In Georgia, or anywhere in the South, his children with Cassie would be considered half-breed mongrels. He had all too often heard the heckling sing-song taunt, "Half-breed from bad seed, half-breed from bad seed."

Ben couldn't risk people calling his children such names. Children with Cassie must wait. Elizabeth could help him wait, he reasoned. His mood always brightened when he thought of Elizabeth. He wished he could see her more often. He could easily imagine Elizabeth sitting in a rocker beside the fire holding their baby—a white baby who would be accepted everywhere. It would be a child with a grand future, but he mustn't think of things like that now.

Zach and Elizabeth were teaching Ben the truth that it's who you know that counts. Some people can do things for you and some can't. If a person doesn't have money and connections, they are useless. Well, at least that's how Zach and Elizabeth had instructed Ben. Cassie could in no way further his career—therefore, according to Zach and Elizabeth, she was meaningless and a waste of time and energy.

Ben was feeling a need for Elizabeth's companionship more frequently than their solitary Tuesday afternoon. Maybe he could arrange a relaxing business trip to Savannah. That would be fun. There were clients they could see there and perhaps, if the stars aligned, one day he and Elizabeth might be a couple. He remembered Zach's warnings about Elizabeth—about her selfishness, but then people could change. Perhaps Zach was wrong. She was certainly desirable and his time with her was always sheer pleasure. He would love to see her several times a week or even every evening, instead of just Tuesday. Perhaps one day she would feel that way about him? Surely, under the right conditions, he could win Elizabeth's heart.

Perhaps Zach was right and a future with Elizabeth was a pipe dream, but he couldn't get her out of his mind. He decided he should go to his room and write his parents and maybe send Cassie a nice letter, too. Yes, he would write Cassie and clear his mind.

6 November 1828

Mr. Lowry made a special trip to bring Ben's letter.

Huff's Boarding House – Milledgeville - 3 November 1828

My Dear Sweet Cassie,

Great news. The votes are counted and I am elected. When I'm sworn in I'll be the youngest member of the Georgia House of Representatives. I wish you could come to the ceremony. We worked long and hard for this day, didn't we? I know you're as happy about my election as I am. I can't wait to begin work on behalf of you and your nation.

Maybe now we can do something, at least in a small way, to help the Cherokee and perhaps even the Africans some future day. I promise you I'll do all in my power. Zach and his father have invited my supporters to a victory celebration tomorrow evening. It will be quite an event. I wish you could share my success. I'll think of you every moment.

It appears General Jackson was elected in a landslide. That's a disappointment but we can hope for the best. Perhaps he'll be a better president than we have foreseen. Since all laws must go through Congress, perhaps he can be restrained when it comes to Indian matters. We can hope the developing civilization of the Cherokee Nation will bode well with the powers that be in Washington City.

With my election, our plans are coming together, aren't they? In four years, when I'm twenty-five, I'll stand for the U.S. House. In 1838, when I'm thirty, I'll seek a Senate appointment where real power resides. That's when I can achieve something substantial for your people. That's in the future, but there is much we can do between now and then. If nothing else, Cassie, I can help the Cherokee leaders know what sinister goings on are being hatched in the backrooms of Milledgeville.

Zach and I have been burning the candle at both ends for months. I'm exhausted. It's been an endless series of social events plus I've been doing a great deal of Zach's legal work. I'm tired of shaking hands and spouting boring pleasantries to men I don't know.

Would you go fishing with me? We'll go fishing without bait. We'll sit on the riverbank with fishing pole in hand and lean back and let the river slowly pass by.

I'll visit soon. I want to spend several days with you and my parents before the legislative session begins. I'm tired—bone tired. Even in my weariness, my last thought when I retire is a vision of you. I miss you terribly. As the French say, 'you are missing from me'.

I want some carefree time roaming the peaceful Cherokee forest. I want to feel the pine needles between my toes, drink cold spring water from a green mossy pool high in the mountains and think about nothing except you and your beautiful smile.

I have a special gift for you. I can't wait to hold you and kiss you again. Until then, my dear Cassie, I want you to know I love you dearly. I shall be holding you in my arms a few days after you receive this letter.

Always yours, Ben, xoxo

Milledgeville – November 1828

"What do you think of our little party for you, Ben?" Zach's father asked. "It's quite an event, isn't it? I can't tell you how proud we are of your dedication. You have represented us well, son. Your election was quite an accomplishment for the firm. Because of you, our bottom line will be significantly blacker this year—significantly blacker. I promise you this won't be the last time I go out of my way to take care of you, young man. Keep doing what you've been doing and I'll see you handsomely rewarded— handsomely rewarded, I say. Everyone knows I always take care of my people."

"Thank you, sir. I appreciate everything you've done. I pledge to do my best for you and our supporters. I want you to know, sir, your hospitality is superb. This must be the most elegant hotel in the South. I love it here, sir, and I'm sure you're proud."

Zach's father slapped Ben on the back with an enthusiasm fueled by too much whiskey.

"I knew from the first moment I met you, Ben, you were the man we needed. Folks like your country boy manner and I don't have to tell you my son Zach has blossomed since you came on board, in case you haven't noticed. He's enjoying his work once again. You two are good for one another. Sometimes we older folks come up with crafty strategies for the success of our offspring, don't we? You've been good for business and for my son. Before you came, I was beginning to wonder if Zach was cut out for the lawyering business, but now he's back to his old hardworking self and I have you to thank for that. Keep up the good work, Ben. Keep up the good work."

"I promise I shall do the best I can, sir," Ben answered.

"Now that you're in the legislature," Mr. Mitchell said, beginning to slur his words, "remember who put you there. Quid pro quo, Ben, quid pro quo. I want every one of our clients to know we have our own man in the legislature. You'll be even better for business now, young man."

Ben replied with a quiet thank you but Zach's father, quite tipsy, paid no attention.

"Ben, put these cigars in your pocket. They're Cubans, but don't tell our Virginia friends. If anyone asks, tell them they're pure Virginia leaf. If you like 'em I'll give you a box. I think these Cubans are superior to anything that comes from Virginia, don't you? I been smokin' 'em since '17 when they lifted the ban. I don't smoke nothin' else."

Ben was listening. He had learned to pay attention to anyone who was talking to him and not let his mind wander, no matter how uninteresting the conversation.

"I've got to mingle now, son," Zach's father said, "but remember how much we appreciate your work. We're looking forward to you bein' in the legislature. When you take your seat, remember who put you there. We've great plans for you goin' forward. Get busy and do your work tonight. Two hundred of Milledgeville's finest are here. They all need a pat on the back from you. Every wife here wants you to speak to her. I know you're tired, but I want our firm to represent every one of them when they need a lawyer. This is your night, Ben. You're the celebrity. Circulate, young man, circulate. After tonight, take a few days off. In fact, I order you to take a few days and recuperate. You've earned it."

"Yes sir," replied Ben.

Zach's father gave Ben a final slap on the back and turned to mix with his well-heeled guests.

"Well—we did it, didn't we?"

Ben turned and there behind him, arm in arm, stood Elizabeth and Zach sporting big smiles and sipping imported champagne.

"I was wondering when you two would get here," Ben said, with relief obvious in his voice. "I was beginning to feel lonely. I owe this night to you two, but I'm not sure I would have gone into politics if I had known how hard this is. Running for public office is harder than farming. Sometimes I think I had rather shake hands with a mule."

"Well," Zach said, laughing and giving Ben another slap on the back, "that's politics, isn't it? You'll get used to it. I'll guarantee you this is easier than farmin'. When this is over let's us three take a nice quiet trip to Charleston. Father was right. Get busy in here, Ben. Tell everyone to come to you when they need anything. Tonight it's all work for you. Your election is money in the bank. Let's keep it rolling in."

Elizabeth leaned up towards Ben's ear and slipped her arm through his. She stood tip-toe and whispered, "Without a doubt, Ben Lowry, you're the most handsome man here. We'll have a good time later. My poor heart skips a beat every time I see your handsome face. I tell Zach all the time how handsome you are."

She pressed her body even more tightly against Ben and gave him a lingering kiss on the cheek. Then, with her lips touching his ear, she whispered once again, "I can't tell you how much pleasure it gives my soul to be this near to you. I'll see you later upstairs. I'll be waiting. Please hurry."

She leaned away, hooked her arm back around Zach's and said louder with a dreamy voice and a playful smile, "I wonder, Ben, if it's this French champagne or maybe it's my growing affection for you, but I'm smitten. When I'm around you I'm as giddy as a schoolgirl with her first beau. You're irresistible. Now that you're in the legislature you've risen even further in my estimation, Ben Lowry. With your election, you've become the most eligible bachelor in Georgia, but don't forget me in the midst of your electoral success. I'm your greatest admirer. I can't think of anywhere I had rather be than on your arm. I'll be the most jealous woman in Georgia if I see you with another woman tonight."

"Bethy," Zach chuckled, "I think you're the most beautiful woman in Georgia. If you think this rustic country boy irresistible, then he must be. I'll defer to your judgment, but I agree he's going to be popular with the ladies, maybe even more popular than I am, and that's sayin' somethin'."

Elizabeth, standing between the two young men, held on to both men's arms and all three laughed so loud those nearby turned to see.

Elizabeth continued in her most seductive voice, "Ben, make sure you find me later, if you're not too tired. I've a special gift I picked up for you in Paris. I've been saving it in anticipation of your victory. I promise you'll love it."

She gave Ben's arm a squeeze and kissed his cheek. Once more on tip-toes she whispered into his ear, "Don't keep me waiting or some other handsome man may sweep me away in my disappointment. When you're finished, come on up. I'll have your surprise waiting in our room."

Ben, tingling from head to toe, responded, "I can't wait. It's my plan to keep you all to myself tonight. I'm not worried about those others and I shall never keep you waiting, my dear."

They parted and Ben immediately engaged his nearest supporter in conversation. As he went about his business, he thought of Elizabeth, their special room and the surprise gift that was waiting. He was envious of Zach's effortless ability to call her Bethy. He wished he had the courage to call her by Zach's pet name—to whisper the name Bethy into her ear when they were alone. Maybe tonight, after enough champagne, he would call her Bethy instead of Elizabeth. He couldn't wait. He couldn't wait until the day he could always call the beautiful Elizabeth his Bethy. He couldn't wait to receive his gift. He wondered what it could be.

9 November 1828

My Dear Cassie,

Everyone is pleased with the election. We had a marvelous victory celebration at Mr. Mitchell's hotel. I wish you could have been there. Everyone stayed late into the night.

Now that I'm a Georgia legislator, I will have access to every office and parlor in Georgia. I can begin to do good things for your people. Everyone of any importance has a home in Milledgeville and the economy is booming. I wish you could be here. I promise to visit soon and tell you everything. New homes and businesses are going up everywhere. Every day is better than the last. Property values are rising—the result of hardworking immigrants coming with skills and money. The United States' money supply has never seen such rapid growth. I think, Cassie, I may have been born for a career in politics and law.

Good news for Georgia and the white culture is not good news for your nation, however. The Cherokee aren't growing in comparison. I don't know where this burgeoning influx of white immigrants will end, but I will promise to do everything I can to assist. Perhaps Ross and the others can stem the tide flowing against them. I hope so.

Until I see you again,

I'm always yours, Ben, xoxo

Chapter XXXVI

1828 - Cassie in the Forest

Chapter 36

13 November 1828 - The Trading Moon - Nu da de qua

Ben came up for the day to celebrate his election victory with us. He must leave before dawn. Tomorrow is my birthday. I wish we could be together all day like last year.

While Ben works in Milledgeville, I'll be working at the Phoenix. I asked Mr. Boudinott if I could write a series of articles about the Georgia constitution and how laws are formulated and passed. The research will be interesting, and I can compare our Cherokee constitution to that of Georgia. I want to understand Ben's work. If this were a different world, I would go to law school. There are no women lawyers—a pity.

I long for the day when I don't have to watch Ben leave down that long, dusty road. I wish he could be here with me on my birthday tomorrow.

16 November 1828

For the rest of my life, my birthday shall remain uncelebrated in a black corner of my mind. I'm glad Ben isn't here.

Mr. Lowry has long wanted me to write about our interaction with whites. I want to forget everything about the whiteside except Ben.

Two days ago the sun was high when I finished at the Phoenix and began my pleasant walk home. I love walking anytime, but I revel in the clear, crisp days of the trading moon after a long, sticky summer. Walking, for us Cherokee, is a time to reflect and enjoy the world around us. We never hurry. Since I was a child I have been told the joy of life is in the journey—each day to be treasured. No one in our community owns a timepiece. Ben says the clock governs the whites. Maybe their dependence on a timepiece is what makes them selfish and irritable. Ben thinks that is so. They never have enough time. I find that a strange thought.

Before the whites came, we had no roads and few horses. We walked everywhere on a multitude of well-traveled paths that would take us to faraway lands. Now, like the whites, we have wagons and horses. We live on farms, but our men still know the old paths. Squatters come, building houses and fences, denying us the use of our own land, despoiling our old footpaths.

Nothing can be done about it, edudu says. We have forced a few squatters to leave, but we are too weak to resist the flood—big wagons are always coming on the wide roads built by whites.

Sometimes Mr. Lowry will give me a ride home in the afternoon. Most of the time I prefer to walk and think about words and writing and what I have been reading. Around New Echota there is a great deal of foot traffic. Sometimes I walk with friends, but this past Friday I walked home alone. I wish I had been with friends.

I wanted to surprise elisi with a big bag of hickory nuts. It's late for hickory nuts, but I know a little hidden valley on the way home where there are dozens of hickory trees with plenty of nuts just waiting to be gathered. I'm sure the squirrels won't mind.

Hickory trees, whites call them scaly barks, are ubiquitous throughout our country. Their tasty nuts last all winter. We make handles for axes, hoes, shovels and pitchforks from its very hard wood. We also make bowls, spoons and other kitchen implements. The hickory's greatest asset is the plentiful nut full of oil. We love the chestnut also. I like the chestnut because we do not have to crack a hard shell. The chestnut has a prickly casing, like a little porcupine, but the nut is easy to remove. I love chestnuts. I never like to gather them.

This day I left the Phoenix carrying edudu's leather bag worn smooth from years of use. I left the main trail for the hidden valley and the tall hickory trees I know so well. I found something I wished I had not.

Straying farther than I intended, I walked down a long hollow on the opposite side of my community. I was out of earshot of anyone. I was alone. I have never been afraid in the forest. I never believed the stories of the dangerous little people in the old Cherokee tales. It was big white people I should have feared.

In the past a Cherokee woman could safely travel alone anywhere at anytime. Anyone finding her would escort her home and defend her from all harm. In these days of frenzied land-grabbing by white immigrants, many have no respect for our property rights—or personal rights. In recent times, danger lurks everywhere.

I heard horses and turned to see three mounted men top the ridge and ride into the broad hollow behind me. I recognized the uniforms. The militia often send mounted patrols through our country looking for runaway Africans. The mounted men followed me through the hardwoods at a distance. They were close enough that I could hear the horses' hooves as they tramped through the thick carpet of crisp autumn leaves. I hesitated thinking the men might be lost.

A White Killing Frost

It was obvious they didn't belong and were well away from any trail. Too late I realized my concern had brought me into grave personal danger.

When I realized I was in jeopardy, I fled in panic. If I could get over the hill I might get within earshot of Cherokee hunters. As I ran under a tall persimmon, my foot snagged on a saw briar. I went down hard cutting both hands and bruising my face on the sharp stones obscured under the deep layer of autumn leaves. My ankle was lacerated and bleeding from the briar. Before I could free myself from the tangled sawbriar vines the three bearded horsemen were upon me.

As I sat defenseless on the ground with my back against the persimmon, the men stared down at me with expressions of amusement. I tried to stand and run but the one closest, the red-headed man, dismounted in one quick motion and grabbed my left bicep. In one rapid motion he pulled me backwards and slammed me to the ground violently. My shoulder and head cracked against stones concealed under the dead leaves. I screamed. I kicked and tried to escape but the man had an iron grip on both of my upper arms. His strong fingers dug deep into my biceps. I continued to struggle as I lay on my back pinned to the ground. The man slapped my face viciously several times in rapid succession. I very nearly lost consciousness. Blood began to run freely from my mouth and nose onto the leaves under my head. After he slapped me I lay stunned—unable to make any noise or scream. I had been silenced. As I began to recover my senses, I once again felt the man's powerful fingers digging painfully into my arms and I cried out. My tears mixed with the flowing blood from my mouth and nose.

"You Indian bitch. Just shut up," the man on top of me said.

He slapped me once again harder than before.

With his last blow, I felt my lower lip split completely through against my front teeth. I felt the hot blood on my neck dripping onto the dry brown leaves under my head.

"She's a hellcat, ain't she, Clement?" the man on top of me said. "We'll tame this bitch, so we will. She'll be a pussycat when we're finished, by god. There ain't no need to fight, you Indian bitch. We ain't goin' to hurt you. We're goin' to have some fun. You don't mind if we have a little fun this afternoon? We ain't goin' to hurt you—we promise. I been lookin' for somethin' like you since I come here and you're a good lookin' thing for an Indian. You're prettier than the last one we did—ain't she, Clement? She ain't nearly so fat and this one's got all her teeth."

I continued to struggle but my attempts to free myself were useless. The man held me even tighter. I could feel the stones bruising my back.

"She's a fighter, ain't she, John? You don't like to give it up easy, do you bitch?"

My struggles were hopeless, but my resistance was reflexive. My eyes were closed.

"Be still. Quit squirming you god-damned Indian—and shut up for god's sake—just shut up."

His sour breath was hot in my face. I heard the sound of his grinding teeth as he strained to keep me pinned to the ground under his heavy body. He slapped me hard once again and shoved me downwards as if he were trying to push me bodily into the soil.

I finally lay still, hardly conscious. I could no longer resist. I abandoned all hope of escape. I was bruised, bleeding and my back was hurting terribly where I had been slammed down on the rocks. I opened my eyes. My fear suddenly turned into a furious anger. In a sudden, raging burst of energy, I struggled with all my might—twisting, turning and kicking the man in his back with my knees as he straddled my torso. My attempt to free myself accomplished nothing except to further infuriate the dirty, smelly man on top of me.

"My word, she's a feisty one, John. All the better, don't you think? I want some lively action, don't you, John? I like a hot saucy woman who makes lots of noise and carries on, don't you? Are you going to make noise for us, bitch? The louder you are the better we like it. Go ahead. Make noise, bitch. Nobody can hear you out here."

The tall man called John dismounted slowly, put his hands on his thighs and leaned down. He stared at me as the filthy red-headed man held me to the ground.

My lips and tongue began to swell. His face was only a handbreadth from mine. In my anger I spit blood and saliva into the red-headed man's face with all the venom I could muster. As my spittle dripped from his bright red beard back onto my clothing, he broke into a smile as if I had given him pleasure. The pain in my back and arms was intense. I could feel a rising nausea from his foul stench. I turned my head and began to retch into the blood-spattered leaves beside my head. I could smell the decaying persimmons under the bed of dried leaves.

As he continued to hold me down, the red-headed man put his lips almost against my ear. His dirty red whiskers brushed my face as he whispered in a deliberate voice, "You're gonna pay for spittin' on a white man. I'm goin' to teach you a lesson, you arrogant Indian bitch, and I'm goin' enjoy givin' it to you. I don't mind you spittin'. I don't mind nothin' you do. You fight and spit all you want to. The more you fight the better. When I'm finished, you'll think twice about spittin' on a white man—you god-damned uppity Indian bitch. I'll put you in your place, so I will."

The red-headed man on top of me slapped my face harder than before.

As I lay on my back powerless to resist, he moved my hands together above my head and held them both in his left hand. He was strong—very strong. As he began ripping at my clothing with his free right hand, I kept my eyes closed. I didn't want to see the men's faces as I was exposed. I knew what he intended.

"Damn you, John, git your lazy ass down here an' grab her arms. I can't do this by myself, you son of a bitch. If you don't help, I'll kick your ass all over these woods when I'm finished. I mean it. Hold her, John. Hold her arms, dammit," the man shouted at his tall companion standing casually next to him.

I could feel the red-headed man on top of me working himself into a raging frenzy. He was beginning to lose control of his speech. I kept my head turned. I began to retch once again.

The man named John hesitated, "I don't know, Liam. I ain't never done nothin' like this. Maybe we should let her go. I don't think she wants us to do this. I don't think I want to do this. Let's go back to the tavern and have another drink. I'm thirsty."

I had a glimmer of hope.

The red-headed man, still holding me to the ground, looked up and snapped, "God damn you, John, you yellow dog. Of course she wants us to do her. It ain't like we was doin' nothin' wrong. We're havin' fun with this thing—that's all. This ain't no white woman. Hell, Indians ain't no different than animals, are they? She's just a damn savage. She'll probably like it anyways, like a brood mare or a nigger woman. God damn it, John, get your lazy ass down here and hold her. Do your part, you skinny son of a bitch, or I'll kick your worthless ass all over these woods. I promise you I will. We done nigger women before, ain't we? She ain't no different."

The man named John hesitated but did as he was told without further objections. He knelt at my head and held my wrists so the red-headed man straddling me could have his way with his hands free. With my eyes closed, I felt the warm afternoon sun shining through the leafless limbs shining directly onto my face.

"You're right, Liam," the man named John said, as he knelt and took my wrists. I never thought about that. This ain't no white woman. I couldn't do this to a white woman, Liam, but she ain't white. Indians ain't like us, are they? They're like animals, ain't they? She ain't no different than a nigger woman. Go ahead and give it to her, Liam. Give it to her like she was a whore nigger woman."

The man named John held my wrists. The tall man, Clement, held my ankles. I might have successfully escaped from one man, but I couldn't escape three. I had no choice but to submit. I wished for some way I could make myself completely unconscious so I would have no memory of what was happening. As the red-headed man had his way, the odor of his breath and the smell of his unwashed clothing burned my nose. I tried not to think as he pleased himself. I kept my head away from his. The red-headed man didn't appear to notice as I once again heaved onto the leaves beside my head. At last I felt him convulse and relax. He was finished. The other two men continued to hold my limbs in their iron grasp.

The red-headed man, now lying motionless on top of me spoke, his face almost touching mine, "John, that was good—real good. I needed that. I ain't had nothin' as good in a while. This ain't my first squaw, but it's definitely the best. You'll like it and she's good lookin' to boot. If she hadn't vomited, it would've been perfect. Hell, she looks better than most white women I been with and she's got all her teeth. I don't like to do a woman with no teeth. Let's come back tomorrow and get more."

He leaned his face down until he was almost touching my nose.

"What do you think about that, squaw woman? We'll be back lookin' for you. We know where you come from. Don't run next time and we won't slap you around so much. I wouldn't a hit you this time if you hadn't run. Don't make me mad. It ain't good to make me mad—an' don't spit on me. I get real angry when people do that. I don't like it when folks make me mad. She's ready for you, Clement. It's your turn."

Before he rose, he lowered his face once again. This time his face and beard pressed hard against my cheek.

He whispered with a haughty chuckle directly into my ear, "I like you, bitch. We'll be lookin' for you right here tomorrow. We know where to find you. Don't run next time and don't make me mad. I don't like it when folks make me mad."

The man named Clement who had been holding my legs spoke, "God damn it Liam, I can't let go till you hold her ankles. She's a hell cat. If I let go, she'll kick my nose off. Come on, Liam, and get her ankles. We held her for you. I want my turn. I had a good view and I'm ready."

"Next," shouted Liam as he stood, with no shame whatsoever, pulling up his trousers. He and the man named Clement exchanged places. Clement straddled me without a thought for decency. As he quickly exposed himself,

I closed my eyes and turned my head again. I wish I had kept my eyes shut from the beginning. Every visual image of that day is burned indelibly into my memory—a part of my mind forever. The second man, Clement, had the same bitter acrid smell as that of his unwashed companion. The man shamelessly satisfied his uncontrolled animal instincts on my bruised, bleeding and unresisting body. I cried softly to myself with my eyes closed. The sun continued to shine through the leafless trees. I felt an ant crawl over my face.

I was physically and emotionally exhausted. I began to think in some kind of confused emotional panic. I imagined I could magically prevent what was happening by averting my mind and my eyes and somehow transport myself to another place. Perhaps this was an evil dream—some ghastly nightmare from which I would suddenly awake and the horror would dissipate like a morning mist in the first light of dawn—a dream I would be unable to remember. It was not a dream. I will remember.

When I finally felt John, the third man, have his way, I tried to gather my senses and save my life. I had the distressing thought that these lawless men might kill me when they finished.

I quietly spoke in English, "Why are you doing this? Please let me go. Please let me go home. I want to go home. Please let me go home."

I reasoned if I spoke softly in English they might have mercy. There is no way for me to describe the confusing mental horror that was exploding inside of my mind at that moment. I was terrified beyond words.

Liam, the red-headed man with the heavy Irish brogue, said, "The bitch speaks English, John. Imagine that. The Indian bitch speaks English. We got us here an educated heathen. Where in the hell did you learn English?"

The Irishman, standing over me, began to shake with rage. He knelt on his hands and knees, continuing to shake with fury, pinning my arms to the ground once again. His face, almost touching mine, contorted into a violent mask of exploding anger as he screamed obscenities in a spray of tobacco-laden spittle—the sharp stones grinding deeply into my back from the pressure of his hands and body.

In his madness he roared his answer to my question. He vented on me an unrestrained, insane wrath directly into my face.

"You want to know why? We like it. That's why. We want to and we can. You're just a god-damned Indian. That's why. We're white and you're nothing—you shouldn't even be here. We do what we want in Cherokee Country. We're the law, you educated bitch. You should know that. There ain't no law again' what we're doin'. You're no better than dog dirt—you're lower than dog dirt."

It seemed with every brutal sentence his face got closer, his eyes wilder, his voice louder and his words more slurred and indistinct. It was as if shouting his insults would insure his words would degrade me and release the evil that sought to escape his tortured mind.

"We can do anything we want to in this damn country. We'll take you and take anything else we want. We're white. We're the law. This is our country now. Nobody cares what we do with the likes of you."

As the red-headed man finished, he spat once more directly on my face from only a hand breadth and slapped me once again as hard as he possibly could. I was overcome with nausea. His saliva ran off my cheeks and dripped off my face. In his mad rage he was breathing hard and fast. He sagged over me as if the voicing of his frenetic outrage had used all his energy. His head was jerking side to side and his eyes flitted left and right. He looked into the woods with a blank stare as if he didn't know where he was or wondered what he had been doing.

"Liam, Liam, Liam, Liam," the man named Clement shouted as he grabbed the back of the red-headed man's shirt and tugged him backwards. "That's enough. Leave her alone. Quit shoutin' at her, Liam. We need to get out of here before somebody comes. You been shoutin' real loud, Liam. That's enough. Somebody might hear you. Get on your horse. We need to get out of here. Let's go now, Liam."

As the red-headed man stood, he looked down and shouted once more, "There, you god-damned uppity squaw. You like to spit in people's faces? Here, let's do it again."

As the other two men mounted their horses, the red-headed man stepped towards me with his horse's reins in one hand. He leaned over and spat directly into my face. I lay semi-conscious with my eyes closed on the hard ground beside the persimmon tree. I began to whimper as I felt the splash on my face. Tobacco-laden spittle mixed with blood dripped onto the dried autumn leaves under my head. I could feel the ants that had been feeding on the scattered persimmons begin to explore my exposed flesh.

"Come on, Liam. We need to get out of here now. Let's go. I don't like this. What if somebody hears? You been shoutin' loud. Let's go before somebody comes. I don't want nobody to see us. I don't want no trouble."

The man named Liam shook with rage as he mounted his horse. I thought of Ben and tried to calm myself and be silent. I felt the cold rays of the afternoon sun shining on my face.

"Liam, let's get the hell out of here. I don't like this."

"We didn't do nothing wrong," Liam muttered as he mounted. "It ain't like she was a white woman."

I closed my eyes as they rode away. I don't remember anything for a long while after that.

When I awoke the woods were perfectly silent. For a few moments I didn't know where I was or what had happened. I was lying partially exposed. I shivered as I lay in the leaves in the evening chill. Suddenly the entire wretched scene came back and I burst into hysterical sobbing. I pulled my knees to my chin and covered my legs with dried leaves. I continued to sob until I lost consciousness once again.

The second time I awoke it was almost completely dark and my mind was numb, as if I were a different person. I remembered everything, but it was as if the horror had happened to someone else or I had read the story in some macabre work of dark fiction. I gained enough mental strength to rise. I moved in slow motion as if my body belonged to another. I watched my dirty hands sluggishly tidy my blood-spattered clothing. As if to erase the violence, I cleaned my body with handfuls of leaves and tried to wipe the dried blood and saliva from my face and neck. I turned for home.

As I mindlessly stumbled towards the river, I often lost my way even though I was familiar with every path. Somehow in the dark I made it to the river. Gratefully, no one was there. Above all I wanted to avoid contact with anyone—especially my family. I could not bear to be seen. I did not want to explain what had happened. I was unable to talk. My only thought was to wash, to wash away the uncleanness—to wash away the brutality. I wanted to cleanse both my mind and my body before I went home. Alone, in pitch darkness and fully dressed, I slipped into the welcoming arms of the cold, friendly water. I wanted the ancient spirit of our compassionate river to cleanse my flesh—to cleanse my soul and restore the balance. The icy water made me shiver, but I did not care. I needed to wash. I wanted to bathe—to be restored. I needed to remove the filth and the memory of the lewdness. I wanted to bathe the inside of my body—to somehow turn myself inside out and let my river wash my soul clean and return me to the uncontaminated person I had been that morning.

I soon realized bathing was a cruel mockery. The white men had written indelibly on my soul with ink from hell. I would be forever contaminated— forever stained. As I stood in the cold flowing river in the darkness, I understood I would never be cleansed of the obscenity that was forever trapped within. No amount of washing could cleanse the hidden crevices of

426

my innermost being. As I felt the icy water flow around me, I realized I would bear my shame forever. I would never be free. Every day for the rest of my life I will be assaulted in my mind once again at the hands of those three white men. Their abuse was never-ending. Those three men will haunt my mind until my last breath. I began to whimper and shiver as I stood in the arms of the flowing river but I did not tremble from the cold.

I vowed to never tell anyone. I especially did not want Five Feathers to learn of my humiliation. My brother would quickly get himself killed avenging my crime and my tragedy would be doubled. I will not tell Ben, edudu or elisi. No one must learn of this horror.

My attackers deserve a retribution in kind but it isn't to be. It will never be. For a moment I wanted evil to befall them, but I remembered the two wolves. I choose not to feed my bad wolf. I had rather die than become haters like them. What a horrible thought—to become like those men. I shuddered and thanked Mr. Lowry and edudu for teaching me not to hate. I will suffer alone and allow the Great Spirit, the judge of all men, to return my world to balance. One day the evil they released will come home to roost above their door like our chickens who come home to their roost every evening. Evil always returns to the place of its birth. I will wait for the Great Spirit to repay. Their evil will return upon their heads one day.

After my encounter, I began my blood time normally. I was pleased about that. At least I wasn't expecting a child. The thought of telling Ben I was with child by unknown men of the Georgia militia was more than my battered mind could bear. How can men do what those three did? From somewhere I must summon strength to bear my shame.

I shall never tell Ben, my brother, Mr. Lowry, edudu or elisi. I shall cope with injustice like we Cherokee cope with everything whites have done to us. I'll remember their words, "It's not like she's a white woman."

Chapter XXXVII

1828 - Ben Speaks to the Council

Chapter 37

21 November 1828

For days I have read nothing while I recover. I sometimes think I should never read white newspapers again. In every newspaper, the arrogant white writers belittle us while exalting themselves. Their self-importance is a constant reminder of my shame and their distain for all things Cherokee.

Copied from the - *Georgia Journal* – Page 2 – 6 November 1828

"…the solemn promise of the United States made in 1802 to remove at their expense the Indians from the territory of the State, is yet to be performed….The rulers of that Tribe, who have since the year 1818 systematically devoted themselves to defeat any attempt to purchase out their permitted occupation of our lands, have as a last resort adopted a Constitutional form of government…a Government professing to be independent, is set up in defiance of the authority of the States of Georgia, Tennessee, Alabama and North Carolina, upon the territory and within the jurisdiction of those States….this attempt will not make any change in the relation in which they stand to the United States….This state of things cannot be endured….Our duty to the people and to posterity requires that we should act. Of the right of the General Assembly to legislate over all persons and all things within our territorial limits, on general principles, a doubt cannot be entertained….Believing that our right is undoubted, that the exercise of our sovereign power is required by the best interests of the State….What disposition is to be made of the Cherokee?...for incorporation, with equality of rights as a part of our political family, they are unfit….I recommend to you to extend all the laws of the State over the territory lying within our limits occupied by the Cherokees…we should unite in fervent supplication to the Ruler of Man and Empires, that he will direct us in all our deliberations, inspire us with a portion of his divine wisdom, and make us the humble instruments of his will, in promoting peace and harmony among the people and in establishing on the most solid basis the prosperity of the State."

John Forsyth - Governor

The Georgia governor believes Georgia's god will direct him and his government in our removal. Is there a god, as the governor believes, who gives blessings only to whites?

30 November 1828

Copied from the Georgia Journal – 24 November 1828 – page 3

Bill to Manumit a Slave

The bill to manumit a slave, Bob, was taken up. Mr. Saffold opposed the bill on the ground, that manumitted slaves generally became a nuisance—and were frequently so old, that they could not make a support for themselves, and thence became a tax on the public, in some way or other—that if people wished to manumit their slaves, they could send them to other States where slavery was not permitted to exist…the bill was laid on the table for the remainder of the session…"

24 December 1828 - The Snow Moon – V s gi ga

The moment Ben's feet touched the ground his mother embraced him with all her strength, and Ben's father, holding the reins of Ben's horse, gave his son a bear hug to welcome him home.

"We have missed you so much," his mother said with tears in her eyes.

As soon as I could, I gave Ben the hug I had been saving. I missed him terribly. I want to put bad memories behind me.

Mrs. Lowry prepared a nice tea. Ben didn't stop smiling from the moment he arrived. Christmas is a happy time and a day for exchanging gifts among whites but Ben would have brought gifts in any case.

After we finished our tea we walked to the council meeting in New Echota. Many of our leaders have known Ben since he was a child. Everyone was glad to see him. Most respect him as if he were a Cherokee himself.

Leaders had been gathering for several days and were anxious to hear the latest news from the whiteside. Ben is perhaps the only white politician our leaders trust. He grew up among us and the men have great respect for Mr. and Mrs. Lowry.

As we walked, Ben's face took a stern look as he spoke to his father.

"I'm afraid I have bad news, Father. The legislature, just this week, passed a comprehensive law pretty much revoking all Cherokee law within Georgia's

429

chartered boundaries. I have the full text and I'll read some of it tonight at the meeting. I'm sorry, Father. I'm very sorry."

Ben's mother and I walked silently behind Ben and his father as they discussed recent events and what Ben would say in the meeting. I'm beginning to think any window of opportunity to save our nation has closed—even with our constitution. Edudu continues to hope good things will come from the hard work of our leaders and men like Ben and his parents.

It seems to me the general government and the states are putting the final pieces in place for a privileged society. In this land of growing white privilege, Africans will continue in bondage and we will be deported. The new president, Andrew Jackson, will see to that, Ben says.

Ben loves the Cherokee casual style of communication and he is especially fond of how we use the moon to mark the passage of time. The whiteside court system requires him to be punctual—but not so here. To be a day or two late for a meeting is nothing of consequence to us. We never hurry. Ben has often reflected our view of time is one of the things he admires most about our culture. He says our serenity may become our downfall when it comes to dealing with the hasty whiteside. Ben thinks the clock is an enemy of society, not only of the Cherokee, but all humankind. I agree.

The three hundred Cherokee sat outside our council house in the cold winter air as I prepared to translate. Mr. Lowry said if I were a man I could work for the general government or the state of Georgia as a translator and earn good wages.

"I have good news and bad news," Ben began quietly, with every eye upon him. "The good news is, in my first year of eligibility, I have been elected to the Georgia House of Representatives. You now have a firm friend in the legislature. That's the good news. However, I am the most inexperienced legislator in Georgia and I have no influence whatsoever among my peers. Nevertheless, I can be your ears and faithfully communicate to you what is happening on the whiteside. You can trust me in that regard."

"The bad news is, Andrew Jackson will be sworn as President of the United States in March of the coming year. He has never been a friend of the Cherokee. I wish I had better news."

As I translated, a muttering went through the crowd. The old grey heads began nodding. They knew what this news meant. Everyone knew of the Creek and Seminole wars and some had fought with General Jackson at Horseshoe Bend against the Red Sticks. Andrew Jackson has forgotten the assistance he received from the Cherokee. Now, most of our men wish they had fought against Jackson rather than with him.

Edudu was first with the talking stick.

"We have heard about Jackson. We know his hatred for the Creek and how he pursued the Seminole and runaway Africans into Spanish Florida. Micanopy's men tell me the Seminole are harassed but manage to evade capture and survive. Tell us about Jackson. What kind of man is the new chief of the whiteside?"

This was not going to be an easy speech.

Ben began, "Andrew Jackson is an American hero. He and his Tennessee Volunteers, and men like him, viciously removed the Cherokee and other tribes from their state, as you know very well. The Overhill towns are no more. Jackson won the battle of New Orleans, smashed the Red Sticks, defeated the Spanish, fought the Seminoles in Spanish Florida twice and has subsequently been proclaimed a military hero in every town in the United States. He and men like him are responsible for the removal of the Choctaw, Chickasaw and other tribes. Whites admire Jackson's courage. Not since George Washington have the citizens of the United States had such reverence for a military leader. Whites love to fight. Whites have great respect for the men who do their fighting.

Everyone listened carefully to the tall, handsome, well-spoken white man.

"Jackson, a fourteen-year-old prisoner, was ordered to clean a British officer's boots. Jackson refused. In a rage, the officer slashed Jackson's wrist to the bone. In 1806, Jackson, six feet tall and a hundred and fifty pounds, fought a pistol duel with Charles Dickenson. Jackson, with ice cold nerves, allowed Dickenson to shoot first without returning fire. Jackson was hit. With a pistol ball near his heart and his left boot filling with blood, Jackson calmly raised his pistol and shot Dickenson dead. That is the kind of cold, calculating man he is. He is the man who insists every person here today should remove outside the borders of the United States and give up their land to white men."

Ben stopped and took a big drink of water to wet his dry mouth.

"In 1813, in a gunfight in Nashville, Jackson was wounded twice. Doctors wanted to amputate his mangled arm, but Jackson's last words to the doctor before losing consciousness were 'there will be no amputation'. Thirty days later Jackson resumed his military command with both arms. In 1814, Jackson successfully defeated the British at New Orleans and became a national hero to the whites. After the battle of New Orleans, General Jackson executed eight men by firing squad in Nashville for desertion. Those aren't the only white soldiers under his command he put to death."

Ben continued, "In 1816, General Jackson's popularity rose again after he ordered an aggressive military incursion into Spanish Florida. At the mouth of the Apalachicola River, well within Spanish territory, a successful, independent African community had become a magnet for runaway American slaves and thus intolerable to white agricultural interests just across the international boundary in Georgia, Alabama, Mississippi and Louisiana."

"The free African community was composed of many escaped slaves and a great number born free. They were supported by the Seminoles. The prosperous African community was under constant pressure by bands of armed white men. The Africans armed themselves and built a secure enclosure for the protection of their families from predatory white slave hunters."

"Jackson devised a plan to destroy the flourishing African plantation. In July 1816, General Jackson ordered General Gaines and Colonel Clinch to sail up the Apalachicola River through Spanish Florida past the African plantations. The naval gunboats' mission was ostensibly to supply Fort Scott in the United States. Fort Scott lay up-river just across the international boundary line in Alabama territory. The United States naval incursion was designed by Jackson to give the United States international justification for military action on foreign soil. Two United States gunboats began a bombardment. During the battle the African's powder magazine exploded within their enclosure. More than four hundred inhabitants, including most of the women and children, were killed instantly. This action ordered by Jackson eliminated any refuge for Africans seeking their freedom in Spanish Florida, especially West Florida, and helped stem the flow of American slaves escaping south. Jackson took credit for destroying the African plantation and thus became even more popular with whites, especially in the South. After this battle, Jackson executed two British subjects found living with the Seminole and Africans. Assisting Africans was a capital offense for a white man—even in a foreign territory."

"President Jackson has one goal. He, and men like him, want an all-white United States. It is clear that the American government will never allow a free African or Indian community. Jackson has acquired powerful followers, especially in the United States Senate. These men are willing to take great risks on his behalf and the vision they share."

The men in council continued to patiently listen to Ben. No one interrupted.

Ben raised his voice once again and continued his bad news.

"I promise to assist you to understand the goings-on in Georgia and Washington. Your Chief John Ross, Major Ridge, Elias Boudinott, George Lowrey and many others will help save your country and they can count on me for accurate information. Other than that, I am powerless. Perhaps the whites can be persuaded to allow you to keep your homes and farms as promised in past treaties."

The assembly was quiet as they listened to news that only confirmed what everyone already knew.

"Jackson and his men have a rifle in one hand and surveyor's tools in the other. They wish to dispossess all Indian cultures and give their land to white farmers. Whites have no intention of living in harmony with you—no matter what government agents promise. They intend to conquer you, seize your land and send you away. They do not want to share your land. They do not want part of your land. They want it all. If you resist, they will destroy you—men, women and children."

Ben continued, "Tennessee Volunteers deported the Cherokee, Choctaw and Chickasaw from their state and came down here to help destroy the Creeks. As I speak the Chickasaw are being removed from the remnant of their land in Alabama and Mississippi. The United States Government is hunting the Seminole like animals in Florida territory. Whites have already taken your best farmland near the rivers. I fear they are preparing to take your beautiful land here in the mountains and hills. You have no army. You have no allies. You cannot resist. I am sorry to tell you these things."

Ben, wishing he was somewhere else, sipped water.

"Above all things they despise your new constitution. They view it as an attempt to compete with their government. Your constitution, and thus your country, will not be allowed to stand."

"There is more bad news," Ben said. "I hope you don't hate me for telling you this. Just this week Georgia passed new laws covering the white counties of DeKalb, Hall, Habersham, Gwinnet, Carroll and others on the white map. On the first day of June this year, Georgia law will take effect in all these counties and all laws, usages, and customs made, established, and in force by the Cherokee will become null and void—as if they never existed. The new Georgia law says no Indian or descendant of Indian shall be deemed a competent witness or party to any suit in any white court. I'm so sorry. By this law, it practically means all white debts to the Cherokee are cancelled. You will no longer be allowed to take a white man to a white court for non-payment of legitimate debts."

"After the first day of June, the Cherokee council will become powerless to govern. The law also says any white court can call up the local white militia to force obedience to the new Georgia laws."

The men understood the storm could not be avoided. We Cherokee are used to bad news but this was bad news piled upon bad news. As I looked over the faces, I knew our national supply of patience was low. We have been beaten down once again.

The next man given the talking stick asked, "Why do they do this? Do they believe us to be animals? Why do they pursue us with no mercy and steal our land? Do they hate our wives and children? Why would they cheat us out of honest debts?"

"It is simple," Ben replied. "Whites believe themselves superior. They cannot understand why you do not want to become white. They hate you because you are not white. They hate you more because you do not want to become white. You can no more resist what is coming than stop the snow from falling or the sun from setting. A harsh winter is coming upon Cherokee Country."

The patient Cherokee men trusted this tall, handsome, honest white man. Although bad news came upon bad news, perhaps this young man, with one foot in Washington, could gain allies for the Cherokee. Perhaps with the hard work of Chief John Ross and others there was a way to avoid the inevitable. Perhaps allies could be found in the northern states. Perhaps the inexorable advance of avaricious immigrants from Europe could be stopped.

Ben sipped water once again. The old men were silent. Everyone knew it was a matter of time before an army of mounted young white men in neat uniforms and hats would come. The once massive Cherokee Nation would be squeezed out of existence—extinguished.

The Cherokee Nation was accustomed to being forced from their homes and farms. Even the Cherokee capital at New Echota was a replacement for the old Cherokee capital destroyed by the whites in Tennessee. It appeared from Ben's news the proud Principle People would be squeezed out of existence.

The next man with the talking stick spoke.

"I do not want to be white. I do not want to speak the white language. It is difficult to believe they are so unfeeling as to force us from the land that eternally comforts the bones of our fathers. I choose to live and die here. Whatever will be, will be. I will keep my family, my farm and my way of life. I will trust Chief Ross. No matter what they demand, I shall never become white."

Ben continued with renewed power.

"I understand your thoughts. Some hope remains. Things can be done. White men can present your case in white courts, and we will. We can print

434

and distribute the Phoenix, and we will. We will continue to demand previous treaties be considered valid—your leaders and others will press the general government in Washington City to honor past treaties. These things we can do. The missionaries and white friends of the Cherokee will not give up, though they be few. You can trust men like my father."

As I translated, I understood our final act of national courage would be to endure our forced deportation. When our deportation came, many of the old men listening to Ben were doomed to die of exposure, starvation and disease and be buried far from home in unmarked graves. It was a gloomy thought.

Edudu, with the talking stick in hand, spoke last, "Beyond the memory of our oldest men, we have been sustained by this land given us by the Great Spirit. These mountains, forests and fields have fed our children from ancient times. Things change. Perhaps we can regain the balance, perhaps not. From across great waters invaders came as numerous as the birds of the heavens. They want this land to belong to them. This land was here long before the Cherokee. This land will be here long after we have gone to be with our ancestors. Whites do not understand. This land has never belonged to us. We Cherokee belong to the land."

After a long pause, edudu continued with every ear tuned to his words.

"One cold autumn morning we will wake. Our feet will crunch upon frozen earth. In the darkness everything Cherokee will have died, covered by a white killing frost."

Without another word, he sat down. No one asked for the talking stick. Everyone left. There was nothing more to say.

Chapter XXXVIII

1829 - Edudu's Puppy

Chapter 38

10 January 1829

Ben arrived with two of the cutest puppies ever. On his way from Milledgeville, Ben found their poor mother lying dead with the two little puppies trying to get milk. He couldn't bear to leave them. He brought them home on the stage in a feed sack.

Ben gave one puppy to his parents' friend. We gave the other to edudu. Edudu has been wanting another dog since his Spinner died. I have not seen edudu with such a big bright smile in a long time. If I had known how much he wanted another dog, Ben and I would have gotten him one sooner. Edudu's new puppy has black and white longish hair, two white front paws and two dark back paws, one eye blue and one brown, a white snout and has become edudu's immediate friend. He follows edudu everywhere and licks edudu's toes every time he sits. He licks our fingers when we hold him. I understand why he follows edudu. If someone gave me bits of bacon all day, I would lick his fingers, too.

11 January 1829

"What will you name your new puppy, edudu?

"I never name my puppies, Walela. It is proper to let a dog name himself. When puppy learns his name, he will tell me. Until then, I wait."

"Edudu, dogs cannot talk. I have never talked to a dog. How can the dog tell you his name?" I said with a laugh.

Edudu petted my head as if I were a puppy.

"My dear Walela, sometimes I wonder if you are truly Cherokee. Perhaps your mother found you under a corn stalk or sleeping in the melons one morning. Perhaps you fell out of Mrs. Possum's pouch?"

Edudu laughed and laughed.

"I think you may be turning white from reading too many white books. Certainly dogs can talk. Everyone knows that. Anyone can hear animals talk if they take time to listen—especially if they understand Cherokee. Animals don't understand the English, but all animals understand Cherokee. You must hold your mind just right to let their thoughts through. Spinner and I talked every day. Do you remember?"

"I remember, edudu," I said, as I thought of the many times I had heard edudu talking to Spinner as if he were a human friend.

"I would sit on the porch and whittle and listen to Spinner tell me about his day and what happened in the woods at night while we slept. When Spinner was finished talking, I would tell him about my day and what I was going to whittle or tell him when we would go hunting next. Spinner was my best friend. He was a very talkative dog, I can tell you. Sometimes Spinner would talk all day and hardly give me a moment's rest, but I didn't mind. He always had something intelligent to say. Sometimes he would ask me to tell him stories. Spinner loved stories. I think he knew every Cherokee story as well as I know them. Spinner was an excellent storyteller. I learned a lot of new stories from Spinner."

"Yes, edudu, Spinner was an amazing dog and a loyal companion. I loved him, too. How did you name Spinner?"

"Walela, you're not listening, are you? Are your ears full of wax? I didn't give Spinner his name. He named himself. When Spinner was a puppy, before he had a name, he chased his tail for amusement. He would see something out of the corner of his eye and would see his tail and the chase was on. Sometimes he would chase his tail until he fell exhausted in a heap like a drunk man. One day while he was lying beside me breathless from chasing his tail he looked up with his brown eyes and told me to call him Spinner. He said he had great fun spinning around and chasing his tail. From that day, I called him Spinner."

"My dear Walela, Spinner told me his name. When our new puppy is ready he will tell me his name. It's important to allow dogs time to find their own name. They're just like people. They need time to learn who they are. This puppy doesn't know his name, but he will learn when the time is right. Sometimes I think animals are wiser than we are. I can tell our new puppy is already thinking about what he wants to be called. Dogs know very well their name is important and not to be chosen lightly. I don't know how long it will be before he knows his name, but he will tell me in due time. We must be patient."

"I guess I'll just have to call him dog until he tells you his name," I said, and we both laughed.

Edudu knows many things. Sometimes I think edudu is being humorous but other times I have suspected he really can talk to animals. People say he is wise above other men. Everyone comes to elisi's porch to hear him talk and listen to his stories. Perhaps he will teach me to talk to animals. I would love to talk to the animals and birds and write their stories. I shall do that one day. I wonder if edudu can talk to fish?

12 February 1829

I love working on the Phoenix with Mr. Boudinott. I like everything about working on our newspaper. I don't mind the long hours, the ink or the tedious proofreading. I learn something new every day from Mr. Boudinott. We published the paper yesterday and the following article disturbed everyone. Can we defend ourselves if our only weapons are paper, ink, words and paragraphs?

The Southern writes about the bill in the House of Representatives of Georgia providing for the extension of Georgia law over our territory.

Copied from the *Phoenix* - 11 February 1829 - page 1

"They are not citizens…They are not the owners of the land they occupy. They cannot be subject to the tax law, to the militia law, or to all the civil laws…the federal government can never induce them to relinquish their present possessions, and that the immediate use of coercive measures alone can possibly prevent the total extinction of the Cherokee, who are constantly pressed on all sides by a constantly increasing white population. We have a large black population, who consider the Indians very little better in point of independence to the whites and as the Indians associate more freely with the blacks…more freely than with the whites…the discontent and envy of the former will be greatly increased. They must be driven from the soil from which they have an inherent attachment, and driven at the point of the sword and bayonet; for they have no right or title to their present homes...The plan is one that might easily be carried into execution by a few divisions of the Georgia militia."

It is clear the English immigrants believe we should be driven from our land by the sword and bayonet. They don't want part of our country. They want it all. We have been here for hundreds of years. They came recently yet they believe themselves the rightful owners. Whites have a strange sense of right and wrong.

14 February 1829

As I came home this unusually warm winter afternoon from the Phoenix, I found edudu sitting on the porch whittling centers for our pine baskets. Oak shavings covered the porch and the ground in front of the porch. His new puppy, curled up beside him, was watching me carefully as I approached.

"Edudu, how are you and dog this lovely winter's afternoon? Have you had a good day?"

"You mustn't offend puppy by calling him dog. You must call him by his name."

"When did you give him his name, edudu?"

"My dear Walela, you don't listen well to be such an intelligent woman. I didn't name him. Dogs find their own name. He found his today and it is the grandest name for a dog I have ever heard—maybe in the whole Cherokee Nation. It was well chosen. He told me today his name is Eagle Killer. Isn't that a splendid name?"

At that moment puppy proudly sat up beside edudu as if he understood us. I was sure puppy smiled at me. As we both looked at him, he barked three times. I had a strange sense that he already understands Cherokee.

"A pleasure to meet you, Eagle Killer. Did you choose your name today?" I asked.

When I said that, he looked up at me and once again barked three times affirming he did exactly as edudu explained.

Edudu and I laughed together. Eagle Killer jumped up on edudu's lap and barked again joining our merriment.

"I have seen he is already a guard dog and loyal. Tell me how he found his name, edudu."

Edudu continued to gently whittle the small piece of oak he was working on for our pine baskets. I could smell the earthy perfume of the living wood as the white shavings fell.

After a long pause, he spoke.

"This morning, Walela, after you went to the newspaper, we went to round up the hogs and check on the piglets and shoats. I wanted to bring them back closer to the house and feed them here. I want to get them used to being close so they won't wander too far away rooting for food. Puppy came with me. I wanted the two farrowed sows closer to home, too."

"I carried only my walking stick. I should have taken my gun. We were deep in the forest searching for our pigs when we came to a clearing and surprised a passel of wild hogs. A grizzled, ugly old boar with long yellow tushes and mean little pig eyes came charging straight for me across the clearing. Before I could run, puppy jumped between me and the hairy old boar and stood his ground growling and snarling. The hair on puppy's neck was standing. The boar looked at puppy with his little nasty pig eyes and stopped.

Puppy, even though he was much smaller than the boar, wasn't afraid. The boar's tushes could rip open big animals but puppy didn't run. Before I had time to think, puppy growled again and attacked like lightening. Puppy sank his needle-sharp little teeth into the boars back leg just above the hock and held on for dear life. I was proud of him, but I knew the boar would turn and attempt to slash puppy. In great pain, the old boar spun, jumped and kicked trying to free himself from the iron grip of the brave little dog's jaws. Finally, old boar shook puppy loose. Puppy sailed across the clearing. The old boar had enough of puppy's sharp teeth. The old pig retreated as fast as he could into the underbrush. Puppy jumped to his feet and chased fearlessly. Puppy stopped at the edge of the clearing, growling and barking loudly, proclaiming total victory. Puppy told everyone in the forest what a coward the boar was for running from a puppy. Puppy said he would give that ugly boar more of the same if he were foolish enough to come back."

I laughed until tears were running down my cheeks. I could see every moment of the confrontation. The little dog was indeed brave. Puppy barked, confirming the truth of the story I had just heard. He is a very smart little dog.

"Walela, when dog saw the boar was gone and wouldn't return, he turned to walk back to me from the far edge of the clearing. High overhead a pair of bald eagles were circling in the blue sky gliding in big circles looking for a lazy rabbit for their dinner. Dog looked up. When he saw the two beautiful eagles far above his head he sat on his hind legs and growled at the eagles— jumping, barking and threatening. He warned the eagles to stay away or he would do to them what he did to the boar. They must leave his master alone. He tried to jump and fly like the eagles. He barked so loudly I think the eagles heard him because they flew away and never returned."

As edudu told his story, I watched the puppy watching us and listening. I looked at the little dog's intelligent eyes going back and forth between edudu and me. I wondered if edudu really did have the ability to awaken in an animal such intelligence as he described. I think perhaps he does.

Edudu continued, "After the eagles flew away, puppy strode proudly to my side, head held high. He sat down beside me, looked up and told me he wasn't afraid of anything that walked, ran or flew. He told me I would always be safe with him at my side and I should never be afraid of wild hogs or anything that flies in the air. He told me his name was Eagle Killer and that he wasn't afraid of anything—even eagles. I told him it was a good name. It is a good name, don't you think, Walela?"

"Perhaps you're right, edudu. Perhaps your dog can talk and you can hear him. Eagle Killer is a remarkable name, I must say. It is the most impressive

440

name for a dog I have ever heard. I don't think we need worry from this day forward. Eagle Killer will protect us from all harm. As I petted Eagle Killer, he licked my fingers. I listened. His voice was quiet and soft but I'm sure I heard him say, 'Thank you, Walela, I like your name, too'."

22 March 1829

Andrew Jackson has been sworn in as the President of the United States. What kind of president will he be towards the Cherokee? Edudu and his friends don't think he will be good for us. I wonder. Is the old fox rejoicing because he has been put in charge of the chicken coop?

Copied from the *Georgia Journal* – 16 March 1829 – page 2

From Andrew Jackson's Inaugural speech delivered in Washington City - 4 March 1829.

"...It will be my sincere and constant desire, to observe towards Indian tribes within our limits, a just and liberal policy; and to give the humane and considerate attention to their rights and their wants, which are consistent with the habits of our government, and the feelings of our people."

28 September 1829

I wonder if this will amount to anything? I wonder what will happen if gold is discovered on Cherokee land? What will the whites do then?

Copied from the *Georgia Journal* – 1 August 1829 – page 3

"GOLD.—A gentleman of the first respectability in Habersham county, writes us thus, under date 22d July: 'Two gold mines have just been discovered in this county, and preparations are making to bring these hidden treasures of the earth into use.'

So it appears, that what we long anticipated has come to pass at last, namely, that the gold region of North and South Carolina, would be found, to extend into Georgia."

12 October 1829

My Dearest Cassie,

Rumors are flying in Milledgeville. Georgia is infuriated by your constitution, but the rumors of gold found in Cherokee Country is worse news, if possible. If white men love anything more than land, it is gold. They love gold more than their soul. The word from the Governor's office is that all Cherokee land where gold has been discovered will be immediately seized irrespective of past treaties. All who do not abandon their land and assets will be imprisoned for four years at hard labor. In addition, Georgia is forming a special militia unit, called the Georgia Guard, to assist their regular militia in enforcing Georgia law in the gold areas.

Every Cherokee family is to be evicted—no exceptions. Every Cherokee farm will be confiscated—no exception. All past treaties will be ignored as if they never existed. You have no avenue for appeal. No matter what government agents have promised, they will permit the seizure of your land. Please communicate this to your grandfather and all his friends. I am not sure what this knowledge will do to help but perhaps it may alleviate some suffering. Appeals to Washington City will be fruitless. The Militia and the new Georgia Guard will turn all Cherokee residents out of their homes. All who stay and attempt to work their own land will be imprisoned. I am so sorry to bring this news.

I cannot wait to see you once again. I am working hard and have so much to tell you in person. Pen and ink are much too impersonal for all that I have learned and desire to share with you.

Loving you always, Ben xoxo

20 December 1829

Mr. Lowry shared another disturbing letter he received from Ben. I cannot believe what I read. We have more cruel news.

My Dear Father,

I enclose an article from the *Athenian*—27 October 1829. I am disturbed—deeply disturbed. Our greatest fears are realized. We have known Andrew Jackson supports Georgia in the removal, but that isn't the worst. Mr. Jackson has given permission to Georgia to prevent white men from assisting the Cherokee. Unbelievably, that permission seems to include missionaries. Apparently, God himself isn't safe from Jackson. Missionary societies have little political power, but they write newspaper articles on behalf of the Cherokee and they are educated. Georgia wants to remove all white benevolent eyewitnesses from Cherokee Country. Take care, Father. Do nothing foolish and do not resist if questioned by the militia. They are a law unto themselves. I do not think you and Mother are in imminent danger, but take no chances, Father.

The new Secretary of War, John Eaton, is a firebrand. He is one of Jackson's most ambitious cabinet members from Jackson's home state of Tennessee. We know what the Tennesseans did to the Cherokee and Choctaw in Tennessee, the Creek in Alabama and the Seminoles in Florida. All I can do is warn you. Beware of the Georgia Militia. They will be the Governor's tool for enforcement. It is rumored Georgia is forming a new police force called the Georgia Guard whose sole task will be to enforce Georgia law within Cherokee Country.

I feel helpless. I wish I could do more. I shall be home for Christmas. I will do my best to arrive on Christmas eve, but I must leave the day after to resume my duties.

I wish a Merry Christmas to my loving parents. Give my warmest felicitations to Cassie.

Always, your adoring son, Ben, xoxo

22 December 1829

Ben's letter disturbed me terribly. I see the sadness in the eyes of my people when we discuss these matters. Each year our sun sheds less light—one day we will live in total darkness. Since gold was discovered, the rush by whites to occupy our land has increased. I regularly hear of whites with no regard for our legal boundaries. Men come from every state and even foreign countries to search for gold under Cherokee land. Ben believes the Georgia government itself is greedy for gold and will soon move against us.

Ben and Zach are right. Money motivates. Easy money highly motivates. We are not citizens of the commonwealth of Georgia and they make no attempt to protect us. Most Cherokee families have already fled their farms in the gold mine area. The Cherokee who lived there have had everything taken from them.

I watch elisi as she prepares our meals, sits spinning or making pine baskets or tending her crops. I wonder what will be her future? What will become of my brother and me. What will become of edudu? Will we be taken to western lands against our will? Sometimes I cry at night when no one sees.

Gold towns grow and we are dispossessed. Whites love our hills and valleys. They love the sound of our whippoorwill in the cool of the pleasant summer's evening as they sit with their families enjoying our soft warm nights. Perhaps one day it will be only white ears that hear the whippoorwill and the hoot owl, and the only stories told by the fireside will be white stories by white storytellers to white children. Perhaps only white children will marvel at the antics of the river otters.

24 December 1829

It is official. All Cherokee land in the gold counties has been confiscated and ordered distributed by lottery to whites. Henry Clay was right, 'If the Cherokee disappeared, the world would not notice.' Whites will never notice our absence. They can't wait to forget us.

The Georgia legislature has passed laws requiring all Cherokee to vacate the new counties. Ben says when Georgia has finished their seizure of the gold lands, they will then turn their attention to our homeland in the mountains. I hope he is wrong. Surely he is wrong. Whites cannot be that cruel. Surely our Chief can preserve a remnant of our country.

On 3 December 1828, the Georgia legislature extended Georgia law into all Cherokee lands and created new counties. Gold, no matter where it is found, is for whites only. We are forbidden to mine our own land. All mineral rights belong to whites. Many of us have been sentenced to four years at hard labor for looking for gold on our own land.

25 December 1829

The following is an excerpt from a bill that passed the Georgia Legislature on 19 December 1829 to go into effect 1 June 1830. The whites have given themselves a generous Christmas gift.

> "...be it further enacted, That all the laws, both civil and criminal of this state, be...extended over said portions of territory respectively, and all persons shall, after the first day of June next, be subject and liable to the operation of said laws ...And be it further enacted, That after the first day of June next, all laws, ordinances, orders and regulations of any kind whatever, made, passed or enacted by the Cherokee Indians, either in general council or in any other way whatever,...are hereby declared to be null and void and of no effect, as if the same had never existed..."

I watch elisi knit. When she makes a mistake, she will undo row upon row of knitting with one tug on the yarn. The offending stitches suddenly lie in an unruly pile on the floor at her feet. One day we Cherokee will be undone.

With one big pull by the whites upon the fabric of our nation, we shall unravel in one horrible episode to be forever discarded. We shall be no more.

Chapter XXXIX

1829 – Cassie's Story

Chapter 39

4 January 1829

"Mr. Lowry, I wrote a little story. I would like for you and Mrs. Lowry to read it and tell me what you think?"

"I would love to read it, Cassie. What's it about?"

"It's an allegory with animal characters. I got the idea from Hans Christian Anderson but mostly from edudu."

"Bring it over this afternoon and share our evening meal. Is it too long to read while you're there? Do you need to leave it?"

"No, sir. It's not a long story. I can read it if you want."

"I'll be looking forward to this afternoon. We've known for a long time you're a writer. I'm sure your story will be splendid."

When I arrived Mrs. Lowry met me at the door with a big hug.

"Come in, Cassie. It's cold. After dinner we'll settle by the fire with a nice cup of tea and you can read your story for us. Come on in."

I agreed. We had a lovely meal. I helped Mrs. Lowry clear the table and we washed up. Mr. Lowry stoked the fire, threw on some wood and pulled up the chairs. Mrs. Lowry served our tea. I was excited and eager.

"Eleanor and I can't wait to hear your story," Mr. Lowry said. "We're quite eager. Is there a preface? We're dying of curiosity."

"I got my idea from edudu. Sometimes he sits for hours whittling with his dog by his side. Sometimes they'll sit quietly. Other times I pass and hear edudu talking to Eagle Killer as if he were a person. I related edudu's stories about talking animals to what is happening in Cherokee Country. One night I couldn't sleep. I began thinking about edudu and his dog and this story came to me. I began writing the story in my mind as I lay in my bed, but I was so excited I got up and wrote it down by firelight. I was afraid I would forget it the way I forget a dream in the morning."

"Well done, Cassie. That very thing happens often when I'm thinking of new homilies. At the most unexpected moment during my repose I'll have an idea. I always leave a pen and paper out for just such a moment. I suppose when we allow our minds to rest we do our most creative thinking. I'm sure your story is wonderful. Eleanor and I are all ears."

"I'll read and when I'm finished, I want to know what you think," I requested. "Please don't tell me it's a good story if you do not truly think so."

An Afternoon with Bentley

"Bentley is my long-time rabbit friend. He lives on the other side of the creek bottom under the ridge by the big red wash just a short walk up from the lake. His warren isn't far from the big muskeedine vines. He is the finest story teller I ever heard, except for edudu. I suppose everything I ever learned about telling stories I learned from those two. I'm sad to confess I've forgotten many of Bentley's stories. Over the years he told me dozens of vignettes of animal life in the forest and humorous stories about himself and his relatives. I can't tell you how many wonderful afternoons we spent together. Most of that time Bentley was telling stories. We would like side by side on a bed of soft pine needles and he would tell his stories and I would laugh till my sides hurt. Bentley told me rabbits have a lot of relatives and thus have a lot of stories. He told me that rabbits like to talk and gossip, especially at family get togethers, but it's always good gossip. Brown rabbits are almost never malicious."

"I should have recorded Bentley's stories years ago, but most of the time when he and I were storytelling, I was laughing so hard I could not have held my pen. My advice is, if you hear memorable stories from your friends, you should write them down as soon as you can in order to remember them later. I never thought I would have so much trouble remembering things."

"Bentley said his mother wrote stories and taught him to write. Bentley said that his mother wrote many stories worthy for publication but she had great difficulty getting her manuscripts accepted. Bentley said not having an opposing thumb makes holding a pen difficult, so rabbits don't copy many books by hand. He said his father and his uncle invented a little device that would hold a pen, much like the way a human holds a pen, and would make writing much easier for rabbits but that's another story and we'll talk about their invention another time."

"I remember one particular story Bentley told me that was especially poignant. The day he told me I wrote it down immediately when I got home. He and I have gone over my manuscript quite a few times making sure it's accurate and that I didn't leave out any important points of history. I'm pretty much telling you the story exactly as he told me. He said he heard this story many times as a young rabbit and, as you know, rabbits have almost as good a memory as elephants. If you look at an elephant's feet you will understand why they have developed a good memory. Elephants don't have fingers. They can't write anything using their feet like we can with our hands."

"Elephants can write very well with their trunks, but I've heard it's nearly impossible for elephants to find a pen big enough to fit their trunk or afford oversized paper to write on. Therefore, they developed a tremendous mnemonic system. Nowadays, I am told, some of the more educated elephants dictate stories to friends who help them get their writings published. You've probably seen their latest work at the booksellers."

"Bentley told me this was a true story and was important brown rabbit history. He said this story was told at every important rabbit get-together. He said the big white rabbits have forgotten this story and never tell it to their little white rabbits. He said only the little brown rabbits, like Bentley and his family, remember this story and keep it alive."

"The following is Bentley's story and pretty much in his own words."

Little Bentley begged, "Papa, tell me the story of the days when the wild brown rabbits lived in paradise on the other side of the Tall Mountain by the Big Waters. Tell me, tell me, tell me please. Tell me that story again. I want to hear that story."

"My dear little bunny," his papa answered, "I'll gladly tell you that story. It's an old story. Life is hard here on the cold side of the Tall Mountain. We brown rabbits work long and hard for food and shelter. This is an unkind land and we don't have much time for recreation. We have little time for story-telling, but it wasn't always so. I will tell you the story, my dear bunny.

For ages upon ages we brown rabbits lived in a paradise like no other on the other side of the tall mountains. Our paradise is now only a memory—a distant memory—old and tired. It's an old story told by old rabbits around a campfire."

"Papa, why did we come to this side of the Tall Mountain? Why did we leave our paradise? Why didn't we stay in our beautiful land?"

"Oh, my sweet little bunny," his Papa said. "Because today is your birthday, I'll tell you the story of that journey and how it is we came to be here on the cold side. It's a story you should hear. I'll tell you of the good days when we brown rabbits lived in a land of plenty in timeless harmony and perfect balance in the land given to us by the Great Rabbit Spirit. Listen well. Every word is true. When I am gone I want you to tell this story to your little bunnies. This is the story I heard from your great-grandfather and he heard from his grandfather."

"On the other side, the grand days of brown rabbit glory continued year upon year—every year better than the last. Every old rabbit I've ever talked to can only recall hearing stories about the good times we brown rabbits had there. Families had all they needed and were happy. We were created to live in that land. We had feasts and holidays when all the brown rabbits would gather with their families. There were aunts, uncles, cousins, grandfathers and grandmothers—so many rabbits, young and old, would come together for our festivals they couldn't be counted. We had wonderful happy reunions at our celebrations. Our delightful rabbit dances, filled with laughter, lasted long into the night. There were piles of fresh clover for everyone and delightful clover cakes and the most delicious drinks. We had the happiest times when our nation was on the other side."

"On the other side of the Tall Mountain by the Big Waters lies the peaceful land—the fruitful land. It continues today a wonderful paradise of fertile lands, endless meadows, wide rivers and rich forests. The only difference is we don't live there. Our land was taken from us.

When we lived there, we had numberless hills and valleys for our warrens. Young rabbits lovers could marry, make a cozy fur-lined warren and raise their family just about anywhere. We were cool in the summer and warm in the winter. We were never hungry. Those were joyous times with thousands of our villages to the north, south, east and west in our wonderland, but things change, Bentley, things change. We don't live there now. Someone else lives in our wonderland."

"What happened, papa? Why did we leave? Why did we come out here where it is so cold and we are hungry all the time? I don't understand? Why did we come across the big mountain and leave our paradise? Who lives in our happy land? Why don't we live there now?"

"I shall tell you how we came across the big mountain and left our land of plenty," Papa said. "This is what happened. The big white rabbits who lived on the other side of the Big Waters learned how to make big boats and they sailed to our shores. We brown rabbits have always been a friendly folk and we welcomed the big white rabbits when they came. The white rabbits marveled at the richness of our land. They asked if they could trade with us. We agreed. They asked if they could tie their big boats to our shore and stay a while. We agreed. They asked if they could build dwellings while they traded. We agreed. They asked if they could bring more relatives, friends, wives and children and build more dwellings while they traded. We agreed. We have always been generous. We like all rabbits no matter what the color of their fur."

"One day, my little one, the big white rabbits told us they were never leaving. They told us the Great One had given them this land. Our land would become the land of the great white rabbits. They liked our land so much they wanted our paradise to be their own. They said they would never go back to their own land.

We didn't understand, but it was too late to stop them. They brought white soldiers and powerful weapons. They brought more and more white rabbits and built multitudes of white rabbit towns. The white rabbits love to build. When they brought their wives and children and built the big towns, we realized they didn't like brown rabbits. No matter what they said, they didn't like us."

"They didn't like our children. They didn't want our brown rabbit sons to marry their white rabbit daughters. They didn't want their bunnies playing with our bunnies. If a brown rabbit married a white rabbit the white rabbits called their little bunnies half-breeds and mongrels. The white rabbits would taunt the children singing, 'half-breed from bad seed, half-breed from bad seed'. Only pure white rabbits had privileges. Only pure white rabbits were protected by rabbit law. The white rabbits were powerful, numerous and hated us. They built town after town beside the Big Waters and forced us to move west."

"We had no choice but to obey. We were too few to fight so we moved away from the Big Waters we loved. The big white rabbits multiplied and took more of our wonderland. Each time they made us move they would promise they would never take more of our land. They always broke their promise. They broke promise after promise. They pushed us farther and farther from the sea until our backs were against the tall mountains. We had nowhere left to go. We realized they would take all of our land, not just part of it. We learned too late we could not trust the promises of the Big White Rabbits."

"When we first saw their big ships, my little bunny, we didn't know they would bring disease, greed and death. We didn't know they would take everything and leave us nothing. The white rabbits worked hard but were never happy. They wanted more. They always wanted more. They wanted our clover fields, they wanted our forests, they wanted our warrens and our villages—all of our villages. They made us go farther and farther and farther—always farther. The big white rabbits were in a rush to acquire more. They must have come from a dark land of selfishness and sorrow."

"The white rabbits formed big villages, lived by a law they brought with them and called themselves civilized. Their law excluded all us brown rabbits. We had been foolish to welcome them."

The smiles Mr. and Mrs. Lowry wore as I began had faded.

"The big white rabbits didn't like us," Papa continued, "and strangely they didn't like each other. We learned they had fought big rabbit wars on the other side of the Great Waters before they got here. Then they fought each other after they arrived. White rabbits love war. They killed one another with dangerous weapons they invented. They told us we didn't know the rules of life or war. They said we were inferior and wild. We finally understood they hated the color brown."

"We brown rabbits were powerless. In their greed they broke all agreements. In their hearts they wanted everything. Their leader in those days, Big White Jack, told us the white rabbits had passed new laws. According to white law we no longer owned our land. If we didn't leave we would be removed. We would be criminals if we stayed. We didn't understand. White Jack told us things change. He said we weren't civilized. The white rabbits said we were lazy. Losing our land was our own fault, they told us, because we didn't want to become white rabbits."

"White Jack told us he would deport every wild brown rabbit over the Tall Mountains for our own good. Then the white rabbits could own all of our paradise—every valley, every river and every meadow. He said removing us was for our protection. I suppose that is what they meant by being civilized—they were more powerful. They believed us to be an inferior race of rabbits."

"Some little brown rabbits in a group of villages in the south decided to fight to stay on their land. Big White Jack and his army came and completely destroyed the wild brown rabbits who wanted to stay. Rabbit bodies were burned or left to rot. Some floated down the river after they cut off their ears to count the dead. I'm sorry to have to tell you this story. After the war against the brown rabbits, signs were put up on all the big trees, 'White rabbits only allowed here'."

"After this, my sweet little bunny, the Big White Rabbits sent soldiers and forced us over the Tall Mountains to the terrible cold land where we live. They told us they were giving us land equal to our magical land, but all they gave us was land they didn't want."

"To this day the white civilized rabbits think our fruitful land is theirs by right. They never tell this story to their little rabbits. They don't believe they did anything wrong. They celebrate the day when the first White Rabbit ship landed and claimed our land for White Rabbit nations. Their little white rabbits must believe when the first white rabbit ships arrived they found an empty land waiting for white rabbit occupants. They must believe we didn't exist."

"But that isn't the only bad thing that happened in our old land by the Big Waters. Big White Rabbits captured black rabbits from a distant land. They forced them to work for no wages. They bought and sold black rabbits among themselves because they didn't want to do the hard work themselves. I think it was the white rabbits who were lazy. What a terrible thing to see. Sometimes a brave black rabbit would escape and live with us. We never judge a rabbit by his mother and father or the color of his fur. The white rabbit soldiers would come looking for runaway black rabbits and take them back to their masters."

"That is the story of the Big White Rabbits who came across the Great Water. We welcomed them but they became powerful and removed us wild brown rabbits and enslaved the black rabbits."

"I heard this story from Bentley with my own ears one day when we were lounging under the pines listening to the wind in the tree tops. Bentley said he heard this story from his father who heard it from his father who heard it from his father, and this is exactly what happened in Rabbit land on the other side of the Tall Mountains. I showed this story to Bentley after I wrote it down and he said I had listened well and this was pretty much correct and that I should let others read it and even publish it if I wanted. I told him I thought it was a sad story. I asked if he was sure he wanted others to hear such sadness. He answered yes. He said there were some things that shouldn't be forgotten even if they were sad. He said if he remembered anything else he would tell me later and I could add it to the story. He said it was important to remember how the white rabbits came to live in the Brown Rabbit Paradise and how the brown rabbits came to be in the Cold Land on the other side of the Tall Mountains. The End."

When I finished reading I looked up. Mr. and Mrs. Lowry had tears in their eyes and said not a word. Together they gave me a big hug and thanked me for my story and said we would talk about it another time when they weren't feeling so emotional. They said I did a marvelous thing and I should write more stories. They said it was a remarkable story and I should have it published.

Chapter XL

1830 – Indian Removal Act - Edudu Goes Fishing

Chapter 40

10 January 1830 - Month of the Cold Moon - Du no lv ta ni

No sign of Ben. I was hoping to see him on his birthday. I know he's busy. I hope he visits soon.

15 January 1830

Newspapers haunt my dreams. Georgia, fearing a slave rebellion, passed a law that any free man of color who comes to Georgia by ship must stay in quarantine for forty days. The quarantined man is forbidden to talk to or give written material to another under penalty of death. How could it be a death sentence to give someone a book? Whites forbid anyone to teach Africans to read. Whites don't like it that we Cherokee have a newspaper. They must know in their hearts what they are doing. They must know, don't they? How did the world get this way?

Copied from the *Georgia Journal* - 9 January 1830 – page 3

"Sec. 10 And be it further enacted, That if any slave, negro, mustizzo, or free person of color, or any other person, shall circulate, bring or cause to be circulated or brought into this state or aid or assist in any manner or be instrumental in aiding or assisting in the circulation or bringing into this State, or in any manner concerned in any written or printed pamphlet, paper, or circular, for the purpose of inciting to insurrection, conspiracy or resistance among the slaves, negros, or free persons of colour, of this state, against their owners or citizens of this state, the said person or persons offending against this section of this act, shall be punished with death."

Reading, writing and learning are pleasures. There are untold thousands of African children prohibited by law from learning. How can whites deny children the pleasure of reading stories—of reading Hans Christian Anderson and nursery rhymes? Whites would punish me for teaching a slave to read and write. I would do it anyway. I would.

"Sec 11. And be it further enacted, That if any slave, negro or free person of colour or any white person shall teach any other

453

slave, negro or free person of color, to read or to write either, written or printed characters, the said free person, of color, or slave, shall be punished by fine or whipping at the discretion of the court; and if a white person so offending, he, she or they, shall be punished with fine, not exceeding five hundred dollars, and imprisonment, in the common jail at the discretion of the court before whom said offender is tried.

WARREN JOURDAN, Speaker of the House of Representatives, THOMAS STOCKS, President of the Senate. Assented to Nov. 22, 1829. GEORGE R. GILMER, Governor.

18 January 1830

It's been unusually warm, but winter has finally come. It has been quite cold the last couple of days.

19 January 1830

Copied from the Macon Telegraph – 16 January 1830 – page 3

"Runaway or Stolen, From my plantation in Bibb county near Tobesafky, on the tenth inst. Four negros, one a negro man about 25 years of age, inclined to be chunky built of a low voice, about 5 feet 8 or 10 inches high; one by the name of Fed, and one a woman Angelina about 18 years of age, tolerable tall and walks lame, Two children one a girl named Dorcas, the other a boy, by the name Bomon about 15 months old. The subscriber will reward any person for the detection of said Negros, if brought to this house or lodged or lodged in any jail so I can get them.

Jan. 14. S 4t.p   ELIJAH NEEL"

I wonder if the Africans will come through our country to escape or head to Florida? Will the Georgia slave patrols catch them?

21 January 1830

As usual Elisi and edudu wanted me to read from the Phoenix. They want to practice pronouncing the Cherokee characters. They improve with each reading. If we had had our syllabary fifty years ago, our entire nation would be literate. I am proud. Edudu asked me to read the following article. He laughed and laughed each time I read. He asked me to read it again and again. We understand the Creeks.

Copied from the *Phoenix* - 20 January 1830 – page 2

"THE INDIAN AND THE WHITE MAN, When Gen. Lincoln went to make peace with the Creek Indians, one of the chiefs

454

asked him to sit down on a log. He did so. The chief then asked him to move, and in a few moments to move farther; the request was repeated till the General got to the end of the log; but the chief still said, "Move farther;" to which the General replied, "I can move no farther."

"Just so it is with us," said the chief; "You have moved us back to the water and then asked us to move farther."

28 March 1830

Ben says Andrew Jackson's new Democratic Party wants control of the United States. Whites are impressed by his military accomplishments. He is brave and reckless in battle. They believe Mr. Jackson can be trusted because he loves to fight, especially against us. It seems all whites are bellicose. None of the tribes trust him. In white newspapers he is praised and described as an Indian fighter. We call him Indian killer. No white man has done more to terminate our national existence than Andrew Jackson.

With the new slave states, Louisiana 1812, Mississippi 1817, Alabama 1819 and Missouri 1821, Ben says Jackson can count on more support, especially in the Senate. Because of opposition from northern states, Jackson needs allies in the legislature to accomplish his agenda.

30 March 1830

Andrew Jackson asked Ben to vote with his party. In return Jackson will support Ben. Ben is in a moral dilemma. He must sail between Scylla and Charybdis. He must learn the political trick of making friends with both the fox and the chicken.

He must not be seen in public with me in Milledgeville, but that doesn't trouble me. Ben has a plan to help us and he must not needlessly offend. If it were known I was his fiancée, his career would be ruined. I am patient. One day Ben and I will marry. Good things will come. We were born for each other. With patience, good things will come.

2 April 1830

Ben has saved for our marriage. I imagine Ben arriving in a four-horse carriage with attending servants to take me to that place where people won't call our children half-breeds. I am willing to wait. I would be just as happy if he took me away on the back of his horse. I will never love another. I am comforted that he loves me with the same devotion.

4 April 1830

Today is Sunday, Mr. Lowry's holy day. I heard him teach about Adam and Eve. They were removed from their beautiful garden home because of rebellion—never to return.

We live in the garden given to the first Cherokee man and woman, Kanati and Selu. Whites want to take our garden to replace the paradise they lost. The white civilizations of Rome and Western Europe, like mosquitoes in summertime, live off the lifeblood of weaker cultures. Now they have come here to take everything we have or will have.

I am weary of being told I'm meaningless, fit only for vanishment.

8 June 1830

Huff's Boarding House - 4 June 1830

My Dearest Cassie,

The news from Washington City is the worst possible. The Indian Removal Bill has passed. It will be celebrated by whites in all states and territories where Indian populations occupy land. The law legalizes the removal of all Indians.

On 28 May 1830 the Indian Removal Act was signed into law by President Jackson.

I suspect the bill was written to please politicians in Georgia, North Carolina, Tennessee, Alabama, Florida, Mississippi and in the new western territories. This bill licenses the government to forcibly remove entire Indian populations—lock, stock and barrel. With this law the deportation of Indian nations is legal and thus no longer offend the white conscience. When their nefarious plans will be accomplished, I have no idea. We can be certain the general government will not oppose any state's removal policy, especially that of Georgia.

I suspect the immediate result of the passage of this law for the Cherokee will be an instantaneous flood of squatters and ne'er-do-wells into Cherokee Country who know their seizure of Cherokee land and assets will not be punished by any white government or court.

The flood waters have been released. I fear before long the Cherokee will be washed away by a cascade of angry white foam. Take great care in your travels, my dear. Be circumspect of all strange white men. Avoid them. I also anticipate an immediate increase in the malicious activity of the militia. Please warn your grandfather.

Perhaps, my dear Cassie, cooler heads shall prevail and the outcome of this disastrous legislation will not be as bad as we fear. I shall do all I am able. I shall visit as soon as I can get away and share everything in detail then.

Until we meet again, I'm always yours, Ben, xoxo

Edudu was sitting quietly in his favorite chair whittling basket centers. Eagle Killer was at his side.

"What have you been doing today, edudu?"

"Not much, Walela. I helped your elisi out back and in the smoke house. I brought water from the spring. Since then Eagle Killer and I have been whittling. Eagle Killer hasn't stopped talking all afternoon. I whittle and think about what Eagle Killer says. When he stops talking I tell him what I think. It's a good day. We have had a good conversation. What have you been doing?"

"I went to school in the morning. I worked at the Phoenix this afternoon. I brought newspapers and I have a letter from Ben. It's about the Indian Removal Act the whites have passed in Washington City. It's not good news, edudu. It's not good news at all. Do you want to hear what Ben has to say about the new laws on the whiteside concerning Indians?"

Edudu paused with the wood in one hand and his knife in the other. He looked at Eagle Killer.

"What shall we do, Killer? Shall we stay here and listen to Walela's bad news or shall I get my gun and see if we can find a squirrel or maybe a fat turkey or would you rather go fishing? What do you want to do, Killer—stay here and listen to Walela or go hunting or fishing?"

Eagle Killer sat up in front of edudu and barked three times. He barked again.

Edudu stood, put his knife away and put the wood he was whittling on his shelf against the wall behind his chair.

"Killer doesn't want to listen to bad news today. Neither do I. I love you dearly, Walela—more than life itself. You read and write in your journal. Read the white newspapers if you want to. Read the Phoenix. Killer wants to go fishing. We shall bring home supper. I don't want to hear more bad things today. I've heard enough bad news lately. Would you like to come with us? I think, my dear Walela, you need to get away from this bad news as much as I do. You read too much. Let's go down to the river and cleanse our mind."

457

"I think that is a wonderful idea, edudu. I shall go fishing with you and Eagle Killer. You have told me how good a fisherman he is, so I shall see. Let's go fishing."

"Yes, my dear. Let's go fishing and forget all this bad news."

Edudu got his gun from above the fireplace and his special leather bag he carries fishing. I carried our basket for the fish and we began the lovely walk down towards the river. It was a beautiful warm day. With the long afternoons of early-summer, we should have plenty of daylight to fish and be home before dark. Edudu told elisi he was hungry for corn dumplings with ramps with our fish. They're my favorite, too. I was already hungry. I don't think anything is quite so tasty as a beautiful piece of fried fish that was swimming in the river about an hour ago.

"Edudu, where is your fishing pole? I thought you said we were going fishing? Are you going to shoot the fish with your gun?"

We both laughed.

"Walela, you're silly. You can't shoot fish. I'm going to talk to the fish. I'll tell the fish to let Killer catch them. You'll see that Killer is a good fisherman. He always catches three fish before he rests. I think if Killer catches about nine fish today, that should be plenty for us and for breakfast, don't you think?"

I continued to ponder the news in Ben's letter as we walked along. As we made our way on well-worn paths to the river, we were surrounded by the glorious summer landscape. I felt a peace flow over me as the living forest embraced us in its loving arms. I am afraid for edudu and elisi. Their souls are bound to this land. Severing the cord that binds them to this beautiful land will simultaneously sever them from life.

I love edudu's closeness to the animals and birds and how he understands our world. When I was a girl, I should have asked edudu to teach me to talk to the animals. I would love to write more stories about animals and perhaps another story about Bentley. I knew edudu talked to Killer and the animals, but I was not aware he could also talk to fish.

"Where are we going, edudu? Where are we going to fish today?"

"I always allow Killer to decide where we fish, Walela."

"You're going to let Killer decide where we fish?"

"Yes," edudu answered, "he's a much better fisherman than I am. He knows all about fish and their habits. Eagle Killer will find the right spot. He knows about hunting, but he didn't want to go hunting today. I think maybe he likes to be in the water when it's warm. He knows where the fish are easy to catch. He likes a nice piece of fried fish and corn dumplings as well as you and I do."

When we got to the river edudu walked slowly downstream following Killer. Eagle Killer stopped at a little cove where someone had built a weir of sticks and stones across the mouth of the little creek not far from where it joined the river.

"Here we are, Walela. Killer says this is the best place today for us to catch all the fish we want."

I could tell Eagle Killer was excited. He was wagging his tale and running back and forth beside the creekbank very near the water. Sometimes he would pause and stare down into the depths and then run back and sit in front of edudu and bark.

"I'm going to close the door to the river and then spread this magic powder over the water, Walela. When I spread this magic powder I have in my bag it will allow me to call to the fish in their language. I'll tell them to swim over to Killer. They'll obey me and jump right into his mouth. With this magic they become obedient fish. In a short time all the fat fish we want will be in our basket."

I laughed out loud.

"Edudu, are you telling me you're going to let Killer catch the fish all by himself? We're not going to use a pole or a net?"

"Yes, Killer will catch them all."

"How can a dog catch fish in the river?" I asked incredulously.

"Walela, it's magical, didn't I tell you? I sprinkle the powder on the water and the fish are under my spell. I talk and they listen. Watch this."

Edudu took some sticks and waded to the middle of the stream where the water was trickling over the crude barricade of stones. He closed the weir using the sticks and smooth stones he pulled from the shallow water. It reminded me of the times Ben and I would spend an afternoon building a dam across small creeks just for fun. Edudu waded back to the shore. From his bag he took several handfuls of a powdery substance and cast it over the still water. He sat down on a rock beside the creekbank and petted Killer, stroking his shiny coat affectionately. Killer, anxious to begin fishing, wagged his tail and barked.

"Now, Killer," edudu said, looking straight into Eagle Killer's eyes, "I want you to get us a fish. Go get us a fish."

Immediately Killer turned and walked to the creek until his front paws were submerged in the perfectly still water trapped behind the newly repaired weir. He moved cautiously to his left and right with his nose almost touching the surface. Suddenly, Eagle Killer dove head first into the creek. When he came up he had a big fish in his mouth. He brought the fat fish back to edudu and dropped it at his feet. The proud dog sat up in front of edudu as pretty as you please.

"See what I told you, Walela. Killer is a great fishing dog. He's probably the best fishing dog I've ever heard about."

Edudu washed the fish in the river and put it in our basket and once again sat on his rock beside the still water. Killer sat quietly beside edudu as if waiting for further instructions.

I laughed to myself. I should have never doubted anything edudu says about talking to his dog or about animals, birds or fish.

"What are you going to do now, edudu?"

"I'll tell Killer to get us another fish. Watch."

"Now, Killer, bring me three fish. I need three fish. Bring three fish."

"How can Killer bring you three fish, edudu? How can he get three fish in his mouth?"

"Walela, you have a lot to learn. Killer will bring me three fish one at a time. Killer can count—especially fish."

Edudu leaned down and affectionately rubbed Killer's ears once again and kissed him on his wet nose.

"Killer, we need you to catch three fish for our supper tonight. Go catch three fish."

Immediately Killer barked his approval. Once again he went to the water's edge looking into the depths—his front paws in the water. He moved to his left and right slowly and carefully—his nose almost touching the surface. Suddenly he stopped, stared at one spot and dove into the water. Once again Eagle Killer surfaced with a big fish in his mouth that he brought and dropped at edudu's feet, except this time, without pause, he returned to the riverbank. In quick succession Eagle Killer caught and dropped three fish in front of edudu. When Killer dropped the third, he sat up proudly looking up at edudu, shook water over the both of us and stood patiently waiting for a word from his master.

"Walela, are you ever going to believe Killer and I talk? I told him to bring three fish and he did? Do you think that a coincidence?"

"I believe you, edudu," I said laughing. "I never doubted your words."

"Watch this," edudu said with a twinkle in his eye. "Killer, get three more fish."

The marvelous dog immediately obeyed. Killer slowly moved up and down the water's edge. In no time at all he had three more fat fish, flipping and flopping, lying in front of edudu. I couldn't help but smile. I washed them and put them in the basket.

"I think, Walela, we'll get us three more fat fish. That will be plenty for tonight and tomorrow's breakfast and enough for us to share with Killer. I just have time to get them cleaned for elisi before dark."

Eagle Killer brought Edudu three more fish. I shall never again doubt edudu and Eagle Killer talk to one another. As we headed back home to clean Killer's catch, I imagined the smell of fish frying in the pan and elisi's corn dumplings just cooked piled high on a plate.

16 June 1830

Today I read part of the law legalizing our removal. Mr. Lowry is afraid. When whites wish to do something, they make it a law. They believe if they make their desires legal, their subsequent actions are just and therefore moral.

Copied from the *Georgia Journal* – 12 June 1830 – page 3

"AN ACT To provide for an exchange of Lands with the Indians in any of the States or Territories and for their removal West of the river Mississippi.

Sec. 1. Be it enacted &c. That it shall and may be lawful for the President of the United States to cause so much of any territory belonging to the United States West of the river Mississippi, not included in any state or organized territory, and to which the Indian title has been extinguished…to be divided into a suitable number of districts for the reception of such tribes or nations of Indians as may choose to exchange the lands where they now reside, and remove there…"

"Sec. 2 And be it further enacted, That it shall and may be lawful for the President to exchange any or all of such districts…with any tribe or nation of Indians now residing within the limits of any of the States or Territories, and with which the United States have existing treaties, for the whole or any part or portion of the territory claimed and occupied by such tribe within the bounds of any one or more of the States or Territories where the land claimed and occupied by the Indians is owned by the United States, or the United States are bound to the State within which it lies, to extinguish the Indian claim thereto."

25 June 1830

Georgia's Senator Forsyth boasted in the United States Congress upon the passing of the Indian Removal Act.

Copied from the *Georgia Journal* - 19 June 1830 - page 1

"...The European doctrine of the right conferred by the discovery of new countries inhabited by barbarous tribes, was, I thought well known. The discoverer claimed the sovereignty over the discovered country, and over everything under, upon, and above it, from the center to the zenith. The lands, the streams, the woods and minerals, all living things, including the human inhabitants, were all the property of, or subject to, the government of the fortunate navigator, who by accident or design, first saw the before unknown country. Such were the doctrines of Spain, England and France. Portugal claimed under a papal bull, which conferred upon the Crown empire and domain over every country newly discovered on the globe, not possessed by Christian people. This papal title was in perfect unison with the prevailing sentiments of an age, in which the decrees of the Roman Pontiff made and dethroned kings, established and overturned empires. All Christendom seem to have imagined, that, by offering that immortal life, promised by the Prince of Peace to fallen man, to the aborigines of this country, the right was fairly acquired of disposing of their persons and their property at pleasure..."

I showed this to Mr. and Mrs. Lowry. We discussed the history of the white mindset towards lesser cultures. Whites, since the Romans, believe themselves superior and privileged above all races—a privilege determined by skin color. A concept that has continued for two millennia.

2 July 1830

Copied from the *Georgia Journal* 26 June 1830 – page 1-2
Wilson Lumpkin's speech to the House.

"...But to those remnant tribes of Indians, whose good we seek, the subject before you is of vital importance. It is a measure of life and death. Pass the bill on your table and you save them; reject it, and you leave them to perish. Reject this bill, and you thereby encourage delusory hopes in the Indians, which their professed friends and allies well know will never be realized...The bill on your table involves but little that can be considered new principle. The only departure...is to be found in that part which extends greater security and benefits to the Indians. The whole of my policy and views of legislation upon this subject have been founded in the ardent desire to better the condition of the remnant tribes...With the Choctaws and Creeks, treaties have also been made, assigning them countries west of the Arkansas and Mississippi. The Creeks have been flocking to theirs, and it is satisfactorily ascertained that they would all go, if the means contemplated in this bill were afforded to the Executive."

"The whole of the Choctaws are not only willing to go but preparing to go...The Chickasaws are anxious to emigrate...The Seminoles of Florida are also desirous to join their Creek brethren in the West...the Indians of Illinois, Ohio and Indiana have been emigrating for many years past, and the cost of their journey has been paid by the government...Our most enlightened Superintendents and Agents have all become converts to Indian emigration: our most pious and candid Missionaries have also added their testimony in our favor."

"Georgia, sir, is one of the good old thirteen states...She claims no superiority...Our social compact upon which we stand as a state gives you the metes and bounds of our sovereignty...our State authorities claim entire and complete jurisdiction over soul and population, regardless of complexion...Her boundaries are not only admitted by her sister States, but by this General Government, and every individual who administers any part of it, Executive or Legislative, must recollect that the faith of this Government has stood pledged for twenty-eight years past, to relieve Georgia from the embarrassment of Indian population...It is known to every member of congress that this was no gratuity to Georgia. No, sir, it was for and in consideration of the two entire States of Alabama and Mississippi."

Whites think edudu, elisi, Five Feathers, Chief John Ross and I are an embarrassment. They seek our removal to possess that which belongs to another, that which they have never worked for, a noble Roman virtue.

A White Killing Frost

21 July 1830

Fifty-five years ago white English immigrants declared political independence from their mother country, Great Britain. They gained liberty by force of arms. Whites love war. For hundreds of years Europe was filled with conflict as it is today. They brought their belligerent passion here. The document declaring their independence from England demonstrates how whites believe they possess the supreme privilege to rule wherever they go in all the earth. All others, like the Cherokee, Creek, Seminole and Africans count for nothing.

Copied from *The Federal Union* – 10 July 1830 – page 1

The United States Declaration of Independence from England

"When in the course of human events it becomes necessary for one people(whites) to dissolve the political bonds which have connected them with another and to assume among the powers of the earth (white powers) the separate but equal station to which the laws of nature and of nature's God entitle them: a decent respect for the opinions of mankind requires that they should declare the causes which impel them to the separation. We hold these truths to be self-evident that all men (white men) are created equal and that they are endowed by their creator with certain unalienable rights that among these are life, liberty and the pursuit of happiness (not for savages or niggers or any race with colour). That, to secure these rights, governments are instituted among men deriving their just powers from the consent of the governed that whenever any form of government becomes destructive to these ends; it is the right of the people (white people) to alter or abolish it, and to institute a new government, laying its foundation on such principles and organizing its powers in such form as to them shall seem most likely to effect the safety and happiness of white people only."

I showed this to Mr. Lowry. He cradled my journal on his lap.

"I'm very, very sorry, Cassie. I wish it wasn't so. I'm so sorry. We whites are an arrogant conceited race, aren't we?"

That's all he said. He closed my journal and handed it back. I think if he had tried to say more he may have wept. Mrs. Lowry said he sat on his porch alone staring into the trees and said nothing to anyone the rest of that day. I suppose he is right. There is nothing more to say.

6 August 1830

The newspapers have been filled with bad news this year. Ben was right. The passage of the Indian Removal Act has given great impetus to the whites to possess our land in its entirety.

Copied from *The Federal Union* - 31 July 1830

"...the president has concluded it proper to suspend the present mode of enrolling and sending off (Indian) emigrants in small parties as heretofore....those who prefer to remove will be supported by the government in their removal, free of any expense to them, and have a full, and just value paid for such improvements as they may leave, that add real value to the soil, and maintained for one year after their arrival in the west, by which time they will have prepared, by opening farms, and otherwise for the support of themselves and families...liberal terms will be extended to them, their limits beyond the Mississippi will be enlarged and all things done for their protection....This suspension of present operations is designed to afford the Cherokee an opportunity to ponder their present situation...The president is their friend. He seeks not to deceive or oppress them. He feels for them as a father for his children. If they leave it will be of their own free will. If they stay it will also be of their own free will. There will be employed no force any way, but the force of reason and parental council, unless it shall be to protect them in their removing."

We can trust white men like a chicken trusts the fox. I do not believe Andrew Jackson thinks of us as his children unless he is a mad father intent upon filicide. Bloody feathers hang from his mouth. Our life's blood stains his clothing.

The Creek war was hopeless, but I understand why they fought. Their motive to fight was to protect their families in their homeland. Their war with the whites was a disaster for the Creek Nation. I fear the Cherokee Nation will fare no better. I hear Edudu and his friends often say they wish they had killed Jackson at Horseshoe Bend instead of Creeks. Under Jackson I fear we Cherokee will fare no better than the Creek.

13 August 1830

Andrew Jackson has been working to establish an all-white culture and consolidate power in the United States Senate. There are only two Senators for each state, large or small. Andrew Jackson's plan is to control the Senate which ratifies all treaties, confirms all judicial appointments and passes all laws. All legislation goes through the Senate.

Copied from *The Federal Union* - 31 July 1830 page 3

"Mr. Wirt, late attorney general of the United States, has been employed by the headmen of the Cherokee to carry their case before the supreme court of the United States. The Cherokee claim to be a sovereign and independent nation....A more wicked and unprincipled project could not have been suggested....it is impossible for two sovereignties to exist in the same district...the sovereignty of the Cherokee could only be asserted by dividing Alabama and Georgia and establishing a new nation....which would be a flagrant violation of the constitution...if sustained, the Cherokee Nation would be viewed as equal to whites....under the pretense of sustaining the pretensions of the Cherokee to sovereignty and independence the opposition are obviously striving to overthrow the State governments and dissolve the union...."

Some days I look at the fluffy clouds passing over our beautiful country. I feel the pure air slide down off the mountains and waft across my face. In the mornings I watch edudu and elisi prepare for their day. I watch them prepare their breakfast and greet the morning sun with joy. I observe my community happily going about their chores unmolested. I hear the children's laughter. They are unaware of the flood of animosity building in the whiteside. They don't read the white newspapers. Soon, very soon, a white dam of loathing will break upon us. We shall be swept away—drowned in a flood of snowy cupidity. The innocent play of Cherokee children will never be heard in these mountains—in the garden given them by their God. Things change, Mr. Lowry says. Things change, edudu says. Things do change.

22 August 1830

The white appetite to possess is increasing. They build fences, barns and houses on our land. They want more. They are never content. The white Democratic political party has passed the law which sanctions the deportation of an innocent, peace loving, people—a people without advocate. They will wash us away to satisfy their longing for racial purity.

Mr. Lowry says white domination stems from the European Doctrine of Discovery and the doctrine of the Right of Conquest. No Indian nation has the strength to stand against white immigrants. If whites had not brought such terrible diseases, we would have the numbers to resist.

Whites want us to speak English, work farms, obey white laws, wear white clothing and abandon our customs. They insist we turn white. White politicians in Georgia consider us an uncivilized embarrassment and we are forbidden to mix with their children.

Most painful is to be named savage—an animal. Whites classify my edudu and elisi among the beasts because they choose not to be white.

26 September 1830

Copied from *The Federal Union* - 11 September 1830 – page 3

"THE CHEROKEE COUNTRY. There is no subject which more urgently imposes itself upon the serious consideration of the people of Georgia than the one with which I have headed this communication. Independent of the just right we have to it's possession, there are other reasons of great weight which demand a speedy change. The peculiar condition of the country at this time –presenting the disgusting scenes of licentiousness, riot, tumult and blood shed—endangering the peace of that portion of the state which lays contiguous to it –requires of our next legislature not only prompt but the most vigorous regulations. It is known that the Indians are utterly incapable of preserving the internal quietude even were the right conceded to them—and that it is totally impractical for the General Government to do so is equally certain...The General Government has acknowledged our right of jurisdiction...The General Government has held out to this unhappy and deluded people the most liberal inducements to prompt them to emigrate—and in return for those friendly overtures she has been met by taunt, insult and derision...The course which and interest both point us to pursue is plainly marked out. Let the next legislature take actual possession of the country—elect the necessary judicial officers...appoint surveyors—have it surveyed and disposed of in the usual manner...Their own good now requires our interference...situated in the midst of the whites their condition will be wretched and degraded—being so completely unfit for the enjoyments of civilized society...we can but deplore that perversity and obstinacy which they exhibit in refusing to embrace the liberal and philanthropic propositions of the Government. Newton."

They say we are unhappy and deluded. For our own good the State of Georgia will help us. Whites are deluded. We are not. They are unhappy because they don't possess our country. We live in daily contentment in our own country. Any words that speak of whites helping us are a cover for avarice.

Whites are pugnacious—never happy. They remind me of proud, hateful mockingbirds. They sing a pretty song but they drive off all other birds from their territory. They cannot share.

29 September 1830

Will dreadful news never end? Georgia will require all white men to be licensed to work in Cherokee Country. Ostensibly, this law is said to protect us. Ben says it is a crafty maneuver designed to remove the only whites who want to see us prosper. Ben says all missionaries will be refused a license.

Mr. Lowry and his wife Eleanor could have gained much wealth if they had chosen a different career, but instead, they chose to devote their lives teaching us Cherokee. Perhaps United States citizens will learn the truth and return stolen property. I fear the white thieves are storing up a horrible day of retribution if Mr. Lowry's story of Naboth is true.

One day, when hearts aren't so cold, someone may read this and shed a tear. Edudu says evil deeds come back upon us like chickens that come home to roost before the darkness descends. Just like roosting chickens, crimes will come home to roost. When judgment comes upon the whites, the white children and grandchildren will have forgotten the crimes of their race. They will think their punishment unjust. I know how they will feel. Perhaps some future day we Cherokee will have a small measure of fairness. Perhaps righteousness, like punishment, will come to us posthumously?

Excerpts from Andrew Jackson's speech in Congress celebrating the Indian Removal Act.

"It gives me pleasure to announce to Congress that the benevolent policy of the government, steadily pursued for nearly thirty years, in relation to the removal of the Indians beyond the white settlements is approaching to a happy consummation. Two important tribes have accepted the provision made for their removal... and it is believed that their example will induce the remaining tribes also to seek the same obvious advantage

"The consequences of a speedy removal will be important to the United States, to individual States, and to the Indians themselves. It puts an end to all possible danger of collision between the authorities of the General and State governments on account of the Indians. It will place a dense and civilized population in large tracts of country now occupied by a few savage hunters. By opening the whole territory between Tennessee on the north and Louisiana on the south to the settlement of the whites, it will incalculably strengthen the southwestern frontier and render the adjacent States strong enough to repel future invasions without remote aid. It will relieve the whole State of Mississippi and the western part of Alabama of Indian occupancy, and enable those States to advance rapidly in population, wealth and power."

"It will separate the Indians from immediate contact with settlements of whites; free them from the power of the States; enable them to pursue happiness in their own way and under their own rude institutions; will retard the progress of decay, which is lessening their numbers, and perhaps cause them gradually... to cast off their savage habits and become an interesting, civilized, and Christian community...Toward the aborigines of the country no one can indulge a more friendly feeling than myself, or would go further to reclaim them from their wandering habits and make them a happy, prosperous people....What good man would prefer a country covered with forests and ranged by a few thousand savages to our extensive Republic, studded with cities, towns, and prosperous farms....and filled with all the blessings of liberty, civilization, and religion?..."

"...Can it be cruel in this Government....to pay the expense of his removal, and support him a year in his new abode? How many thousands of our own people would gladly embrace the opportunity of removing to the West on such conditions!"

Andrew Jackson, President of the United States

Perhaps someone will read this journal—perhaps not. On the day of our coming vanishment everything Cherokee will dissolve into unremembered oblivion when English immigrant farmers cover our land like a killing white frost.

Chapter XLI

1830 - The Quilt – The Enemies of Georgia

Chapter 41

2 October 1830 - Month of the Harvest Moon – Du ni nv di

I'm beginning to understand the southern states' feud with their General Government. Every southern newspaper talks of nullification and deunionization. The quarrel is growing. Where will it end? I wouldn't be surprised if they fight. Whites have a long, belligerent history. They love battle. Their Secretary of War reminds me of our old Red chief. Whites have a fondness for combat. I think that's why they elected Andrew Jackson.

27 October 1830

I haven't attended Mr. Lowry's school as I would like since I began working at the Phoenix. On the days I work, I miss his school room. I miss teaching little children and I miss the books—oh, I miss the books. As often as I can, I help younger students. I am always learning at the Phoenix. I dream I might one day have my own newspaper and school. I want to be in a schoolroom. Ben's father says I am a born teacher. It would be marvelous to have Ben as my husband, a school and a newspaper. I would then have everything I love and be the happiest of women. I crave the daily challenge of learning new things. I feel I have wasted a day when I don't read.

I love my conversations at the Phoenix and with Mr. and Mrs. Lowry and their visitors. Helping Mr. Lowry keeps my mind active. I love it when he tells me I'm the most inquisitive student he has ever had.

Ben's mother believes it only a matter of time before Ben will formally propose marriage. She always has a cup of tea ready when Mr. Lowry and I come for lunch. The two of us always find time for intimate discussions about family matters. She has a mother's instinct and wants the best for her son. I love our long conversations. She believes I will make Ben a good wife even though I'm Cherokee. I don't know of any whites, even among other missionaries, who approve of a mixed marriage. She and Mr. Lowry are the only ones.

Eleanor is curious about my relationship with Ben but respectful and would never pry. I try to tell her everything because I trust her. It's comforting to have a friend who can keep secrets. Edudu says a friend who keeps your secrets is a true friend, indeed.

29 October 1830

Yesterday Mrs. Lowry was not talkative. When I arrived she was unconsciously worrying her apron—an action that always betrays her mind. I knew something was wrong. When I asked if everything was alright she said nothing, smiled and gave me a warm hug. There was a tear in her eye.

"What is the problem, Mrs. Lowry?"

"Everything's good," Eleanor said, but with no smile.

"I'm a blessed woman today. I'm sorry for my uncontrolled emotion. I had every intention not to cry in front of you. I do have something to tell you, but let's wait till after school. Everything is good, Cassie. I promise."

Eleanor gave me another hug before I left, but it was an embrace with no words. I sensed she was concealing something of importance.

"Finish the children's lessons, Cassie, and get your work done at the newspaper. Wilbur and I have a surprise for you this afternoon. Everything is good. I assure you Mr. Lowry and I are quite content. Don't worry. When I think of you, Cassie, my happiness overflows. Can you be patient until this afternoon? I promise I'll tell you everything. Today is a good day. Please do not worry."

"Of course, I can wait and I promise not to worry," I said.

If there is one thing we Cherokee have learned, it is patience. We know how to wait. I finished teaching at the school and my work at the newspaper. When I returned to the Lowry's home Eleanor had a nice tea ready for us. As before, I sensed something wrong, but the source of the problem was impossible to guess. It wasn't a Christian holiday or anyone's birthday. It wasn't the Fourth of July. No one was ill and I knew the latest from Ben was good. What could this be? Mrs. Lowry was in no hurry to share. She set out fresh cream, hot bread, lovely little delights made with smoked ham and a plate of sugar cookies. This was an unusually nice tea. Something must be wrong.

As we shared small talk, Mrs. Lowry gave no clue to the problem or surprise that I knew must be coming. I would let her talk and share in her own time. I waited patiently. Having tea with Mrs. Lowry is always pleasant. I could tell she was happier this afternoon. I hoped the tears I had witnessed earlier were not a harbinger of bad tiding.

At last, the last cookie disappeared and our cups were filled for the last time.

471

"My dear Cassie," Mrs. Lowry said, "you are the daughter Wilbur and I longed for but never had. You are a gift—a special gift from heaven. It has been our pleasure to have you in our school and our home. We want you always in our lives. Wilbur and I watched you grow from a cute little precocious child into a brilliant young woman of great intellectual standing. Even if you and our son were not in love, we would still cherish you as our daughter. If your mother and father were alive, they would be so very proud of you. We count it an honor to have known you and a double honor for you and Ben to be together."

I felt tears coming. I could see the same in Mrs. Lowry's eyes. I felt her growing emotion.

"You helped Wilbur in school for years, and you and Ben,…well, it's obvious you and Ben were meant to be together, which is a bonus for us. We couldn't be more pleased. I can't wait till you two are married and give us grandchildren. I couldn't wish for a better daughter-in-law."

Mr. Lowry, who had joined us partway through our tea, had not said a word—not a single word and that, too, was unusual. Mrs. Lowry paused. I was about to learn what Mrs. Lowry had hidden from me.

"Cassie, I shall share with you now the source of my disturbed emotions you witnessed this morning. I know you are troubled. We have heard rumors out of Milledgeville—terrible rumors," Mrs. Lowry said. "Wilbur and I are afraid for your nation, the school and our future. Ben warns of sinister things afoot in Georgia now that Andrew Jackson is president. We're afraid, but we shall trust our Maker and do what is right. We'll never abandon you, Cassie. Of that you can be certain."

Eleanor paused, wiped her eyes, glanced over at her husband. Her hands were working with nervousness in her lap.

"Missionary work is all Wilbur has ever wanted or will ever want. That's one of the things that made me fall in love with him all those years ago."

She glanced again at her husband and gave him a smile and a pat on his arm that reflected a lifetime of devotion.

"Before I was born my parents sold all their belongings when they emigrated as newly-weds," Mrs. Lowry said. "They had money for passage and little else. They began a new life in this new world and had no regrets. Wilbur and I have no regrets—none whatsoever. Sometimes, Cassie, I miss Mother and Father terribly. I think about them every day."

Mrs. Lowry dried her eyes with the corner of her apron as Mr. Lowry, still without speaking, held her tight. I had never seen Mr. and Mrs. Lowry so emotional. I was speechless in the presence of such strong sentiment.

"I have only three things my parents brought from Germany," Mrs. Lowry continued softly. "I have Mother's tea service, Grandmother's wedding quilt and my parents' wedding rings. That's all. Wilbur and I chose mission work as our vocation and have accumulated little according to this world's standards."

Mrs. Lowry paused and smiled at her silent husband once again and continued, "Cassie, we've laid up another kind of wealth in a place more secure than any bank—a place where thieves can't break through and steal. Wilbur made it clear when we married we would never be affluent. Wilbur believes a person can't take wealth with them when they pass, but we can send it on ahead. That's exactly what Wilbur and I have done. We've been sending our treasure on ahead and we don't have one regret, Cassie—not one."

With that speech Eleanor lost control and sobbed quietly for a few moments. Mr. Lowry, with his arm around his wife's shoulders, held her but said nothing. Mrs. Lowry quickly regained her composure, sat up straight and dried her eyes on her apron once again. She took a deep breath and with her hands clasped tightly in her lap continued speaking softly, "Wilbur and I want to give you something, Cassie."

She looked at her husband.

"Now?"

He nodded. Eleanor rose slowly and disappeared into the back room. She returned with a huge parcel wrapped in plain brown paper.

"Wilbur and I want you to have this," she said, once again with tears filling her eyes.

"Take it, Cassie. Open it. Open it now. It's yours. It's our gift to you. Open it."

I couldn't speak. I untied the twine and inside was a colorful quilt. It was crafted with a most exquisite original design and finest needlework I had ever seen.

"I don't know what to say. I don't know what to say," was all I could manage. I recognized the quilt. It was Eleanor's own wedding present she had often displayed on her bed. I was overcome.

"It's yours. It's our gift to you," Ben's mother said. She gave me a happy kiss on the cheek.

"This is the quilt my maternal German grandmother gave my mother for her wedding just before my parents emigrated. It's the quilt my mother gave me when I married Wilbur and now we want you to have it as an advanced gift for your wedding—with Ben, of course. Wilbur and I say the same thing to you my mother said to me. Let this quilt be a reminder of our love that will forever keep you warm."

"We also want you to have this tea service, Cassie. From this day forward it belongs to you, but if you don't mind, I'm going to keep it for just a while longer. We shall enjoy it together, but it's yours from our heart to yours. We'll give it to you at the appropriate time. It reminds me of my mother and grandmother. One day you can give the tea service and quilt to your daughter on her wedding day. We love you dearly, Cassie. We hope in some small way these gifts communicate the depth of our affection."

Eleanor couldn't continue.

We paused, embraced, wept and dried our tears. I have no words to express how good these people are and how much I love them.

After a nervous silence Mr. Lowry spoke quietly for the first time.

"Cassie, according to Ben strange things will begin happening soon. Ominous rumors are coming out of Milledgeville. While we have yet a measure of peace, we decided to communicate our love to you. Our hearts have been entwined with yours since you were a little girl and will be forever."

I was completely overcome. Tears rolled down my cheeks.

After we regained our composure once again, Mrs. Lowry spoke with her hand on my arm, "Cassie, this quilt has reminded me of my mother and grandmother every day since I married Wilbur. It's yours. If one day we're separated, let this quilt remind you our hearts are beating with yours. If my mother and my grandmother were here, they would love you as we do."

As I held the quilt, Mr. Lowry put his arms around both Mrs. Lowry and me with the quilt squeezed between. I wondered if this tearful moment would ever end.

"Stay with us a while longer, Cassie," Mr. Lowry said. "Let's go out on the porch. I have news. As much as you read the newspapers, you may already know what I'm going to say, but I want to share the latest from Ben that provoked the giving of these gifts.

When we were seated on the porch, Mr. Lowry set his face and began.

"Cassie, Ben has confirmed the rumor that all white men here in Cherokee Country will be required to swear an oath of allegiance to Georgia. We will be required to apply for a license to work and reside in Cherokee Country. There will be no exceptions. Georgia has claimed sovereignty over all Cherokee land within its chartered limits. Milledgeville doesn't want you or your people to receive encouragement from anyone, especially educated white missionaries with a developed sense of justice. The new law is an obvious pretext. The governor referred to us missionaries as the enemies of Georgia. It appears I will be forced to discontinue my work."

"How can that possibly happen, Mr. Lowry? How? How can they do that?"

"I don't know, Cassie. I've pondered that question. How can it possibly be we missionaries are considered the enemy in this enlightened century?"

"I cannot believe that to be the truth," I said. "Calling you the enemy is beyond anything I can imagine."

"I know. I know," Mr. Lowry said staring at the clean floorboards of the porch. "Ben is certain of his sources and he is worried. Georgia doesn't want anyone assisting you, Cassie, not even God. I believe Georgia is afraid of missionaries. That tells me something about the conscience of politicians. This is not a Christian country—not even close. I thought it was, but it isn't. This government's integrity is an assumed veneer covering the commercial self-interest of the well-to-do. They want your land and what may be under your land. The Good Book isn't something they care about. They wouldn't be offended if they were accused of having a modern brotherhood with the Sadducees."

"Cassie, we asked you here because it's entirely possible Eleanor and I will be forced to leave without warning—perhaps in the very near future."

I was troubled and answered quickly.

"It cannot be anyone would consider you their enemy. Even the Militia wouldn't do that to you, would they? Why would they force you to leave? I don't understand."

Mr. Lowry answered slowly.

"My dear Cassie, Ben says I shall be forbidden to do God's work here in Cherokee Country in order to hasten your removal. He says I will be arrested if I persist. I have served my God faithfully and I shall continue to serve him no matter what law is passed in Milledgeville. I can't imagine they'll put me, or anyone, in jail for being a missionary. I hope this is a political bluff, but if they are serious, I will stand with God against the state of Georgia. Ben thinks Georgia will act soon so Eleanor and I decided to give you the quilt today. You and your people are at the center of our heart. Consider these an early wedding gift."

Mr. Lowry continued in a most serious tone.

"The governor's office is acting under the influence of an insatiable avarice which has guided Georgia since the day of their charter. I, and a few friends, will refuse the oath. We'll sign nothing. We'll submit to God alone. Other missionaries have said if push comes to shove they'll sign and leave. I don't blame them. I don't know the future, Cassie, and I don't know what the Guard or the Militia will do, but I know I labor for someone with infinitely more power than the pitiable government of Georgia. Nonetheless, unfolding events may be unpleasant. I don't know how long Eleanor and I will remain in our home. If God wouldn't spare his own son, we can't demand special treatment, can we?"

I felt myself beginning to cry again as I considered the enormous import of what Mr. Lowry was saying.

"Since the discovery of gold, greed has flourished. We humans behave in the same greedy way powerful humans have always behaved when they desire the possessions of another—they take what they want. Our government possesses the same self-indulgent appetite as the Romans. Georgia covets the possessions of its weaker neighbors and vindicates their corrupt desires with law. I fear Eleanor and I will be taken in spite of our prayers. I'm embarrassed to be white. I'm ashamed of Georgia. I'm humiliated by the actions of our United States. White folks are good to white folks and I guess that's where it ends."

Mrs. Lowry gently rubbed her husband's neck and massaged his tense muscles. I could see the look of affection and tenderness as she spoke to me and yet continued to admire her husband.

"Cassie, when I was little my mother tried to teach me to speak German. I'm afraid I was a poor student. I wanted to speak English like all my playmates. I was embarrassed to admit my German heritage and tried to hide my German accent. However, I do remember some things from my mother's patient lessons. I have remembered one thing more clearly than the rest—brought to my memory by current events."

Mrs. Lowry turned to face me and spoke softly.

"My mother said when she and Father arrived in Savannah they used the two German words liebestraum and lebensraum to describe their joy. One word means 'dream of love' and the other 'room to live'—both of which they were seeking here in America. I fear our fellow immigrants have decided, in order to fulfill their dreams, they must possess the entirety of the Cherokee Nation. They want your land, Cassie—they want it all. They have chosen to grow and be happy at your expense."

"I'm afraid Eleanor is correct, Cassie, but we asked you here today to assure you that Eleanor and I will never abandon you," Mr. Lowry said.

I was unable to respond. I understood only too well the truth I was hearing.

Mr. Lowry continued, "One day I shall stand in the dock before the judge of all men. I shall be required to give answer for my actions. I don't have to tell you, Cassie, that I'm understandably nervous about that meeting. I trust his judgment. I do not trust Georgia. I will not bend to their will—not one iota. As flawed as I am, I shall obey my Lord. I have made up my mind. I can do no other. I will not accede to cynical, pernicious demands from Milledgeville."

Mr. Lowry paused again, staring down at the rough-cut wooden planks of his porch. One large teardrop fell from his cheek leaving a large, perfectly round moist stain on the clean dry floor boards.

"Our many letters have been ignored," he said, "and probably turned the government against us. When we're gone, you'll be alone, Cassie—isolated in a sea of angry white foam. Indians have been accused of atrocities when the real outrage was perpetrated by Europeans in a blind quest for fee simple land at no cost to themselves. I fear there is no one left to prevent a bitter winter descending upon you."

As Mrs. Lowry and I listened, I felt our hearts breaking in unison. Mr. Lowry, staring into the distant trees, continued to share his distressing news.

"The Cherokee, like the Choctaw, Creeks, Chickasaw and Seminoles are doomed. I see it now. The writing is on the wall."

I thought Mr. Lowry would break down. He took my face gently between his big, calloused hands. He looked into my eyes and spoke with the deepest love and affection I have ever heard.

"Wherever you go, remember us. If one day you find hope impossible, wrap yourself in this quilt and recall our love for you. Our love shall follow you all the days of your life."

Mrs. Lowry put her arms around me, kissed my cheek and whispered, "My dear Cassie, Wilbur and I have a third thing we want you to have. You have the quilt. It will keep you warm in our absence. We're going to give you the tea service for your refreshment. It will cheer and refresh your soul. The third gift we will give you when the time is right—but not quite yet. Wilbur and I want you to have our wedding rings. When you have our rings, you will possess everything our parents brought from Europe and everything Wilbur and I hold dear on this earth. Our life will then be completely merged with yours."

I was overcome. I objected.

"I can't take your wedding rings. That wouldn't be right. You need to keep your rings."

Wilbur and I have talked about it, Cassie. That's how we wish it to be. For the time being, don't be too hard on us if we continue to wear the tokens of our eternal love, but one day soon when appropriate we'll give you both the tea service and the rings. We want to keep them for a little while yet. My dear Cassie, we're not going to need them where we are going."

That was the end of the conversation. We sat quietly on the porch listening to the little song birds flitting to and fro and watching the squirrels play hide and seek around the red oaks. We watched the high fluffy clouds moving slowly across the blue sky. There were no more words.

I shall not sleep easily tonight—perhaps not for many nights. I have never experienced emotion as I did today with Mr. and Mrs. Lowry. I have never experienced the depths of such love as was poured upon me. I wish only good things for my dear friends. I hope Mr. Lowry's fears never come to pass. I will let my heart speak through my pen.

The Quilt
Thread and needle,
Colorful remnants of precious cloth,
Cleverly stitched with love,
Warmth and affection,
Covering, protecting,
Enfolding, surrounding,
Reminding,
Warming tea cups,
Sugar and milk,
Fondness and devotion,
Nourishing my soul,
Family and friends forever.
Splendor of gold,
Circles of love,
Eternal affection,
Timeless bonds,
Extending far beyond today,
Unto forever.

12 November 1830

"Cassie, I did it again. I've been re-elected to the Georgia House. This is my second term."

"I'm so proud of you, Ben. I was worried that your connection to your father and the Cherokee would have reflected poorly on your re-election, but I guess not."

"I was elected by a wide majority. Zach and Elizabeth worked hard for this election, Cassie. They've built a strong base for me. Now comes the hard part. I've got to repay all these folks who voted for me."

"What do you mean? How do you repay all the people who voted for you? They didn't loan you money, did they?"

Ben laughed.

"No, they didn't loan me anything. Folks give me their support during my election campaign and they tell their friends to vote for me. They may even contribute money to my re-election but, in return, I have to do them favors after my election. When they need something they come to me. I do my best to make them happy. Quid pro quo in legal terms."

November - 1830 – Mitchell's Hotel – Milledgeville

"Well, Ben, here we are and I'm as happy as a pig in sunshine. We did it again, didn't we? You, Zach and Elizabeth have done a great job—you three have worked hard. I can't tell you how pleased we are."

"We're all proud of you, Ben. Keep up the good work, son. Take these cigars like I gave you last time. This could become a habit—a very pleasant habit and a profitable one if you keep gettin' re-elected."

Ben, Zach and Elizabeth celebrated once again an election victory. Ben's re-election moved him one step closer to the grand prize—an appointment to the United States Senate and once again Elizabeth presented him with an election night surprise. Life was good for Ben in Milledgeville. He had become a leader in the white community—a man of privilege.

Chapter XLII

1831 - Roses Transplanted – Missionaries Jailed

Chapter 42

11 March 1831 - The Windy Moon – A nu yi

As Mr. Lowry feared, the law requiring all white men to be licensed in order to work in Cherokee Country is in effect. Ben says it will apply to all professions, including missionaries. I am worried—terribly worried.

Ben rode up yesterday. We spent the afternoon shoeing Mr. Lowry's horses and talking about the new law with his parents. I love to watch Ben and his father together, especially when they're working. They behave like best friends. That thought makes me smile. There is something special about the friendship of a father and son. I want to be friends with my children the way Mr. and Mrs. Lowry are friends with Ben.

I watched Ben shoe his father's horses this morning. Farriers amaze me. It is interesting how they hold the hoof, prepare it and nail the shoe. All the while the animal stands patiently on three legs.

Mr. Lowry sat on one of the hickory stumps holding the halter rope while Ben shoed the horses. I sat on the other stump.

"Cassie, you want to try this?" Ben said. "You're good at everything. You might enjoy shoeing? We'll show you how. You can do it if you try."

I laughed and shook my head, "I have never had a desire to get under a sweaty horse and work on their stinking feet. You and Mr. Lowry reek for two days afterward."

Mr. Lowry laughed.

"You're right, Cassie. There are only two requirements for a horseshoer and you don't possess either."

"What are they?"

Ben's father laughed again.

"A farrier needs only two things—a strong back and a weak mind. Shoeing other people's crazy horses for a living has to be the worst job in the world. I can't imagine why anyone in their right mind would want to nail shoes to the bottom of horses' feet to earn their bread."

"It looks impossibly difficult to me," I said.

"We shoe our own horses for economy, Cassie. I only keep horses easy to shoe. Ben can tell you that. I learned long ago to sell any horse difficult to shoe. We may not have the best-looking horses around, but as far as shoeing is concerned, they're the finest. Our horses stand quietly while being shod. If we were wealthy, we would hire a farrier. Considering we shoe every four to six weeks when we're using an animal, hiring a farrier would be expensive. You can't work an animal without shoes, but you know that, don't you? Ben also knows I only buy horses with dark feet. Dark hooves hold a nail much better than white hooves."

Ben, working under the horse with horseshoe nails sticking out of his mouth, could only grunt in reply.

"Mules have the best hooves of all," Mr. Lowry continued as we watched Ben work, "but I guess I'm too proud to ride a mule or have one pull our carryall. Mules are fine for plowing or snaking logs, but I like a good-lookin' hoss' under my saddle and pulling my carriage—if you can call my old carryall a carriage. Mules are fine for hard work—for pullin' heavy loads in big wagons, but otherwise, I want a good lookin', well-configured horse. I absolutely avoid all horses with white feet. The dark hooves hold the shoe longer, don't they, Ben?"

Ben grunted again. Ben was under the front of his father's saddle horse, back bent double, head towards the rear and the hoof squeezed tight between his thighs as he worked quickly to prepare the hoof for the shoe. Ben's legs and thighs were protected by a thick leather apron that covered him from his waist to his knees.

"If these horses are so easy to shoe, Mr. Lowry, why do you wear that thick leather apron?" I asked.

Ben, holding the horse's ankle, let the foot down slowly and stood upright even more slowly stretching out his back muscles gradually with an ugly grimace.

After a few moments stretching, Ben stood up straight and took the nails out of his mouth.

"Cassie, the leather apron protects the front and inside of my thighs in case the horse jerks his foot away unexpectedly. My leather apron is split in two right up to the belt buckle. I tie the apron around my waist and then tie the thick leather around each leg with rawhide. If the horse yanks his foot from between my legs before I have time to twist off a nail, I'm protected by the thick leather. Without this apron, I could have a really bad day."

Ben laughed, put the nails back in his mouth, picked up the foot again and went back to work. The horse stood quietly on three legs while Ben worked quickly—almost in a frenzy. He worked as if being bent double at the waist was the most natural position in the world for the human body. I watched him

481

place the shoe and drive one nail on each side. When the nail had seated and the shoe was firmly secured, quite a bit of the sharp end of the nail was sticking out the side of the hoof. Ben immediately twisted off the nail excess that had gone through the hoof in a quick, almost invisible motion with the claws of his little horseshoe hammer before driving the next nail. He then bent the nail stubs down using his clench bar and hammer—firmly securing the shoe to the horse's foot. I had never seen Ben, or anyone else in my life, doing any kind of work so quickly—in such a flurry of motion.

After Ben had one nail in each side of the shoe, he once again let the horse's foot down by holding the horse's ankle until the hoof rested flat on the ground and the horse was standing comfortably on all fours. The way Ben lowered the horse's foot seemed like a delicate, slow maneuver and unnecessary. I wondered why Ben didn't just drop the horse's foot?

"Why did you stop, Ben? Why did you put the horse's hoof down before you had all the nails in and why so deliberate? Why didn't you go ahead and finish?" I asked quizzically.

"Do what?" Ben asked, standing and stretching out his back and taking the nails out of his mouth in order to answer my question.

"Why did you put the horse's foot down slowly before you were finished? Why didn't you go ahead and drive all the nails while you had the foot up and the horse was standing still?"

Ben caught his breath and stretched out his back once again.

"Well, Cassie, from experience I know how long I can hold the foot off the ground before the horse gets tired and snatches it away. I could do the whole shoeing job without resting myself or allowing the horse to rest but that would get me hurt. If I hold the mare's leg up too long, she'll get tired and pull her hoof away with a jerk. That unexpected jerk could cause a serious injury. Father and I never allow our horses to do that. We never allow them to pull their foot away prematurely under any circumstance. We pick the horse's foot up and work quickly. We put the horse's foot down before they tire even though we're not finished. Breaking the shoeing job into segments makes the job take longer but we don't have to worry about getting hurt. Any horse that continues to snatch his foot away unexpectedly, we sell. Since we shoe our own horses, we don't want any unpredictable horses when it comes to shoeing—or anything else really. I had much rather have an ugly horse that's easy to shoe than have the best lookin' horse in the country that's crazy when it comes to shoeing. It's not nice when a horse snatches its foot away, especially when there's a big shiny nail stickin' out the side of the hoof wall. That's why I wear this apron—just in case. If the horse jerked his hoof from

482

between my legs, the result could be nasty to certain parts of my body without this apron."

Ben looked down between his legs to indicate the area of his body that might be damaged, made a terrible face and we all laughed.

"How do you know where to drive the nail?" I asked. "I've never understood why the nails don't hurt the horse's foot. That doesn't make sense to me."

"Come here, Cassie. I'll show you. It's simple—really simple."

I leaned against Ben and watched as he picked up the horse's front hoof and brushed the dust from the bottom.

"First," he explained, "we take the horse to the blacksmith and have him turn a set shoes to exactly fit front and back. Horses are like people. Their feet are different sizes. The front shoes are always a little bigger than the back. We keep two or three sets on hand for each horse just in case they throw a shoe and we can't find it. Normally, we'll reset each set of shoes several times before they're worn out."

"I understand that. I've been to the blacksmiths with edudu."

"This isn't complicated. When I'm ready to start working on a hoof, I clean and trim the bottom with this hoof knife. I dig out any small stones I find in the crevices or in the white line. I trim the frog and the scaly part and inspect the foot to make sure it's healthy. Then I use these nippers to trim the excess growth of the hoof wall to the proper length and angle. Using the nippers is pretty much like trimming your fingernails. You don't want to trim your fingernail down to the quick, do you? And we don't trim the horse's hoof too short either."

I watched Ben trim the excess hoof with quick, neat motions of his nippers. The excess was removed in one long neat piece that the Lowry's dog immediately snatched away as if it were a treat. I've never understood why dogs eat the discarded pieces of a horse's hoof, yuk.

"Now that the hoof has been cleaned and trimmed, watch this."

"I'll rasp the hoof perfectly smooth and at the correct angle to the horse's leg so the shoe will fit perfectly. There must be no gaps between the hoof and the shoe. It's important to maintain the natural angle of the hoof. You wouldn't want your horse up on tip-toes or set back on their heels."

Ben pulled me close beside him with the horse's front foot securely between his legs and once again began his explanation.

"Here's how you know where to drive the nails, Cassie. Look closely. See this clean white line that runs around the middle of the hoof wall? It's easy to see now after I have rasped the hoof smooth, isn't it?"

"Yes, I see it—I see it," I said eagerly. "The white line goes all the way around the bottom of the horse's hoof. It's plain as day. No one has ever shown me that before. How interesting."

"Yep, that white line represents the border between the sensitive part and the dead part of the hoof. Outside the white line has no feeling for the horse. Inside the white line the horse's foot is sensitive. If I drive a nail into the outside dead part of the hoof and the nail bends outward, the horse will never feel a thing. If I get a nail too close to the white line, I'll quick the poor horse and tomorrow he'll be limping. When I quick a horse, and I've quicked a few over the years, I have to pull that shoe off, identify the offending nail and re-nail the shoe correctly. The horse isn't happy and I'm not happy. I've learned not to quick a horse, as you can imagine. Shoeing once is hard enough without doing it twice. Now you know everything I know."

"How do you know where the nail will come out? Why doesn't the nail just go straight up or turn inward? What makes the nail come out the side of the hoof?"

"Good question, Cassie. You are the inquisitive one, aren't you, but that's why you know so much about everything. Would you believe I use magic nails?"

"No, Ben, I wouldn't believe you use magic nails. How do you get the nail to come out the side of the hoof so predictably?"

Ben laughed and continued, pulling me over once again to his side.

"We farriers have a secret. It's like magic. Look at this nail. See how the tip is beveled on one side? You put that beveled side towards the inside of the hoof and the nail will always bend outwards away from the sensitive part. You might say that bevel works like the rudder on a ship. If you drive the nail in backwards—well, we don't want to think about that, do we? A farrier will only drive a nail into a horse's foot backwards once. After they get him down from the top of a nearby tree, he'll remember never to do that again."

Ben and his father laughed so hard they had to stop and get their breath.

Ben continued, still chuckling.

"The metal in horseshoe nails is soft. The nails bend easily as they go through the hoof. Additionally, the nail head has a depression on one side so when I'm in a hurry I can feel with my finger which way the nail should be driven through the shoe without looking. The instant I touch a horseshoe nail, my fingers know which way it goes into the hoof—which way it will bend."

After Ben and his father finished with the horses, they exchanged small talk as they rested on the hickory stumps. It was a beautiful day. Mrs. Lowry brought a bucket of cold spring water and the dipper. Tonight, as I write in my journal, I see Ben in my mind, resting on that old hickory stump in the dark shade of the tall chestnut tree—sweat dripping from his hair and off the end of his nose almost in a stream. I watched him drink the cold water his mother brought from the spring. I watched him pour several dippers over his face and head. After watching Ben and his father shoe their horses, I understand why no one would want to shoe horses for a living. That was the hardest and fastest I have ever seen anyone work in my life.

When Ben cooled off, he began telling his father about the new license laws.

"I knew something like this was in the works, Father. I've been hearing rumors. The law is in effect, but no one knows how strictly it'll be enforced."

After a long silence Ben's father spoke quietly.

"A few of my fellow missionaries are unbending, son. They won't swear allegiance. A few intend to continue to work here without a permit but most are going to pack up and leave. Maybe this will blow over—maybe not. I don't trust the Guard. They're a law unto themselves up here and a bad lot. Everyone has stories about them. They get away with everything. Our complaints fall on deaf ears. The rumor is the Governor himself encourages the Guard to harass the Cherokee and missionaries. Georgia wants the Cherokee to give up and emigrate. They want us missionaries gone, too."

Ben took another long drink of cool spring water from the dipper.

"The truth is, Father, no one in Milledgeville cares one way or the other about what goes on up here in Cherokee Country. What you heard about the collusion between the Guard and the Governor is probably true, as far as I can tell. Cherokee injustice is a non-issue in Milledgeville—always will be, I'm afraid. They think more highly of their horses than they do of the Cherokee."

"I understand too well, son. Some of my fellow missionaries are frightened. The older ones are packing up now. They intend to remove to Brainerd to continue their work or give up and go back north altogether. Your mother and I are staying. We don't work for the Governor. Georgia doesn't pay our salaries. We'll not submit to patent wickedness, for that's what this is."

Mr. Lowry put his arm around his wife.

"We'll stay, son. Under no circumstances will we be intimidated. We'll never accede to anti-religious laws and forsake our duty. Your mother and I made a pledge long ago. It wasn't an oath to the State of Georgia. It was a much higher promise."

Mr. and Mrs. Lowry kissed Ben and me on the forehead. It seemed that their kiss was the seal of the truth of Mr. Lowry's words. I was honored they were thinking of me as one who would be abandoned if they were forced to leave. The thought of faceless men in distant cities making decisions to ruin the lives of these two unselfish people was insufferable.

"Father, the missionaries have been a burr under the governor's saddle for a long time. The Governor will act. I'm sure of it. From what I'm hearing, he will strictly enforce this law. The missionaries' letters to the general government and newspapers defending the Cherokee and their right to remain has stirred up a hornet's nest in Milledgeville. Most of all they despise the fact that you teach the Cherokee to read and write. They have convinced themselves the Cherokee people are incapable of education and that the Phoenix is the work of white men."

Mrs. Lowry said quietly, "What a strange world in which our own government believes only white folks should read and write."

"Yes, Mother," Ben continued, "what is worse, Georgia believes you missionaries have been influencing Ross and others to defy Georgia's demand for emigration."

Mr. and Mrs. Lowry were sitting on the same hickory stump, side by side, arm in arm, listening to their son's sober words.

Mr. Lowry nodded to Ben to continue, "The governor needs a scapegoat. He wants it to appear as if the missionaries are traitors. John Eaton, Jackson's Secretary of War, has assured Governor Gilmer you and the others deserve no special treatment. The word in Milledgeville is missionaries prefer savages to white folks. Since Jackson's removal bill has become law, the talk about enforcing the Georgia Compact has increased tenfold. I'm sorry, Father, but you're eminently correct. The writing is on the wall. You are the declared enemy of Georgia—that's the Governor's very words."

Ben's father rested on the stump with his good wife beside him. They listened patiently. I could see this news cut deep.

"Greed for land and greed for gold has fueled this law, I suspect," Ben's father said.

"I think so, Father. The discovery of gold has provoked Georgia to de facto claim all Cherokee land in defiance of all past treaties. They've set in motion the final legal land lotteries. The end is coming. All the remaining unsurveyed land in the northwest of Georgia's chartered boundaries they have lumped together calling it Cherokee County. It won't be long before all Cherokee land from the Tennessee River down through these mountains will be surveyed and given away—every acre. All past treaties are defunct—dead. There will be no negotiations with Chief Ross and the Cherokee leadership. Georgia is acting from a position of military strength. They will seize all

Cherokee land because they can. I don't know when this will happen, but the wheels are in motion. It won't be long. Tennessee, Alabama and North Carolina are doing the same thing—seizing all Cherokee land holdings. One day soon the state of Georgia with the assistance of the General Government will send soldiers to remove every Cherokee family."

After Ben's speech we sat silently under the big chestnut tree for a long time in the cool afternoon shadows behind their little house. No one spoke as we digested Ben's news. It was a magnificent day that betrayed nothing of the darkness looming just over our national horizon. The birds were singing on every side. The white dogwoods were beginning to flower. The canopy of the tall deciduous forest, newly awakened from its winter sleep, was turning that special color of green only seen in early spring. The weather was warm, even for March. Today, all was as it should be.

Ben's gloomy news turned my thoughts inward. I shivered to think what will happen when Georgia sends its soldiers. Since I was a little girl I've had the recurring dream of ghostly white riders appearing out of the darkness grabbing Cherokee children like a hawk swooping upon an unsuspecting rabbit. They wear enormous hats. Their uniforms have great silver buttons. Their horses snort fire and showers of sparks fly from their hooves. The white, faceless men with long arms reach down to snatch children and carry them away. I'm terrified. I run but I can't escape. A rider is coming fast from behind. I turn to look as a young white soldier grabs my hair. His eyes are empty black holes.

Ben continued, his voice was hardly above a whisper.

"The new laws stop complaints, Father. These new laws eliminate reliable white eyewitnesses and at the same time provide a convenient whipping boy. That's the bottom line, Father. Georgia doesn't want anyone of character to witness their actions. Out-of-sight—out-of-mind, that's the purpose of this law. They're removing all sympathetic eyes. That's my opinion."

17 March 1831

Today is St. Patrick's Day in Savannah. We don't celebrate Christian holidays. Ben says St. Patrick's Day is important to the Irish who remain loyal to their Pope in Rome. I have no good memories of the Irish. I wish they would go back to Ireland and take the English.

18 March 1831

Mrs. Lowry left word she had something important to share with me. She had the cruelest of news.

"Cassie, the Guard came yesterday. I was thankful Wilbur was with me. Wilbur greeted the young men respectfully. Their young officer was no older than Ben. He dismounted quickly without giving a return greeting. He informed Wilbur we had been declared enemies of Georgia and must swear allegiance to the state of Georgia and leave Cherokee Country or be arrested. The young officer said if we choose to stay our assets will be seized and Wilbur will be arrested and tried as a criminal. If convicted, he would serve four years hard labor. I cried in the doorway. I knew Wilbur would be stubborn. I feel helpless, Cassie. I'm afraid."

I put my arms around Mrs. Lowry. I had nothing to say.

Mrs. Lowry continued, "The young officer was bold. His tone was unfriendly. He said, 'The Governor has given you one month to remove or face imprisonment. I suggest, sir, you take this warning seriously. The Governor will not be lenient with you and your turncoat friends. You will no longer be allowed to hide behind a Bible. I suggest you make plans to leave today. There will be no further warning. The next time I see you, you'll be arrested, chained, transported, tried and convicted. Good-day'."

"With that terse warning the patrol left for the next missionary home."

"I'll be here when you need me. I promise," I said.

"In some strange twist of fate, Cassie, we have become the enemy of our own people. In a thousand years I would have never believed Christian missionaries would be considered the enemy. When the soldiers said they were doing this for our good, I laughed at the irony. As I stood on the porch listening to the horrible words of that young man, I felt a kinship with you and your people I have never felt. Wilbur and I are finally one with the people we serve. What a price we have paid for that privilege."

"I am so sorry, Mrs. Lowry."

"I know, dear. I know. Thank you for saying," Mrs. Lowry said. "Cassie, they're getting ready to seize your country and they want us out of the way. I should have known this would happen when I read President Jackson's speeches about Indian removal. Wilbur is right. If God wouldn't spare his own son, why should he spare us? I don't like what's coming, but I'm prepared. I shall not shirk my commitments to you, your people, my husband or my God."

Eleanor dried her eyes. We held one another and didn't say a word. We couldn't speak.

Mrs. Lowry continued in a whisper.

"Wilbur didn't say a word to the young officer as he quickly delivered his message and went on his way. I watched my husband's eyes follow the soldiers down the road and out of sight. Even after the soldiers were gone Wilbur stood on the front steps staring into the distance holding the single sheet of paper signed by Governor Gilmer. I put my arms around him from behind. All I could think about was the sudden end of my husband's work represented by a single stroke of a pen. The Georgia governor has ended my husband's career and destroyed the Cherokee's best friend. May God forgive him."

Mrs. Lowry began to sob uncontrollably. I held her as she wept. I had no words of comfort.

After she recovered, she could only speak in a hoarse whisper.

"I suppose this is our last spring here, Cassie. Our future is in His hands. We've done everything we can. I know how you feel."

"Wilbur rode to visit the other missionaries to talk about our future. I asked him to send for you. He told me he might not be back for a couple of days. Come on inside and have a cup of tea. Please stay with me. I need your company."

21 March 1831

Three days after being served by the Governor's office, a dozen tired missionaries met at New Echota for a somber meeting to discuss the law requiring them to swear allegiance to the State of Georgia and to be licensed to work in Cherokee Country. They knew their application to be licensed would be denied.

"We discussed Georgia's law and our responsibility, Eleanor," Mr. Lowry said to his wife when he returned. "Most are frightened and are leaving. A few are determined to stay. We prayed and turned it over to God. That's all we can do. I'm staying. I'm not signing anything. I agree with the apostle Matthew. 'Seek ye first the kingdom of God and his righteousness and all these things shall be added unto you. Take therefore no thought for the morrow for the morrow shall take care of itself. Sufficient unto the day is the evil thereof'. My entire life I have served one master and that master isn't the governor. I'll go to jail defending my right to share my faith with the Cherokee."

"I was hoping you would say that Wilbur, but my heart is heavy. I want you to know that whatever happens I'm at your side. I've been your helpmeet in the years of plenty and I'll be at your side during the lean years."

Mr. Lowry took his wife in his arms.

"Eleanor, I love you dearly. I could not have gotten this far in my life without you. I'm going to need you now more than ever. However, it's only fair to tell you what I've learned. We can expect no help from the north nor from Washington City. We have been vilified in all the white newspapers. We have been abandoned. Our trust is in God."

"In any case, we'll write everyone we can think of and you're welcome to help. How ironic our own government should find it necessary to remove Christian missionaries. The new law makes me think of thieves who sneak around in the dark so no one can witness their theft. With the missionaries gone, no one of character will be left in Cherokee Country to tell the truth."

24 March 1831

Whites boast about the magnificent accomplishments of their great civilization. A nation isn't virtuous because they have an army, laws, lawyers, judges and courts. No one believes Rome to have been righteous because of their wars. I'm reading Gibbon in a new light.

25 March 1831

Yesterday Ben brought more bad news.

"I feel helpless, Cassie. Even though I'm in the legislature, there's nothing I can do. The Georgia House is behind Governor Gilmer one hundred percent. I must vote with my peers. If I voted against them they would impeach me instantly and run me out of town on a rail."

"I know, Ben."

"I want you to come with me to Mother's house," Ben said. "We're going to dig up her roses and take them to your grandmother, if she wants them. Mother can't stop them from seizing the house, but she doesn't want the Guard to have her roses."

We spent the afternoon transplanting Eleanor's beautiful roses to the front of elisi's porch by her front steps. Elisi was thrilled. These are the first roses she has ever had. For many years edudu has protected the dogwoods and redbuds that surround our house and fields making the surrounding woods look like an expansive garden in the springtime—like a rich man's estate. The roses will be a wonderful addition to her summer color.

Mrs. Lowry told us this wasn't the correct time to transplant, but that cannot be helped. We dug up as much of the root system as we could and with plenty of water they should survive, Mrs. Lowry said.

It was a simple thing, to transplant roses, but I saw between my elisi and Mr. and Mrs. Lowry something the entire world would be proud to witness. Elisi gave Eleanor a huge embrace. I would not have thought a few rose bushes could generate so much emotion. Elisi had tears in her eyes. The simplest action can sometimes bring untold joy. Mr. Lowry told edudu to prune them each year and occasionally bury fish heads around them and they will do fine. We have plenty of fish heads.

After we transplanted the rose bushes, I spent the rest of the day with Ben. We sat close to one another in the overarching gloom that dampened our mood. The emotional strain of recent news was heavy on our hearts. I would prefer a romantic picnic, but that didn't seem right today. I felt Ben's powerful body next to me and wished I could change the course of history. I thrilled at his tender kisses as he left. My heart was heavy as I watched him disappear around the bend. He sat tall in his saddle, erect and proud, as he headed back to Milledgeville and his responsibilities. Things change, echoed in my mind. Things change. I wondered what those changes would bring, but as long as Ben is near I am content.

17 April 1831

Today I walked to the Lowrys'. When I arrived my worst fears came to pass. The Lowrys' door stood open hanging on one hinge with odd things scattered about the porch. The unswept yard was in disarray with hoofprints everywhere. A frightened possum ran out when I entered their home. The Lowrys' personal things were gone, but the larger items of furniture were still there. This note was pinned to the mantelpiece:

Our Dearest, Dearest Cassie,

Mr. Lowry has been arrested, chained and transported to Milledgeville for trial. The soldiers are making him walk the entire way. I must leave here immediately. I will load what I can in the carryall and follow. I am so sorry, but I have no time to find you. I have no idea where they are taking Wilbur. I doubt if he and I shall ever return. I am at my wits end. Please forgive me for not saying goodbye personally. Please write general delivery Milledgeville. The soldiers seized our other horse and all our tack—everything.

Please take the chickens and their feed to your grandparents. I turned them out so they could get water, but you can catch them when they roost. Take everything you find in the house, sheds and smokehouse before the Guard come. Please take everything. I am so sorry this has happened. Please forgive me for not saying goodbye properly. I feel as if I am abandoning you. I love you dearly and will to the end of time.

Until we meet again under better circumstances, you will be on my mind—night and day.

Mrs. Wilbur Lowry

18 April 1831

Edudu and I moved everything we could from the Lowrys' home. We easily caught the chickens in the evening. We found a cow lowing miserably in the meadow behind the Lowrys' empty home—her sack distended. We milked her right there to give her relief. She must have belonged to another missionary who was taken suddenly. I dislike the Guard with all my heart.

27 April 1831

My Dearest Cassie,

My news is not good. By now you know that exactly thirty days from the date of the signing of the law Father was arrested, chained and transported to Milledgeville for trial—he refused to sign the document affirming his allegiance. Mother has taken a room at my boarding house. Father's arrest and transport was a shock to his mind. He is not the same. He has stopped communicating. I don't know all the details of his arrest and transport, but he was horribly treated. He was beaten, deprived of sleep, proper food and drink and was quite bruised when I saw him. He and one other were bound and forced to walk the entire way. I would have never believed missionaries would be treated as criminals. His trial date has been set. His trial will be a political sham. I have no hope of justification The State has made it clear they will make an example of Father to deter others.

Georgia has legally seized Father's house in New Echota as compensation for his arrest. It will become the headquarters for the Georgia Guard. How ironic a house built as a refuge for the uplifting of the Cherokee should become the headquarters of violence and cupidity. Your edudu is right. Things change, don't they?

I tried to persuade Father to sign the oath and remove to Brainerd as most of the others have done, but he will not sign. He stubbornly remains in prison. He is completely uncommunicative. I can't say I attach any blame to him for his actions. Father has never feared the consequences of doing what is right. I have always admired his sterling integrity. Unlike others, Father has been true to his word. I will keep you informed and come to you when duty allows.

Loving you Always, Your Ben, xoxo

5 May 1831

My Dearest Cassie,

I am so sorry. In a brief trial this morning Father was sentenced to four years hard labor. As I suspected, Georgia has made him an example to dissuade others. Nothing could be done. He would not sign the oath nor would he defend himself before the judge. Georgia is firm in its intention to remove the Cherokee and anyone who assists them—especially white men. How ironic my father was imprisoned for preaching Christianity without a license. I would have never thought a license would ever be required to preach the gospel. I think it has been clearly demonstrated who is and who is not civilized. Georgia behaves like Imperial Rome rather than the modern Christian culture they profess to be. Mother is as well as can be expected. She asks about you daily. She visits Father every day allowed. I will visit as I can. Beware of uniformed white men ranging about in Cherokee Country. I fear their numbers and activity will increase with the removal of the missionaries.

Take care, my dear Cassie. Loving you more every day,

Ben xoxo

26 May 1831

One day, perhaps, someone will do something on our behalf. Perhaps someone can right an old wrong. I wonder if the wrong committed against our nation will be quickly forgotten or even worse, one day considered justified by whites. What will the whites do to us if they treat their own like Mr. Lowry?

28 May 1831

We are told our land is being given to the civilized and progressive people who deserve it. I read this speech by an Indian chief. The arrest of Mr. Lowry will forever show the duplicity of whites.

Copied from the *Southern Recorder*

"...before the governor and assembly of Pennsylvania, by the chief of the Menomonies...Brother--we see your council house-

-It is large and beautiful. But the council house of the red man is much larger. The earth is the floor--the clear sky is the roof--a blazing fire is the chair of the chief orator, and the green grass the seats of our chiefs. You speak by papers and record your words in books. But we speak from our hearts and memory records our words in the hearts of our people."

I want Ben. I wish he were here.

Chapter XLIII

1832 - Ben's Father Released – Ben Elected to US House

Chapter 43

8 January 1832 - Month of the Cold Moon - Du no lv ta ni

Georgia is giving away more of our land in another lottery. They mandated a third of the 160-acre lottery portions to be designated as gold districts and divided into forty-acre lots distributed in a separate lottery. The drawing will be 22 October through 1 May 1833. Our leaders can do nothing to stop the high-handed seizing and giving away of our land. We are helpless. Maybe we should give up and remove now, as a few have. Elisi and edudu want to be buried beside their ancestors. I shall stay with them. I don't want to be buried in strange soil. Where they go, I shall go. Where they die, I shall die.

9 January 1832

Edudu and some visiting friends asked me to read the newspaper. Alabama has taken over all Cherokee land by extending Alabama law over all land within its borders allowing whites to settle at will. Edudu has many friends who live around Turkey Town. This is bad news but edudu said he expected nothing less. Alabama is following Georgia's footsteps.

Copied from the *Southern Recorder* - 5 January 1832 – page 2

Tuscaloosa. Dec. 24

In relation to white settles on Indian Territory, and State Jurisdiction.

Resolved by the Senate, and House of Representatives of the State of Alabama in general assembly convened, That this state recognizes a power in no one to dispossess white persons who have, or may settle on any lands knows as Indian territory, not occupied by any Indian or Indians.

Resolved, that all territory within the boundaries assigned by the United States, and accepted by the Convention of Alabama as the boundary line of this state, is within the ordinary jurisdiction thereof, and subject to all its laws, civil and criminal.

Resolved, That any exercise of jurisdiction on the part of the United States, by their courts or otherwise, over any portion of territory aforesaid, in the possession of any Indian tribe, which it could not constitutionally and legally exercise over that portion of territory, which is in the possession of the citizens of this State, is an usurpation of power on the part of the United States.

On the same page was this article about removing free people of color to Liberia. Whites want nothing to do with Africans socially, slave or free. Whites insist upon racial purity and shun any person with features or skin color unlike Europeans. They want to deport all Cherokee and free Africans. They want a pure white culture.

Copied from the *Southern Recorder* – 5 January 1832 – page 2

North-Carolina. -A Bill has been introduced into the Legislature to raise a fund for the removal of free people of color to Liberia, (proposing to lay a tax of ten cents for that purpose on every black poll in the state.)

10 January 1832

I thought my heart would burst when I heard Ben's voice after his long absence. His visit was a wonderful surprise. I wish I could see him more often. I loved his greeting.

"My word, Cassie, you're more beautiful than ever," Ben said. "I have missed you. I don't know why I don't take the time off from my work to come up here more often. You are a sight for sore eyes."

"I missed you too."

"Cassie, I can't tell you how good it is to have your arms around me. I just want to look at you. Has anyone told you today that you have the most beautiful eyes in the world?"

"No one but you."

We both giggled. I am always giddy when Ben first arrives.

"I need you, Cassie. When you're close, everything is right in the world. When I'm near you, problems melt away. Let's walk. I've a lot to tell you."

As we walked to the river Ben bubbled with excitement reminding me how much he missed our country and my company.

"I can't express how happy I am to be here, Cassie. I've thought of you and this place ten thousand times in the last few months. My fondest memories are here where I spent my boyhood—where I met you. I close my eyes and walk these hills in my mind. I smell the air and feel my toes sink into a soft carpet of pine needles. I feel the touch of your hand. I imagine your lips on mine. Things change, don't they, Cassie? No matter how hard we try to keep things the way they are, things change. The world changes. Our lives change. Riding up here knowing Father is locked in prison is a horrible experience. I don't ever want things to change here or to change with you and me."

I held his arm and pressed myself tight against him.

"You're right, Ben. Some things change but you can be assured my love for you will never change—never."

We continued walking slowly towards the river, arm in arm, enjoying one another.

"I understand about change, but elisi and edudu are still with me," I said. "Our community is here and our leaders work hard on our behalf, but I miss your parents. When I pass the old school house, I think of your father and a million other thoughts. I can't believe he's gone. I can't believe how badly your parents were treated by the militia. Lately we've had more trouble with the Guard."

"How are your mother and father doing, Ben?"

"That's what I wanted to talk about, Cassie. I have good news—very good news. I just came from Brainerd. Our new governor released my stubborn father from prison."

I couldn't help but interrupt.

"That's wonderful news, Ben. I'm so pleased for you but why did you wait to tell me?"

"I'll tell you in a moment why I delayed. It's not all good news. As you know, Father wouldn't sign the oath even after being sentenced to four years hard labor. He's hardheaded. Governor Lumpkin agreed to release Father with concessions and signed an executive order. I think having a Christian missionary in prison was becoming an embarrassment to the Governor's office. The primary concession for Father's release was his immediate and permanent removal to Brainerd—leaving Georgia altogether. Father agreed, or at least they said he agreed. I'm not so sure that's actually the case. I don't believe anything they say. I think they released Father for political reasons to take pressure off the Governor's administration. I've got reason to believe Father didn't agree to anything or sign anything."

As we walked, I could feel Ben's tension and the emotional pain recounting this news to me was causing him.

"I wish I could have been there with you, Ben."

"I wish you could have been there too. Mother and I met Father at the prison gates upon his release with a carriage packed and ready to travel. I immediately drove the both of them to Brainerd before the Governor could change his mind. I wanted to get him into Tennessee and away from the Militia and Guard as quickly as possible. When we left Milledgeville everything my mother and father owned in this world I could carry in my arms. What a shame after all these years and Father's hard work."

"I would love to see your mother again. Could we go up sometime?" I asked.

"I would like that," Ben replied quickly. "The first time I can get away for any length of time I'll take you up to Brainerd."

"The folks at the mission are wonderful, Cassie. They gave Mother and Father a little one-room house. It's old but solid and has a good roof. My parents are finally out of Georgia for good. I'm grateful for that. That's the good news, Cassie."

"What's the bad news, Ben?"

"Father wasn't doing well in prison—not well at all. Mother and I are worried—very worried. That's the bad news."

"I was troubled about your father being in prison, but no matter what the circumstances, his release is wonderful news. I'm happy he's safe."

"That's what I wanted to talk to you about, Cassie."

I could tell more bad news was coming.

"Father has been released, but he's still in prison."

"What do you mean, Ben? What's wrong? What have you not told me? How can he be free and yet in prison?"

"Father seems to have lost much of his mental faculties, Cassie. He hardly eats. He's thin as a bean pole. His hair has turned pure white since his arrest. He doesn't talk—not even to Mother. He never says a word—not a word—not one word. When I try to talk to him he just stares at me as if he doesn't know me or know what's going on around him. Mother helps him dress and eat. Something happened to Father in prison, Cassie."

"I am so sorry, Ben."

"I know."

"I wish I knew what the Guard did to him. Father's tortured soul has fled to some dark corner of his mind. Mother takes care of him as best she can. Father can't be left alone for a moment. He's wandered away from Mother several times and frightened her terribly. She doesn't think he knows who he is. That's why I'm certain Father did not sign an agreement to leave Georgia. The Governor wanted rid of Father."

"I'm so sorry, Ben. I don't mean to cry. I don't know what to say. This is terrible."

I couldn't say anything else. When we reached the river bank Ben sat quietly and held me while I cried against his shoulder. We watched the river flow by for a very long time. The water, gently flowing by our secret place, whispered its comfort as I thought of poor Mr. Lowry imprisoned in his madness. His insensibility induced by fellow white men. I cannot imagine Mr. Lowry, so intelligent, happy and full of life, bereft of rationality.

"I don't know what the future holds, Cassie," Ben said quietly after a long silence. "I'm standing for the United States House of Representatives this autumn. Perhaps when I'm elected I'll be able to do something in Washington City for the Cherokee, but a member of the House has little influence. It's several years yet before I qualify for a Senate appointment where the real power lies. Zach is working hard for me to get that appointment. Zach and his father want me in the Senate, but that's not what I want to talk to you about, Cassie."

Ben turned and faced me and held me tightly.

"Cassie, I have more bad news. The word is Georgia will seize the remainder of Cherokee Country soon. They can't be stopped. I know you and your grandparents want to stay, but Georgia will make that impossible."

Ben held me by both arms and stared into my face.

"I'm begging you, Cassie. You and your grandparents must go to Brainerd immediately and prepare to remove west with the next group. You can't stay. It's not safe. Ross and the other leaders are going to be ignored. Georgia won't let your grandfather keep one acre of his farm and you know the Guard. Things will get out of hand. You see what they did to Father and he's white. I know your grandparents don't like the removal party, but they need to get out of here before the trouble starts."

"They won't leave, Ben," I whispered.

"They need to leave now."

"I know, but Elisi won't leave."

"They have to leave, Cassie, before terrible things happen. If they won't leave, you'll have to leave without them."

"I couldn't go without them, Ben."

"If you don't leave you'll be at the mercy of the Guard."

"Elisi won't leave and edudu won't leave her. I've told her again and again what will happen but she won't listen."

"Tell her what I've told you."

"She won't go, Ben. Her parents, grandparents and all her relatives are buried here. She doesn't understand. I don't think any of the Cherokee understand. She's not going to leave her little house. She won't leave unless our Chief tells her to leave. She's loyal. Everyone here is loyal to our chief."

"He's wasting his time begging in Washington City," Ben said quietly.

"That's what edudu says, but we're not going to leave."

"You and your grandparents should leave but I understand."

"Ben, I want to stay. I want to stay with elisi and edudu and work on the Phoenix. Our newspaper is important. Chief Ross and the others are depending on us. I couldn't leave now in any case. I guess we're as stubborn as your father."

I could sense Ben's growing anxiety as we talked.

"I understand perfectly, Cassie. If I were you, I probably wouldn't leave either. Your work on the Phoenix is important. Your newspaper is the best thing the Cherokee have done. Editors everywhere read it and I'm surprised the Guard let it continue. Georgia understands the power of literature. That's why it's illegal in the South to teach Africans to read. I hear talk. Folks in Milledgeville liken the Cherokee to Africans and hate your newspaper. One day they'll stop the Phoenix. Mark my words."

"We're afraid of the Guard but there's nothing we can do."

"I'm afraid too, Cassie, but I have more news. President Jackson is up for re-election. He's promised to support me if I support him—quid pro quo. I don't particularly like Jackson, but if I want to be elected I must support him. I have no other choice. No one who opposes Jackson can be elected. The business of politics is complicated, isn't it, Cassie? Don't think ill of me if you hear I've supported Jackson. I'm doing the best I can, but I'm only one voice. I dare not say a word in opposition if I want to be elected."

"I'll be patient, Ben. Do what you can."

"I will."

"Remember I'm yours, Ben. I long for the day when this conflict will end and we can be together in peace. I'll wait as long as I need to, but could you come up more often? You can stay at our house overnight. Elisi will make you a bed. You need to get away from Milledgeville and I need to see you."

22 January 1832

I haven't heard from Ben since he was here on his birthday. I worry about Ben's father and Mrs. Lowry. Georgia would not grant a license to missionaries, but they have given hundreds of uneducated white men license to live here and despoil us. Georgia is doing everything they can to force our emigration. We are forbidden to conduct our government and enforce our own laws. Edudu must go to Tennessee for Cherokee meetings. Since the missionaries left, edudu receives constant reports of the theft of our horses, cattle, hogs and other property. Roving gangs of white men, calling themselves the Poney Club, and certainly sanctioned by Georgia, are behind much of the robbery.

> Copied from the *Cherokee Phoenix* – 21 January 1832 – Page 2
>
> "...a band of white men who are distinguished throughout the country by the appellation of 'The Poney Club' were located and permitted to reside upon Cherokee lands by...Georgia—and it is notorious that these men are visited by others of their own class from all quarters and many cases have occurred of their dismounting Cherokees off their horses in the face of day and escaping with them,--also of driving off whole gangs of Cherokee cattle and hogs from the woods where they range...it is an incontrovertible fact that the country is now more infested with this description of settlers than ever and the woods and public highways are almost alive with them..."

In that same issue of the Phoenix is the text of the Georgia Law dividing Cherokee land into forty-acre gold lots to be distributed by lottery. Only white men may enter the lottery. Since gold was discovered, thousands of whites have invaded. Georgia has seized more land. It is simply Victori Spolia. The two self-serving words mean today exactly what they meant in Rome—the powerful take everything—the defenseless keep nothing. Georgia passes new laws to salve their conscience and justify their ill-gotten gains. Soon, if my count is correct, we will have had eight separate lotteries giving away Indian land. How long can this continue? The surveyors come in direct violation of past treaties—treaties now meaningless. My hope has fled. We are undone.

22 April 1832

> Copied from the *Cherokee Phoenix* – 21 April 1832 – Page 3
>
> "Georgia has commenced her survey of Cherokee Country notwithstanding the decision of the Supreme Court of the United States. Our country is now overrun with surveyors, laying off the land into small sections about two hundred acres—The gold region is to be laid off into lots of forty acres. There are, we believe, about ninety-two districts nine miles square. One company of surveyors are sent to each district, consequently there are not less than five hundred and fifty men, employed in survey, under the authority of Georgia...marking trees or otherwise doing the thing which is expressly forbidden, by the

act of congress of 1802—If the intercourse law, and the treaties were carried into effect, which the president is constitutionally bound to do, these men, who are now employed in surveying the land would suffer the just penalty of the law...the fifth section of the law alluded to..."that if any citizen shall make a settlement on any lands belonging to or secured, or granted by treaty with the U. States, to any Indian tribe, or shall survey or attempt to survey such lands, or designate any of the boundaries, or otherwise, said offender shall forfeit a sum not exceeding one thousand dollars and suffer imprisonment not exceeding twelve months." In the same section the president is armed with full power to take such measures and to employ such military force as he shall judge necessary" to carry the law into execution."

23 May 1832

I read this passage in Ben's father's Book:

"Remove not the old landmark and enter not the field of the fatherless for their redeemer is mighty. He shall plead their cause with thee."

They must not know their own Book. Does this mean the weak and fatherless will have the white god as their advocate in a court of law? Will the white god be concerned for us Cherokee? Is he a white redeemer only? Is he blind to Cherokee injustice?

18 June 1832

Copied from the *Southern Recorder* 14 June 1832 – page 3

"J.J. Audubon, Esq. the celebrated Ornithologist, and his two assistants, arrived at this port yesterday, in the Revenue Cutter *Marion,* in excellent health, after a tedious tour through the Florida Keys. We are informed they have succeeded in taking 500 different species of Birds, some of them entirely unknown heretofore—besides several specimens of Minerals, Shells, Rocks, &c. (Char. Cour.)

1 July 1832

This a most remarkable quote by Lord Bacon. Reading is good, talking about what one has read is even better and writing about what we have read makes one accomplished. I want to read more of Lord Bacon's writings.

Copied from the *Southern Recorder* 21 June 1832 – page 1

"Reading maketh a full man; conference a ready man; and writing an exact man; and therefore if a man write little he had need have a great memory; if he confer little; he had need have a present Wit; if he read little he had need have much cunning, to seem to know that he doth not….Lord Bacon."

3 July 1832

I read this article to edudu and he laughed. He doubts if anything will be done to help the Cherokee in North Carolina. There is nothing we can do to get rid of whites when they squat in our country. We cannot use violence. Perhaps this time good will be done, but I doubt it.

Copied from the *Southern Recorder* 21 June 1832 – page 3

"STAUNTON, (Va.) June 8, Col. Armstead and Capt. Gardner, of the United States Army, were in this place a few days ago, on their way to North Carolina,---We understand their business is to expel some Georgians (said to be about 200 in number) who have entered on the Indian lands, in that State, to search for Gold. Representation of the fact, we learn, was made by the Governor of North Carolina to the President of the United States. Two companies of troops are on their march from Charleston, South Carolina, to the scene of action.

30 August 1832

There is division among us. Elias Boudinott has resigned from the Phoenix. He and Chief Ross disagree about the political future of our country. It is a sad day—a sad day indeed. Chief Ross wants our nation to remain where we are now. Mr. Boudinott favors national removal. Elias and his wife and I are good friends. I love every one of their children. It seems nothing is simple. Life becomes more complicated as things change.

30 September 1832

The Black Hawk War is over. We know the outcome of every war between whites and Indians. Many Sauk, Fox and Kickapoo were killed. Whites rejoice over our loss as if we were the incarnation of their devil.

12 November 1832

Ben was elected to the United States House of Representatives by a wide margin. He is achieving his life's goals. I am proud. I can't wait until his next visit. Maybe he can one day do something for us.

Milledgeville November 1832

"Ben, here we are celebrating another victory. This has become a pleasant habit. You were elected easily in '28 and '30 and here it is '32 and you're Georgia's newest representative to Washington City," Zach's father said enthusiastically.

Ben smiled at the compliment.

"Young man, I'm so proud of you I'm about to bust my buttons. I can't wait till you take your seat in the United States House of Representatives. Won't that be a grand day? You can bet I'll take the trip up to watch you take your oath. Everyone is so pleased. I can't tell you how much this means to me and the firm."

Zach's father gave Ben a big slap on the back that took his breath away.

"Yes, sir. This is a grand day," Ben answered, thinking how good it felt to be elected once again to public office.

"This is the third time I've decorated this hotel's ballroom for you, Ben. We're proud as a peacock. I'm superstitious. I planned this third victory celebration exactly like I did in '28. I'm wearing the same suit of clothes, I invited the same people, with a few additions of course, and we're having the same food, champagne and the same cigars. Put these in your pocket for later. I remember how proud I was of you that first night, Ben. I'm ten times prouder now. You've help make us the most successful law firm in Georgia, and maybe in all the South. Because of you, everyone knows where to come to if they need something from the government. You, Zach and Elizabeth have turned a lot of government business our way."

Ben was smiling and waiting for a chance to say thank you. It would have been impossible to interrupt Mr. Mitchell in any case.

"Ben," Zach's father continued without a pause, "I have a little gift you'll appreciate. It's the kind of gift you can take to the bank—the only kind of gift that counts. It will be on your desk when you get back to the office. I've been generous this year—more generous than last. Keep up the good work, son. This is the beginning. We're in Washington City now. Next will be the Senate for you. I'm working on that right now, but tonight enjoy yourself. You've earned it."

"Thank you, sir. I appreciate your consideration."

"Keep doing good work, son. I'm as proud of you as I am of my own son."

"Thank you, sir," Ben replied respectfully.

504

As he listened to Mr. Mitchell, Ben mused that things were working out well indeed. He was saving more money than he thought possible, consolidating his career and planning his future. Things couldn't be better and, like the last election, Bethy had invited him up to the suite for her traditional victory gift. She had ordered his gift specially from Paris and assured him he would enjoy it far more that the last. How could this gift be better? But then Elizabeth was always full of surprises. He couldn't wait.

9 December 1832

More bad news. Georgia has created ten new counties from seized land: Cass, Cherokee, Cobb, Floyd, Forsyth, Gilmer, Lumpkin, Murray, Paulding and Union. Whites are forbidden from taking possession of land won in the lottery if we still live there. The problem is, most whites don't read and to what court would we appeal when whites seize our farms? The Guard support whites in all disputes. We have no advocate. Whites have evicted and continue to evict many families from their homes and farms. The white map is expanding. Our Cherokee map is shrinking.

10 December 1832

Copied from the *Federal Union* - 6 December 1832 - page 2

"Resolved: That the measures pursued by the President of the United States, for the purpose of inducing the Cherokee Indians to remove beyond the limits of the state of Georgia, are in a high degree acceptable to this legislature, and deserve the approbation of the people, as founded on the most liberal, just and generous policy: Which was unanimously agreed to."

If they lived with us they would see what their policies are. They would fight to the death if someone treated their families as they treat us.

10 December 1832

Copied from the *Georgia Journal* – 6 December 1832 – page 2

"The Electoral College of the State of Georgia assembled yesterday at twelve o'clock, in the Representative Chamber, every member being in attendance, and deposited their ballots for Andrew Jackson, for President, and Martin Van Buren for Vice-President of the United States."

United States government is complicated and much different than that of England, France or Germany. Andrew Jackson is president once again.

Whites boast about his military career and his ability to fight Indians. We have no hope. With his election I fear we are completely undone.

13 December 1832

In the United States only those 'Free, White and Twenty-One' vote.
Copied from the Georgia Journal – 10 December 1832 – page 2
"...Mississippi...revised their Constitution...ARTICLE 3, Legislative Department. Sec. 1, Every free white male person of the age of twenty-one years or upwards, who shall be a citizen of the United States and shall have resided in this State one year...preceding an election...may vote for any state or district officer, or member of Congress..."

18 December 1832

I imagine the wonder of unlimited access to books. I am happy as a Cherokee woman, but study is difficult when whites have all the privileges and we have none. Mr. Lowry wanted me to go to college, but that shall never be. Every day I study Greek, Latin and French, but since the missionaries left, I have access to fewer books. If I were white and male, I would attend the University of Georgia. Whites reserve all privilege for their children.

Copied from the *Federal Union* - 13 December 1832 - Page 1
"University of Georgia. The Faculty of Franklin College ask the attention of the public to the following statements: For admission into the Freshman Class, a candidate must have a correct knowledge of at least nine of Cicero's Orations, the whole of Virgil, John and Acts in the Greek Testament, the whole of Graeca Minora, English Grammar, and Geography and he must be well acquainted with Arithmetic....Strict attention is paid to Composition and Declamation by all the Classes. Every candidate for admission into the Freshman class, must be, at least, fourteen years old ...The rates of tuition, the Library fee, and servants' hire, are thirty-eight dollars per annum...All who desire it, will have opportunity of studying Hebrew, Spanish, German and Italian for which no additional charges are made...Board can be obtained in respectable houses at from nine to ten dollars per month."

A young white man can have anything he wants. A Cherokee man, much less a woman, will never be admitted to the University of Georgia.

18 December 1832

From the *Georgia Journal* – 13 December 1832 – page 2 President Jackson's acceptance speech to congress.

"...the hostile incursions of the Sac and Fox Indians necessarily led to the interposition of the government...the Indians were entirely defeated, and the disaffected band dispersed and destroyed...Severe as is the lesson to the Indians, it was rendered necessary by their unprovoked aggressions; and it is to be hoped that its impression will be permanent and salutary....I am happy to inform you that the wise and humane policy of transferring from the eastern to the western side of the Mississippi the remnants of our aboriginal tribes, with their own consent, and upon just terms, has been steadily pursued, and is approaching, I trust, its consummation...the conviction evidently gains ground among the Indians, that their removal to the country, assigned by the United States for their permanent residence, furnishes the only hope of their ultimate prosperity. With that portion of the Cherokees, however, living within the State of Georgia, it has been impracticable, as yet, to make a satisfactory adjustment...I directed the very liberal propositions to be made to them...they cannot but have seen in these offers the evidence of the strongest disposition, on the part of the government, to deal justly and liberally with them. An ample indemnity was offered for their present possessions, a liberal provision for their future support and improvement, and full security for their private and political rights....They were however rejected..."

How were the Fox and Sac provoked? Invaders from another continent seized their land by force of arms. That would provoke anyone. Everyone should understand our hesitancy to accept the white's 'liberal and just' terms? Not one treaty with any Indian tribe has ever been honored by whites. How can they expect us to trust them? The fox is trying his best to persuade the chickens to unlock the gate. Those would be foolish chickens.

19 December 1832

Fortunate drawers, assisted by the Guard, have evicted many families on the Coosa river. When mounted white men with rifles tell us they have a legal deed to our property, we have no choice. I have heard that story repeatedly.

Perhaps we should go west now? Once again whites go back on their word and we are dispossessed.

21 December 1832 – Milledgeville
My Dearest Cassie,

I fear this year will not end well. I heard the Governor's address to the legislature. The State of Georgia has been prospering beyond the hopes of even the most optimistic, according to Governor Lumpkin. It is true. Zach and his father are making more money than expected. I'm saving as much as I can. Since Father can no longer assist Mother in any way, I send Mother money for a servant. Father is failing and Mother, the eternal optimist, doesn't expect his immediate recovery. It breaks my heart.

I include an excerpt from the governor's speech which illustrates Georgia's optimism and my pessimism:

"The territory embraced in Cherokee county should be divided into counties of suitable size, and form, to promote the convenience of that portion of our population who may inhabit that section of the State; and the organization of such counties should be provided for without unnecessary delay."

I wish, my dear one, I had better news but, unfortunately, truth does not come in season. I shall do my best to visit around Christmas time. I am not certain when my responsibilities will release me or how long I shall be at Brainerd helping Mother. I would wish to see you more often. I remind you once again in the strongest terms to encourage your grandparents to remove to Brainerd and go west with the next detachment. I promise to help them liberally if they remove. You cannot trust the misguided optimism of Chief Ross.

I am wishing you every happiness this joyous season. I think of you every day.

Yours Always and Forever, Ben xoxo

Chapter XLIV

1833 - Final Lotteries - Georgia Sends Surveyors

Chapter 44

19 January 1833 – Month of the Cold Moon – Du no lv ta ni

Will the lotteries never end? With these last lotteries, Georgia has defacto seized our every house, farm, barn and field. There will be no more lotteries for there is no more land for them to take. The last lottery bill passed 24 December. They have taken our land. Soon they will take us.

These splendid mountains will be here long after we are gone. This land doesn't belong to the Cherokee. This land never belonged to the Cherokee. We belong to the land. I wonder if we will be remembered?

21 June 1833 - The Green Corn Moon - De ha lu yi - The longest day.

We have learned to the victor go the spoils. We are too few to resist the greedy immigrants.

Our fate will be the same as past cultures who were to weak to defend themselves. We shall be vanished into the dark, unvisited corners of history. They believe their actions justified. They will not tell their grandchildren what they have done.

22 June 1833

Wisely, my brother and his friends have not returned violence for violence, even when provoked. Such actions would only serve to bring white wrath upon the innocent. I wish my brother did not harbor hatred, but I understand his heart. Whites have earned our animosity. I understand why he and his friends want nothing to do with the white culture. If it wasn't for Mr. and Mrs. Lowry, Ben and the other missionaries, I would feel the same way.

Above all, we detest the overarching symbol of white arrogance, the surveyors, sent to partition our forests, fields, mountains and farms into ever smaller parcels. They measure and squeeze until we can be squeezed no more. When we see surveyors we know another portion of our heart will be cut away. We're like crawfish in a creek bed—always moving backwards to escape. The surveyors, with their books, chains, numbers and drawings are the precursor establishing their white, fee simple, laws.

Our young men sometimes harass them. Most of the time we do nothing. The surveyors work unopposed protected by the Militia. There is nothing to be done against loaded guns and the faceless horsemen wearing uniforms and big hats.

23 June 1833

We never needed paper promises to know who owned our land. We did not need a piece of paper registered at a courthouse. We Cherokee, Choctaw, Chickasaw, Seminole and all the others knew very well who owned our land.

Whites insist that laws and paper prove ownership. For our continued happiness they insist we must abide by their laws—white laws. A piece of paper is a contract that cannot be broken. How silly. True contracts are made in the heart. Their heart is too small to safely hold promises.

Since the day they arrived, they ignore their promises and the papers we signed. I understand why our men hate white law and loathe the surveyors. If it wasn't for my brother's love for his family, he would be in a white prison or dead. I worry about the thoughts in his heart. If he retaliates in a moment of passion, I will understand.

26 June 1833

I spent the morning talking with edudu about my brother and two of his friends. What they did was not good but I am proud of him.

As he spoke to me, edudu stared out into the trees, "When I was a child, Walela, I saw men return from the hunt with buffalo and elk. I haven't seen a buffalo since I was a boy. I haven't seen an elk in many years. Before the whites came, our children experienced endless days of plenty. We lived beside the rivers where the soil is dark. We grew more corn than we could eat. We caught baskets of fish. There were buffalo, elk and deer as numerous as the stars in the sky. It is not so now."

"Whites care nothing for the forest or the animals. They cut all the trees and kill all the animals. A white evil is creeping upon us from the east consuming everything. They are like hungry pigs at the trough, never looking around, gobbling up everything with their bellies distended."

I listened patiently as Edudu continued, "I wonder if whites know anything about caring for the earth that sustains them? What will happen when they find themselves with nothing? Will they find another land of plenty and take that land away from innocent people and consume it also?"

"We cannot change things by wishing. We cannot live another's life. We cannot feed the good wolf of another. We can only feed our own good wolf.

I have found great peace in my soul by living my life and allowing others to live their life and understanding the difference. I let tomorrow worry about itself. I have enough to occupy my mind without borrowing tomorrow's burdens."

I listened quietly and patiently. I love how edudu will tell me the truth about what he is thinking. Edudu continued once again after thinking to himself for a long while, "Walela, don't be concerned about your brother. He has been gone too long, but I know why. Your brother loves you dearly. His love for you will keep him alive. He will not be foolish. It is his love for us that prevents him from returning evil for evil. He does not want to bring retribution upon our heads. Five Feathers told me something he did. He did what I would have done were I a young man."

"What did he do, edudu? Tell me. Please tell me."

"Walela, I trust you. Your brother trusts you. I shall tell you everything. Your brother and I meet at a secret place when Five Feathers hunts. He gives me the game they have killed. Five Feathers will not be here for a while. He doesn't want the Guard and Militia to see his face. I don't know how long he will be gone, but do not worry. Your brother makes good decisions."

When edudu and I talk on our front porch, we sit close. He holds me in his arms as he has since I was a little girl. I love the sound of his voice and the smell of his clothing. His mind is full of life. I love the clever way he uses words when telling stories. He has seen much. He continued recounting Five Feathers' adventure.

"When I meet Five Feathers, we talk about good things. Your brother asks about you and elisi and sometimes asks about Mr. and Mrs. Lowry and Ben. Your brother has a noble heart. He cares about the future happiness of others. He will certainly be chief."

"Yes, edudu. My brother walks with grace and peace, but can be quick like a mountain lion. I am never afraid when he is near. If an angry bear should come, I would not be frightened with my brother near."

Edudu laughed.

"When Five Feathers was a boy, your elisi and I made his bed from the skin of the mountain lion to help him grow powerful and quick. Your brother does indeed move with the grace and power of the big cat. He has the keenest sight and smell of all the young men. He is the best at ballplay. No one takes the ball from him."

"Yes, Edudu. Like you, he has been gifted. I have known he will be a great white chief or perhaps a red chief if we ever need one again. He may be the chief of our entire nation. We can trust Five Feathers and his wisdom. He will protect us."

My mind is filled with words, writing, history and ideas, but my brother's mind is filled with the forest, hunting and the joy of providing. He is in tune with the heart of our people, with the animals of the forest and the earth itself. Even Mr. Lowry believes my brother will make a good chief and should learn to speak better English. I agree, but my brother does not like the white English-speaking people who have covered our land like a killing frost on a cold winter's morning.

"Yes, Walela, I understand your brother," edudu continued. "He thinks like a Cherokee man of long ago. He is powerful and men follow him easily. He has the power of Dragging Canoe. I am proud of him."

Edudu paused for a very long time. As he began to speak once again he put his arm around me and pulled tight against himself. He stroked my hair like he did when I was a little girl.

"Walela, your brother is hiding but he did no wrong. Five Feathers acted in the name of our nation. His deed was not retribution but duty—an honorable act of courage that will help return the balance."

"Tell me the story, edudu. Tell me of his valiant deed. What happened? What did my brother do?"

Edudu held me and we looked into the forest. I waited quietly for him to continue. I felt secure.

"Walela, surveyors divide our land into their white counties and into their 160-acre lots for their fortunate drawers. They add our Cherokee Country onto their white maps as if we didn't exist. They increase. We decrease. They are ticks that suck our blood until they burst. Whites take our land and give it to strangers from across the sea. They hate our children and speak of us with foul names. Our land is covered with white parasites who thrive on Cherokee blood."

Edudu paused again and I waited.

"The Guard came for Mr. Lowry," edudu said. "The missionaries were removed because they were helping us. Soldiers will come for us soon. Only a corrupt people would imprison a man like Mr. Lowry."

"They have no respect for goodness," I said. "Ben believes the whites who win land in the lottery are waiting for their army to remove us. He says some whites even now are acquiring large sums of money by buying and selling our land. What can we do? We cannot resist. We cannot return evil for evil or the Guard will kill us all."

Edudu held me tightly. I could smell his clothes.

"Yes, Walela, things are worse. When our chief, John Ross, returned from Washington City, he found fortunate drawers had occupied his house on the Coosa. Whites had given his property to strangers in his absence. When he arrived home the white men who took his farm threatened his family at gunpoint. Even though he is Chief, there was nothing to be done—nowhere to appeal. Our chief lost everything because he is not white. We can't prevent fortunate drawers from taking our land. We can't get a white sheriff to defend us. White justice is for whites. Such unfairness makes young men like your brother boil with anger."

As I listened, Eagle Killer was lying quietly by edudu's chair. Sometimes I think Eagle Killer understands edudu's stories as well as I do. His eyes, one blue and one brown, seem to have a human intelligence. He is a beautiful, obedient animal. I love the way Eagle Killer will lay his head on his crossed paws and watch us. Yes, I think he understands everything we say.

"Walela, one day they will live in this house, too. We will never be more than savages in their eyes. To them, we are animals, like the buffalo and elk. Before the whites came, we never needed police or law courts. Now the balance is gone. We will never again be the Principle People. We shall, in the end, Walela, be pushed and pushed until we tumble off the end of the earth and fall into discarded mountains of white meaningless paper."

Edudu paused and said nothing for a long while. I was quiet and thinking about his words. Finally, as he was stroking my hair, he kissed my forehead and began his story once again.

"Walela, this is what happened. Your brother and two friends were hunting in the mountains to the west towards Alabama. It was a cold, rainy spring day with the wild north wind whipping the dead leaves through the mountain forest as they followed the trail of the white-tailed deer down the mountain's backbone above Rising Fawn's mountain. To their left and right, as they traveled the crest, the low leaden rain clouds filled the valleys below. Your brother and his companions had a deer and two turkeys in their slings."

"As they came around a tall, lichen-covered boulder as large as a house, they found themselves directly in the path of three armed Georgia surveyors who instantly threatened them with loaded guns at close range. Your brother was in the lead. He stopped still. He was not afraid. He made no move to flee with the guns of the white men pointing at him. He stood his ground. He did not retreat. To his right, a bowshot away, your brother saw the men's tethered mounts and pack animals tied in a dense grove of scrubby black pines to protect them from the blustery north wind. The white men had been sheltering under the overhang of the huge bolder beside the path."

"You need to get out of here and head west," the white man in the lead said to Five Feathers. "Go down into Alabama and you won't be harmed. We promise not to hurt you, but drop the game. Do as I say and get out now. Leave the game here for us."

The leader motioned with the barrel of his gun in the westerly direction down the mountain and into Alabama. Your brother did not move or look away from the white man's face."

The white man spoke louder.

"Do you understand English? Drop the game and get out of here. Do you understand?"

The leader of the white men, his coat soiled with dirt and tobacco stains, put his thumb on the hammer of the gun and slowly pulled it to full cock. The sharp metallic sound communicating to everyone the unmistakable presence of mortal danger.

The nervous tobacco-chewing men, their weapons also now at full cock, faced the three Cherokee men and held their ground. Beads of moisture from the intermittent mountain mist condensed on their beards and their long hair curled from under their hats. It was cold that day. Occasionally, larger drops of water from the limbs above dripped onto their coats and leaf bed with a single audible thump.

The leader spoke again with undisguised hostility.

"If you linger, you'll be shot dead. Drop the game and get the hell out. I know you understand English."

The red-headed leader paused to transfer his quid to the other cheek and spoke even louder.

"We don't want you god-damned Indians around here. We got surveying work to do. Get the hell out. It was a good thing you came by. Now we can have fresh meat. You can consider it payment for our work here in Indian country. We'll count it as rent."

The three men laughed, amused to see the three, wet, cold Cherokee men standing in front of them who would be forced to surrender the hard-earned results of their successful hunt.

"We're goin' to survey every inch of this state," the talkative red-headed man continued. "We been told you don't like surveyors. They told us to look out for you. We're loaded and ready. We'll shoot you where you stand if you don't get a move on."

The red-headed man held his gun stock tight against his mid-section with the end of the barrel just a few feet from Five Feathers. At point-blank range there would be no need to aim.

"One wrong move and we'll kill all three of you where you stand and leave your bodies for the varmints, won't we, Clement?" the leader growled to his friend behind him. "We'll kill 'em right where they stand, won't we?"

The man named Clement grunted in agreement.

"You tell him, Liam. We won't put up with no funny business, will we? You tell 'em, Liam."

The red-headed man squinted in the mist and shoved the barrel of his gun towards Five Feathers in a threatening manner.

"Do you understand English, you god-damned Indian?"

Five Feathers nodded slowly in reply, never taking his eyes from the red-headed man. Your brother answered the white man. He didn't shout. In the gusting wind, he spoke with just enough force for the white men to hear.

"I understand your words. I understand your words perfectly."

The three white men, becoming more tense and nervous with each passing moment, were ready for trouble. Afraid of an ambush, their eyes flitted this way and that searching for unseen Indian adversaries sneaking up the mountainside behind them.

"You reckon there's more of 'em? Why don't they leave like you said?" the tall white man said, as he looked left and right.

Five Feathers and his two friends had one unloaded musket, their unstrung bows, hunting knives and leather slings—all useless against the three loaded smoothbores at close range, plus handguns each of the white men carried—all loaded, primed and ready. Five Feathers carried edudu's old war club in a sling on his back—useless against a gun fired at close range.

Five Feathers held his ground. His two hunting companions would take their cue from him and would follow Five Feathers' lead no matter the consequences. If Five Feathers chose to fight, they would fight. They knew any attack against the white men could mean instant death.

The white men expected, after a short stand-off, that the three Indian hunters would retreat, leaving their game behind for the surveyors, and once again Five Feathers would be dispossessed by white men.

The deadlock continued. The white leader motioned impatiently once again with the barrel of his gun for Five Feathers and his companions to move down the mountainside.

Five Feathers stood still. He did not obey the command nor take his eyes from the red-headed man. He might as well have been a glistening statue cast in bronze as he stood in the mist on the mountaintop staring at the face of the red-headed man. To the white men and even to his companions, Five Feathers seemed to grow larger every moment.

Five Feathers spoke once again just loud enough for the men to hear. "We will not leave this mountain, English. You white men should go home. We will not harm you if you leave now. You should leave our country. Go back to the whiteside. It is cold on this mountain top. This is not a good day to die on a lonely mountain path far from your home. Go back to your warm fires and your wives and your children. You should go home."

Five Feathers stood firm in the middle of the mountain path that snaked for endless miles along the narrow mountain crest. Water droplets dripped from the leaves and the branches of the surrounding trees making occasional distinct sounds as if someone were dropping pebbles into the leaf bed from the tree tops. The white men were tense and afraid.

This fearless Cherokee man, who continued to stand in their path, caused them to think he must have companions hiding nearby ready to pounce upon them from behind. The longer Five Feathers stood his ground, the more the white men became jittery and uncomfortable. They scanned the woods around them for danger from an ambush yet at the same time afraid to take their eyes off this Indian.

It seemed to them the tall, handsome, muscular Indian with the expressionless face was carved from stone and possessed no emotions and felt no fear. He seemed to stand taller than even a few moments ago, completely unaffected by the wind and weather. Except for his brief speech, Five Feathers had not moved or made a sound since he surprised the surveyors.

Was this Cherokee man not afraid of death? Was he crazy? The uneasy surveyors sensed his strength—which seemed to swell. Even though they possessed far superior weapons, they found the confrontation unnerving. Perhaps the Indian didn't understand. They didn't want to kill an unarmed man, even an Indian. Five Feathers, his face and arms glistening in the dampness, was standing slightly more than an arm's length from the leader—the man with the red beard and the intense blue eyes.

"Let 'em go, Liam. I don't like this," one of the men said.

"We don't need their game. Tell 'em to git. Let's do our business. I tell you, Liam, I don't like this. You don't have to be a god damn hardheaded Irishman and have your way all the time. Tell them to keep their deer and git the hell out. Let's get the work done we was hired to do and git back home. I don't like this. I don't want no trouble."

Five Feathers, with the wind gusting around his leggings and his face shimmering with the mist, spoke again in a perfectly controlled voice—just loud enough for the men to hear.

"We are staying on our mountain. We will hunt today in our country. You will not take our game. You will not survey this mountain today. You three should go back to the whiteside. Take your animals and your equipment. Ride to your homes in peace. We allow you to leave. Go to your children and sit by your fires. Enjoy your hearth. Be happy. Go home and live many years and play with your grandchildren. We will not harm you. You should go now."

With every word Five Feathers spoke, the red-headed man seemed to grow more angry. As Five Feathers finished speaking the red-headed man spit on Five Feathers' feet.

"Who the hell do you think you are? You're nothin' but a god damned Indian and I'm going nowhere. You're never goin' to tell me what to do. You're the one goin' to leave. I'll see to that."

The red-headed man motioned with his gun again towards the path down the mountainside.

"If you know what's good for you, you'll git down that mountain and leave us alone to do our work or I'll shoot you where you stand. I ain't afraid of you."

Five Feathers paused for a moment as the men nervously watched one another. Five Feathers continued, "If you do not go, white man, you shall die here today on this cold, wet mountain and the busy ants will consume your eyes. They will crawl into your dead ears and nose and feast on your flesh. If you do not obey me and leave this mountain, this very night the possums will feast upon your cold white body. Your wives and children will await your return forever."

When Five Feathers finished speaking, he stood as if carved of stone, as if he were not breathing or blinking. He never took his eyes from the leader with the red beard. The three white men didn't like this strange man standing unmoved in front of them threatening them with such a horrible end, even if he were powerless to carry out his empty threats. Surely he said these bold things because there were others lurking hidden somewhere on the mountain? Is that why this man exhibited no fear?

The white men, although somewhat uneasy, continued in their arrogance, pretending to be courageous. Each with his gun at full cock and his finger on the trigger. The Cherokee men in front of them were helpless.

The white leader, doing his best to match the courage and physical presence of Five Feathers, spit another stream of tobacco-laden spittle onto Five Feathers' leggings without taking his eyes from the tall Cherokee man.

"We got guns," the leader said arrogantly. "You got nothin'. We got the Militia behind us. We're goin' to take your game, Indian, and we're goin' to survey this mountain. I fancy a nice turkey leg tonight, don't you, Clement?"

The dirty red-headed man continued his speech.

"We don't want trouble, but we'll sure give trouble if you don't leave—and I mean now. I'm tired of you standin' there looking at me like a dumb-ass. I don't like you. I don't like you at all—in fact, I don't like any god damned Indian," he spat his last words bitterly. "If you don't drop that game and get the hell out of here, I'll kill you and cut off your hair for fun. Do you understand what I'm sayin', you god damn Indian, or are you stupid?"

The red-headed man laughed.

The two white men, standing close behind their leader, continued to glance around nervously. They were beginning to believe with certainty that more Cherokee men were hidden in the underbrush and they were outnumbered. What else could explain the bravery of the tall Indian standing in front of them who disregarded every order he was given and was ready to give up his life for a dead turkey and a dead deer as a matter of principle in the middle of nowhere.

Liam, with the red hair and beard, continued his superior tone. The nervousness and volume of his voice increased.

"We're going to survey this land. You god damned Cherokee should get the hell out of Georgia and go west where you belong. This is our land now. You're trespassing. We got a job to do. Don't you understand nothin' I'm telling you?"

As the surveyor spoke, it seemed each word became louder until by the end of his speech he was shouting. Although Five Feathers was standing almost close enough to touch the barrel of the white man's gun, he was unmoved by the surveyor's words. Liam's voice finally rose to a hysterical scream as if the force of his words alone would remove the Indian from the mountain top. Five Feathers could see the white man's finger on the trigger. The white man's shouting had no effect—the stoic Cherokee man had no intention of backing down.

The surveyors were unprepared for an encounter like this. They didn't want to kill the defenseless Cherokee men, but their pride wouldn't let them retreat. It was a standoff. Five Feathers had been in this situation before. He knew exactly what he was going to do this time.

The handsome, muscular Cherokee man was dauntless. His behavior wasn't a put-on bravado, but a tested courage that came from his soul tempered by hundreds of years of Cherokee experience. The three white men began to think they would be forced to kill this Indian if they wanted to survey the mountain.

The leader spoke again. His voice had risen into a mad scream. Flecks of spittle flew onto the barrel of his gun and Five Feathers' clothing.

"There's nothing you or your two Indian friends can do to stop us. I'm not standin' here all day. We got a job to do and we're going to do it. This is your last chance. If you don't leave, you'll regret it. You won't be the first Indian I've kilt. Pretend to be brave, you god damned savage, but we got guns and we're goin' to do our job. I think you're just stupid."

"I don't like this," one of the white men said to their leader.

"Let them go and let's get out of here. We can survey here tomorrow. I don't like this. I want to leave."

The red-headed man paid no attention to his companion and continued wildly shouting at Five Feathers.

"You'll leave or you'll die right here with lead in your belly. Now, for the last time, get the hell out of here and drop that deer and turkey."

By the time the red-headed Liam had finished his speech, he was yelling at the top of his voice so loud that his spittle drooled off his red beard onto his own clothing.

The two companions laughed nervously. They stood a little more upright believing they were in a position of unassailable strength yet they didn't want to shoot the three Indians in cold blood who had done nothing but stand in the path.

The red-headed man continued, "You're goin' to drop your game and run like the chicken-shit Cherokee always do—like a yellow dog with its tail between its legs. I done decided. If you don't go, I'll put a bullet in you right now—right there where you stand, you god damned statue of stone. Why the hell do you stand there lookin' at me. Do you think I'm afraid of you? I wouldn't be afraid of ten of you. I've kilt the likes of you. Your hair won't be the first I took. It won't bother me to kill you and get my bounty. This is it. You're done."

Liam slowly began to raise his weapon to his shoulder and aim at the middle of Five Feathers' chest. The two white men just behind, believing Liam had at last decided to kill the Indian, took an awkward step backward over the dead leaves, branches and uneven rocky ground on the mountain path.

At the exact moment the two men stepped backwards, a huge buzzard caught an updraft in the valley below and soared up and over the mountaintop directly above their heads. Like an evil apparition, the huge, black buzzard with wings outspread seemed to mysteriously appear gliding silently across the mountaintop—almost brushing the treetops. The massive bird's sudden appearance caused the three white men to flinch. Their upwards glance caused the white men to take another unconscious step backwards.

Five Feathers was watching their eyes. When the white men looked upwards and moved backwards towards the security of their pack animals, Five Feathers moved with blinding speed against the red-headed leader who had threatened him.

Five Feathers was much too quick for a response from either of the three men. Attacking without a firearm, Five Feathers moved quicker than lightning. The instant the white men were distracted, he reached the war club on his back and threw it at the center of the forehead of the man with the red beard. The heavy end crashed into his skull before he could pull the trigger. He crumpled to the ground in a heap, instantly unconscious—blood flowing through his red beard onto the damp soil under his head. He lay still on the mountain path. As he fell, his rifle discharged harmlessly against the lichen-covered boulder at their side. The sound of the bullet's ricochet echoed off the mountainsides into the valley below. The other two men were caught completely unawares by Five Feathers' attack and were paralyzed with fear. Both men hesitated. Their delay was deadly. Before they could think or squeeze their triggers, Five Feathers disarmed them both. In a single flurry of movement before the two white men could make any move to flee or defend themselves, Five Feathers threw them both to the ground. Quick as lightening the powerful Indian broke their arms over protruding rocks in the leaf-bed— their arm bones shattering with loud splintering sounds like the breaking of dead tree branches. As quickly as it began, Five Feathers' solo attack was over. He stood staring down at the three surveyors sent by the state of Georgia to divide his land and give it away to others who spoke only English. Five Feathers, breathing normally and with no expression, stared down at the three helpless men at his feet. Escape was impossible.

The red-headed man lay unconscious, blood running onto the damp leaves from the deep gash in his forehead. The other two lay with broken arms, terrified, immobile and moaning in intense pain—whimpering, begging for mercy from this strange Indian, bigger than life, who had somehow overpowered them without modern weapons.

"Please, please, please, please don't hurt us. Please don't hurt us," the two men pleaded, groveling in the leaves at Five Feathers' feet. With their arms broken, they were unable to rise to a sitting position or stand. Their only hope of survival was to elicit some measure of compassion from the stoic Cherokee man who had, so far, shown no pity or weakness but who they knew understood their English.

"We weren't really goin' to hurt you," the tallest white man said. "Tell him, Clement. Tell him we ain't like Liam. We ain't bad."

The man named Clement said, "John's right. We wouldn't let Liam hurt you. Please don't hurt us. We're good men. We'll go home. We got wives and children. We'll go home."

The man named Clement began to cry.

The tall man named John begged.

"It was Liam. He's crazy. Please let us go. We promise we'll go home and never bother you again. We won't never come back. We promise. We like Indians. We've always liked Indians. We never meant no harm. We were just havin' fun. Clement was right. We weren't really goin' to shoot you. I ain't never shot nobody. We wouldn't do that. Liam never did shoot nobody, neither. We like Indians. No one will ever come again. We promise. Please don't hurt us.

As the two men lay writhing on the damp rocky ground on the mountain top path, they continued to beg for their lives as the expressionless Cherokee man stood above them saying not a word and giving no indication of what he was thinking or what he would do next. Five Feathers' companions were as stunned as the white men. They, too, continued to stand quietly watching the bizarre scene unfold in front of them. Who was this hunting companion of theirs, this Cherokee warrior who had risen to be larger than the mountain itself?

Finally, Five Feathers moved. Slowly and deliberately he knelt beside the unconscious Liam and took his worn leather pouch from his shoulder. He dumped its contents onto the path. Just a few feet from the two conscious white men and in their full view, Five Feathers knelt, scraped back the dead leaves and scooped the empty leather bag full of soft damp loamy earth—never once looking at the pitiful men continuing to moan and beg an arm's length away. They stared at their attacker wondering what was their fate. What was he planning? With their arms broken and lying at crazy angles and their eyes wide with pain, they watched as the Cherokee man filled the leather bag full to overflowing with the dark damp soil—Cherokee soil taken from the path on the top of a Cherokee mountain.

Five Feathers put the leather strap of the worn leather pouch across his shoulder and hung the leather bag across his chest, rolled the red-headed man onto his back and knelt with his full weight on his torso. The two white men watched.

Five Feathers, still without any facial expression, spit on the unconscious man's face. Five Feathers' spittle, mixing with the blood still flowing from the red-headed man's wound, dripped onto the damp path beneath his head.

"You would spit on me? You would kill me? You would take our land and make our wives and children homeless? You would kill those who never did you harm?"

Five Feathers continued to speak to the unconscious man lying on his back under him as if he could hear.

"You want to give our land to your friends? You wish to take everything we possess? You would take the land from under the feet of our children? I shall give you what you want. I shall give you all the Cherokee soil you can eat and breathe. You shall have our land. I shall freely give to you the Cherokee soil you have desired. You shall take our earth to that place I shall send you today. I will fill you with good Cherokee soil for your journey."

Five Feathers, kneeling on the unconscious man's chest, took a handful of soil from the bag and began stuffing the unconscious man's mouth with the black moist earth. The man wakened suddenly, opened his eyes wide in panic making choking noises as he tried to breathe. Wildly staring upward at the Cherokee man he had intended to kill, he began to flail with his arms and legs to free himself from the crushing weight on his chest.

Five Feathers ignored the man's attempts to free himself and continued forcing soil into his mouth—packing the damp earth deep into his throat. The red-headed man thrashed and writhed but in vain. Five Feathers continued to hold the wounded man to the ground. He stuffed his mouth with black soil until saliva and soil mixed came out the red-headed man's nose in great black bubbles as he made a final gasping choking noise and breathed his last.

The white man with the red beard lay dead—motionless—his sightless blue eyes staring up into the grey rain clouds moving slowly above the mountain path. Another buzzard glided low across the mountaintop. The gusty wild wind whipped dead brown leaves onto Liam's ashen face and his red beard. The other two white men began blubbering incoherently, begging for their lives.

Five Feathers' companions were as stunned as the white men and still had not moved or spoken since Five Feathers had sprung into action. When the first man quit breathing, Five Feathers turned to the other two struggling on the ground nearby, their broken limbs useless for defense or escape. Unable to stand, they struggled with their legs to slither on their backs between the rocks and trees and somehow slide down the mountainside away from this powerful mad-man they believed would do to them as they had seen him do to their leader.

Five Feathers knelt beside the two men and spoke to them quietly, "You want our land? You came up this mountain to take our land from us. You want us to leave our country. You want to live in the homes we built for our children. You want to turn my elisi and edudu out into the forest so you can sit at their fire, work their fields and eat from their smokehouse. You want to eat our deer and turkey. You want the Cherokee's land. I shall give you the Cherokee soil you so desire."

The two white men, in intense pain, were watching as Five Feathers, kneeling between the two, spoke again.

"You English crossed the sea to take our country from us," Five Feathers continued quietly—patiently. "You should have listened to me and you would be on your way home to your children. You want to send us away from our country to a place far away. Instead, I shall send you away—to a place from which you shall never return. I shall send you to the place where you belong."

The two pathetic men, trying to dissuade this Cherokee man from his intended task, began to cry and plead and sob, hardly able to enunciate their words, their tears mixed with spittle dripped from their beards as they continued to beg, "We don't want your land. Please, please, please, please, we're sorry. We shouldn't have said those things. We won't say that again, will we Clement?"

"He's right—we'll do anything you ask. We won't come back," the other man said. "We don't want your deer. That was Liam. We don't want you to be homeless. We'll leave and never come back. Please, please don't kill us. We always liked Indians. We don't want your land. We never did want your land. Please don't hurt us. It was Liam. We like Indians. We meant no harm—honest. We'll leave and never come back."

"From your own mouth you speak truth. You shall leave today and never return."

The two surveyors continued to whimper, but Five Feathers paid no attention to their appeals and spoke no more. Without pity, he knelt on the next man's chest. With one hand holding the man's head in place, he slowly forced small handfuls of the soft moist black sandy earth into his mouth until the man, his back arching and kicking madly, tried to free himself in one final unsuccessful muscular spasm until he, too, blew black, gritty bubbles out of his nose. He choked, aspirated the mixture in his mouth and his breathing stopped. He lay motionless, his mouth filled with the Cherokee soil he had coveted, his eyes glazed like Liam's, staring sightlessly at the scudding grey rain clouds flying low across the lonely Cherokee mountain.

Five Feathers' two friends shivered in the cold mist as if they would be next. Their shiver wasn't prompted by the cold but by what they were witnessing. They had never seen anything like this. Motionless, they watched Five Feathers execute his judgment against the last white man. Five Feathers squeezed the man's mouth open with one hand and slowly forced the earth in until the man coughed and choked on the black dirt and he, like the other two, foamed black bubbles of Cherokee earth out his white nostrils and thrashed in a final panic-stricken death throe like an animal caught in a steel trap.

The three men lay dead, staring with sightless eyes at the iron-grey sky above the mountain path. Trailing from the mouth and nose of each was a mixture of Cherokee soil and saliva. The raindrops, beginning to fall in a steady drizzle, began to wash their faces clean.

Five Feathers ordered his companions to throw the bodies, saddles, bridles and all their equipment into a nearby pit. He cautioned his companions not to keep one thing belonging to surveyors sent by the state of Georgia. He told his companions to thickly cover the men and their equipment with laurels and finally to throw the deer and turkey carcass on top. If someone happened by, they would discover the decomposing animal carcass and investigate no further. The horses and mules, minus their saddles, bridles and burdens would soon find new masters. The three white men would never be heard from again. Their employers would assume they had decided to head west themselves.

"Our people were kind to the white men when they first came to our land. If white men had not brought so much disease, Walela," her edudu said, "we would have many like your brother. We could defend our homes. Those like your brother are few. We cannot resist. Do not worry, dear one. Your brother will not abandon us. He will not go to prison or be hanged for his deed. Your brother will come back when it is safe and care for us. He would never leave us to face the English alone."

"Edudu, I cannot feel sorrow for the three who died coveting our land. I understand my brother. I do not want to feed my bad wolf, but I am not sad for them—especially for the man named Liam. The Guard are being repaid in kind. They should have listened to my brother and they would be holding their children this very day."

Chapter XLV

1834 – Ben Learns the Truth

Chapter 45

4 January 1834 - Cold Moon - du no lv ta ni

It has rained day after day for two weeks without pause. The water of the flooding river rushes high above my special place. I'm weary of grey skies and continual dampness. Today it turned cold. We had snow, but at last I see a blue sky. I love the white mantle of snow covering our land. I dread the thaw.

5 January 1834

Yesterday's light snow melted quickly. The ground is soggy. Mud is everywhere.

Our world has turned cold. It isn't just us who suffer. The Choctaw are being arrested and moved by the army. No one sees. No one cares. Like us, the Choctaw are powerless. They will be vanished—heard from no more. No one tells their story. Edudu says the Choctaw are invisible far out on the American frontier. The whites care nothing for their plight. We understand.

Copied from the Federal Union – 1 January 1834 – page 2

> "About five hundred artillerists, of the United States Army...passed through Milledgeville on the 24th of December...A part of them are destined for Fort Mitchell, a part for Mobile, and a part for Choctaw country."

6 January 1834

How blind we humans can become to the needs of others. How does one come to believe Africans are of no more worth than a cow? How can Africans be valued only for their labor like an ox or a mule? Whites view themselves infinitely above us.

Copied from the *Southern Recorder*, 1 January 1834, Page 1

> "Sales of land and negros, by Administrators, Executors, or Guardians are required by law to be held on the first Tuesday of the month between the hours of ten in the forenoon, and three in the afternoon at the courthouse in which the property is

situated.—Notices of these sales must be given in a public gazette sixty days previous to the sale.

Copied from the *Southern Recorder*, 1 January 1834, Page 1

"The undersigned, having purchased of General LaFayette the township of land in Florida granted to him by the congress of the United States, offer the same for sale. This land is situated in the immediate neighborhood of Tallahassee, and is believed, for fertility of soil, and local advantages to be more valuable than any other land in the territory. The southwestern part of the township adjoins the city of Tallahassee..." William B. Nuttall, Hector W. Branden, William P. Crane

While Osceola resists, they give away his land. The Seminoles are angry. The army has made it known that all captured Seminoles with African features will not be transported west when captured, but sold as slaves—including the children. Africans families will be broken up and sold."

26 January 1834

Tennessee, imitating Georgia, has seized our land above the river. Tennessee extended its laws over all our land within its boundaries. We are being squeezed. Tennessee and Georgia have nullified our constitution. Soon they will nullify our bodies.

Copied from the *Cherokee Phoenix* – 25 January 1834

"From the *Knoxville Republican* Sec. 1. Be it enacted by the General Assembly of the State of Tennessee, That the laws and jurisdiction of the state of Tennessee, be and hereby extended to the southern limits of the State, of that tract of country now in the occupancy of the Cherokee Indians..."

Elijah Hicks, our editor, reprinted an article from the Palladium that says what everyone knows about President Jackson, his administration and the government of Georgia. I included an excerpt of Andrew Jackson's speech. As I walk, I watch mothers and children at play. Whites believe everyone who isn't white must be miserable. Like a horse with a broken leg, they have tasked themselves with putting us out of our misery.

Copied from the *Cherokee Phoenix* – 1 March 1834 – page 2

"...they have neither the intelligence, the industry, the moral habits, nor the desire of improvement, which are essential to any favorable change in their condition....(the Cherokee are) established in the midst of another and a superior race and without appreciating the causes of their inferiority or seeking to control them, they must necessarily yield to the force of circumstances and ere long disappear."

I hope Andrew Jackson disappears.

16 May 1834 - The Planting Moon – A na a gv ti

Our beautiful newspaper has closed. We cannot buy paper and ink. Our money is exhausted. We have no money for postage or wages. President Jackson has stopped government payments owed us according to treaty to force us into poverty. They want to force our national emigration. What can we do? We can't fight. We will soon be vanished—somewhere out west we will disappear into nothingness.

It has been an honor to work on the Phoenix. I cherish every memory. With the closing of the Phoenix, I'm as sad as if my friend died.

I am proud that our newspaper survived this long. We exist in a sea of hate, surrounded by the Georgia Militia and Guard. Since the 1830 Indian Removal Act, our nation has been increasingly squeezed, invaded and dispossessed. The flood of whites is worse every year threatening our freedom.

I need Ben. He must come soon. He must come and take us out of this hate, misery and pain.

17 May 1834

I haven't seen Ben in weeks. Edudu told me a story.

"Walela, I think you should gather some strawberries. While you are gathering them, think of Ben. It is time you learned how to draw to yourself the man you love."

"How do I accomplish that, edudu? What do you suggest? I have written letters and he doesn't come to me."

"Come sit with me on the porch and I'll tell you the story of the first man and woman and how they solved their problems when distance came between them."

"I would love that, edudu. I would like that very much."

We sat together, edudu in his straight-back chair and I on the floor beside, as I did when I listened to edudu's stories as a little girl. I wanted to look up and feel the security I felt years ago. With edudu near, nothing in the world can harm me—not even white men.

"When the first man and woman came together," edudu began, "they lived happily for a very long time. They loved one another dearly. For some reason, the man became angry with his wife and the woman turned her face from him and left her husband. She traveled towards the land of the Sun in the east. Her husband was heartbroken. The Sun asked the husband if he wanted his wife back and he said he did. He missed her terribly. Could anything be done?

The Sun caused a patch of the finest huckleberries to grow in her path, but she was not interested. The Sun raised up a great patch of blackberries directly in front of her as she walked along, but she cared nothing for the blackberries either. There were some other fruits she passed, but nothing was of interest to her. Her heart was sore and her husband's anger caused her hunger to disappear completely."

"There were trees with beautiful red service berries, but she seemed not to see their beauty with the pain that was in her heart. Then, right in her path there was a lovely patch of ripe strawberries. She had never known strawberries. These were large, juicy and sweet. They were soft and ripe. She smelled their wonderful fragrance from a distance. After she ate a few strawberries, she turned her head to the west and into her mind came the memory of the husband she loved. Because of her memories, she could no longer travel east—away from her love. She sat down with her mind filled with images of the man she loved and she determined to return to him. She gathered her bag full of fine, beautiful strawberries for her love and as fast as she could, she ran towards the west—towards her husband and home. He met her on the way and arm in arm they traveled back to their home together. The strawberries erased the pain and brought the two lovers back together. From that time, strawberries were important to her and her husband. They never left one another again."

"What a lovely story, edudu. I do love strawberries."

"I think, my dear Walela, you should go gather ripe strawberries and all the while think of Ben. The strawberries may well cause your heart and his heart to search for one another."

18 May 1834

The Guard wants to frighten us into emigration. Since the missionaries were removed, they have been commissioned to dispossess and steal. Georgia passed laws so we cannot bring suit against a white man. If we resort to violence, the Guard will kill us or burn our houses. No one sees or cares. Justice has departed our country. We are alone. Who can oppose the likes of Curry and Butler sent by the Governor himself to make our lives difficult.

Our crime is simple. We are not white.

The president and the newspapers talk constantly of removal. Lewis Cass, Jackson's Secretary of War, thinks we are not fit to own land and must emigrate for our own protection. The general government assigns agents to help us. We are not benefited by their white help. We are harassed and dispossessed at every turn. The future may become worse, but how can it be worse? They have taken all the good farmland in the river bottoms. Soon they will come for us in the mountains. Some have lost hope and plan to remove as demanded, but edudu and elisi will not leave. None of their friends will leave. They are loyal and wait for word from our chief, John Ross. They hope he can persuade the general government to allow us to stay. We shall see.

Ben is the light in my life. One day he and I shall be together and these dark days will vanish in glorious happiness with my first view of his face when he comes for me. He will come. I know he will come. I wish it were tomorrow. I miss him every day and I think of him every night. He is my only hope. I know he will come.

2 June 1834

Our situation is bad, but the Africans' lot is worse.

Copied from the *Federal Union*-1 January 1834.

"Two Hundred Negros arrived and for sale of both sexes consisting of good cooks, washers, and ironers and seamstresses and chamber maids, blacksmiths, carpenters and a large supply of field hands and plough-boys. Persons wishing to purchase would do well to call early as convenient and examine for themselves. Oliver Simpson, H.H. & S.F. Slatter, John Lane."

They offer 200 Negros for sale as easily as cattle. Like cattle, I have seen slaves disfigured for easy identification. Owners cut a notch out of their ear or put a scar down the cheek or knock out a tooth. A runaway can be brought back from a non-slave state by United States law if proven they are escaped property. Unscrupulous slave hunters lie to authorities in non-slave states. White authorities care little for the plight of Africans in any case. Slave patrols sometimes beat our men to force betrayal of Africans.

Chattel is movable property such as furniture, animals or slaves, to be distinguished from land or buildings which cannot be moved. Whites believe Africans void of emotions or that they have no filial love? How can Africans be denied the right to marry and love their family? Whites have a great deal to answer for.

The whites say, "The slave has no rights…he or she cannot have the rights of a husband or wife. The slave is a chattel, and

chattels do not marry. The slave is not ranked among sentient
beings, but among things and things are not married."

I must not feed my bad wolf. Like edudu, I will trust the Great Spirit to
take care of things beyond me. One day I will pass this life. All that will be
left of me will be this story—my strokes of ink made on paper with the pen
Mrs. Lowry gave me. I will be gone, but the white God and the Great Spirit
will remain. Judgment will come. Perhaps this story will help right old
wrongs. I hope one day to see Mrs. Lowry come around the bend to visit with
me. What a glorious day.

4 June 1834

I often take my journal and quilt to our special place and write as I watch
the water silently glide by. I listen to the river's gentle voice speak words of
inspiration. I think how things change. I think about Mr. and Mrs. Lowry. I
think of Ben and the life he and I will have and I write. Hurry the day when
Ben takes me to himself.

Things change,
Time is uncertain,
One day calm,
Another day storms,
One day rain,
Another day snow,
One day sadness,
Another day joy,
One day loneliness,
Another day Ben,
Together forever,
Never to change,
Never to separate,
Each day growing,
A lifetime together,
Never to change.

June 1834 Milledgeville

"Ben, things are bad for the Cherokee, aren't they?" Zach said, looking
sideways at his friend.

"Yes, it seems for the last few years things have gone from bad to worse
for them," Ben answered.

"I know what you mean," Zach said. "First, the Indian Removal Act, then
gold was discovered, then the Georgia Guard was formed and your father and

his missionary friends were forced to leave. Now Georgia has canceled all Cherokee law. Yep, I would say it couldn't get much worse. To be honest, Ben, it won't be long and the Cherokee will be gone. They can't hang on much longer."

"I think you're right," Ben answered quietly. "The writing has been on the wall for a long time. Things are bad for the Cherokee and it gets worse every day."

Zach nodded and listened.

Ben continued, "The Cherokee councils meet in Tennessee now to avoid the Guard and now Tennessee has extended its laws over Cherokee Country. The end is coming. I think you're right. Terrible things are happening in Cherokee Country mostly because of the lotteries and Georgia's failure to honor past agreements."

"Well, Ben, you won't have to worry long," Zach said in a lighter voice. "Everything's comin' to a head and it's about time. I hear a lot of Cherokee have had enough. They're packin' up and emigrating. The Guard finally shut down the Phoenix and it's about time. That god damned paper was run by white folks anyway. Those lazy, illiterate Indians couldn't have kept that paper running for as long as they did without white help. An Indian newspaper was a big waste of time, wasn't it?"

Ben didn't know what to say. Ben had long ago decided never to argue with anyone in Milledgeville about the Cherokee or Africans, but he did feel Zach's pessimism about the future. There was no way the Cherokee could hold their unraveling nation together. Zach was probably right. It was time they left. If they were to go quietly it would be better for everyone. Both Georgia and Tennessee were pressuring them to emigrate. The Cherokee were being squeezed from all sides. How could they resist the ever increasing influx of white settlers who coveted their beautiful country? White expansion could not be stopped.

"Ben, I asked you here today because I need to talk to you about something. I've got some men working up in Cherokee Country. As you know, Father and I have been doing some speculating in lottery land. The details don't matter, but we got a couple of crews of men up there takin' care of business. We're going to make a lot of money when the hardheaded Cherokee finally get wise and leave, but that's not what I want to talk to you about. I like you Ben. We're friends, aren't we?"

Zach paused, smoked his cigar, sipped his whiskey and waited for Ben's response. Ben was puzzled but had learned to be patient when the long-winded Zach was talking.

"Yes, of course we're friends," Ben answered as he studied Zach's face. "I know we don't see exactly eye to eye on the Cherokee, but you're the best friend I have. I trust you, Zach—I do. What do you want to talk to me about?"

Zach studied Ben's face for a moment and blew a cloud of silvery smoke towards the ornate ceiling.

"Ben, a couple of days ago I got some news from Cherokee Country that bothers me. This news concerns you and that's why I asked you here today. I didn't want to talk about this in the office. I've been thinking about what my man told me and I decided it was something you should know. Have you talked to Cassie recently?"

"Yes," Ben replied—his mind instantly at attention. Zach never talked about Cassie or his relationship with her and he rarely talked about the Cherokee.

Ben shot back, "What about her? Is she ok? What is it, Zach? What news have you heard?"

Zach calmed his fears.

"Cassie is good, Ben. She's fine—fit as a fiddle as far as I know, but I heard something I decided you should know—something I needed to tell you. Don't worry, Ben, like I said, Cassie is well, but the next time you see her, ask her if something bad happened to her a couple of years ago that she never talked about with you."

Ben was visibly upset.

"Zach, you must tell me what you're talking about. I must know what it is you know. You must tell me."

Zach put his hand on Ben's shoulder.

"Ben, I'm your friend. You know that. For now let me say I heard something, but I don't know anything for sure. I hear rumors all the time. What I heard may or may not be true. I don't like to spread hearsay, and this certainly isn't first-hand information. You understand?"

"Please tell me, Zach. Please tell me what you heard," Ben begged.

Zach sat down and continued, "What I heard may be no more than malicious gossip. I don't want to put evil into your mind based on tittle-tattle, but there was enough in it I decided I should mention it and let you decide what to do. If roles were reversed, I would want to know."

Ben stared at Zach without responding.

Zach puffed his cigar and continued in a lazy voice, "My men are up in Cherokee Country. They heard about an incident that happened near New Echota some years ago concerning the Guard and a young Cherokee woman who worked at their damned newspaper. When they mentioned the Indian newspaper, I put two and two together and thought you would want to know. I know you've known that Indian woman friend of yours since childhood. I promise you, Ben, you'll never have a better friend than I am. I would want you to tell me if you heard something about Elizabeth, but right now, what I heard is only rumor. I don't know if it's true or false."

Ben felt immediate conflicting emotions at the mention of Elizabeth's name. He didn't need to be thinking about Elizabeth and Cassie at the same time.

"Whatever this was happened a long time ago, Ben. I thought the best way for you to handle this would be for you, yourself, to ask Cassie what happened. Let Cassie tell you and you'll get the truth straight from the horse's mouth and be done with it. That's the right way. Perhaps what I heard is nothing but rumor. This may be hearsay or just a couple of drunk soldiers boasting about things they never did."

Zach took a puff from his cigar and pointed the burning tip at Ben as he spoke, "You ask her and see what she says. It's not my business to tell you gossip."

Ben, in some distress, begged again, "Won't you tell me what you've heard?"

"No, Ben. It wouldn't be right. I don't want to do that. You do the right thing and ask Cassie what happened and we'll both discover the truth, won't we? To be honest, I'm curious myself about what really happened. I've thought about this the last couple of days. I even asked Elizabeth's opinion about what I should do. Elizabeth and I agree. You should talk to Cassie. That's the only way."

Ben was looking at Zach and said nothing.

"I'm going home now, Ben. I've had enough to drink. You go home and get a good night's sleep and don't worry."

As Zach put down his glass and prepared to leave the hotel he turned to Ben, "I figured you would want to leave straightaway so I arranged for you to take some days off. Leave in the morning and stay gone as long as you want. Father agreed with me. Count this as a well-earned holiday. You've been workin' hard. Father wants to keep you fresh. We got some big plans coming up and we need your help. Take care of business with that Indian friend of yours and come back with a clear mind and we'll make more money than ever. I'll take care of everything at the office while you're away. Goodnight, Ben. I'm exhausted and a little drunk. I'm going home and get a good night's sleep and you should, too."

Zach gave Ben a friendly slap on the back and walked unsteadily to his waiting carriage. Ben watched Zach's negro driver help his drunk friend up into his seat and off they went. Ben wondered what the news could possibly be, but he would have to wait. He didn't like thinking about the possibilities. He left for New Echota before dawn.

9 June 1834

It was wonderful to see Ben, but he asked me about the men who attacked me. I hoped I would never have to share that experience ever again with anyone, especially Ben.

"Cassie, we need to talk. Let's go down to the river to our place. Bring something to eat and we'll spend the afternoon there. I want to listen to the river and we can talk there in peace."

"I think I would rather spend the afternoon with you beside my river than travel the world with kings," I answered.

"Aren't you curious about what I want to talk to you about, Cassie?"

"Of course, I'm curious, but I am patient. You'll talk when you're ready. The longer you are away, the more I learn patience."

When we arrived at the river, we sat quietly without talking. I could tell Ben was preparing himself for an important conversation. I wondered what he was thinking, but I have learned to let others think when they don't want to talk. I playfully pulled him to me on our blanket. We kissed.

"I may be patient when it comes to waiting for you to speak what's on your mind, but I'm not very patient when it comes to your kisses," I said playfully. "Those I wait for impatiently. I always want more. I never have enough. I wish you would give me more kisses, Ben—and give them more often."

Ben put his arm around me and kissed me gently on the forehead.

"Cassie, I do have something serious to talk to you about. Zach told me a story that troubled me. That's why I'm here. Zach and his father have men working all around Cherokee Country. One of Zach's men heard a drunken story from a couple of soldiers in a tavern. He told Zach."

Ben looked at me and paused a moment, but I was silent. My worst fears were realized. The thing I most dreaded had come upon me.

"Zach wouldn't tell me what the story was that his men told him, but he did say they described events that happened several years ago up here in Cherokee Country. Zach wouldn't tell me the details—not one word. He insisted I should ask you what happened. He said this was personal between you and me. I want to know what happened no matter how bad it was or how

534

embarrassing. I love you and I want to know. Please tell me what happened if you can. I'll continue to love you just as I always have. Did something bad happen? My mind hasn't been able to rest one minute since Zach spoke to me."

As I gathered my thoughts, I was troubled thinking about that horrible day and what happened. It was a day I had tried to bury. I had long known that I would eventually have to tell Ben.

"Ben, I love you dearly—more than my own life. Yes, something bad did happen several years ago. It was terrible. I had hoped the day would never come when I would have to tell you, but I will tell you everything if you want to know."

"Yes, Cassie. I want to know. I must know. You must tell me."

"You are my darling, Ben. I've often wondered if you would ever find out. It was horrible. I still have nightmares about that day. I had good reason not to tell you—or anyone. I had good reason to forget."

"I don't care, Cassie. I must know. Please tell me. Will you tell me?"

"Yes, I will tell you, my love. When I tell you, you must promise never to tell Five Feathers or edudu or anyone. You must promise. You must promise, Ben."

"I promise I'll tell no one," Ben immediately replied.

"I was afraid that if I told you what happened, it would get you killed," I said in a whisper. "I couldn't bear that. I was afraid if my brother heard, it would get him killed. I love you, Ben, more than my own life. I would simply die if anything bad happened to you."

I told Ben the entire story of that hideous day the men attacked me. I left nothing out. It's the only time I've ever seen Ben truly angry and lose control.

"Cassie, I promise I'll find those men. I'll see to it they're punished. They don't deserve to live. I'll kill them with my own hands. I'll tie them to a tree and castrate each one slowly and listen to their screams as they bleed to death. I promise I'll find them."

I took Ben's hands in mine and kissed each of his fingers. I looked into his eyes and spoke as lovingly as I could.

"My dear Ben, your response is exactly the reason I didn't tell you years ago. What's done is done. I love my brother, I love my edudu and I love you more than life itself. I didn't tell anyone because I knew what the reaction would be. You can't undo what they did. Killing those men wouldn't change what happened. I can't live without you. You must not do anything foolish or you will double my pain."

We sat silently there on my rock in our special place listening to the patient water slide by. Ben held me close. I had my arms around Ben and pressed the side of my head tight against his chest where it belonged.

"Do nothing foolish, Ben. Please, please do not speak to anyone about this. Five Feathers must never know. If my brother found out, he would surely get himself killed."

When I finally looked at Ben's face, my arms still around his chest, I could see his eyes were full of murder.

"Ben, I couldn't live without you. Nothing good can come from revenge. Those worthless men who assaulted live worthless lives. Leave them alone to wallow in their worthlessness. That can be their punishment. I want you. I want you in my life forever. I want you to keep your job. I don't want my brother to die. Do you understand?"

"I understand Cassie. I'm angry, of course, but I understand."

Suddenly, Ben's eyes softened and he spoke gently, "I would never do anything to compound your pain. You know that. I adore you."

"Ben, I am forced to live with my horror. Let's let this end—here and now. Even if you were to exact revenge and get away with it, I would still have to live every day with the horrible thing done to me. Let this go. Let your father's God take care of justice. You do believe your God will take care of this one day, don't you?"

Ben didn't say anything. I did my best to make certain he saw the wisdom of my words.

"Ben, if you take revenge and are discovered, it will end your career. You might even hang. The Guard have friends everywhere on the whiteside—even in the Governor's office. Do you remember what your mother and father taught you? Don't let them suck you into their disgusting world. Think about us and our children's future. You wouldn't want me to suffer a second time, would you?"

Ben smiled for the first time.

"No, Cassie. I don't want to increase your suffering. I promise I'll forget about this. I promise."

"Ben, I've borne my shame for almost six years. Not a day goes by when I don't remember that horrible day and those filthy men, but it would bring no joy to have those men punished if I lost you. Remember the two wolves, Ben. Remember what your father taught you about forgiveness. Feed your good wolf as I have. Justice will come from another quarter. The Great Spirit will take care of those men. Balance will come. These men will reap what they have sown."

"I believe that, Cassie. I believe that but it still makes me angry. I can't describe the anger that I feel."

"Ben, promise you will let this go. I'm begging you with every ounce of my being. I want to hear you say out loud you will not take vengeance on these men and you will let this go for my sake—for our sake—for our children's sake. Tell me Ben. I want to hear you say the words."

After another long silence, we listened to the water gurgling by my rock. Ben kissed me and sighed. I knew he was thinking about what I had said.

"Cassie, you're right. I knew you were right from the beginning. Those men aren't worth the powder and shot it would take to kill them. I promise I'm not going to let them into our lives a second time. I promise."

"Promise me, Ben. I want to hear you say the words."

Ben looked deep into my eyes and held me by my shoulders.

"Cassie, from this moment I'll forget what happened and you and I shall move on. I love you dearly and you're right. I promise to forget."

June 1834 Milledgeville

When Ben returned to Milledgeville, he asked Zach to meet that next evening. When Zach was settled, Ben got straight to the point.

"I saw Cassie, Zach, and had a long talk with her. She told me everything. She told me about three uniformed Guard who raped her. I guess that's the story you heard. Her account was the most horrible thing I've ever heard. Since she told me, I haven't been able to think about anything except retribution. I want those men to pay. I want them to suffer—to suffer horribly. I want to be the one to inflict their pain—weeks of pain so I can hear them beg me to stop their torture. Is that the story you were talking about, Zach? Is that the rumor you heard?"

Zach took a sip of whiskey and smiled. He looked at Ben over his glass.

He responded almost in a whisper, "Yep, that's what I heard. A couple of our men who do contract work for us were up in Cherokee Country. Three drunken guardsmen were boasting what they had done to a young Indian woman near New Echota. The woman they described sounded like the woman you know. I wasn't sure. When men are drunk, they'll say most anything both true and false. I knew if this were true you would be angry. You do have an exaggerated sense of justice, but I like that about you. You must have spent a lot of time with a soft-hearted mother."

"Yes, my mother and father were soft-hearted," Ben replied.

"The three guardsmen told my men they had been assigned to harass the Cherokee newspaper—the Phoenix. They boasted that they had followed an attractive Indian woman from the newspaper office and caught her alone in the woods. They were surprised to hear her speak perfect English. When I heard that, I knew I would have to tell you. I'm sorry, Ben. I thought a long time about not telling you, but if it were me, I would want to know, but don't forget that Cassie isn't white. What happened to her isn't good but it isn't the same as if she had been a white woman."

"Thanks, Zach, I appreciate you telling me," Ben said a little sarcastically. "You're a good man for telling me."

"After Cassie told me the story," Ben said, "she was relieved. I told her that she and I are closer than ever before. I must confess, Zach, I would love to take care of those men myself. Since the moment she told me, I've tortured and killed them a thousand times in my mind. I wake up in the middle of the night thinking about ways to increase their pain."

Ben laughed a little wry laugh and said in a distant voice without looking at Zach, "I don't know if I have ever enjoyed thinking about anything as much as their slow painful death. I surprised myself. I lie awake thinking what I would do with a sharp knife—slowly—or maybe a dull knife would be better. At the least, I want to tie them to a tree and castrate them like pigs and listen to them scream as I watch them bleed to death—then leave their sorry bodies tied to the tree to be eaten by animals. Thinking about what they did to an innocent woman has driven me crazy."

"I know exactly what you mean," said Zach.

"I came back here to regain equilibrium. I need to let this go. I know I do," said Ben finally.

"Ben, our work in the legislature is important. Our work comes first. Forget this thing. Our plan for the Senate is going well and I figure by the time the next election comes you'll have just about enough votes in the house for a Senate appointment. You don't lack too many now. We don't need any trouble."

"Yes," Ben agreed, "it would be a mistake to ruin my career and everything you and I and Elizabeth have worked for. Cassie is good now, but I could still kill them with my bare hands. I don't think it would be a good idea for me to ever know their identity, Zach. If you ever find out who they are, keep that information to yourself."

"If I find out, you can wager I'll never tell you. I promise you that, Ben," Zach said forcefully. "Don't forget, Ben, those men have friends in the Governor's office. What happens to Indians is of no concern to the Governor or anyone in Milledgeville. Don't forget that. Folks would think you a strange bird to get upset over anything the Guard or Militia does."

"Yes, I guess you're right. I know too well what people think."

"I thought about retribution myself," Zach said. "Even though she ain't a white woman, I thought about taking care of those men and never saying a word to you till it was over. Father and I have connections and it could be done, but she isn't white and these men have friends. That damned Bishop knows everyone in the state. We got bigger fish to fry, Ben."

"I know all about Bishop and the Guard and what they've done in Cherokee Country," Ben agreed. "He's a loose cannon."

"If those men died, suspicion would eventually come to us or to the firm," Zach continued. "We should give this one a pass, Ben. Revenge could cost us everything we've worked for. Even if we could prove their crime, no judge would convict them. It's not a crime anywhere to assault an Indian. I told my men to keep an eye out for these guys. Who knows, maybe the right situation would present itself and they would disappear one day."

"You're right, Zach. That's the same conclusion I've come to five hundred times a day since I talked to Cassie. No one thinks it a crime to assault an Indian."

"Ben, we've worked for years to get where we are. We don't want to risk everything we've worked for on some momentary emotional satisfaction over something that isn't important. Those men aren't worth the rope it would take to hang 'em. Ben, let this go. Can you do that? Can you bury this and never talk about it again? That would be best, don't you think?"

Ben's eyes met Zach's and Ben nodded his agreement. At that moment Ben was too emotional to risk speaking.

"One last thing before we drop this," Zach said, "for your good and for the good of the firm, this conversation shall never be mentioned again. It ends right here. I never told you about anything and you never had a conversation with an Indian woman. Do you understand me, Ben? You know nothing about what three drunk Georgia soldiers did. We don't want the Governor thinking we're sticking up for Indians."

"I understand. I promise I'll never bring it up again," Ben said.

"I understand, Zach. This conversation is erased from my mind. I'll never bring it up again."

June 20 1834

Copied from the *Federal Union* – 11 June 1834 – page 2

"CREEK INDIANS.—Many Creek Indians, who have sold their land in Alabama, have assembled in Paulding county; and their number is daily increasing. They are unwilling to remove...;

they have no lands…they say that they are determined to remain in Georgia…If these destitute and indolent savages are permitted to remain in Georgia they will prove disagreeable and troublesome intruders. Having sold their lands under regulations established by the War Department, with a view to their removal to the West they are now under peculiar care of the Federal Government; and we have no doubt that the president will adopt prompt measures to rid us of the intrusion. Should it become necessary for Georgia to act, she will easily remove these trespassers from her borders, but a call to the field would be inconvenient and irksome…"

31 July 1834

Copied from the *Federal Union* – 23 July 1834 – page 2

Cherokee-Injunction Case, Judge Warner's Opinion, Delivered at the Convention of Judges, July Session, 1834

"This is a…contest between the rights of the state of Georgia and…the Cherokee Indians…The state claims the right to limit the Indians…In…1730 six of the principle chiefs of the Cherokee Indians…went to London, and acknowledged themselves subject to the king, in the same manner as were their white brethren of South Carolina. During the war of the Revolution, the Cherokee Indians took part with the British Crown…the American cause was victorious and the Indians conquered….Each state within its respective limits retained all the rights which belonged to the crown…From the Declaration of Independence up to the time of the adoption of the constitution…each state had the right to manage all affairs with the Indians within its own limits…The Cherokee Indians have never been recognized by the Government as a sovereign people…The states before the adoption of the Federal Constitution, having the exclusive right to manage the affairs of the Indians within their respective limits, and not having delegated this right, the conclusion is irresistible, that it yet remains in the states….That the Government of the United States "solemnly guarantied" to the Cherokee Indians the lands in their occupancy, within the limits of the state, is admitted; but the State of Georgia contends that she had prior and paramount right to all the land within her limits…It is plain to...everyone...the territorial rights of the states were to be considered sacred...It is therefore clear that the Cherokee Indians have not derived any vested rights to the soil within the limits of Georgia by virtue of the several treaties made with them and the Government of the United States...The supreme court of the State of New York...have exercised an entire supremacy over all the Indian tribes within the State, and have regulated by law their internal concerns, their contracts and their property"

12 November 1834

Great news. Ben has been elected to the U.S. House for the second time.

Chapter XLVI

1835 – Council at Running Waters – Schermerhorn

Chapter 46

9 January 1835 – Month of the Cold Moon – Du no lv ta ni – Friday

Beginning last night and all day today, the frigid north wind has been whipping down the mountains bringing frozen rain and snow. We have been listening to the sleet make music against the windows and the wind whistling a tune in the chimney blowing a smoky downdraft. Even though it is so cold, I love every moment of a winter storm. I feel sorry for edudu carrying in our wood and tending to the animals. Elisi and I put more straw in with the chickens. The poor things are so cold.

The storm was a surprise. Edudu said he never expected a storm from the northeast. The entire landscape is covered in its beautiful winter coat with drifts in many places as high as my knees and other places with hardly any snow at all. I feel sorry for the animals and the birds. I walked down to the river. It has much ice floating, but it is not frozen across. I wonder where the river otters are? How do they stay warm?

24 January 1835

Copied from the *Georgia Journal* – 20 January 1835 – page 2

"...within the present limits of the State, lies the Cherokee tribe...From whence does the State derive the right of jurisdiction? I answer—by charter from the Crown of Great Britain—the right which Great Britain had to these limits she acquired by discovery and conquest...Such rights are recognized among nations...and is not now open for discussion...as a question of international law the right is established.

This writer could write for the Romans about establishing Roman jurisdiction over foreign lands. Our land was divided among white Europeans and then we were conquered. It is interesting how they gave themselves the right to dominate those who wish to remain independent.

28 June 1835

In North Carolina it is a criminal offense for free Africans to educate their children. African fathers must not teach their children. I am grateful for Mr.

and Mrs. Lowry who think education is for all. I think about them every day. Mr. Lowry would hate this new North Carolina law."

1 July 1835

Whites are afraid of slave uprisings like the Turner rebellion in Virginia or the huge Jamaican rebellion. Whites don't want Africans reading. They are terrified the increasing numbers of Africans who do all the hard work will unite. There are almost as many Africans in Georgia, South Carolina, North Carolina and Alabama as whites. Whites hated our newspaper for the same reason they deny Africans the right to literacy. I can't express in words how much I dislike and fear the Guard and the Militia. Even when a man of colour is free, he is not permitted to teach his own children to read and write. What an asinine, fatuous law that denies life to little children?

Copied from the *Federal Union* - page 3 - 3 February 1835

"North Carolina has decided by a vote of fifty to thirty-eight that a free man of color shall not be permitted to educate his own children or cause them to be educated."

4 July 1835

If our ancestors had known the future, they would have drowned every white man before he came upon dry land. I never will understand. I read this to edudu and three of his friends. They were not happy.

Copied from the *Federal Union*-23 June 1835-page 2

"Our Cherokee Affairs: The terms of the treaty lately offered by General Jackson to the Cherokee are marked by unparalleled liberality to that misguided and unfortunate people and paternal solicitude for their welfare. It secures to the tribe a good and permanent home, and provides for distribution to each individual Indian...for their removal...Notwithstanding the magnitude of the price, the extraordinary liberality of the government has been approved by the American people....The assent of the chiefs to these treaties has generally been acquired by direct bribes...To the pure and inflexible patriot now at the head of the government, has been reserved the honor of reforming this corrupt and corrupting habit; of restraining the inordinate cupidity of the chiefs and of securing justice to the poor, weak and obscure Indian....Many of the most intelligent Cherokee are anxious for the confirmation of the treaty; but it is seriously apprehended that John Ross will resort to the most criminal measures to prevent its acceptance...that Indians of the Ross party, after the commission of the most flagrant crimes, may set at defiance, or may evade our constables, and sheriffs; that they may hold in contempt the array of our juries, and the authority of our judges."

"For a long course of years Andrew Jackson has evinced a steady friendship and a paternal benevolence for the Cherokee...The president has long been the faithful friend of Georgia and at the same time, with guardian care, he has attempted to provide for the real welfare of the Cherokee...These two men will not be censured for their measures in relation to the Cherokee, except by those who are determined to encourage these victims of delusion in their foolish rejection of the liberal offers of the President and their obstinate determination to violate the laws of the state and to oppress the friends of emigration...the honor of Georgia will sustain governor Lumpkin in his determination to maintain the authority of her laws for protection, from the ruffian violence of (Chief John) Ross and his savage myrmidons."

"Thank you, Walela, for reading to us. We know how things are. We know what the whiteside has always thought. Georgia hates us for no reason other than a wish to possess that which belongs to another. Our good John Ross has never advocated violence in any form—never at any time. He has been a hard-working representative to the white governments and promoted peace at every opportunity. Andrew Jackson says evil things about him because John Ross cannot be purchased."

One of Edudu's friends spoke, "I have not heard of a single crime committed by our chief or any of the men who work with him. Chief Ross tells us every time I hear him that we shall not use violence in any form. You read the white newspapers, Walela. What do you think?"

I spoke to the men, "I read the white newspapers. I know what they are saying and why. These accusations of Cherokee violence are not true. The men who control the newspapers write lies intended to inflame the wider white populace over time—to bend public opinion to hate us. White readers receive and believe every bad thing said about us—even the stories that have been invented. Whites want to believe bad news about us because they want our land. White politicians find it easy to deceive because it's in their best interest."

The men nodded and edudu spoke, "Robbery, theft, intimidation, fraud, murder and rape have been committed against us for decades by whites. It's useless for us to complain to white authorities. Every year it gets worse. They steal our livestock and anything else they want. Just a month ago I watched a group of white men take most of my hogs. Even though I was standing there and told them the hogs were mine, there was nothing I could do. They laughed as they drove my hogs away. They know white judges will not convict a white man for a crime committed against an Indian."

"One day, perhaps, our story will be told," I said. "I will write as long as I can hold a pen. Men can kill with a lead bullet, but there is no rifle powerful enough to kill a noble idea once written."

Edudu spoke once again, "You keep writing, Walela. Maybe that will do some good. A grand council meeting has been called at Running Waters. It will be held on John Ridge's farm. We are going to be asked to vote by Mr. Schermerhorn and Mr. Curry on the disbursements of annuities. We will be asked to decide whether the money goes to individuals as the Ridge and Curry people want or into the national treasury as our chief prefers. Schermerhorn and Murray, friends of Ridge, want the money to go to individuals—to their friends, of course. The removal party is doing their best to gain broad support among us at the expense of Chief Ross. I don't like this. It's appears Ridge and Curry are going behind our chief's back intentionally—like thieves sneaking around in the night."

"What do you think will happen, edudu?" I asked.

"I shall let you know, my dear, when I return from the meeting. I will listen and learn. I will listen and learn."

When edudu returned from the meeting at Running Waters, I couldn't wait to hear what happened.

"What happened, edudu? Tell me. Tell me."

"Our chief is a good man," Edudu said, with a smile. "Even when the whites and the removal party sought to go behind his back, our people remained loyal and strong. Ridge, Schermerhorn and Major Curry were defeated in their attempt to undermine our chief's authority. They were defeated badly. I have a great suspicion, Walela, that Ridge and his friends are interested in acquiring wealth at our expense and they'll continue to work to defeat our chief. I find it hard to believe that Ridge and his friends hold the best interest of all Cherokee in their hearts—especially the poor Cherokee."

I was unusually impatient, "Please tell me what happened. I can't wait to hear."

"My dear Walela, you should have come with me. It was a magnificent meeting. Everyone behaved. There was almost no drunkenness and no violence whatsoever. We had dances, ballplays and wrestling and I talked with all my friends and told stories. I told a lot of stories late into the evening. We heard the speeches by Schermerhorn and his friends and we finally voted. The vote was big in favor of our chief. I am pleased. Perhaps we may be allowed to keep our farm, perhaps not, but at least the removal party was soundly defeated."

"That is wonderful news, edudu."

Edudu looked at me and this time he didn't smile.

"I know a great deal about this world," edudu said after a long pause. "We can admire a colorful smooth stone lying on the ground, but pick that stone up and we discover slimy, slithering things living underneath. Life is like that. I know a great deal about the removal party. I hear things. I think about things. When they talk it appears they have everyone's best interest at heart. Almost every day someone tells me what is going on down by the Coosa river, up at the Agency and other places. If someone damns the stream in one place it will overflow in another. I fear the defeat of the removal party at the meeting has only delayed the flood. The removal party is defeated for the moment, but I know they are secretly planning things with the whites. Whites want rid of us and they don't care how. They will use the removal party as a tool if they can. I hope for the best, but my sad heart tells me Ridge and the whites will conspire. We shall be washed away by waves of white water."

28 July 1835

Good news. John Ross is going to move our silent printing press and all our printing equipment to Red Clay. We can begin publishing the Phoenix again. I will do anything to assist our newspaper. If I live in Tennessee and work on the Phoenix, Five Feathers can care for elisi and edudu while I'm away or perhaps they would come with me. What wonderful news.

6 August 1835 - ga lo nii moon--the end of the fruit moon

It is hot, sticky and dusty. We need rain. The dust and heat make elisi's cough worse. She does not sleep well. The days and even the nights are hot like an oven. The pleasant summer winds have been stilled. The house never cools. Elisi and I are impatient as we wait for the hot summer sun to retreat south. We're eager to feel the cool breath of autumn spread over our land. We will rejoice with the trees as they don their colorful garments.

24 August 1835

Horror. Without warning the Guard took our printing press, destroyed all our supplies, burned our building and scattered our precious syllabary type. It is rumored someone, perhaps Stand Watie, told the Guard about our plans to move the printing press north outside of Georgia. I don't want to believe any Cherokee man would betray his own nation, but edudu has heard things. I cried all afternoon. Our ability to send our newspaper throughout the United States has been destroyed forever. The right to speak truth—the right whites cherish above all is for whites only. Whites did not want us to begin printing again. Mr. Lowry was right. The powerful men in Milledgeville understand that words are more powerful than lead, powder and iron.

Perhaps we should remove to western lands to escape. Edudu, elisi and their friends are too old. They should be buried in their own country with the bones of their mothers and fathers.

Where is this promised land? How would we get there? How would we live? If forced from our home, elisi and edudu will not survive.

I fear edudu's words will prove prophetic. One cold morning the sun will reveal everything beautiful in our country frozen and lifeless—covered by a white killing frost.

21 November 1835

When I finished reading this article to edudu he looked at me and said nothing. I could read his face. Our chief continues to work to help us keep a remnant of land. Tennessee and Georgia are working together for our defeat. I should stop reading white newspapers.

Copied from the *Federal Union* - 13 November 1835 – page 3

"We have just had an interview with some gentleman on their return from the council from Red Clay, from whom we learn that the proposals, made to the Cherokee by the United States Government have met with final rejection. The two parties, whose views and actions have been so diametrically opposed to each other, met to confer on the possibility of so modifying the proposed treaty as to meet the conflicting views of the parties; and although the treaty and all its provisions were rejected, the parties so far united as to appoint a delegation, composed of both Ridge and Ross men, to meet and confer with the commissioners of the United States. Whether this conference will take place in the Cherokee Country, or at Washington, is not yet settled; but it is presumed they will meet at Washington: We leave to others to say whether this course of Ross is or is not finesse. But it appears to us that he wishes to gain time, and thereby see what regulations our present legislature will adopt towards the lands now occupied by the Cherokees, within the limits of the State.

If the present legislature should not provide for granting, indiscriminately, all the land in Cherokee Country, it is more than probable that he will still continue to reject the most liberal offers of the general government. But if the States of Tennessee and Georgia will adopt proper measures, there can be no doubt, but that they will, be forced to accept arrangements for their speedy removal West of the Mississippi river. Let Georgia grant all her lands, and Tennessee prevent their removal thither, and the result is obvious. –Cassville Pioneer, 30 ult."

Our chief and John Howard Payne have been arrested in Tennessee by soldiers from Georgia. What is our chief's crime? He stands for our Cherokee people and for that he is persecuted beyond the borders of Georgia. They destroy our printing press. They arrest our chief. I can only imagine what will come.

Copied from the *Federal Union* – 20 November 1835 – page 2

"There are four Cherokees in Milledgeville, who state, that in the absence of Col. Bishop, the second officer of the Cherokee Guard, with a detachment crossed the boundary of the State, proceeded to the residence of John Ross in Tennessee, seized him, and brought him a prisoner into Georgia. They state, that this outrage was perpetrated at the suggestion of Shermerhorn and Currie, agents of the United States, and that its motive was, to keep Ross from going to Washington, to represent the Cherokees with the Federal Government.... Mr. John Howard Payne also, a gentleman well known to the literary world, has been arrested under the suspicion of his having conspired with Ross, against the welfare of Georgia, and it is said his papers give evidence of the fact."

26 November 1835

My Dear Cassie,

I dashed off this letter in a mad rush to make the afternoon post. I want you to read the latest first hand. I include an article from today's newspaper, the Federal Union, 20 November 1835, from page two and three. Perhaps John Ross can perform miracles and your people may have a tiny homeland in the corner of Georgia, but I fear there are, even as I write, backroom negotiations. Zach thinks the same. He would know.

My guess is Shermerhorn has a hidden agenda straight from the War Department or the White House. Treachery is afoot. Zach warned me not to trust Jackson. Shermerhorn has written asking the President to refuse to negotiate with John Ross and the national party. The President and Shermerhorn have planned to cause strong divisions in the Cherokee leadership and sign a treaty with a portion of the delegates. When that clandestine treaty is signed it will be immediately pushed through the United States Senate before Ross can mount objections. Chicanery of this kind is not uncommon with Jackson and Cass—even among whites. Georgia will cooperate with Shermerhorn and Curry and the removal party. I don't like this, Cassie. I don't like this at all. Please share this with your edudu and his friends. Perhaps the looming disaster can be averted. I will do my best to communicate this to John Ross himself. This letter is for your eyes only. Do not let it out of your possession.

Loving you more every day, Ben xoxoxo

"New Echota – 31 October 1835

Col. John H. Lumpkin

"...The Red Clay council has closed and the result of their deliberations have been of vast consequence to the Cherokee people—I considered that the Indian controversy now to be closed. The Ross party and the Treaty party have united, and have agreed to close the Cherokee difficulties by a general treaty. To effect this object the people in general council assembled, have elected twenty delegates, with full powers to treat at Washington City. Those delegates, to wit: John Ross, John Ridge, John Martin, Elias Boudinott, Charles Vann, Soft Shell Turtle, E. Hicks, John Baldridge, John Benge, James Daniel, Sleeping Rabbit, Joseph Vann, Richard Fields, Richard Taylor, Lewis Ross, Thomas Foreman, Jesse Bushyhead, Peter of Aquohee, James Brown and John Hass...the appointment of this delegation clothed with full power to treat, was ratified by the people....there were upwards of one thousand men signed the power of this delegation. This delegation then commenced a negotiation with Mr. Schermerhorn and as they could not procure from him positive terms, they have adjourned over to meet at Washington City, on the 20th of December next, to treat at headquarters….against Mr. Schermerhorn's official labor I have nothing to say; he has served his government with zeal and energy. But candor requires me to express my fears, that his zeal will carry him away from the true course which the government ought to adopt. I believe that he has written letters to the President to reject the Delegation at Washington, and contrary to the will of all the parties of the Indians, has appointed the 3rd Monday in December to hold a treaty with the people at the New Echota….I feel a great desire to avert the great calamity of a people expelled out of their houses in winter, which leads me to make this appeal in behalf of my people….to the correctness of these views, I pledge to you my sacred honor. Your Friend, John Ridge

Why is Schermerhorn meeting in New Echota? Cherokee national meetings have been forbidden in our capital. I do not like this meeting when our chief is in Washington City. Georgia permits the removal party to hold meetings in Cherokee Country but John Ross and the national party must meet in Red Clay. A terrible storm brewing—a terrible storm.

Chapter XLVII

1836 – Disputed Treaty Ratified – Gen. Wool Appointed

Chapter 47

2 January 1836 - The Cold Moon - Du no lv ta ni

I miss Ben. Sometimes he comes to me after visiting his parents in Brainerd. His job is important. I understand why his visits are less frequent. Perhaps I'm foolish to wait, but I want no other man. At night I smell his fragrance. I feel his arms. I hear him whisper as we compose ourselves for sleep.

3 January 1836.

Big trouble is coming. On December 29 ult in the absence of our chief, Major Ridge, Elias Boudinott, John Gunter and seventeen others of the removal party signed a treaty in New Echota with the representative of the general government. Things happened as Ben predicted. Why didn't they wait for our chief? Why the rush? Edudu believes there will be trouble. J. F. Schermerhorn, the Jackson representative, negotiated the treaty. He persuaded the small removal party to sign away our entire nation without our chief's presence and against John Ross's expressed will. This could be the beginning of the end. They should not have signed without our chief. Something is not right. Why did they go behind our chief's back? Was their concern to preserve their personal wealth? Why did Schermerhorn accept the signatures without our chief and without a general council? Edudu thinks Schermerhorn purposely waited until our chief was absent or worse, arranged our chief's absence. Schermerhorn knew Chief Ross would not agree to any treaty that would cede our entire country. Edudu thinks Schermerhorn was acting under direct orders from President Jackson.

Ben is right. Whites, like the Romans, know how to divide et impera. Divide and conquer, as Roman generals knew well, is the proven way to defeat one's enemies. We are certainly their enemy.

John Ross, in Washington City, works to influence the general government so we can at least have a small share of our land. All our chief's work is in doubt. Will the white congress ratify this sham treaty? I hope not. This fraudulent treaty may be the first out of scores of previous agreements the general government honors. It gives away our land in its entirety. They are like that. They have what they want—our vanishment.

4 January 1836

I asked Harriet why her Elias signed the treaty. She thinks his friends pressured him. She and I think some men, including Elias, think Chief Ross is wasting his time. They believe it would be better to exchange our land and start a new life across the Mississippi rather than continue to struggle and perhaps lose everything. Some have left for the west, but most of us remain. We want to stay in the land the Great Spirit gave us. Why would we leave? The land doesn't belong to us. We belong to the land.

None of my friends want to go west. Perhaps our chief can work a miracle. Perhaps Major Ridge is right and we should leave. How could they sign our country away for money when our Chief wasn't here? The land belongs to all of us. The removal party represents a small portion of our people. There will be trouble over this, big trouble.

According to the piece of paper they call a treaty, every Cherokee family must leave within two years. The approaching evil comes inexorably. Edudu and elisi will not talk about the treaty or the removal party. They trust our chief. Everyone should trust him. I am confused but I hope for the best. I wish Ben would take us away.

Why can't I stay with my friends and family in the land of my nativity where my father and mother are buried? Why can't they stay on the whiteside like they promised?

February 1836

The *Camden Journal* says South Carolina is sending mounted regiments to Florida to pursue Seminoles and take them west. They talk about how we violate the rights of white people. We didn't go to Europe and take their land. We were born here and they are Europeans by birth. I don't want to be known as an American. Americus Vespucci was an Italian explorer. How odd our land should be named after an Italian sea captain by the whim of a German cartographer and given away to Europeans by a Catholic Pope who lives in Italy. How did they come up with such a convoluted scheme?

I am Ani yu wiya, the Principle People. I am not European, American, English or Italian. The name whites give me doesn't change who I am, who they are or what they want. Schermerhorn and his foreign government have schemed to separate us from our land since the day they arrived.

What will become of the Principle People? Will we disappear like a morning mist swallowed by a summer sun?

27 April 1836 – Soon the Planting Moon - A na a gv ti

The blackberry blossoms tell us spring has arrived and soon we'll plant corn and vegetables. For one more year we'll enjoy squash, beans, cucumbers, pumpkins, watermelons and ramps. I love Dla-ya-de-i, polk-salad in English, gathered when young and tender. Edudu and I love them with an egg scrambled—so does Five Feathers. We gather the dark purple polk-salad berries for a rich dye when we're making pine baskets.

Soon we will pick blackberries. If Mrs. Lowry were here, I would take her a basket of blackberries and help her bake them with wheat flour into a beautiful pie.

I miss the Lowrys. Ben never talks about his father's arrest or his father's weakness. He never mentions the wonderful relationship he had with his father. I miss my parents too, even though I don't remember them. I imagine how different my life would have been if my parents had lived. I imagine the untold joy that would have been mine with my parents and elisi and edudu. Things change in this world. Things change.

May 1836

I just came from Harriet and Elias' home. Their seventh child was stillborn today. Harriet is ill. She is sleeping. She will survive. We will bury her child tomorrow. Perhaps Harriet will come to the burial if she feels well enough. Five Feathers and his friends will build the little coffin and dig the little grave. I cannot imagine the pain of losing a child after carrying it to the final moment of promise. My heart is with Harriet and Elias. I can think of nothing today but their loss. I cry often.

12 June 1836

Bad news. The Schermerhorn treaty has been ratified by the United States Senate despite objections from Chief John Ross. Maybe we will stay—maybe not. The newspaper says we will be transported. What does transported mean? I asked edudu. He said nothing—not one word. He took his gun from over the mantlepiece. I watched him and Eagle Killer as he walked slowly up the hill into the woods, his back bent like an old man. He leaned against a hickory sapling for a long while before he disappeared in the trees.

Being transported will be terrible. The news becomes more ominous with every passing moon. I threw the chickens their scratch feed this morning. I watched them eat. They don't read the newspapers. They're not afraid or have nightmares about armed men on horses. Every morning the little brown sparrows come and sneak the smaller bits of the cracked corn. Will the sparrows be transported also?

Copied from the *Georgia Journal* – 7 June 1836

"The treaty lately concluded the Headmen and Chiefs of the Cherokee Indians…for the purchase of all lands owned, claimed, or possessed by the Cherokees East of the Mississippi, as ratified by the President and the Senate of the United States has been officially published…The Indians are to be transported by the United States to the West of the Mississippi…"

13 June 1836

John Brewster and friends can't wait to make a profit.

Copied from the *Southern Recorder* – 2 June 1836 – page 1

"Central Bank – AND CHEROKEE LAND AGENCY.

The undersigned offers his services to the public as an Agent for the transaction of business in the Central Bank, and in selling Cherokee lands. His fees will be for Agency in discounting or renewing each Note in Bank one dollar; for effecting sales of Land, five dollars per tract under one hundred dollars, and five per cent. for all above that sum. His late residence in the Cherokee Country and present station in the Surveyor General's Office, peculiarly adapt him for this agency. All communications must come post-paid, or they will not be taken from the post-office. Milledgeville April 26, 1836. JOHN BREWSTER

14 June 1836

Copied from the *Federal Union* - 9 June 1836 – page 3

"…it is the part of prudence to observe the Cherokees with a watchful and suspicious eye, even though they may appear to be quiet and peaceable…they have in fact given strong indications of hostility, which cannot be safely be overlooked. Since the failure of the Florida campaign, and the temporary success of the Creeks in Alabama…the Cherokees in Murray, and other counties in which they are numerous, have become sulky and insolent in their demeanor, and have declared that they will burn the houses of the whites, and do as much damage as possible.

The Ross-men say, that Ross has told them that their land should never be sold; and that rather than leave it, as required by the treaty, and by the laws of Georgia, they will die fighting on it...should the Cherokees...commit any acts of hostility thousands of brave and generous Georgians...will rush to the assistance of their exposed fellow-citizens. An avenging storm, with desolating fury will beat upon the heads of the infatuated race. Woe to the Cherokees, if they should shed the blood of any of our people!

18 June 1836

Whites say they are frightened of us Cherokee. Edudu knows nothing of planned violence against whites. Cherokee violence is the invention of white newspaper writers meant to inflame white readers and justify white greed.

Copied from the Southern Recorder – 14 June 1836 – page 3

"...Rumor states that Cedartown has been laid in ashes and from 12 to 16 families butchered by the Cherokees...that the Indian force now collected is computed from 3 to 500—that they insolently demand provisions from the whites, and are robbing them of their cattle...Therefore we anticipate that our volunteers...will receive orders...to protect their own homes, as the present seat of hostilities is only about a day's ride from here.

There is no Indian force in Cedartown. There is no violence. No one is demanding anything from white settlers. No one has been murdered. No cattle have been stolen. There is no name attached to this article. What do the thousands of white newspaper readers think? I know what they think.

7 July 1836

Copied from the *Southern Recorder* – 5 July 1836 – page 2

"...we believe the Cherokees will remain quiet, at least for the present...the President has made a requisition for a brigade of troops on the governor of Tennessee, which will make its Head-Quarters at Athens, Tennessee, on the borders of Georgia, and adjacent to the Cherokees."

11 July 1836

We are a tame and peaceful people. We build houses. We plant our crops. We feed our chickens, cows and pigs. We raise our families. We have no army. We have no weapons. We have been preyed upon for a hundred years, yet the United States and Georgia speak of us as a nation characterized by savage perfidy and violence. We are not the ones who disregarded treaty after treaty. We have not broken promise after promise and taken that which belonged to others. Their perfidy, not ours, will be infamous. Whites believe they have never done wrong. Lewis Cass, Jackson's Secretary of War, understands war. He studies war. He pursued and destroyed Indians in Michigan before he came to Washington City. He and Jackson are two peas in a pod.

Copied from the *Federal Union* – 30 June 1836 – Page 2

"The following letter from the secretary of War to the Georgia Delegation in Congress…shows that the Federal Executive has adopted, and is executing energetic precautionary measures to preserve the lives of our citizens and to guard the peace of our Cherokee counties against the dangers of savage perfidy and violence.

War Department, June 18, 1836

"Gentlemen—It may be agreeable to you to know, that with a view to prevent or suppress any hostilities among the Cherokee Indians, a Brigade of Tennessee Volunteers, amounting to one thousand to twelve hundred men, one half mounted, one half infantry, will rendezvous at Athens on the 7th of July, and proceed immediately to Cherokee Country. Brigadier General Wool has been assigned to the command, and has been authorized, should circumstances require it, to call for additional force, and to take all measures necessary for the suppression of hostilities among those Indians, should any occur and for their immediate removal.

Very respectfully yours, your obedient servant,
Lewis Cass

2 September 1836

In the *National Intelligencer*, a Washington City newspaper, whites want their wives and daughters to wear the latest fashions from Paris while, at the same moment, they send their armed young men to remove us to a country we know nothing of. Who is barbarous and who is civilized?

Copied from the *National Intelligencer* – 27 August 1836 – page 1

"F. Taylor will receive subscriptions for the Journal of French Fashions…Each number will contain numerous colored engravings of fashions from the Parisian magazines, which are regularly shipped from France to the editors of this work a week before they are made public there…Subscribers will therefore have the advantage of receiving the fashions direct from Paris every two weeks instead of waiting several months…"

Copied from the *National Intelligencer* – 27 August 1836 – page 2

"…In East Florida…this section of the country has been constantly menaced by inroads of savage infuriated Creeks, struggling to escape into Florida to join the Seminoles; and frequently have harassed our volunteers who have been obliged to march into Georgia to oppose these new enemies…this duty falls upon…a few whites engaged in the labors of the field, and embarrassed with a large colored population, who can add nothing to their active force…All experience has shown that the only sure way of defending a frontier against Indians is to carry on an offensive war into their country…destroy their crops, capture their families, and force them to submit."

My last glimmer of hope of a future on our ancestral land has faded. Whites will not rest until they control everything.

3 September 1836

Whites have begun constructing new military roads throughout our country. The rumors are true. Georgia plans an offensive war against both the Seminoles and us.

6 September 1836

It has been terribly hot. I'm anxious for the cool days of autumn. Bear Paws' mother came to see me today. The whites have been selling more whiskey than ever and Bear Paws has begun drinking again. Our men asked the white whiskey sellers to leave, but they laugh at us. The soldiers drink a lot of whiskey.

"Walela, I am heartbroken," Bear Paws' mother said, almost in tears. "I thought my son had stopped drinking whiskey, but once again he is causing terrible disturbances. I don't know what to do. I have been listening to the missionaries. Will you write a letter to my Bear Paws for me?"

"Of course I will, my dear Adsila. I have paper and pen. I can write now."

"I want him to know I have asked both the white God and our Great Spirit to help him stop drinking whiskey. Please write in Cherokee."

I wrote for Adsila:

My Dear Bear Paws,

I would give anything to save you from whiskey. You have been my joy since you were a happy baby.

Someone taught you to love whiskey more than you love your mother. Breaking my heart has become easy for you. This did not happen in one day. I do not blame you.

You are willing to wreck everyone's life for the pleasure of drinking whiskey and then you don't remember. You and your bad wolf will both soon perish if you continue.

My son, I have a new prayer. I no longer pray for your safety or that you come home to me.

I will pray that the Great God of all brings you to himself no matter the cost. My dear Bear Paws. This is your mother's prayer:

God of heaven and earth I beseech you,

My son, Bear Paws, cannot stop drinking whiskey. In the past I asked you to keep him safe. I withdraw those prayers. I give you permission to do whatever it takes to get him to stop drinking whiskey. If he will not stop, you have my permission to rescue him from his madness and bring him home to yourself. You have my permission to use pain, suffering, or even death to rescue him—his death or mine.

I give you permission to break my heart if need be. I withhold nothing. I love my son. Please bring him to his senses. I wish nothing good for men who sell whiskey. They vend sorrow and pain. I leave them to your judgment.

I give you permission to do anything you wish with my son or with myself—be it life or be it death.

This is my prayer, Adsila

My Dear Bear Paws,

I shall offer up that prayer every day to the Great Christian God and our Great Spirit until you stop drinking whiskey or the Great Spirit takes you to himself.

I have given permission to spare you from nothing—to spare me from nothing. I no longer pray for your protection. I pray for your rescue.

If someone brings news of your death, I will know you have gone home and are finally free from the evil of whiskey and your bad wolf.

If I hear of your death, I will know where to find you. One day I will join you there. We shall be forever free of those who sell death. I love you more than my own life,

Your mother, Adsila

I gave Adsila the finished letter in Cherokee. She said she would give it to Bear Paws. She said he would probably come by to have me read it to him. When she left, I cried.

15 October 1836

Dear Harriet was on this earth for only thirty-one summers. She passed while still young and vibrant. Sometimes things change slowly and we hardly notice. Other times changes crash into us.

My friend leaves behind a husband and six beautiful children. Harriet suffered at the hands of her own family and now the final human indignity—premature death. I want to experience endless days laughing again with Mrs. Lowry, teaching with her husband and sitting during long, carefree afternoons with my dear Harriet. I want to watch her children play. Things change. Things change.

26 October 1836

Elias is sending the children to Harriet's relatives. Eleanor, Mary and Sarah are going to stay with their aunt, Mary Brinsmade, the sister who stood up for Harriet when she married. The boys, William Penn, Frank Brinsmade and Elias Cornelius will go to school in Manchester, Vermont. I hope they get a good education and will not be taunted as half-breeds.

We will help Elias even though he signed the Schermerhorn treaty. I cannot forget the good work Elias did as editor of the Phoenix.

Edudu and Five Feathers do not understand how Elias could betray his chief and will never forgive him. I wonder what will happen? There is much division concerning the Schermerhorn treaty. What will become of us? I am afraid. I am afraid of the Georgia Guard. I miss my friend Harriet.

14 November 1836

Ben is elected once again to the U.S. House—his third term. Martin Van Buren will be president. Andrew Jackson will be gone, but I wonder if anything will be different. Ben's political future is bright and getting brighter. I wish I could see him more often. One day we will be together—it must be. Surely it must be so. It will be so.

Milledgeville – The Grand Ballroom - Mitchell's Hotel

"Ben, here we are again. I don't know about you, but I'm getting well used to our success. Third time's a charm. Next election will be the Senate. Everything is moving along as we planned. We've done well—very well and I'm grateful as usual. There will be a nice token of my gratitude on your desk when you return to work—better than last time—much better than last time," Mr. Mitchell said with an alcohol fueled, red-faced grin."

"Thank you, sir. I am grateful—very grateful," Ben answered. "These last eight years seem like a dream. Your business has grown. We've prospered beyond expectations. I have you, your son and Elizabeth to thank."

"Elizabeth and Zach have been busy, haven't they? I wonder where they get the energy? I guess it's the energy of youth," Mr. Mitchell said with a wry smile.

"Ben," Zach's father continued, "there's something I've been wanting to talk to you about and this is as good a time as any."

"Yes, sir. I'm all ears."

"You're becoming an important man in Georgia and in Washington City, Ben. More and more people are taking notice of you. More folks are coming to you for advice and help with their business. You're popular and I couldn't be more pleased. I've been thinkin'. It's about time you bought a few slaves. We need to let it be seen publicly that you're a proud Georgian and you believe in our rights, states' rights, the right of us Southerners to own property free and clear. The House of Representatives is one thing, but when you're in the Senate you'll have to toe the line. The Senate is another kettle of fish entirely. We've been puttin' the word out that we want you in the Senate, as you know. Folks like you. All my friends believe you will represent them very well in Washington City, but if they're not sure you are a slavery man through and through, you don't have a chance in Georgia. There's goin' to be a lot of pushin' and shovin' in the Senate in the next few years. Folks have to be sure where your heart is on this matter, if you know what I mean. You have to be clearly seen to be on the correct side of this issue."

"Yes, sir. I've been thinking about that. I'm been telling everyone that I'm fully committed to the rights of folks both north and south to own property. That's not a problem with me, sir. Slavery is an institution that was here when the old thirteen became a nation and it can stay as far as I'm concerned."

"Good for you," Mr. Mitchell continued. "I have my ear to the ground. Just the other day one of my wife's friends was wondering why she never sees you with your slaves. She wanted to know why you're always doin' for yourself. Not many folks know you don't own a single slave. That's going to be a problem if you want to be a senator. You can't say one thing and do another. If you're going to support slavery, you're goin' to have to own slaves. That's what I want to tell you. It's time to act."

"Yes, sir. I've thought of that," Ben answered. "Zach has often suggested I buy slaves, but I don't know how to handle them or how to pick out a good one."

"Ben, you've made us a lot of money and you're going to make us a lot more. Quid pro quo. Here's what I'm going to do. You need some slaves. Zach tells me you and Caesar get along quite well. He's heard you two talking French and Latin. That's a waste as far as I'm concerned. We don't need nothin' around here but English. I talked to Caesar this morning. How about I give you Caesar, his wife, son and daughter as an election gift? They'll be another token of my gratitude. You've got plenty of money now. You can buy yourself a little house near the office and use Caesar as your personal servant, his wife as your house keeper. Everyone of any importance knows Caesar from my private dining room. When they see him with you they'll know you're a true Southerner. I hate to give him up but givin' you Caesar is the best way to solve this problem, don't you think?"

"Yes, sir. Caesar is an excellent servant. I see your point, sir."

"If I give you Caesar, everyone in Washington City will know you own slaves—besides, you need the help. Caesar's daughter is a seamstress and his son, Horace, is a farrier. You can make extra money hiring them out if you don't have enough for them to do. What do you say?"

"Sounds good to me, sir. I've always liked Caesar. I'll do whatever it takes to get that Senate seat. You know that, sir. I think it would be a wise decision, under the circumstances. It would be a very wise decision for me to acquire slaves.

Chapter XLVIII

1837 – Extinguishment Planned – Gen. Wool Removed – The Quilt

Chapter 48

8 March 1837

On 4 March, Martin Van Buren was inaugurated as the new president of the United States. Will he continue Andrew Jackson's policies? He says he will in his acceptance speech.

Copied from the *Federal Union* - 4 April 1837 - Page 3

"More of the Creeks. The *Mobile Mercantile Advisor* says:-- Three Steamboats--the John Nelson, the Chippewa and the Bonnets O'Blue--have arrived from Montgomery with 1,900 Creek Indians, on their way to the far west. The John Nelson had 660--the Chippewa 800--and the Bonnets O'Blue 450. There are about 1000 yet to come, to complete the entire Creek Nation."

I read this to edudu. Without saying a word, he looked at me and shook his head. He got his gun. He and Eagle Killer didn't come back till the next day. I know his thoughts. They are the same as mine. The Creek Nation, once happy, numerous and proud, has been erased. They have vanished like the buffalo and the elk. Whites live in the Creek houses, plow their fields and work their corn. Chestnut trees will never again shade Creek children as they play their games. Not one Creek village remains. One day soon it will be our turn to be herded onto steamboats like frightened cattle—removed from the sight of our invading benefactors.

I have been told steamboats now operate on all the rivers. John Ross and his brother Lewis have a ferry, stores and a trading post at Ross's Landing. For many years elisi and I traded our pine baskets with them. One day white steamboats will carry us away as they now carry away the Creeks. On that day white newspapers will celebrate with the news, "All Cherokee Removed".

30 March 1837

Edudu and the other leaders of our nation have received a letter from General Wool warning of our removal. I remember Mr. Lowry quoting from his Book, 'the writing is on the wall'. This letter is not good news—not good news at all. Edudu said he will never trust a white general. He will trust our chief. He will not betray his nation.

Army Headquarters
New Echota, March 22, 1837
CHEROKEES:

It is nearly a year since I first arrived in this country. I then informed you of the objects of my coming among you. I told you that a treaty had been made with your people, and that your country was to be given up to the United States by the 25th May, 1838, a (little more than a year from this time,) when you would all be compelled to remove to the West. I also told you, if you would submit to the terms of the treaty I would protect you in your persons and property, at the same time I would furnish provisions and clothing to the poor and destitute of the Nation. You would not listen, but turned a deaf ear to my advice. You preferred the counsel of those who were opposed to the treaty. They told you, what was not true, that your people had made no treaty with the United States, and that you would be able to retain you lands, and would not be obliged to remove to the West, the place designated for your new homes. Be no longer deceived by such advice! It is not only untrue, but if listened to, may lead to your utter ruin. The President, as well as Congress, have decreed that you should remove from this country. The people of Georgia, of North Carolina, of Tennessee and of Alabama, have decreed it. Your fate is decided; and if you do not voluntarily get ready and go by the time fixed in the treaty, you will then be forced from this country by the soldiers of the United States.

Under such circumstances what will be your condition? Deplorable in the extreme! Instead of the benefits now presented to you by the treaty, of receiving pay for the improvements of your lands, your houses, your cornfields and your ferries, and for all the property unjustly taken from you by the white people, and at the same time, blankets, clothing and provisions for the poor, you will be driven from the country, and without a cent to support you on your arrival at your new homes. You will in vain flee to your mountains for protection. Like the Creeks, you will be hunted up and dragged from your lurking places and hurried to the West. I would ask, are you prepared for such scenes? I trust not. Yet such will be your fate if you persist in your present determination.

Cherokees: I have not come among you to oppress you, but to protect you and to see that justice is done you, as guarantied by the treaty. Be advised, and turn a deaf ear to those who would induce you to believe that no treaty has been made with you, and that you will not be obliged to leave your country. They cannot be friends, but the worst of enemies. Their advice, if followed, will lead to your certain destruction. The President has said that a treaty has been made with you, and must be executed agreeably to its terms. The President never changes. Therefore, take my advice: It is the advice of a friend, who would tell you the truth, and who feels deeply interested in your welfare, and who will do everything in his power to relieve, protect and secure to you the benefits of the treaty. And why not abandon a country no longer yours? Do you not see the white people daily coming into it, driving you from your homes and possessing your houses, your cornfields and your ferries? Hitherto I have been able to some degree, to protect you from their intrusions; in a short time it will no longer be in my power. If, however, I could protect you, you could not live with them. Your habits, your manners and your customs are unlike, and unsuited to theirs. They have no feelings, no sympathies in common with yourselves. Leave then this country, which after the 25th May 1838, can afford you no protection and remove to the country designated for your new homes, which is secured to you and your children forever; and where you may live under your own laws, and the customs of your fathers, without intrusion or molestation from the white man. It is a country much better than the one you now occupy; where you can grow more corn, and where game is more abundant. Think seriously of what I say to you. Remember that you have but one summer more to plant corn in this country. Make the best use of this time, and dispose of your property to the best advantage. Go and settle with the Commissioners, and with the emigrating Agent, Gen. Smith, receive the money due for your improvements, your houses your cornfields and ferries, and for the property which has been unjustly taken from you by the whitemen, and at the appointed time be prepared to remove. In the meantime, if you will apply to me or my Agents, I will cause rations, blankets and clothing to be furnished to the poor and destitute of your people.

John E. Wool

Brg. Genl. Comdg.

9 April 1837

Copied from the *Federal Union* - 4 April 1837 - page 3

"FROM FLORIDA: The prospect of war being closed becomes brighter and brighter. It appears that Micanopy has come in, and we learn verbally that Phillip has said he will not remain out if Micanopy surrendered."

"The steamer Duncan MacRae, Captain Philbrick, from Black Creek bring us a cheering letter--which we give below-- also a slip from our correspondent of the *Darien Telegraph* with the *Jacksonville Courier* of Thursday last from the editors...We congratulate them and the country at large on the prospect of a speedy termination of a war which has cost the country some of her best blood and expended so much of the treasury of her citizens. Fort Heileman, March 23"

"TO THE EDITOR: An express arrived a few moments ago from General Jesup, who states that Micanopy, in conformity with the treaty, came in on the 16th, of course you know before this that he is to be retained as hostage, until the whole tribe is removed...however what these redskins say is not to be depended upon."

I would be curious to know if the ignorant white man who wrote this believes what he has written? Do they believe their own lies? I fear it is so. When edudu heard me read, he was so angry he spit on the newspaper in my hands and shouted, "Who are these people? They have been lying to us for a hundred years."

Without an apology, he took his gun and he and Eagle Killer disappeared once again into the forest and he didn't return for three days this time. He was as angry as I have ever seen him. When he came back, he apologized for spitting on my newspaper. He doesn't like to talk about such things. I am worried. Elisi and Edudu are old. Edudu's hair is white and his back is bent. In the last couple of years he has begun to look like a fragile old man. Since the Shermerhorn treaty, elisi gets up often in the night to go out back. When I hear her get up, I make certain she is safely back in bed before I sleep. Sometimes I find her sitting on the front porch in the middle of the night. She is fretful and I am afraid for her. I am troubled, too. There is so much bad news. I wish Ben were here.

15 April 1837

Copied from the *Federal Union* - page 3 - April 11th 1837

"The *Southern Patriot* of the 6th inst. says, our informant adds that the troops were rapidly moving to Tampa Bay. Part of Alligator's Jumper's and Micanopy's tribes had gone. It was rumored at Black Creek that Osceola sent word to General Jesup that if government would pardon him he would come in. He had sent in his tribe and drawn rations. It was considered by most intelligent officers at the seat of hostilities that the war was over."

The army wants to deport Osceola, as they do us, to some land out west they have never seen. The Americans want the Florida territory to themselves. They are cleansing the land like elisi sweeps the dirt from our house. They will sweep Florida clean of Seminoles and so shall we Cherokee be swept away.

Sometimes I wish I didn't know how to read. Sometimes I wish my mind was concerned with entertainment and frivolity.

Copied from the *Federal Union* - 18 April 1837 - Page 1

"UNIVERSITY OF GEORGIA - Athens March 23rd 1837 "At the commencement in the first week of August next, the trustees of this institution will elect a Professor of Moral Philosophy and Belles Letters, to fill the vacancy occasioned by the death of Professor Pressley. Salary 1,600 per annum. Asbury Hull Secretary."

Philosophy means lover of wisdom in Greek. Georgia seeks to remove us and the Seminole at gunpoint while their University seeks a Lover of Wisdom to teach young men morality. Do they love wisdom? Can they appoint a man who has an understanding of human morality? Whatever it is they teach at the University of Georgia, it is white European philosophy.

30 April 1837

Copied from the *Federal Union* 25 April 1837

"No white man, not in service of the U.S. is allowed to go south of a line East and West through Fort Drane from the St. John's river, to the Gulf of Mexico, on any pretext whatsoever. All vessels arriving at Tampa Bay are to be immediately

566

examined, and no one permitted to land, except those having business with the military authorities on shore. The negros are to be sent to St. Marks under charge of Lieutenant Vinton, where their owners must go to claim them.... unprincipled white men will tamper with the Negros of the Indians, and thus lead to a renewal of the hostilities."

Copied from the *Federal Union* 25 April 1837 page 3

"Headquarters - Army of the South, Tampa Bay, 5th April 1837. ORDERS No. 79. 1st The Commanding General has reason to believe that the interference of unprincipled white men, with the negro property of the Seminole Indians, if not immediately checked, will prevent their emigration, and lead to a renewal of the war."

1 May 1837

Edudu and elisi wanted me to record this article about curing bacon. Edudu said this autumn he was going to try this when he killed his next hog. Like elisi, I think skippers are disgusting—absolutely disgusting. The sight of them, knowing what they eat, makes me want to vomit.

Copied from the Federal Union – 25 April 1837 – Page 1

"A writer from Mississippi, states, as a preventative against skippers, bugs, &c. in curing bacon, tobacco smoke; the tobacco is put in the fire when smoking the meat with wood. He says, 'Last year, my bacon was, by, I may say accident, smoked pretty smartly with tobacco, so much so, that I apprehended it would have been spoiled by tasting and smelling of the tobacco smoke, but, was agreeably disappointed, it neither tasted or smelled of the tobacco and neither skippers or bugs, or anything else troubled it...'"

3 May 1837

Ben says General Wool is to be replaced. He has been friendly with the removal party but has protected our rights on rare occasions.

My Dear Cassie,

I take pen in hand briefly to communicate the news that General Wool is to be replaced. The rumors are the general government and the governors of Alabama, Tennessee and South Carolina want rapid and immediate action regarding the Cherokee removal. They believe Wool has been dragging his feet and is unsuited for the task. It is also rumored General Wool will face charges, probably a court martial, over actions in Alabama. In any case, the word is Colonel Lindsay, currently serving in the Seminole War, will be transferred to New Echota. He will be given temporary command of the army and have the cooperation of the governors and their militias.

Be doubly careful when you see strangers, Cassie. No one is sure about the general government's plans but nothing bodes well for the Cherokee. I am as certain as I can be under the circumstances that come May next the army and militia will act in concert to remove the Cherokee Nation in its entirety. I wish I had better news.

I remain busy with my duties as a lawmaker and with the law firm and with my upcoming Senate bid. If you need anything, please let me know. I plan to visit you soon. I shall endeavor to see you after I visit Mother and Father who remain in Brainerd. Once again, I beg you to persuade your grandparents to emigrate. It is of the utmost importance for your personal safety that you remove from Cherokee Country as soon as possible. Please persuade them to accept the benevolence of the white authorities. Ross cannot be trusted to accomplish anything of merit for the Cherokee.

Your Loving Ben, xoxox

22 June 1837

Edudu is going to the big council meeting Chief Ross has called at Red Clay. I would love to go and see everything and talk to edudu's friends and listen. Thousands will be there. Maybe we'll learn if we are going to be allowed to stay another year. I wish the Guard would allow us to have councils here in New Echota. I want to go, but I must stay with elisi.

11 August 1837

Edudu and Eagle Killer returned from the meeting at Red Clay. Edudu is ill with a high temperature and coughing. I am worried. After he bathed in the river, I put him to bed and gave him broth. I have never seen him so ill. It rained unceasingly the last few days of the council and everyone was soaked. Edudu said it was almost impossible to keep a fire going or for anyone to stay dry. It was most difficult for the several hundred families who attended. Edudu said everyone was patient and few left early.

12 August 1837

When edudu recovered, I asked about his trip.

"How was the council? Did anything important happen? Is there good news?"

"Be glad you didn't go, Walela. I don't think anything much was accomplished. Our future is not good. It was wet—terribly wet. You would have been miserable. Everyone was miserable. I wish we weren't forbidden to have meetings here at New Echota. Because of the Guard and Militia, we are forced to go to Red Clay to get beyond Georgia's reach."

Edudu hacked, coughed and sounded terrible but managed to continue.

"At my age the traveling and the bad weather was too much. I wanted to hear all the latest news and listen to the speeches. I wanted to see my old friends. This may be the last time I see them if the whites do as they say. There were storms every day at the end of the meeting. I felt sorry for the families. There were maybe four thousand people and no real shelter."

"Was there any trouble, edudu?"

"There was no trouble. It was peaceful and we had plenty to eat thanks to Chief Ross. He spoke about his delegation's visit to Washington and Arkansas. He reminded us of the general government's intention to force our removal. There wasn't much new. It was good to see old friends."

"What did you learn, edudu?"

"I learned nothing new. The meeting didn't give me any hope, to tell you the truth. In the rain on the last day, the government's Mr. Mason delivered his address in English. It was translated. Most of the men listened respectfully and that was the end. Everyone went home."

Edudu coughed once again, bending double and spitting up terrible things from his lungs. When he was breathing normally once again, he continued.

"I felt so sorry for all the families. Many had no more than a blanket stretched over a limb to shield them from the downpours. No one wanted to go home before the end of the council even though the weather was terrible.

The men tried valiantly to keep their fires burning but with little success. I'm still cold."

13 August 1837

If ten thousand people a month are coming into New York from England, I wonder how many are coming into all the ports? No wonder whites want our land. Immigrants want land and don't care where they get it or who they take it from—especially if it is free to them.

Copied from the *Georgia Journal* – 8 August 1837 – page 2

"Emigration.—The average number of emigrants to New York is estimated at 10,000 per month. As far as numbers go, we can easily spare them....If we take £15 as the average of what...the emigrants individually carry out, we shall have nearly £2,000,000 in specie, carried to America each year, without receiving anything for it. It is so much gold drawn from the producing capital of the country—so much thrown into the resources of America. Liverpool Mail, of the 24th ult."

11 October 1837 - The Harvest Moon – Du ni nv di

My Dearest Ben,

I cannot express in words how much I miss you. I only hope you think half as much about me as I think of you. I know you're doing your best for us. I know you're busy. It is said we will lose our nation. Our last hope is said to be that each family will be allowed to keep a little farm—enough for our pigs and chickens and a small corn field. Chief Ross believes we still have a chance for that, but I don't think so. Edudu and his friends wait on word from Chief Ross in Washington City but no news is forthcoming.

Your father would say the writing is on the wall. I am not surprised to learn the final plans for our deportation are being made in Milledgeville. A few families have removed, but most will stay until Chief Ross tells us we must leave. I read the newspapers and I understand, but my people are unable to comprehend the consequences of the dark wings of the approaching malevolence.

Whites believe themselves to possess the power and beauty of the eagle. In truth they are fussing buzzards with ugly featherless heads, pushing and shoving to consume the remnants of decaying flesh on the bones of our dismembered carcass, regurgitating carrion to repel their enemies with its foul stench and all the while believing themselves to be the noblest of all creatures.

My friends, in their innocence, continue to plant and prepare for another year as if everything will be normal. Sometimes I wonder if your father's God is a white invention to justify their venal, grasping actions, as if everything they do was approved in heaven. They believe, as does James F. Cooper, that we, like the Last of the Mohicans, should disappear. We should cease to exist and make way for the superior white culture. That would suit the whites nicely.

Perhaps edudu is correct and this evil is a test. I wish Hans Christian Anderson would send a fairytale prince to our rescue. I fear no valiant prince will appear to destroy our oppressing dragon. In my heart, you are my prince and I belong to you no matter what comes. The one thing that will never change in this world is my love for you.

You are my valiant prince forever, Cassie oxoxo

13 October 1837

Copied from the *Georgia Journal* – page 1 – October 10, 1837

"...*The Cherokee Land Lottery* will contain all the names of all the fortunate drawers in the Land Lottery, and their residence, up to the first of January 1838, with an engraved map of each Land District in the Cherokee Country, immediately preceding the names in each district. *The Cherokee Land Lottery* will contain about five hundred pages, royal octavo size, will be printed on good paper, neatly bound and delivered to subscribers by the first of March 1838 at five dollars a copy..."

The last of our farms will soon belong to Georgia's fortunate drawers. They will have a printed map of every acre of our land. When we are removed, there will be no one left who remembers. Whites will never keep our memory alive. Henry Clay wished we would disappear. That would be best for all concerned, he said. Our vanishment shall soon be accomplished.

19 October 1837

Huff's Boarding House – Milledgeville - 14 October 1837

My Dearest Cassie,

I feel guilty for not writing more often. Immediately upon receipt of your wonderful letter I took pen in hand. I miss you. I miss you extraordinarily. Count on me to visit soon—probably before the end of the month. I need to get away from my work and refresh my mind. I can't wait to hold you once again and be reminded of what is important. I want to spend an entire day looking into your sparkling eyes. I must get away from this job that consumes my energy with constant compromise.

Things are busy and confused. I fear your political assessment is correct. No courageous prince will rise to slay the dragon. Everyone thinks Ross's continued attempts to persuade the general government to nullify the 1835 treaty are the cause of all the problems in the peaceful emigration of the Cherokee. I fear the general government will allow the removal to go into effect even if it means military action. The white population in the several states surrounding Cherokee Country has grown sufficiently large to support the removal. The consensus of all the whites surrounding the Cherokee is that their government should immediately seize and occupy all Cherokee land. The government will fund the task. I'm embarrassed to say that everyone here is quite eager to accomplish your vanishment. Soon, Cherokee Country will be no more. I wish I had better news.

I trust you are well. I shall write again soon. You are my heart and soul. Once again, I beg you to persuade your grandparents to emigrate immediately. Somehow you must coax your grandparents to take advantage of the benevolent offers of the state of Georgia to aid their relocation. It's for their own good. Trust me.

Yours Forever and Ever, Ben, xoxox

19 October 1837

When Ben's work takes him to the north of the state, he often visits his parents at Brainerd. Mr. and Mrs. Lowry have been a loving mother and father to me. Ben's beautiful father has never recovered since his release from prison. He has lost all enthusiasm for his work—even for life. He must have been abused unspeakably by fellow whites. He has hardly spoken, even to his wife, in years. I feel deep sorrow for Eleanor. They have no assets. They depend on the generosity of the mission and the charity of their good son. Who are these people who would do this to their own kind?

Will Ben continue to love me? With each infrequent visit, Ben brings darker news. He warns we should not wait until soldiers force our removal. Edudu, elisi and their friends will not leave until told by our Chief. I will never leave their side. I wish Ben could protect us. I wish, I wish, I wish.

28 October 1837 - Month of the Harvest Moon – Du ni nv di

Today was the best day Ben and I had in a long time. He and I had a wonderful day talking incessantly amidst the colorful trees. We enjoyed the cool air after a long, hot summer. We talked about everything like old times—like we did when the world was new. I know he loves me. I do so wish he could come more often. I'm sure he will. I hope he will. I know he will.

"Cassie, I can't tell you how nice it is to be here with you. I've been incredibly busy. I needed this relaxation. I enjoy the city, but I can't forget my boyhood home. I think this is the most peaceful spot on earth. No one's in a hurry here."

"We're never in a hurry here. You should come up more often."

"I think I shall. I need too."

"If you would come and see me more often, you could relax and do better work. We could be together for life like the bluebirds and never migrate."

"I know what you mean, Cassie. Not one of those flowery Milledgeville women, wearing Parisian fashions and smelling of French perfume, can compare with you. As soon as a city girl opens her mouth, I'm disappointed. You're not only beautiful, but I love you—every part of you. I love your mind, body and soul. I love your intelligence, your clever wit—you have substance. There is no one like you in my life and never will be. I should see you more often. I will come more often—I promise."

"All you have to do is get on the stage and come."

"I know."

"You could come anytime."

"I know I could, Cassie," Ben paused and drew circles in the bare earth with the toe of his boot in front of us.

"You are so good for me. This is the only place I can relax. You're the only woman I've ever met I can talk to and who understands. You're still my woman, aren't you?"

"I will always be your woman. You've known that since we were in school together."

"I've always known that too," Ben said.

I laughed and held him close.

I whispered into his ear, "I'll never change, Ben. I have loved you and always will. You're my man—my only man. That will never change. I'll never change."

"I know you'll never change. That's one of the things I love about you. You have a solid character. I can trust you."

"Thank you, Ben. You can trust me but I've been worried. You're busy, but I want to see you more often. I need to see you more often. Perhaps you could take me to see your parents again? I loved our trip to Brainerd. It was so nice being with you for those days. I loved having you all to myself."

"Mother asks me in every letter to bring you up again," Ben said. "She says your visit is the only thing that seems to brighten Father. He still hasn't said a word in months. He may never speak again. Who would have thought my father, the smiling, laughing, confident man who taught others every day, who preached the gospel every Sunday—the man who made his living by talking, would end up a dumb mute. When I visit, I look at my father huddled in the corner or sitting on his bed. His face bears a tortured look. I think he's still being persecuted by the devils of hell unleashed by the Guard and Militia. I can't tell you how that makes me feel. I've been reticent to speak of such things, but I wanted to share that. I needed to share that."

"You can tell me anything, Ben."

Ben paused and held me for a long time. I could tell talking about his father was bothering him deeply. I petted the hair on the back of his head and neck and waited for him to speak when he was ready.

"I should take you to him, Cassie. I promised Mother I would bring you soon."

"We need to do that," I said quietly.

"I'm going to see them again sometime around Christmas or the New Year. I'll let you know," Ben said. "Would you like to ride up with me then?"

"I would love to ride up with you anytime," I answered quickly. "You don't need to ask. That would be wonderful. A visit with your parents would be the best gift you could possibly give—other than our marriage, of course."

Ben smiled and kissed my forehead.

"We're agreed. Let's plan on that," he said, still holding me tight against his chest.

"Every time I'm with you, Cassie, I realize how much I want you—how much I need you. One day I'll figure out a way we can be together—I promise."

"I know."

"We'll be married."

"I know."

"I'll come for you one day. I will."

"I know," I answered again.

"The way people feel about a relationship is strange, Cassie. If we wanted to live in France, we could live in peace."

"I would love to live in Europe. We would be accepted there," I answered.

"I know we would," Ben replied. "How odd that is when you think about it? Europeans come here and take your land, but we must go to Europe to find acceptance."

We were quiet for a long while watching the sunlight on Mrs. Lowry's roses. Busy squirrels were chasing one another on the nearest tree trunks paying no attention to Ben and me.

"Whites will take our farm, won't they Ben?"

Ben didn't answer my question.

"You would love Europe, Cassie. I could practice law there. Maybe that's what we'll do. Would you like to live in Paris? You would love Paris. You already speak French. Perhaps we could live in Germany. Would you like to live in Berlin? They say it's a marvelous city with all kinds of cultural activities."

"I would love to live in Berlin," I answered. "I would love to live in Paris, Berlin or London. I would love Madrid, too. I've been reading Spanish—Don Quixote. I wish I could see the world as he does. It's a marvelous book."

"You've been reading Don Quixote in Spanish?"

"Yes. Spanish is easy since I know French and Latin. It's quite simple, actually—much easier than French."

We watched the squirrels. I felt the gentle wind blowing across the porch. I wondered how long this peace would last?

"I'll live anywhere with you, Ben. That's all I care about. It doesn't matter where we are."

"You're good with language, Cassie. We could travel anywhere."

"I don't know much German," I said, "but you do. It wouldn't take long for me to learn."

Ben looked up at the sky. He was silent for a long time. We held one another.

"We can figure something out," he said.

"The easiest thing would be to emigrate west," I answered. "Some have already gone. We could make a good living in the western territories. We're young and strong. You could practice law and I could teach children and women."

"I would love to teach like my father did," Ben mused quietly.

"We could live with my Nation."

"I could do that."

"We wouldn't have to worry about much," I said. "Wouldn't that be a good life?"

"It would."

"We could persuade your parents to go with us. We could leave now. I think elisi and edudu would go if you and your parents were to come with us."

"I don't know. I have a lot to do. I'm running for the Senate."

"We could have a good life. A very good life," I said quietly.

"That would be a good life, Cassie. You could have a house full of babies and they would be smarter than both of us."

Ben held me close. It was a good day—a very good day.

"I want a houseful of your children."

"Your babies would come from your womb with a book in their hand, I'm sure."

We laughed.

"I could teach as I've always wanted to and maybe start a newspaper," I said. "You could teach, too."

"We could do that," Ben said, watching the playful squirrels. We watched the bluebird pair on the eve of the house. The male had a spider in his beak. He tried to give it to his mate but she refused.

"We could emigrate west and be happy together and no one would call our children half-breeds. We could do that, Ben. We could do that now before the troubles begin."

"We could go west, Cassie, but I don't want to live in poverty the rest of my life excluded from civilization beyond the pale. I need to save more money first."

"If I'm with you, Ben, I would be rich—anywhere. Let's go now."

"Let's wait till the right time, Cassie. Let's wait till I have saved enough so we can live comfortably. That's the right thing to do."

Ben held me and said softly, "I'm sorry, Cassie. I didn't mean that rudely. You know what I mean. I have things I must do before we can live together."

"Yes, I know what you mean, Ben," I said in a whisper.

"I'm standing for the Senate."

"I know," I answered.

"I've saved some, but if you can wait, I can acquire sufficient so that we won't have to worry about anything. I'll earn and save enough so that we'll be very well off."

"I never worry now, Ben—not with you."

"We can live anywhere—even Europe, but you need to be patient, Cassie."

I watched him as he thought about our future.

"I am patient," I said quietly.

"After my Senate appointment I can do anything I want."

As I listened, I could read between the lines. Ben was unaware how far he had moved from his boyish innocence since becoming a lawyer. He had forgotten the foolish promises of boyhood. I know Ben thinks of me as his friend and confidant—when he is here with me. I don't believe he thinks of me in Milledgeville as he used to.

When he is with me, he returns to the boyish character of the carefree young man living in his father's house accepting his parents' moral compass. In a protected corner of his mind, Ben retains his boyhood—an untouched secret fantasy world reserved for me and his parents—like a special room in a mansion house reserved for one's relatives who will never visit again. Ben's life of choice, I suspect, is his heady life of law, politics and intrigue in Milledgeville and Washington City—an exciting life lived exclusively among the upper level of privileged whites.

577

Our relationship is a nostalgic boyhood remnant. I knew Ben's two lives existed side by side. One waxing—one waning. One old life lived long ago in Cherokee Country and a new stimulating life in Georgia's capital. I have often wondered if his other life includes Elizabeth. I know a woman like Elizabeth must exist. Ben is much too handsome not to be involved with women when he is away from me. I don't care about that. I just want to be with him one future day. When all is said and done, I want him to choose me. I want him to choose me as I have chosen him.

"Let's go back to the river today, Ben. Let's have a romantic picnic where we had our first kiss. I want to spend every moment with you."

"I love your spot by the river, Cassie. I think about it often."

"Do you remember how we pledged our lives to one another so many years ago?" I asked. "Do you remember that day?"

I was watching Ben's face. I knew he remembered.

"I remember every detail," I said. "I remember the weather. I remember the clothing you were wearing. I remember what elisi said to me that evening after we parted. Do you think of that day as often as I do, Ben?"

"You don't have to answer that question," I said.

Ben didn't answer my question.

"I would love a picnic in our spot, Cassie. I'm always amazed how soothing life is here—especially by the river. I would love a picnic by the river—by our river—in your spot. I remember you said white folks were always trying to find happiness and the Cherokee were already happy. I've pondered that thought many times—especially in Milledgeville where everyone is working so very hard to be happy."

We were quiet for a few moments. I could see Ben reflecting in his mind.

"You're right, Cassie. Life in Milledgeville is exhausting—truly exhausting. No matter how much I accomplish in a day, it isn't enough."

I could feel what Ben was saying.

"In Milledgeville my soul is pushed, pulled, stretched and tugged in a hundred different directions at once—from the time I get up until I retire. Everyone wants more. You're right, Cassie. You're very right. Whites want more—more of everything."

I laughed to myself and Ben heard my cynical chuckle.

"You're right. They want everything we have and they're in a mad rush to get it," I answered.

"I know. I know," Ben replied. "I remember you said the clock is humankind's worst invention—after ten years a lawyer, I agree. I've learned to hate my watch."

"When we get married, I'll throw your watch away, Ben."

"When we get married, I'll let you. I often think how no one up here worries if it's nine in the morning or three in the afternoon or even what day it is. They don't care."

"Wait here on the porch for me, Ben. I'll get our picnic ready."

I returned with the quilt Ben's mother had given me and the pine basket containing our picnic. Today would be special. I could sense it. I could feel Ben's pleasure being back with me where he grew up as a carefree boy. It seemed every moment he was here he was looking younger and fresher and more alive.

I put my arms around Ben and looked up at his face—in that moment he was just a little boy who had grown taller.

"It is nice to be in a place where folks are never in a hurry and everyone speaks to everyone," he said.

"Our country has always been a place of safety for anyone in trouble," I answered. "Perhaps one of these days you'll have your fill of the hustle and bustle and we'll live happily ever after just like one of Hans Christian Anderson's stories. You don't have to stay with me all the time, Ben, just most of the time."

When I said that, Ben pulled me close to him and we laughed as I tossed my hair. With the blanket and picnic, we walked hand in hand to our special place—the most peaceful spot in the universe.

I was happy—the most content I had been in a long while. Maybe today would be a turning point in our relationship. Maybe after today I would see Ben more often.

As we walked, Ben reflected and chatted. I could tell he was at peace.

"You know, Cassie, I wish I could go back to the years I spent here as a boy. I wish I could turn back the calendar."

"Those are marvelous memories for me as well," I said.

Ben continued, "I recall endless days hunting—sometimes alone and sometimes with my father—sometimes with your brother or other Cherokee boys."

"I remember those days, Ben."

"I remember wonderful days spent with my father cutting our firewood. There's not a thing about those days that isn't wonderful in my memory."

As we walked along, I listened to Ben reflect upon his serene childhood. I didn't dare say a word and interrupt his thinking. I didn't want to disrupt such a wonderful and cathartic rehearsal.

"I learned the Cherokee have respect for everyone, regardless of where they're from. Your people don't care if one's parents are white or African or a mixture. Here everyone is loved and respected. There are no half-children here—no mongrels or half-breeds—just fathers and mothers and friends—and you know everyone by name."

I loved listening to Ben talk. The timber of his voice reminded me of his father and mother.

"My people never think about things like that, Ben. There are no half-brothers or half-sisters here. There are no half-breeds, mestizos or quadroons. No one here is one-quarter Cherokee or one-eighth African. All are accepted with full citizenship. There are no half-citizens, half-brothers or step-children here. We don't have second-class people like on the whiteside."

"How wonderful that is, Cassie. I'm tired of seeing and hearing that distinction in Milledgeville. My parents always looked at people as whole people and they were right. Your people are right to believe and practice that."

"Ben, sometimes I think you've become a Cherokee at heart. Your thinking is good—wholesome. You understand."

Ben stopped, turned and looked at me—studied me really.

"I think you're right, Cassie. I feel as if I have shed a great weight from my shoulders when I come up here. I do."

I laughed, squeezed his hand and we began walking again.

"From the moment you arrive here with me," I said, "I can see you begin to relax like you're shedding your Milledgeville skin. I want you to have everything good in your life. My life is yours, Ben. I have waited for you ten years and I'll wait ten more years, if need be. Remember one thing, you'll never meet a woman who loves you more than I love you. You'll never meet a woman who will take better care of you, and you'll never meet a woman who is as good for your soul as I am. I was created for you—for you alone, Ben Lowry. I believe that."

Ben was looking at me as we walked along. I wanted him to know how I felt inside.

"We were meant to be together," I said. "I was born to take care of you the rest of your life."

Ben gave a little laugh as he put his arm around my waist and pulled me closer.

"I know that, Cassie."

"You do?"

"In my better moments, I know you're the only woman for me. I have to remember that when I get to Milledgeville. The minute I get off the stage, my busy life becomes a hectic madhouse. I must learn to remember you're waiting here for me. I've got some things to sort out in my life. I need to prioritize, don't I, Cassie?"

"I've been thinking about that, Ben. I know you work hard and I know things bother you. I know you have the desires any young man has. That doesn't bother me. Those desires cannot be ignored. I'm not jealous."

Ben didn't answer.

"I know you don't think about me every moment you're not here. Just remember, my dear Ben, anytime you look into the sky and see our moon, be it day or night, know there is someone not far away looking at that same moon wishing you well, wishing all good things will come your way—someone created just for you."

"What a lovely thing to say, Cassie."

Just at that moment we arrived at our place. Ben held me tight as we stood on our special stone by the river leaning against one another watching the water flow slowly.

"I'll do that. I promise," Ben said. "When I look at the moon, I'll think about you up here looking at that same moon—that same Cherokee moon."

With that promise, we kissed tenderly and held one another for a long time.

Ben changed the subject.

"I was hoping we would picnic today, Cassie. All the way from Brainerd I was excited about seeing you. For some reason, I knew this would be a special day."

"Every day with you is special," I answered softly.

"The last few months have been difficult, very difficult," Ben said, with a pensive look.

"They've been difficult up here, too."

"I know. I don't like to avoid certain topics but, yes, I have been working hard—much too hard. The imprisonment of the missionaries, my father's illness and the impending removal of your nation is weighing upon me. Sometimes I feel terribly guilty that I can't do more for the Cherokee."

"I know."

We stopped talking and I pulled him to me with both arms. I looked up at his handsome face."

"Come to me when you're unclean," I said. "I'll wash your guilt away. I shall wrap you in myself and cleanse your soul."

Ben smiled. We kissed tenderly.

"I know I shouldn't worry, but I do. I have great anxiety thinking about you and your grandparents. The removal will happen, Cassie, but I had hoped it would be delayed. Ross thinks there will be some eleventh-hour reprieve. I hope he's right.

"Our Chief is a good man. A very good man. He always hopes for the best. No one could work harder for us than he does," I said, still looking up at Ben's face.

"Somehow, with you here in your place, all those horrible things seem distant," Ben said.

He pulled me to himself—tight against his body. We embraced and he kissed me passionately—more passionately than I can remember.

He pulled me down and we sat pressed tightly against one another on the quilt by the river's edge enjoying the afternoon and holding hands. It was an unusually warm day for late October—a perfect day for a picnic.

"Ben, I study your face when you come here. After just a little while in our special place you're smiling. You relax and begin to laugh. All the corruption of Milledgeville falls away.

Ben didn't speak.

"And the best thing—you look at me like you used to. In your eyes I see that boy I fell in love with in that little schoolroom. Perhaps you should consider a change in your life for your mental health?"

Ben looked at me and grinned. We laughed together at that idea. We both knew Ben would not be leaving Milledgeville. He loves his work and political life.

Ben pulled me down. We lay together on the quilt still holding hands.

"Cassie, I love these autumn days without a cloud in the sky—a sky so blue it hurts your eyes to look up, and air so clear it's as if I could reach out and touch the mountains."

"I know, Ben. I know."

"Cassie, the air's so soft today I can't tell where the air ends and my skin begins. I feel like I'm part of some huge piece of artwork. I feel as if my body is a fluffy cloud floating on a blue canvas sky."

"What a lovely thing to say, Ben. You should write poetry. That was the most beautiful use of language I've heard lately."

We sat up and slowly ate our little picnic. After we finished we sometimes talked and sometimes lay beside one another in silence. It was a special afternoon.

Without words, Ben pulled me to him and kissed me. I was more than ready to be held, to be kissed—to be desired. I dream of his kisses—of his arms around me.

He kissed me but this time neither of us were prepared to end the kiss. Our kiss seemed as if it were eternal. I wanted more, much more, and he did, too. I wanted everything this man had to give—both now and forever. I wanted to be part of him. I wanted to merge into his mind and life. I wanted us to become one. He kissed me with passion. In that single moment I wanted to return the lifetime of love stored in my heart—love overflowing for him alone.

I hoped when he understood the depths of my passion he would give all of himself rather than a portion. I wanted the power of my longing to reach to Milledgeville and capture his heart.

The day and our kisses could not be controlled. That was as it should be. Kisses should never be controlled.

After all these years of waiting for Ben, it was time. My world achieved its long awaited balance that afternoon on our big flat stone by the river's edge, lying on the quilt his mother had given us as our wedding gift. The kisses became passionate—then consuming. Our hunger led us into a never-ending embrace as we explored one another with the yearning only soulmates can achieve.

We were alone on the quilt under the perfect sky on a perfect day. It was a perfect moment. We were one.

As Ben held me, he whispered how much he loved me, how much he had always loved and wanted me. He whispered of my beauty and of his longings.

I yielded to the man I adored. I gave myself to the one I had chosen years ago as the father of my children.

My years of patience were rewarded in one glorious afternoon. Our lives joined as we had always planned. Our love was consummated as my hair fell about his head and our bodies quivered with unfettered desire. We held one another oblivious of the murmuring waters beside us, the birds singing above us or the dozen squirrels playing on the opposite bank. We were blind and deaf to everything, save our beloved.

I was the sole object of his passion as he was of mine. I was the delight of his soul. He was the joy of my eyes. My happiness was complete. Perhaps now he would know I alone could make him happy, that I alone could fulfill his deepest craving for a lifetime of satisfaction. I was born to fill his dreams, his mind—his world. I wanted this moment to endure. I was his to do with as he wished. I would deny him nothing—not today, tomorrow or any day. Ben is my sun, moon and stars. I am finally and fully his. He is mine.

Ben and I, in love since childhood, shared the ultimate pleasure in the physical union of a husband and wife. Our lives are now complete, the two becoming as one, as his mother and father had foreseen and welcomed.

How could I preserve this moment? Was preservation possible? Is it possible to relive this day? We are one, united and now sharing everything good and bad, and Ben felt the same. He will never experience a friendship or relationship stronger than ours. We could want no greater. What we have consummated will grow and flower into eternal magnificence—ever growing, ever flowering.

As we lay holding one another, wrapped in the quilt, we looked through the limbs of the trees on the riverbank into the clear sky and saw nothing but our glorious future together—forever inseparable.

"My love for you will never end, Cassie. I need you. You are special."

"You are special, too. You've always been special."

"You are the most beautiful woman in the entire world. I have missed you. From this moment forward, Cassie, you can count on me. One of these days I'll come for you. We'll be together always."

"I know that. I've always known that, Ben. I know you'll come."

Ben kissed me again.

"I knew it before, but I promise I shall love you till the last day of my life. My last thought in this world will be how much I have loved you."

We fell asleep in one another's arms caring nothing for others who might disturb us by chance. We had arrived in heaven.

I woke in Ben's arms.

With Ben sleeping beside me, I thought how he had wonderfully reverted to the young man who had lived in New Echota with his parents. He was again the boy I loved—the boy who loved me.

Ben woke as I watched him sleep. We gathered our things. As we walked back up the hill the reality of Ben's departure back to Milledgeville loomed. The pain of that parting would be sharper than ever before. As we walked up the hill I could feel his mood swing back to occupy the form of a successful Milledgeville lawyer and politician.

I felt myself begin to cry. Ben didn't notice.

"Cassie, this next year is a big year for me. Things will happen that will determine the direction of my political career—maybe for the rest of my life—for our lives."

"I'll keep waiting. I'll wait for you forever, Ben."

"I'll do everything I can for you and your grandparents."

"I know you will."

I could feel the tension re-enter Ben's body as he spoke with a more formal tone.

"Once again, let me urge you in the strongest terms. You and your grandparents should leave soon. Do everything you can to persuade them. If you leave, I can help. I can give you money for your journey. I can even pay for a servant. If you choose to stay until the army comes, I won't be able to do much—maybe nothing. No one is exactly sure what will happen during those last days. All I know is if you stay it won't be good. I hear talk. The removal will be a logistical mess—of that I'm certain. I don't think anyone in government understands how big Cherokee Country is and how many Cherokee there are to be moved."

"I know, Ben. I know. I know."

"Do your best, Cassie."

"I'm going to explain everything to them again. They know if we leave soon we could be in place for the spring planting, but I doubt they will leave. They're too old."

"Do your best to persuade them."

"They're set in their ways. They walk by the graves of their relatives every day. How can strangers from across an ocean expect them to sever those ancient ties?"

"This country has power over the Cherokee mind. I'll grant that," Ben said.

"It's true, Ben. We belong to this land. The land doesn't belong to us. We can't deny who we are. Leaving is the same as forfeiting our lives. It will be difficult but I'll go anywhere with you. I belong to you."

Ben's voice had lost the softness I had heard by the river. His tone was almost harsh as he spoke of his plans.

"This coming year, if I'm appointed to a senate seat by the legislature, I can write my own ticket. Zach, Elizabeth and the firm have promised to endorse my candidacy. We've been working for ten years for this appointment."

"I know you have."

"The Senate is the big prize."

"I know it is."

"One six-year term in the Senate and I'm set for life. I'll have achieved everything I've worked for. I'll be in a stronger position to do something for the Indian nations."

Ben's mind had changed. His attention had left me and my place and our picnic and our love. He was somewhere else. He was someone different.

"I'll take care of you. Don't worry about that. I'll take care of you, Cassie. I promise."

"I know you will."

Ben left early in the afternoon. He promised to be back before the first of the year. Things will be clearer in Milledgeville then, he said.

I wonder what life has in store for us—for the Cherokee? Will Ben be able to take us away before the coming of the white killing frost? What part do Zach and Elizabeth play in his life? Life has many uncertainties. Whatever may come, today I had the best day of my life with the man I love.

21 November 1837

My time passed. I told elisi what Ben and I had done that day by the river. She is certain I'm carrying Ben's child but we will not know for sure for another month. She and I are happy. I want ten children and dozens of grandchildren for Ben. I have my beloved living inside of me. I thought loving

Ben was the greatest pleasure on earth, but giving him a child brings even greater happiness.

The thought of my beloved's seed growing inside of me is the happiest thought I could imagine. Even with all our problems, life has become brighter and our future more certain. I trust Ben. He will find a way. He will love his child. I am impatient to see Ben holding his child, to see elisi and edudu hold our baby and see Eleanor's face when she sees her first grandchild. Maybe, when Ben's father holds his first grandchild, he shall return from that terrible place he has been.

Chapter XLIX

1837 - Ben's New Job – Bear Paws

Chapter 49

25 November 1837 - The Trading Moon – Nu da de qua

Ben came to see me on his way back from visiting his parents and conducting business in two of Georgia's new counties, Murray and Walker— land that until recently was part of Cherokee Country.

He came to see me in order to tell me personally he has taken a new job assisting the government with our removal. We didn't have a picnic or walk to the river. I do not have the courage to tell edudu, or anyone, about Ben's new job. Ben is a good man. Perhaps it is a good thing Ben was given this job.

When Ben and I were settled on the porch after his arrival he took my hands and spoke in a business-like tone, "I have news, Cassie. I've been troubled thinking how to tell you, but I must. That's why I came by to see you today. I've been offered an important job working for the state of Georgia and I've accepted. This isn't a job I would have chosen. You must understand I accepted this job because I didn't want someone unfriendly to the Cherokee in the position. At least now I'll know what's happening in Cherokee Country and I can keep you informed. Gilmer himself sent representatives to persuade me. I was flattered. I couldn't refuse. This job will be good for my future."

I didn't say a word. Ben continued his business-like speech.

"I'll supervise the final settlement of the new counties before, during and immediately after removal. They want the new counties integrated into Georgia with fully functioning county governments. The most important thing is the registration of deeds at the courthouses. That's where my work will be. Georgia wants the Cherokee land settled quickly. That's the job. With this work, the state will gain full control of all the land within its chartered boundaries. It gives me no joy to tell you that, but you knew it was coming."

Ben waited for me to respond. I couldn't answer a word. He was uncomfortable but he continued.

"I will have nothing to do with the removal. I want no part of that. My job is not military. I'm a civilian in state government like I've always been. This is an ordinary, honest job."

I watched his face as he struggled to justify himself. I wondered if he was trying to persuade me or persuade himself.

"I'll oversee surveying, registration of lottery winners, establishment of functioning county seats, assist in initial judicial appointments, assist the governor with law enforcement and elections—everything that has to do with proper county government. Most of my work will be with land. That's my expertise—land."

"I know, Ben."

"They're going to take it all, Cassie. Every farm. I've told you before. This isn't new. When this is over, Cherokee Country will be white—all white. They're not going to allow any Cherokee land holdings—none at all."

"I know. I know."

"I told you this would happen, but now it's being planned in detail."

I looked out into the woods thinking about Ben's news. Two squirrels were chasing one another around the big white oak.

"I wouldn't do this, Cassie, if it were up to me. I took this job for your sake—for the Cherokee. I wanted to tell you about it first-hand. I didn't want someone else to tell you or you see my name in the newspaper and get the wrong idea. Please don't think I have betrayed the Cherokee. It's not like that. It's not like that at all. I'm a friend of the Cherokee. You know that. I'll do right by you and your people. I will."

"I know, Ben."

Ben paused. We sat close to one another holding hands. Ben was uncomfortable, but I had nothing to say. My heart was heavy. I wasn't going to make his confessions easier. I felt numb as I thought of elisi and edudu being forced from our home. My heart was heavy.

"Cassie, things are going to happen fast after the weather breaks this spring. The date is still the twenty-fifth of May. I've a lot of work to do in a short time, but the governor's office has been liberal. I'll be supported by the military when I need their help—civilian chores, of course."

"I thought you would have nothing to do with the military?"

"I will have nothing to do with the removal. The military will help me facilitate setting up the local governments and help maintain law and order—that's all."

I looked at him. Ben was tense and nervous but determined to finish his explanation.

"That doesn't sound good, does it?" he said.

"No, it doesn't."

"I promise I'll be good to the Cherokee. I will, Cassie. You can count on me. That's why I came by today—to promise I'll do my best for you and your people. I haven't forgotten what I learned here. I didn't want you to hear this news from someone else."

I wanted to say something but I couldn't respond. Ben could see I was troubled. He continued his recital as if rehearsed. It probably was rehearsed.

"The May date is set in stone, Cassie. This time they're going full steam ahead. They're impatient."

I was quiet. He looked at me and continued more softly.

"This job is an honor—a big honor. Please don't think ill of me for accepting. I'll be good to the Cherokee. I promise. I haven't changed. I'm still a good man."

"I know you're a good man. I still love you, Ben."

"I hope so."

"I'll always love you no matter what happens."

"I know."

As we sat close, Ben continued telling me things I didn't want to hear. I thought of elisi and edudu. I imagined what would take place here on our little porch when young white men, wearing uniforms and hats and riding big horses, came for us.

"They needed a lawyer familiar with the Cherokee."

"You're a good lawyer. They're right about that. You know a lot about the Cherokee."

"I'm sure I was chosen because of my friends—especially Zach and Elizabeth. They have influence. This job will be a feather in my cap. It will help me get the Senate appointment I've been workin' for. This is my big opportunity, Cassie—our big opportunity, I mean. Things will change after this. I promise."

As Ben held my hands I could feel his discomfort. I tried to believe things will somehow work out for us—that Ben and I will be together somewhere, someday.

"Remember I'll wait for you, Ben."

"I know you will, Cassie."

"One day I'll look up and see you coming for me. We'll go somewhere and be happy," I whispered.

"Yes, we will," Ben answered, also in a whisper. "I promise to come for you one day."

We held each other's hands. As long as I am touching him, I'm happy. After a long pause Ben continued his business-like voice.

"Because I understand the Cherokee, they believe I can persuade some to emigrate before the deportation begins. That would make everyone's job easier. I hope I prove helpful. They said working with the Indians will serve me well when I'm in the Senate where all treaties are ratified. They said I would be chosen for important committees and probably be an advisor to the War Department in my first term. That would be a great honor, wouldn't it, Cassie? When I'm a Senator, I can do wonderful things for the Cherokee and the other tribes, can't I?"

"I always thought you would do wonderful things, Ben."

I surmised Ben was leaving out the more distasteful aspects of his new job, but Ben is right. It would be better to have him in this job than a white man who hates us—who cares only for the whiteside.

I heard elisi and edudu moving about in the house. Ben took his pen-knife from his pocket and fiddled with it.

"They needed a man like me to ensure a smooth transfer of land to white ownership. They want to avoid retaliatory violence by whites. When it's over, they want this whole thing to have been a non-event and avoid newspaper coverage as much as possible. That's why they wanted me. I'm sure that's what you want too, Cassie. No one wants trouble. No one wants a war. That's why I wanted you and your grandparents to emigrate early—to avoid all these problems."

Ben was wearing expensive new boots, new trousers, with a stylish coat and hat. He was riding a perfectly groomed horse. He would be well paid for the job he had described. I could imagine the compromises he would be required to make in exchange for his pay. My heart sank lower thinking of our removal and what my beloved would be asked to do. It wasn't fair for us or for him.

I remained silent.

"It's critical between now and the end of May hostility be avoided," Ben said. "Georgia doesn't want undue national attention. Some accuse us in the legislature of ulterior motives, but that's not true, Cassie. Most men in Milledgeville mean well—they do."

"You're the only man in Milledgeville I trust. I don't trust any of the English."

"I'm not English. I'm American," Ben said flatly.

"Same thing."

"Not really."

"They all speak English."

"Well, of course we do."

"They all want our land. They all came from Europe. They all hate us. They're all the same."

"Cassie, you know the difference between Americans and the English. We're not the same as the English. Americans aren't British. We're not the same. We're a completely different country."

"Tell me one thing that's different."

"I don't want to talk about that, Cassie. Some bad things have been written about the Cherokee in the newspapers, but that's water under the bridge. Those days are gone."

I looked at Ben's face. He had no idea of how he was different.

"Things have changed. The motives of those I work with are honorable, for the most part—not like the old days of the Georgia colony. White men in government now are progressive. The Cherokee are not their enemy. Georgia has the Cherokee's best interest at heart. They genuinely want the Cherokee to prosper. That's what I'm going to work for."

"Do you really believe that, Ben."

"Well, yes I do. I've seen people change in Milledgeville since I've been there."

"I haven't seen any changes up here—not with the whites—not at all."

"Cassie, there's no way we can right every old wrong."

"I would like to see them right one old wrong, but that will never happen. After they take our land they'll forget everything. Extinguish is the right word. They'll forget what they've done," I said somewhat sarcastically.

"That's not true, Cassie."

"They'll forget. They'll never right even one wrong. They think only of themselves."

I was annoying Ben. I shouldn't be petulant, but I couldn't help being skeptical of the motives of the rapacious men in Milledgeville. Rapacious is the right word. I laughed a cynical laugh under my breath as I thought of the true meaning of the word."

Ben continued and didn't pay attention to my spite.

"A peaceful exchange will serve everyone's best interest—ours and yours. After all these years of struggle, your people deserve a happy outcome. Out west the Cherokee can prosper. You'll be insulated from the destructive pressure of white civilization. You'll be safe there."

"They'll eventually come for us there."

"No, they won't, Cassie."

"They always come. They'll take everything. We'll never be safe."

"Cassie, you must be positive. I'll do my best to try to persuade Ross to agree to a voluntary national emigration. If Ross doesn't agree, he's increasing the danger for everyone. At this point, the state is doing the Cherokee a favor. The government is being kind to the Cherokee."

"Do you believe that?"

"One day, when your nation is settled out west, they'll be grateful. I promise you, Cassie, I'm going to do my best for every Cherokee family. I promise. What we're doing is for their own good."

"I don't mean to be cross."

I had never felt so depressed in Ben's presence. What had happened to the little boy and little girl who had met in Mr. Lowry's schoolroom? Have our dreams vanished? Ben is assisting in that vanishment. There is no hope now—none. I knew exactly what Ben was saying. I held his beautiful strong hands as he continued his recital.

"I'm only doing what the Cherokee agreed to. It's not my fault the removal party signed that treaty. None of this is my fault, Cassie. I'm not to blame. I'm an honest man doing an honest job. I've always been an honest man. None of this is my fault."

I was glad no one was around to hear Ben's terrible news.

My beloved continued, "A few disgruntled Indians, influenced by Ross, could start a war—as bad as the Creek or Seminole war. I don't want to think what an angry white mob would do up here if that happened."

"We know exactly what angry whites do. We see it all the time."

"I know, Cassie. I'm talking about the removal. I want you to be ready. It's written in stone. The removal can't be stopped."

I held Ben's hand and leaned my head against his shoulder as I watched our bluebird pair perched on the eave of house. I didn't care about anything

593

he was saying. It was as if he was talking to a tree. I wanted this to be over so Ben and I could be together in peace.

"In any case, I'm glad I was the one chosen for this job, Cassie. I'll do my best to see the Cherokee are treated fairly. Perhaps Zach and Elizabeth were right, and I'm headed for the Senate. This job is certainly a stepping stone. It will almost guarantee my Senate appointment. That's really what I came to tell you. Imagine what I can do when I'm in the Senate? Perhaps I can undo some of the bad things. You understand that, don't you? I'm doing all of this with you and your people in mind. I'm thinking of you."

Ben paused once again. I heard the bluebirds twittering. I suppose Ben is correct, but what I saw in my imagination was a horror.

"Colonel Lindsey will continue to oversee the military aspect of the removal. It's rumored General Scott, old fuss and feathers, will replace Lindsey before too long. Scott's a good man, I hear—very fair. All I want is the best for everyone and this removal to proceed peacefully. It's the best thing for your nation."

Ben waited for me to say something—to say something to help him deal with his guilt over taking a job that would assist whites in taking our land, but I found it impossible to speak. I wanted him to stop talking. I wanted him to hold me—hold me forever—and stop talking.

Ben was determined to finish what he came to say.

"Georgia is continuing to build removal forts and roads. I hate the fort they built here—right in the middle of town. It's a monstrosity, isn't it?"

"It's terrible," I said.

Ben paused again waiting for me to say more but I had no desire for conversation. I didn't want to talk about removal forts, the army, the Militia or anything concerning the removal of my family from our home. To Ben this was just a job—a well-paying job.

"I'm sure it's the last thing you want to hear, Cassie, but the Militia and Guard will be in charge of the round-up. That's the main reason I want you to emigrate early. You can avoid the worst. I don't want you to have anything to do with the Militia or the Guard. I have nothing to do with that. I can't help you in any way when the removal begins."

I was shivering inside. I couldn't look at Ben's face. I felt as if Ben were talking to himself.

"They're saying not one family will be left behind. This is the government's solution to their long-standing problem. I had to come by and tell you. I couldn't bear to write this in a letter.

"I'm glad you came. I'm always glad when you come."

"I would consider myself a coward if I didn't tell you face to face. I hope you don't hold this against me. I'm doing this for the Cherokee. I wanted this job so I could at least do something to make the removal easier. I don't like this any more than you do, but what was I to do? I couldn't refuse, could I? I couldn't stand by and do nothing for the Cherokee. I couldn't allow someone in this job who hated you."

"They all hate us in Milledgeville. I read the newspapers. They want us to disappear—to vanish."

"Well, that's why you should emigrate now. I'll be in a position to take care of you when this is over. This job will require an enormous amount of work and it'll be lucrative for me—for us. I'll have enough to buy a place—a nice place."

"What did they promise to give you for this work?"

Ben sat silently for a few moments. He looked away.

"I'll be paid in gold and receive a bonus of two thousand acres of bottomland if we have a peaceful conclusion. That's quite an incentive, isn't it? The governor has held back quite a few acres from the lotteries for rewards like this. I'll have money when this is over, Cassie. I promise I'll take care you. I promise I will."

"I don't care about the money, Ben."

"If I get the Senate appointment, I can take care of you, your grandparents and Five Feathers."

Ben was excited to get the job. A Senate appointment would mean he would be away for six more years. I could feel his excitement but I was feeling abandoned. All I could think of was our national misery. All the families I knew throughout our country would suffer the same fate. I wish I knew nothing about his job or the events in store for us. I wish he and I could go west this very day.

"When this is over, I can sell the land they give me and buy a farm and build you and your grandparents a nice little house out west. I had to take the job, Cassie. You see that, don't you? I had to take the job. It was the only thing to do."

"I understand. I'm glad you came to see me."

595

I don't know how, but I'm certain Ben and I will be together. I will bear his children. Somehow, we will be together. Happiness will be ours.

Milledgeville November 1837

Ben returned to Georgia's capital pleased he had been honorable and had spoken to Cassie face to face. He could now concentrate on his job without a nagging sense of guilt. There were things about his job he didn't like, but life was like that. At least the bottomland he would receive could be held as an investment or sold for top dollar at the right time. After this job he would be set. If he was careful he could fund his retirement, his parents' retirement and even buy Cassie a little place out west. This job was the opportunity of a lifetime and then on to the Senate, but first things first. If he handled this job well, Zach and Elizabeth assured him the Senate seat was his. If he were a senator, he was sure that Elizabeth would accompany him to Washington City. He was sure of it.

Ben was unaware of his moral transformation. He had allowed the crisp black and white principles of youth to blend with the colorless ethics of law and politics, coating his soul with indistinct layers of grey preventing him from identifying truth or detecting a lie. Unknown to himself Ben had become a puppet, a caricature, faintly resembling his previous self, controlled by political marionettes whose strings attached directly to his compromised integrity, all sustained by hollow promises of money, power and pleasure.

Ben reflected on his meeting with the governor. The task he had been given was formidable, but he was told he wasn't to worry about budget or staff. Governor Gilmer would personally take care of his every need as long as the job was done quickly and efficiently. Ben was determined he would do his job. He would do a good job. He would worry about Cassie and her grandparents another day. She was a strong woman. She and Five Feathers could handle any problem. They would survive, come what may.

As Ben rode back to Milledgeville, he thought fondly of his future Senate appointment. This job would get him noticed. If he could complete it successfully, and he was sure he could, it should put the icing on his political cake. He might even end up more popular in Georgia than Crawford. He was gaining a political reputation as a master of compromise and he could count on Zach and Elizabeth to work behind the scenes to ensure final success. They were as excited about going to Washington City as he was—perhaps more so.

The closer he came to Milledgeville the more he thought about Elizabeth and less of Cassie.

He wanted to see Elizabeth tomorrow. The thoughts of her at the hotel, her smile, her fragrance, walking with her up the long staircase and being alone with her in her private suite gave him a sudden moment of intense pleasure but also renewed that familiar empty ache in his chest that was only relieved when she was physically near. He was impatient. He didn't realize how much he had missed Elizabeth until this moment. He thought again how impressed she would be with the gold and the land he was promised. She was exactly the kind of woman he desired—a woman who understood a man's world and was comfortable in it. This job was coming at the perfect time in his career. It would be his crowning achievement. He was doing the right thing. What a pleasure it would be to have Elizabeth on his arm in Washington City.

In the end the Cherokee would thank him. Their problems were self-inflicted—a direct result of the shortsighted, bullheaded Cherokee leadership personified in the stubborn John Ross. The removal party had rightly seen the pragmatism of early emigration. Cassie needed to be out west, not in the United States. The removal would be in her best interest. She would see that eventually. Two cultures had clashed and the weaker must yield. None of this was his fault. Sometimes for no reason bad things happen to good people. Removal was required for the good of the Cherokee. Cassie would come to understand emigration was the only path.

Ben's relationship with Cassie would be a problem. He would be personally in charge of giving away her community, but it must be done. He had warned her repeatedly. The removal wasn't his fault. The refusal of Ross to budge an inch wasn't his fault. Ben was innocent.

It is true Cherokee Country had been the land of their ancestors, but didn't they see the writing on the wall? Didn't they understand they couldn't stand against the solid, legal rights of the United States and the needs of its people? He didn't understand the Cherokee obstinacy. The Cherokee had been given a beautiful country out west where they could prosper without white pressure. They should be grateful. Many important whites had gone out of their way to protect the Cherokee future by facilitating their national emigration. It was foolish to believe the Cherokee should have their own nation in the east. It was not practicable. It had become impossible. Everything east of the Mississippi was white land now. Everyone knew that.

In any case, the Cherokee did not have the intellectual ability to maintain a modern nation. Indians were inferior. Theirs was a sub-culture—a stone age society of short-sighted illiterate hunters and gatherers. That didn't matter now. The Cherokee were finished. They were leaving as they should—as they must.

Ben's thoughts drifted to his parents and their years of work in Cherokee Country. He felt a nagging guilt about the change in his political and social views since becoming a lawyer but that couldn't be helped. His parents had paid a high price for standing up for their beliefs. Ben worried about his father—his mind shattered by his imprisonment. The years his parents had spent working for the Cherokee had been a waste. They were living on charity and no more than existing at the Brainerd Mission. Life was unfair but none of this was his fault. Against good advice, his father had stubbornly provoked the authorities and brought poverty and mental illness upon himself. He had provoked his own arrest. He had been well warned of the consequences of opposing Georgia law. Civilization exists where the citizens remain civilized. If folks ignore the law, anarchy results. His father knew that. The rule of law must govern all aspects of a progressive society.

The same was true of the obstinate Cherokee who were being removed because of their hardheadedness. It wasn't his fault he worked for the state. It wasn't his fault he would oversee the giveaway of Cassie's village. He was doing what was right for the situation. Situational ethics, he had read recently, taught that right and wrong should be judged on a case-by-case basis. There was no black and white truth in the modern world. The United States was building a new world—a vibrant, modern, progressive world where things changed every day. This new world needed modern ideas and ethics to match. Five-thousand-year-old morals crudely etched in stone must be discarded.

If Ben had been truthful with himself, he would have realized he had adopted the epicurean ethics of Zach and Elizabeth. He had slowly become a devotee of sensual pleasure. His life had increasingly become a life in which he chose self-interest as primary in all situations.

Ben understood, as everyone should, Indians would always remain savages. The word was harsh, but correct. The Cherokee were destined to disappear just like Cooper's Chingachgook in *The Last of the Mohicans*—a prophetic novel indeed, Ben thought. The Cherokee would be swallowed by the progressive white tide rolling across the North American continent from sea to shining sea. Like the Delaware, the Cherokee would and should disappear. Cherokee land would be developed by an enlightened white culture—a culture of education, science, music, agriculture and industry. Georgians wouldn't allow themselves to be hindered by weak-minded hunters and gatherers with no agriculture, science, art or written language. Wide roads and great cities would replace the undeveloped forests of the benighted Cherokee.

The Cherokee must go. It was his duty to serve the state of Georgia. After all, he was free, white and twenty-one. It was his duty to be part of the developing white culture, implementing social reform and strengthening the economy for the benefit of all.

As he thought about it, everything he did was for the Cherokee's own good. He should be commended—probably would be. Cassie would be better off west of the Mississippi and the sooner the better. He saw that clearly now.

26 November 1837

The Surveyor General in Milledgeville has maps of our Cherokee land with all the information needed for the fortunate drawers. John Ross is in Washington working for us. Whites continues to give away our country.

Copied from the *Federal Union* - 14 November 1837 page 1

"Printed Maps of the LAND DISTRICTS IN CHEROKEE. Representing the Water Courses, Numbers, Names and Residences of the Drawer of each Lot.--For sale at the Surveyor General's office at $5.00 each. Persons requesting a Map of any District enclosing Five Dollars will be furnished without delay by mail. James F. Smith Milledgeville September 7, 1837."

29 November 1837

Copied from the *Federal Union* - 14 November 1837 - page 2

"Whereas, the time stipulated in the treaty with the Cherokee tribe of Indians for their removal...is approaching, and as it is the universal opinion of those best acquainted with...their removal, that difficulties will occur...which will endanger the lives and property of the citizens...without preventive measures being taken by the government...Be it therefore enacted, That his Excellency the Governor be, and he is hereby authorized to accept...four volunteer companies of mounted men, to be stationed, one in each of the counties of Lumpkin, Union,

Walker and Murray, for the protection of the citizens of those counties..."

Edudu believes the Guard has mapped the location of all our homes in order to arrest us quickly when the time comes. There is no news from our Chief in Washington. I have heard nothing from Ben. I am frightened—terribly frightened of the white soldiers. I never go to New Echota.

28 November 1837

Once again Ben wrote asking that we make immediate plans to emigrate. He says if we go now it will be safe to travel. He will personally take care of all our expenses. He says if we stay here there will be confusion and he cannot guarantee our safety. I'm sure he is right, but I shall stay with my family. I go where they go. I sleep where they sleep. I shall be buried where they are buried.

Letter from Ben - 22 November 1837 – Huff's Boarding House

My Dearest Cassie,

Events in Georgia are heading to a climax. Let me beg you in the strongest terms to persuade your grandparents and Five Feathers to emigrate immediately. It is reported that most Cherokee families are planning a crop this spring. That is a mistake—a big miscalculation. There will never be another Cherokee harvest in Georgia. There will be no Green Corn Festival this year. The general government will never give in to Chief Ross. The treaty of 1835 will stand.

At the end of May troops will remove every Cherokee man, woman and child—old and young. Every Cherokee family will be gone. I don't know what else to say. If you love me and trust me you will persuade your family to leave immediately. I love you and care about your grandparents. If you delay I cannot guarantee your safety or comfort. It could even be a matter of life and death. I do not have a high opinion of the discipline of the patchwork United States army, much less the various militias or the Guard or the myriad of civilian contractors who will be hired by the government. Please heed this warning. I am privy to much information. I can assure you what I have communicated is accurate. If you emigrate now you will be in place for a crop this year out west. It's your only hope.

I miss you every day we are apart. I wish you and yours all the best in every way. Do not ignore this warning.

Your Loving Ben, xoxoxoxo

I read Ben's letter to edudu. He spoke quietly to me.

"My dear Walela, your Ben speaks truth, but perhaps our chief can persuade Washington City to allow us to work a small plot of land among the whites as if we were white landowners. If they take our country perhaps they will at least allow us to keep our little farm. We are almost like whites now, aren't we? My dear Walela, what do you think? We are civilized, aren't we?"

"Edudu, I don't know what to think. I cannot imagine leaving. I love these hills. This is the land given us by the Great Spirit. It is written in the white's holy Book that their first man and woman were cast out of their paradise for rebellion and never allowed to return. Now whites want our paradise to replace the one they lost. I don't know what is right, edudu. Some have left to find peace in the western lands, but my life is with you. I will be the happiest of women to be at your side. I will never leave you or forsake you. Where you go, I go. Where you sleep, I shall sleep."

Edudu looked at me for a few moments.

"Your elisi and I have talked about removal many times, Walela. We will not leave until our Chief tells us to go. Perhaps he can arrange for us to be buried here where we should be buried. I am old. My ears cannot hear the songbird's music. My eyes cannot see the squirrels play. My bones ache when I lie down and when I rise up. I stumble when I walk. I can hardly carry a half a bucket of water from the spring. I have one last wish, Walela. I want to be buried here with my ancestors in my best clothes."

"I promise you shall be buried properly, edudu. I promise."

"I don't want to go to a strange land. I have my burial clothes ready. We are staying, Walela. One way or another, we shall be buried here in Cherokee Country—in the soil of our ancestors. I think, Walela, you and I shall never speak of emigration again."

9 December 1837

We rose early as usual this morning. The birds were singing. Killer was anxious about something. He was unsettled. Edudu let him out to see what it was. Immediately we heard Eagle Killer begin barking in the front of the house. He had found something. Edudu and I found Killer on the ground at the end of the porch pawing the ground. He was alternating between barking at something and running back towards us to tell us to come and see what he had found.

"He's probably got a possum cornered under the porch," edudu said. "I suspect Mrs. Possum smelled those fish heads I buried around the rose bushes yesterday. She should have taken her babies and gone to her den before the sun came up. If she tries to get away now Killer will hurt her. I'll hold the dog. You get a stick and run Mrs. Possum out from under the porch so Killer won't hurt her or have her babies for breakfast.".

I picked up a long stick and kneeled down to look under the porch so I could frighten away Mrs. Possum. Instead of a possum I saw something I'll never forget.

I jumped backwards and leaned both hands against the corner of the house and began to retch.

"Edudu, hold Killer tight," I said. "Don't let him go. Please don't let him go."

Edudu looked at me with a puzzled look.

"Is the possum dead, Walela?"

"Don't let Killer loose, edudu. Look under the porch. Don't let Killer loose. Please don't let him go."

I retched once again.

Edudu kneeled down and saw what I had seen.

Bear Paws was lying on his back just under the porch up against the house. He held a bottle in one hand. His blank eyes were staring up at the floor boards. Ants were crawling over his face, in his nose, mouth and eyes. He had drank too much whiskey and choked to death on his own vomit. He had soiled himself. He smelled horrible. I'll never forget that pathetic sight. I cannot understand why men make and sell whiskey. Since white men have taken over our country they sell whiskey, get men drunk and steal their money and possessions. Why would anyone want happy little boys to end like this? I hate whiskey. There isn't one good thing about the consumption of alcohol for pleasure.

I called Five Feathers and we pulled Bear Paws out and laid him on the end of the porch. With difficulty Five Feathers pried the half full bottle from Bear Paws cold fingers. It was as if even in death Bear Paws didn't want to be released from his curse. The bottle had the markings of the white traders—traders in death. Five Feathers muttered a curse and smashed the bottle against the white oak tree in front of the house. Elisi covered Bear Paws with her best table cloth.

"Go tell Adsila, Walela. His mother should know before anyone else tells her the bad news," edudu said.

"I will. I'll go now."

I thought to myself how terrible it will be for her to hear the news about her son. I hate whiskey and those who sell it. There's not one good thing to say about whiskey.

I told Adsila her son had died in the night at our house. I didn't tell her everything. I didn't tell her where we found him. When I left her, I cried.

Chapter L

1838 – Ben's Surprise - Removal Forts - Ben Stands for U.S. Senate

Chapter 50

10 January 1838 – Ben's Birthday

Great news—I will be like other women. I will have a baby—Ben's baby. Nothing could make me happier. Even in the midst of our troubles I'm pleased to be the mother of Ben's child. I wish I had been the mother of Ben's babies long ago. I love the feeling of eager anticipation. My future is known. I am already impatient for the child's arrival. I shall be a mother.

When Ben learns he is to be a father, he will think more of us and our future. Ben is a good man. He will become a better man when he learns a child shall spring from our eternal love.

Ben's mother will be thrilled beyond words. I cannot wait to see her face when I share with her my joy, but I must tell Ben first. I hope he comes today—on his birthday. This would be the best of all days to share my news. Perhaps he visited his parents in Brainerd. Our child will be a handsome boy and look like his father. I hope Ben comes today.

13 January 1838

Ben came yesterday after visiting his parents. We had a lovely morning. He told me the latest about his parents and the news from Milledgeville. The reports are not good.

"Ben, do you have time to walk to our special place? I'll put a few things together for a picnic. Would you like that? You love our spot by the river. It will be like old times. Would you like that?"

"You know, Cassie, I'm bone weary and that's exactly what I would like to do. Let's do that. I want to sit on your big rock all day with nothin' to do but listen to the water gurgle past, hold you close and lay back and watch the lazy clouds drift by. I would like that immensely. What a good idea."

On the way we talked about this and that. He shared the news about his parents.

"Father remains trapped in some distant corner of his mind and is declining."

"I'm sorry, Ben. I truly am."

"I know."

"How is your mother?"

"Mother was asking for you. I told her you were well. She's increasingly worried about Father and showing her age. The folks at the mission provide them with a cabin. It isn't nearly the comfortable house they had here, but it is a roof over their head."

"I miss her terribly."

"I know you do. She misses you, too."

"I hope your father gets better. I miss him, too."

"I do, too, but I don't know. He's worse than the last time I was there. Father can't do chores so a small place is easier for Mother. They have a well and a pump. Mother doesn't have to walk to the spring like she did here."

"I'm glad she has a pump."

"Me too. I send money every month to Brainerd. They supply my parents with milk and eggs."

We arrived at our spot by the river. It was cool. I brought my quilt. I put out the things from my pine basket. We sat hand in hand without talking and listened to the water burble and gabble as it slid past our rock whispering its blessing to the two welcome lovers above. I was happy.

Ben held me. It felt as if the river lifted its arms and caressed my face, assuring me all would be well. My two dear friends, Mr. and Mrs. River Otter, passed swimming lazily downstream. They swam past both on their backs taking note of everything in their watery domain.

When they were half a stone's throw away, they saw Ben and stared at him as they drifted with the current. Finally, with a knowing, sagacious nod of their heads, they gave Ben permission to rest with me beside their river as they continued their journey.

It was time, but I was nervous. I knew now was the moment.

"Ben, I have something important to share. I am a happy woman—a very happy woman. In fact, I'm the happiest of women—much happier than the last time you were here."

"You are always happy, Cassie. I think you're the happiest person I know."

Ben smiled. His smile helped me.

"You make me happy. I have loved you, Ben Lowry, since the day I first met you in your father's little schoolroom. You're the most wonderful man in the world. I'll never love another."

As I studied Ben's face, I saw in his eyes a reflection of the youthful passion—the look I see when Ben and I are in our special place. I thought I would burst. I had to share the good news.

"Ben, I'm going to have a baby, our baby, your baby. Is that not wonderful news?"

I felt Ben's entire body instantly tense. I had hoped it would be joyful news to him. I watched him gather his thoughts. I knew I must allow him time to think.

"Cassie, are you certain?"

"I'm certain."

"Are you sure? You're definitely going to have a baby? Are you positive? Is it possible you're mistaken?"

Perhaps I should have told him another way, perhaps never told him, but I was glad he finally knew.

"Ben, I'm sure. There is no doubt. I've had no issue in two months and elisi says it is definite—no mistake. I am with child. Everything has changed within. I can feel it. I'm going to have a baby, Ben—our baby."

Ben said nothing. I could feel his continued tension. There was no sign of joy on his face.

"I'm happy—very happy. I want you to be happy, too," I said quickly.

Ben looked at me.

"I know we intended to wait," I said, "but I want you to be pleased. Some things don't come in season. I want you to be happy—as I am happy. I want us to be happy."

We sat in the very spot on the very quilt where Ben and I had conceived—the quilt his parents had given me. I knew he was thinking of what people would say if they knew he had a child by a Cherokee woman. His friends in Milledgeville would call our baby a half-breed, but that didn't concern me.

"I'm sorry, Ben, but I'm happy. I want you to be happy about our baby—your baby. Your mother will be happy."

When I mentioned his mother, I felt him start. He looked at me. As I watched him considering my news, I wondered if he felt the same way about marriage to a Cherokee woman as he used to?

I began to cry.

"I am so sorry, Ben, I don't mean to cry. I know you wanted to wait until after we married to have children. I wanted to tell you I was expecting our baby—the child you have given me—given us, and I wanted more than anything for you to be pleased. I want this to be a happy time. I want this to be our baby. I want you to be happy, too."

Ben pulled me close and held my head tight against his chest. His chin was resting on my head. I felt his heart beating. I couldn't control the conflicting emotions that filled my body. I had allowed unspoken thoughts to build and now I couldn't prevent their release. Telling Ben was such an instant relief I couldn't stop the tears—tears of joy, gladness and hope.

Ben relaxed and began to rock me gently.

"I am happy, Cassie. I am happy. Don't cry."

He held me against his body with one arm and with the other he entwined my hair with his fingers spread wide, pressing my head even more tightly against his chest. Still without speaking, he rocked us gently with the rhythm of the river.

"Oh, my dear Cassie, forgive me. Please forgive me. I should have responded differently. I'm so sorry. I'm happy for you—for us."

"Are you really happy, Ben?"

"I'm happy. You're going to be fine, Cassie. Don't cry."

I could feel his breath in my hair.

"Please don't cry. Everything is good between us. Your baby will be fine. You'll be a good mother and I'll be a good father. Everything will be good with the child. I'll see to that. I'm delighted for you, Cassie—for us. Let's allow this to be a happy moment."

"Thank you, Ben."

I kissed his chin and put my head back against his chest.

"Forgive me, my dear, for my unthinking response," Ben said sweetly. I'm ashamed of myself. You'll make a wonderful mother. It will be a beautiful child. How could it not be beautiful if you are its mother? Will you please forgive me, my dear?"

"I forgive you."

Ben squeezed me and began rocking me tenderly once again. He slowly wiped my tears with the back of his hand. Still sniffling, but much happier, I held him tighter.

"Dear Ben, there is nothing to forgive. I am so happy you are here. I know you'll be a good father. I want you to be happy—happy for us."

We listened to the birds, the water and the gentle wind sighing in the tree tops. Without speaking we watched the squirrels frolic on the opposite bank. The river otters swam by once again. Ben continued to gently brush away my tears. I was happy in his arms with my head against his chest listening to his soothing heartbeat. I wanted to stay next to him forever.

"I'm going to be busy with my new job, Cassie. I won't be able to come up as often as I would like, but don't worry. I'll come often and check on your progress. Zach and I are putting together my bid, a strong bid, for a Senate appointment. I told you about that. He thinks '38 is the year for sure—the culmination of ten years hard work for us."

"I know."

"I'll be incredibly busy, but I promise to see you as often as I possibly can. Write if you need anything and I'll take care of you. I promise I will. I won't forget you."

"I'll let you know. I promise," I answered. "I'll let you know if I need anything for the baby."

"Don't worry about anything Cassie. I've saved. I can take care of you and the baby. Just let me know what you need. I promise I'll help."

I felt drained. I wanted to sleep. I wanted Ben to hold me like this for the rest of my life and allow me to sleep without dreams. I felt as if my body would be renewed by pressing against him. I knew we would walk back to the house, he would mount his horse and be gone for a very long time. But now he was here. I was happy.

"There's more news, Cassie. It isn't good, I'm afraid.

"I know," I answered. "It's all bad news lately. I read the newspapers."

"The army is transferring more troops. They say as many as 15,000 troops may be in and around Cherokee Country soon. They're afraid your people might resist removal like the Creeks did in Alabama. Some troops will be United States Army. The rest will be Tennessee, Georgia, Alabama and North Carolina Militia. Forts are being constructed all over Cherokee Country. I guess you know that."

"I know. I've seen the soldiers and their wagons. They're everywhere."

With my head still against his chest, Ben continued. I could feel the vibration of his chest against the side of my head.

"I'm told there will be more than fifteen forts in Georgia alone—maybe as many as thirty all around Cherokee Country. The general government will go through with your deportation this time. Ross is beatin' a dead horse in

Washington City. They allow him to talk and deliver his memorials and petitions but the die is cast. The removal is coming. The Rubicon has been crossed."

"Chief Ross is a good man."

"He is a good man but he's wasting his time," Ben said quietly.

"He's a good man," I said in a whisper once again.

"I know he is," Ben said, "but I wish he would agree to a national removal. That would save everyone a lot of trouble."

"I've been reading the papers," I said. "I know you're right. It's hard to believe they're taking everything from us and nothing can be done."

"I know, Cassie. It isn't fair. It truly isn't fair. I've done everything I could. I promise I have."

"I know you have, Ben. I know."

As Ben continued speaking, he held my head tight against his breast. I felt the comforting vibration of his voice and I wanted this moment to endure without end.

"Father and men like him have done everything they could over the years, but it's not enough. In retrospect, it was never going to be enough. The removal is coming whether we want it or not. They want the land."

"It's coming. I know it," I said in a whisper.

"Georgia is building new roads and strategically placing the removal forts. If you and your grandparents don't emigrate, you'll be arrested and deported. It won't be pleasant. Van Buren may be president, but the energy of the Jackson administration drives the removal. Once the orders are given, it will come like a storm, I'm afraid. It's going to happen. Your grandparents and Chief Ross can't wish this away. They can't avoid it any longer."

"I know, Ben. I know. I know. Edudu and I never go to New Echota. Soldiers are everywhere there. The fort in the middle of our beautiful town is the saddest thing. So many have been dispossessed—everything taken and whites living in their houses. When white settlers take someone's farm, our people go somewhere and begin all over with nothing. It happens all the time."

"I've seen it, Cassie. I know. I know what these last few years have been for the Cherokee. Stay close to home. It will get worse before the removal."

"We never go anywhere now. Every time I hear hoofbeats, I shiver. Everyone's frightened of the Guard and the Poney Club."

"I've heard about the Poney Club, Cassie. I don't trust the Guard and the regular Militia's not any better."

"I'm afraid, Ben. We hide when we see the English."

"They're not English. They're Americans. You know that."

"There isn't any difference."

"Yes, there is."

"Tell me what will happen to all the children, Ben? Do you know? What will happen to elisi and edudu? What will happen to all the old folks? I never thought they would do this."

Ben held me tight.

"Cassie, the removal will begin and end quickly. You'll have no warning. I have information the military wants to surprise everyone to prevent escape. They don't want to allow anyone to get away—not one family."

"Edudu says they have maps of all of our farms and houses. They know where every Cherokee family lives."

"I'm sure that's true," Ben said. "I doubt if I'll be told when the removal begins. Only the big-wigs will know that. All I know is, it will be at the end of May and early in the morning. That's all I know. The military, thank goodness, has nothing to do with me. They tell me nothing. I could never be a part of that. It rather nauseates me to think about it."

"Ben, I know you won't be involved. I know you wouldn't be involved with anything like that."

"No, I'm a civilian. I have nothing to do with the military."

"No one in Washington City is listening to our Chief," I said. "I know that, but we won't go until our Chief tells us. Until then, we'll plant our corn and squash. Edudu is putting out his martin gourds like he does every year. Perhaps Chief Ross can persuade the government to allow us to keep our little farm and become citizens."

"Take my word for it. That will never happen."

"I talked to my brother, Ben. Five Feathers has promised not to react violently if the soldiers do come for us. I believe him. He and his friends could cause a lot of trouble, but he is wise like edudu. He knows what would happen if they were violent. He will be a chief one day—when we get out west Five Feathers will certainly be Chief."

"Yes, your brother is wise. He will be Chief one day, perhaps."

"Ben, I think it would be better to die fighting than die of starvation and disease—slowly choking to death in a western prison. Maybe we should fight like the Creeks, die honorably and be buried here where we belong."

28 January 1838

Whites admit duplicity. They sign treaties and break them. They value honor among themselves but arrest us under a white flag. Who would believe the white government to be other than devious? They want to maintain white privilege. Why would we trust them?

From the *National Intelligencer* – Friday - 5 January 1838

"The deputation of Cherokees, ...with the full concurrence of the War Department undertook to act as mediators between the Seminole...and the U. States....Those chiefs who had come in under the Cherokee flag of truce were made prisoners of war and...imprisoned...There are some further rumors as to the treatment of Micanopy and the other Chiefs who came in with the Cherokees desiring to effect a peace. It is said they have been threatened with death in the event of any blood of the whites being spilt by those Indians who still hold out...the Cherokees have protested against the violation of the flag of truce."

February 1838

The Dahlonega mint has begun production of gold coins. Europeans have taken our land by right of discovery and right of conquest. They have taken everything under it and are about to take everything upon it. They claim they are honorable because everything they do is legal. What we believe legal and what whites believe legal are different things. Things indeed change.

12 February 1838

Copied from the *Federal Union* – 6 February 1838 – page 2

"Speech of Mr. Lumpkin IN SENATE, Monday Jan. 22, 1838. CHEROKEE TREATY. Mr. Lumpkin said...While Mr. Ross continues to protest...the Government considers the treaty the supreme law...much has been done towards the execution of the treaty which cannot be undone...is not now far distant, when my course of policy of these people, from first to last, will receive the general approbation of all those who are well informed on the subject...Mr. John Ross and his associates...are laboring under great misapprehension, in regard to the true state and condition of these people...I have in my possession a document written by Mr. Elias Boudinot, late Editor of the Cherokee

Phoenix, and one of the principal agents who negotiated the late treaty of 1835...a reply to the allegations contained in the writings of Mr. Ross...the Cherokee people are kept in a state of delusion and misapprehension in regard to their present condition...They unfortunately believe...Mr. Ross is here doing something to abrogate...the late treaty...this is a ruinous delusion...The time for their final departure is...May...and when the time arrives they must go: no power can...overturn this treaty...these people...ought to yield to the advice of better friends...who stand ready...to take them by the hand and lead them forth to their promised land of rest, where I trust these people will cease to be troubled by the white population...that it might be shown...that the Government was resolutely determined...to carry out with this people its benevolent policy...without which it is impossible the race can be preserved.

13 February 1838

The courageous Osceola is dead.

Copied from the Federal Union – 6 February 1838 – page 3

"OSCEOLA, THE INDIAN WARRIOR...departed this life at Fort Moultrie...Thursday evening last...For years...his name and character has been familiar...the master spirit of this long and desperate war. He was the savage, treacherous, murderer of General Thompson...for which act, as well as...others, of like cruel character...he should have suffered the tortures of death more painful and ignominious than was reserved for his fate by an all-wise Providence. He was...consistent in hatred—dark in revenge—cool, subtle and sagacious in council. Osceola will long be remembered as the man, who with the feeblest means, produced the most terrible effects."

1 March 1838

I wonder about the future? What will come of the white's determination to dominate both us and the Africans? Did these two men pay the ultimate price in an attempt to free Africans from bondage?

Copied from the *Federal Union* – 27 February 1838 – page 2

"Execution of Read and Evans. ….Jas. Read and Thos. Evans on the 9th inst. for Negro stealing. The unfortunate men…were convicted upon the clearest testimony. They were both strangers among us, and we believe in the State. About 1 o'clock the Sheriff, followed by a large crowd, started to the place of execution…"

6 March 1838

Copied from the *Federal Union* - 27 February 1838 – page 3

"…a letter was received last evening from an officer of the Army at Indian River…Gen. Jesop had captured three or four hundred Indians, men, women and children…Gen. Jesup is now near Jupiter…twenty-one Indians and one hundred and three negros have come in…It is also said that a considerable body of Indians are on an island southwardly, and are hemmed in by some of our troops…Gen. Nelson has killed fifteen Indians and taken nineteen prisoner."

The white army scours Florida for Seminoles. If our forefathers had known what the whites were planning, they would have drowned them before they reached shore and burned their ships. Maybe we should have gone over there and taken their land away from them. Edudu said he should have killed Andrew Jackson himself during the Creek war.

Free Africans were captured with the Seminoles and their families broken apart and sold. The Seminoles are being deported. Every Seminole with African features is sold into slavery even though born free.

12 March 1838

Long ago Mr. Lowry asked me to write about things that trouble me or my nation. I shall never forget the Lowrys' love. Unlike most, they were never two-faced. They never said one thing and did another.

Mr. Lowry's Book spoke of a man who was God and man—who lived when Rome ruled the world. Mr. Lowry said his fellow whites revere that Book. I would never tell Mr. Lowry he is wrong, but perhaps whites should read their Book more carefully. Maybe whites don't know the word hypocrite means actor in Greek—a person who pretends to be one person but who is actually another.

Copied from the *Federal Union* - 6 March 1838

> "...In every possible situation we might find an example in Jesus Christ for us to follow. Let us, then, show our love to him by a faithful adherence to his precepts remembering the test of Christian character: By this shall all men know ye are my disciples, if ye love one another."

The white men in Georgia love their fellow white men. They don't love us. The man who wrote these words is a white citizen of Georgia. His government has constructed military forts throughout our country to facilitate our vanishment.

Do whites believe their Book is a white book? Mr. Lowry read, "By their fruits ye shall know them."

If we had a fruit tree that made us sick we would burn it.

March 20th, 1838

I miss our dear Cherokee newspaper. I am weary of reading white newspapers full of hate. They will never know us. They despise us living near. Perhaps we should leave, as Ben suggests. I shall ask elisi again if we should flee the brewing storm, but I know her answer. She will never leave. She wants to be laid to rest in the country the Great Spirit gave us.

21 March 1838

Throughout history one nation dominates others by conquest, deportation, absorption or destruction. The stronger thrives. The weaker disappears. Whites believe we should disappear and that they are ordained to rule the world.

Copied from the *Federal Union* - 13 March 1838 - page 1

> "What will this union be fifty years from now? The morning of 1887 will dawn upon this nation doubled in extent...fifty millions of freedmen will look upon the light of that morn and glory in the name...GREAT NATION. Splendid cities will then exist where now the Indian, the Lord of the dark forest around him, lies prone upon his copper face, dreaming of the happy hunting ground of his fathers, with whom must soon dwell the whole Indian race. On that day, a mere handful will be lingering on the borders of the great deep that must at length engulf them...the present dwellers of the earth will have then ceased

their bustle...a new race of men--our children and our children's children will then manage the machinery of the world...and may the heavens permit us to continue our glorious career until all the nations of the earth become as we are."

They believe they deserve to flourish. I hope the final arbiter is as Mr. Lowry says. I hope one day the English stand before the bar Mr. Lowry told us about.

5 April 1838

The English love their racial purity. Can virtue be transmitted by blood? Elisi sneered at the newspaper advertisement.

Why must we be deported? Why must they possess everything we worked for? Sometimes edudu and I will catch our chickens at dusk and take them to our special roost tree in our enclosure for chickens. We stand under the tree in the twilight and toss the chickens into the lower branches where they stay for the night. After a few nights, our chickens come home to the same tree to roost without our help.

Elisi says the evil the whites have released on our world will come home to roost over their heads. Evil, like our chickens, always returns to the owner. The deeds perpetrated against us will come back upon them in their twilight. Darkness will descend on their culture. On that day, they and their children shall understand injustice and be afraid.

From the newspaper,

"RUNAWAY...a bright mulatto boy named Alfred...about seventeen years of age...He so nearly white that he no doubt intends to pass as a white man and when he is discovered he will be with a white man...a liberal reward will be given to any person who will recover him and put him in my possession or in any safe jail."

Whites believe it a crime to pretend to be white when one is not. Can privilege only be transmitted by pure white blood?

Copied from the *Federal Union* – 10 April 1838 – page 2

"In the Senate – Monday, March 26, 1838

CHEROKEE TREATY – Mr. SOUTHARD presented a memorial...signed by the deputation of Cherokee Indians, now in Washington...in regard to their situation under the late treaty, and praying Congress in some mode to interfere for their relief...with signatures of 15,665 persons of that nation.

Mr. Lumpkin said: I must express my deep regret at the introduction of this subject...the Senate should...put to rest all...hopes of the Cherokee people, that John Ross can effect the slightest change in the determination of a branch of the Federal Government, to execute the Cherokee Treaty of 1835.

"...this...treaty...was negotiated by a highly qualified and competent delegation of the Cherokee...the treaty was thoroughly discussed in this Senate and received its ratification...nine-tenths of the intelligent Cherokees have emigrated...or are preparing to go...There is no difficulty in regard to the executing of this treaty with the intelligent portion of the Cherokee people...the opposing Indians are ignorant and uninformed and these would...have cheerfully yielded...but for the wicked...operations of this man John Ross...Unfortunately he has been permitted to hold too much correspondence with the Executive officers of this Government...The twenty-third of May next...these people, so far as Georgia is concerned, must go, and go quickly. The citizens of Georgia hold grants for the lands on which these Indians now reside in that State, and the grantees are legally authorized by the laws of the State, as well as by Treaty, to take possession of their lands on and after the twenty-third of May next; and, sir, possession they will take; and the Indians will then be truly forced out of house and home...We have treated the Indians with all the kindness and forbearance which their interest required. But, sir, whatever conflict may arise, after the 23d of May, Georgia must, and will, be speedily relieved from this long-standing and vexatious perplexity...They must go or evil will come of it...all the combined powers of the Federal Government cannot abrogate or change this treaty, without the consent of the States interested, and that consent will never be obtained."

The writing is on the wall. Our good Chief is wasting his time in Washington City. I admire his courage. One day he will be honored but not now.

28 April 1838

Ben's predictions are true. We will soon be deported. Whites continue to think of us as deluded savages. They expect submission as if we were animals. How would they react if they were forced from their homes by invaders—invaders who believed them inferior because they have white skin?

I have warned edudu and elisi of our impending removal, but they continue to wait for our Chief. Five Feathers and I would leave today if we were alone. Most of our neighbors don't believe whites can be so heartless.

Copied from the *Federal Union*-Excerpt from page 2

"Major General Scott has made a requisition…for twenty companies of Militia of this state to be employed in removing the Cherokee…these companies are to march immediately to New Echota…This force, in addition to that made upon the states of Tennessee, Alabama and North Carolina and the regular troops will present a body of…seven or eight thousand men…sufficient to strike terror to…these deluded savages as are induced to resist the execution of the treaty."

"And earnest determination on the part of the government to have them removed is manifested, which…will be sufficient…to satisfy these Indians that Ross will not be able to have the time prolonged for their removal…Their remaining without evidencing any inclination to prepare for their removal indicates…it necessary that they shall be forcibly carried off…we sincerely hope that every leniency may be exercised by our fellow-citizens and that their removal may be accomplished without loss of lives of any of our people, or the fatal consequences which would ensue to the Indians from their commencing hostilities."

Copied from the *Jacksonville Republican*

"All accounts received from the Cherokee Nation heretofore, concur, in stating that the Indians were making no preparations for removal…they were planting corn and making other arrangements for a crop the ensuing season…Ross, we learn, has been solicited by those, whose feelings and opinions he should respect; but preserving in his obstinate and reckless determination to bring ruin upon his nation, he refuses to return, and replies, that his countrymen expect him to remain in Washington to attend to their business."

We trust our Chief. We will wait for him. I hope against hope our Chief will be successful. If not, I choose suffering with my people. I shall not flee in fear.

29 April 1838

At last a letter from Ben. I hope he can visit before the end of May. My heart aches for him.

> My Dearest Cassie,
>
> I have been incredibly busy with my job and preparations for my Senate bid, but I think of you and your condition often. You are constantly on my mind. I'm sorry I haven't been to see you. I will have business in your area soon and I look forward to visiting towards the end of May. We can spend some relaxing time together and perhaps take several days to ride up to Brainerd to see my parents before you are too far along, if I can manage to be away from my duties. Mother asks for you in all her correspondence. Let me know of anything you might possibly need to help in your condition. I will help you any way I can. All you have to do is ask.
>
> Thinking of you and your baby, take care,
> Your Loving Ben, xoxoxo

30 April 1838.

From the *Athenian:* Mounted militia units from Alabama, Georgia, and North Carolina have formed and are on their way to New Echota to join the general government in the removal. White militia units are also on alert for runaway blacks hiding among us.

5 May 1838

No word from Ben. Troops are moving all around us—mounted men are everywhere. We are afraid to leave our house. There are many reports of our people being robbed.

11 May 1838

Terrible things are written about us in the newspapers, but I saw this and it made me smile. It's not often I read the white newspaper and smile.

Copied from the *Southern Recorder* - 8 May 1838 – page 1

"Stars – Stars are sparks of fire, stricken out from chaos by the hoof of the winged horse of Time in his journey to eternity. W-h-e-w!!"

12 May 1838

Today we received a letter from General Winfield Scott by special messenger. Copies of this letter are being sent to every Cherokee community. General Scott, who replaced Colonel Lindsay, is adamant every one of us shall be removed.

I am filled with dread. I do not expect Scott's army will treat us as he promises. Whites have never been considerate, honorable or kind. Should we suddenly begin to trust? No one expects General Scott to give us what we need. Whites are takers, leeches and parasites who suck the life from our bones and wish us removed from their sight. We trust whites like a chicken trusts the fox. If they cared about us, they would leave us in our own land. Does the sly fox call the chicken his brother just before he consumes him— feathers, blood, bones and all? Osceola died in prison, arrested by General Jesop under a white flag. I don't trust the United States nor do I trust General Scott.

"Major General Scott, of the United States Army, sends to the Cherokee people, remaining in North Carolina, Georgia, Tennessee and Alabama, this ADDRESS:"

"Cherokee--The president of the United States has sent me, with a powerful army, to cause you, in obedience to the treaty of 1835, to join that part of your people who are already established in prosperity, on the other side of the Mississippi. Unhappily, the two years which were allowed for the purpose, you have suffered to pass away without following, and without making preparations to follow, and now, or by the time that this solemn address shall reach your distant settlements, the emigration must be commenced in haste, but I hope without disorder. I have no power, by granting further delay, to correct the error you have committed. The full moon of May is already on the wane, and before another shall have passed away, every Cherokee man, woman and child in those states, must be in motion to join their brethren in the far west."

"MY FRIENDS--This is no sudden determination on the part of the President, whom you and I must now obey. By the treaty, the emigration was to have been completed on or before the 23rd of this month, and the President has constantly kept you warned, during the two years allowed, through all his officers and agents in the country, that the Treaty would be enforced. I am come to carry out that determination. My troops already occupy many positions in the country that you are to abandon, and thousands, and thousands are approaching from every quarter to render resistance and escape alike hopeless. All those troops, regular and militia, are your friends. Receive them and confide in them as such. Obey them when they tell you can remain no longer in this country. Soldiers are as kindhearted as brave and the desire of every one of us is to execute our painful duty in mercy. We are commanded by the President to act towards you in that spirit, and such is also the wish of the whole people of America."

"Chiefs, headmen and warriors--Will you then, by resistance, compel us to resort to arms? God forbid! Or will you, by flight, seek to hide yourself in mountains and forests, and thus oblige us to hunt you down? Remember that in pursuit it may be impossible to avoid conflicts...Think of this, my Cherokee brethren. I am an old warrior, and have been present at many a scene of slaughter, but spare me, I beseech you, the horror of witnessing the destruction of the Cherokee."

"...make such preparations for emigration as you can, and hasten to this place, to Ross' Landing or to Gunter's Landing, where you all will be received in kindness, by officers selected for the purpose. You will find food for all, and clothing for the destitute, at either of those places, and thence at your ease and in comfort, be transported to your new homes, according to the terms of the Treaty."

"This is the address of a warrior to warriors. May his entreaties be kindly received, and may the God of both prosper the Americans and the Cherokee, and preserve them long in peace and friendship with each other.

Winfield Scott, Cherokee Agency, May 10, 1838."

They have broken every promise except the one promising removal.

17 May 1838

I found elisi crying to herself this morning.

"Walela, I am troubled—very troubled. Everything I hear brings fear to my soul. What will become of us?"

"Elisi, we are all worried. I don't know what to say to comfort you. We will take each morning as it comes. I promise I will never leave you. Where you go I will go. Where you sleep I will sleep. Five Feathers will be with us also. He has promised."

"I know. I know you will not leave me but I cannot but worry. I don't like all the soldiers," elisi said with a tremor in her voice.

As we sat on the porch holding one another, I looked over our little house and farm where she and I were born.

"I do not know what will happen, elisi. Today you are loved. Tomorrow you shall be loved and every tomorrow after that. Edudu, Five Feathers and I love you. This house and our Country loves you. That devotion is constant and will never fail."

Elisi looked up.

She saw something and smiled for the first time.

"Walela, look at our bluebirds feeding their little ones," elisi said happily.

For a long time we sat silently and watched the bluebird pair coming and going under the eave of the big wooden shingles at the top corner of the porch.

"They aren't worried," elisi said. "If our little birds are not worried, I shall not be worried."

"You are correct, elisi,"

I smiled watching the beautiful bluebird pair coming and going feeding their young.

"We shall take the days as they come just as the little bluebirds do. They don't worry about tomorrow. They need not worry nor shall we."

She and I watched a small hole high up in the corner of the eave. As we watched, a bluebird flew into his little hole with something in his beak. We walked quietly away from the house and sat with our backs against the big white oak so we could leave the bluebird pair undisturbed and watch as they fed their babies. Their color, rich and pure, was bright and lovely in the quilted pattern of sunshine as it filtered through the trees in the early morning. Bluebirds are such carefree creatures. We sat for a long time and watched the birds.

"Walela, I wish we could be free to come and go as these birds."

"I do too."

"I wish we had as little to worry about."

She held me tighter as she spoke. We sat with our arms around one another like young lovers as we watched the bluebirds.

"Your edudu said the bluebirds built their nest close to the porch so they can listen to his stories."

We laughed.

"I like to think about things like that. I like his stories, too."

"Everyone loves edudu's stories."

"I think they nest here because I feed them all the skippers I find," elisi said, with a smile.

"I do not understand why whites must have our farm," she continued. "Perhaps they are jealous. Perhaps they want to sit here against this tree and watch the bluebirds come and go in the spring or perhaps the soldiers will pass us by and allow mother and father bluebird to remain for another year."

"I hope so," I answered.

18 May 1838

Elisi asked me to record this in my journal. I hope next year I will help her with the churning—right here in our little house.

Copied from the Southern Recorder – 15 may 1838 – page 2

"BUTTER.—When the "butter will not come" owing to the cream being too sour, if you dissolve a large teaspoon of soda or pearllash, in a pint of warm water, and pour it in, churning at the same time, it will change in a moment, and gradually form into a beautiful, solid lump of sweet butter."

19 May 1838

Copied from the *Georgia Journal*-15 May-1838-page 2

"Governor Gilmer - Gen. Charles Floyd to the command of the Georgia forces in Cherokee Country. The number of companies amount to thirty-one—Eleven hundred are mounted gunmen. The whole number of his command will be from 2,500 to 3,500 men. Gen. Floyd is required to repair with his staff, to New Echota and to report to Gen. Scott at Athens (Tennessee).

24 May 1838

Renatus Floyd has arrived in New Echota with troops. He commands the Middle Military District with New Echota as his headquarters. Our time is short. Soldiers are everywhere. I want Ben. I want Ben to care for me—protect me. Where is Ben? I am more frightened than I can communicate. I heard elisi sobbing again last night in her bed. Edudu comforts her, but he knows his words are empty. He knows her fears will soon be realized. Crying is all we have. When I heard her crying, I got into her bed and held her all night.

The end will come soon. I imagine within days. We shall be removed to some place we have never seen—to a distant place unwanted by whites and far from their presence. Perhaps, even then, they will break their promises and steal it from under us, pushing us farther and farther until we finally fall into endless darkness, falling forever off the end of the earth searching for a home we shall never find.

Copied from the *Southern Recorder* – 8 May 1838 – page 3

"We learn, that the Georgia quota, are organized, and many of the companies on the route…to Cherokee. A fine spirit has characterized the country…and we feel great pleasure in saying, that probably a finer body of men, that that which will compose the Georgia Brigade, belongs to no service."

"…Gen. Charles Floyd, has been ordered to the command of the Georgia Brigade…"

"All that prudence, sound judgment and the most untiring devotion to the interests of the country…has been done. We can now only repeat our hope…that the removal of the Cherokees may be accomplished, and the rights of humanity, and the peace of the country at the same time maintained."

Chapter LI

1838 – One Day in May

Chapter 51

26 May 1838 - Month of the Planting Moon – A na a gv ti

Our world has collapsed. At first light armed men burst into our house front and back. We were terrified. Three came in the front and three came in through the back. They ordered us not to move.

"You're under arrest," one said. "You must come with us now."

The soldiers were young, nervous and all were white. They seemed angry.

"You must not delay. Bring only what you can carry. You cannot bring dogs or any animal. You must come immediately."

"What are you doing? Why are you here? Where are we going?" I asked in English.

Eagle Killer was growling at the intruders from under the table. The hair was standing on his back. His teeth were bared in a snarl. Edudu ordered him to stay under the table and be quiet or he would have attacked immediately.

Six polished bayonets glowed bright orange reflecting the flames from the fireplace.

"Colonel Lindsey has ordered your arrest. You're to be brought to Fort Wool immediately. The treaty is being enforced. You are being removed."

The soldier in his new blue homespun uniform made a motion with his bayonet indicating we should move to the front door.

Another soldier spoke with surprise.

"Well, what da' ya' know, Bill. The damn squaw speaks English good as you. Why would a Indian woman want to learn English so good?"

The two soldiers on either side of the mantelpiece were putting edudu's little wooden animals in their pockets.

Eagle Killer continued to snarl. Edudu warned him again to stay under the table.

"Look here, Dan. Look at these old newspapers. There's some of them god damned old Cherokee newspapers, and look at all these books. What in the hell do you keep these papers and books for, squaw—for kindlin? What would Indians do with books?"

The soldier laughed a nervous laugh.

624

My initial terror changed to indignation. I should have stayed quiet, but I was suddenly outraged. I felt my resentment building at the soldier's insult and crass comments. Suddenly I wasn't afraid. I should have been afraid.

"Those are my books," I answered proudly.

"I read them," I said. "I read them all. I read all the newspapers, too, and those are our things on the mantelpiece the soldiers are stealing like common thieves. They shouldn't steal our things."

My brother's eyes were observing everything. He was calm. He wasn't afraid. He carefully watched each soldier's movements. He put his hand on my shoulder. With the pressure of his fingers, I felt him ask me to stay calm. He was right. Nothing could be done. Resistance was impossible against six nervous men with loaded weapons and bayonets. I should have listened to my brother.

"Well, well," the soldier in charge said sarcastically, "a god damned educated Indian and a squaw at that. That's like puttin' pearls around a sow's neck. An educated Indian is 'bout as useful as tits on a boar hog, ain't it, John? All this learnin' wasted on god damned ignorant Indians."

In a single motion, the soldier grabbed a handful of newspapers and threw them into the fireplace. Without thinking, I jumped to rescue my precious newspapers—each one a dear friend.

As I sprang to the fireplace, a soldier slammed my back with the butt of his rifle driving me to the floor. My brother lunged to my defense and another soldier crashed his gun butt violently into the back of my brother's head with a terrible thud. Five Feathers fell unconscious on elisi's once clean floor, now dirtied with red clay tracked carelessly into elisi's clean house by the soldiers' dirty boots.

With a snarl, Eagle Killer ignored edudu's warnings and leapt to our defense. He buried his teeth deep into the thigh of the nearest soldier, pulling and tugging with such force both dog and man fell to the floor. The soldier began screaming in agony from Killer's sharp teeth driving ever deeper as Killer thrashed left and right seeking to subdue his enemy and defend his master's home.

As I and my brother lay defenseless on the floor, a soldier, in one swift motion, ran his bayonet clean through Eagle Killer just behind his front legs pinning him helplessly to the white oak floor.

The bayonet went through the dog's body, the sharp point of the bayonet buried deep into the oak floor boards. With a quiet moan and the silent exhalation of his breath, Eagle Killer let go of the soldier's leg. The wounded dog lay quietly, pinned to the floor—blood quickly beginning to puddle under his body.

The soldier calmly put his boot on Eagle Killer and tugged his bayonet free. He wiped the blood with elisi's clean towel lying on our table. With a laugh, he threw the bloody towel into the fireplace, now blazing with newspapers.

Eagle Killer, lying on the floor in a growing pool of blood, looked towards edudu whimpering. He tried to move his front legs.

The white soldier bitten by Eagle Killer stood and examined his leg. Shouting obscenity, the soldier kicked the brave Eagle Killer hard with the toe of his boot. The dog slid under the table and never made another sound.

Edudu knelt to see to his dog under the table. One of the soldiers grabbed edudu by the neck and slammed him back against the wall violently. Edudu hit the wall so hard his breath left him. Edudu slid down the wall into a sitting position gasping for air. The other soldiers watched unconcerned.

"Leave the god damn dog alone, old man. I told you. You can't bring dogs. That dog ain't goin' to live no-how. Good thing, too. We ain't feedin' no dogs where you're goin'."

"You Indians should have left when you was told. This is your fault—not ours. We ain't responsible for nothing. This is all on your head."

As I lay on the floor, I began to regain my senses. I could see Eagle Killer lying paralyzed with his eyes looking towards his master. The puddle of dark blood under him was spreading.

I was glad Five Feathers had been disabled. My brother would certainly be dead if he had not fallen unconscious from the soldier's blow. He would have attempted to best all six soldiers and suffered the same fate as poor Eagle Killer. I was foolish. I almost caused my brother's death. I would be more careful with these dangerous men in the future.

As I rose, elisi, shivering and weeping in fear, helped edudu to his feet. Elisi and edudu, white-haired, bent, slow and barefoot in their little home cringed against the wall before the young white soldiers. The first light of dawn had reached the tree tops. A rooster crowed just outside the back door. A young soldier took the bacon elisi had laid out for us. He wrapped it in newspaper and put it in his pouch.

Edudu and elisi had never done a bad deed in their lives. These young white men were forcing them to abandon the only home they had ever known. Ben had warned us this would happen. I couldn't believe anyone could behave like this. Surely this was a bad dream. This was some kind of hallucination that would disappear with the morning sun.

When my brother regained his senses, he slowly helped me to my feet so we wouldn't provoke the nervous soldiers to further violence. We were ordered once again out the front door with the threatening motions of the deadly bayonets—the polished metal reflecting the bright orange light from the roaring fireplace that was consuming my beloved newspapers.

Before we left, elisi, thinking clearly, quickly bundled a few utensils along with my journal, pen and sketch book into my quilt. In just moments from the time the soldiers first burst in, we were pushed out our front door and onto the road to New Echota. We left Eagle Killer under the table as we went out the door. Edudu was in tears.

Four soldiers escorted us away from the house. The two remaining soldiers broke out our windows, piled our bedding, furniture, books, newspapers and all of elisi's pine baskets into the middle of the room over the table completely covering Eagle Killer. From outside the house I imagined I heard one last muffled cry from Eagle Killer for his master.

The soldiers shoveled the hot coals from the fireplace onto the pile of combustibles in the center of the room and left the doors open. Before they were down the front porch steps, orange flames filled our house and were licking at the ceiling.

As we were forced away, I saw the first tongues of red flames come through the wooden shingles. Clouds of smoke billowed from the doors and windows and from under the eaves.

The soldiers had orders to make certain we would not return. They had done their job.

As I watched the flames, I noticed Mrs. Lowry's red roses in front of the porch in full bloom—brilliantly red in contrast to the dense grey-white smoke.

Under the eave our three baby bluebirds, their little pin-feathers just beginning to grow, fled the choking smoke and flames boiling up through their nest.

They awkwardly exited their sanctuary under the roof at the top corner of the house. As I watched, their perch burst into flame. The three fledglings were instantly denuded—their soft pinfeathers singed away in a moment. Their skin turned black. The three little birds fell helplessly from the eave beating the air madly with featherless wings. As they hit the bare earth, I saw a puff of dust raised from each impact.

627

A wisp of smoke curled from their blackened little bodies—their useless wings extended at crazy angles. They lay still. I turned away. I could bear no more.

Using their bayonets as prods, the young men ordered us onto the road to New Echota without delay. Elisi, the only one of us who kept her head, carried our only possessions over her shoulder in my quilt like a sack of grain. Later, we would regret not gathering more things in the few moments we were given—most of all, our precious shoes.

An unforgettable morning of heartbreak unfolded as we and our neighbors were marched to our incarceration—babies, mothers, fathers, the aged—all at bayonet point.

Soldiers arrested Cherokee families in their homes, men and women in the fields, women on their way to the spring—wherever we were found. None were allowed to return home for any reason.

My cousin, Red Bird, born deaf, saw the soldiers and fled in terror. They shouted for him to stop, but he kept running. They shot him in the back. When we passed his body, his eyes were glazed, staring at nothing as he lay in a gathering pool of blood where the soldiers had pushed his corpse out of the roadway.

I thought of Mr. Lowry and the white holy book. He said whites believe the first man and woman, Adam and Eve, were expelled from their perfect garden—never to return. We Cherokee have lived in our garden until today. We have been expelled by whites who lost their paradise and want to possess ours.

As we trudged towards our old capital, I thought how this beautiful land where my parents are buried will soon be emptied of everything Cherokee.

Never will a smoking Cherokee chimney welcome us to its friendly hearth. Never will our children run to the river or play under the chestnut trees. Never will our young men bring game to thankful households. Never will we fish our rivers or gather the plentiful fruits and nuts of the forest. Never again will I spend long joyous hours making pine baskets with elisi or sit by the river in my special place or watch the squirrels on the white oak tree in front of elisi's porch.

Never again will we pick cucumbers, squash, okra and beans and prepare meals for the ones we love. Never again will edudu put up his martin gourds. Never again will I feed our chickens, lock them in at night and sell their eggs. Never again will edudu tend his hogs and fill our smokehouse. Never again will I gather poke-salad. Never again will edudu tell stories on elisi's front porch. The bluebirds have gone. We have been vanished—our land cleansed. We have been replaced.

Big empty wagons driven by white men waited on the roads. They waited for the soldiers to remove the Cherokee families. By the time we had been herded to New Echota, the wagons were loaded high with household belongings from Cherokee homes. The white men knew we would be leaving. Like hordes of buzzards, the white scavengers were stripping us of everything—even our memories.

With soldiers before, behind and on either side, our column of young and old was goaded along with coarse language. I tried to memorize the familiar landscape we were passing. One future day I wanted to describe to my child the beauty of the meadows, hills and mountains—the land that loved me. I will never enjoy another day here—in the land given to us by the Great Spirit. I wanted to memorize this last vista.

Perhaps we can heal in the western land, if there is indeed such a place. Perhaps they'll throw our bodies into a lonely pit and be done with us. They boasted if we disappeared the world would not notice. After we are gone, whites will fill our land and never think of us again. They will live as if the land had always been white, always theirs, a European birthright from time immemorial.

With our backs to the warm morning sun, our wretched group was herded towards our detention. Our national darkness enveloped me making my thoughts blacker than midnight as we silently plodded towards a black, featureless future. Although not yet noon, our Cherokee sun had permanently set, never to rise again. Arm-in-arm elisi and I cried bitter tears and not for the last time, I could be sure.

All was quiet. Even the children were quiet. No one spoke as we walked along in the eerie silence—a trudging column of human misery that grew constantly as soldiers added more families taken suddenly from their homes. My brother supported us every step. Blood stained his clothing but thankfully the bleeding had stopped. Elisi tended his wound.

As we were forced along, a soldier goaded a man's child to move faster—piercing the child's back with his bayonet. The infuriated father struck the soldier with a stone.

The father was arrested. When we arrived at New Echota they stripped the child's father to the waist, tied his hands above his head and flogged the man a hundred lashes with a cat-o-nine tails—punishment reserved for Indians and Africans. He was punished for hitting the soldier with a stone.

The sound of his screams echoed throughout the camp. The man fell unconscious, flesh hanging from his back. The soldier continued flogging the unconscious man until he had been given the full hundred lashes. The child's father did not survive.

I spoke to my brother. I was worried—terribly worried.

"I know your courage, Five Feathers. I know you are not afraid to die."

"I am not afraid, Walela, but I will not die for nothing. I will take care of you and our elisi and edudu."

"Please remember we need you."

"I will remember. I don't mind dying—but not yet. I will see you safe to the west."

"I foresee terrible times and you are our only hope. I beg you not to be foolish. If we survive, we will need your strength and wisdom."

I knew he heard me. He is never impulsive. He thinks about everything.

"Be patient, Five Feathers. These men will gladly kill you. Travel with us to the west. Be patient. Become our chief and help build our nation anew."

"Perhaps I will be chief. Perhaps not, but I promise to take care of you. I will not give my life away for nothing."

"I need you to take care of my son and teach him to hunt. Will you promise to do nothing foolish, no matter what you see or how these men provoke you? You can accomplish nothing violently against these men. If you retaliate, my baby and I shall perish. Our future is in your hands."

"My dear sister, I shall take care of you and your son. We shall live. Wherever they shall take us, I promise we shall live."

I cried on his shoulder. As we walked along, he supported elisi and me.

My brother, with an expressionless face, was silent but after I spoke, he gave me the first smile I had seen since the soldiers came. In my brother, we have hope—hope for me and hope for our nation. Perhaps we can start a new life. My brother is wise and understood my plea—he will be a magnificent chief.

When Ben heard the removal had begun ahead of schedule, he left immediately for the Cherokee capital. As he neared New Echota, he saw families of barefoot Cherokee under guard carrying their meager possessions—their faces masks of fear and confusion. He should have gotten here sooner. He hoped Cassie was well. When he finally arrived at New Echota, what he saw was a shock. The once peaceful Cherokee capital was overrun with soldiers, contractors, wagons, animals—squads of militia were coming from all directions escorting small groups of despondent Cherokee families. It was a madhouse.

Ben had tried to persuade Cassie and her relatives to emigrate early and avoid this mess. He had known it was coming. The stubborn Cherokee, fanatically loyal to the hardheaded Ross, could not be persuaded to disobey their chief. Her grandparents were determined to stay till Ross told them to leave. Ben had explained to Cassie circumstances would be out of his control once the removal started but his good advice was of no avail. Now they must suffer the consequences. It wasn't his fault. None of this was his fault. The Cherokee were to blame for everything.

If Cassie and the rest wanted to be stubborn, so be it. Any problems they encountered from now on were of their own making. He refused to allow himself to feel any guilt or culpability. No one could blame the government or soldiers. He told the Cherokee they couldn't stay. Cassie read the newspapers. She understood precisely what would happen and when. If they had left last year, he could have arranged for them to travel comfortably, paid for everything and even provided a servant. It made him angry to think about the inconsiderate selfishness—both of Cassie and the entire Cherokee Nation. The bullheaded Ross was the root cause of all these problems—not white people. The Cherokee unwisely listened to their stiff-necked chief. The Cherokee were a stupid people.

As Ben rode along slowly, he knew he would do what he could, but it was probably too late to do anything helpful for Cassie and her family. With his job, he didn't have time to take care of everyone. He felt an angry wave of impatience with Cassie rise within himself. She knew better. She should have thought about him and not caused him so much inconvenience.

As he passed the old Cherokee burial grounds, he was appalled. A dozen white men were madly unearthing every Cherokee grave searching for valuables. The cemetery was well over a century old—probably much older. The graverobbers had thrown the remains carelessly everywhere on open ground. Ben said something to a soldier, but the men told him exactly where he could go—in coarse language. Ben knew they would loot every gravesite searching for valuables the Cherokee had buried with their loved ones. There was no one to stop them. The removal of the Cherokee made even their gravesites fair game for scavengers.

Even the recently deceased had been disinterred, their partially decomposed bodies lay abandoned, tossed aside like so much rubbish. The militia ignored the graverobbers. It was none of their business. Graverobbing and its accompanying desecration, although not officially sanctioned, was allowed to rid the land permanently of Cherokee—both on it and under it. This country would be white—everything above it, on it and below it.

It suddenly occurred to Ben that this scene would be common in every old Cherokee graveyard from North Carolina through Tennessee and Georgia into Alabama. Beginning today the white culture would dispossess the Cherokee—both living and dead.

Ben couldn't stop his mind from retracing its previous line of thinking. How could the Cherokee ever think they could coexist with the superior white culture? The removal was a problem, start to finish, caused by the irretractable Cherokee mind. The very fact that they resisted the removal that was for their own good showed they were unfit to live with or near whites. For decades, the surrounding whites had been patient. History would show how the white culture flourished and the backward Cherokee had declined—overcome not by violence but by the racial superiority of the forward-looking white culture.

The pigheaded Cherokee should have recognized they could not keep this beautiful land simply because their ancestors happened to have hunted here. Things change. The Indians were naïve—supremely foolish. They were benighted children of the forest—a decaying culture collapsing of its own ineptitude—a moldering anachronism in a modern, progressive, white world. They had demonstrated themselves to be a sub-standard culture with a sub-standard mentality—incapable of civilization. He hated to admit it, but if the truth be told it was good riddance.

On his way to New Echota Ben had seen wagons fully loaded with household goods—all driven by whites. He saw one white man and his teenage boys driving a large herd of hogs, Cherokee hogs, to who knows where. These were not good times, but it would all soon be over and this corner of Georgia would be fully civilized.

Ben passed his father's old home, now the local officer's quarters for the Georgia Guard, with newly constructed stables and outbuildings. He couldn't believe how things had changed. Ben wanted this moment in Georgia history to pass quickly. He was perplexed. What should he do? What could he do? All he knew was he must continue to do the job the state of Georgia had hired him to do and let the military worry about the Cherokee. The removal wasn't his business. It wasn't his fault. Cassie was out of his hands. Helping set up the new counties was his business. He was a civilian. The military and their actions, or inaction, was not his concern.

As Ben rode into the old town, things were certainly changed from his boyhood when New Echota was a thriving Cherokee town. The military had leveled most of the original Cherokee structures and constructed the grotesque Fort Wool—the symbol of white ascendency dominating the Cherokee capital where friendly council fires had once burned. A couple of the stronger Cherokee buildings had been reinforced for use by the military but most Cherokee structures were gone. The building that had housed the printing press was gone. The council buildings were gone. The State of Georgia now owned New Echota. How ironic the once noble center of Cherokee culture and government had been transformed by whites into a Cherokee prison.

Fort Wool was so out of place. Like all of the hastily constructed removal forts, it was built for storing military supplies, but mostly, he had been told, it was constructed to reassure the growing white population within Cherokee Country that their government in Milledgeville was committed to the security of white settlers. The removal forts were wooden monuments built to reassure fortunate drawers of their government's commitment to cleanse the land of every single Cherokee family.

As Ben rode up to the first checkpoint, he was recognized immediately by the captain.

"Hey, Ben, good to see you again. Did they send you up here to check on our handiwork? Nice to see a friendly face. We've been busy this morning. I was just getting ready to do an inspection. I would be honored if you would ride with me. I need to have a look around. I have to check on the prisoners being brought in. I'm sure you're curious. It'll be some show. I'll give you a guided tour and you can fill me in with the news from Milledgeville and Savannah."

"It would be a pleasure to ride with you, sir, and I am curious about what's going on here. I've never seen anything like this."

"Well, Ben, this is a mess for sure. We weren't sure what was goin' to happen. We're doing the best we can. I need to make sure everything is working properly. I'm praying we don't have an Indian uprising like the Creeks in Alabama. That's the only thing I'm afraid of. Ride with me, Ben. It'll take maybe an hour or less. I'm proud of what we're doing here. We've put in a lot of hard work. I'm pleased that at last Georgia is standing up for our rights. We're doing what we should have done years ago, Ben. You'll never see anything like this again, I'll wager. I'm as proud as I can be of these hard workin' men."

Ben accompanied his friend on his inspection tour. Ben needed to know what was going on with the military and, in particular, in this county. He could ask the captain key questions and get the answers he needed to help him with his job. Murray, Cass and Floyd counties just to the south would be teeming with new white settlers looking for the property they had won in the lottery or bought from someone who did. The removal was one of the things he had to pretend to like. Quid pro Quo, Zach would have reminded him. Life was full of compromises if one wanted to get ahead.

"After our inspection, I'll treat you to some refreshment in my quarters," the captain said with a laugh. "You're a bigwig now. I need to take care of you. What would people say if I let a man like you leave hungry and thirsty?"

The captain laughed again as he urged his horse forward. Ben thought about the refreshment. After the long ride, refreshment would be welcome. He had gotten used to being waited on in Milledgeville. Thinking about food and drink brought his mind back to the hotel and Elizabeth. He couldn't wait to see her again, but this wasn't the time or place to think about Elizabeth.

As Ben and the captain passed close beside the western side of Fort Wool, the captain said, "Ben, this is what I wanted to see. We're holding all the Cherokee here before we take them north to Ross's Landing for removal. I wanted to see how the detention was progressing. We began the roundup long before sunrise to catch 'em by surprise."

"How did you know where to find them?"

"The Guard supplied us with detailed maps of every Cherokee house in our area. We know where to find them. We've got most of them already. They don't have anywhere to go. A few might get away, but we'll round them all up in a few days. They're stupid like sheep. Our plans have worked pretty well so far today. We already have a couple of hundred in custody."

"Has anyone been hurt? Has there been any resistance like the newspapers warned?"

"Thankfully, there hasn't been much violence. No resistance has been reported thus far. We had to horse-whip a few Indians for misbehavior, but that's all I know about. There's been a few shootings reported but no organized violence like some feared. These Indians aren't smart enough to come in out of the rain. If they had enough sense to organize, they would have left here long ago. It just goes to show how dumb they are. In a few days, we'll have 'em all—no problem."

Ben and the captain rode around the large open area roped off for the Cherokee detention and patrolled by several dozen armed pickets—all with loaded weapons and bayonets shining in the afternoon sun.

"Ben, Ben," someone shouted from inside the detention area.

Ben continued without acknowledging he had heard anything.

The shout came again, "Ben, Ben."

Once again Ben ignored the shout.

The captain gave Ben a sideways look and asked, "Do you know any of the Cherokee in there? I know you lived here when you were a boy. You have my permission to go inside if you wish. You'll be safe. They've been disarmed. All the fight has gone out of 'em."

"No, I don't think I'll go inside," Ben answered. "My father knew a lot of older Cherokee when he had his school. He left seven years ago and he's never been back. I don't really know anyone up here. There's no telling who might know my family in there."

He didn't mention to the officer that his father had disobeyed Georgia law and spent months in prison at hard labor. That wasn't something Ben wanted everyone to know. Some things were best forgotten.

27 May 1838

Everyone has been arrested. We are being held in the open under heavy guard. I cannot describe my hopelessness.

When the Guard destroyed our print shop they scattered our syllabary lead type everywhere. I found one small piece in our compound today. Finding that little piece of lead type was painful—reawakening our loss of the Phoenix. That little piece of lead I found tells me Georgia will discard us with the same careless abandon.

How long will we be in the open with no shelter, no food and no way to care for our bodily needs? Where are we going?

It is rumored we are going to Ross's Landing to be put on steamboats. How long will we be without things we need? Whites treat their animals with more care. We have nothing. Many are sick. It's almost dark and we haven't been given water or food. Two have died and are being buried at the edge of the woods as I write.

28 May 1838

As we were arrested, elisi bundled some utensils in my quilt along with my journal and sketch book. That is all we have. We have been given nothing.

We need shoes. I should have been wiser the morning we were arrested. Instead of worrying about my newspapers and books, I should have thought about our future needs as prisoners. We will need shoes—perhaps we will be given shoes? I doubt it.

We had two dozen laying hens penned behind the house and two hogs hanging in the smoke house. Elisi, Five Feathers and I had planted our fields and edudu had more than two dozen hogs running over towards the forest— all now the property of whites. When we reach the western lands, the general government will give back what they took. Forgive me if I don't believe them. They have lied to us for over two hundred years. I expect their duplicity to continue. I wonder if they lie to one another like they lie to us?

The soldiers took our guns and knives. We have been given no rations. Everyone is hungry. We are helpless. Even though hungry, the children have been quiet. A few brought food but most are hungry. I wonder what the children think in their frightened minds. Some say we will be given rations today. We have no fuel. Few have anything to cook with. There are perhaps three or four hundred of us now. More will be brought in today. The soldiers are scouring the countryside to make sure they get rid of us all.

We are not allowed outside of our compound to relieve ourselves. We have no tools to dig latrines. The smell is worse than an unkept barnyard in summertime. I helped my poor elisi today relieve herself in full sight of white men who seem to find pleasure in our embarrassment. We have little water and no means of personal hygiene. Our situation will become worse.

Surely we will be given food soon. The rumor is we will be given corn meal and salt pork this evening. The sky is our roof. The soil is our bed. We cannot wash. Our drinking water is dirty. Some say we will have tents, food and blankets when we get to Ross's Landing. I suspect it is a lie to placate us.

All night there is a constant noise of the restless, the ill and uncomfortable, sick children. The night air magnifies every sound. No one can sleep. I dread another night listening to the wretched, sick children cough constantly. I lay with elisi, edudu and my brother. My mind will not rest. I must express my mind. I must write of the blackness that pursues me.

Night and Day
Lies, betrayal, perfidy,
Day, night, despair,
Treachery, deceit, torment,
Grief, anguish, misery,
Hollow, empty eyes,

Reflecting blackness,
Confused children,
Desperate mothers,
Hopeless men,
Staring into nothingness,
Weary, hungry, thirsty,
Dust, filth, stench,
The soil our bed,
The sky our roof,
Herded somewhere,
Driven into oblivion,
Never to return,
One day in May,
We vanished.

The young white soldiers obey orders. What would I do if I were a white soldier with a young wife and children? If I were a white man ordered to do what they are doing, I would probably do as they do. They can't disobey orders. May they be forgiven. They don't know what they're doing. They have no idea of the horror they are party to. I hope they enjoy our land. They will soon forget us. Their injustice will be forgotten.

They will possess every valley, home, meadow and mountain. Not one Cherokee family or free African will remain. The Africans hiding with us will be sold back into slavery. The Creeks will be captured. Andrew Jackson in his retirement in Nashville must be gratified thinking of the fulfillment of his dream of a unified white country cleared of Indians.

It is sixty miles to Ross's Landing. I hope elisi and edudu can make the journey.

An old woman and a child were carried out as I write. They were wrapped in their own clothing. Five Feathers said they have a few discarded slabs to fashion a coffin. They will be buried in unmarked graves near the edge of the woods.

"Thanks for the refreshment," Ben said to the captain and meant it. He was grateful for something nice to drink after a long day.

"With your permission, sir, I would like to ride over to the Cherokee community near the river and see what's there."

"Ben, the Cherokee are gone. Every family has been arrested," the captain said. "They're all here now. There's nothing to see. I was there myself just a few hours ago. All property has been confiscated and some homes burned.

Some houses are already occupied. Everything has been cleaned out—tables, chairs, lamps, furniture, tools, stores—everything. They've cleaned out every smokehouse and rounded up all the livestock—even the chickens."

The captain laughed.

"I know. I saw it coming in. It looked terrible, to tell the truth," Ben answered quietly.

"It's not that bad, Ben. Everyone knew this was coming. The looting can't be helped. The Indians will be reimbursed out west if they suffer any loss. Besides, I look at what the Indians have left behind as rent for all the years they lived here free and clear."

Ben didn't speak.

"I am doing my job," the captain continued. "You understand that. I have orders. Besides, they don't have much worth anything. They're just Indians. They know how to do without."

"Everyone knew it was going to happen. That's true," said Ben.

"My mission is not to take care of the Indians. I've been ordered to remove them," the captain said, defending himself. "These stupid Indians had two years to leave. This is their fault—clear and simple. This just goes to show you how dumb these damn Indians are. I don't feel sorry for a god damned one of them. They ain't got sense enough to come in out of the rain."

Ben replied with no emotion, "I guess there's no need to ride over. I was curious. I haven't been there in a long time. I just wanted to have a look around."

"Ride anywhere you want, Ben," the captain said as Ben turned his horse away. "You're safe here. We've seen to that. It's been a pleasure to see you again."

"It's nice to see you again, too," Be replied. "Thanks again for the refreshment. If you don't mind, I think I'll take a ride down to the river before I head back."

Ben left the captain and rode to the one place he wanted to see, the spot he and Cassie had picnicked many times, her secret place by the river where he had made love to her on her big rock, the spot where she became pregnant with his child, the child she was carrying at this moment.

He arrived with his escort and his servant, Caesar. He told them to wait on the rise and he rode down to Cassie's big rock still obscured by thick laurels and exactly as he remembered.

Nothing had changed. It looked exactly as it did the last time he was here with Cassie. He strangely expected to see Cassie appear from behind the laurels as he rode to the opening.

How foolish he was. He mustn't let sentiment cloud his thinking. He must be realistic. As he sat his horse there in the opening just a few feet from the water, the memories flowed. Against his will he relived that afternoon with Cassie—the day, in retrospect, he regretted fiercely. He wasn't ready to become a father.

There was no question of marriage—not now. Above all he didn't need some self-righteous government official to discover he had fathered an Indian woman's child.

He shouldn't have come to Cassie's spot. There were too many memories. He would think about Cassie and her baby another time—not now. He turned away unsatisfied and rode back towards New Echota wishing he had never visited the spot beside the river.

As he walked his horse up the hill, he passed a white man dressed as a civilian—a new settler probably. He carried two dead river otters by the back legs, one in each hand. Their heads left little furrows in the dust.

Ben was not prepared for what he had seen even though he knew the removal was coming and pretty much knew how it would unfold. New Echota had been his parents' home—his boyhood home. It was a place filled with nostalgic memories of his youth. A kind, friendly place where he had played, worked and hunted with his Cherokee friends. A place where he and Cassie had spent long enchanting afternoons in conversation walking about the countryside sharing their magnificent dreams. He had no ill will towards the Cherokee—none. If he would allow himself, he could see their side of the problem, but he didn't like thinking about that. That was water under the bridge. He couldn't think about that and do his job. He would think about that when this was over and Cassie was out west somewhere.

He couldn't believe the state of her community, completely stripped of inhabitants with white families already beginning to occupy vacant Cherokee homes.

As Ben rode back up the hill into town, he stopped at Cassie's homeplace and felt a sudden wave of black emotion. It was old log home where he and Cassie had spent quiet afternoons on the porch talking about everything under the sun—the porch where Cassie had spent endless days reading newspapers and writing in her journal—the porch where he had listened to Cassie's

639

grandfather tell his colorful Cherokee tales and laughed his head off at her grandfather's witty humor.

He was shocked. Nothing was left but a pile of smoldering ashes under the scorched white oak limbs of the huge old shade trees that surrounded the home. He noticed the nubs of his mother's charred rose bushes he and Cassie had transplanted. He remembered their beautiful show of color when they bloomed bright red in front of the sturdy little house. As Ben looked around, he thought how the ashes of Cassie's home symbolized the end of his father's work. Everything his father had lived for was now literally in ashes—gone. Cassie's house, her community, her nation was gone forever. It was a gloomy thought—even to the prosperous, white lawyer turned politician from Milledgeville. For an instant, Ben allowed himself to glimpse what had actually happened. He was witnessing the sudden collapse of a centuries old culture—a collapse orchestrated by an invading army of educated white Europeans greedy for land—fee simple land. He was a part of that orchestra, but he would think about that later—not now.

Ben's expensive chestnut mare stood patiently in the warm Georgia afternoon sunshine of late spring quietly swatting annoying insects with her perfectly groomed black tail. She lightly stamped her feet to frighten away the maddening yellow horseflies in their never-ending attempt to light on her legs. She obediently and patiently waited for her master's next command.

Ben had never felt smaller or his life so out of control as at this moment. What was he doing? Why was he here? What was happening? How could this have happened in this happy land of contented people? How could he have been a part of what had been done this day?

As he sat his horse in front of the pile of smoldering ashes, his thoughts came full circle. He thought about the Cherokee's hardheaded refusal to leave. The treaty had been signed, and even though disputed, they should have seen the writing on the wall. They couldn't be that stupid, could they? The remnant of that little carefree boy inside of Ben understood that no matter what the white political rationalizations of the removal, what he was seeing wasn't fair. Everything about this was ugly.

It wasn't fair the Cherokee should be treated this way, but it also wasn't fair they could cause him such problems by their refusal to take the advice of a benevolent government—a government committed to the Cherokee welfare. They should have known their future was out west in the land generously given them by folks who were concerned about their future. Not every white man was greedy.

The Cherokee Nation, the silly Cherokee constitution, the useless Cherokee newspaper and fruitless attempts to teach an illiterate culture to read was humorous. He thought of the wasted trips to Washington City by the Cherokee leadership, pursuing a vain attempt to mimic white civilization and gain acceptance—an impossible task for such a backward people. They were never going to be white. They would never achieve equality. It made him laugh. They were like a donkey who wanted to become a racehorse. It would never happen. They brought all this upon themselves.

The Cherokee leadership should have known they had no choice but removal. If they were smart they would have left in 1830 or before and kept their assets. The Cherokee were stubborn, Ben thought. They were getting exactly what they deserved.

29 May 1838

Over four hundred of us are now imprisoned. It is ironic we are held captive in our own capital. I hate the Militia and the Guard—the two wolves aside—I hate them. We are confined where our elders met and where we printed the Phoenix. White men destroyed our Overhill towns and our old capital in Tennessee and now whites have captured our new capital and we have been evicted once again.

Whites have come for us again. One day in May our vanishment is complete. Three more died from ague and fever. More are sick.

One Day in May
Our symphony concluded,
Performed never again,
One day in May.
The strings, brass, woodwinds have gone silent,
Oboes and bassoons will never more sound,
The melodies of our flutes have ceased,
Our crescendo past,
One day in May.
The last bar rang through our valleys,
Echoing our lament,
One day in May.
Our final performance,
Our finale,
Performance concluded,

A White Killing Frost

Terminated by Compact,
Our harmonies extinguished,
Our music erased,
Our orchestra silenced,
Our symphony complete,
One day in May.
The principal people vanished,
Our chorus erased,
Never to grace these valleys,
All chords severed,
Never to be heard again,
One day in May.

30 May 1838

Before sunrise we were wakened by the soldiers. At dawn we were ordered to begin walking north. Our destination is Ross's Landing. With soldiers on all sides we walked all day in light rain. We camped in an open field beside the road with a creek a few hundred yards away. At least we have fresh drinking water. There is no spare clothing. There are almost no tents or blankets. They say we will be supplied when we reach Tennessee. Most are wearing the poor clothing they were wearing when arrested. We build fires to dry our clothing. We sleep on wet ground. We have no shelters, no beds, no food and no hope. It will be a long night. Five Feathers brought two old blind men to dry at our fire.

We were told after dark no one should leave the perimeter or they would be shot. We must relieve ourselves where we camp.

Chapter LII

1838 – Extinguished – Elisi and Edudu

Chapter 52

1 June 1838 – Month of the Green Corn Moon – De ha lu yi

The second day of our forced march to Ross's Landing has ended—a lonely parade of unwanted humanity. Many are ill. The soldiers want us to walk fifteen miles a day. Elisi and edudu are in the wagons with the elderly and the sick. We receive no help. We suffer quietly. Who will populate our country? Who will tend our fields of ripening corn? Who will enjoy the hams and bacon hanging in edudu's smokehouse?

I watched Five Feathers this morning as he helped lay two little children in shallow graves on the edge of our campsite before we were ordered to resume our trek.

At Ross's Landing I will be just a few miles from Mr. and Mrs. Lowry. Things change. Mr. Lowry told us there is One who will lift the fallen and restore the years the locust have eaten. We have been forgotten and forsaken. If Mr. Lowry's God remembers us, he will be the only one.

My baby is growing. Walking is becoming difficult. I am grateful for my brother. I am weary—so terribly weary. I want to rest—to rest for days. I want to go back to my bed and sit on our front porch and listen to the birds.

The soldiers have allowed some men to leave to persuade relatives in hiding to turn themselves in. Soldiers hold the man's family hostage, under close guard, until he returns. I don't think the whites have our best interest at heart as they claim.

2 June 1838

I woke next to Five Feathers with a mist of rain in my face. Our clothes were damp and clammy. When we rest we lie unprotected under the firmament with no shelters—no tents. We are homeless, helpless and hopeless. As I look at the starless, leaden sky, I wonder what was our crime. It's been bone dry and ordinarily the misty rain would be welcome.

We walked all day. We will arrive at the river tomorrow. I am tired—exhausted. I worry about edudu and elisi packed into the bumpy wagons with

643

the sick. All day they are tossed about on these horribly rough roads. What must they be thinking? How will they survive?

At least I can write. East of Ross's Landing, at the Brainerd Mission, is a woman who is praying to her God for our safety. All I possess is Mrs. Lowry's prayers and her quilt. My prayer is that Ben will take us away. Where is Ben? What is he doing? Is he busy with his job?

We were joined in the afternoon by another group of Cherokee prisoners. A woman from that group delivered her baby beside the road. After she delivered, the militia forced her to rejoin the column and continue. When we made camp this evening, my brother and his friends dug a grave for the woman and her baby girl. The Militia graciously supplied the tools for the men to dig the grave.

3 June 1838

The shadows were long as we arrived at Ross's Landing. Everyone is exhausted—our energy consumed by mere desire for survival. We were herded into an enclosure by the river, penned on all sides with ropes and pickets as in New Echota. We were not the first occupants. There was a horrible stench of human urine and feces. We are not allowed to leave our enclosure for any reason—even to relieve ourselves.

We need shelter. We have no building materials or tools. There are few tents or blankets. We have no possessions, few utensils, no soap and no extra clothing. Our water is dirty. Many have no shoes. We have no proper food for our children and babies. The only thing the whites allow us to keep is our patience. That precious commodity will soon be depleted. Then we shall close our eyes and die.

I am too tired to think—unable to escape the odors and clouds of flies breeding in the mountains of manure lying everywhere around this military madhouse that used to be the quiet village of Ross's Landing. Several have reported measles. Fever and dysentery are common. The children are lethargic. Every morning there is a burial. There are no sounds of play or laughter—no friendly conversation. We wait silently—nowhere to go—nothing to do.

I have had my first glimpse of a steamboat. I remember wishing Ben and I could ride a steamboat on a romantic river excursion. The name of the first steamboat I saw was the George Guess, the English name of Sequoyah, who invented our syllabary. How ironic whites would use a steamboat with a Cherokee name to remove us from view.

At least my unborn baby is for now protected from this misery. Civilian contractors dole out our meager rations of corn meal and salt pork. We have often eaten partially cooked food for lack of fuel and proper cooking utensils. To whom should we complain?

We are exhausted and dirty but at least we will not be forced to walk again tomorrow. My back aches. This afternoon elisi and I were in the line to receive our rations. I was impatient to get my ration and lie down. Elisi was ahead of me. The white contractor asked, "Flour or cornmeal?"

Elisi, embarrassed and afraid to make eye contact, whispered to the contractor, "Seluesi."

Seluesi means cornmeal in Cherokee.

The white man growled, "We speak English. If you want to eat, use English or go hungry you god damned Indian."

Elisi cowered before the man and whispered something inaudible. Standing just behind her, I interrupted. I spoke politely in English.

"Sir, she is asking for cornmeal."

The man stared at me for a moment. His face contorted into an angry mask.

"You uppity Indian bitch. Who do you think you are? I didn't ask you. This ain't none of your god damned business. I'm white. Speak when spoken to."

He leaned from his seat beside the wagon and slapped me to the ground with all his strength. I lay on my stomach with my knees to my chest. Blood streamed from my nose.

The young soldier next to the contractor watched with disinterest. Two soldiers standing behind the wagon laugh loudly about something. The contractor spit on me as I lay beside him next to the wagon wheel.

"You dumb bitch," he snarled down at me. "Why can't you Indians learn English. Get the hell out of my way both of you. Nothing for you two. You god-damned Indians don't appreciate what we do for you. You lazy bastards are always wantin' somethin' for nothin'. This is your fault. You god damned Indians are nothing but trouble. Get the hell out. Nothing for you two."

Elisi pressed a corner of her shirt against my nose and helped me to my feet. We slowly walked away.

I knelt on the ground. After a while my nose quit bleeding. We went back to our place. It won't be the last evening we go hungry. I wish Ben were here. If Ben were here it would be better. He would take care of us.

Two children were buried this evening. One corpse wrapped in a tattered shirt and buried in several pieces of a discarded puncheon. When I saw the men carry the little body, I touched my stomach and comforted my child.

4 June 1838

When I woke this morning my elisi was dead in my arms—her body cold and stiff in the pre-dawn starlight. I wept. I held her to my breast until the eastern sky began to lighten before I woke Five Feathers and edudu.

My beautiful elisi was always clean and neat and bright with a smile and a good word for everyone. She would have given anything she had to anyone in need—even whites. As we prepared her rigid dirty body for burial, I noticed her torn, soiled clothing stained with my blood from the previous evening. Her white hair was dirty and disheveled. She would have been embarrassed to be seen this way, but there was nothing we could do. I cried as I held her for the last time.

Five Feathers and I did our best to prepare her for burial. We had only her dirty clothes for wrappings and no coffin. Things I could have never imagined a few weeks ago, I now witness daily. I wish the white congress could see the result of their compassionate laws and watch us being escorted west in comfort.

Shall we die before this ends? I am frightened—more than I have been in my life. Just after noon soldiers brought more families into our enclosure. They had walked for three days from Fort Cummings at Lafayette. One woman told us they had received no food since the day before. Another woman had two small children and was as big with child as I am. She said in Lafayette an old Cherokee woman had fallen in front of a heavy wagon that drove over her unconscious body. The soldiers dragged her out of the way. She was buried beside the roadway.

Like us, the new prisoners brought little more than the clothing they were wearing when arrested. There is no joy, no laughter, no conversation—just lifeless eyes staring from gaunt faces—all emotion washed away by the Militia. I see that same face everywhere. It's the face I wear—a mask to conceal the grotesque wretchedness that thrives within us.

Everyone was soaked to the skin. We used blankets as best we could to shelter from the intermittent light rain. General Scott assured us we would be escorted west in comfort. Does Winfield Scott believe in the white man's hell?

Five Feathers and edudu helped bury four others this morning along with elisi. More are sick and afraid. The sick are everywhere.

Ben, immersed in his work, learned the prisoners from New Echota had been marched to Ross's Landing. Feeling guilty, he left to take care of business in Gilmer and Murray Counties. Along the way he would visit his mother and find Cassie if he could and then head down to Lafayette for more business in Walker County. This removal was a complicated nuisance. He could try to get Cassie released into his parents' custody, but Georgia had no military authority by the river. Ross's Landing was in Tennessee. The entire military operation was being overseen by the United States Army. General Fuss n' Feathers Scott would not be likely to allow any deviation from orders. Ben had to be careful what he asked for. Perhaps the best thing would be to leave this alone—to ask for nothing. He had warned Cassie for several years she should emigrate. He would do what he could, but she should have gone west with the rest of her people when she had the chance. This was her fault— nothing to do with him.

Ben was tired. He decided to try and find Cassie before visiting his mother and father at the Brainerd mission. He quickly found the compound where the prisoners from New Echota were being held. He left his escort and black servant at the gate. The soldiers granted the well-dressed Georgia politician from Milledgeville immediate access to the camp.

When I saw Ben, the sun began to shine and birds began to sing for the first time since our arrest. Although we hadn't bathed since we had been taken into custody, I couldn't resist throwing my arms around Ben. At that moment, I didn't care that I would soil his new coat. Ben didn't return my embrace. I quickly regained my composure. My brother and edudu stared at Ben from some distance with no words of greeting. I knew what they were thinking.

"Elisi died this morning, Ben. She was so sick. She had been coughing for three days."

I began to cry.

Ben didn't know what to say.

"When I woke this morning, she was dead in my arms." I said.

My tears stained the sleeve of Ben's new coat.

"Elisi didn't understand, Ben. We weren't allowed to bring anything. They marched us up the road and burned our house."

Ben said nothing and made no attempt to hold me or kiss me. I suppose he was embarrassed in front of his militia escort.

"Elisi fell ill that first night," I continued. "We slept on the ground at New Echota with no shelter. She began coughing and never recovered. Her spirit was broken, Ben. She gave up."

"I'm sorry, Cassie," was all Ben could say.

"I know, Ben. I asked for a doctor yesterday but the guards laughed. We washed her face this morning. Five Feathers made a coffin of a few slabs. We buried her this morning with the others."

Once again my tears fell on Ben's coat.

"I am so sorry, Cassie," Ben replied, "I'll do what I can. I promise. It's awkward for me to be here, I'm sure you understand, but I'm glad to see you're well."

"I know you are."

"I don't know what to say," Ben said. "I warned you to leave, but that can't be helped now. I was afraid it would be like this, but I never dreamed the army would keep you in this filth, but I understand how difficult this operation is. I'm sure they're doing the best they can. I'll speak to the men in charge. They can do better than this. There's nothing I can do right now, Cassie. I have to do my job."

"I know you do. I'm not angry with you," I said.

Ben looked left and right to see if he was being observed.

"Can you get us out, Ben? Is there some way for you to help us?

Ben didn't answer.

"We could stay with your parents in Brainerd. We wouldn't cause any trouble. Please, please—help us get out of this terrible place, Ben."

"I'll do what I can, Cassie. This is an Army operation. I have no authority here. The Georgia Militia has no jurisdiction. No one from Georgia has anything to do with Ross's Landing. This is Tennessee soil and, in any case, all these soldiers are under orders from General Scott. He's United States Army. They obey his orders."

"It's terrible in here, Ben. You can't imagine how terrible this is."

Ben looked around to see if anyone was watching him talking to the young, pregnant Indian woman. He wanted to leave.

"I did ask the captain if he would parole you into my custody," Ben answered, "but he said he had orders not to let anyone out no matter who they were."

"Could you ask him again?"

"I will ask again. I never imagined the removal would be this unpleasant, but I'm sure they'll get things right soon. You'll have what you need. In no time at all you'll be in your new home out west and everything will be good. I'm sure this is a temporary inconvenience. This is a complicated operation. General Scott is a good man. He has a good reputation. He'll set things in order quickly. I'm sure of it."

"I don't think it will get better, Ben. The soldiers hate us."

"It will get better. They'll get supplies, tents, food and doctors here. They're probably on the way now. I wouldn't worry if I were you."

"It's too late for doctors. Elisi is dead."

Ben paused for a moment and looked around again before speaking.

"I'm sorry. There's nothing I can do. I was worried about you, Cassie. I see you're good now. I'll do my best to get you out of here. I'll do what I can. I'm sorry about your grandmother."

I saw Ben glance at my stomach. It was obvious it wouldn't be long before the baby, his baby, would be born. I wondered what he was thinking. I wondered if he was embarrassed by his own child? He probably was.

Ben, tall, handsome and finely dressed, looked dramatically out of place in our pigsty. I understood his embarrassment. I tried to refrain from touching him again. Ben is a good man at heart and wouldn't do anything intentionally to harm anyone. I know he means well. I don't think he understands.

"Please help me get edudu and my brother out, Ben. People are dying here every day. You can't imagine how bad it is here. There are no medicines or doctors. We drink filthy water."

I tried not to cry.

"I'll do what I can," he said quietly so no one could hear.

"We have no latrines. I'm hearing terrible reports about the groups who have been removed ahead of us—dreadful things. I don't know what to believe. The news coming back is horrible. I'm worried for our baby. I want to go home, Ben. I want to go home."

As I cried, I once again began to soil his coat. Ben was annoyed. He took a step backward. I couldn't control my tears.

Ben loved Cassie, but what was he do? Events had taken a course of their own and he couldn't swim upstream. He had warned her. It wasn't his fault. He had a job to do with the state. He must fulfill his contractual obligations. That was only right. He would help the Cherokee where and when he could, but that wasn't his job. All he could think of at the moment was that he needed to get out of this stinking place before someone figured out why he was here. He had been there quite long enough.

It was time to leave. He didn't want his security detail to suspect his past relationship with Cassie and he didn't want to soil his expensive trousers and smell like a barnyard for appointments later in the day. He was annoyed that he would be forced to unnecessarily change or clean his clothes.

I stood on tiptoes and whispered into Ben's ear, "I'm sorry if I have embarrassed you. I'll never do that again, Ben. I know you don't want them to know this is your baby."

"I know you would never intentionally shame me, Cassie," Ben answered. "I know that."

"I'll never humiliate you, but please don't forget us," I said. "I want to go home, Ben. I want to go home. Please help us. I want to go home. Your mother will take us in. I know she will. Tell the soldiers your mother will take us. Please help us. Your mother will take us."

I continued to beg as if my insistence would insure our release.

A soldier approached.

"Sir, the contractors are preparing to distribute the daily ration. Sometimes it gets nasty—pushing and shoving and that kind of thing, sir. It's nothing bad, but you don't want to be in here, sir. The Indians ain't violent but I wouldn't want you to get pushed around. Indians don't have no manners, sir. They got no respect at all. It's ugly in here, if you know what I mean, sir."

The private observed the frown on Ben's face.

"Everything's ok, sir. The Indians won't be here long. Don't you worry your head about them savages, sir. We take good care of 'em. They'll be leavin' soon and everything will get back to normal like it should be."

"It ain't like they're white folks, sir. They're used to things like this. They don't mind. We'll get rid of 'em quickly, sir. This dirt don't bother them none. That's what they're used to, sir. It won't be long an' they'll 'ave disappeared—gone completely. Everthing will be normal again. You'll see, sir."

Ben didn't answer. He didn't know what to think. It was as if he was in some kind of mental daze watching himself from a distance as he went through the motions of speaking. He knew the soldier's assessment was correct. Very soon the Cherokee would be gone and that would solve a lot of problems.

Despite every care, Ben's new boots and trousers legs were soiled. He would have to get Caesar to clean his clothes before his next meeting. This

650

whole removal was obscene—nothing but trouble. He couldn't wait to get out, but it wasn't only the filth or the acrid stench he wanted to escape. Ben wanted to flee Cassie and his unborn child and the nagging thought of his indiscretion which made him feel far more uncomfortable than the odor of stale urine and uncovered human feces. The memory of uncontrolled passion and foolish promises came to his mind—memories he had pushed into the far corners of his mind. Ben's soul felt as dirty as his new boots with a grime no boot brush could remove.

"I promise I'll do everything I can to get you out of this camp."

He looked into my eyes—eyes he used to say were the most beautiful he had ever seen. I wondered if he thought that now?

Ben, embarrassed to embrace Cassie, gave her hand a parting squeeze. He was reminded, even in the midst of the filth, Cassie was exceptionally beautiful. Perhaps he should do more to get her out, but then again, he couldn't draw attention to her condition and their relationship. Someone would put two and two together and it would harm his future—maybe destroy his career. He couldn't let word get back to Milledgeville and ruin his chances for a Senate appointment. He had risked enough just by coming for this short visit under the guise of an inspection. He had a Senate seat to think about. He would figure out some other way to help her, if he could. His primary responsibilities were to Zach and Elizabeth and to the firm. He must think about his obligations and political future.

A Cherokee woman married to a white man was exempt from the removal. Ben knew that, but marrying Cassie was entirely out of the question. Marriage was not an option—at least not a marriage with Cassie—an Indian. He would think about her and her baby later. How simple things would have been if the Cherokee had agreed to emigrate. Cassie would be eight hundred miles away—out of sight and out of mind and safe with her own people. Could they not understand the times? John Ross, the National Party and the other Cherokee leaders had brought this misery upon themselves—that's for sure. The pragmatic removal party had been proved right. They alone, although a small minority, had seen the futility of trying to maintain a Cherokee homeland within the chartered boundaries of Georgia. This unnecessary wretchedness could have been easily avoided. It wasn't his fault and it wasn't the fault of the government. It wasn't Jackson's fault or the fault of the army. Blame lay squarely upon the bullheaded Ross and the Cherokee leaders who stubbornly couldn't think for themselves. They should have never tried to keep their land. The Cherokee had no ability to think realistically in our modern world. They were an anachronism. They would always be backward and uncivilized—inherently unfit to live in the modern world—forever unable to adjust. He understood that clearly now. He was no longer a schoolboy under the influence of his father's Utopian dreams. He should have known he and Cassie were doomed to a star-crossed future.

"I have to go, Cassie. I'll do everything I can and I'll be back soon. I'll see what I can do.

"Please get us out of here, Ben."

"I'll do my best," Ben said.

"You're an important man. You know people. Please help."

"I'm sure I can do something for you," he said again. "Don't worry."

"I'm not worried now, Ben—now that you've come. I knew you would come."

"Everything is going to be good in the end. The army will get things right. You'll see," Ben said.

He gave Cassie's hand one last squeeze as she instinctively lifted her lips for a goodbye kiss. Ben, ignoring Cassie's expectation of a parting kiss or an embrace, turned away quickly and immediately headed for the exit—head down. Walking fast, Ben passed the contractor's wagons preparing to distribute the daily ration of cornmeal and salt pork. Ben was uncomfortable, disturbed and wished he hadn't come in the first place. He was definitely in the wrong place. At least now he could tell his mother he had seen Cassie and had done what he could. If he had looked back, he would have seen Cassie crying on her brother's shoulder.

Ben gave my hand a little pat as if I were a pet dog and then he was gone. No kiss—no embrace—no final words of hope but I understand.

It was wonderful to see Ben again even if the meeting was brief and his mind preoccupied. I know in my heart he loves me. He's a wonderful little boy caught up in a complicated adult world—a world much too complicated for us. I was happy to see him healthy and prosperous in his new job. He is a good man. He will do what he can. He's a good man.

5 June 1838

I awoke to edudu's labored breathing. He was weak and had soiled himself during the night. He couldn't stand. I knew yesterday, in my heart, he would not survive long after elisi died—the love of his life. I saw in his eyes that burying the woman he loved would be too much for his kind heart. His

652

life had been inextricably entwined with hers for over sixty years. With her gone he had nothing to live for—nothing whatsoever. He had no reason to live without his bride.

Illness, exacerbated by filthy conditions, exposure, poor nutrition and nonexistent medical care, had taken its toll on the elderly—on my edudu. I waited at the gate. The moment the white doctor was allowed in I begged him to examine edudu. When I spoke he stared at me for a moment. Perhaps, because I spoke excellent English, it influenced him to grant my request.

He agreed to examine edudu.

I described edudu's weakness and told the doctor his wife had died the day previous. As the doctor was examining him, edudu opened his eyes, looked at the physician and whispered to me in Cherokee.

"What did he say?" the doctor asked.

"He said you look like a kind man and you should help someone else. He said he will be fine without your assistance."

The doctor closed his bag.

"Tell your grandfather he is very kind and he should rest. He needs immediate hydration and nutrition. Broth would be good."

"Where will I get broth in this place, doctor?" I whispered.

The doctor motioned for me to follow him out of edudu's hearing.

"I understand, dear. I know very well what you're up against."

The doctor looked tired—very tired.

"I would give you what you need myself, if I could. I've already given away all my money. I have no resources and few medicines. I wish I could do more. I promise I'll do everything I can for your grandfather. Let me introduce myself. I am Dr. Uriah D. Thweatt, at your service. Please ma'am, may I ask your name?"

"I'm Cassandra, sir, but everyone calls me Cassie. A pleasure to meet you, Dr. Thweatt. Thank you for treating edudu."

When I mentioned my name, the doctor's head rose and a light entered his tired eyes as they locked onto mine.

"And a pleasure indeed to meet you, young lady," He said crisply, continuing to look into my eyes with more energy than before.

"Do you happen to know a Mr. Wilbur Lowry and his wife, Eleanor?" he enquired quietly, never looking away from my face.

"Why, yes sir. I know them quite well, sir. Mr. and Mrs. Lowry lived at New Echota for many years. I attended Mr. Lowry's school. He, his wife and his son are dear friends. Do you know them, sir?"

653

"I know them quite well. Mr. and Mrs. Lowry and their son have been friends of our family for many years."

"I knew them from up north. In fact, I was somewhat involved in their first meeting and subsequent marriage. Mr. Lowry was a friend of my wife and Eleanor was my assistant for a short while. My wife arranged for them to meet at our home one evening over dinner and the rest is history. As soon as I heard about the removal I volunteered to assist the mission at Brainerd."

I was overcome. I felt myself beginning to cry for joy.

"I talked to Mrs. Lowry this morning. She asked me specifically to search for you as I made my rounds. She described you and your family in detail. It was providential to find you in this madhouse, my dear. I knew locating you would be like finding a needle in a haystack. I think perhaps, young lady, our meeting was ordained. Mrs. Lowry has been intervening fervently on your behalf daily. Perhaps this is the answer to her ardent supplications."

"I'm glad to meet you Dr. Thweatt."

"I'm so sorry I didn't recognize you sooner, young lady," Dr. Thweatt said. Mrs. Lowry told me how bright you are and about your advanced language skills."

Dr. Thweatt paused and his voice took on a more serious tone.

"I've encountered a great deal of resistance among the Cherokee because I'm white. Most don't want me to treat them at all. Some would prefer to die than submit to a white doctor, which sentiment I can fully understand. One only has to look around at what has been perpetrated against these people to understand their reluctance. We haven't done the Cherokee many favors lately, have we?"

I nodded. I didn't know what to say. I was so tired I didn't feel like talking.

"If you will permit me to change the subject," Dr. Thweatt continued, "I'll tell you that I could do a great deal more good for your people in the camps if I had someone like you to assist me. It was Mrs. Lowry's suggestion."

I was listening carefully now.

"She suggested you could interpret for me. She said you are reliable, honest and quite the linguist and would be trusted by your people. She assured me I would not regret acquiring your able assistance. I suspect we shall only need Cherokee and some Creek, but she said you were equally proficient in French, Latin and Greek—both koine and classical. Those skills will help with the necessary medical nomenclature and perhaps you can help me research my medical books and journals."

654

The doctor smiled and continued without pause. I was too tired to speak.

"Mrs. Lowry suggested I could use your brother to help tote and carry. The two of you, as assistants, would greatly increase the likelihood of the suspicious Cherokee allowing me to treat them—your assistance would greatly increase my effectiveness as a healer. But, my dear, she didn't mention you were expecting. I'm not sure this activity would be best for your unborn child. You will be immersed in sickness and death all day and then there would be the constant exertion."

Tears were coming into my eyes as I answered, "I would very much like to work for you, Dr. Thweatt. I would be far better off with you, sir, rather than mired in this filthy pig pen with no chance of exit. Nothing could be worse than this and no where would I be exposed to more illness than here. This camp is filled with disease. I would count it an honor to work with you and I think my child would be better off to have a physician watching over the both of us, sir."

"Well spoken, my dear. I see your wisdom and I must say I agree with your conclusion. These camps are filthy. There's no sanitation, the food is terrible and the water polluted. I received news today that the situation is perhaps worse up at the Agency, if that can be imagined."

I remained silent as the doctor continued, "I have even better news. In case I did find you, I have already arranged for your parole into my custody. I will vouchsafe for you and your brother with the army and there will be no need to provide a hostage."

Dr. Thweatt smiled and held me by the shoulders, "That would mean, my dear, in my custody you and your brother would be allowed to spend your evenings with Mr. and Mrs. Lowry."

I couldn't believe what I was hearing. Had I just heard the answer to my prayers? I could feel the tears begin to roll down my cheeks.

"In answer to my query, would you like to be my aide, Cassie? I would be honored. If you do accept, would you please ask your brother if he would also assist?"

I began to cry for happiness and relief. I felt as if I were dreaming.

"I fear your work with me will only delay your removal," the doctor continued, "but you can stay at least a week or two longer in better circumstances and, in addition, stay at the mission each evening with Mr. and Mrs. Lowry instead of this pig sty. What do you say?"

This must certainly be the answer to Mrs. Lowry's prayers. I was so moved I was almost unable to voice my response. With tears streaming and

655

my voice so choked with emotion I could hardly make a sound, I answered, "Oh, yes sir, yes sir. My answer is yes. We would be honored to assist you, sir. Yes, we will help you."

How ironic Ben's mother, isolated and miles away from Ross's Landing at the Brainerd Mission, had become our savior while her son, the powerful connected politician, could do nothing to relieve one moment of our despair—not even to provide us with a shovel to dig a latrine.

The doctor smiled at my answer and picked up his bag.

"It's done then. All is agreed," he said crisply. "I have much to do. I'll be back here to your camp this afternoon to check on your grandfather. I'll come for you at first light on the morrow to begin our work. I'm afraid it will be a long day but certainly better than being here."

"We are ready, sir."

"If you'll permit me, I'll send word to Mrs. Lowry to expect you about sundown or later, if that's agreeable? Unfortunately, my dear, I have been working on the sabbath—no rest for the wicked. The late hours I keep can't be helped and working on the Lord's day can't be avoided when the ox is in the ditch. I think I have that proviso by good authority. Reverend Buttrick doesn't agree with my caveat, but that can't be helped. My conscience will not allow me to act otherwise."

"We shall be ready, sir," I answered tearfully. "Thank you so much for everything."

Dr. Thweatt left and I and Five Feathers did our best to make edudu comfortable. Later that afternoon our edudu called us to his side and whispered his final wishes.

"My sun sets. My beloved waits. She beckons. I must join her."

"You must rest now, edudu," I said.

I don't think he heard me when I spoke to him.

"Please lay me to rest close to my dear one," edudu continued. "Care for your brother and your baby after I am gone, Walela. They will need you. You are strong. In some ways you are stronger than most men."

Edudu closed his eyes and I thought he would sleep but after he rested for a few moments he spoke again.

"My beloved is impatient. I must go. One day you and I and Five Feathers shall reunite with your elisi. We shall tell stories to the bluebirds and laugh. Keep writing, my dear Walela. Your elisi and I shall see you one day. It will be a meeting of great joy. I must go."

Five Feathers and I held edudu in our arms between us. We cradled his feeble body supporting his head as he spoke his last words, "I have lived long and well. I have loved and been loved."

Edudu looked at my brother, "Five Feathers, I go to my beloved. Care for Walela. Teach her baby our ways. When you become chief, care for the Principle People. Help them remember who they are."

With those words edudu breathed his last. Even in death his face bore the indelible stamp of wisdom, taking on a youthful glow as he left us to be with his bride. I found it difficult to believe him gone. But then I realized he was not gone. In my mind I had decades of memories and conversations I could recall. I could seek his advice and listen to his endless Cherokee stories at will. He would never be gone. I shall always hear his words echoing in my ears, "Walela, things change. I go to my beloved".

Soldiers do not provide coffins. We are allowed to use offcut sawmill slabs to make something resembling a coffin so we don't have to throw dirt in the face of our loved ones. We do what we can without tools. Men are constantly moving to and from our Cherokee graveyards. We have abandoned our traditional burial customs. We clean and wrap the bodies as best we can with what cloth we have. There are no eagle feathers.

I wonder if we will ever resume our ancient way of life and bury our dead according to proper customs—washing in lavender, wrapped in a clean white sheet and laid in a proper wooden casket with a single eagle feather. Will a man's widow ever have a seven-day mourning period again? Practicing our customs is impossible. Perhaps we will never be allowed to resume our life— an existence so odious to whites. Must we become white or die?

Our existence is one of constant lamentation. Death resides with every family. Will that dreaded specter with his inky black wings ever depart? Will that deadly shadow travel with us on our journey west and consume us entirely?

Chapter LIII

1838 - Cassie and the Doctor – Reunion

Chapter 53

Around edudu's grave were dozens of mounds of fresh turned earth. Each mound marking the last resting place of a Cherokee father, mother or child. Each mound of soil destined to disappear with the next rain. When we have been finally removed to the west, we will leave behind hundreds of graves—graves never marked, visited and never to be honored by the new occupants of Cherokee Country.

As I watched my brother throw the last soil on edudu's grave, Dr. Thweatt arrived in his carryall. The doctor waited respectfully until Five Feathers finished. The contractor took the spade.

The doctor put his arm around me.

"I'm so very sorry, Cassie. I'm so very sorry," the doctor said. "My heart is with you, my dear."

"We have nothing here, sir. My brother and I are alone. Five Feathers and I are free to go with you. Elisi and edudu shall remain forever a part of the land to which they belong—as they wished. We can work any time we're needed."

"I understand, Cassie. I'm so sorry for your loss."

"Thank you, sir."

"I'll come for you both on the morrow, just after dawn. I will vouchsafe your parole with the Army. You two will be released into my custody. I know you and your brother can be trusted not to violate your parole. You will have freedom of movement as long as you are with me and I return you to the army when required."

"Thank you, sir. I can't tell you how grateful we are."

"It's Mrs. Lowry you need to thank, my dear. I'm afraid I work long, difficult hours, but I'm sure anything will be better than waiting all day in this fetid place. If you get tired, you can always rest in the carryall. Be aware that working with me means you must be prepared to go at first light."

Without another word, the doctor left to continue his busy schedule caring for the hundreds of Cherokee suffering illness.

6 June 1838 – First day with Dr. Thweatt

As promised, the doctor met us at the entrance to our camp as the muggy Tennessee dawn was beginning to turn the sky pink over the missionary ridge. As promised, the sleepy soldiers allowed us to accompany him without hindrance. It was wonderful to get out of the camp—an elation I could not express, but my heart was with the hundreds of my fellow sufferers who remained confined in miserable conditions here and other places. As we left the camp, I felt guilty, as if it were dishonest for me not to share their misery.

In the half-light of dawn, Five Feathers helped me into the doctor's carryall.

"I appreciate you and your brother's help more than I can say, Cassie. I apologize, but I will not be able to compensate you two for your service. I will see you are fed, clothed and housed. That is all. I'll take care of you to the best of my ability. I promise. That's the best I can do for you. I wish I could do more. If I had money I would pay you for your services."

"Extracting us from that devilish camp will be pay enough, doctor."

"For the next little while, Mrs. Lowry will provide your morning and evening meals," the doctor said. "She will provide your sleeping quarters and do any washing you may require. I don't know how long I'll be allowed to use your services before you're deported, but I hope quite a while. We'll do some good work for your people. We'll do our best. That's all I can promise."

"We're grateful, Doctor Thweatt, and we promise to be the best assistants we can possibly be."

I began to cry with emotion thinking of the kindness of this man and the possibility to see the Lowrys this very evening. Five Feathers, silent and observant as usual, held me as I quietly wept. Dr. Thweatt waited to speak until I composed myself.

"My dear, the fact that you and your brother speak Cherokee and Creek will allow me to reach many more people effectively. You two are a godsend to my work here."

"We think you are the one sent by God, Dr. Thweatt."

Dr. Thweatt smiled and patted my hand affectionately as the morning light began to reflect off his white hair.

"Whatever the case, I couldn't have special ordered two better assistants. As you know, your people are suspicious of whites. Your presence will give me some credibility. I'm grateful for that."

"Here we go," Dr. Thweatt said, as he flicked the reins to speed up his old mule. "Let's get to work and do something good today for your people. I want to visit both camps here at Ross's Landing today and there are a couple of smaller camps over towards the Brainerd Mission I need to visit. I want to visit the poor Creeks. I fear they have been abused and neglected even more than the Cherokee, if that is possible. We'll certainly not have enough time to visit them all, but we'll do the best we can."

"We're ready, doctor. My brother and I will do the best we can to help you and our people."

"I know you will," the doctor answered. "Forgive me my old carryall, Cassie. It's about as old as I am. It's small and uncomfortable, but it will have to do. I wish I had a proper carriage but it's all I have. I brought some breakfast for you two. Look in that pouch at your feet, Cassie. The food is for you and your brother. I've already eaten. It's not the best in the world, but it's filling and better than you would receive in the camp. At least it isn't salt pork and its been cooked properly."

I found the pouch and shared with Five Feathers. I couldn't believe we were eating good food—fully cooked. I almost cried again at the taste of the simple breakfast.

"When we get out of the camps we're never going to eat salt pork again," I said softly.

"I'm tired of it myself," Dr. Thweatt said firmly as his carryall bounced on an especially rough part of the roadway.

"The roads around here are rough and full of ruts and potholes. In your delicate condition, I'll do my best to avoid the worst of the humps and bumps but I'm afraid an uncomfortable ride can't be helped."

"You're doing fine doctor. After what we've been through, I feel like a princess."

"Well, I'll drive my old mule as carefully as I can. We'll be there in less than an hour. Thanks again for you two giving me your service," Dr. Thweatt said kindly.

"You're most welcome."

"Let me know if my driving gets too rough. Sometimes I get in a hurry and take little care. It's quite rare that I must consider the comfort of passengers."

"I will, sir. I promise."

The rest of that day passed in a confusing whirl. By the time Dr. Thweatt was finished with his rounds, Five Feathers and I were exhausted. The emotion required to talk to the suffering and then to translate medical terms continually was grueling. Dr. Thweatt was tireless. We were pleased to be with him and would never complain from the long hours.

The doctor worked all day at the camps near Ross's Landing treating a variety of complaints of those who could be persuaded to allow a white doctor to treat them. I translated and Five Feathers and I comforted the ill as best we could. My brother did the heavy work—lifting and turning and carrying patients—and helping to prepare the deceased. Most Cherokee prefer traditional remedies and don't trust white doctors or white medicine. As Dr. Thweatt predicted, Five Feathers and I were able to persuade many who would otherwise not have allowed him to treat them. I struggled with my emotions all day going from sickbed to sickbed almost without pause—from one miserable situation to another. For those beyond help, we did what we could to make them comfortable in their last hours. As we arrived at the gate of the second camp just before noon, a child was being carried out for burial, having died of a bloody flux. The wretched little body was wrapped in nothing but an old shirt and lashed to a slab with twine. One emaciated arm, no bigger than a stick of kindling, was hanging out of its dirty, ragged shirt—dangling grotesquely. It was only the first of many lifeless Cherokee bodies we would see being prepared for burial.

By the time we arrived at the Brainerd Mission shortly after dusk, we were drained—completely shattered. I felt unable to take one more step.

As the doctor's old mule plodded into the mission, I saw Ben's mother running to meet us. I have no words to describe my joy to see Mrs. Lowry once again. She was as welcome as the angels of heaven. As she came near, she almost leapt into our arms as we embraced. We wept upon one another. Even my stoic brother was emotional. I apologized for our horrible appearance and our unwashed condition but my apologies were instantly dismissed amid smiles and tears and long embraces. Even in the midst of the death and sickness we had witnessed earlier in the day that yet hung over us like a dismal gloom, the reunion with Mrs. Lowry was one of the happiest moments of my life. I have missed her terribly. Mrs. Lowry received us with a childlike, giddy emotion. I have never seen a more beautiful sight than her face. Dr. Thweatt sat quietly in the high seat of the little carryall and watched our reunion with a patient smile. I was sure I saw a tear in his eye.

"I've been waiting on you two all day," Mrs. Lowry exclaimed. "I am so happy to see you. I knew you wouldn't be here till now, but I've been watching for hours."

We were so emotional and crying so often we had great difficulty talking. Mrs. Lowry wouldn't let go of my hand. I couldn't believe we were finally at her home.

"I can't tell you the pleasure I have to see you two again," Mrs. Lowry finally said as she composed herself, still holding my hand.

Mrs. Lowry gave Five Feathers a big, long hug—an embrace Five Feathers returned heartedly.

The doctor was smiling.

"I'll see you two in the morning bright and early," the doctor said. "Be ready by first light. We have a lot to do tomorrow. I want to take advantage of you two while I have you."

"We'll be ready, doctor."

With that the doctor, still smiling, flicked the reins and the tired old mule ambled away.

"We'll get you both a nice warm bath, dear, before your bedtime," Mrs. Lowry said cheerily. "I have clean clothes for the both of you already laid out and your quarters for the night are the best I could arrange. I expect they'll be at least moderately comfortable, considering what's going on around us. I'll do your washing while you're out with the doctor tomorrow. Come with me and I'll show you and Five Feathers your sleeping quarters."

Five Feathers and I were speechless. We were weary and glad Mrs. Lowry was talking. It was as if her words were a warm bath welcoming us home. Both Five Feathers and I were humbled.

"It's the best we can do under the circumstances, I'm afraid," Mrs. Lowry explained. "The mission is crowded with desperate people coming in daily, as you can imagine. We house everyone we possibly can. Sometimes soldiers demand accommodation. When that happens we must turn others away. Because of the soldiers, your sleeping arrangements are not what I would prefer, but you'll have a roof, it's dry and it's as clean as I can make it."

Mrs. Lowry led us to a small corner stall in the little old stable behind her cabin. The structure was old and leaned a bit to one side, but it looked sturdy enough—like a grand manor house after what we had been through.

"I had one of the men put up a few boards and enclose the wall to the top so the mules in the next stall won't bother you. We put a floor in one side for your beds so you won't have to sleep on the bare ground. It's not much. I'm sorry we have to put you up in a stable."

"It's so much nicer than where we were last night," I answered. "You can't imagine."

"Yes, dear. I can imagine. I've been down to the camps on numerous occasions with Dr. Thweatt. I know exactly what you've been through."

I watched Mrs. Lowry as she was showing us our sleeping quarters with the animals. I watched her nervously wringing her apron and remembered her doing the same the day Ben left for law school. I began to cry once again and once again Mrs. Lowry held my hand as she continued to tell us about our accommodations.

"I had all the manure removed and you have fresh sawdust on the floor and clean straw under your beds," she continued, as if apologizing. "It will still smell like a stable, I fear, but that can't be helped—at least it's a clean stable."

"According to Mr. Lowry, better people than us have slept in a stable on occasion," I answered.

"Still, I wish we could do better, dear," Mrs. Lowry said apologetically.

"The two beds have clean bedclothes. You'll probably find the animals quieter company than your crowded camp. It's as nice as we could make it."

"It's a palace, Mrs. Lowry. It's wonderful. Five Feathers and I will sleep like infants tonight. It really couldn't be better."

I couldn't help giving Mrs. Lowry another long embrace.

Mrs. Lowry, again worrying her apron, said in a low voice, "Our outhouse is just behind the stable so that will be convenient. We do have lime so the odor shouldn't be disturbing."

I thought of the filth we had been forced to endure. This was such a relief.

"I am so sorry, but it's the best we could do on short notice. I would put you up in our little cabin, but it's overcrowded—soldiers, you see. We have no choice. I'm afraid you'll have to let Missy sleep with you. She's our cat. We feed her here in the stable to keep all the little visitors away. She does her job very well. She's a good cat. She'll be good company. Sometimes when things get hectic I come out here and bring her a saucer of milk and sit with her a while. I tell her my troubles. She doesn't mind at all. She purrs and cuddles around my ankles and reminds me of a world that once was normal."

Mrs. Lowry took a deep breath, looked up at me and Five Feathers, twisted her apron once again and smiled—a beautiful relaxed smile.

"For the time being," she continued, "we have three Georgia Militia officers who demand we put them up while they're here. You'll be safe here in the stable. No one will disturb you. You'll probably rest better here than our little house, to tell the truth. I found both of you another change of clothing. I hope they suit. I've laid out your clean clothes in the washing shed behind our kitchen and your bath water will be warm shortly. I've heard the vermin have been increasing in the camps but we won't talk about that. After you've bathed and changed, I'll have your supper ready. While you're gone tomorrow, I'll wash your clothes for you. I'm so glad to see you two. I'll prepare all your food while you're here. You can take your meals with us when the officers aren't here. When the soldiers are present, I'm afraid you'll have to eat out back. They have made it clear they don't have much use for Indians but I guess that can't be helped with white soldiers. I'm so sorry."

I nodded my agreement with her assessment.

Mrs. Lowry twisted her apron.

"I can't express how happy I am to see you two."

With those words, both she and I broke down once again. We had to sit to regain our composure. Even my normally passive brother had a tear in his eye. While she and I were sniffling and snuffling, Missy purred and rubbed our ankles reminding us everything would be good this evening.

"I'm so sorry, Mrs. Lowry. I can't keep from crying."

"Neither can I."

"We can't tell you how much we appreciate all this," I said quietly. It's been terrible since the soldiers came for us."

Once again, there in the stable, Five Feathers gave Mrs. Lowry a hug. I could tell he was emotional even though he didn't show it outwardly.

Eleanor smiled and swallowed and began worrying her apron again and smiled—a bright, warm smile that warmed my heart.

"At least for a while, my dear," Mrs. Lowry said with a touch of joy in her voice, "we shall enjoy one another's company like old times. I am determined to make every moment of your time here pleasant."

Mrs. Lowry paused.

"I'm so sorry to hear about your elisi and edudu. You have my deepest sympathy."

"Thank you," I answered.

"I am so sorry, my dear. I feared greatly for them when I heard the arrests had begun. Many of our older Cherokee friends have not been strong enough to withstand their arrest, the forced journeys and the inconveniences—many have succumbed, I'm afraid. Here at the mission we're called on to bury the elderly and children every day, but I don't want to talk about that now. I can't tell you how much I have missed you since Wilbur's imprisonment, but now you two are here and this is the happiest day I can remember in months and months and months."

"It's our happiest day, too," I answered.

"If you two will come with me now to the shed behind the kitchen, I have the water heated for your bath. I know you're exhausted, but after that we'll eat and talk just a bit till you're ready for bed. I wish I had something special to feed you like old times. We have a good oven, but it's on the other side of the property and we don't bake every day. I fear all I have for you tonight is a plate of beans with fatback, day old cornbread and a nice jug of buttermilk. When I heard you were coming, I saved a couple of fresh onions—they're not as good as the ramps you used to bring me, but they're fresh. There's plenty of cornmeal and fatback around here these days, but not much in the way of fresh vegetables, milk, eggs or butter, but I'm sure it's better than what our stingy government has been giving you."

I was loving listening to Mrs. Lowry's voice. I felt myself longing to lie down and rest my weary back, but I wanted to listen to Mrs. Lowry forever. Being here with her was like a dream fulfilled. I couldn't bear to tell her that we were tired and I needed to lie down.

"I'm afraid the doctor will be calling at first light," she continued. He works long hours, but he's a good man and everyone loves him dearly. You'll love him too, when you get to know him. He's precious."

"I can tell that already. He's been a perfect gentleman," I responded.

"He's one of the kindest men I've ever known," Mrs. Lowry said. "He's doing the best he can to help your people and he's madly writing a book about Cherokee herbs and medical practices. I told him you could help him with that. I know you and your grandfather were knowledgeable in that area and, of course, your Latin studies are far advanced. I remember Mr. Lowry boasted about your skills often. You two sleep well and I'll wake you in the morning in plenty of time for your breakfast before the doctor calls. Breakfast won't be much, but it will be nourishing. The doctor and I always put together something to take for his lunch."

I couldn't keep the emotion from my voice.

"Thank you so much for everything, Mrs. Lowry."

"What you have prepared for us is a palace and a feast compared to what we've experienced. Thank you—thank you. There is no way to tell you how grateful we are."

"It was the least we could do."

Mrs. Lowry's hands began to twist in her apron once again.

"We would have done more if we had more time."

She paused. I saw a look of consternation come across her face. My mind flashed back to her cabin in New Echota. Something was bothering her.

"I guess you're wondering about Mr. Lowry."

"Ben told me about him. I have been afraid to ask," I answered.

"I'm sure you're wondering why he hasn't greeted you. He's in his bed. He stays in his bed most of the time."

"I'm so sorry, Mrs. Lowry."

"Thank you. He doesn't get up much these days. Sometimes he'll stay in bed all day—sometimes days on end. He never talks. I'm never sure if he knows where he is or even who he is. Sometimes when visitors come to the door I find him hiding under the bed. I'm so sorry, Cassie. I wish you didn't have to see him like this. Doctor Thweatt says one day he may just snap out of the mental state he's in and be his old self, or he may never recover. Since his imprisonment he hasn't been the same. I can't imagine the horror the Guard and the Militia put him through. I'll tell him you're here and maybe tomorrow evening you can visit with him for a little while. At least you can sit and talk to him even if he doesn't respond. Your presence may help him remember something. I hope so. I've been hoping your visit might be good for him. He always thought the world of you and Five Feathers."

7 June 1838 - Second day with Dr. Thweatt

Our night in the stable was our best night's sleep since our arrest. The animals had very good manners during the night. Compared to the camps it was quiet and Missy kept us company. Her purring was a welcome tonic. She slept curled up beside Five Feathers' head most of the night. Five Feathers and Missy were immediately best friends.

Mrs. Lowry's breakfast was the best meal of our life compared with the revolting food of the camps. We had bacon fried just right and a poached egg. We had proper biscuits, a day old but that didn't matter, with a taste of butter and sorghum molasses to finish. It was a feast. Mr. Lowry was still in his bed. When I greeted him, he looked through me as if I were a stranger or not even there. He didn't say a word or acknowledge my presence. I can't imagine the mental anguish the poor man must have suffered.

Dr. Thweatt arrived just before dawn and we were quickly off. The first camp we visited was indistinguishable from the two we had visited the day before. The camp had the same problem with widespread measles along with the ever-present ague and fever, dysentery and bilious fevers as the camps we had visited yesterday. No wonder, with the unsanitary conditions. I wonder how men like Dr. Thweatt handle the emotional strain of so many ill people under such trying conditions day in and day out. I wonder what he thinks of at the end of his day? Even with scanty supplies, nonexistent pharmaceuticals and dreadful conditions, a physician present and interested in their condition brightened the spirits of most.

"There's a measles epidemic, Cassie," Dr. Thweatt said. "There's nothing I can do. Measles is a terrible disease. It spreads quickly under these filthy, crowded conditions. It's a dreadful disease—dreadful."

"It was all in our camp. It was terrible there, too. Many died," I said.

"I wish I could do more," The doctor said. "Poorly nourished children and the elderly are most vulnerable but with the measles I've seen strong men succumb. The army has crowded all the families together without proper housing and sanitation. They were asking for trouble."

"We didn't have proper latrines," I said quietly.

"I know. I've seen," the doctor said in a whisper. "If the measles itself isn't fatal, the pneumonia that follows often brings death. We can bleed them and administer an emetic, but that's about all that can be done. It's a terrible disease and one of the most contagious. I wish I knew why, Cassie, but this disease seems to strike down the Cherokee more than whites."

I was too tired to talk.

"The army has squeezed you together with no sanitation, poor food, contaminated water and grossly inadequate shelter. I have to control myself. What are they thinking? Farmers wouldn't keep pigs in conditions like this. I agree with Reverend Butrick—the government has chosen an expensive method of killing Cherokee children and elderly. May God forgive them. We'll do what we can to make them comfortable, Cassie. I thank you and Five Feathers from the bottom of my heart for your help."

During the day Five Feathers helped bury six adults and two children. Many were beyond help and would pass soon. Five Feathers was busy.

8 June 1838 - Third day with Dr. Thweatt

Dr. Thweatt told us he has been called to Fort Cass to aid the doctors there and report. We're to leave before dawn and be prepared to stay at least three days away from home in rough conditions. Dr. Thweatt smiled at us when he said we can sleep in the carryall on the trip. I don't think anyone could sleep in a bumpy carryall.

We worked long hours today. I don't feel like writing tonight. My baby is stirring. Dr. Thweatt says my pregnancy is progressing perfectly and I'll deliver a healthy child. He thinks, by the way I'm carrying, it will be a boy.

Five Feather helped dig seven graves. Two children and five adults.

9 June 1838 – Fourth day with Dr. Thweatt

We left for the Agency long before daylight. Doctor Thweatt said we'll make the forty-five-mile journey easily in one day with a fresh horse at the military stage along the way. He wanted to get there as quickly as possible. Dr. Thweatt was ordered to visit Rattlesnake Springs, Bedwell Springs, Mouse Creek number one and the East Mouse Creek camps and report to Fort Cass.

The doctor thinks two or three days will suffice to survey those camps and make his report while treating all we can. When he completes the assignment, we will return immediately to Ross's Landing. I haven't been to Charleston, the Agency or even Red Clay in years. Things change, as edudu said.

There are several thousand imprisoned near the Agency. I recognize little of the countryside from my previous visits. So much is different with the army, the camps and the contractors and the ubiquitous wagons. We traveled all day, a day which dawned hot and muggy without a breath of wind. I could feel the sweat on my body as if I had been dipped in molasses. My clothing stuck to my skin. Rivulets of sweat were constantly running down my face and back.

There is no sign of rain to settle the choking dust. The water in Chickamauga Creek is the lowest in memory. We need rain. Dr. Thweatt said the drought is so bad the steamboat traffic on the Tennessee River is stalled. Steamboats cannot pass the shoals south of Ross's Landing and only those of shallowest draft can make Knoxville upriver.

We traveled all day. It was a bumpy but a pleasant ride in the carryall. I enjoyed the rest from our duties with the doctor and took great pleasure in the countryside along the way. We passed several groups of men repairing the bumpy road surface. We changed horses early in the forenoon and then again at noon and once again in the afternoon and had a quick meal at the army depot. We arrived at Rattlesnake Springs camp just at twilight, much too tired to work. We immediately retired. Five Feathers and I slept on the ground under the carryall. Dr. Thweatt slept in the officers' quarters. It is the first day Five Feathers has not dug a grave.

10 June 1838 – Fifth day with Dr. Thweatt

Dawn revealed our location adjacent to a camp of upwards of a thousand Cherokees guarded by armed soldiers in a broad open expanse. It wasn't nearly as crowded as the camps at Ross's Landing. I could tell many of the families had not been in the camp long. I have no idea where they are from—I suppose North Carolina. We began work at first light. As we arrived at the gate we were immediately taken to an old man lying in the bed of an old wagon with a tattered covering. He had a quick, weak pulse, dry hacking cough and was spitting up mucous streaked with blood.

Dr. Thweatt, already sweating profusely, turned away, leaned against the wagon, wiped his brow and whispered to me, "The old man has consumption—much advanced. He's not long for this world. Make him as comfortable as you can, Cassie. There's nothing more we can do for him. Follow me when you're finished."

As I comforted the old man, Dr. Thweatt turned to the young woman lying beside the old man. Dr. Thweatt bowed his head. She had expired not long before we arrived. She had recently delivered an infant and it, too, was dead in her arms. Dr Thweatt called for Five Feathers to remove the bodies and help her family prepare her for burial. I was overcome. I couldn't help but stare into the young woman's glazed eyes and wonder about my own condition and my future. A busy green fly crawled on her face. Her hair was dirty and disheveled. I brushed the fly away from her face. Without a word to the doctor or my brother, I ran to an open space and was sick. I could never be a doctor and deal with this daily. How does Dr. Thweatt manage?

My brother helped bury 4 adults—3 children. When we finished, Five Feathers and I slept under the carryall once again. Dr. Thweatt slept with the officers.

11 June 1838 - Sixth day with Dr. Thweatt

The dawn broke hot and sultry—no sign of much needed rain. Dr. Thweatt brought us a nice breakfast from the officers' tent and I felt a guilt for all those around me who wake and have nothing. From the beginning Dr. Thweatt had asked me to keep notes and statistics to give to the director of medicine upon our departure.

The weather continues hot and dry. The sky is brass. The sickness, especially at Calhoun on the Hiwassee, is worse than ever. Our days pass in one long, revolting haze of misery upon misery—the faces of the damned blending into one indistinguishable nightmarish vision. Each night hapless specters come to me in my dreams pleading for assistance—assistance I am never allowed to give.

Today was no different than any other—a parade of disease, fever, vomiting, diarrhea, coughing, retching and death as we assisted men, women and children. This evening I feel as if I have been bathed in some kind of permanent impurity. How will I ever forget? How will I ever be cleansed of this infectious pollution of both body and soul?

Dr. Thweatt gave me a copy of the *Southern Recorder*. I was exhausted but eager to read the first newspaper I had seen since our arrest. The news continues as before. The white writers believe their government's actions righteous. I am weary. My emotions are so depleted I am unable to shed tears. What the white writers describe and what I have lived through are two different events.

Copied from the *Southern Recorder* - 5 June 1838 – page 3

"...the rights of Georgia will never be compromised...We are likewise happy to be enabled to put before our readers the report of Col. Kenan, of the admirable conduct, and most successful operations of Gen. Scott, to whom was confided the critical duty of executing the treaty with the Cherokees. Our readers will perceive, that Gen. Scott has greatly added to his honorable renown, by the admirable efficiency with which he has performed the duty assigned him; and that he has found a most efficient right arm in our own Floyd—and what, above all, will be the most gratifying intelligence to the patriot and philanthropist, the simple announcement, that without the shedding of a single drop of blood, there remains not a single Indian in Georgia, except those who are in the keeping of the army and ready for instant removal to their home in the West."

Copied from the Southern Recorder - 6 June 1838 – page 3

"To his Excellency, G. R. Gilmer:

Sir:--Having just arrived from the scene of operations in the Cherokee Country, I avail myself of the honor of communicating to your Excellency, the movements of my Chief, General Scott, within the limits of Georgia. Upon the 24th ult., he placed the Georgia Volunteers under the command of Gen. Floyd, in position; and on the 25th commenced operations. General Floyd, in person, commanded the first detachment that operated. The promptness and ability of his movement, gave the commanding General the highest satisfaction, while it presented to the balance of the command, the most salutary example.

The number of prisoners on Tuesday last, was about 3000; and by this time, I do not think there is a wandering Indian in the Cherokee Country, within the limits of Georgia. The captures were made with the utmost kindness and humanity, and free from every stain of violence.

The deportment of our Georgia citizens, resident in the Cherokee counties, has been marked by a forbearance and kindness towards the Indians, that must win for them the admiration of every philanthropist. Permit me to conclude with the congratulation of our rights being so promptly and peacefully secured.

With the highest regard, A.H. Kenan
Volunteer Aide-de-camp to General Scott."

It's official according to Mr. Kenan. The Cherokee Nation is erased. Not one of us resides freely within the chartered limits of Georgia. Our vanishment is complete. The kindhearted and philanthropic Georgia citizens are happy their rights have been secured and their soldiers have made room for their expansion—lebensraum is the German word, Mrs. Lowry once said.

There is nothing more to write. Perhaps out west I can write about happier events with my brother and my baby. Georgia has what they wanted. We have been removed.

Five Feathers buried an old woman, two old men, a young man and woman and their two children.

12 June 1838 – Seventh day with Dr. Thweatt

I cried myself to sleep. It seems I cry myself to sleep most every night since our arrest. We have treated many children for Cholera infantum. It is a terrible disease with vomiting, diarrhea, thirst, and muscle cramps. I do not like to see parents tending their children and observe the helplessness in their eyes. Parents should not be required to bury their own children.

It was all I could do to assist the doctor today. We found an old man with no family lying abandoned in the weeds beside a fence. He had been left under a bush to fend for himself in his last hours. He was lying on a scrap of cloth in his own filth with another scrap of cloth over his middle and a piece of bark about three feet long his only cover from the elements. The old man was unable to turn, relieve himself or communicate. He could only look into our eyes as we attempted to relieve his distress. Dr. Thweatt said he would not last long and we should endeavor to make him comfortable—that was all that could be done. We did what we could. His eyes followed us as we left him. How do I bear these indelible images?

We met Dr. Grant, also working in the camps. He confessed he was a dentist and not a trained physician. The army recruits who they can and pays them the lowest of wages. I suppose that's better than nothing.

Dr. Thweatt says more will die with the unsanitary conditions, dirty water and poor nutrition. Ben said General Scott would take care of the problems. Things are not better. They are worse.

Few have proper cooking utensils, proper shelter is non-existent and fuel scarce. Every day we see families eating partially cooked food. Civilian contractors hired by the government have sometimes distributed spoiled rations. The drinking water is contaminated from many sources including animal and human feces. No one seems to care—certainly not the soldiers. I see weariness and apathy in the young, white soldiers' eyes. They are weary. Like us, they want to go home. The authorities want this to end quickly. Everyone in authority wants the removal to end so they can return to their homes. They have a home. Will we ever have a home?

Dr. Thweatt says at least half of all infant children have already died prematurely or will soon succumb. A large percentage of the elderly aged sixty and older are dead after almost three weeks of imprisonment. The elderly fare poorly living under such harsh conditions exposed to the elements. I think Reverend Buttrick's comment is accurate. The army has chosen an expensive way of putting us to death. Perhaps this madness will end before we perish entirely.

I counted thirteen children and seven adults taken for burial today in total. Measles is rampant. Five Feathers fell asleep instantly tonight—utterly exhausted.

13 June 1838 – Day eight with Dr. Thweatt

We watched two small children die of convulsions today and two of yaws—an ugly disfiguring disease common where children have inadequate hygiene. I have always enjoyed books and learning but I'll never want to be a doctor. I've learned all I want to know about pain, suffering, disease and death. My emotions are frayed like an old, worn rope. How does Dr. Thweatt process the daily wretchedness? I admire him more than I can say. Doctor Thweatt tries to assist the very things everyone else ignores. He is one of the best men I have ever known.

When the doctor bleeds patients, I cannot watch. He assures me it's for their good. He performs his surgery with a steady hand in every case, even when fatigued.

Five Feathers never speaks when he assists the doctor, but he cannot disguise his emotions. My brother has a strong sense of human worth. He will be a good chief—a great chief. Sometimes at night I think about our removal and how it has all been accomplished legally to assuage the white conscience.

Dr. Thweatt was given a copy of *The Boston Recorder*. The northern newspapers quote the southern newspapers. The north is being told we are emigrating of our own free will with the gracious assistance of the army. Perhaps no one will ever read this journal. Is all my work futile?
I am weary of recording deaths. Five more died today.

14 June 1838 – Day nine with Dr. Thweatt
Dr. Thweatt has been ordered back to Ross's Landing tomorrow. We are exhausted both mentally and physically. All our medical supplies are spent. We have nothing left in the carryall. Typhus is spreading. It is a nervous condition with trembling and great agitation, inflammation of the lungs, coughing and complete incontinence of both bowels and urine. Typhus has a ghastly appearance. I had a difficult time helping the doctor today. The patients in the final stages take on a wild look and mutter incoherently. When they reach the point of confused rambling nothing can be done, the doctor said. Death is imminent. I wish to never see that disease again in my life.

Today, like yesterday, was dreadful. I expect nothing less tomorrow. I witnessed several more children carried to their burial. The children seem to always be wrapped for burial in someone's old shirt and tied onto a wooden slab with their little faces covered by a piece of bark. I find myself this evening devoid of emotion—unable to weep.

I didn't get an exact count in my notes today. The graves are becoming more numerous. Will be any children left when we reach the west?

I recorded five dead of dysentery and six of nervous fever.

15 June 1838 - Day ten with Dr. Thweatt

We arrived bone tired at the Brainerd Mission long after sunset. We were exhausted beyond words. I had never traveled so fast and far in my life, changing horses every ten miles. Five Feathers drove and allowed the doctor to sleep in the back. Unusually, Mrs. Lowry was not out front to greet us. I roused Dr. Thweatt. We found Mrs. Lowry in bed, shaking violently from head to toe. I was frightened. Doctor Thweatt said she was suffering from the ague and fever—alternating between shivering and high temperature. The doctor recommended she evacuate both stomach and bowels. He administered quinine. He told her she may experience a headache, nausea and some roaring in her ears, but that was to be expected from the quinine. I helped her with the doctor's instructions until she was sound asleep. I fell into my bed. I don't think I could have taken one more step. Five Feathers was already sound asleep with Missy purring gently curled beside his head. I felt like we were home.

16 June 1838 – Day eleven with Dr. Thweatt

The doctor, Five Feathers and I returned to the mission in the late evening after a long day. Mrs. Lowry, weak but much recovered, met us at the stable and handed an official looking letter to Doctor Thweatt. I was overjoyed to see her up and about. I had been worried all day. She had better color and her lovely smile was back.

The doctor put the letter in his vest pocket and began to care for his horse and methodically put his things away. All three of us stood and stared without offering to help. He stopped, put his hands on his hips and looked at each of us in turn with an expression of some defiance.

He patted his vest pocket and looked at each of us in turn.

"You three want to know what's in this letter, don't you?"

"Well, I was going to wait to read it until after I put away our things and fed the horse and I could sit and relax with a nice cup of tea, but I guess if you three are so impatient, I'll read it now."

We crowded around him.

"And I suppose you want me to tell you what this letter contains?"

We didn't say anything. We squeezed so close around him he hardly had room to take the letter from his pocket. Neither of us said a word as we waited.

He held the letter in his hands and turned it over and over, looking at it from all sides as if to divine its contents unopened. His delay was maddening.

"It's from the army," he said at last.

He sat down on the crossbeam stepover under the door leading into the tack room. Missy immediately hopped up into his lap, curled into a ball and began purring.

As we crowded around like children waiting for a treat, Dr. Thweatt opened the letter with a torturously deliberate slowness, as if wishing to prolong our anxious impatience for his pleasure. Mrs. Lowry and I pressed even closer, not wanting to miss a word from this important letter from the military.

I had never seen an official letter from the army.

Doctor Thweatt slowly opened the folded single page letter, scanned its contents and looked up at us slowly. His fallen countenance revealed the news.

"The news isn't good, Cassie. A company of about twelve hundred Cherokee left four days ago for the western territory. Your detachment is being organized to leave tomorrow morning," the doctor said in a whisper.

I felt a stabbing pain in my heart.

"The parole I have arranged for you and Five Feathers has been revoked and I must deliver you back to your detachment by first light tomorrow.

Mrs. Lowry put her arm around me.

"I am sorry. I am so sorry, but I must keep my pledge," the doctor said. "I obtained your parole on my honor. You must report to your detachment first thing in the morning. I'm sorry."

Dr. Thweatt's shoulders sagged. It was all he could do to sit upright. He suddenly looked much older than his years, bent and timeworn. His wrinkled hand, still firmly grasping the open letter in gnarled fingers, fell between his legs as if he had suddenly lost the strength to hold up his arms. It appeared the doctor's tired, old body would melt into the sawdust of the stable floor.

The news was as disappointing to the good doctor as to us. At that moment, I felt sorrow for the good doctor. I could feel the genuine agony he felt for us. He was indeed a good man and, if possible, had risen in my estimation.

"I am to return you at first light for immediate deportation. I regret having to share this news with you," the doctor whispered.

"We're grateful for everything, doctor," I said. "It's not your fault."

"You and Five Feathers have been assigned to assist the white doctor who will accompany the detachment. That's all the letter says. I'm so sorry. I have been called back to Charleston and then called to report to Mission headquarters in the north. I was hoping in my heart this day would never come. I wish we could continue together. I'm sorry. I'm so sorry," the old doctor said pathetically.

I watched a single tear run down the creases of the doctor's old cheek. Missy, still curled into a ball, continued to purr in his lap. The letter fell from the doctor's fingers and lay on the sawdust between his legs.

Chapter LIV

1838 – Cassie's Goodbye

Chapter 54

16 June 1838

United States Army Officers' Quarters – Detachment Headquarters - Ross's Landing

The Captain charged his officers the evening before their departure to escort approximately seven hundred fifty Cherokee prisoners eight hundred miles west.

"Our mission, under orders from General Winfield Scott, is to escort the prisoners outside the borders of the United States as efficiently as possible. I want to be moving when the first ray of sunshine hits the river."

"The water level is too low for steamboats. We'll travel overland. We are not allowed to pass through white settlements or towns. We will cross improved farmland only with permission. All damage incurred to private property will be paid for by the Indians through their conductor. Indians will pay the cost of all ferry crossings. Indians will have a daily ration provided by army contractors."

"Do you understand?"

The captain scanned the young faces of his subalterns. In unison each young white officer responded.

"Yes, sir."

The captain continued, "You are to protect the white citizenry from the prisoners and you yourself should abstain from unnecessary contact. No fraternization or assistance shall be given. The Cherokee are not to be trusted—especially the young men. You'll have to keep a close eye on them. Watch closely for any sign of rebellion. Do you understand?"

Again, in unison, the young officers responded.

"Yes, sir."

"This journey will take approximately eighty days, depending on the weather. You must be vigilant night and day.

677

Anyone neglecting his duties will be severely punished. We do not want trouble of any kind. I want to finish this assignment and get back to the proper job of the Army."

"Do you understand?"

They understood.

"One last thing. The Indians are not allowed to leave the detachment for any reason. They are not allowed to buy, sell, trade or hunt. We especially want to keep them from whiskey. As you know, white men are constantly trying to sell them whiskey."

Every young white soldier was listening carefully.

"The Indians must be kept within the column under close guard at all times. The general government is providing everything required for the journey—including wagons for the sick and elderly. All others must walk."

The captain continued, "Hunting is forbidden. They will eat the food we supply—nothing else. You must prevent Cherokee men from wandering. Watch them carefully. Don't trust them. Since we're holding the women and children hostage, any men who stray will most likely come back. I don't expect problems from the older Indians, but the young ones will be tempted to stray. Hunting must be prevented. If they are allowed to wander the countryside, the lazy bastards will steal everything they get their hands on. That must not be allowed. Do you understand? We must protect white civilians."

"Yes, sir."

"Remember, I want each of you on your station and I want to give the order to move just after first light. I expect to make ten miles a day. We travel rain or shine."

17 June 1838 - Pre-dawn at the Brainerd Mission

As we said our last goodbyes, Eleanor and I sobbed uncontrollably in one another's arms while Dr. Thweatt waited patiently in the carryall. He was required, on his personal honor, to return us to the army before dawn.

"I'm so sorry, honey, I'm so sorry, I'm so sorry," Mrs. Lowry said, beginning to cry—gasping for breath as she choked back sobs. She was clutching my shoulders in her small gnarled hands, her old finger joints swelled and disfigured by the ravages of arthritis. I held her tight. I was afraid she would collapse to the ground.

Her bonnet was askew and her grey hair mussed. In the pre-dawn darkness, she looked so much smaller and older than her years—life had not been kind to her. If Mrs. Lowry had seen herself, she would be embarrassed. She was exhausted emotionally and I thought how both she and her husband, just as much as we Cherokee, were victims. Like us, they had become expendable objects of pity.

In the morning dimness Mr. Lowry was silhouetted in the doorway standing tall and still in his nightshirt. His uncombed shock of coarse white hair glowing and unruly—sticking out on every side. Expressionless, he blankly stared into the distance with no indication he was aware of who he was, who we were or what was happening. I wondered again to what hidden crevice of the mind Mr. Lowry had fled for safety. Ben and his father throughout Ben's youth had been the best of friends—more brothers than father and son. No wonder Ben's mother looked frail. Her husband had been taken from her as surely as if he were dead and buried. As we said our last goodbyes, Mr. Lowry urinated off the side of the porch in full view oblivious that we were near.

The thought of what was being done to these people who had given everything they possessed or ever would possess to help us made me cry anew. I could not comprehend the law that gave white men this right.

Mrs. Lowry gathered herself, wiped her cheeks with the back of her hand and straightened her carriage.

"I'm so sorry, my dear. Please forgive me."

"There's nothing to forgive, Mrs. Lowry," I said.

"Forgive my weakness and my failures," Mrs. Lowry continued. "We tried to get you released into our custody but to no avail."

"I know. I know you did your best."

"The authorities will not listen to anyone here at the mission. They care nothing for your marvelous educational achievements. Their only thought is to send every Indian west. I enjoyed your presence the last few days more than I can say. You and Five Feathers were a gift from heaven. You answered my prayers. I feel as if my life has been renewed."

"You may have saved our lives, Mrs. Lowry. You rescued us."

"Your stay here has been good for both of us," Mrs. Lowry said. "I want Wilbur and me to go west with you, Cassie. He never answers when I ask about that, but perhaps we will come later—perhaps one day. I'm sure he would prefer to spend his last days with the Cherokee out west than here or in any white community. Maybe the trip west is what he needs. You and Ben are our only family, Cassie."

"I'll be waiting on you, Mrs. Lowry. Please write and let us know when you're coming—oh, please come. Please do come."

Mrs. Lowry pressed the flat of her hand gently against the underside of my distended stomach as if to cradle my unborn child—her grandchild.

"I wish I could be there when our grandchild is born," Mrs. Lowry said wistfully. "I'll talk to Dr. Thweatt and perhaps, somehow, we can take Wilbur west at some point and be with you, your brother and our baby. Perhaps the journey would bring Wilbur back. Perhaps when Wilbur sees me holding our grandbaby, he will come back to us."

"I hope you can come. I do hope you can come," I said.

"Cassie, I love my son and I wouldn't trade him for anything, but I always wanted a little girl. If I ever had a little girl, I would have wanted her to be just like you. Cassie, you have become my little girl. You are the daughter I always wanted."

I stood helpless and speechless. I didn't know what to say. In the emotion of the moment I had no words. We both began to cry again. Dr. Thweatt and Five Feathers were waiting patiently—stoically.

"Mrs. Lowry, years ago while Ben was at law school he made a sketch book—sketches of me—parts of me actually—my nose, my feet, my eyes, my hands. There are a couple of dozen sketches. They're a bit tattered now, but they're precious to me."

Eleanor was looking at me with a strangely perceptive look.

"I know dear. They're lovely sketches. I loved them," Mrs. Lowry said with quiet emotion.

I took a deep breath and continued, hoping I wouldn't cry, "This sketch book was a token of his love to impress upon me how much he missed me the fourteen months he was in Connecticut. I'm sure we will be together when this is over, but I want to ask you a favor. Ben has lost perspective, I think, with all that's going on and the pressure of his job. Would you please give these sketches to Ben for me? I want him to remember. Would you do that for me?"

With hands shaking, Mrs. Lowry took the little sketch book from my hands.

"Of course I'll give it to him, dear. I won't let him forget you. He has been busy and distracted. He's young, but he won't forget you. You can count on me. He will remember you. I won't let him forget."

It seemed to me this parting would never end. We held one another quietly once again and the ever-patient doctor and my brother continued to wait beside the carryall.

Wilbur, the once powerful, robust man who in days past had an ever-ready smile and a good word for everyone, continued motionless in the shadow of the doorway. In his madness, his limp feeble arms hung useless at his side. His once powerful sunburned hands were now withered. His long, yellowed nails and white hands resembled the claws of a great bird.

Suddenly, Eleanor smiled—a bright engaging smile.

"Cassie, I promised you the tea service years ago. It's time. I know you must go."

She took me by the hand and pulled me to the carryall. She pulled back the oilcloth and showed me a small wooden flour box tied securely with twine tucked in the corner.

"Last night Dr. Thweatt and I packed the tea service in old rags and sawdust for your trip. The box is sturdy."

"Your tea service should survive the journey. All I ask is every now and then when you have a cup of tea in your new home, you think of us and remember our wonderful days in New Echota. Remember that the cup you hold in your hand I once held in mine. I shall remember you every day of my life, dear. I never drink a cup of tea when I don't remember you and pray for you. Perhaps one day our country shall return to normal and return your people to their proper place. Perhaps you and I and our new grandchild shall share a cup of tea once more under happier circumstances not long hence. In any case, this tea service is yours."

Mrs. Lowry put her hand on the doctor's arm.

"I'm so sorry, doctor Thweatt. I know we're taking much too long to say goodbye but I may never see my Cassie ever again and I can't seem to let her go"

The doctor's face was sympathetic. He is the most patient man I've ever met.

"You ladies take all the time you want," the doctor said. "If I have to drive Cassie out west myself to keep my promise to the army, I'll do it. You take all the time you want to say your goodbyes."

Mrs. Lowry thanked the doctor and looked again at me.

"I know you must go but I've one last thing to say. I've been saving it for last," Mrs. Lowry said.

I couldn't imagine what she was talking about.

"The quilt and the tea service are the most precious things I have from my mother's family in Germany. They're yours now, dear."

"Remember us. Let our quilt keep you and your baby warm. Let our tea service nourish you and our baby. We have done everything we can to help you. Please don't forget us."

"We'll never forget you, Mrs. Lowry. We'll always remember."

"I shall pray for you every morning and every evening. And perhaps one day you'll give the quilt and the tea service to my grandchild on the occasion of her wedding and tell the child of happier times in Cherokee Country— wonderful stories of our glory days."

"I'll remember all the stories. I'll write them down for us," I said.

"I didn't realize it then, but when we were there in New Echota we weren't very far from heaven, were we my dear?" Mrs. Lowry said.

"Those were the best of days. I thought they would never end," I answered.

Mrs. Lowry smiled and patted my arm as she used to do.

"Just as Wilbur used to remind us, 'the joy is in the journey'."

Mrs. Lowry paused a moment and stared at the ground.

"There is one more thing I promised you. I suspect you have forgotten."

With that statement, Mrs. Lowry withdrew a tiny silk purse with a twisted silk drawstring from the pocket of her apron. She withdrew an equally tiny box from the silk purse and opened it. There were the two plain gold bands, polished and shining in the predawn starlight. Mrs. Lowry handed them to me.

"They're yours, Cassie. I don't know how or where, but I trust the Almighty that you will reach your destination and you and Ben will be united."

"I believe so too. Ben and I will be together," I said.

"I know that will happen. You and Ben will wed. I want to be there that day," Mrs. Lowry said. "Wherever you are, Wilbur and I will be there with you with these rings. Take them, dear. If at this moment I could take my very heart from my body and give it to you, I would. Go with God and take the heart that beats within my breast with you. Take these rings and on your wedding day remember us."

"I'll never forget you, Mrs. Lowry—never—never," I said.

Tears rolled down my face.

Mrs. Lowry kissed my cheek and said through her own tears, "I will never forget you. I will miss you every day until our reunion, if not on this side, then one day on the other. I have loved you more dearly than can be said in words. Your visit with me these past days has been one of the greatest joys of my life."

We wept once more in each other's arms, gathered ourselves and Mrs. Lowry patted my stomach gently once again.

"Take care of my baby. Write the moment you arrive. I will compose a return letter the very hour we receive a letter from you. We'll do everything we can, Cassie. I'll talk to Ben and give him the sketch book. He's a good boy and he'll do right by you. I know he will."

"I know he will, too," I said.

"I'll see that my son doesn't forget you, dear. Don't be surprised, young lady, if you look up one day and see Wilbur and me coming round the bend to see you in your new home out west. I love you dearly."

Mrs. Lowry gave Five Feathers and me a final embrace as we mounted the carryall. Dr. Thweatt made sure we were settled and gave the reins a twitch. The old mule nodded his head, gave a little snort and we were on our way with a clatter of hooves. I couldn't believe our time with Mrs. Lowry was over.

Dr. Thweatt turned the old mule's head towards Ross's Landing. I heard the crunch of the mule's shoes and the ring of the iron tires on the dry, hard-packed gravel roadbed.

The sound reverberated in the morning stillness against the wooden buildings.

A rooster crowed.

I waved to Mrs. Lowry until we turned the corner by the graveyard and she was lost to sight. I wish with all my heart she and I will meet again. I have left behind someone who loved me more than life itself. I have been blessed with a friendship few in this world enjoy—I am most grateful.

In the pre-dawn darkness of a Georgia Militia encampment near Ross's Landing, Ben felt a hand gently shaking his shoulder and a distant voice from above quietly calling him to consciousness. According to his own orders of the previous evening, Ben was awakened well before dawn. It was his servant, Caesar, above him. For a moment Ben didn't know where he was. As he lay in the dim light of Caesar's lantern, he suddenly remembered he was at the Georgia Militia encampment near Ross's Landing and had an exceptionally busy morning planned. It seemed in the last two months he had been in a different camp and a different bed every night. He had slept fitfully. As he swung his stocking feet to the canvas floor of the uncomfortable tent, he looked around, remembering he was at the foot of the ridge east of Ross's Landing. There was nowhere in this crowded encampment to find a place for rest—night or day. There was no end to the odd noises of men and beast that seemed to be amplified by the darkness. It would be good, very good, to get back to Milledgeville and quiet nights in his own bed in Huff's boarding house or better yet at the hotel with Elizabeth. As his servant helped him into his trousers, he thought how he would prefer to be at the hotel. He was impatient for this job he had taken with the government and this cursed removal to end. He mustn't torture himself and think of Elizabeth—of his Bethy. He had responsibilities.

Ben, dressed and ready to go, sat on the edge of his cot and sipped the refreshingly hot coffee put in his hand by his resourceful servant. They hadn't brought coffee. Supplies were scarce in this madhouse but Caesar was capable. He must remember to thank him. He probably had bought this with his own money or perhaps carefully borrowed it during the night.

Ben sipped and reflected how he had been working all over Cherokee Country to oversee the distribution of newly vacated Cherokee property. He had been dealing with fortunate drawers, surveyors, the ubiquitous ignorant and arrogant squatters and the seemingly inexhaustible supply of inexperienced officials in the new county seats that tested his patience at every turn. His was a confusing and complicated job. It seemed as if he was the only person who knew what to do. Everyone wanted his advice. His days were filled answering questions by inexperienced, near illiterate men deficient of the mental ability to find their way home much less to read and understand simple straightforward government documents.

As his servant helped him complete his toilet in the dim light, he reflected on his awkward visit with his mother the day previous. He shouldn't have gone. Visiting his parents was a mistake. His mother, prematurely grey, was a shell of her former self—barely able to care for his father. Ben was worried. His father, a complete invalid, was incapable of understanding the simplest instructions. Ben suggested once again to his mother that she should bring Father to Milledgeville. He would put her into proper accommodations with servants and perhaps they could find doctors who could help, but she point-blank refused. It was their duty to support the work at the mission, she insisted. So be it, Ben thought. He couldn't force his mother and father to do the right thing. If his mother insisted on continuing the sham of his father's pointless work, there was nothing he could do.

Ben's mind suddenly came back to the reason for his early call. He had received news that Cassie's detachment would be leaving this morning and he must see her off. How utterly inconvenient. His mother would never forgive him if he didn't say goodbye to Cassie. Saying farewell to Cassie was at the top of his list of unpleasant tasks in a job that had an endless series of disagreeable chores. He wished there was some way he could at least postpone seeing Cassie this morning. He threw the last of the coffee into the corner and handed the cup roughly to his servant. This was something he would just have to go and do. He might as well get this over with.

Ben washed in the small white porcelain washbasin, dampened and combed his hair in the scrap of a mirror attached to the wooden upright and tidied his clothing. He stood thinking as Caesar brushed his coat and helped him with his boots—boots Caesar kept shined to a mirror finish. He was expecting another extremely long hot miserable day. The god damned Indians continued to be a bother. He couldn't wait till they were gone and this was all over. For the thousandth time Ben thought how stupid and greedy the Cherokee were for trying to keep all this good land.

The hostler quietly held his mare as Ben swung his tall frame into the comfortable saddle in one effortless motion. At least his ride on his well-trained saddle horse was a welcome beginning to his dreadful day. His mare had become a friend—a silent friend and confidant who listened patiently, never criticized and instantly obeyed his every command. He could count on her to never ask difficult questions or second guess his orders. She would wait all day and never complain. As they rode along, she obeyed the slightest motion of the reins, pressure from his legs or even a shift in his weight. Ben smiled to himself. Riding his mare was the highlight of his job with the state of Georgia. What a strange thing to think of this morning.

The sun was still well below the horizon with just the faintest hint of lightness tinting the eastern sky behind the big ridge—the ridge running north and south everyone called the missionary ridge. Stars were twinkling. There wasn't a cloud to be seen in the morning sky. It would be another beautiful, cloudless day—hotter than hell.

Without thinking, he tugged at his tight collar remembering the heat and sweat of the day previous, wishing once again he didn't have to perform his first task in obedience to his mother's wishes.

685

He leaned slightly to the left and his mare obediently turned onto the road towards Ross's Landing and Cassie's departure point. As he slowly rode west, he noticed once again the low water level in the normally big, free-flowing Tennessee River. There was hardly any current. The big river that usually ran wide and deep and often flooded in late winter and spring. This summer it was the shallowest he or anyone had ever seen. The little creeks, tributaries and marshes in this area were all but dry. This would be a terrible year for farmers in the Tennessee Valley.

Head down, Ben's tall chestnut mare walked slowly towards Ross's Landing, her ears flicking occasionally left or right. Ben wasn't in a rush. He marveled how the once sleepy Cherokee outpost and ferry crossing he remembered as a child had exploded into a bustling center of activity—a veritable city. Ross's Landing had certainly changed.

When he was a boy this ferry crossing just upstream from the big moccasin bend was on the edge of nowhere. In the last two years Ross's Landing had magically mushroomed into a busy town and military center. He correctly reasoned it would soon blossom into an important city with its strategic location on an important navigable river joining Tennessee, Alabama and Georgia. There was no doubt this part of Cherokee Country had been coveted by the white population for quite some time. The government had recognized the importance of controlling the Tennessee River valley. Facilitating trade and commerce in the South made a necessity of removing the Cherokee. His father would have surely drawn the parallel of the white government's coveting of Cherokee land with that of King Ahab and Naboth's vineyard, but that was his father's view and this wasn't a Sunday morning sermon. Things change. The once tiny Cherokee trading post and ferry was this morning an all-white burgeoning town. The Cherokee right to possess land had been legally extinguished. They were a backward bunch, Ben thought. Everything that had been done with the Cherokee had been legal and aboveboard.

Ben halted on a rise. Below him a panoramic vision of the entire morning scene was unfolding. The vista spread out before him was magnificent. The morning sun was beginning to brighten the eastern sky behind him. The picturesque Tennessee River to his right was smooth as glass with a few small busy boats out on early errands.

The steamboat docks, with several big paddle wheel steamers with barges lashed to their sides, were quiet. The river level was far too low to allow for their passage. The two main prison camps, still obscured in the morning mist, lay below him and to his right towards the river. To his left up the hill and as far as he could see, were an endless sea of tents and hastily constructed, low-slung wooden structures occupied by the United States Army, various military units, militias, hundreds of contractors and their wagons, their animals and mounds of supplies stored wherever they could find shelter. Mixed among all that and on the periphery were hundreds of recently arrived civilians—mostly ne'er-do-well scavengers to Ben's mind.

Even the north side of the river, the old whiteside, had far more activity than he remembered. Columns of smoke were beginning to rise from hundreds of fires in every direction. They seemed to climb straight to heaven as if invisible chimneys were conducting the smoke skyward in perfectly transparent glass cylinders. The rising smoke in the still morning air gave the appearance of a giant forest of trees whose trunks reached to the stars. These fires would soon provide breakfast for some twenty thousand souls scattered as far as he could see. After the men were fed and watered, everyone would soon be out and about on the business of the day making Ross's Landing appear from his perspective on the crest of the hill like a gigantic disturbed anthill.

Ben continued to delay. As the summer sun rose, Ben's morning view was breathtaking. The human occupation displayed below him was like some detailed mural on a huge museum wall. Ben, unwilling to move on at the moment, sat still on his mare. He hooked his right knee around the saddle horn and lounged backward against the cantle observing the remarkable vista. His mare waited patiently. The eastern sky behind him began turning a brighter shade of pink.

Invisible below him were several thousand Cherokee under guard. He was told there were several thousand more at the Agency at Charleston along with a number of smaller Indian camps guarded by the militias. There were numerous encampments of the contractors. As far as he could see in every direction there were symmetrical groups of wagons laid out below him resembling the play toys of a giant children's game spread across an equally gigantic table top.

He had never seen so many wagons, horses, mules and oxen in one place in his life, not even in Milledgeville or Savannah. In addition, Ross's Landing had attracted hundreds of curious civilians anxious to benefit from Cherokee misfortune. It was more likely, Ben thought in a cynical moment, that the civilians would add to Cherokee misery. He mused how the government had quietly allowed looting, probably encouraging it if the truth be known, as a

687

means to ensure the Cherokee would have nothing to return to even if they were of a mind to escape and return to their homes.

In no hurry to meet Cassie, he continued to rest with his leg hooked around the saddle horn. Ben knew he would never see anything like this ever again. From his vantage point he could make out a dozen groups of fifty or sixty soldiers guarding Cherokee prisoners. Some Tennessee militia and some Georgia militia. All the North Carolina militia would be at the Agency and the Alabama militia would be down at Fort Payne, Gadsden and Guntersville. The United States Army dominated and seemed to be everywhere. According to what he had heard the night before, the military believed most of the Cherokee had been rounded up. Patrols would capture the stragglers easily. In a week or two there wouldn't be a single Cherokee family left anywhere. Georgia now shared a clean, unobstructed border with Tennessee, Alabama and North Carolina. He gave a wry smile thinking of the term—clean border. He wondered if folks ever thought about what had been cleaned away to facilitate the burgeoning interstate commerce and the rapid development of modern white agriculture. Very soon the backward Cherokee would be gone and the way would be cleared for a progressive culture and the continued explosive economic development of the United States.

Continuing to procrastinate, Ben braced his hands behind his back on the cantle. He would do anything to delay his visit with Cassie. He would sit here and enjoy the view as long as he could and make his inconvenient visit with her as brief as possible. He heard his black servant stir behind him on his mule but Caesar was of no concern. His slave could take care of himself—let him wait.

Tennessee and Georgia could now get on with the business of building a nation—a great nation of perfectly united states. Tennessee, Georgia, Alabama, North Carolina and South Carolina were now ethnically pure— quite an accomplishment for the last forty years. Those states were prepared, at the behest of the general government, to develop militias that would defend the gulf coast against foreign invasion.

While Ben was musing, the first ray of the morning sun cleared the eastern ridge and in that single brilliant moment illuminated the largest of the Cherokee prison camps in a sudden explosion of light. In a moment, the vista before him changed. The predawn mist cleared. It was like scales falling from the eyes of Saul of Tarsus—as if Ben were viewing the scene below through his father's eyes—eyes friendly towards the Cherokee.

Against his will, as Ben saw what his father had taught him to see—man's inhumanity to man. The last few miles of his morning's journey towards Cassie's detachment stretched out before him as clearly as if he were viewing a theater's well-lit stage from the front row. At the far end he could see the steamboats and their docks. Their smoke stacks quiet and unattended, reflecting brilliantly the sun's first rays. This side of the moored steamboats he saw Cassie's detachment being prepared to begin their eight-hundred-mile journey—humans and animals moving like tiny figures in a drawing.

Against his will Ben shivered. It was as if he had been given divine insight. Instead of witnessing the lofty development of a progressive white culture, it was as if he were viewing some macabre painting—a caricature portrayed in garish colors by the brush of a fiendish madman depicting scenes taken straight from Dante's circles of hell.

The scene below was the result of a disturbed underworld anthill—an evil subterranean realm belching depravity to the unsuspecting surface, spreading corruption over everything in sight—suffocating every living being in layer upon layer of iniquity. Ben saw men and animals wading through mountains of putrefying injustice. His mind recoiled.

It was as if Winfield Scott was directing a massive stage play written in hell and choreographed by Satan himself—a dramatic farce manipulating hordes of foul actors controlled by an insanity vomited from the pit, a production widely applauded, received with great acclaim by white audiences everywhere. The thought made him feel soiled and unclean.

"This isn't my fault," he said to himself. "I've nothing to do with this. I'm not responsible. If I had something to do with this mess, I would see they were treated better. I'm not responsible. None of this is my fault. This isn't my responsibility."

Ben looked away and tried to free his mind of unwanted images. He kicked his mare into a steady determined gait and rode down the hill to the staging area beside the river. He was determined to get this meeting with Cassie over and done with and get on with his business in Lafayette. He had no wish for further observations.

He was not looking forward to this meeting with Cassie. Her love for him, once joyous, he now found cloying, sticky, inconvenient—demanding. He needed to get back to Milledgeville as soon as he could and away from Ross's Landing, the removal and Cassie. He wished he were anywhere but here. Why did he take this job? It wasn't worth the money, at least not now. It would be nice to spend time at the hotel with Zach and Elizabeth when this was over.

He wished he were there now with Elizabeth, drink in hand. He must remind himself that his Senate appointment would make all this worthwhile. That was why he was doing this. He wondered how Zach and Elizabeth were progressing with their behind the scenes influence on his behalf for that coveted appointment?

As he neared Cassie's enclosure, he reminded himself he was laying the groundwork for the rest of his political career. He couldn't help it if she was Cherokee. The momentary discomforts the Cherokee were suffering had nothing to do with him. He would do what he could for her, but he couldn't spend time worrying. Events were beyond his control. In the back of his mind, in order to salve his conscience, he would take time off and make certain Cassie and her baby were taken care of. That thought relieved him of immediate responsibility. Maybe he would buy her a little house when she arrived in the west and provide her with a modest income. He could do that secretly. No one would know.

Ben, leaving his servant at the gate, was given permission to enter Cassie's camp, but he was cautioned the visit was to be limited to ten minutes. The Indians were being formed into a column and they were already late. Ben assured the officer he would be out of their way quickly.

The area where the Cherokee were imprisoned reeked of stale urine, uncovered feces and, even at this early hour of the day, was swarming with flies. Ben hated the god damned flies. They were breeding all around Ross's Landing in the mountains of manure produced by the thousands of draft animals. Flies buzzed on everything and everyone—another reason to get away from this place.

Near the entrance, Ben spotted a woman with a quilt draped over her shoulders—a quilt he recognized immediately as his mother's. The woman turned and looked towards Ben. It was Cassie. Late in her pregnancy, Cassie's face, normally healthy and brown, was gaunt and drawn. Her hair, usually bright and shining, was disheveled and dull. She carried herself with a stoop as if bearing a heavy load. Her expressionless face told the story. Her eyes, once filled with youthful dreams, were vacant dark holes void of emotion.

Ben was glad he had left his servant and accompanying guards at the entrance. He didn't want them to observe his meeting with Cassie. He didn't want anyone to see her pregnant and put two and two together.

17 June 1838 – Ross's Landing

Ben came to see me this morning after Dr. Thweatt returned us to our camp. I loved the sight of him walking towards me. I remember his smile, eyes, his shoulders, his powerful arms—I love everything about him. Ben will do good for us if he can. I know he will. It wasn't today, but one grand day he will come for me and his child and take us away. We will be together.

When I saw him I began to cry. I was so tired and frightened. To see his face gave me hope. I was hoping he had come to take us away.

I knew Ben was embarrassed of me because of his job. That didn't matter now. I don't care what Ben's job is. What is happening isn't Ben's fault. I'm sure he has done what he could. The only thing that matters in my exhausted mind is that Ben is actually standing before me. I could finally reach out and touch him, hold him and look at his face.

I am proud of Ben. I will never tell anyone Ben is the father of my child. I know it would not be good for his career if people knew he fathered a half-breed. Perhaps Ben and I shall be blessed with the happiness that is our destiny when we get out west.

When Ben thought about Cassie, he rationalized he could do a lot for her and the Cherokee at some future time, but not now. A United States Senator has wide-ranging power. With the help of Andrew Jackson and his progressive democratic party, he had an excellent chance to be appointed to the Senate. He could do anything he wanted for the Cherokee then. He could change the course of history. His Senate appointment seemed like a sure thing. Zach and Elizabeth had assured him of his success.

When Ben arrived he hesitated, took my hands and looked at me. I waited for the embrace that never came. I'm sure he didn't want to embarrass himself by showing affection.

"Cassie," Ben said lamely. "I'm so glad to see you. I talked to Mother yesterday and she told me you might be leaving this morning. I wanted to see you before you left. I've talked to the captain and he will personally make sure you are taken care of properly. He promised he would keep a special eye out for you. You can trust him, Cassie. He's a good man."

In that moment, my heart fell at my feet. My last hope was shattered. I am alone. Ben was not going to help us.

My heart turned to Five Feathers and our journey. My brother and I must somehow survive and rebuild our lives out west. We must survive without Ben's help.

There was another awkward pause as Ben and I stood motionless looking at one another. There was nothing to say, but even in my despair I was glad Ben was beside me. I knew he was uncomfortable and I understood. It would not be good if his superiors knew of his relationship with an Indian.

Ben's voice was wooden.

"I'll come to see you as soon as this is over, Cassie."

"I know."

"I'll see you are taken care of when I'm finished with my job with the state of Georgia. I promise."

"I know you will."

"In a few months I'll find you and your baby. If things go really well and I'm appointed to the Senate, I'll send for you and we will make a life in Washington City or somewhere you'll be welcome."

I wanted to believe Ben's words. I don't think he would intentionally lie to me. Ben, his hands holding my biceps under the pressure of the moment, was thoughtlessly exerting far too much force—bruising my arms with the pressure of his fingers.

I remembered the last time a man had bruised my biceps and I strangely felt that same humiliation. I had no words and no feeling left. I am mentally and emotionally fatigued—too exhausted to cry. Anything I might say to Ben at that moment would stick in my throat.

Ben realized he was hurting me and relaxed his grip.

"There's a lot of work for me now that the Cherokee are emigrating," he said.

"I know, Ben. I know you're busy."

"My staff and I are working night and day. This job will promote my career and my ability to help the Cherokee in the future. For the future good of the Cherokee, I need to do this, Cassie."

"I know you do, Ben."

"I took this job for the Cherokee. Really I did, Cassie. None of this is my fault. My entire career has been devoted to the Cherokee. You know that."

"I know you're not involved in the removal, Ben. I know that. I'm not angry. I'll never be angry with you."

Ben continued looking into my eyes persuading me of his good intentions. He reminded me of when he was a boy.

"If I go to Washington, I can mitigate some future injustice and help the Cherokee in the west. Someone must do this job and I would rather it be me

692

than someone who didn't care. There is much I can do in politics in the future."

"You'll be a good Senator."

"I will be. I promise."

He paused. I couldn't speak. I looked into his beautiful blue eyes—eyes I had loved since I was a girl. I felt a sorrow of heart to see the young man before me swept along in a direction opposite that which he had intended. As I looked into his face, I realized he believed his own words. He still had a measure of his youthful innocence. This beautiful June morning might be the last time I would see the man who would mean everything to me till my dying day.

"I wish you were going with us, Ben."

"I wish I could go, too"

I knew he was lying.

"The soldiers will allow you to come, but I know you can't. I know you have an important job. You can't abandon that. I wish you could come with us."

I paused again, never taking my eyes from Ben's face. He continued to hold my arms and I was overcome with the same loving emotion I had felt years ago when we sat by the riverbank and talked for hours and held one another. Irrationally, I loved him as dearly as ever—perhaps even more. There was nothing my mind could do to relieve the ache in my chest—an ache that would only be removed by my beloved. Love, I had learned, can't be controlled or extinguished. It can't be manufactured or denied by effort of will. Love isn't that simple. Love exists outside the control of the lover. Love cannot be created or destroyed by one's volition—no matter how intense. Human love exists independently of human decision. As hard as I might try, no rational thought of my mind could erase my love for this beautiful man.

"I will be thinking of you every day, Ben."

"I'll be thinking of you, too."

"I have never wanted anything but the best for you. Five Feathers and I will take care of our baby. Someday, Ben, when things are different, you and I shall be together. I have always known that you and I will be one. Your mother thinks so, too. If it's a boy, I'll name him after you. I hope he looks like you."

Ben smiled.

"You're sweet, Cassie. We'll be together one day. I promise."

Ben spoke the right words but without conviction.

Our arrest and deportation wasn't his fault. I knew that. I would gladly share the fate of my nation. That was as it should be. I was pregnant because I loved a man. I will have his baby and teach our child to love his father. That was as it should be, too. I wasn't angry with Ben.

"I will wish you well every morning when I rise and every night before I sleep," I said.

"I'll do the same, Cassie. One day we'll be together. I promise."

I looked up at the tall, handsome, well-dressed man before me. He was the picture of success.

"Ben, I am pleased you came."

"I'm glad I came, too," he said.

"I know you must go. Do you remember our promise about the moon?"

I could see he didn't remember.

I reminded him of our mutual promise, "The moon that shines over Georgia is a Cherokee moon. Remember our promise to one another when you went to Milledgeville?"

"I remember," Ben said.

"When you look up at our Cherokee moon," I said, "remember there is a woman who loves you looking at that same moon."

"I'll remember. I promise."

"Remember me and remember your baby when you see that moon."

Ben winced. There wasn't a day that went by when he didn't try to forget his indiscretion. A lapse in judgment committed on this very quilt draped about Cassie's shoulders. What was done, was done. He couldn't marry Cassie. Marriage to an Indian woman would ruin his career. The straightforward black and white morals he had been taught by his mother and father had little by little, without Ben realizing, turned to meaningless swirls of gloomy grey.

Cassie needed to find a Cherokee man. She should find the child a Cherokee father. He did not want the infant. The child should be raised by Indians, among Indians with an Indian family. That would be best—as it should be. It was best that Cassie was leaving Georgia and going west. That solved many problems. Cassie and the child would be happy. With her gone he could continue his career. Perhaps he and Elizabeth would find a life together in Washington. She would look grand on his arm.

Ben was determined to say something kind to Cassie and leave. He had been here long enough.

"I'll personally speak to the Captain about you and Five Feathers."

694

"Thank you, Ben."

"The captain is a good man. He'll listen to me. They've put a lot of work into this, Cassie. I know it doesn't look like it now, but the army is genuinely concerned for the Cherokee. If there are problems, the army will soon put them right."

"I hope so."

"Write when you arrive. When you're settled, send me your address."

"I'll write the moment I arrive," I said.

At least he was thinking of me in some way and I loved it, but Ben had changed. I sadly thought that there is none so pathetic as the man who believes his own lies. Perhaps one day he would see the truth.

Not for the last time Ben thought it a good thing for the Indians to be removed. True, there would be some discomfort in the removal, but out west Cassie, her baby and the Cherokee would have their own nation and be left alone by white men. The removal was in the Cherokee best interest. Georgia needed the new counties. Georgia needed space to grow. The Cherokee had to go. It was that simple. They were in the way.

A sergeant informed Ben it was time. He must go.

Ben looked down and pressed my hand.

"Goodbye, Cassie. I have always loved you. Write when you arrive."

With those words, he pressed my hand once again and turned away without an embrace or kiss and quickly strode towards the exit never once looking back.

I would never again see Ben, Mr. and Mrs. Lowry or my community. In a few moments young, white men speaking a European language will, at bayonet point, force us to an unknown future. The last act of the Cherokee tragedy is complete. The drama has ended. The stage is cleared. The curtain has fallen—the theatre emptied.

Chapter LV

1838 – Ben's Denial - Cassie Deported

Chapter 55

Ben, relieved to get away, strode toward the exit without a backward glance. He wanted out of that stinking place. He wanted to be as far from the sights, sounds and smells of Ross's Landing as he could. He would never come back. He couldn't wait to mount his horse and leave.

He felt as if he had done something wrong—terribly wrong, but in his heart he knew he was doing the best he could. What was he supposed to do? Every job had conflicts. He had been doing good work—very good work. On several occasions he had intervened with the authorities on behalf of the Cherokee, but there wasn't anything he or anyone could do to help the Cherokee Nation or Cassie. Everything was out of his hands. The benighted Cherokee had chosen to listen to Ross. They must bear the penalty of their foolish decision. Government warnings had been clear. If there was injustice in the camps, it had nothing to do with him or even the government. The Cherokee had brought this unpleasantness upon themselves. Their misery was self inflicted. The army was doing the best they could with the hardheaded, backward Cherokee. They had been warned—well warned. What was happening was not the result of anything he had done or not done. He shouldn't feel bad, but he did.

Ben, walking with long strides and with head down, saw nothing and was trying not to think. He wanted to get onto the road to Lafayette and into the fresh air of the quiet countryside as rapidly as possible. He badly wanted this day to be over. He wanted to get away from the river and the raucous confusion that reigned all about him. He wanted to be back in familiar surroundings. What he wouldn't give at this moment for a quiet drink with Zach and Elizabeth, but he mustn't think about Elizabeth. It wouldn't do to think about Elizabeth. That would be torture.

He felt sick to his stomach. His next appointment that afternoon was in the new county seat of Walker County—just a nice ride south. He couldn't get there fast enough. He couldn't wait to get to a place where the Cherokee had been removed—completely removed. He didn't want to see another

Indian for a long time. It would be a lovely ride through Walker County if he could ever get out of this damn camp and into the saddle.

As Ben reached the exit, one of the young Georgia soldiers recognized him. The sentinel gave Ben a long look. Ben was quite a curiosity. His fine clothes and expensive boots were out of place in the midst of the removal at Ross's Landing.

The young soldier spoke in a loud voice.

"I know who you are. I seen you in New Echota. You're that Indian lovin' lawyer from Milledgeville, aren't you?"

Without breaking stride, looking up or thinking, Ben shot his answer back in a brittle, impatient voice.

"You're mistaken. I'm not that man. You've got me confused with someone else."

Ben had no interest in pausing for conversation with anyone, much less someone who may have known of his past relationship with the Cherokee or with Cassie. Increasing his pace with his accompanying three guards and his servant, Ben turned left and continued the short distance up the hill to the enclosure where his horse was being held. Ben couldn't wait to feel the familiar comfort of the smooth polished leather of his comfortable saddle, the reassuring rhythm of hoofbeats and the power of a highly-trained animal under him—an experience that always brought a heightened sense of tranquility—of purpose—of normality. He wanted to be part of the serenity of the countryside. He wanted to inhale the pleasant smells of honeysuckle instead of stale urine, manure and unwashed bodies. He wanted to be away from the river—far, far away from the river.

Ben found it impossible to raise his eyes from the path. He had seen enough to last him the rest of his life. He didn't want to see anything else. He wanted no more haunting visual memories. There was nothing he could do for anyone here and no reason whatsoever for a backward glance. Everything behind him was just where he wanted it—behind him forever. Just like his employer, he wanted to extinguish the problems of the Cherokee—all of their problems. He wanted them gone, vanished and forgotten out west. When the Cherokee were gone his problems would disappear. He could finish his job in peace, his mind could rest and he could get on with his career.

Another soldier leading an especially handsome brace of coal black matched mules in full harness approached Ben. The mules, with the double tree hanging from the harness and trace chains jangling, came down the hill to join the detachment behind him to be hitched to some contractor's wagon

697

for the journey west. Ben stepped aside to let the young man and his mules pass.

As the man passed Ben, he took note of the well-dressed man so out of place.

The young teamster spoke loudly.

"I know you. Your parents were missionaries down in Cherokee Country—down at New Echota. I seen you down there."

Ben wasn't paying attention.

"You're the one with that good lookin' Indian girlfriend, aren't you? What ever happened to her?"

The young teamster laughed.

Ben couldn't get away fast enough.

"She had that baby yet?"

The driver laughed again as Ben passed. Everyone had heard the loud voice of the driver and was watching Ben to see his reaction.

For a second time, and with an even louder voice, Ben denied the teamster's accusations.

"No, that wasn't me. You're confused."

Ben continued, "I'm not that man. That wasn't me. I tell you I'm not that man."

With that encounter Ben descended into an even darker mood with an even blacker scowl. He felt like an animal being pursued—like a coon being chased by a pack of hounds. He didn't like that metaphor. A coon would soon be up a tree and unable to escape—trapped and treed and have his hide tacked to the barn wall. He didn't like that thought, but that's exactly how he felt— as if he were being pursued with no means of escape. All he wanted was to get away—to flee—to be alone. With the crowd around him it seemed he was making no progress whatsoever to get back to his horse and make his escape.

None of this was fair. This was so unpleasant. He had thought his long-time relationship with Cassie would be unknown at Ross's Landing. He wanted his past to be forgotten.

In just the few moments since he had left Cassie he had encountered two impertinent men who knew who he was, knew his family, his father and his relationship with Cassie in New Echota. Ben was in a near panic to mount his horse and forget what was happening—to avoid forever all contact with anyone at Ross's Landing. He wanted to be anywhere except here. If he could just get away from this place quickly, the soldiers would forget him. He would once again become the anonymous, faceless employee of the state of

Georgia—an unidentifiable, unnamed man doing his job in the shadows—just the kind of job he wanted.

Immediately to Ben's right, up the hill a short distance from where Cassie's detachment was being prepared for departure, was a small white tent. Under the tent was a small table with a stack of neat papers and a couple of Georgia militia standing a lazy guard. Behind the tiny table was a well-dressed jovial official with a big black handlebar. The dapper man, like Ben, was over-dressed with black boots shined to a mirror finish and a high white starched collar. The little sign on one of the posts of the tent read, 'Fortunate Drawers Here—State of Georgia'.

With permission of General Scott, Ben had ordered this tent at this location. General Scott had been ordered to cooperate with the governors of the surrounding states. Thus, Ben was allowed the table for men coming down the river and surrounding area who wanted to take possession of their lottery winnings within the chartered boundaries of Georgia. The smiling dandy with the handlebar worked for Ben. On Ben's orders, scores of these Lottery Tents were manned throughout newly vacated Cherokee Country in the new counties and would be there for the next few weeks—maybe longer. They were needed to accommodate the flood of men rushing into the land vacuum created by the Cherokee's sudden emigration. The tents provided necessary information to the lottery winners and those who had legitimately purchased Cherokee land from them. Everyone needed to know how to register their new deed at the new courthouses.

Ben heard the man behind the small portable desk singing the old song,
> 'All I ask in this creation,
> is a pretty little wife and a big plantation,
> way up yonder in the Cherokee Nation.'

In apparent obedience to the old song, thousands of white men were hurrying to occupy the newly abandoned Cherokee lands they had acquired in the lottery. Others were hoping to avoid the courthouses and squat on unoccupied, unclaimed land. Everything was fee simple. Each new courthouse in all the new counties was a beehive of activity daylight to dark. It was important to the Georgia government, and thus Ben, to act swiftly to control this undisciplined flood of humanity. The legitimate landowners must be helped to occupy their legal landholding as quickly as possible. The Georgia economy would get a huge boost from the settlement of this land. There were profits to be made by those smart enough to take advantage of the forced Cherokee exodus.

699

In no time at all the Cherokee and the military would be gone. Law and order must be maintained in their absence. That was the purpose of organizing the counties. It was still early enough in the year to get some crops in—especially the crops left in the many fields planted earlier by the industrious Cherokee—fields now abandoned and badly in need of attention.

Ben's job was distasteful but it was a clear path to advancement and a Senate appointment. With a successful conclusion, he would win even more friends in Georgia and Washington. According to Zach, his success was inevitable, but that's the way it is in all aspects of life when one works hard, Ben thought. A rising tide lifts all boats, he had been reminded often.

As Ben walked past the lottery tent, he continued to fume with impatience. He felt as if he would burst if he couldn't get away immediately. Each delay was maddening. He needed to get on the road away from the sights and sounds of the mass of humanity being herded west from Ross's Landing.

Because of the congestion and the activity of the departing detachment, Ben, in his haste, had progressed only yards from the entrance to Cassie's camp. He nodded to the man with the handlebar under the little white tent and continued towards the nearby enclosure where their horses were being held. The Georgia militia stable was hard by the fortunate drawers' tent. He was almost there. Ben gave a welcome sigh of relief as he took his reins from the hostler. His mare stood patiently as he mounted. Instantly, as Ben swung his leg over the saddle and settled in, he felt a sense of security. The hostler led Ben's horse through the crowd by the stable towards an unobstructed path up the hill to the main road south and out of the melee. Ben's escort and servant would follow.

Another teamster assigned to the removal was noisily leading a fresh pair of draft horses in full harness down the hill.

He called to Ben in an extra loud voice, "I know you."

The young teamster shouted up at Ben humorously, "I know you. You're that damned Cherokee lawyer. We sent your father to prison for helping the Indians."

Ben was trying to ignore what the young man was saying.

"You're the one with that pregnant squaw woman," the teamster continued.

Ben was sitting in the saddle high above the crowd around him. Everyone around and in the fortunate drawer's tent heard the driver's words and turned to watch and listen to Ben's response.

700

The teamster's remarks touched Ben's last nerve. He lost all control. This was too much. It wasn't fair. Why should he be singled out for anything? He wasn't guilty of anything. He was doing his job and he was doing a good job. He always did a good job. This was unfair. He should have ignored his mother and not said goodbye to Cassie. It was a mistake to come to the river this morning of all mornings. Ben had been tense for days with the pressure of his job, his visit with his mother and father and this visit with Cassie this morning. He was always moody after seeing his father's condition. He was wound tighter than an eight-day clock.

This morning saw a climax of ramped-up tension that exploded like madness personified. This unexpected third accusation, coming hot on the heels of the first two, struck his every exposed nerve worn raw by weeks of repressed tension and worry exacerbated by his forced visit with Cassie. Ben's persecuted mind shattered in a sudden vicious release of tormented fury. For the first time in his life, Ben lost all restraint and discipline. He exploded. With his hands and body shaking with the unexpected intense emotion, he stood in the stirrups, leaned towards the young teamster's face below him and shouted his childish tantrum at the top of his voice. Ben's facial muscles contorted into a cruel mask as he bellowed at the young soldier, only yards away. For the third time Ben denied knowing anything about Cassie or any association with the Cherokee.

"God-damn it to hell you son-of-a-bitch. Just shut up," Ben screamed, standing in his stirrups. "Why don't you just shut up and leave me alone."

Ben's voice got louder.

"I'm not the man. Don't you understand? I-am-not-that-man."

As Ben shouted his denial, everyone turned to watch as if Ben were providing entertainment.

"I don't know what you're talking about," Ben continued in an uncontrolled shriek. "Shut your god-damned mouth. I-am-not-the-man."

Ben was drained. He was weary of the unfair questions. Why couldn't they leave him alone. His outburst was a surprise, even to himself, but he was now drained of mental energy. He felt as if something wicked was pursuing him as he sought his escape from this damned river of human misery in which he was required to wade. He was fatigued. He felt trapped. The soldier deserved the harsh words and more besides.

Ben's third denial and bellowing oath reverberated off the temporary wooden structures on the hill above Ben. His shouts of denial echoed back over Cassie's detachment and even as far as the river bank below. Everyone heard his frenzied explosion of angry words. In curiosity, onlookers, guards, soldiers and Cherokee alike turned to see this angry, well-dressed man shouting crude obscenities at the top of his lungs. Obscenities weren't unusual—delivering obscenities while being well-dressed was.

Ben was embarrassed. For the first time since he had walked away from Cassie, Ben looked back. He saw Cassie looking straight up the hill at him. Their eyes met. She had heard him clearly—every word. Everyone had heard him. Her upturned face wore no expression. She held Ben's gaze for a moment. Ben watched as she turned away leaning against her brother's shoulder.

After weeks of imprisonment, deprivation and fear, Cassie had no reservoir of strength. She was used up. Ben's shouts of denial were the culminating blow. Ben's shouted words had taken from her the very last thing she possessed. She collapsed into her brother's arms just as the soldiers gave their final order for the detachment to begin their westward journey.

The meeting with Cassie, their awkward goodbye and his denials were too much, even for Ben. He felt the callousness of his outburst swell his chest to the bursting point as his horse walked up the hill towards the road that led south away from Ross's Landing past the old Cherokee post office and settlement where Chief Ross had his home. The old road that continued straight down into Walker County and the new county seat at Lafayette. He felt as if he would cry, but it was over and done with now. He felt relief. He had other things to think about. He must think about something else and not about Cassie. He shouldn't have shouted those words. It was unfortunate if she had heard him, but none of this was his fault. Even his shouts were not his fault. He was to blame for nothing. He had a lot of work to do before his return to Milledgeville, and then his election campaign and, hopefully, it would be on to Washington City and his new Senate appointment. He needed to think about that. Zach had taught him to have a thick skin when it came to his political critics and hateful criticism. Zach had taught him to think of criticism dispassionately, like water off a duck's back. He would think about Cassie and her reaction to his words another time. He knew it had been a bad idea to say goodbye to Cassie. He should not have come, but none of this was his fault.

17 June 1838 – First day on the trail west

Immediately after Ben's visit, the soldiers completed the formation of our detachment. We shall be deported but at least on the road we will escape the filth and vermin. I have never felt so unclean. I feel sorrow for the people to be brought in after us.

Our first day is done. I'm exhausted. We walked all day—morning till evening. Where will this end?

I hope someone preserves this journal. I hope they tell our story. Perhaps the whites who move into our country will learn how we were moved out for their convenience and remember us.

Many children unwell.

Five Feathers helped with the burials. He is the strongest of the men—he doesn't mind digging.

Buried Corn Tassel's child. Buried Flax Bird. Buried White Bird.

18 June 1838 – Second day on the trail

Our second day is complete. Elisi and edudu are gone. Mr. and Mrs. Lowry are silenced. I have seen my Ben for the last time. I am ready to go anywhere. It doesn't matter where they take us. My baby, my brother and I shall have a new home somewhere. We shall survive. I am determined to live.

I am glad the river is too low for steamboats. I had rather walk. I remember edudu's frightening stories of the Suck, Boiling Pot and Skillet and the dangerous Muscle Shoals below the Moccasin Bend. If I'm going to die, I had rather lie down under a tree. I do not want to choke to death on water. Whatever will be, will be. Perhaps as we travel we can somehow clean ourselves properly and be rid of the incessantly biting vermin that infest our bedding and clothing. I have never felt so unclean.

Our parade has been eerily silent. No one waves us goodbye. There are no conversations or happy calls from children. It is curious to observe the young, healthy, tall white soldiers—all wearing sturdy boots.

We are dark, with black hair and not one of our men has whiskers. As we walk I hear the same never ending sounds—the iron wheels, the horse's hooves, the clinking of trace chains and the creaking of the wagons. The birds remind me of home. What birds will we find out west?

Our journey will be eighty days but already the wagons are filled with sick and elderly. Many have no shoes. Some carry burdens. How will this end? Where will it end? Will we be transported to a land of perpetual twilight with no sun or moon—a land deserted by animals where justice has been suspended, where time no longer exists, conveniently outside the white consciousness?

It was a long, hot, miserable day. My feet hurt and my back aches.

Buried Big Field's child. Buried old Chesnut. Buried Four Killer's child.

19 June 1838 – Third day on the trail

Five Feathers and I help our white doctor. We have no infirmary and almost no medicines. We translate. The doctor's expertise is animal husbandry—an appropriate choice by the government since they think of us as animals. How much help will he be to eight hundred of us and most of us afraid of a white face? He has no cure for lice. My neck and torso are covered in welts. Since our arrest none have changed clothing or washed properly.
Buried Grass Hopper's child. Buried Johnson.

20 June 1838 – Fourth day on the trail

We try to help the sick but most choose to bear illness quietly rather than suffer the indignity of treatment by a white doctor who evidently brought an ample supply of whiskey. His inattention doesn't matter. We Cherokee are practiced in dying without complaint.

Soldiers understand the importance of taking care of their live stock. The army frequently stops to rest the draft animals. All the soldier's horses have shoes. Many of us do not.
No burials today.

21 June 1838 – Fifth day on the trail

Yesterday was the midsummer solstice. It's the day in Latin the sun stops, and an evil omen for our nation. Perhaps our days this year will get shorter and shorter until we have no day. Perhaps in the land where they take us we shall exist in the eternal darkness of the damned—thrust there forever by those who despise us.

I cannot forget Ben's denial, but I forgive him. He, like us, is afraid. He fears his friends. In his heart he is a good man—a very good man. When this is over he will come. I want him. I need him. I believe in Ben. In his better moments, when this madness has passed, he will do what is right and choose his baby. What joy to see him hold our child.
I am weary.
Buried Nancy's oldest child. Buried old Otiah. Buried Smith's child.

22 June 1838 – Sixth day

This morning we left behind three mounds of fresh turned earth that will disappear after the first rain. Their travail has ended. Today they shall rest. They shall weep no more. They have been vanished.

We have left a trail of fresh turned earth—a sorrowful trail watered by our tears. If you want to find us, follow our trail of tears.

I passed an old woman I knew from New Echota sitting alone in the dry, dusty grass beside the road. She held her old grey head in her withered hands. We stopped to assist. A soldier ordered us to keep going. When we stopped for the night I checked the trailing wagons. The old woman was nowhere to be found.

Buried another of Nancy's children. Buried Tallassah. Buried Mary.

23 June 1838 – Seventh day

Another hot day. The birds sang to us this morning. I am tired.

The soldiers caught my brother returning from hunting. They tied him to a wagon wheel and horsewhipped him. He was told not to leave the column or he would get worse. He didn't make a sound during his punishment.

Five Feathers helped dig this evening.

Buried Anderson's child. Buried The Goose's wife and her stillborn child. Buried old Standing Turkey.

24 June 1838 – Eighth day

This afternoon twenty Cherokee joined us who had escaped a previous detachment. They said their group was famished. During one period they had nothing to eat for two days. They told of an old woman too weak to walk down the hill to board the ferry. A soldier kicked her onto the ferry boat. After they landed on the other side, she was never seen. They said their old women cried like children as they were driven west.

Buried Tobacco John's wife. Buried Nancy's youngest daughter. Buried Young Duck.

Chapter LVI

1838 – Five Feathers Hunts Again - Whippoorwill

Chapter 56

25 June 1838 – Evening – Ninth day on our trail west

I am determined. We shall not be erased. Our nation shall not be obliterated by unbridled white avidity. We will endure. I have no idea of our destination, but I will not let them decide our future. My brother and I will rise above this.

Moses and Sally, an elderly brother and sister from New Echota, both died today one after the other. I watched Five Feathers shovel soil onto the bark covering their faces. Buried Hopkins' youngest child.

26 June 1838 – Tenth day on the trail. The Green Corn Moon - De ha lu yi

The celebration of our Green Corn Moon should be the happiest of times. Our celebrations, dances, ballplays and story-telling are memories this year—memories that come from another lifetime.

I am too tired to write. Ben's baby lies heavy within me. No one mentions the past happiness of our festivals. I wish I was home. Five Feathers continues by my side every step. He never leaves me. He will be chief after we arrive in the west. He is strong—strong and tireless and always helping with the children. I don't know how he manages to stay so strong on such poor fare.

Every morning I have nausea. When we arrive and are free, I promise the morning star I will never eat salt pork again. I won't allow it in my house.

The soldiers have tents and a cook. We sleep on the ground and our food is terrible—our water filthy. If General Scott were here, would he describe our experience as comfortable?

Five Feathers buried Falling Blossom's new baby that came early.

27 June 1838 – Eleventh Day on the journey west.

The older ones never complain. They wait for whatever comes, good or ill.

Agents told us we would be given credit for everything we leave behind, or like will be replaced with like. I'm sure they will keep their word just as they kept their word with all the past agreements. If we make it with our lives, I shall be pleased.

The soldiers stopped early today to shoe. When I watched the farriers, I thought of Ben.

I'm tired. The extra rest time is welcome. There is a stream close by. I want to bathe.

Buried another of Nancy's children. Buried July. Buried Tusla.

28 June 1838 – Twelfth day on the journey

Last night as I slept, I was transported in my dreams to elisi's porch and a Cherokee sky filled with stars. Like an old dear friend from long ago, the soft summer night welcomed me with open arms and we embraced.

As I sat on our familiar porch, I smelled once again the soft nighttime fragrance of the honeysuckle. The velvety night caressed my face whispering love into my ear.

From out of the darkness my dear friend, the whippoorwill, welcomed me home with his friendly call—his lonesome call—his glorious call that fills me with joy as I write about it. We talked. I told him how happy I was to be back home. He told me of the lonesome days since I had gone. I promised I would never leave again. He was overjoyed. To celebrate my return and our friendship he shared a poem he had written just for me. He gave me his gift to comfort me in my loneliness, so far from home. In my dream, his words echoed from the forest surround. His magical voice flew straight into my soul and resides there still—the gift of the whippoorwill.

I awoke in the darkness. The dream had flown. I was no longer in my childhood home but a prisoner lying on the hard ground under a foreign sky, but the gift I was given remained.

Immediately I found my pen. In our silent camp in the midnight blackness the gift of the whippoorwill continued to echo clearly in my mind. I remember every word lovingly spoken to me by my old friend as if his words were engraved on a stone monument. His song celebrates my childhood, reminds me of home and our nation. He reminds me of everything good and right—of all the lovely things I can't now see but things that shall always be—whether I see them or not.

The stars were bright in a cloudless sky as I rose. The soldiers on night guard paid me no mind. The moon had set. By the golden light of the last embers of the dying fire, I wrote the words my nocturnal visitor sang just for me. I wish to have that vision every night. Mr. and Mrs. Lowry would love this poem.

Whippoorwill

I hear your call in the lonely night,
From seasons long past,
You fetch me home on your glorious cry,
Whip-poor-will
I heard you bid me in the night,
Wake me from my sleep,
Calling me to renew our friendship,
I come to your cry,
Your call clear and bright,
Whip-poor-will
From the shadows you invite,
Out of cool summer's mist,
From the warm silence of deep night,
From beside the river we love,
Deep and wide—our ancient home,
Whip-poor-will
All is still but you and me,
Sing to me your song of home,
Your call comes on invisible wings,
Clear as I listen under the stars,
Your dark forest surrounds cozy and safe,
Whip-poor-will
What say you this night?
All is well with you and me?
You invite me to your tour,
To join your pleasant walk,
Whip-poor-will
You call me home,
To all that's good and right,
You call me to childhood,
To my protection once again,
Even in darkness with no light,
I am secure in your night,
Whip-poor-will
Nothing shall harm in your place,
Your voice not forlorn,
Time is yours this friendly night,
Naught is lost,
Your call restores that which vanished,

Whip-poor-will
You guard the night,
You guard my soul,
You are my light,
My gentle bed,
Whip-poor-will
You and owl stand sentinel,
We cavort till dawn,
You are my nightly joy,
Spellbound I listen to your call,
Whip-poor-will
Shall you come again another lonely night,
To grace my dream?
Will you bring my childhood,
Once again on tiny wings?
Whip-poor-will
Shall I hear your voice once more?
Will you bring back that which is lost?
Will I see you once again,
And hear your lonesome call?
Whip-poor-will

Today was difficult—overly tiring. I was near collapse when we were allowed to stop by a flowing stream. The soldiers are tired. My baby is active. I want to lie down. I am drained, weary. I don't want food.

My brother and I observed a soldier shouting at an old woman who did not understand the soldier's commands. My brother held his temper. He knows he is my child's only hope. I need him desperately. I fear one day he will become angry and a soldier will kill him. Five Feathers is not afraid to die. Perhaps it would be best for a man like my brother to die defending his people. I would not be ashamed of him if he died fighting—if he died in a valiant moment of honor, but I want him to help me with my baby and help us on this long journey. In English, I heard a woman ask a soldier, "Why do you do this?" The soldier laughed in return. He spat his words back the way a snake spits venom, "Because we can."

Buried Amachanah. Buried Denis Woff's child. Buried the child born untimely to Ahyoka. She did not bring happiness.

29 June 1838 – Day thirteen of our journey

I feel a weariness deep in my bones. I want to write, but I have no strength. My baby is growing. It is difficult to walk. I move slowly. Will we walk forever? The white soldiers have no sympathy for their enemy.

I have nothing good to write. There is no joy among us. Whites now possess what they longed for. They live in houses we built and work fields we cleared and planted. Will a lonely white girl find my special place beside the river? Will my old friend the whippoorwill sing for her? The world will not miss us. No one will remember. We have been erased. Our vanishment is complete.

Buried old Dirt Thrower. Buried Feather's wife.

30 June 1838 – Day fourteen of our journey west

We stopped early today beside a rock filled flowing stream. The happy water is welcome. The soldiers are tired. We are exhausted. I miss home. I miss all my friends and our river. We must prepare to begin a new life. Will there be a river?

My time is approaching. I wonder if Ben knows his baby will be born under a wagon or beside the road or under a tree—to be reared in a strange land? I pray our child will come into the world and have a good life. I want the child to look like his father. I hope Ben finds us.

I will send him a lock of his baby's hair. As he reads the description of his baby, his love will rekindle. Ben will come. I know he will come. He is a good man in his heart—a very good man. One day I will look to the horizon and see him coming to me. I know he will come.

My ankles are swollen. My back aches. Maybe there will be no mosquitoes tonight. I smile. Every spring edudu put out the martin gourds. I am glad my brother helps. I could not make another day without him.

I think every day of our story, of our old newspaper and of New Echota. Perhaps the story of us Cherokee will not be lost. Perhaps Mr. Lowry was right and perhaps my story will be read one day.

Buried Sarah Raincrow. Buried McDonald's youngest child, Sinda.

1 July 1838 – Day fifteen of our journey west

Unobserved, we walk. No one sees us weep. We make one more day. We bury our dead. To find us, you need only to follow the trail of fresh turned earth. Follow our trail of tears.

No fresh water today. We drank stale tepid water from dirty containers—the same containers we share with the animals.

I am unwell. My brother and I walked together. Sometimes I'm so weak he almost carries me. Without his support I would go bouncing in a wagon and surely die with the rest. I watch the children with their mothers. They do not know they are prisoners. They do not know they have no future. I wish I was a child. My only desire is to see my child walking with them. I watched Five Feathers carry a tired child on his shoulders. As he walks along, I watch him play with the children, diverting their minds—teaching them about the birds, trees and animals. Five Feathers will be a good chief.

My brother watches over me. Even without proper food, my brother is strong and still the most handsome man I have ever seen, except for Ben. When I behold my brother, I have faith our nation will survive—be renewed.

I want us to make it successfully to the land we have been so kindly given. I want to wake and find the soldiers gone. I want to see my brother holding my baby.

We survive on corn cakes. Every morning I am sick. Since the day I conceived, the smell of pork as it cooks makes me ill. Sometimes all I eat is a bit of cornbread. I need to eat for my baby. I'm doing the best I can. Our baby will come soon. I am joyous. At last I will be a mother.

No burials today.

2 July 1838 – Day sixteen of our journey west

Today was hot and our trail long. I'm exhausted. We camped early by a welcoming stream. It is an oasis. The little creek, shaded by tall trees on both sides, is filled with smooth stones with the languid water running from one puddle to another. The children immediately began jumping from stone to stone playing games, shouting and laughing. The water was no more than knee deep anywhere. Watching the children play games in the water in the cool of the afternoon is the most pleasant sight I have seen since our arrest. We are blessed to have the innocence of children among us. I want to see my child join their games. I must become more like children.

I sat on a stone beside the water. I stretched my legs before me, resting my swollen feet in the cool water listening to the enchanting sounds of the river as it ambled over and around the smooth rocks. Everyone's mood is lighter. Even in our distress, a serenity has fallen upon us. Tonight I shall sleep next to this bubbling creek. I shall close my eyes and listen as it sings its gentle lullabies throughout the dark night. I am exhausted, but the thought of the clean, fresh water invigorates my soul. I am giddy with the thought of washing my clothes and body—to feel my skin clean and my hair fresh after the heat and sweat of the past days and escape from the vermin. Under the stars I will make my bed beside the mellow course. I can almost forgive the soldiers for bringing us to this marvelous place. I wish we could stay.

Hunting is forbidden, but occasionally my brother sneaks away and brings back a turkey or rabbit. Sometimes he slips away at night and returns with a chicken. When the soldiers catch a man hunting, they whip him mercilessly as if he were a disobedient African. We are ordered to stay away from whites and their property. We are forbidden to hunt.

My brother saw rabbit signs this morning. No white farms are near. He said he would bring me a rabbit or turkey. I won't have to eat salt pork this evening. I would love fresh sweet meat with no salt.

My brother can escape from the soldiers any time. He could easily make his way westward and be free, but he chooses to stay with me and my child. He promised to care for me and my baby. My brother always keeps his promise—unlike whites.

Walking with our detachment is torture for him. I see him look longingly towards the forests as we pass and feel his yearning to roam.

The soldiers took our guns, bows and knives, but Five Feathers, like most of our men, can bring down a rabbit or turkey with his leather sling. Our men played a game of accuracy with their slings and a wooden disc. Someone would swiftly roll the wooden disc through an open area. The men would compete to see who could hit it with a stone from their sling. My brother was always the best.

All morning my brother searched for smooth stones for hunting. When the soldiers were out of sight, he kissed my forehead and told me he would bring a fat rabbit for my dinner. I felt our spirits unite as I watched him disappear silently into the underbrush. I could feel my heart roam in his freedom.

The baby feels heavy. Will my time be soon? I miss elisi. She would know what to do to make certain my baby is healthy. I want Five Feathers to come back early tonight.

Five Feathers, reveling in his temporary freedom, quickly discovered rabbit signs and soon had two fat rabbits tied to his belt. He was enjoying the silence of the cool shade under the forest's dense summertime canopy and the simple ability to go where he pleased instead of where he was told.

He would walk a mile or two more under the fluffy early afternoon clouds, enjoy his freedom and slip back into the column unobserved and prepare the rabbits for his sister's evening meal. On this pleasant day, there was no need to do anything except enjoy the forest and his momentary freedom. For a few moments at least, life was good for this tall, handsome Cherokee man.

Five Feathers discovered a dry creek bed running parallel to the road. During the rainy season the little creek would be a mad, tumbling, noisy stream impossible to cross, but today, after weeks of bone dry weather, there was no water flowing—none at all. The remaining water in the narrow creek bed had gathered into occasional shallow stagnant puddles filled with happy tadpoles and delicate water spiders skating merrily on the glassy surface. Big flat stones filled the creek bottom as if someone had conveniently placed them to allow Five Feathers to walk effortlessly from stone to stone.

Walking on the flat stones of the creek bed meant he could avoid the thick underbrush and stay out of the tangle of laurels and travel unobserved. The dark green laurels on both banks were woven closely. Their thick foliage provided perfect cover for anyone in the creek bed not wanting to be seen. It was as if Five Feathers were walking down his own private hallway in his own paradise with solid green walls.

A sudden noise behind caused Five Feathers to stop instantly and turn. A short distance behind him were two armed hunters, both white. They had stepped into the creek bed with their long guns raised. They shouted for Five Feathers to halt. The men, less than a bow shot away, shouted once again ordering Five Feathers to stand. Five Feathers was not going to be detained by two clumsy white hunters. He saw an opening in the laurels to his left and instantly leapt like a mountain lion.

Five Feathers remembered the last time a white man wanted to steal his game and these men would not have the rabbits intended for his sister. With a powerful athletic move, Five Feathers leapt upward and sideways for a small opening at the bottom of the solid wall of laurels lining the creekbank. If he could reach the opening and escape the first salvo the men fired, he could slither through the base of the laurels and easily escape the pursuit of these slow, clumsy men.

The moment Five Feathers jumped, both men fired. These weapons weren't the inaccurate smooth bore muskets Five Feathers was accustomed to. These were rifles that made the lead bullet spin and hold its intended line with uncanny accuracy.

In the middle of Five Feathers' leap, a single bullet struck his back. The large caliber lead bullet passed through the upper part of his chest just under his right shoulder slamming Five Feathers' body down against the bare soil of the creekbank just short of the opening and his intended escape under the laurels. Unable to move, and bleeding profusely from the exit wound in his upper chest, Five Feathers lay still against the creekbank. His head and neck were lying at an awkward angle to his body, his left cheek pressed against the cool, damp earth and his left arm extended above his head as if he were reaching for a handhold.

Before the dense cloud of gun smoke obscured the men's vision, they saw the Cherokee man fall. Terrified of a counter attack, the two hunters knelt on the smooth stones in the middle of the dry creekbed and frantically reloaded their weapons.

When the smoke cleared, the nervous men, their reloaded rifles at the ready, saw the wounded Cherokee man lying face down perfectly still with his right arm at his side, palm open, and his left arm extended above his head. He was motionless and probably wounded.

As the two men slowly and carefully neared, a small rivulet of blood ran from under the Indian down the near-vertical creekbank turning the small stagnant puddle below a bright pink.

The nervous men approached cautiously one step at a time—rifles ready. Five Feathers was lying awkwardly. He had not moved since he fell. As the two men reached the wounded Indian, they saw the location of the entrance wound, a round, black hole in the back of the Cherokee's leather shirt.

The first man to approach the prone form of Five Feathers leaned forward and carefully examined Five Feather's back.

"Hank," the first man said, "that was a good shot. This 'un ain't goin' nowhere in a hurry. You got him good, didn't you?"

His companion answered, "That was some good shootin', wasn't it?"

"Watch him, Hank," the first man said again. "Don't take your eye off him and keep your finger on the trigger. He may be playin' possum. I don't trust these god damned Indians."

Both men, chewing tobacco and standing within a yard of Five Feathers, spat on the unconscious man's back. The brown spittle ran down Five Feathers' leather shirt and dripped into the puddle mixing with stagnant pink water below.

"Well, John, it looks like this 'un's done for," Hank said. "He's shot clean through, ain't he? The bullet come out the other side, I think. You step back and watch him and I'll make sure he's dead."

Hank, with his rifle at the ready, held the muzzle of his weapon just inches from the Indian's body. With the toe of his boot the man named Hank kicked against Five Feathers' leg. The white man immediately jumped backward as if he expected the wounded Indian to suddenly leap upon them.

Even after the violent kick from the white man there was no movement from the prone Cherokee warrior. He was unconscious—or dead. The men didn't care which.

The first curious man, now emboldened, gave Five Feathers' leg a second vicious kick and jumped backwards once again, but still no response from the Indian.

"John, I think we got us here one dead injun. You keep your rifle on 'im. I still ain't so sure he's not playin' possum. He may not be dead now, but he soon will be. If he so much as twitches, give it to him right through the heart. Watch his hands. If he moves, pull the trigger."

The man named John, following instructions, nervously aimed his loaded rifle at the prone Indian lying on his stomach on the slope of the creek bank. The man named Hank laid his rifle carefully on a large stone out of the reach of the unconscious Indian in case he suddenly revived. Kneeling beside the wounded Cherokee warrior, the man named Hank unsheathed his razor-sharp skinning knife and roughly grabbed a handful of Five Feathers' glossy, short black hair at the crown and jerked it tight upward and backward. As Hank pulled Five Feathers' head and neck backwards, the warrior's unconscious body began to slowly slide down the near vertical creekbank. As Five Feathers' face-down body slid, the man continued to hold Five Feathers' hair in his left hand. Five Feathers' feet slowly slid into the puddle of pink water below him disturbing the tadpoles. The white man repositioned himself for his intended task, straddling the Indian's body. Once again, the man yanked Five Feathers' head backwards away from the red soil of the creekbank.

With his skinning knife in his right hand, the man named Hank made a deep horizontal gash in the flesh of Five Feathers' head just above his right ear. In almost one motion and using all his strength, the sharp knife circled all the way around the Indian's head cutting deep—the blade making an audible sound as it ground against bone. The man named Hank completed his grisly task. With the rapid strokes of a skilled hunter, he quickly separated the hair and flesh from the skull. When the white man severed the last bit of flesh from the skull at the back of Five Feathers' neck, the Indian's face made a thud as his head and cheek slapped against the damp soil of the creekbank. The man named Hank was left holding the Indian pelt in his left hand. As Five Feathers lay there, it looked as if he was wearing a skullcap of exposed, bloody animal flesh. With a beaming smile, the man named Hank held his prize high to be admired by his companion.

"By god, John, I've always wanted to do that. I've heard about it and I've seen 'em before, but I never thought I would have the chance to get one. We're lucky to get this 'un, ain't we? I thought all the injuns were gone," Hank said, once again holding up his prize.

John uncocked his rifle.

"I thought he was goin' to git away, didn't you, Hank? Yep, I thought he was goin' to git clean away. I sure did. Did you see how that chicken shit injun jumped for cover, like a scared rabbit? We got 'im, didn't we? We got 'im. He didn't get away from us, did he, Hank?"

The man named Hank washed his trophy in the pink puddle surrounding Five Feathers' feet.

"We got him, by god, John. We got the last one, I reckon. We'll be famous, won't we? There won't be no more after these are gone. Yep, we'll be famous. We kilt the last injun."

Hank, tucking his prize in his belt, continued with a broad grin for his hunting companion.

"Ain't nobody around here ever got one of these that I know of. I ain't never seen one in these parts. Can't wait till I get back and show ever' body what we got. They'll all wish they had come."

"We'll be famous, Hank," the man named John replied.

Hank laughed, "Now all I got to do, John, is get me a bear."

"It's a shame you can't turn that pelt in for a bounty like they used to. My daddy's old uncle said he used to make a lot of money on bounties for dead Indians in the old days—that and chasing runaways from the plantations. He had some stories to tell when he was drinkin'. Keep that pelt and maybe you can sell it. Let's get the hell out of here, Hank, before the soldiers come. We ain't far from them soldiers. They probably heard the shots."

"I wouldn't worry, John," Hank said. "Them damn soldier boys ain't goin' to do nothin'. It ain't again' the law to kill an Indian. I ain't never heard of nobody goin' to jail for shootin' an Injun—never. It ain't like he was a white man. Hell, they'll probably give me a reward. Killin' that injun gives you a good feelin', don't it?"

The man named Hank cleaned the blood from the blade of his knife on the back of the unconscious Indian's leather shirt. He cut the rabbits off Five Feathers' waist band.

The two men, with a final look of satisfaction, headed back the direction they had come—away from the column. Not once giving a backward glance to the wounded man they left lying in his own blood against the cool earth of the creekbank.

The resilient Five Feathers continued to breathe in quick shallow breaths hanging desperately onto life as he lay on the slope of the creekbank in the cool shade of the evergreen laurels with his feet in the shallow puddle of pink water.

Five Feathers finally regained consciousness.

Weakened by loss of blood, he was unable to lift his head or even open his eyes. He couldn't move his right arm. It was paralyzed from the passage of the rifle bullet. Hardly moving and eyes still closed, Five Feathers slowly explored with his left arm trying to find a handhold or exposed root to give purchase to pull himself into the brush and get out of sight. He needed to obscure himself in the cover of the laurels to allow time to recover. He needed to rest. He must rest. After several unsuccessful attempts to pull himself upward, Five Feathers was utterly exhausted from loss of blood and too weak to move. He lay still. His eyes remained closed—his breathing labored. He felt the welcome coolness of the damp soil on his cheek. He decided he would rest quietly where he was for a little while longer and try again when he had gained strength. He never moved again.

2 July 1838 evening

Five Feathers did not return. I heard two gun shots in the forest. I am worried. I have a bad feeling about those gunshots. They came from the area where Five Feathers was hunting.

Buried Bigbear's grandchild. Buried Dreadful Waters. Buried Oolanheta.

3 July 1838 – Day seventeen of our journey west

My brother can easily hide from the clumsy soldiers, but when I heard the two gun shots ring out in my brother's direction yesterday afternoon, I was alarmed. My brother's failure to return has confirmed my fears. I am alone. I am alone with my baby. I must find strength and survive. My baby and I will begin a new life in the west. We must. I will protect my child. I will tell my child the stories of our village, our nation, edudu, elisi and Five Feathers. I will tell my child of the owl and the whippoorwill and teach him about ballplay. Somehow, my child must hear the stories—all the stories. We will endure. My child and I shall outlast those who seek to destroy us. I will not die. I will live. My baby will live. Our nation shall live. It must.

Buried Rainfrog's daughter. Buried Charles Timberlake's daughter, Alsey.

4 July 1838 – Morning – Day eighteen of our journey west

I am up before the sun. I am unwell. My discomfort increases. I feel my baby heavy within. Soon I shall be unable to write. My waters haven't broken but he is ready to come.

My baby must overcome. Our nation must live. I am determined. I will live. Whites will not defeat me. Whites can take our homes and corn fields but I will not be discarded like so much rubbish. They can take our life but I shall not give them my soul. My baby shall grow into a Cherokee man. I will tell him stories about Five Feathers, elisi and edudu.

I cannot walk. Without Five Feathers I must bump along in the dreadful wagons. I feel my baby coming. I shall write again after my precious comes. I am impatient to write of my joy. I will give my things into the care of my friend—my journal, pen, quilt and tea set. After the baby comes I shall write once again and tell our story. Today my baby shall be born. Today my tears end. Today my child and I begin our new life. Today is the most wonderful day of my life. As I write a mockingbird sings to me from the top of a nearby tree. The clever bird shares my joy. All is well. I await my joy.

Chapter LVII

1838 - First Johnson Reunion Planned

Chapter 57

The Johnson Family Farm – Tennessee

Abner cupped his white porcelain mug of steaming black coffee in both hands and looked over the rich bottomland stretched below him. Most of what he saw was his. He inhaled the aroma of the delicious coffee slowly as if it were a delicate perfume and quietly stared at the steam rising from the black liquid his wife had just put into his hands.

"Martha," he said after a while, "there isn't anything in this world I can think of that rivals my love for you."

She beamed hearing those words. She loved it when Abner was romantic. He wasn't romantic nearly enough, but that was alright with her. She was a happy woman and felt fortunate to have him for her husband. He was a good man—a very good man. They had a good life on their farm in Tennessee.

"…but this coffee might just come close."

He gave her a big grin. Their eyes met for a moment of shared intimacy. He adored her—always had. He couldn't imagine a day of his life without her, or what he had done before they married.

"I'm a bit lazy this morning, Martha. Since tomorrow's the Fourth of July, I'm going to take the morning off and help you get ready for your get-together with your relatives."

"That'll be nice, Abner. You don't take much time off."

"I'll get my chores done this afternoon," Abner said quietly. "I want your first family reunion to be a success."

His wife's face brightened once again. She knew he loved her, but sometimes the endless days of unremitting labor left her with an empty feeling—both a mental and physical exhaustion. There were times when she needed him and needed his attention—like today. She was grateful.

"I want everything to go right. I want everyone to have a good time," Abner said, still looking out over this property.

"You know how important our family is to me," his wife said.

"I know, Martha. We'll have a great get-together. We will. I'll make sure of that. But Martha, I can't tell you how much I'm enjoying sitting here with you and having nothing much to do just now. I worked late yesterday to give you, to give us, plenty of time together today—to relax while we prepare. It makes it feel like we got two Sundays in one week, don't it?"

Martha nodded and smiled.

"You're a special woman, Martha. I want you to know that."

"I think you're special, too, Abner."

Abner looked away from his farm and directly at his wife's face. He held his coffee in one hand and laid his free hand on her bare forearm tenderly.

"Everything I do is for you," Abner said, still looking at his wife's face. "I don't say that enough, do I? Too many mornings, you sweet woman, I'm in the fields working before the sun comes up and ever' mornin' when I'm out there I think I'd rather be here with you—just sittin' right here like now drinkin' coffee and lookin' at your sweet face."

"I think about you too, all the time," Martha said, lowering her eyes and blushing slightly at the marvelous unexpected compliment.

"Well, thinkin' about you is a much nicer thought than lookin' at the backend of a mule all day, don't you think?" Abner said.

They both laughed.

"You're so pretty this mornin', my dear," Abner said, giving her arm a squeeze.

Even as obtuse as Abner could be at times, he realized telling his wife she was beautiful immediately after talking about the backside of a mule wasn't exactly a choice endearment. Martha understood her husband's intention and took no offense. She would never be offended by him no matter what he said. She loved him more than her own life and blushed like a schoolgirl at his compliment. They had been married over three years now, but her face would still turn red when her husband gave those unexpected compliments. She loved them. He didn't give them nearly often enough.

She sat motionless beside him in the fresh, warm, early morning air and watched the mist-filled valley begin to clear as the orange sun began to peek his nose over the distant eastern hills behind them. The rising sun had sent brilliant streaks of red and pink against the almost invisible cirrus clouds high over their heads.

Martha snuggled up to her husband. While he sipped his coffee, they enjoyed their mutual contact in the breaking July dawn—a welcome respite from their exhausting summertime routine. Neither spoke for a long time as they enjoyed the unrivaled majesty of the rural Tennessee sunrise.

She refilled his coffee. She felt secure and safe with him and even when he didn't pay her attention, she knew she could count on her husband for the rest of her days to provide for her and the new baby that would be here soon. Abner was a good man and a hard-working man. She could trust him. He wasn't the most handsome man in the world, not by a long shot, but he was scrupulously honest and reliable. She could count on him in any circumstance. He would always be there for her and their new baby. She felt a wave of sentimental emotion sweep over her which almost brought her to tears. Her love for him seemed to grow daily.

"I want to thank you again for the dinner bell, Abner. It's beautiful, isn't it? I love it."

They both looked up at the new bell proudly displayed just behind them.

"Now I won't have to shout for you to come in for your dinner. It's the best gift I've ever had. Thank you."

"You're welcome, my dear," her husband replied. I enjoyed gettin' the bell and enjoyed puttin' it up for you."

Martha leaned on her husband's shoulder and said quietly, "I love comin' out here and ringin' it when I got your dinner on the table. I love the bell. I think it's the most beautiful bell I've ever seen. I know it was expensive, but it's so pretty and I love the sound. It has such a beautiful ring. I love you, Abner. Don't you love the bell, too? It's somethin' I'll use every day."

Abner studied the black polished bell he had mounted attractively on a tall shaped cedar pole inside of a perfectly mitered cedar frame. It was a perfectly cast bell with the design of a waving American Flag on each side and it looked just the part there by the cabin.

His wife had mentioned she wanted a dinner bell last year to call everyone in from the fields. She deserved it. She worked as hard as any man. Her long hours preserving food for the winter and cooking for everyone was miserably hot work that verged on drudgery. On top of that was the washing, managing the house slaves, taking care of the chickens and fattening hogs and keeping the house clean. Abner was glad he wasn't a woman. She deserved the bell and more besides. Perhaps he would build her a whole new kitchen with the big cast iron water reservoir he had seen in a catalogue in town. Yes, he thought to himself, that's exactly what he would do. He would order that reservoir and surprise her with a new kitchen out back next year for her birthday. He smiled to himself at the thought of pleasing her and the joy the surprise would bring. He loved her dearly.

Abner stared at the bell for a few moments thinking about his wife.

721

"You, my dear, are much prettier than that ole' bell. I want you to know that. I think you're the prettiest woman in this county, to tell the truth."

Martha blushed again. This had been Abner's father's farm and his grandfather's before that. Everything on the farm his family had built with their own hands and with the help of slaves. Abner couldn't afford to hire an overseer. His farm wasn't that big. He only had eight slaves—four male and four female. Only two of the field hands were old enough to put in a proper day's work. His wife took care of the females. She trained them and made sure they were kept busy. Niggers were an expensive investment—a very expensive investment, but he needed the extra hands to work the extra acreage he planted each year if he wanted to make the big profits, plus he made extra money hiring them out during slow times. The government was always hiring niggers for their various projects.

His thinking came full circle. This bottomland he was lookin' at was good to him and in a few years he would have enough laid by to purchase more land and more slaves. He could see in his mind the big house he would eventually build for Martha. She deserved a proper house instead of their tiny old log house. He would build her a respectable kitchen separate from the house with a big brick oven and a proper cookin' hearth with a high ceiling. He would make sure she always had enough house slaves so she wouldn't have to sweat over an open fire all day. He couldn't imagine how anyone could have a proper house without slaves. There was just too much work for one man and one woman. Slaves were a necessity. Help for Martha would be important with the new baby coming. He would put the female slave quarters not too far away out back so she could call on them anytime day or night.

The female slaves were a great help to Martha and since all four were still of childbearing age, he would have yet more slaves to work the farm, job out or sell. Healthy male slaves, even young ones, brought good money—even more if they were skilled. Young female slaves, if properly trained, would also bring good money when he got ready to sell them. He could depend on Martha to give the slaves in her care the very best of training. She knew how to teach manners so the slave girls would have the skills necessary to wait on the wealthiest, most demanding buyers. Martha knew exactly what to do. With luck, in a few years, Martha's slave girls would produce quite a few children. He could sell a few, buy more land and furnish her new house in proper style. Life was good here in Tennessee—very good.

In his last visit to his neighbor's farm to the north, Abner had seen a big muscular field hand. He would suggest to Martha they could arrange a temporary swap with his neighbor for his slave's services till all his female slaves were pregnant again. The bigger the male slaves, the more they were worth.

Abner was always thinking about ways to make more money. Money was hard to come by. They either made or grew pretty much everything they needed. When they went to town the only thing they ever bought was sugar, flour, salt, coffee and tea and most of the time they bartered for that. Their house, barn and sheds had been built with their own hands and slave labor, of course. He had been buying a lot of ready-made fabrics. Home spun was a waste of time, as far as he was concerned. Spinning took far too much work for what it saved.

With good luck, he could see building that new house on the hill in a couple of years—maybe less. He already had the plans laid out in his mind—every room, door, fireplace and window. He could see every inch of it. It would be a beautiful home. He knew exactly what he needed for Martha's new kitchen, too. Maybe he would take a trip to Nashville and see what newfangled things he could get that would make her life easier.

Abner continued to sit on the log bench silently enjoying the peaceful dawn and sipping his coffee. The bench they were sitting on was Abner's handiwork, too. He had a knack for working with wood and spent what spare time he had sitting on this very bench with Martha. Like most things he did, he saw the finished bench in his mind before he ever began to shape it. He had wanted a graceful artistic resting place in front of the cabin for his wife and himself. His father would have loved his woodwork. There wasn't a day that went by he didn't think of his mother and father and miss them. His father had always taught him to go the extra mile when creating something and add touches of beauty to anything, even if it was a corn crib.

The bench was their favorite outdoor place to pass time together. He had even spent a lot of time thinking about the right place for the bench. He put it in a spot that would catch the first rays of the early morning summer sun but would be in the shade the rest of the day. Abner enjoyed working with his hands and figuring things out. He thought, once more, how he loved this farm and the rural life here. He wouldn't want to live anywhere else. When he had the time, especially in the winter, he loved to roam the woods hunting and fishing. He loved to coon hunt—mostly because he could do that at night and it didn't take away from his work. This was indeed a beautiful part of God's wonderful creation—like a Garden of Eden. Yes, he thought to himself again, the Garden of Eden couldn't have been any nicer than his part of the world.

After sitting silently for a long while, Abner pulled his wife closer with his arm around her waist. Once again, Abner thought what a glorious morning this was. He noticed Martha's stomach again. It was round. She was expecting their first. He and Martha had just about everything two human beings could wish for and soon they would be a family—this child would be the first of many, he hoped. Life was good out here on the Tennessee frontier. They lived in the most scenic and fruitful land one could imagine—certainly the best he had ever seen—even when he was back east. Yes, it was just as good as any Garden of Eden.

"You know, Martha, we've been blessed here. We have this farm and all the bottomland a man could want. We own our place and no one can take it away."

"I do love it, Abner."

"It's paid for and we have the deed," Abner said. "Not even the government can take it from us so long as we pay our taxes. My father and grandfather worked the same soil I work. I'm proud of this place."

"I know, Abner."

"We have a connection to the earth. We have security, don't we, Martha? I have you and we're going to have a baby."

"I couldn't be happier bein' here with you," Martha said.

Abner looked out over the farm at the crops that would be ready for harvest before long.

"Life is good, isn't it, Martha? What more could a man want? I wish my father and mother could have lived to see this day and be at your reunion tomorrow."

Martha laughed to herself, suddenly remembering the strange way Abner had proposed to her and that first meeting with his parents when they announced their engagement. He had asked her out one Sunday afternoon after church. They had picnicked on the creekbank and on the way home Abner had stopped by the churchyard and led her into the graveyard.

"What are we doin' here, Abner. I never really heard of folks courtin' in the graveyard?"

"Well, there's something I want to show you. I want to ask your opinion."

She smiled as she remembered what he did next. He led her to the family's plot, set aside with a simple wrought iron railing with plenty of room for additional family burials.

"Martha, these are my grandmother and grandfather's graves—God bless 'em. I remember the day when I was a little boy when we buried them. I miss them ever' day."

"And, next to them is where my momma and daddy are buried."

"And right here next to my mother and father is where I'm goin' to be buried."

"What I want to ask you is, Martha—what I want to know is, would you like to be buried here next to me?"

Martha remembered that day with fondness. Perhaps it wasn't the most romantic way for a man to ask a woman to marry him, but she had accepted and they had laughed about that day often, and everyone in the valley knew the story. Abner is a good man, she thought again, and she was so glad she had married him. They would have a good life together.

"I'm looking forward to your family comin' over tomorrow," Abner said. "We'll have a good time. I'm lookin' forward to the holiday. I got the tables built and we're ready for everything. I'll put the pig in the ground later this mornin'. He'll be ready well before noon tomorrow. It won't take my boys two shakes to dig him up."

Abner's slaves had dug a pit about three feet deep and big enough for his two-hundred-pound pig to fit easily with room on the sides. He filled the hole with wood and was letting it burn down until there would only be a bed of live coals and no flame or smoke. He prepared the pig; filled the insides with onions and apples. Later that morning he would level out the hot coals, throw in a thin layer of soil and then lay in the pig. He had another fire beside the pit that had also burned down to hot coals. He would shovel the hot ashes on top of the pig then a thick layer of hot coals and then cover everything with a foot of earth. This time tomorrow he would dig it up, clean it off, and my word would they have some good eatin'. He couldn't wait. He had already given the entrails and offal to the slaves—tomorrow they could have the head, ears, feet and tail. His mouth began to water just thinking about the tenderloin and chops.

"We're going to have some good eatin' tomorrow, Martha. Your brothers and their wives will bring some food and we'll have the biggest celebration we've ever had since we been in Tennessee."

"Yes, we'll be eatin' high on the hog," Martha said and laughed at her reference to Abner's pig in the ground.

"I'm hungry as can be jus' thinkin' about it and my watermelons did well this year, too. They're the biggest I ever raised. Can't wait till we cut them tomorrow. I got four big ones down in the spring."

His wife gave him a long sideways look and marveled once again how much she loved him. She was proud of her husband—proud of his hard work. She thought that was quite a speech for a man who normally didn't have a lot to say and usually kept his feelings to himself. He was excited about his morning with no work to do.

She didn't mind she was married to a quiet man. She had learned to read his moods and body language, but she loved it when he shared his mind with her. She laid her head on his shoulder and gave his arm an affectionate squeeze as they watched the sun rise. She wanted him to know she was pleased with his little speech.

She thought to herself that she had everything she could possibly want on this farm—or could ever want now that she was pregnant. She put both hands on her swollen abdomen and gave a smile. She felt the baby kick.

Oh my, she thought to herself, not for the first time. I hope this first child is a boy. Abner wants a boy so badly. We have plenty of time for girls, but I hope he doesn't decide to come today.'

She quietly released her breath not wanting to worry her husband. She wondered what he was thinking as he looked over the beautiful summer landscape and the head-high corn in the fields below almost ready for harvest. He was deep in thought. Her gaze, as always when she sat on this bench, slowly traveled from horizon to horizon, left to right involuntarily. The view was breathtaking. That's why Abner's grandfather had built on this particular spot up on the hill. The panorama never failed to amaze her. She loved the view of the two peaks on the ridgeline on the other side of the valley and, like always, thought how their shape had the uncanny resemblance to some giant woman's breasts.

She mused out loud, "This is a most beautiful land and the most beautiful of days, Abner. We have family and neighbors who would do anything for us if we asked."

"We got kin all up and down this valley."

Abner was listening and smiling and let her talk without answering.

"We have each other and we're going to have a baby. We are blessed, aren't we? Why would anyone want to live anywhere but here? We'll never leave this valley, will we?" Martha asked, laying her head on her husband's shoulder.

Martha's rhetorical questions were interrupted by the distant sound of horse's hooves coming from the southeast towards the farm—unusual any time but especially this early in the morning. The sound was getting louder each moment. Travelers didn't come this way every day—certainly not a group of travelers on horseback. Without a word, Abner got his rifle and bag. One never knew when a gun would be necessary. Abner would never take anything for granted, especially out here on the frontier.

Abner wasn't worried. Rural Tennessee had been safe for a long time. Andrew Jackson and his Volunteers had made sure of that. He walked down the hill a bit and stood on the narrow wagon track that was the main east-west road through the valley. Six mounted United States Army cavalry appeared over the rise walking their horses up the road toward Abner's farm. They wore the blue uniform Abner had seen before.

They rode up to Abner and respectfully informed him they were the advanced scouting patrol for a detachment of Indians being escorted across the Mississippi. The detachment would pass this farm on the morrow, they informed Abner.

"It's about time we got rid of them damn Indians," was Abner's immediate response.

Abner occasionally had problems with small groups of Indians coming up out of Alabama wanting to trade, but they hardly ever caused a problem. He had missed a few chickens, but that was about it. He was more worried these days about disease with his wife pregnant. He had heard terrible stories, everyone had, how easily disease spread among the Indians. They were cursed. He could protect her from most everything, but he couldn't protect her from disease. He didn't have any use for Indians in any case. He had never liked the dirty shifty look of them. The lazy, sneaky bastards knew not to come around his place. He wasn't afraid and his threats weren't empty. He wouldn't hesitate to shoot. It wouldn't be the first time he had killed an Indian who wouldn't listen and it wouldn't be the last if they bothered him again. Shootin' an Indian wasn't a crime in Tennessee.

When Indians came it would always mean a few sleepless nights afterward guarding his farm and stock. He didn't want the no-count Indians coming back stealing or breaking into his barn. It was high time they were taken care of once and for all—ever' last one. They were a big nuisance and today's news was welcome—most welcome.

The July morning was already muggy and Abner's shirt, along with the uniforms of the soldiers, was already stained with sweat. Abner invited the patrol up the hill to the shade of the big red oak beside the cabin. The invitation was more than politeness. Abner wanted news. These men would have a great deal of recent information, both of the army and from things back east. The big news concerned the final removal of the Cherokee. He wanted to hear every detail. He had heard rumors, but the last reliable news he had was over two weeks old. As soon as the soldiers dismounted and were properly introduced to his wife, she offered refreshment. The young men politely accepted.

As he watched the young soldiers cool themselves and rest in the shade, he wondered why any young man would want to join the army and put themselves through that misery for thirteen dollars a month. A strong young man who wasn't afraid of hard work could make thirteen dollars a week most places.

Abner's wife ordered one of her girls to bring the men some lovely sassafras tea sweetened with some of their precious sugar. The sweet, cool tea was everyone's summertime favorite. Abner had expanded their root cellar just behind the house. It was in just the right place. It was always cool and dry as a bone even in the winter. They used it to store vegetables and such and to keep milk and butter cool in the summer.

Abner's wife marveled how young these soldiers were—hardly old enough to grow whiskers. She felt a mother's compassion and her first thought was somewhere there were six mothers of these six boys hoping their sons were being fed properly and had a clean shirt. It broke her heart. She touched her stomach again and felt the baby kick. She didn't like that lonely emotion. She knew one day she would feel the same for her children when they were older and far from home, but that day would be a long time coming. She wouldn't think about that now.

The young men accepted the sweet sassafras tea eagerly.

Martha made sure the young men had their fill. After Abner heard all the news from back east and it had been discussed with the appropriate amount of small talk, the Corporal addressed Abner in a more formal tone.

"Sir, tomorrow a contingent of United States Calvary escorting about eight hundred Indians, all on foot, will pass this farm headed west."

"We're takin' them outside the borders of the United States across the Mississippi River on orders from the War Department."

"We want you to know, sir, there will be no danger and you'll have no trouble. They're all Cherokee, sir, and they haven't caused a problem since we left Ross's Landing on the seventeenth. We haven't had the slightest difficulty. You and your family will be quite safe here, sir, as we pass." We assure you of that, sir."

"Thank you, men," Abner said formally. "I appreciate you comin' by and lettin' me know. I appreciate what you're doin'. Thank you for your service. It's high time we got rid of the god damned Indians and I don't care if they're Cherokee, Creek or Choctaw. I want them out of here. They need to be gone."

"That's what we're doin', sir."

"They ain't been nothin' but a nuisance since I've lived here."

"That's what everyone says, sir."

"Our entire country will thank you when you get rid of 'em."

"Thank you, sir," the young corporal said. "I must advise you, sir, it would be a good idea if you were to round up your stray animals, just for tomorrow."

"We haven't had any problems, but you never know. It would be a good thing to keep your stock away from the Indians, especially chickens and such—we don't want to temp 'em, sir."

"We feed them well. They get plenty to eat. We make sure they get everything they need."

Abner nodded in agreement.

"And also, sir, we wanted to ask your advice. We've scouted this area, but we want to ask you the best route west. We're bringing the Indians through here on foot."

"May we ask, sir, which is the easiest route to take through this valley. What's your advice, sir?"

Abner thought a moment and responded firmly, "I don't want those damned Indians anywhere near this farm or my wife, do you understand?"

"Yes, sir. We understand."

"I don't want you to bring them damned savages through here. They can go around our farm."

"Yes, sir. We can do that."

"Do you see that tree line on the other side of that big cornfield?" Abner pointed out the direction to the soldiers.

"Yes, sir. I see the tree line."

"Just on the other side of that cornfield and that tree line is a creek running the length of this valley east and west and on the other side of that creek there's an old wagon track that will work just fine for your column. You can take that."

"When you come down this road, turn left here at my fence line. You'll come to a creek with a ford over there in the tree line. Ford the creek and turn

729

right down the wagon track—that'll take you west and out of this valley. I want all the Indians on the other side of that tree line and out of this valley by nightfall."

"Yes, sir. We can do that, sir," the corporal answered respectfully.

"There's no white folks over there and no cultivation and you can't get lost. You'll have easy goin'. Don't bring them Indians through my farm."

"No sir. We won't bring them through your farm."

Abner continued, "Don't take down any fences and don't go through any of my fields. Do you understand?"

"Yes, sir. We understand perfectly, sir."

"You do not have permission to cross my property or take down any fencing."

Abner said all this firmly, never once taking his eyes from the face of the young officer and making his points by slamming his fist into his open hand.

Abner raised his voice and spoke again to make his point, "I don't want the god damned Indians anywhere near my place. For all I care, they can all go to hell."

"Yes, sir. In fact, sir, those are our orders from the Captain and General Scott. We're happy to oblige, sir. You can count on us, sir. We are here to protect the white citizens. The Indians will go through here peacefully, sir. They go where we tell them. They know we're doing what's best for 'em. They're like a bunch of sheep since they were arrested. They do whatever we tell 'em to, sir."

The corporal turned to Martha with a polite bow and touched his cap.

"With your permission, ma'am, we'll be heading back to camp now. We're thankin' you for the tea. That's most kind of you, ma'am. We haven't had anything like that since we left Ross's Landing. The tea reminds us of home, ma'am. Thanks again."

The corporal turned back to Abner.

"We have a lot of work to do this afternoon, sir. We need to be headin' back."

Abner nodded.

"Expect our full contingent tomorrow as early as we can get 'em here—maybe two or three hours after sunup," the corporal said. "If we can get those lazy Indians movin' and don't have to dig too many graves, we'll have 'em here early—well before noon."

"I would appreciate that, corporal. The sooner the better."

"I promise we won't bother you when we pass, sir. We'll keep the Indians on the other side of the valley as you have instructed. When we get here to your property line, we'll turn to the left and follow your instructions. Thank you, sir."

The soldiers rode back up the road the way they came.

"I wish the Indians weren't coming tomorrow, Abner. I don't like Indians. Tomorrow's the Fourth of July and you know my four brothers and their families are coming to celebrate with us. I was looking forward to a happy day."

"I wouldn't worry too much, Martha."

"I hope these Indians don't ruin our get-together, but I guess there's nothing we can do about it," Martha said, with a worried tone in her voice.

"Don't you worry about anything, Martha. I'll take care of everything. I'll make sure you have a good reunion."

"I hope so, Abner. All five of us children haven't been together at one time since our parents died and my brothers are sayin' they want to start gettin' together every year on the Fourth."

"I would like that," Abner agreed.

"Next year we'll invite all your people, too, Abner. Wouldn't that be fun to have both families here for the reunion?"

"I would like that, too," Abner agreed once again.

"In a couple of years, think of all the children. Won't it be fun? Can we have both sides of the family here next year."

Martha suddenly frowned again.

"I do hope the Indians don't ruin our plans tomorrow, Abner."

"Don't worry, Martha. You can't trust Indians but you can trust the army. We may have to put off our get-together till a bit later in the day, but the Indians aren't coming near our place. I'll see to that. You start getting things ready, but don't put anything out till after them god damned savages pass. Those Indians aren't getting' one damn thing from me. I don't trust them. I'll make sure none of them wander up here. Maybe this will be the last we'll ever see of Indians. I hope so.

Chapter LVIII

1838 – Abner's Nightmare

Chapter 58

4 July 1838 - Johnson Family Farm – Tennessee

Abner slept poorly. He rose long before sunrise with the first crow of their old rooster. The stars were still shining brightly with no sign of dawn. He wanted to double and triple check his preparations for the hundreds of Indians coming by his farm later that morning. Abner went to the lean-to shed on the back of the barn and shook his boys awake. He would make sure they were vigilant. They would mind Abner. They usually did, especially the older ones. They knew what he would do if they disobeyed.

Exactly as forecast the leading soldiers escorting the Indians rode slowly up the road towards the farm in the late morning. The detachment was traveling at a snail's pace. Even before the leading horsemen came into sight, Abner ordered his wife to go inside with the girls, bar the door and not let anyone in. It would take a while for the Indians to pass. He wasn't going to take any chances. He had one of his boys watching the house, the pigs and chickens and the others down at the barn watching the stock he had penned up in the back lot. His farm and belongings were as secure as he could make them.

Abner rode his saddle horse up the road to meet the detachment. He didn't like what he saw. There were too few soldiers to control too many Indians, but there didn't appear to be anything out of order. Everyone was coming down the road peacefully. Other than a shortage of soldiers, he didn't see anything that especially worried him at the moment. He hoped the savages would mind their manners when they passed. If they didn't, he would give them what for.

The lead group of mounted soldiers, along with the Indian spokesman for the detachment, halted in front of Abner. The courteous Indian representative, a Cherokee himself, politely requested passage down the valley straight through Abner's farm. He said it would be much easier on the tired Indians if they were allowed to travel straight down the valley rather than detour around Abner's farm. The detour was five miles out of their way and the detachment would be required to unnecessarily ford the creek twice. The detour would be unreasonably difficult, Abner was told, since all the Indians were on foot and many without shoes.

"I humbly request, sir, that we be allowed to walk straight down the valley. We'll take down and return all fences exactly as we found them."

The Cherokee representative continued politely with perfect English.

"Any damage incurred to fences, crops or property of any kind will be paid for on the spot in gold. You yourself, sir, can be the judge of the monetary damage."

"We have families, women, children, and elderly folk, sir, and they're all on foot. It would be a relief and a Christian blessing if you would suffer us to pass straight through."

Abner looked hard at the Cherokee man. Indians would get no Christian blessing from him—today or any day. The Indians weren't Christian. They deserved no good will from his God or any god. They didn't deserve anything as far as he was concerned. He was glad they were leaving. He would just as soon they disappeared completely. He knew the army had clear orders not to bother landowners. That's the way the government had always handled Indian removals. Andrew Jackson and the rest of the Tennesseans stuck together and took care of business. He was proud of the Volunteers. They took care of their own. Abner didn't want any of the sick, thieving, sneaky Indians anywhere near his land or his wife. He wasn't going to risk allowing them to pass through his place. They could detour around his farm. They were well used to being barefoot.

"No. Absolutely not," Abner answered in a hard voice. "You'll not pass through my farm. I reckon you'll have to go down by the creek and cross at the ford. You can take the road down on the other side of the tree line and head down the valley like I told the soldiers yesterday. You won't have to take down any of my fences or go near my corn fields. You can keep your money. I don't want Indians comin' through my place."

"Yes, sir," the Indian representative said in a low voice.

"There's good water on the other side," Abner continued. "If you follow that road, there's a ford across the creek for the wagons to get over and another ford for them to get back again at the bottom of the valley. I told you yesterday. I don't want Indians anywhere near my place."

"We understand, sir."

"You most certainly do not have my permission to pass through this farm and you do not have permission to stop or camp anywhere in this valley—for that matter. All us landowners want you out of this valley before sunset. You can camp up in the hills beyond the valley."

The sad-faced Indian representative was well used to denial. He knew it was useless to debate with this white man, typical of the white settlers who owned every farm they came to. White men owned everything now. Every Indian farm had been taken. He knew Abner's mind was made up and the tired soldiers didn't care either way. The soldiers were here for their pay. The convenience or inconvenience of the Cherokee detachment was not their concern.

The soldiers allowed the Indians to rest only when they rested the draft animals. Cassie, near the head of the column and the entrance to the farm, suddenly doubled over with the pain of a contraction. Her water broke, soaking her legs and feet. She fell to her knees with the pain of the contraction. Her friends supported her. They knew she would travel no farther this day.

On the heels of the first contraction came another. Cassie's companions helped her to the side of the road and the welcome shade of an old white oak tree. They laid her on the quilt—the bed on which the child would struggle to enter the world—the quilt given her by Eleanor.

The soldiers had orders to be especially vigilant during rest stops and prevent anyone from straying. Anyone who could not continue on foot would be unceremoniously thrown into a trailing wagon with the elderly, sick and dying. The army did not permit stragglers. There were no options.

There was one doctor for everyone, but he spoke no Cherokee, had few medicines and no way to care for or transport the ill or minister to a woman in labor. Cassie's situation was desperate. She and her friends were on their own. Ready or not the child was coming.

After the discussion with Abner, the soldiers ordered the column to resume their journey—turning to the left across the creek and away from the Johnson farm as instructed. The July morning, already miserably stuffy under a cloudless sky with no wind, promised the exhausted Cherokee another stifling day of dust, sweat and tears. The soldiers led the detachment around Abner's farm exactly as instructed.

Abner, leading his horse back up to the hill, saw the knot of Indian women gathered in the shade of the big white oak down by the road. He immediately shouted and waved indicating they should get back in the column and get on the move. None of the Indian women understood or paid him attention.

Waving his arms, Abner shouted again at the Cherokee women.

"Get the hell out of here, you god damned Indians. Get the hell out of here. Get back onto the road and don't leave that thing here. Take it with you."

Abner wanted the detachment to pass his farm as quickly as possible—the entire detachment. He wanted the soldiers to take care of these stragglers. He was angry that Indians would stop near his place for any reason. He mounted his saddle horse and galloped the short distance to big white oak. He found four Indian women comforting a fifth woman lying on a quilt on the backside of the big shade tree. As he approached he shouted again but to no avail. Cassie, in intense pain and beginning her delivery, couldn't be moved. Her friends intended to stay and help, but Abner intended otherwise.

The angry farmer, in an irrational panic, fired a shot into the air as he threatened the frightened Cherokee women. The passing Cherokee walking on the road some distance away stared with expressionless faces at Abner and continued walking. Two weary young soldiers turned their tired horses away from their escort of the slow-moving column and walked slowly back towards the irate, gesturing farmer who was demanding their immediate attention. Escorting Indians day after day was a thankless task for these young, underpaid soldiers. Dealing with unreasonable white farmers was almost as bad.

Abner was terrified his wife might contract some terrible disease or the Indians might decide to camp overnight beside his property.

"I want these god damned Indians out of here now."

"Yes, sir."

"Get them out now. Do you hear me?" Abner said in his most demanding voice. Get the god damned Indians away from here. Do your job like you're supposed to and remove these Indians—now, right now."

"Yes, sir," the young soldier patiently replied once again.

In obedience to the farmer's demands, the young soldiers turned their horses slowly towards the four Cherokee women under the old white oak tree. With gestures easily understood, the soldiers ordered the frightened women back into the moving column. When the women hesitated, the soldiers used the power of their horses and their boots to push the women back to the trail toward the main column which had almost passed the farm. The friends of the woman in labor would not be allowed to stay—not here beside this white man's farm.

Cassie was alone.

The abandoned Cherokee woman, now in great pain, lay on her quilt obscured from the view of anyone on the road by tall grass and weeds and the trunk of the large tree.

As she lay there, she thought of Ben and his mother and wished Ben could be there with her. She wanted his arms around her once again. She did her best to look up the road hoping to catch a glimpse of Ben coming to help.

Ben didn't come.

Alone, under the big white oak tree on a hot July morning, Cassie delivered her baby.

Abner followed the soldiers and pointed back at the white oak tree, shouting at the young white soldiers.

"What do you expect me to do with that? You can't leave that thing here on my property."

The soldiers said nothing.

"You said you would take care of these Indians. What am I supposed to do? I don't want this thing here. Take it with you," Abner demanded.

The soldiers were hot, tired and bored.

"Sir, the trailing wagons are comin' by shortly. They pick up all the stragglers. They'll get her sure. If they don't, she'll catch up as soon as her baby's born. I reckon she's Tennessee's problem for the time bein', sir. I can't carry her on my horse. You'll have to wait for the wagons to get her, sir. That's what they're for."

"I want her out of here now—this instant."

The tired young soldier continued, "I have orders to keep these Indians moving and get them out of this valley before we camp for the night, as you requested, sir. We've a long way to go before nightfall unless you want the whole bunch to camp right across the creek and wait for this one."

"No, I want them gone from here," Abner said flatly.

"Then I have to get on with movin' them, sir. We don't leave anyone behind. I seen women like her have babies before, sir. When she's done, she'll catch up with the others in no time. They usually do. After the baby's born she'll be up like a cricket. If she don't recover, you'll have one less Indian to worry about. She's no concern of ours, beggin' your pardon, sir."

"Well, I don't like this one bit."

"She ain't goin' to bother you none under that tree, sir. These Indian women are as tough as a lighter knot. They're used to a hard life. They're strong, sir."

"I hope you're right. I don't want her around here—not with a baby," Abner said quickly.

"We're only doing ten miles a day, sir. She'll catch up in no time. Good luck, sir."

The young soldier turned away with his fellow to rejoin the detachment. They had sympathy for the farmer. They wouldn't want Indians camping on their property, either. No one wanted Indians around.

Abner was furious. He was enraged with the army that he had been left to deal with the Indian straggler lying beside the road under his white oak tree close to his home. He was infuriated at it, whatever it was. It wasn't fair that he should have to deal with this on the day of his wife's reunion, of all days. The Indians couldn't have picked a worse time to pass. God damned Indians.

He went back up the hill and ordered his wife to stay inside a little while longer. More than half of the Indian detachment had crossed the far side of the creek and were heading down the valley and were almost out of earshot. It wouldn't be long and all the Indians, the contractor's wagons and the soldiers would be out of sight down the valley leaving one Indian woman behind to test Abner's patience.

Abner was tense and irritable.

"I'm going to stay up here by the cabin with my rifle till every last one of these god damned savages is gone. I don't trust the sneaky bastards."

"I'm glad you're here, Abner."

"Don't you worry, Martha."

"I'm not worried with you here, Abner."

"Good. I'm here and there won't be any trouble. I'll see to that. I'm going to stay here and make sure you're safe. Soon as they're gone, we'll start gettin' ready for your reunion."

He didn't mention to his wife about the unwanted thing under the tree. He wasn't sure how he would take care of that problem. He hoped the soldiers were right. He hoped the woman would catch up to the slow-moving column soon after she delivered.

"Abner, can I open the door? It's really hot in here. I got things cookin' for the reunion."

"Sure, sweetheart, open the door. I'm here and the Indians are mostly gone. You can leave the door open and come outside as long as you stay close. I'm goin' to sit right here till they're out of sight."

"I'll get you something to drink," his wife said sweetly.

Abner watched the last of the Indians moving south on the other side of the Creek and then to his right down the valley to the west, just as the soldiers said they would. By noon, maybe before, they would be out of sight—long gone, just as the soldiers said they would be. He could dig up the pig and get ready for their guests and his wife's Fourth of July reunion. He was looking forward to a relaxing afternoon with no work—something that didn't happen very often.

"Abner, my brothers and their families will be here before long and you still have to dig up the pig."

"I know."

"I hope everything is good and these Indians haven't caused my brothers a problem."

"The damn Indians won't be a problem."

"Do you think it's alright if I start getting things ready? I need to put the tables out. The girls and I have a lot to do if we're going to have our celebration. I want everything to be perfect."

"I'll take care of everything, sweetheart."

He wasn't thinking about his wife's reunion.

"Don't you worry. I got everything under control. We may be a little late, but that's ok. I got one more thing I need to do before I begin helping you, dear. You go take a rest and let your girls tend to the cookin'. I'll be back before long and take care of everything. Gettin' the pig up won't take the boys two shakes. Don't you worry about nothing."

"I'm not worried, Abner. I'm not worried in the least with you here."

Abner turned towards his wife and stared at her blankly for a moment. Martha could tell something was bothering her husband. Abner didn't want to cause his pregnant wife any problem. He took her in his arms and held her there on the bench for a moment and kissed her on the forehead gently. He was concerned about his wife and their baby. Martha was going on nine months and Abner didn't want her to go into labor prematurely. The local doctor said he would make sure he was close by until she delivered. Abner would send one of his boys on their fastest horse the minute she began her labor. Abner didn't want to deliver that baby himself—not today or any day. He held his wife for several more minutes.

The sound of the Indians and the draft horses' clanking harness and trace chains had gradually faded into the distance towards the west. His farm was quiet and secure once again. All was normal in his scenic Tennessee valley.

His Garden of Eden once again belonged to himself alone—except for one thing.

"I'm goin' to go check around and see what's going on down on the road."

"I'll make sure the stock and fences are good. I won't be gone long."

"Be as quick as you can, Abner. I want everything to be perfect for our first reunion. Nothing is more important than family."

"As soon as I get back, I'll help. We'll have a good time today—I promise. I'm not going to let a bunch of no-count Indians spoil your reunion."

"Don't you worry about nothin'," Abner assured his wife.

"I won't worry, dear," she answered.

"Don't do too much. Don't pick up anything heavy. You make your girls do all your liftin'. That's what I bought 'em for."

Abner looked at his wife and thought that he loved her more at this moment than ever before. He hoped the unwanted problem under the tree would be gone by the time he arrived. He wanted everything to be good for his wife's special day. She deserved to have a carefree, happy day with her family.

"I can't wait till my family gets here, Abner. We haven't seen them in such a long time. The children will have grown. I want to see my brothers and their wives. I miss every one of those children. I hope they remember their aunt Martha."

"With the last of the Indians gone from Tennessee, we have something extra to celebrate this year, don't we, Abner?"

"You're right, dear," her husband agreed. "We got a lot to celebrate this year. We've had a rough morning, but this will be a good day—a real good day. Next year we'll invite both sides of our family."

His wife went into their little house to rest. Abner immediately went down the hill to see if his problem had gone. From his cabin, a little rise obscured his view of the base of the trunk of the white oak. When he walked over the rise, he could see the Indian woman was still there. The trailing wagons had missed her, hidden in the weeds behind the trunk of the big tree. He didn't like this. He felt his anger rising once again. This was unfair. He was fuming—beginning to lose control.

He walked over to the Indian woman and examined her carefully. She was lying half on her side and half on her stomach—her face turned away from him. There was no movement. He gently shoved her shoulder with the toe of his boot disturbing a small yellow butterfly that had been resting on the woman's black hair. Abner watched it as it fluttered upward through the limbs of the oak towards the brilliant July sun.

He pushed her again with his boot—harder this time, but still no response. Unwilling to touch filthy Indians with his hands, Abner rolled her over with the butt of his rifle. When the Indian woman rolled over he saw her wide open unblinking eyes glazed in death, staring upward as if following the disturbed butterfly. The busy ants had found her face.

The only sound in the deep shade of the white oak was the loud buzz of large green flies. Shocked and dazed, Abner stumbled backwards, tripped and fell to the ground. In a panic, Abner continued to scoot backwards on his behind away from the unexpected horror that suddenly overwhelmed his mind.

He didn't need to see this and certainly his wife in her condition didn't need to know anything about this. Still breathing rapidly, he recovered from his shock. Half running and half stumbling, he ran up the hill to get his pick and shovel from the shed behind the house. He had to bury the Indian immediately. He didn't want his wife or the slaves to see this. He didn't want anyone telling his wife what lay down by the road—that someone had died just down the hill from their house. A woman dying in childbirth would be a bad omen. He wanted to take care of this himself immediately. If he asked his boys to help, word would get back to his wife. He couldn't risk that. He would have to do this alone.

"What are you doing, honey?" his wife asked innocently, leaning out the back door.

"I'm burying some carne the Indians left. Stay in the cabin and rest. I'll dig a hole and bury it and be back in two shakes. I won't be long. You rest. Let me take care of this. I'll be right back and we'll get started."

He muttered to himself as he half-ran and half-walked down the hill.

"God damned Indians. They never cease to be trouble."

"They're trouble even when they're dead."

"I'm glad they're gone—god damned Indians."

"It's about time they was gone."

"We should have gotten rid of them long ago. They been nothin' but trouble."

The white settler, angry because of the morning's events, the inconvenience and the horror of the work he was required to do found it impossible to think clearly. There was no way he was going to dig a proper grave for this inconsiderate savage. Why did they leave her here?

She should have died somewhere else if she wanted to be buried properly. Indians didn't deserve a Christian burial anyway. They were savages—little different than animals. The dead Indian was an animal and would get an animal's burial. If it was a white woman, he would dig a proper grave and have a proper Christian burial. They would say words over her and show respect—but she wasn't white. There would be no words. The truth was she wasn't any different than a dead possum. He would dig a shallow grave in the nearby wash and throw some dirt over her. That would be good enough for an Indian. In a fit of irrational anger, he spit a stream of tobacco juice on the dead woman's face disturbing the ants. Serves her right for being here in the first place. She should've died somewhere else.

Digging furiously with his shovel and pick-ax, Abner quickly scooped out the wash next to the body deep enough to adequately cover the Indian. Not wanting to touch the body with his hands, he decided to pull the quilt, woman and all, until she rolled into the shallow depression. He would throw the quilt over the body, cover it with a layer of earth, throw flat stones on top and that would do. He could go back up the hill and get ready for their visitors. His wife would never know.

Abner got on the other side of the hole he had dug and pulled the quilt so that body, quilt and all, would fall into the depression he had hollowed out. As Abner pulled, the limp body rolled into damp soil of the shallow grave with a thud. The body rolled into the hole face upwards. It seemed to Abner her open eyes were staring directly into his, accusing him of carelessness—or worse—blaming him for her death.

As Abner leaned to fold the blanket over the body and hide the accusing face, he was shocked once again. Beside the woman and not quite in the grave, was a tiny baby almost obscured in a fold of the quilt. He had to look twice to understand that he was looking at the form of an unclad newborn still connected to its cord. It had fallen out of the Indian's clasped arms when he moved her. The baby had a perfectly formed little face surrounded with a shock of black hair.

He felt a burst of nausea and turned away. On his knees, with his back to the Indian and her baby, he rocked backward and forward and dry retched. He had never seen anything as disturbing—as sickening in his life. Still on his knees, his stomach revolted at the vision he would never forget.

He wanted someone else to finish this job. It was all wrong. This was unfair to him and his wife. This was a holiday, a United States holiday commemorating the union of states. He and his pregnant wife should be celebrating the fact that they lived in the greatest country in the world. He shouldn't be here. Indians were nothing but trouble. This was his land and his country. Indians should have never been here. They should have been taken care of long ago.

The infant's body had not quite fallen into the shallow grave with the mother's body when Abner had dragged the quilt. With the toe of his boot, Abner pushed the little body of the dead newborn. It rolled into the grave beside the corpse of its mother on the quilt. Its tiny little arms stretched above its head as if reaching to be held. It looked as if it were still alive. It was a little boy.

Abner wanted this to be over. This wasn't fair. This wasn't the same as burying a dead possum. He had shot a horse once. That was awful. This was worse. It wasn't right he should have to do this. This wasn't his fault. He wasn't responsible for this. He hated this disgusting mess. He hated Indians.

Impatiently, he pulled the quilt over the two lifeless bodies, once again disturbing busy ants and green flies. He didn't want to be looking at the thing he would cover as he shoveled dirt. As he pulled the quilt one final time to cover the bodies completely, it looked as if the dead baby was pressing against its mother in an embrace—as if it were alive and moving its little arms and fingers as it searched for its mother. Abner lost control. This was too much. With that final vision, Abner's world collapsed on itself.

Throwing the shovel aside, Abner fell to his knees in a fit of mad lunacy shouting incoherent obscenities at the ungrateful thing under the quilt. With spittle dripping off his chin and continuing to spout unintelligible vulgarities, Abner, using both his hands and feet, worked wildly to cover the insanity under the quilt as quickly as possible with a thin layer of soil, sticks, leaves and grass. Cursing all the while, the crazed farmer kicked and flailed anything within reach to cover the indecent atrocity whose continued exposure to the light of day seemed to threaten his existence.

Abner knew he must erase the ugliness of what he had seen. He must protect himself and his family from what he was covering as if, when covered, the dead Indian pair had never existed. With their burial, they and their memory would disappear—vanish from the earth forever. They would be completely removed from his consciousness and from any connection to his farm, family and life. They would disappear.

When Abner finished covering the bodies, he was exhausted—physically and mentally. He was completely drained. He sat on a nearby stump, elbows on his knees, head between his legs, sweat dripping off his face and nose in

Chapter LVIII

1838 – Abner's Nightmare

Chapter 58

4 July 1838 - Johnson Family Farm – Tennessee

Abner slept poorly. He rose long before sunrise with the first crow of their old rooster. The stars were still shining brightly with no sign of dawn. He wanted to double and triple check his preparations for the hundreds of Indians coming by his farm later that morning. Abner went to the lean-to shed on the back of the barn and shook his boys awake. He would make sure they were vigilant. They would mind Abner. They usually did, especially the older ones. They knew what he would do if they disobeyed.

Exactly as forecast the leading soldiers escorting the Indians rode slowly up the road towards the farm in the late morning. The detachment was traveling at a snail's pace. Even before the leading horsemen came into sight, Abner ordered his wife to go inside with the girls, bar the door and not let anyone in. It would take a while for the Indians to pass. He wasn't going to take any chances. He had one of his boys watching the house, the pigs and chickens and the others down at the barn watching the stock he had penned up in the back lot. His farm and belongings were as secure as he could make them.

Abner rode his saddle horse up the road to meet the detachment. He didn't like what he saw. There were too few soldiers to control too many Indians, but there didn't appear to be anything out of order. Everyone was coming down the road peacefully. Other than a shortage of soldiers, he didn't see anything that especially worried him at the moment. He hoped the savages would mind their manners when they passed. If they didn't, he would give them what for.

The lead group of mounted soldiers, along with the Indian spokesman for the detachment, halted in front of Abner. The courteous Indian representative, a Cherokee himself, politely requested passage down the valley straight through Abner's farm. He said it would be much easier on the tired Indians if they were allowed to travel straight down the valley rather than detour around Abner's farm. The detour was five miles out of their way and the detachment would be required to unnecessarily ford the creek twice. The detour would be

"I promise we won't bother you when we pass, sir. We'll keep the Indians on the other side of the valley as you have instructed. When we get here to your property line, we'll turn to the left and follow your instructions. Thank you, sir."

The soldiers rode back up the road the way they came.

"I wish the Indians weren't coming tomorrow, Abner. I don't like Indians. Tomorrow's the Fourth of July and you know my four brothers and their families are coming to celebrate with us. I was looking forward to a happy day."

"I wouldn't worry too much, Martha."

"I hope these Indians don't ruin our get-together, but I guess there's nothing we can do about it," Martha said, with a worried tone in her voice.

"Don't you worry about anything, Martha. I'll take care of everything. I'll make sure you have a good reunion."

"I hope so, Abner. All five of us children haven't been together at one time since our parents died and my brothers are sayin' they want to start gettin' together every year on the Fourth."

"I would like that," Abner agreed.

"Next year we'll invite all your people, too, Abner. Wouldn't that be fun to have both families here for the reunion?"

"I would like that, too," Abner agreed once again.

"In a couple of years, think of all the children. Won't it be fun? Can we have both sides of the family here next year."

Martha suddenly frowned again.

"I do hope the Indians don't ruin our plans tomorrow, Abner."

"Don't worry, Martha. You can't trust Indians but you can trust the army. We may have to put off our get-together till a bit later in the day, but the Indians aren't coming near our place. I'll see to that. You start getting things ready, but don't put anything out till after them god damned savages pass. Those Indians aren't gettin' one damn thing from me. I don't trust them. I'll make sure none of them wander up here. Maybe this will be the last we'll ever see of Indians. I hope so.

unreasonably difficult, Abner was told, since all the Indians were on foot and many without shoes.

"I humbly request, sir, that we be allowed to walk straight down the valley. We'll take down and return all fences exactly as we found them."

The Cherokee representative continued politely with perfect English.

"Any damage incurred to fences, crops or property of any kind will be paid for on the spot in gold. You yourself, sir, can be the judge of the monetary damage."

"We have families, women, children, and elderly folk, sir, and they're all on foot. It would be a relief and a Christian blessing if you would suffer us to pass straight through."

Abner looked hard at the Cherokee man. Indians would get no Christian blessing from him—today or any day. The Indians weren't Christian. They deserved no good will from his God or any god. They didn't deserve anything as far as he was concerned. He was glad they were leaving. He would just as soon they disappeared completely. He knew the army had clear orders not to bother landowners. That's the way the government had always handled Indian removals. Andrew Jackson and the rest of the Tennesseans stuck together and took care of business. He was proud of the Volunteers. They took care of their own. Abner didn't want any of the sick, thieving, sneaky Indians anywhere near his land or his wife. He wasn't going to risk allowing them to pass through his place. They could detour around his farm. They were well used to being barefoot.

"No. Absolutely not," Abner answered in a hard voice. "You'll not pass through my farm. I reckon you'll have to go down by the creek and cross at the ford. You can take the road down on the other side of the tree line and head down the valley like I told the soldiers yesterday. You won't have to take down any of my fences or go near my corn fields. You can keep your money. I don't want Indians comin' through my place."

"Yes, sir," the Indian representative said in a low voice.

"There's good water on the other side," Abner continued. "If you follow that road, there's a ford across the creek for the wagons to get over and another ford for them to get back again at the bottom of the valley. I told you yesterday. I don't want Indians anywhere near my place."

"We understand, sir."

"You most certainly do not have my permission to pass through this farm and you do not have permission to stop or camp anywhere in this valley—for that matter. All us landowners want you out of this valley before sunset. You can camp up in the hills beyond the valley."

The sad-faced Indian representative was well used to denial. He knew it was useless to debate with this white man, typical of the white settlers who owned every farm they came to. White men owned everything now. Every Indian farm had been taken. He knew Abner's mind was made up and the tired soldiers didn't care either way. The soldiers were here for their pay. The convenience or inconvenience of the Cherokee detachment was not their concern.

The soldiers allowed the Indians to rest only when they rested the draft animals. Cassie, near the head of the column and the entrance to the farm, suddenly doubled over with the pain of a contraction. Her water broke, soaking her legs and feet. She fell to her knees with the pain of the contraction. Her friends supported her. They knew she would travel no farther this day.

On the heels of the first contraction came another. Cassie's companions helped her to the side of the road and the welcome shade of an old white oak tree. They laid her on the quilt—the bed on which the child would struggle to enter the world—the quilt given her by Eleanor.

The soldiers had orders to be especially vigilant during rest stops and prevent anyone from straying. Anyone who could not continue on foot would be unceremoniously thrown into a trailing wagon with the elderly, sick and dying. The army did not permit stragglers. There were no options.

There was one doctor for everyone, but he spoke no Cherokee, had few medicines and no way to care for or transport the ill or minister to a woman in labor. Cassie's situation was desperate. She and her friends were on their own. Ready or not the child was coming.

After the discussion with Abner, the soldiers ordered the column to resume their journey—turning to the left across the creek and away from the Johnson farm as instructed. The July morning, already miserably stuffy under a cloudless sky with no wind, promised the exhausted Cherokee another stifling day of dust, sweat and tears. The soldiers led the detachment around Abner's farm exactly as instructed.

Abner, leading his horse back up to the hill, saw the knot of Indian women gathered in the shade of the big white oak down by the road. He immediately shouted and waved indicating they should get back in the column and get on the move. None of the Indian women understood or paid him attention.

Waving his arms, Abner shouted again at the Cherokee women.

"I hope you're right. I don't want her around here—not with a baby," Abner said quickly.

"We're only doing ten miles a day, sir. She'll catch up in no time. Good luck, sir."

The young soldier turned away with his fellow to rejoin the detachment. They had sympathy for the farmer. They wouldn't want Indians camping on their property, either. No one wanted Indians around.

Abner was furious. He was enraged with the army that he had been left to deal with the Indian straggler lying beside the road under his white oak tree close to his home. He was infuriated at it, whatever it was. It wasn't fair that he should have to deal with this on the day of his wife's reunion, of all days. The Indians couldn't have picked a worse time to pass. God damned Indians.

He went back up the hill and ordered his wife to stay inside a little while longer. More than half of the Indian detachment had crossed the far side of the creek and were heading down the valley and were almost out of earshot. It wouldn't be long and all the Indians, the contractor's wagons and the soldiers would be out of sight down the valley leaving one Indian woman behind to test Abner's patience.

Abner was tense and irritable.

"I'm going to stay up here by the cabin with my rifle till every last one of these god damned savages is gone. I don't trust the sneaky bastards."

"I'm glad you're here, Abner."

"Don't you worry, Martha."

"I'm not worried with you here, Abner."

"Good. I'm here and there won't be any trouble. I'll see to that. I'm going to stay here and make sure you're safe. Soon as they're gone, we'll start gettin' ready for your reunion."

He didn't mention to his wife about the unwanted thing under the tree. He wasn't sure how he would take care of that problem. He hoped the soldiers were right. He hoped the woman would catch up to the slow-moving column soon after she delivered.

"Abner, can I open the door? It's really hot in here. I got things cookin' for the reunion."

"Sure, sweetheart, open the door. I'm here and the Indians are mostly gone. You can leave the door open and come outside as long as you stay close. I'm goin' to sit right here till they're out of sight."

"I'll get you something to drink," his wife said sweetly.

Abner watched the last of the Indians moving south on the other side of the Creek and then to his right down the valley to the west, just as the soldiers said they would. By noon, maybe before, they would be out of sight—long gone, just as the soldiers said they would be. He could dig up the pig and get ready for their guests and his wife's Fourth of July reunion. He was looking forward to a relaxing afternoon with no work—something that didn't happen very often.

"Abner, my brothers and their families will be here before long and you still have to dig up the pig."

"I know."

"I hope everything is good and these Indians haven't caused my brothers a problem."

"The damn Indians won't be a problem."

"Do you think it's alright if I start getting things ready? I need to put the tables out. The girls and I have a lot to do if we're going to have our celebration. I want everything to be perfect."

"I'll take care of everything, sweetheart."

He wasn't thinking about his wife's reunion.

"Don't you worry. I got everything under control. We may be a little late, but that's ok. I got one more thing I need to do before I begin helping you, dear. You go take a rest and let your girls tend to the cookin'. I'll be back before long and take care of everything. Gettin' the pig up won't take the boys two shakes. Don't you worry about nothing."

"I'm not worried, Abner. I'm not worried in the least with you here."

Abner turned towards his wife and stared at her blankly for a moment. Martha could tell something was bothering her husband. Abner didn't want to cause his pregnant wife any problem. He took her in his arms and held her there on the bench for a moment and kissed her on the forehead gently. He was concerned about his wife and their baby. Martha was going on nine months and Abner didn't want her to go into labor prematurely. The local doctor said he would make sure he was close by until she delivered. Abner would send one of his boys on their fastest horse the minute she began her labor. Abner didn't want to deliver that baby himself—not today or any day. He held his wife for several more minutes.

The sound of the Indians and the draft horses' clanking harness and trace chains had gradually faded into the distance towards the west. His farm was quiet and secure once again. All was normal in his scenic Tennessee valley.

738

His Garden of Eden once again belonged to himself alone—except for one thing.

"I'm goin' to go check around and see what's going on down on the road."

"I'll make sure the stock and fences are good. I won't be gone long."

"Be as quick as you can, Abner. I want everything to be perfect for our first reunion. Nothing is more important than family."

"As soon as I get back, I'll help. We'll have a good time today—I promise. I'm not going to let a bunch of no-count Indians spoil your reunion."

"Don't you worry about nothin'," Abner assured his wife.

"I won't worry, dear," she answered.

"Don't do too much. Don't pick up anything heavy. You make your girls do all your liftin'. That's what I bought 'em for."

Abner looked at his wife and thought that he loved her more at this moment than ever before. He hoped the unwanted problem under the tree would be gone by the time he arrived. He wanted everything to be good for his wife's special day. She deserved to have a carefree, happy day with her family.

"I can't wait till my family gets here, Abner. We haven't seen them in such a long time. The children will have grown. I want to see my brothers and their wives. I miss every one of those children. I hope they remember their aunt Martha."

"With the last of the Indians gone from Tennessee, we have something extra to celebrate this year, don't we, Abner?"

"You're right, dear," her husband agreed. "We got a lot to celebrate this year. We've had a rough morning, but this will be a good day—a real good day. Next year we'll invite both sides of our family."

His wife went into their little house to rest. Abner immediately went down the hill to see if his problem had gone. From his cabin, a little rise obscured his view of the base of the trunk of the white oak. When he walked over the rise, he could see the Indian woman was still there. The trailing wagons had missed her, hidden in the weeds behind the trunk of the big tree. He didn't like this. He felt his anger rising once again. This was unfair. He was fuming—beginning to lose control.

He walked over to the Indian woman and examined her carefully. She was lying half on her side and half on her stomach—her face turned away from him. There was no movement. He gently shoved her shoulder with the toe of his boot disturbing a small yellow butterfly that had been resting on the woman's black hair. Abner watched it as it fluttered upward through the limbs of the oak towards the brilliant July sun.

He pushed her again with his boot—harder this time, but still no response. Unwilling to touch filthy Indians with his hands, Abner rolled her over with the butt of his rifle. When the Indian woman rolled over he saw her wide open unblinking eyes glazed in death, staring upward as if following the disturbed butterfly. The busy ants had found her face.

The only sound in the deep shade of the white oak was the loud buzz of large green flies. Shocked and dazed, Abner stumbled backwards, tripped and fell to the ground. In a panic, Abner continued to scoot backwards on his behind away from the unexpected horror that suddenly overwhelmed his mind.

He didn't need to see this and certainly his wife in her condition didn't need to know anything about this. Still breathing rapidly, he recovered from his shock. Half running and half stumbling, he ran up the hill to get his pick and shovel from the shed behind the house. He had to bury the Indian immediately. He didn't want his wife or the slaves to see this. He didn't want anyone telling his wife what lay down by the road—that someone had died just down the hill from their house. A woman dying in childbirth would be a bad omen. He wanted to take care of this himself immediately. If he asked his boys to help, word would get back to his wife. He couldn't risk that. He would have to do this alone.

"What are you doing, honey?" his wife asked innocently, leaning out the back door.

"I'm burying some carne the Indians left. Stay in the cabin and rest. I'll dig a hole and bury it and be back in two shakes. I won't be long. You rest. Let me take care of this. I'll be right back and we'll get started."

He muttered to himself as he half-ran and half-walked down the hill.

"God damned Indians. They never cease to be trouble."

"They're trouble even when they're dead."

"I'm glad they're gone—god damned Indians."

"It's about time they was gone."

"We should have gotten rid of them long ago. They been nothin' but trouble."

The white settler, angry because of the morning's events, the inconvenience and the horror of the work he was required to do found it impossible to think clearly. There was no way he was going to dig a proper grave for this inconsiderate savage. Why did they leave her here?

She should have died somewhere else if she wanted to be buried properly. Indians didn't deserve a Christian burial anyway. They were savages—little different than animals. The dead Indian was an animal and would get an animal's burial. If it was a white woman, he would dig a proper grave and have a proper Christian burial. They would say words over her and show respect—but she wasn't white. There would be no words. The truth was she wasn't any different than a dead possum. He would dig a shallow grave in the nearby wash and throw some dirt over her. That would be good enough for an Indian. In a fit of irrational anger, he spit a stream of tobacco juice on the dead woman's face disturbing the ants. Serves her right for being here in the first place. She should've died somewhere else.

Digging furiously with his shovel and pick-ax, Abner quickly scooped out the wash next to the body deep enough to adequately cover the Indian. Not wanting to touch the body with his hands, he decided to pull the quilt, woman and all, until she rolled into the shallow depression. He would throw the quilt over the body, cover it with a layer of earth, throw flat stones on top and that would do. He could go back up the hill and get ready for their visitors. His wife would never know.

Abner got on the other side of the hole he had dug and pulled the quilt so that body, quilt and all, would fall into the depression he had hollowed out. As Abner pulled, the limp body rolled into damp soil of the shallow grave with a thud. The body rolled into the hole face upwards. It seemed to Abner her open eyes were staring directly into his, accusing him of carelessness—or worse—blaming him for her death.

As Abner leaned to fold the blanket over the body and hide the accusing face, he was shocked once again. Beside the woman and not quite in the grave, was a tiny baby almost obscured in a fold of the quilt. He had to look twice to understand that he was looking at the form of an unclad newborn still connected to its cord. It had fallen out of the Indian's clasped arms when he moved her. The baby had a perfectly formed little face surrounded with a shock of black hair.

He felt a burst of nausea and turned away. On his knees, with his back to the Indian and her baby, he rocked backward and forward and dry retched. He had never seen anything as disturbing—as sickening in his life. Still on his knees, his stomach revolted at the vision he would never forget.

He wanted someone else to finish this job. It was all wrong. This was unfair to him and his wife. This was a holiday, a United States holiday commemorating the union of states. He and his pregnant wife should be celebrating the fact that they lived in the greatest country in the world. He shouldn't be here. Indians were nothing but trouble. This was his land and his country. Indians should have never been here. They should have been taken care of long ago.

The infant's body had not quite fallen into the shallow grave with the mother's body when Abner had dragged the quilt. With the toe of his boot, Abner pushed the little body of the dead newborn. It rolled into the grave beside the corpse of its mother on the quilt. Its tiny little arms stretched above its head as if reaching to be held. It looked as if it were still alive. It was a little boy.

Abner wanted this to be over. This wasn't fair. This wasn't the same as burying a dead possum. He had shot a horse once. That was awful. This was worse. It wasn't right he should have to do this. This wasn't his fault. He wasn't responsible for this. He hated this disgusting mess. He hated Indians.

Impatiently, he pulled the quilt over the two lifeless bodies, once again disturbing busy ants and green flies. He didn't want to be looking at the thing he would cover as he shoveled dirt. As he pulled the quilt one final time to cover the bodies completely, it looked as if the dead baby was pressing against its mother in an embrace—as if it were alive and moving its little arms and fingers as it searched for its mother. Abner lost control. This was too much. With that final vision, Abner's world collapsed on itself.

Throwing the shovel aside, Abner fell to his knees in a fit of mad lunacy shouting incoherent obscenities at the ungrateful thing under the quilt. With spittle dripping off his chin and continuing to spout unintelligible vulgarities, Abner, using both his hands and feet, worked wildly to cover the insanity under the quilt as quickly as possible with a thin layer of soil, sticks, leaves and grass. Cursing all the while, the crazed farmer kicked and flailed anything within reach to cover the indecent atrocity whose continued exposure to the light of day seemed to threaten his existence.

Abner knew he must erase the ugliness of what he had seen. He must protect himself and his family from what he was covering as if, when covered, the dead Indian pair had never existed. With their burial, they and their memory would disappear—vanish from the earth forever. They would be completely removed from his consciousness and from any connection to his farm, family and life. They would disappear.

When Abner finished covering the bodies, he was exhausted—physically and mentally. He was completely drained. He sat on a nearby stump, elbows on his knees, head between his legs, sweat dripping off his face and nose in large drops onto the freshly disturbed earth—each drop of sweat making an audible sound as it struck the ground.

After a short rest he raised his head and blindly looked through the limbs of the white oak at the cloudless sky for long minutes, unmoving, unthinking, unseeing, as if paralyzed, hardly remembering the task just completed, not thinking about anything. His mind was numb.

He gradually returned to normal. He moved slowly, dragging large flat stones onto the top of the soft earth to prevent animals from disturbing the remains—just like he would do if he buried a possum. He could never allow that body to be uncovered for his wife's sake—for his sake. No one must ever see that sight again. What had happened here must be forgotten—erased. No one must ever see that thing he had buried. He would permanently remove from his mind the events of this day. He would forget. He must forget. He would make himself forget. He would never remember this day ever again—never speak of it to anyone.

This wasn't his fault. None of this was his fault. The god damned Indians were to blame. Indians had caused his family problems from the beginning. Everyone hated them. He would erase from his mind everything that had to do with Indians. He would cause the Indians and even their existence to vanish.

Abner leaned on the long handle of his shovel and spit tobacco juice on the flat stones as a mark of finality. The Indians were gone. It was as if the entire nation of Indians were dead and buried under those heavy flat stones. He would see to it their memory was buried with them. The entire Cherokee Nation, and every other Indian nation as far as he was concerned, was dead and buried. Good riddance to a bad lot.

Leaning on his shovel, his breathing returned to normal as he stared down at the flat stones. He suddenly remembered Martha waiting for his return to help her get ready for her long-awaited reunion. He must pull himself together. He had a lot to do this afternoon. It wasn't easy but he had finished a most unpleasant task. His life could return to normal. The Indians were gone. Balance was restored once again to his life. All was as it should be. This would never happen again. His life, his community, the state of Tennessee and his nation were finally rid of everything to do with god damned Indians. Tennessee was white—pure white.

Before he went inside, he washed his face and hands—and then washed them again. He wondered what it was that made his soiled hands so difficult

743

to clean. Martha mustn't see him till he freshened up and removed the burial from both his flesh and his mind. He washed again.

For years afterward, Martha Johnson would be wakened in the middle of the night to pitiful, sobbing moans and terrified screams of her tormented husband huddled on the floor in the corner behind the bed, sobbing and writhing under his nightshirt, whimpering, arms above his head, trying to escape some pursuing nocturnal horror as he cried, "Take it away. Take it away. Take it away. Not here. Take it away. Take it away."

Chapter LIX

1838 – Ben's Reward

Chapter 59

26 September 1838 – Milledgeville – Ben Lowry's Law Office

With the removal of the Cherokee, a flood of immigrants poured into the northwest corner of the state. Cherokee Country, long coveted, was now fully surveyed. Every acre of land within Georgia's chartered boundaries was now free of Indian occupation. The new counties had been mapped, county seats established, officials appointed and many thousands of eager white families had moved in and begun a new life. The entirety of Georgia's chartered limits was now in white hands. Ben's work with the state of Georgia was finished. Georgia's vision was a reality.

Ben had a meeting with government officials in his well-appointed office in Milledgeville. It was time to receive his reward. The successful conclusion of the removal was a feather in his political cap and another step towards his appointment to the Senate.

Everyone was pleased the Cherokee disturbance was over. The fear of a war with the Cherokee, like the recent Creek war in Alabama, had been averted. The Cherokee's claim to land had been legally extinguished and Ben received his due share of the credit. The Cherokee were gone lock, stock and barrel. The few Indians who had escaped General Scott's roundup could be easily apprehended and deported. They had nowhere to hide and nowhere to go. Everything was as it should be. At long last, the agreement of 1802 had been fulfilled by the general government. Life was good in the state of Georgia.

A few thousand Cherokee remained in prison camps in Tennessee near the Agency awaiting cooler weather to complete the removal. The hardheaded John Ross had grudgingly agreed, finally, to the peaceful self-removal of the entire Cherokee Nation. That huge operation in Tennessee was winding down, but Georgia had already been cleared. Every Cherokee family had been rounded up and removed—sent off to Ross's Landing and the Agency. Georgia was free of its Indian population for the first time in its history, both Creek and Cherokee. Osceola was dead and the stupid Seminoles on Georgia's southern border would soon be deported en masse by the efficient

United States Army. Life in Georgia couldn't be better thanks to Andrew Jackson and the Indian Removal Act.

Georgia could get on with the economic development of the entire state within their chartered boundaries and not just the Piedmont. With the removal of the Cherokee, Georgia could take its rightful place as leader among progressive southern slave states—the largest state east of the Mississippi and one of the ole Thirteen. More than a hundred thousand new acres of prime farmland had been opened in a matter of weeks, not to mention the vast tracts of virgin timber that were immediately available for harvest. Wide roads were being built to connect to its sister states of Alabama, Tennessee and North Carolina and all without the nuisance of paying tolls on Cherokee ferries and paying to travel overland on Cherokee roads. The removal of the Cherokee had been good for business. It should have happened years earlier. With the Indians gone, Georgia would grow more quickly than ever before.

Andrew Jackson's 1830 Indian removal bill had played out precisely as envisioned. Missionaries could complain, but the Cherokee were gone. No use crying over spilt milk. John Ross and his allies were silenced, defeated, deported—never to return. Ben's work had been a complete success.

Plantations, roads, railroads, canals and bridges could be built. Excited entrepreneurs and forward-thinking governments were already raising money to develop the new idea of building railroads to connect widely separated population centers. The railroads, powered by steam locomotives, could ignore the river system that was currently the only means of the long-distance transport of goods and people. With the advent of the railroads the great inland cities politicians had envisioned could be developed. All this was possible because of the removal of the benighted Indians and their stupid belief they had title to land. For the first time in its history, Georgia had complete geographic integrity.

In the few short months since the removal began, everything Cherokee had been removed—even their bones. New Echota, the once proud Cherokee capital, was sub-divided and given to fortunate drawers, most of whom had already taken possession. The Cherokee had been rounded up. The last remnants of the irresponsible Creeks from their war in Alabama had been apprehended. African runaways had been captured and returned to slavery. Africans could no longer count on escaping to Cherokee Country or to the Florida territory and sanctuary with the Seminole. Now the Georgia Guard, created to manage white security in Cherokee Country, were out of a job.

Ben was looking forward to the meeting with the personal representatives of former president Andrew Jackson. He was excited thinking about the next step in his political career—a United States Senate appointment. Jackson, although retired, was still the driving force behind his democratic party and Ben's appointment depended on his favor. This meeting was all-important.

For the last couple of months Ben had been puzzled by the absence of Elizabeth and Zach and their lack of communication. Ben had been out of town and consumed by his duties. It seemed no matter how hard he tried, their paths didn't seem to cross. He had been so incredibly busy the last three or four months there had been no time to visit with Zach or Elizabeth. Ben had lost touch. He had no idea what was going on behind the scenes in Milledgeville.

The week previous, after his return to Milledgeville, he sent Elizabeth a note asking to meet her later that afternoon—or perhaps on their regular Tuesday. She had scribbled two words on the returned note—Not Today. Ben was puzzled. It was strange that Elizabeth and Zach hadn't been in contact. Something was wrong.

He sent a second note asking Elizabeth to dinner, but once again the note was returned with only the two words, Not Today, scribbled on the back. There was no signature and no explanation.

Ben was confused. For the last year he had been under the impression Zach and Elizabeth were in the final stages of arranging his Senate appointment—that everything in their relationship and partnership was progressing nicely. True, he had been busy and out of touch, but that was all part of their plan for his success, he had been told. Elizabeth should have contacted him by now and Zach had been away from the office on business since Ben's return. Something was amiss. Something was very wrong. Ben was anxious to get his relationship with Elizabeth back on track.

Ben was aware he had fallen for Elizabeth. He was in love with her—head over heels. Every thought he had of her was accompanied by a terrible ache in his chest, an ache that could only be removed by her physical presence—her loving touch. He was missing her terribly. Now that the removal was over, she had become the center of his thinking. He needed her.

Why were Elizabeth and Zach not in contact? Surely she cared for him—at least a little? She had been such a carefree lover and indicated on many occasions the two of them were destined for big things. He must see her. He must. Somehow he would figure out a way to be with her—to have her in his life. Maybe she would answer another note. He certainly wasn't going to give up.

He would have to think about Elizabeth later. At this moment he had business to attend to with the two presidential envoys who had been assigned by the War Department during the removal as liaison between Georgia's governor, the President, the War Department and Ben.

The men entered Ben's office and Ben instantly perceived something was amiss. The men had an unusually cool manner. Something had changed. Something wasn't right.

"Mr. Lowry, we're pressed for time so we shall get to the point."

"Both the President and General Jackson thank you for your invaluable service to your nation and the state of Georgia."

"Well, thank you, sir," Ben answered politely.

The government's messenger continued, "You did a splendid job assisting in the removal—quite a splendid job. We were not disappointed. You were indeed the man for the task at hand."

"Thank you, sir," Ben answered politely once again.

"President Van Buren commends you for the successful completion of your mission and will recommend to the Governor of Georgia that you be given the highest honor for service to your country. We will recommend you be compensated generously."

The official continued but his tone changed, "However, we must convey that at this moment it is not convenient for President Van Buren to receive you in Washington City. He will let you know when your visit will be appropriate."

Ben sensed that everything was not as good as he thought previously.

"In addition, President Jackson asked us to inform you he will send an invitation to the Hermitage when he deems it appropriate—perhaps sometime after the election."

In that instant, Ben realized he had been played—played for a fool.

In so many words, the officials of the general government were dismissing him like a naughty schoolboy.

He had been used. The postponement of his visit with President Van Buren was the same as being told he would never be invited.

He had become persona non-grata. The Senate endorsement he had been promised was obviously canceled. Without the support of Van Buren and Jackson, he couldn't get elected to the city council. Only Jackson's men had a chance in Georgia politics.

It suddenly became clear. He had been used. How could he have been so naïve? It had been rumored Jackson and Van Buren would give their support to one of Ben's young, up-and-coming opponents, but he had refused to believe it. Now he knew it to be true. Confirmed by these two men, his political ambitions had been quashed in one fell blow.

He now understood the unexplained absence of Zach and Elizabeth. They had abandoned him politically. They had thrown their lot in with someone who better suited their ambitions. Ben and his career had been sacrificed for who knows what. Zach and Elizabeth had moved on. He had been replaced.

He suddenly saw himself as Elizabeth's intrepid knight. In return for all his time and trouble he had received the coup de grace on her big chess board—brazenly sacrificed in her vain, egocentric gambit for advancement. He was yesterday's news. How could he have not seen this coming?

He had noticed Zach and Elizabeth had not been in regular contact during his frantic weeks working with the removal and now he knew why. They had found someone else to assist them in their quest for power and wealth. Ben was now no more than a successful local lawyer—nothing else. His magnificent political aspirations were crushed. Nullification—that was the word being bandied about in the newspapers. Now it applied to him. He had been nullified. If he were to turn the three steps to the left as he entered the foyer at the hotel he wouldn't be surprised to find his young, handsome opponent sitting with Zach and Elizabeth at this very moment drinking expensive whiskey distilled at the Hermitage and smoking expensive Cuban cigars. The handsome young man would be spellbound by French perfume and tempted with visions of state dinners in Washington City. He would be dreaming of a beautiful, carefree woman who would occasionally give him the most wonderful gifts in her private suite. He knew the routine. He had been a dupe, a puppet, a buffoon. He had in no way resembled a valiant knight. He had been an oaf, a miserable pawn. He was a dullard fit only for the most menial of tasks.

Throughout Georgia he would be considered a jackass by his peers who knew of his past relationship with Zach and Elizabeth—perhaps people had known all along he was a fool. He had been warned, but he remembered his clear decision to have a peek over that elusive edge of the big stone mountain his mother had warned him about. He had discovered by bitter experience that the edge of the mountain didn't exist.

After the brief meeting and curt goodbyes, the men from Washington City left for their next appointment. As Ben stared out the window, seeing nothing, his messenger returned with the third note he had sent Elizabeth just this morning. Ben was asking for their Tuesday meeting and dinner or any meeting. As she had twice before, she scribbled only two words, NOT TODAY, across the bottom of the note. Third time was a charm Ben thought to himself. He would never see her again. He should have listened to Zach. He should have listened to his mother and father. He had played the fool. He had thrown away the best years of his life in pursuit of a fantasy—a fool's illusion. He was a laughingstock. He felt as if he would explode.

Ben leaned back in his expensive upholstered black leather chair and stared at the note in his hand with a sense of complete hopelessness. A burning pain filled his chest as he realized his love for Elizabeth would be forever unfulfilled. Even after this third rejection he knew in his heart he loved her more than ever. He should have heeded Zach's advice. He loved Elizabeth. He loved her with all his heart. He always would. He wanted desperately for Bethy to be in love with him.

Even now Ben's mind sought some as yet undiscovered clandestine method by which he could win her heart. His mind began to spin dizzily looking for the solution to the impossible puzzle that would finally bring her to him. She couldn't be that cold and insensitive, could she? For a few moments Ben felt his entire body filled with the pain of his unrequited desire for his lover—the woman he had mistakenly fallen for.

Ben leaned back in his chair and for the first time understood clearly that he would never see Elizabeth's face again. After the visit of the two envoys, it was obvious his law career was all he had and all he would ever have. His political career was over. He would never again be elected to public office. He would probably lose a great many of his clients. Andrew Jackson, the governor of Georgia, Elizabeth and Zach had used him just as they had used hundreds of other eager politicians. Their glorious promises turned out to be arrogant vanities filled with insignificance. Their visions of promised wealth had vanished in the stark political reality of the moment. Their promises had disintegrated into nothingness, like the clouds of backroom cigar smoke from which they were born. The ambitions of his years of tireless labor were gone. The expected taste of victory had turned to ashes in his mouth.

He would never again walk up those three stairs. The glory of Tuesday was gone. He would never again walk up the hotel's magnificent central staircase to spend heavenly afternoons in her private suite. He would never again smell her rich perfume, feel the softness of her hair or the tingle of her touch. All that remained was a suffocating pain in his chest that grew with every evil thought. He had been a self-absorbed simpleton. He had disregarded all warnings.

Ben couldn't stop his thought process that dwelt upon his failure and his love for Elizabeth. His mind was trapped in a vicious downward spiral of malevolence.

As Ben stared through his white linen curtains into the busy street, he contemplated the reality of his circumstance and let fall his engraved notepaper returned from Elizabeth. Nothing mattered now. His life was over. His bolt was shot.

He looked at the hand carved chess set on the corner of his desk Zach had given him not long after he went to work for the firm. He remembered their conversations about how Zach and Elizabeth played their game with human chess pieces recalling how Zach had cautioned him not to lose his heart to her. He had ignored the advice of his mother, father and his friend Zach. He had literally become that replaceable chess piece on Elizabeth's board—a knight sacrificed by her in her well-planned gambit.

What a mockery his life had become. With one bitter sweep of his arm Ben sent the expensive mahogany chess pieces flying against the far wall with a crash. His attraction to Elizabeth must have seemed comical to his peers. Behind his back he must have been viewed as a laughing stock—a droll burlesque character in a ridiculous farce. They would have thought his misplaced love for her laughable, silly—the actions of a naïve schoolboy. He was an object of pity—ludicrous and embarrassing to his clientele. Perhaps he would even be let go by Zach's father.

As he leaned back in his chair and stared out the window, the mist cleared. He could see clearly. For the first time in years, he could see his life and his decisions as they really were. He had given up things more beautiful than any man could hope for in exchange for a meaningless pursuit of wealth and power. His life-choice had been a delusion—a mirage—never a thing of substance for him to keep.

Cassie had gone west and taken the baby with her. He would probably never see either of them again. His father's health was ruined and he would never teach again. The Cherokee were gone. His political career was derelict. His reputation was ruined.

Like the smoking ashes that had been Cassie's home, so was his life. He had selfishly given up everything he loved for something he could never possess. He had spurned the most beautiful of women for an egocentric vanity—a chimera—an illusion impossible to achieve and never worth possessing in the first place. What could he possibly do? How could he possibly find joy or purpose now? His life's ambitions were shattered.

In the blinding light of merciless self-analysis Ben realized, in truth, he had become a sleazy reflection of Zach and Elizabeth. He had become a user himself—no better than the foul, bribe-taking politician in the back streets of Milledgeville he had become familiar with while in the halls of power.

As he stared out the window through the crisp white linen curtains, he realized he had put himself first at the expense of everyone who loved him. For the first time in years he thought of his mother's advice the day he left for law school and the warning about trying to look over the edge of the big stone mountain. He had gaily chosen the forbidden. Suddenly, without ambiguity, he could see his father telling him about the dangers of the thin end of the wedge. He had absolutely nothing to live for. Perhaps he should fall to a well-deserved death at the foot of the stone mountain—and add his grave to those other foolish young men who believed lies—young men who insisted on finding out for themselves. Perhaps to cease to exist would be best.

Into his mind came his father's old quote from Macbeth.

"Life's but a walking shadow, a poor player that struts and frets his hour upon the stage and then is heard no more, it is a tale told by an idiot, full of sound and fury signifying nothing."

He examined the new twenty-two caliber Derringer pistol Elizabeth had given him for a birthday present last year. It was a beautiful pistol. The precision weapon, with its modern percussion cap firing mechanism, had been ordered straight from the Derringer factory in Pennsylvania. Elizabeth, he now understood clearly, had tempted him into an utterly empty life for her own selfish benefit. She had manipulated him from the day they met and when he had served her purpose, she had, without a qualm, sacrificed him for personal advancement.

He didn't want the life she offered. He would never want that life. He didn't want anything she or Zach had to give. He saw that now.

He didn't want wealth, power or Elizabeth. He wanted things of substance. He wanted the things he had discarded and now longed for as a thirsty man longs for water in a dry and barren land. He wanted the things his mother and father had taught him to love.

He had thrown away gold and kept ashes. Like Esau, who carelessly sold his birthright for a mess of pottage, he had despised everything worth having for momentary gratification thinking only of himself. Oh, that he could go back and live his life over again.

Engraved in a beautiful flowing conjoined script on the handle of the little pistol were the names Elizabeth and Ben. Ben laughed cynically. The handgun was an appropriate gift. He wondered if she had foreseen this moment. This pistol was the only thing he had left from his relationship with her—all he would ever have. How fitting.

How appropriate that the only thing Elizabeth had ever given him of any worth was an instrument of death. He stared at the pistol in his hand and faced again the bitter truth that he was no different than Elizabeth and Zach. His life was as pointless as theirs. He was worthless. His life was empty—signifying nothing. He had over time deliberately disposed of his past and now he had no future.

Ben, seeing nothing—thinking nothing—stared blindly out the curtained window as he placed a percussion cap in the loaded pistol and cocked the hammer.

Chapter LX

2016 - Katie Brings Closure

Chapter 60

I have finished transcribing Cassie's journal. The edited manuscript has gone to the publisher. It will be in print soon. At last, after all these years, her story can be read. With all my heart, I wish I could rewrite this story. Cassie wrote a long time ago, and I shouldn't let the ending of her story bother me so much, but it does. I can't help but cry occasionally.

When I think of Cassie, I'm often reminded of the old woman's question in Tahlequah, "When does the thief legally own that which he stole?"

Since the journal first came into my possession, I have thought of nothing but transcribing this story to honor Cassie and her people and, as I was told in my dream, to tell her story. My task is complete. I did my best.

Her journal deserves to be published and read, but there remained one last task to perform to give closure to Cassie, her journal, her journey and the Johnson family, and allow Cassie and her baby to finally rest in peace.

I asked Greg if he wanted to ride with me to the Johnson farm. He said he would rather not and I thought that a good thing and, in fact, I really didn't want him to go with me when I thought more about it. It occurred to me it might be best if he could find himself a nice girl who understands a global, capitalistic, market economy, loves water sports, drinks beer and thinks it humorous when someone talks about a place where we keep our Indians. I think it's about time Greg and I seriously re-evaluated our relationship.

I left about ten the next morning and pretty much followed the route Cassie would have walked when she was deported from Chattanooga in 1838—the route of our nation's embarrassing ethnic cleansing—an operation conveniently executed immediately before the advent of common photography.

I drove slowly, stopping by the roadside often, thinking about the journal the entire time. From the moment I started my car, I was troubled by incessant dark thoughts boiling through my mind. When I stopped occasionally beside the road, I would stare out the car window and imagine the laboriously slow progress of Cassie's detachment down the very road I was driving. Every one of the deportees were on foot and most without adequate footwear.

I shouldn't be thinking so much about Cherokee history, but I can't help myself. I searched for places the soldiers would have considered a good spot for the hundreds of Cherokee prisoners to rest or to camp. I noticed where the road ascended making a long, difficult climb for the weary Cherokee carrying burdens and the draft animals pulling heavy wagons. I imagined the detachment fording streams and stopping to water the draft animals and allowing them to rest for thirty minutes. I drove slowly, visualizing Cassie's column stretching for the best part of a mile. They were under the command of our own United States Army with the Georgia and Tennessee Militia pressed into service. I have two young cousins in the military. I had a difficult time picturing my own cousins ordered to do such a thing anywhere, much less right here on American soil, but that's exactly what our young soldiers did. They obeyed orders like young men do.

I must have an overactive imagination. When I stopped at a likely resting spot for Cassie's detachment, I could see her sitting on a rock ledge in the shadows. As I stared and imagined, I saw her glancing over my way—nodding her head as she acknowledged my finished work on her behalf.

I laid my head on my steering wheel and cried several times during that trip to the Johnson farm. This journey is different than my first. This time I know the truth. I know who lies under that old white oak tree under the anonymous headstone.

The drive to the Johnson farm, less than two hours with modern roads and bridges, would have taken two weeks or more for Cassie's detachment. As I reflected, I recalled my original excitement when I was searching for the two mountains hoping to find anything to confirm the text of the journal. The old woman was right. There are things about this story I do not like—things I wish I had never learned.

Today was different—much different than my first trip to the Johnson farm. I guess I was depressed by the visions made realistic in my mind by months of in-depth research. I could close my eyes and literally see the long column of men, women, children, grandmothers and grandfathers trudging down the road silently. I could see the mounted, uniformed men prodding them along as if they were a herd of cattle.

I didn't like re-living those events. What was worse, I am part of a nation who has officially chosen to forget—to forget and justify. I feel a burden. Since the day I was born, I have enjoyed the fruits of the land taken from Cassie. I and my family have personally profited from Cherokee loss. In that regard I share the guilt of my relatives. My great-grandparents, grandparents,

parents and I have enjoyed the fruits of a land stolen just as surely as a robber who enters a convenience store with a pistol and takes all the money and ten cartons of cigarettes. Does that money and those cigarettes ever become the rightful property of the robber, his children or grandchildren? Are my parents the rightful owners of their property in Walker County? Well, they have a deed and I guess in today's world that's all that counts.

That's a good question, isn't it? I've asked a few people that question and you might be surprised at their reaction. What would you say if you owned property in northwest Georgia?

The Cherokee ethnic cleansing has been forgotten. The Cherokee and their sister tribes have been turned into cartoon-like athletic mascots by my white culture that displaced them—like Florida State's mascot, the Seminole Chief Osceola, or in our nation's capital, the Washington Redskins, in the very town where Andrew Jackson's Indian Removal Act became the law of the land in 1830.

I arrived at the Johnson farm just after noon. There were no holiday decorations and no cars parked out front this time. When I arrived, I redid my makeup as I sat in my car in their beautiful long driveway preparing my mind for what I was going to share hoping I wouldn't begin crying all over again.

I rang the doorbell. Mrs. Johnson, her daughter Ann and her granddaughter Cassie all answered the door together. They remembered me and graciously invited me in with warm greetings. They were as pleased to see me as I was them. I couldn't restrain the tears when they gave me a big hug.

"What's the matter, Katie?" little Cassie said with concern. "Is something wrong?"

"No," I answered. "I've been thinking about my research and the Trail of Tears. I guess the emotion of seeing you when you opened the door was a bit much. I'm so sorry if I upset you. Please forgive me. I didn't mean to cry. Please forgive me."

Cassie's mother, Ann, answered, putting her arms around me and walking me into the living room, "Don't you worry, Katie. Come on in and sit down and we'll get you a glass of ice tea and you cry all you want to."

"Cassie and I are spending the weekend with Momma and Daddy," Cassie's mother continued, "and we're more than pleased to see you. We've talked about you often since the day of the reunion and we're dying to find out what you have learned. Come on into the living room and sit down."

As I gathered myself, I noticed the two of them looked just the same as the day we first met at the Fourth of July reunion earlier in the year. I thought of Ann's story about the voice on the day she conceived her daughter and how the voice wanted her to name her daughter Cassie. That story meant so much more now that I had finished reading the journal. I now knew who was buried under the white oak tree.

Mr. Johnson joined us and when we were settled in the living room with a nice glass of ice tea, I began.

"I have some news for you—good news, I think."

Everyone was listening. I could tell I was a welcomed guest.

"As you remember from my visit here the day of your reunion on the Fourth," I continued, "I'm a journalist and I'm interested in the Trail of Tears and the detachment of Cherokee that passed this farm in 1838 and I'm interested in the grave here on your property down by the road."

"If you recall," I continued, "I shared information I had about a Cherokee woman's journal. She kept her journal, the journal I have in my possession, from 1820 until 1838, the year of the Cherokee Trail of Tears."

"I'm finished with my research and with the transcription of the journal. It will soon be in print. I was wondering if you would like to hear some of the details of that research—especially as it pertains to the Johnson family and this farm?"

"Yes, please," little Cassie said quickly and the others were nodding in agreement. I had their full attention.

Little Cassie continued, "I brought some library books home from school about the Trail of Tears. I've been studying them all summer since your visit. I've learned a great deal—some of it not so nice. I'm the only one who knows much about what happened then. All they talk about around here is football, huntin' and the Civil War. They never want to talk about Indians."

"What did you learn, Katie?" little Cassie asked. "Tell us. Please tell us what you learned."

Little Cassie was excited and I could tell her mother and grandparents were also keenly interested. They all were watching and waiting.

I took a deep breath and began.

"I can't tell you how many hundreds of hours of research I've put into the journal and its transcription. Here are some things I've learned, especially as they pertain to you here on this farm."

"A Cherokee woman, her English name Cassie, lived in Cherokee Country near New Echota—near modern day Calhoun, Georgia—quite close to I-75. I discovered she was indeed the journal writer I've spoken about."

"She was arrested in late May of 1838, probably on May twenty-sixth, and marched to Chattanooga with all her friends and neighbors to Ross's Landing. She was in the very last of the large summer detachments that were forced west before Chief John Ross agreed to the national self-removal."

No one said a word.

My heart was pounding. I took another deep breath and a sip of ice tea and continued, "Immediately after her group of about eight hundred left Chattanooga, Chief John Ross gave up all hope for a Cherokee homeland. He asked General Scott if he would allow the Cherokee people to remove peacefully as soon as the weather cooled in the autumn and traveling was not so dangerous. General Scott agreed."

Everyone was listening. I had a captive audience.

"After Cassie was deported in late June from what is now Chattanooga, it is estimated that about fifteen more detachments left for Oklahoma in the autumn. Most of those left from the Agency in Charleston, Tennessee, near Cleveland. After being held prisoner in New Echota and Chattanooga, Cassie was forced once again onto the Trail of Tears around the middle of June 1838."

"I have strong evidence Cassie, expecting a baby any day, never made it past this farm. I will present the evidence I have in a moment. I came today because I thought you would want to know what I have learned."

"Oh, please do continue," Ann and little Cassie said almost in unison. They were quite impatient as they waited for me to tell them what I had discovered.

I looked directly at little Cassie's grandfather.

"First, Mr. Johnson, I learned something about the bow you have over your mantle. This may be a bit melodramatic, but may I hold it again please?"

"Yes, of course you can, young lady," Mr. Johnson said. "I remember very well that day you were here and your interest in the bow at that time. I've never forgotten you, young lady. I remember you asked me all sorts of questions I couldn't answer."

Mr. Johnson retrieved the bow from its expensive velvet-lined shadow box over the mantelpiece and handed it to me.

I held it in my hands. I felt a queer, tingling sensation as if the bow had some hidden inner life. I remembered Five Feathers' edudu said the bow was made of living wood and would continue to live and be faithful to the hand that held it. With the bow made of living wood in hand, I continued my rehearsal.

"I have transcribed the entire journal the Cherokee woman kept for eighteen years. I also acquired supplementary material from a friend of hers who was also in her detachment. I'm still not sure of her name but I'll probably figure that out before too long. I was quite fortunate in my research."

"The transcription of the journal is with the publisher and I brought a copy of the manuscript—an ARC, advanced reader's copy, and you're in it, Cassie. I'll leave this copy with you when I go. It's yours when I'm finished here. You can read the passages about you, your mother, grandfather and your family reunion I visited this past July."

"For now, would you like to read a passage for me from Cassie's new book about a bow her brother made himself? It's about a bow very similar to this one I'm holding in my hand."

"Of course, I would love to read for you, Katie," little Cassie said. "I love to read out loud. The teachers let me read out loud all the time."

I handed Cassie the open book.

"Please begin reading at the blue pencil mark," I instructed.

She began:

"Five Feathers and edudu prepared for the hunt in proper Cherokee fashion observing every ritual. Just before they went to bed that evening, edudu handed Five Feathers the bow and said, "Look at your bow, Five Feathers. What do you see?"

Five Feathers examined it carefully and smiled. Just above the grip the young man saw the delicate carving of five eagle feathers in a curious and clever design. He loved it. Just below the handle was an equally artistic carving of the bust of a big male deer and proud antlers.

"Edudu, the feathers are beautiful and I love the deer and his antlers. It is our clan. I love what you have done with my bow and my name. Thank you, thank you, thank you."

"Five Feathers, you and Walela are of the deer clan. I thought this would be a special gift to carry with you the rest of your life. This is your bow."

Cassie finished the passage I had marked and I took the manuscript from her. Without a word, Mr. Johnson, who had been sitting on the couch walked over and slowly and with a sense of reverence, very gently took the bow from my hands. He stood beside me examining the carving carefully as if seeing it for the first time.

No one spoke. Everyone was staring at the bow in Mr. Johnson's hands and occasionally they would glance towards me and my book.

Finally, Mr. Johnson spoke to no one in particular, "I wonder if this is the bow that belonged to that young Cherokee man?"

"I have more information, sir," I said quietly. "Five Feathers, the young man your little Cassie read about just now, was the brother of the woman who died on the Trail of Tears—the woman named Cassie. I think we can safely say the bow described in Cassie's journal is the very same bow you're now holding in your hand, Mr. Johnson. There's more to the story about the bow, but I'll come back to that in a minute."

"Secondly," I said, bringing everyone back from their thoughts about the bow and its original owner, "I went to Nashville and obtained a copy of the final report by the forensic pathologists on the examination of the remains found in the grave by the road. I brought a copy of their report, which I will leave with you."

"In the report, it says the remains of the mother and child were wrapped in a quilt. The quilt, according to the pathologists, was handmade with unmistakable German cultural characteristics and made from fabrics available only in Germany. The quilt was very likely hand-crafted in Germany and brought over by immigrants. I suppose most everything in those days was hand-made."

"The original forensic report deduced the woman and baby to be of European decent. They were sure until they read the excerpts from Cassie's journal."

I asked Ann if she would like to read. She nodded and took the book from my hands. They were all interested and paying close attention. Ann's hands were shaking as I handed her the book.

"Ann, I want you to read this excerpt from the journal of a woman who was on the Trail of Tears with Cassie and passed this very spot in July of 1838. This will shed some light on what we already know. This woman and her journal made it the entire way to Park Hill in what is now Oklahoma."

I asked her to read the passage that described the physical location, the peaks on the ridgeline, the tree, the quilt and the baby.

Ann began:

> "4 July 1838 - Walela was in labor all morning, but something was wrong. The baby did not come. Walela was in

great pain and discomfort. Our detachment stopped by a big farm across from the twin mountains to the south that resembled the breasts of a woman—the right taller than the left. As we waited for permission to continue, Walela's waters broke. We laid her on her quilt in the shade beside the road under a big white oak tree.

Soldiers forced us to leave her. My daughter and I hid across the road waiting for the soldiers to leave. An angry white man came shouting for the soldiers to take Walela away. The soldiers laughed at him.

From our hiding place, we watched the white man go back up to his cabin, shouting angrily at the soldiers following the wagons.

When the man was gone, we crossed the road to help. Walela and her little boy were both dead. I cut off a corner of the quilt to remember her. She told me she and Ben had conceived her baby on this very quilt. So many of us have perished. So many children have died. I hope my children and I make it to the west and the man in the house will bury Walela and her baby."

When Ann finished no one spoke. Finally, with no expression on her face, she said to me, "That's the grave on our property, isn't it? It's the grave under our white oak tree, isn't it?"

"Cassie is Walela, isn't she?"

"Cassie is the woman buried there, isn't she?" Ann asked.

Ann's eyes were filling with tears. Her voice was cracking. She was having difficulty continuing. I was tearing up too. I knew this was going to happen but I was still unprepared.

"The Cherokee woman and her baby boy are buried here, right here on our farm, aren't they?" Ann continued, "The woman buried under the tree wasn't a white woman at all, like they thought? Cassie and her baby were Cherokee."

I nodded in agreement and held out a remnant of old cloth for Ann to see.

"I found this in the pages of the second journal I found in Oklahoma. The forensic folks said it was an exact match—there is no doubt. The woman in the grave is the Cherokee woman, Walela. Her English name was Cassie. The woman in the grave is the author of the journal. There is no uncertainty."

Little Cassie said again, "We know the name of the mother, don't we?

"Yes, we pretty much know everything now," I answered. "Because we have her journal, we know everything that happened leading up to her arrival here. We know she was going to name the baby Ben, if he had lived."

I paused to gather myself. It was an emotional moment. No one spoke.

"And that's not all," I said. "In the grave, according to the forensic folks, they found two gold rings—most probably wedding rings. I understand you have the two rings here in the house, Mr. Johnson?"

"Yes, that's right, Katie," Mr. Johnson answered. "My mother and father thought they should keep them here. Mother couldn't bear to part with them. I'll go get them. They've been in the top drawer of mamma's chifforobe since momma passed."

He returned with the rings and handed me the little case which I opened.

"According to the journal, Mrs. Lowry gave Cassie two wedding rings the morning they left Ross's Landing. Those rings belonged to Mr. and Mrs. Lowry. According to the forensic folks, the woman was holding the rings in her hand when she died."

"These are the rings that would have been used in her wedding if she had married her fiancé, Ben."

No one spoke.

Mr. Johnson, muttering to himself, walked to the window that overlooked the big white oak tree down by the road.

"We're going to have to put up a new gravestone," he said to no one in particular as he stared out the window. "I'll do that tomorrow."

"We'll have to have a new gravestone," he mumbled once again.

Mr. Johnson, continuing to stare down the hill to the gravesite, muttered once again, "We're going to have to put up a new gravestone. I'll do that this week. I have to put up a new headstone. I'll do that this week."

Ann, her mother, Cassie and myself were crying.

"Now I know whose voice that was I heard, don't I? Ann said between sobs. "Now we know who was responsible for the dreams. I shall never forget that voice. Thank you so much, Katie, for all your work to bring us the truth," Ann continued. "It wasn't right that woman should lie there all this time in an unmarked grave after what she went through. It wasn't right. We'll have to put up a headstone. We can't deny the truth."

I nodded.

"We owe you a big debt," Ann said quietly. "Cassie owes you a big debt. The Cherokee Nation owes you a debt. Thank you, Thank you, Thank you."

With those words Ann broke down into a fit of crying—her shoulders heaving up and down—gasping for air between each pathetic sob. Her daughter's arms were around her shoulders and little Cassie, too, began crying. I couldn't help but join. Ann's mother was crying, too. As we all cried there in the living room on the hill above the grave, I couldn't help but think that finally Walela had some measure of closure. It occurred to me that this little gathering in the Johnson living room was the only memorial service Walela and her baby ever had. I was pleased her story had been told. Ann, her daughter and grandmother and I ended up on the couch wiping our eyes and blowing our noses. It took us quite a while to finally gather ourselves. It was an emotional moment.

I heard Mr. Johnson, still standing transfixed at the window, whisper again to himself, "Cassie and her baby are buried down by the road. Her brother's bow has come home to be with his sister. I didn't choose this bow—it chose me. We're going to have to put up a new headstone, aren't we? I'll do that this week."

I thought of the end of the Cherokee woman's life and the life of her baby boy just a few yards down the hill from where we were sitting. I knew in my heart I had accomplished the wishes of the voice and now the story had been told as requested. I hope I have told it honorably. I did the best I could.

Now that I know who owned the voice, I wonder if perhaps one day I will hear that lovely voice again, perhaps in another time and in another place and under more joyful circumstances. I hope so. I would love to hear that voice again.

I have never been terribly religious, but in that moment I hoped that Cassie's Great Spirit would bring the long-delayed justice to her and her people. I want very much to meet the woman who wrote the journal and whose bones, along with the bones of her baby, were buried under the lonely white oak tree down by the old road—the road that led through this Tennessee valley towards unknown western lands and outside the borders of the United States.

I wanted to hold her and hug her neck and tell her everything was going to be ok.

In that moment I knew I must name my baby Cassandra Eleanor. We would call her Cassie. That would be my final token of respect.

Chapter LXI

2016 – Johnson Reunion Remembered

Chapter 61

The Johnson family now knows Cassie and her baby are buried in the grave under the old white oak tree and that her brother's hunting bow hangs over the mantelpiece as if standing permanently as a sentinel. As I left the Johnson's and walked to my car, the long, quiet shadows fell across the quiet rural Tennessee landscape. Everything was at peace—in balance. Cassie's story was delivered to the publishers. I had brought closure to the Johnson family, to myself, to Cassie, her brother and her nation—at least in some small measure.

As I opened my car door, I saw my old cane lying on the back seat and I was transported back to that Fourth of July reunion I attended here just a few months ago. Every detail of that day remains sharp in my mind.

I recall this driveway full of late model cars and fancy four-wheel drive pickups, each with a gun rack in the back window. I could see the tons of food and all the happy families milling around the house, pool and patio.

I turned the corner at the end of the driveway and the last rays of the afternoon sun reflected off the simple granite gravestone there to my left as I slowly drove away. The engraving just legible from the road, 'Mother and Child'.

I could trust Mr. Johnson to have another headstone in place soon. The low afternoon sun shone across the fertile fields of the picturesque Johnson farm—the landscape little different than it was a hundred and seventy-five years ago when Cassie last viewed this valley. I reflected on the baby boy born beside the road on that day. I shivered. Unbidden, my mind rehearsed the old woman's words in Tahlequah, "I think, my dear, the story may be pursuing you."

She was right. The story had been pursuing me. I knew that now and it was a pursuit I welcomed. It was my privilege to have obeyed the voice and told her story. I felt a sense of relief and gratitude as I began the drive back to Chattanooga.

The last resting place of a brave Cherokee woman from New Echota lay behind me in the long shadows as I gently accelerated my Camry past the old white oak towards Chattanooga and my small apartment off of Vine Street.

A myriad of emotions poured over me as I pondered the life and death of the woman who had allowed me, nay, chosen me, to transcribe her journal. I was going to cry once again. The visit with the Johnsons had been supercharged. I needed to decompress. My mind had been thinking too much about the things I had learned. I needed immediate relief. I pulled over just up the road from the Johnson farm, laid my head on my arms and sobbed uncontrollably one more time. When I finally got control of myself, I looked up as a small yellow butterfly landed on the hood of my car.

That little yellow butterfly had been sent. I suddenly realized that last of all it was I who had been granted closure. The little butterfly confirmed that my task was completed. All was resolved.

Since I have completed my research I have a different view of life in our United States. I understand who it was who lived here before the Johnson family was given their federal land grant. I know who the people were who lived in Walker county before 1838. I know now the meaning of the word Mrs. Lowry shared with Cassie—lebensraum. I know only too well. My father's farm and everyone around me are living on land taken from the Cherokee.

As my mind traveled back in time, I could see dozens and dozens of Cherokee towns up and down the network of rivers in Cherokee Country. I can see Cherokee mothers caring for children, fields of ripening corn, squash, pumpkins and beans—martin gourds all around the perimeter of their villages. I can see Cherokee families and their old folks sitting on their little front porch in the evening twilight whittling and telling stories and listening to the whippoorwills in the gathering dusk and the trills of the mockingbirds in the tops of the trees. I had a vision of the joy accompanying the Cherokee Green Corn festivals—the food, the families and the renewal of relationships—the connection with their past that maintained the balance.

Things change, I mused to myself. Things certainly change. Things change.

I thought about Ann Johnson and the voice that told her to name her baby Cassie. I thought about the Johnson family enjoying the fruits of the Tennessee soil and how their land was acquired.

I remembered Ashley sharing her story about her M.R.S. Degree and how happy she was to be a part of the extended Johnson family. I recall her excitement to renew relationships at their reunion and once again be included in a warm, loving extended family at their annual celebration.

I remember Ashley, happily married and pregnant, saying to her aunt, "I'm so glad we live in Tennessee. It's so full of promise and today is our country's Independence Day. We have nothing to fear, do we? I'm so thankful my child will grow up in the land of the free. We have life, liberty and the pursuit of happiness, don't we?"

After her patriotic speech, I remember watching Ashley and her Aunt Ann quietly survey the landscape, as we all did, and thinking of their happiness and security. I can hear her aunt musing out loud as she looked over her ancestral farm, "What could be better than this?"

Memories of that July Fourth reunion continued to flood my mind.

I remember watching Ashley kiss her aunt's cheek and whisper, "I wouldn't want to have my baby born anywhere in the world than right here."

I found a tissue in my purse, wiped my eyes and blew my nose. I needed to get control of myself and drive home. I had thought about this enough for one day—for a lifetime really. I needed to finish my degree.

I regained my composure and glanced over at Cassie's journal lying in my passenger seat—a copy of the very book that had come down this road all those years ago. As I drove east on the trail on which they wept, I heard a voice from somewhere say clearly, "Thank You, Katie—Thank You—Thank You."

The End

Postscript I - Katie's Postscript

It's been a labor of love reading and transcribing the things Mr. Lowry encouraged Cassie to write in that old accounting ledger all those years ago. I loved every moment of my work. I couldn't really call it work. I feel more like an artist or a sculptor—but, of course, Cassie is the artist.

I was curious and tested my DNA to determine my heritage. I had been told part of me was Cherokee.

As it turned out, eighty-five percent of me came from somewhere in the United Kingdom—probably English, ten percent from western Europe—probably Germany from my grandmother's side and I'm six percent Scandinavian. I'm solid white.

From my research I have learned that from the very moment my relatives stepped ashore here on the North American continent, they began a process of ethnic cleansing that eventually spread from sea to shining sea—Mexico and Canada included. Hundreds of ethnic groups, cultures and languages were removed, most of them violently, by my land-greedy relatives searching for lebensraum.

Our collective white memory is short and selective. We don't talk about what happened in our history any more than we talk about a family member in a mental institution. We justify our behavior, don't we? 'It wasn't my fault' is a phrase we all learned early in childhood. I'm not nearly as proud of my country as I was before I began my research.

Cassie's book is finished. The transcription is complete. Her wish is fulfilled. I am not the same person I was on that day in Tahlequah when I first met the old Cherokee woman and held that mysterious old book in my lap wondering what it contained.

Yours Sincerely,
Katie
xoxo

Postscript II - Author's Epilogue

One evening I mentioned to a dinner guest I was writing a historical novel about the Cherokee Trail of Tears. He was interested. My comment caused my guest to immediately share a story from his military experience.

He re-counted how in 1970, as a young serviceman stationed at Fort Sill, Oklahoma, he and a fellow soldier were driving through the rural countryside. The landscape suddenly changed. My friend asked his buddy about the curious change in the landscape—unlike the normal farmland they were familiar with. Why did the landscape look so different, he inquired.

His army buddy behind the wheel replied, "Oh, that's where we keep our Indians."

In 1970, two young, white United States Army soldiers observed what is for most of us a forgotten political-cultural oddity. They drove past the continuing results of our Federal Government's ethnic cleansing during the nineteenth century when score upon score of unwanted Native American tribes were forcibly removed from all parts of these United States, east, west, north and south, to small parcels of land in Oklahoma—all the unwanted crowded in together, side by side. Originally, when the Native Americans were moved, Oklahoma was outside the borders of the United States. Our government got rid of its unwanted Indians.

I used that soldier's 1970 retort to lead into my novel. The following is an excerpt from a letter from John Ross, Principle Chief of the Cherokee, to Job R. Tyson of Philadelphia. The letter was written one year before the Cherokee deportation.

> Washington City – 6 May 1837
>
> "…we asked that if we were to be driven from our homes and our native country, we should not also be denounced as treaty breakers, but have at least the consolation of being recognized as the unoffending, unresisting Indian, despoiled of his property, driven from his domestic fireside, exiled from his home by the mere dint of superior power. We ask that deeds be called by their right names.
>
> We distinctly disavow all thoughts, all desire, to gratify any feelings of resentment. That possessions acquired, and objects

attained by unjust means, will, sooner or later, prove a curse to those who have sought them, is a truth we have been taught by that holy religion which was brought to us by our white brethren. Years, nay, centuries may elapse before the punishment may follow the offense, but the volume of history and the sacred Bible assure us, that period will certainly arrive. We would with Christian sympathy labour to avert the wrath of Heaven from the United States, by imploring your government to be just."

Cassie's grandfather would say in more colorful use of language, "One day their chickens will come home to roost".

Chief John Ross, well acquainted with the Christian scriptures, would have been quite familiar with the old Hebrew story that goes like this:

King Ahab wanted the beautiful vineyard next to his palace. He wanted it for an herb garden. The problem was the beautiful piece of property he had his eye on was owned by someone else.

The owner of the vineyard, Mr. Naboth, wouldn't sell.

The king said, "I'll trade or I'll give you money. Tell me what you want. I must have your vineyard, Mr. Naboth. Please sell it to me."

Mr. Naboth, quoting longstanding law, respectfully told the king it wouldn't be right for him to sell his ancestral land. He was sorry but he couldn't conscientiously sell the family farm. No deal.

Jezebel, the king's wife, was incensed when she heard of Mr. Naboth's refusal. She found Mr. Naboth's gross selfishness incredible. How could anyone refuse the king? How could a common man insist on keeping his family farm against the wishes of the king? Everyone knew the king came from a family that possessed privileges normal folks didn't have. Jezebel thought no one should refuse her husband, the king—the highest authority in the land.

Jezebel had a plan. She hired men to swear Mr. Naboth had committed crimes against the state. Jezebel arranged for Mr. Naboth to be arrested, tried, convicted and executed—all according to the letter of the law. Everything was done publicly and legally before a judge. The problem Mr. Naboth had caused by wanting to keep his own land was taken care of quite legitimately. King Ahab was a law-abiding man, even if he was king. Everything was done legally and above board—well, mostly.

The Naboth's Vineyard Removal Act passed and became law. So, the proud King Ahab took possession of Mr. Naboth's beautiful vineyard, and it was about time.

And so, Andrew Jackson was finally rid—oops, sorry, a slip of the pen. I meant to say, King Ahab was finally rid of the Cherokee—darn it, there I go again with that slippery pen. I meant to say, Ahab was finally rid of his selfish, inconsiderate neighbor, Mr. Naboth. Now the king had legal possession of the beautiful land being misused by Mr. Naboth. King Ahab was happy. He understood, even back then, if you want something that doesn't belong to you, it must be taken legally. You can't steal things from others like the uncivilized barbarians do. Civilized folks do things legally in congress or in a court of law. Doing things legally also makes them moral and right, doesn't it?

So, Ahab proudly took possession of the beautiful next-door vineyard and everyone lived happily ever after—right?

Nope.

Not exactly.

Ahab got what he wanted but he didn't live happily ever after—neither did Jezebel.

Ahab had a lingering problem that came with his crafty use of his country's legal system. He had forgotten there was a higher authority than the president—I meant to say—there was a higher authority than the king, his wife, Jezebel and their judges. I just can't seem to control my dodgy pen, can I?

John Ross had been told by missionaries that there is someone who keeps a record of human injustice—even a record of obscure things that governments sweep under big, heavy rugs. Coincidentally to our story, that someone who keeps a record sent a man named Elijah to have a talk with King Ahab just at the very moment he was taking possession of his new vineyard.

I can see Elijah walk up to the king there in Naboth's vineyard and point his bony finger in the king's face.

Elijah said to the happy new landowner, "Where the dogs licked the blood of the innocent Naboth, so shall the dogs lick your blood and dogs shall also consume the flesh of your wife Jezebel."

White English immigrants shared their precious Authorized King James Version with Chief John Ross. Perhaps that old book King James authorized all those years ago was and is meaningless. Maybe it's just a collection of well-meaning Jewish stories. Maybe that old book is full of myths intended for old women and impressionable children. What do you think? Do you think John Ross's fear, expressed in his letter to Mr. Tyson, is nostalgic nonsense—

just wishful thinking? Or is there, perhaps, a higher authority who takes injustice seriously and remembers? Are we above such authority?

You can bet Ahab was hoping Elijah was blowin' smoke. How could anyone oppose the president and congress—oops, darn it, there I go again. I meant to say, how could anyone oppose the king and his government and not expect to get stepped on? The king rules by divine authority—right?

Oh dear, according to this old story and according to what Chief John Ross said in his letter, what goes around, comes around and bites you in the A**, doesn't it?

If you're interested, the library may still have an old, dusty copy of that out-of-date King James Version somewhere that has that story. If you can't find a copy of that old book in your local library, you can borrow the old one the Chief Justice of the Supreme Court has. The Chief Justice used a King James Version to swear in George Washington. If you happen to be in Washington D.C., go see the United States Chief Justice and read the story in I Kings chapter twenty-one.

Today our United States Federal Government holds title to 63% of all land west of the Mississippi. Where did they get that land? What do they do with it? All those folks our government crowded together in Oklahoma know where the Federal Government got their land both west and east of the Mississippi River. The rumor is the Federal Government will soon turn it all into a giant presidential herb garden.

John Ross said that if the United States wanted to take the Cherokee land by force there wasn't anything the Cherokee could do about it, but according to the white man's own sacred writings, someone higher up than the president and congress is taking notes.

If I were the President of the United States, I would keep an eye out for a man named Elijah just in case he might be spotted walking up Pennsylvania Avenue.

In books and films produced for white amusement in the United States, Native Americans are portrayed as backward, violent, irredeemable—brutal savages deserving of a violent end—deserving extinction.

White writers created stories for our entertainment like *Roy Rogers, Gene Autry, Hopalong Cassidy, Gunsmoke, Bonanza, Cheyenne, Wagon Train* and *Rawhide.*

Films, like John Ford's *The Searchers,* validate white ownership of the American frontier—every acre. In *The Searchers,* Indians are portrayed as immoral savage animals. Shoot on sight was John Wayne's mantra. These stories were written long after the fact and justify our seizing ownership of the entirety of the North American continent. It's obvious to everyone that America should be white owned and operated, isn't it?

In 1826, James Fenimore Cooper's *Last of the Mohicans* portrayed his white protagonist, Natty Bumppo, better known as Hawkeye or Deerslayer, as the champion of a superior white culture in the malevolent frontier world of sneaky, heathen redskins. Hawkeye, representing our superior white race, defeats the irredeemably wicked Indian, Mauga.

Native Americans, in James Fenimore Cooper's *Leatherstocking Tales*, are violent savages wholly without human kindness. The single exception is old Chief Chingachgook and his son. They alone demonstrated a civilized Indian character by their submission to higher white culture and their decision to allow their own race to expire—as our Henry Clay suggested should happen.

Mauga disappears. The Mohicans conveniently abandon the frontier for the benefit of the superior white Europeans.

Indians simply disappeared from these United States, didn't they? That's what we're told.

In 1838, while Cassie was being deported, one could hear a Beethoven symphony in New York or take an excursion on a steamboat down the Hudson. Whites deserve to own Cassie's land by virtue of their superior intelligence and culture, don't they?

There exists in Washington DC over 600 treaties ratified by the United States Government with Native Americans. Not one treaty has been honored.

Even our government's ethnic cleansing has been cleansed. This very day we worship the image of Andrew Jackson on our twenty-dollar bill as the consummate American hero, Indian fighter and president. Andrew Jackson, along with George Washington, Abraham Lincoln, Ulysses S. Grant and Benjamin Franklin reside in our political Cooperstown. Yes-sir-ree-bob, right there on our twenty-dollar bill is the image of our nation's number one Indian-killer and ethnic-cleanser. He was quite a man, wasn't he? Quite a hero, isn't he?

Modern politicians rail about the despicable perpetrators of ethnic cleansing on other continents. We won't stand for that horrible injustice against those poor innocent people, they say. No-sir-ree-bob. We're the good guys. We wear the white hats. We'll bomb the hell out of anyone who chooses to ethnically cleanse their neighbors—like they did in Bosnia.

The moment British colonists arrived on these shores they began to get rid of the Indians by offering a bounty for a dead heathen savage. Since it was inconvenient to bring the entire body to the authorities to collect their reward, the bounty was paid if just the hair and skin of the head were brought—as if it were an animal pelt. The authorities in Massachusetts and other colonies offered a reward for the evidence of the death of a male Indian and also for that of a woman or child.

The offering of a bounty for dead Indians worked. Native Americans, like the buffalo, were quickly hunted to extinction. All free Native Americans are gone now—vanished like the last of the Mohicans and we have their land—except in Oklahoma, of course, and we'll probably have that before too long.

It wouldn't be until 1990 that the Federal Government passed the Native American Graves Protection and Repatriation Act. As late as 1990, Native American pelts were on display in white museums beside the remains of the extinct hairy mammoth and the dried bones of the Tyrannosaurus Rex.

I have heard Harriet Tubman's portrait will be placed on the front of our twenty-dollar bill and Andrew Jackson moved to the backside.

How ironic. The most powerful white supremacist, Indian killer and ethnic cleanser in American history will be displayed on the same twenty-dollar bill with Harriet Tubman. How paradoxical. Only our benighted Federal Government, the same government that passed the Indian Removal Act of 1830, could find such a juxtaposition innocuous.

A bill will soon be introduced in Congress to begin returning substantial portions of Cherokee land to Cherokee ownership—and other tribes—to return that which was taken. The primary restoration will be the return of the old Cherokee Capital of New Echota located near Calhoun, Georgia and also the nearby Chattahoochee National Forest along with the Smoky Mountain National Park. All illegally seized in 1838.

If you want to help Cassie and her people, contact your congressman and give your support to both the removal of Andrew Jackson from the twenty-dollar bill and the restoration of Cherokee lands in Georgia and the Smoky Mountains. Perhaps this can be a beginning. Perhaps the other civilized tribes, along with the Cherokee, will have justice at last. Perhaps we white folks can avoid the consequences of John Ross's warning. Perhaps Elijah won't be sent to 1600 Pennsylvania Avenue after all.

In the words of the wise old woman in Tahlequah:

"When does the thief legally own that which he stole?"

Postscript III - A Story

A man inherited a thousand-acre farm complete with equipment, outbuildings and a magnificent, modern 6,000 square foot home. The farm could be traced back five generations. What a wonderful family legacy.

The proud son took possession of his ancestral property—a property filled with decades of family memories. It was the farm where he grew from a boy into a man.

One day, as he was organizing in the library, he discovered a secret drawer in his great-great-grandfather's old desk—a drawer never before opened. To his surprise, the secret drawer contained documents relating the details of how his great-great-grandfather had obtained the farm.

The secret documents told how his great-great-grandfather had gained possession of the property by intimidation, violence, lies, deceit, bribery and the brutal eviction of the rightful owners—forcing the family to transfer legal ownership into his name against their will.

He examined the papers carefully. He did research. His great-great grandfather's actions were easily documented. The facts were there. The evidence would, even at this late date, be provable in a court of law. His great-great-grandfather was a crook and had acquired the farm by grossly illegal means. His great-great-grandfather wasn't great at all.

As he read the secret documents, the man realized he knew the descendants of the dispossessed family. While his family had thrived in the midst of prosperity, the dispossessed lost their station in the community and lived less than modestly beyond the rail yard in a rental property.

As the young man read the secret documents, he found himself in a moral dilemma. His great-great-grandfather was a crook. That was a fact. He had inherited a farm that had been stolen. That was a fact.

In light of his great-great-grandfather's crime, he had to decide if he would ignore history or consider righting an old wrong. Should he tuck the incriminating papers back into the secret drawer? Should he dismiss the new evidence? Should he enjoy his inheritance no matter how it had been acquired? Didn't he possess the legal deed to his beautiful property?

Should he allow himself to entertain the question:

When does the thief legally own that which he stole?